THE DRAGON CHILD

THE DRAGON CHILD

Dragon's Quest

JARED NESCHER

Dragon Child Publishing

ISBN: 979-8-9907975-0-5 (Paperback)
ISBN: 979-8-9907975-1-2 (Hardcover)
ISBN: 979-8-9907975-2-9 (E-Book)

Library of Congress Control Number: 2024923180

Published in Grants Pass, Oregon

First edition: 11/12/2013
Second edition: 2/18/2014
Series edition: 12/2/2024

Interior Illustrations by Shastina Maya

Cover Editing by Christopher Teskey

www.thedragonchild.com
Dragon Child Publishing

Contents

To God, for giving me the imagination and the love for storytelling; and to my family, for supporting me, when all others said writing stories was a foolish thing.

Author's Note

Imagination is a great thing; it allows mankind to develop in so many different ways. The human imagination allows us to think outside of the box. As it helps an artist to draw what is not there, it also helps a scientist find solutions to his problems. Because of our imagination, the human race has come far as a species; we have even touched the moon, which generations before thought impossible. Yes, because of our imagination, our technology and achievements have gone beyond our understanding. However, as a race, we are failing; there is so much left undone. There are children suffering, wars of conquest are still being fought, and religious fanatics are still killing innocent people. We claim to be a sophisticated species, but there are animals that know more about the meaning of life than we do. Humanity severely needs to look at itself.

The Dragon Child is a book series. If anything, it allows people to view humanity with nonbiased eyes, gives them a chance to step back and see what we were meant to become. Though it is a Christian-based fantasy, The Dragon Child has much truth for the human race. I encourage nonbelievers to read it in the hopes that they will acknowledge humanity's shortcomings. If anything, they will share in an adventure of a lifetime, and come to love the characters.

However, I would like to impress my concern upon the believers as well as the nonbelievers. The Dragon Child is a fantasy novel—although fantasy does have some aspects of reality, and this novel has plenty of that. The book is meant to be taken to heart, not to be taken into reality. The Dragon Child was not meant to be a retelling of history or an add on to the Bible. It is especially not meant to become a new religion. I humbly ask readers to simply enjoy it and learn from it, as well as share it with others, in the hope that we can make this world a better place not only while we live here but also for future generations to live in.

Prologue

Many people say that they have learned something that has changed the way they think, but what I have learned has changed more than just the way I think, and it is better that someone knows what I have learned than if I let it slip away into the void. So I will tell you what I know. But first, I must ask a question. Why do we tell stories? Because they are a gift, they teach us many things, if we only have the ears to hear them. They show us our past, present, and future. They help shape our world. Some are poorly written, some are exaggerated, and others are not even true (this we call fiction). But the question is, are they really fiction? To answer that question, I will tell you something that will shake the very foundations of fiction.

The phrase "worlds within worlds" was not only meant for fiction. For example, even though we cannot see them, the cells in our bodies are there, and they have a life of their own. We would be foolish to think that we are alone and that we stand separate from the universe.

We do not see that we are a part of everything, like nature; everything has a part in the balance. Everything merges one thing with another. Every fantasy is so real yet so different that we don't truly know how factual it is. Just what makes a fantasy a fantasy? Fantasy is something we do not have, yet we desire it. Like a light at the end of the tunnel we can see it, but not touch it. However, with every tunnel, there are two ends. So the light you are seeing is either the light of the future or the light of the past. In the light of things to come, there are infinite possibilities for what might be. In the light of things that have come and gone, it is similar to a painting that has faded with time. We can no longer see its true form or even come close to seeing what it might have been.

After seeing two open tunnels, our imagination does not hesitate to soar. Some say we need to stay in reality; however, they are the people who are empty and dry. Some of the greatest inventions of our time were made by people who dreamed of doing the impossible when others told them it could not be done. The present cannot exist without the past or future. God has given us the imagination to fill the void. It is a gift we need to use. So in saying that, I ask you to listen to what I'm going to tell you and let your imagination soar.

Fairy tale is another term for fiction. Why? Do you truly know the answer to that question? If you don't, then let me answer it for you. Fairies are the keepers of tales; they are the true historians. Read a hundred books, and I'll bet you will never hear of this. Because historians don't like to be known. They prefer to work in secret. There are thousands of fairies for everything: fairies for leaves, for rain, for wind, and for fire. There are good fairies, bad fairies, mischievous fairies and even just boredout-of-their-mind fairies. The greatest of them all are the historians. They have another name, but I cannot pronounce it. They were one of the first creatures ever made, even before the elves. Historians are the most powerful of all the fairies.

Unlike most fairies, who were given power over their charge (though sometimes they have more than one charge), historians were given power over many things because they had to be everywhere and see everything to be the living record. It was said that they even had the ability to touch heaven's gates and speak to the Creator himself. Instead of going to nature, they went to the Creator to get their orders as to where they needed to be. Very rarely did they influence the world around them. Their life's desire was to keep the past alive. Those who forget the past are condemned to repeat it, and some things should not be forgotten.

So what does this have to do with fiction, you ask? If you say nothing, then you give our imagination too much credit. How were stories told in the ancient days? They didn't have books or TV. Stories spread by word of mouth, and the imagination filled in the rest. Stories spread from person to person or from fairy to person. That's right; they are the real storytellers. Even past the year 2000 and on, our stories don't belong to us. The fairies sit on our shoulders, hidden from our sight, whispering into our ears. For their lives to have meaning, they must find someone to pass the stories on to. Each person a fairy talks to has been chosen for a reason. So I am telling you that every ancient story told is based, in part, upon truth.

Some stories are truer than others. The reason for that is some people do not like the stories they hear. Instead of giving the stories the respect they deserve and writing them down correctly, they change them to fit their own opinions. So how many stories are truer than others? I don't know, and it doesn't matter. Though there are many great stories and talented authors, they don't matter. Don't get me wrong; I am fond of many authors. I hold several authors in great respect and admiration. I could never do what they have done. Many of their books have captivated our hearts and minds for generations, and the stories as well as the authors deserve respect. Nevertheless, like the rising and setting of the sun, when it goes down, we know that one just as good, yet different, will come tomorrow.

However, the story that has come to me is like a sun that will never set. What do I have that is better than the other authors? Absolutely nothing! I am simply educated and cannot compare to the other authors. What I have is the oldest of all the fairies, and she carries the greatest tale ever told. She rejected, for thousands of years, every author she found. Why? Because the story she carries is so great, it cannot be altered in the least. She chose me based on the fact that I am no scholar; the words that I carry are those of an average man. All that I pray for is that I do right by her and do the story justice in the telling. I am honored alone by her presence and the knowledge of her and the tale. The story she brings is different in a way that most stories exist within themselves. Each land creates its own habitat, therefore creating its own story. Although people travel to distant lands, they still have their own stories. Never has a story ever merged from one into another. Like you have never heard of the Greek gods meeting the Norse gods. Every story has its own time and place.

The story I am about to tell you is like a shadow. It exists in every story ever written, hidden from our eyes, the reason being that everyone in the land was so wrapped up in their own story that the greatest tale just walked on by. It was like the wind in the trees: you know that they are being moved, but you cannot see what's moving them. Never before or after has anyone ever walked on every corner of the earth. So with her whispering gently into my ear, let us begin.

***

Concerning dragons, what we think we know about them is all wrong. There are hundreds of books that talk about dragons. However, those books are based on humans, elves, and other creatures. Dragons are but a passing whisper; it is not their story. The dragons' tale is a bit different than others. There are even guidebooks to dragons, which clearly have nothing to do with dragons at all! Like idiots, we categorize dragons like we do dogs, trying to stereotype their characters. Humans have even gone far enough to separate them by color.

Well, I am here to tell you that you are wrong. If anything, they are a lot like us. Their wings, horns, and bodies will never grow the same as another's. Their scale color will never match another dragon's. Also, their lifestyles will never be the same, for some will be good, some evil, some will be happy, and others sad. I hate the way that dragons are mostly portrayed as being vicious and evil. Even Christians themselves have always told me that dragons are evil. However, I have yet to find proof that they are.

Like humans, they live both physically, mentally, and emotionally. We don't give them enough credit for who they are. They have even achieved more than us, for they are not prejudiced against color. For it was known that they had families of many colors. If there was a separation among dragons, it was in their hearts. The only thing dragons and man do not have in common is that dragons live from their emotions, not their physical instincts. That gives them a greater power to live by. This is one of the gifts that we were given yet forgot long ago. So if the dragons are greater than man, why are they all gone, you ask? Why did they simply disappear and only the dinosaurs' remains were left behind?

Good question. I will tell you why. However, to do so, I must take you back to the beginning. Unfortunately, by that, I mean the beginning of everything! So get comfortable wherever you are and keep an open mind. Whether you believe in God or the Big Bang, it doesn't matter. Life simply started, and something had to help it. So man isn't the center of the universe, as he believes; there is something greater than us! Also, we were not the first lifeform; sadly, we came last—even behind the monkeys.

The Alliance

It was heaven on earth, one giant landmass and beautiful gardens where perfection and balance ruled. Even the Creator walked among the gardens and loved all that he had made. One of his favorite creations was the dragon. Dragons were the most beautiful and majestic of all creatures, gifted with both knowledge and wisdom. They were even given temporary guardianship over the other creatures. The Creator even walked and talked among them. But as time moved on, the Creator had finished all that he intended to make, ending with his most precious creation—man.

The dragons welcomed us and loved us the way they loved the Creator. However, all that changed the day the Creator gave guardianship of the earth and all creatures on it to humans. That was the start of the rift between us humans and dragons, and it didn't end there, though I wish it did!

Some of the dragons respected the Creator's wishes; others didn't and became jealous of man. They believed man to be a weaker race than dragons and that man did not deserve what the Creator gave them. And as though a log had been added to the fire, things were destined to get worse. Not only was there a rift between dragons and man, but now they were divided among themselves. They were on the verge of chaos, which was when the Deceiver took advantage of the situation.

Not much is known about the Deceiver, and the dragons that knew about him did not speak of what they knew. All that was known was that he was the first of the Creator's servants and was very powerful. It was said that his pride in that power led to his downfall. His real name does not come into the story at this time; they called him the Deceiver because he got a man to betray the Creator. In so doing, the world would never be the same. It was said that the Deceiver was the first ever to betray the Creator. It was also said that the Deceiver wanted man to fall to separate the Creator from man, opposing the Creator's plan. In response to the Deceiver and man's betrayal, the Creator sent all creatures from the gardens, and even the earth erupted in anger against man. For what was once one land split into many, and oceans became the divide. Chaos was inevitable; the dragons blamed man for taking away what they had loved so much—the Creator and the peaceful gardens.

Of course, the race of man blamed the dragons for their fall, foolishly mistaking them for the Deceiver. This was the start of the Great War, and without fail, the Deceiver had more fuel for this fire. From the depths of darkness, he unleashed his forces upon the earth. Creatures that he twisted to his design— creatures like orcs, goblins, trolls, and many more. He gave them a thirst for carnage and destruction that would never be quenched. Oddly, every now and then, some would come forth with a peaceful nature. However, it was rare, for they were designed for evil. So they were spread throughout the earth. Wherever there was peace, the Deceiver bolstered his forces.

The war raged on for hundreds of years, until one great army comprised of elves, dwarves, and dragons made their last stand. They sacrificed themselves so that the rest of the world may know times of peace. No one who entered that last battle of the great war ever came out alive. However, neither did the enemy; that last stand produced an end to the Great War; twelve hundred years after the fall of man, it was finally over. Many of the dark creatures disappeared from the face of the earth only to become legends; it was even said the Deceiver disappeared on that battlefield and was never seen again. Orcs seem to be the only creatures left to cause any problems, but they never mobilized big enough to become a great army again. Many wished they could say there was peace after the end of the Great War, but that was not true. Even thousands of years after the last battle, the races continued to fight one another as if hatred were the only thing that they knew. For not only did good and evil fight, but good fought good and evil fought evil. There was no peace between the races. They only fought together for a common enemy, and when it was defeated, they went back to fighting each other. Even on the other side of the world, the races that had forgotten where they came from and the meaning of the war still felt disdain for one another. The light of hope was almost put out until one man made a different choice than his ancestors. What he did started the ripples in the pond.

Jorn was no great king. He was a simple farmer with only a mind for good, tilled earth. He was a stout, light-skinned man of six feet with reddish-brown hair and blue eyes. A well-built man with strong arms not a person for miles around would fight him. With his deep voice and a hint of stubbornness, he seemed almost overpowering. However, he had a gentle touch; even the plants seemed to grow in his hands. Jorn wanted a simple life with a small farm, a wife, children, and a future, but even that seemed impossible with the ever-growing darkness threatening to overtake the world. Though he was a man of peace, he too knew that if he did not fight to defend his land, it would burn. The memory of losing his parents to orc raiders when he was young was still very clear in his mind.

Jorn did not think he would ever leave his little village; he never dreamed he would fight in a grand army, but life had a different plan. It all started one day when a band of orcs attacked his village. Jorn was able to rally the villagers and defend their peaceful home. However, something did not seem right to Jorn; he had a deep feeling that something was wrong. When he looked at the dead orcs, it confirmed his feelings. This was not a simple band of forest orcs looking to cause trouble. They were heavily outfitted with armor, swords, shields, and helms; they were a band of orcs prepared for war. With that information, he convinced his villagers to go check on the other nearby villages. They secured their home in case of another attack, and Jorn left half of the men there to defend it. Once the village was prepared, Jorn set out with the other half of the men in search of answers, hoping for the best but expecting the worst. Jorn did not know that would be the last time he would ever see his home.

When Jorn and the men that followed him reached the next village, they arrived just in time to ward off an attack from a band of orcs. Jorn was somewhat relieved to know that his feelings about the orc attack were not wrong; however, at the same time, he was worried of what that meant to his village and the surrounding area. He shared that information with the villagers, and they all came to the same conclusion: that this was not a simple attack and something needed to be done. Jorn wanted to continue to check the surrounding villages and make his way to one of the bigger cities to see if they were aware of the problem. He was surprised when many of the villagers agreed with him and wanted to go along. So like what they did with their village, they secured this village and moved on to the next. Once again, Jorn took half of the male population, doubling his fighting force. They were able to save and secure three other villages, each time adding to their fighting group. On their journeys, they only found one village that was destroyed with no survivors. That only made Jorn hasten his pace to one of the major cities further east.

When they arrived, they were shocked to see the city completely surrounded by an orc army. Even though the city had giant walls, it was not faring well under the siege. Jorn and his villagers were greatly terrified, considering they were outnumbered by more than ten to one. However, they were determined to do what they could to save the people in the city. Since it was dusk, Jorn had an idea and organized his men to stay hidden until dark. As night fell, it seemed as if life itself was on their side. That night, there was no moon, and the fields around the city were completely dark. Jorn knew there was a risk in this maneuver, but it was the only thing he could think of. The band of villagers made their way to the back of the orc line and started attacking. Because the battle was so fierce and loud, most of the orcs could not distinguish cries of battle from cries of death. So the orcs did not catch on to the fact that an enemy was among them until half of their army was destroyed. Even then, they could not distinguish who the enemy was and create a rally to fight them off. Eventually, the orc army ran, not knowing who had attacked them. Surprisingly, Jorn only lost a few men in that risky maneuver; they almost lost more trying to convince the city guards that they weren't there to attack them. Still, the city would not open up its gates until morning to properly see the surrounding area, so Jorn and his men set up camp a ways back from the field of carnage. They didn't get any sleep, concerned that the Army of orcs would return, but they were able to get some rest before dawn. When the sun rose, everyone could see the extent of the carnage, and they realized how lucky they were to have survived. Jorn's plan not only saved the city but his band of men as well. When the city gates were finally opened to the rescuers, it was like the old tales of glory. Jorn and his group were met and led through the gates with cheers and applause from all the survivors in the city. Once again, life took the choice away from Jorn to return home and swept him once again into the title wave that was coming. He did not realize that he was becoming a symbol of hope for the people. The king of that city was not liked by the people; he was selfish and mostly took care of those that he favored. When Jorn arrived, there was a shift among the people, and the king was quick to recognize it. He knew that if he didn't act fast, the people and his own guards would turn on him. Recognizing that Jorn was not a man who sought power, the king did the only thing available to him: he swore his allegiance to Jorn, and in doing so, he maintained his position of power. Jorn, however, did not recognize this; his only thought was hunting down the remaining orcs and stopping them from destroying other villages and other cities. So he didn't linger long in that city, gathered what he needed, and went out to make sure others were safe. The only difference was that when he left that city, he was no longer the leader of a group of villagers; he was the leader of an army. From there, the story of Jorn grew and continued to inspire hope everywhere he went. He was thinking that he'd only hunt down a few remaining orcs and that would be the end of it, but that was not the case. With each city or village they reached, they were just in time to save them from what seemed to be a growing army of orcs. That, however, did not stop Jorn; for every place he saved, his numbers grew. Many of the human cities swore their allegiance for the same reason that the king in the first city did. There were only a few human kings that were truly loyal to Jorn and had faith in him, and they took protecting Jorn very seriously, knowing that he was important to their survival. Unlike most leaders or kings, who would send others to die in their stead, Jorn was the first to fight. He would not sleep until his men were well cared for; this was not a trait of a king of men. This had a powerful effect on his men. His status was elevated even higher when his army saved several elven cities and several dwarf strongholds. The elven and dwarven leaders took these deeds to heart and swore their lives and their armies to Jorn's cause. This made the story of Jorn more powerful when it was spoken thousands of miles away. It seemed as if humanity was given life again, for people flocked in great numbers to join Jorn's cause. More than a hundred a day came to join this great army. Gathering more than a million strong, the greatest army marched upon the earth. Slaves, farmers, soldiers, and even kings all came to fight. Their need for freedom from darkness was a powerful dream, and they all wanted to live it. However, there were occasions when some great leaders desired power and tried to take leadership from Jorn. Even though he was more than eager to give up his position and return to his farm, Jorn had no choice in the matter. All in the army had undivided loyalty to him and would not let even their own sovereigns take the leadership.

After a year of battling what seemed to be a never-ending flood of orc armies, Jorn and his army all gathered in a large plain, just south of what was thought to be the last remnant of the great gardens. In addition, it was not far from what was believed to be the center of the dragons' empire. Since the army had been there for several weeks, the elven and dwarven craftsmen built a nice cabin designed to be the leader's war room, and on this day, it was packed full. All the kings and generals of Jorn's army were in attendance for this meeting. In the middle of this cabin was a fire pit surrounded by stools where all the leaders could eat and discuss their plans. Jorn, however, was in the back corner listening to others talk; even though he called this meeting, he was not eager to speak. The two that were speaking and holding everyone's attention were an elf and a dwarf. Both were considered the highest in command among their own kind and were greatly respected by all who were there. It was rumored that if Jorn were ever to die, both of them would take command of the army. The dwarf king was called Red Helm; he was a big dwarf, standing a little over 4 and a half feet tall. What he was named at birth, no one could recall everyone called him Red Helm because he had dark red hair braided back in the shape of a dwarven helmet. It was rumored that he never washed it so that it would always keep its perfect shape. As for the elven king, he was the complete opposite, reaching over 6 feet tall, having long silver hair, and looking as if nothing was out of place. Everyone called him Ravelle because they couldn't actually pronounce his full elven name; even some of the other elves had trouble pronouncing it. He never disliked the shortening of his name; in fact, he rather preferred it, as if a shorter name gave him more authority. Red Helm and Ravelle were getting the meeting started with the usual banter that everyone had become accustomed to.

"That last battle was intense," Red Helm shouted. "It was so crazy, I almost thought Ravelle might actually get his hands dirty."

"Now remember our deal, Red; if I get dirty, you must take a bath," Ravelle retorted, earning himself a few laughs among the crowd.

"Not on your life, elf boy!" Red Helm snapped as he let out a long belly- shaking laugh. After he stopped laughing, everyone could tell by the look on his face that this was going to be a serious gathering. "All joking aside, that last battle was a lot more than we expected. I'm surprised we didn't lose more men than we did."

"Don't forget we have women soldiers fighting with us too," one of the generals chimed in.

"Shut it! You know what I meant. We should've lost more in that battle. Up until now, our tactics are what have set us apart from our enemy. Sooner or later that's going to change. Hasn't anyone noticed that with every battle, we win; yet their numbers don't diminish. Something doesn't seem right."

"Red is right," Ravelle spoke up.

"You hear that lads, I'm right, so don't forget it," Red Helm shouted back in an attempt to lighten the mood just a little.

Ravelle knowing the need for a good laugh, waited for those who found it funny to quiet back down before he started up again. "Red Helm is right; logically, we should start to see a diminishment of numbers. However, for some reason that has not happened; for every thousand we kill, we see two thousand on the next field of battle.

Something does not feel right about this, as if some great force were against us as if someone were toying with us."

"It's the Deceiver; he's behind this," someone shouted from the crowd.

"That's enough of that," Red Helm shouted. "We want realistic ideas, not rumors and fairy tales! There's no evidence that the Deceiver ever existed! We're fighting real armies, and we need real answers! I'm not going to send my dwarves chasing ghosts!"

"No one said we were going to chase ghosts," Ravelle replied, setting a hand on Red's shoulder to calm him down. "You're right, we need answers, and we need ideas. I have a feeling someone already does. Jorn, you've been hiding in the shadows long enough. Come forward and speak your mind."

Jorn slowly made his way through the crowd to the center of the room. He stood across from his two greatest leaders so he could look them in the face. He knew that out of anyone, he had to convince these two of all the importance and need for his plan. "Friends and fellow leaders," Jorn said loud enough for everyone to hear, but he never took his eyes off Ravelle or Red Helm. "I called this meeting together for this very reason. Most of you are smart enough to know that we're winning battles yet we are not gaining any ground. The more we fight, the more we see that it is not just orcs that we are fighting. The number of orcs has not diminished yet they have swelled their ranks with goblins, trolls, and fell things. I don't know what's controlling them or what's driving them on, but I do know this: it's only a matter of time before they find something big and bad to join their side."

"If you're referring to the rumor about a dragon, that's just it; it is only a rumor," replied the human general that oversees the network of spies. "We haven't been able to verify whether that is true or not. If you ask me, it's no different than the Deceiver; it is nothing, but myths and legends, dragons don't exist."

"I will disagree with you," Ravelle stated. "Dragons do exist; I just haven't seen one in a long time. But that is not the point; what Jorn is getting at is that they are gaining more allies and stronger ones. If we do not follow their example, we will be overrun and outmatched. If we were further south, you might be able to gain a few more Elven armies."

"Forget that," a dwarf king spoke up. "We need more dwarves, filthy, mad, and armed for battle. Any word from Shieldholt?"

"No, King Ronnar believes they can wait out this problem, and they've locked the doors and sealed themselves in the mountain," replied Red Helm. "And the next dwarven city is farther away than the elves; I'm sorry to say we have no more dwarven allies coming."

"So how are we supposed to gain more allies and stronger one?" an elven king asked.

"I've already thought about that," Jorn spoke up quickly, trying to regain the attention back on him. "I've been thinking about this for a long time; I just never wanted to voice my opinion until I had more information. We do need more allies, but not elves and dwarves; I thought if they might have a dragon, we should have one too."

"Are you mad?" one of the human kings snapped. "Dragons are evil beasts; they will destroy us without a second thought!"

"That is not true!" Ravelle shouted, trying to reduce the chatter rolling through the crowd. "Elves remember more than all of you. Yes, occasionally there are bad dragons, no different than there are bad humans. What those dragons do is scar people's memories for hundreds of years, but that does not mean that all dragons are bad. Elven histories tell of dragons that fought for good and that they hid themselves away."

"Ravelle speaks the truth," Red Helm added. "Us dwarves have had more dealings with bad dragons than you humans have ever had. Still, even our histories speak of the time when dragons and dwarves fought together. I do not think that both elven and dwarven histories could be wrong. What concerns me is why they hid themselves away."

"Why is something we will not figure out here; let Jorn continue so we may see what rattles inside his head," Ravelle said.

"Thank you, Ravelle. The truth is, I've been thinking about contacting the dragons for quite some time, which is why I brought the army here to this location."

"So you do believe in the rumors of the Dragon Empire?" Ravelle said, a little surprised by his leader.

"So, you brought us close to a potential enemy without telling any of us," one of the human kings snapped. With that proclamation, the gathering broke into an uproar, with everyone wanting their opinion to be heard.

After a couple of minutes of nonstop yelling, Red Helm had enough. "Shut it!" he shouted above the ruckus, so loud it seemed to shake the building. When everybody quieted down, he continued in his normal tone of voice as if nothing had happened. "Have you all lost faith in Jorn that quickly? When has he ever led us astray? Now, that doesn't mean I like his idea; however, we're running out of options. If the enemy has dragons, we're in a lot more trouble than we think. We're all the way up north, so we might as well strike up a conversation with them if they even exist. So I will hear no more argument on that subject; if you don't like it, there's the door." Red Helm waited a moment to see if anyone would dare walk out the door. Everyone looked around to see if someone would walk out, but no one did. "Good, with that settled, let's move on to the next problem. How in the world are we supposed to contact the dragons?"

Before anyone could answer, Jorn spoke up: "I thought of that as well. I cannot ask anyone to sacrifice themselves for my crazy idea; I will go and speak with them myself."

"No!" Ravelle yelled. "You are the leader of this army; you cannot put yourself in that danger."

"I will not argue this," Jorn shouted. It was not as loud as Red Helm shouted but it had a power of authority behind it. Since Jorn rarely raised his voice, everyone went silent. So Jorn calmly continued his train of thought. "It makes no sense to send anyone else. If dragons are as wise and powerful as Ravelle believes they are, then it is rude to send anyone of lesser authority. I will also not risk the message that I have spent months preparing in the hands of anyone else."

"All right, so you're mad," Red Helm replied. "Where do we go from here? How do you make contact with the dragons? Because I'm pretty sure no one here can speak the dragon language. You might as well walk up and wave your underpants, showing that you crapped yourself in their presence."

"Actually, that's not a bad idea," Ravelle said.

Red Helm slapped his hand on his forehead. "Great, the both of you have gone mad."

"I wasn't referring to his undergarments, Red; I was thinking about a flag. Jorn could carry a flag, and that flag could represent the need to speak to them. We don't need to worry about him being able to understand them; I believe the dragons would be able to understand Jorn fine."

"Ravelle, you're not making me feel any better. What type of flag would represent the need to speak? What color would it be? What symbols would we put on it?"

"I believe the color of the flag should be white," Ravelle continued. "White is a neutral color, and it can represent light or purity. I can also write the old elven rune for friend; the dragons should recognize it. Since Jorn is determined to go by himself, this should be the end of the conversation. We have a lot to prepare for not just supplies for Jorn to take on his journey but also for his absence. It would be no good for the army to fall apart in his absence." With Ravelle's final words, there was a muttering of agreement among the crowd, and they began to disperse and go their own ways.

"I still think you're crazy," Red Helm said as he smacked Jorn on the back. "The moon should be full by the next couple of nights; if you're not back by the next one, I'm taking a group and coming after you."

"Deal," Jorn replied as he shook Red Helm's hand. Then he left the meeting hall to collect his things for his journey.

"I hope you're good at drawing runes; he's going to need all the help and luck on earth to survive this." Red Helm stated as he stood next to Ravelle, both looking at Jorn as he left the building.

"I have a strange feeling that this was meant to be," replied Ravelle almost in a whisper.

It took only a couple of hours for Jorn to pack up all the supplies he needed and for Ravelle to make the white flag with the Elven rune on it. They didn't want to make a big deal of him leaving, so Red Helm, Ravelle, and Jorn met quietly at the North end of the camp. Ravelle handed over an eight-foot pole with the flag on it.

"Now you're sure it says, friend?" Jorn sarcastically asked. "Because I hate to be eaten over a mistake in one word."

"It says, friend, I'm not that bad at writing the old language," Ravelle replied with a smile on his face and a look of worry in his eyes. "Come back to us, friend, in one piece."

"I still think you're both mad," Red Helm added. "I bet you both a drink of ale that this is the last time a white flag is ever used to make a truce. This is what happens when an elf and a human have an idea together. If you die, do I get all your belongings?"

"No, you have to split them with Ravelle."

"I don't like the deal, but I'll take it. Since I'll come after you if you don't come back, it looks like Ravelle gets your stuff and mine."

All three of them chuckled for a moment, enjoying the camaraderie. Then they went silent, acknowledging the seriousness of this moment. The three of them looked at each other and nodded in agreement at what had to be done. With that, Jorn turned and walked away from the camp, leaving his friends to stare after him.

Jorn had never seen a dragon, nor did he want to, but he knew something had to be done. So he summoned every shred of courage he could find and marched toward the dragon city, alone. For days he traveled north, away from the plains. He passed over valleys and hills and soon found himself traveling on rolling mountains. Jorn knew he was getting close to the dragons, when he noticed the condition of the forest that covered the mountains. The trees were great giants; a man couldn't even put his arms around one-fourth of their base, and the undergrowth was so thick that he could barely move. He wondered if even animals could pass; obviously, only creatures that could fly could pass through this forest. For a long time, he pushed through the thick underbrush, wondering if he would ever see the other side. Eventually, he saw an enormous mountain through the trees. Still a long way off, he caught a glimpse of a figure flying around the mountain. Too big to be a bird, he thought.

"I now know where my journey ends," he said, his voice breaking the silence of the forest. He looked back at the forest and then continued to squeeze through the brush. His time was almost out before Red Helm came after him. Tired and weary, he finally reached the doorway to the dragon city. Even at the opening, he felt insignificant against the might of the dragons.

Jorn stared up at an endless mountainside. Even as he was standing at the mountainside on his way to the city, nothing seemed higher than the mountain where the dragons dwelt. Like a tree looming over an ant, there was no mountain on earth that could compare to this one. It was as if the Creator made this mountain for one specific purpose—to shelter the dragons. The mountain was so high that the clouds touched its sides, and the snow would not melt. When Jorn was done being in awe of the size of the mountain, he turned his attention to the doorway, which was a single tunnel leading into the mountainside. The tunnel itself had a sense of greatness to it. It was perfectly rounded, yet it looked natural, as if the Creator made it.

The opening stood twenty times higher than Jorn's height, and as he drew closer, his blood grew cold. On each side of the opening, there stood a black-scaled dragon, standing straight on its hind legs. The dragons were about one-fourth the height of the tunnel. They had in one hand a shield, and in the other a long spear. They both had on a beautiful silver breastplate with rubies and emeralds on it. As Jorn walked closer, he noticed that the pole he was carrying, which held the white flag of truce, was shaking. He gripped the pole harder, trying to steady it. He stopped in front of the dragon guards, equally spaced between the two, standing firm and holding the pole close to him.

To Jorn's surprise, the guards did not do anything to stop him or harm him. He noticed that one of the guards had a look in his eye, like that of a hungry man staring at food that he couldn't eat. So he slowly turned to the other guard and said, "I need to see your leader."

The guard glared down at him and then turned to the tunnel and roared. Jorn stepped back a little, startled by the roar and how it echoed through the tunnel. Shortly after, a dragon roared back through the tunnel, followed by light footsteps.

Jorn saw a small dragon figure emerge from the tunnel. It stood a couple of feet higher than him and had purple scales. The small dragon walked on two legs and had no arms, just wings and claws in the middle of the wings at the joint. The wings were folded tightly behind his back as he stood straight up.

"We have been waiting for you, human," the dragon said arrogantly. "It took you longer to get to us than we expected."

"You were waiting for me?" Jorn replied. "How did you know I was coming?"

"Nothing escapes our eyes in our lands, human! Now come, the king of all dragons wants to see the man foolish enough to set foot here."

"How do you know my language?" Jorn asked, letting more of his confused questions come rolling out.

The dragon let out a chuckle before he answered. "We know all languages, even ones as pathetic as yours. Let me get this straight. You ventured into our territory not even knowing our language or how you could communicate with us. You are a bold one. No wonder the king wants to see you. It's either that, or it's time for his snack."

The dragon quickly gestured to Jorn's flag and asked, "And what is with that ridiculous white flag, is that supposed to mean you surrender to us? Also, whoever tried to write the elven words for friend did it wrong."

"Aaaaah, it's supposed to symbolize a truce," Jorn muttered, a little embarrassed.

With that, the dragon's face took on a sinister smirk, and then he turned and quickly stomped into the tunnel. Jorn laid down his flag and followed, eager to get out from underneath the guards' hungry eyes. Halfway through the tunnel, he stopped and turned back, longing for the sight of his farm. He wondered if anything was ever going to be the same again. He knew there was no turning back now, for a new wind was about to blow that would change the lives of many. Taking a deep breath, he turned and continued into the dragons' domain.

On the other side of the tunnel, his eyes opened with astonishment when he saw the inside of the mountain was hollow. Half of the mountain's interior was a city made of stone, mostly of different colors of red and brown marble. It was almost the full height of the mountain, and as he looked up, he noticed that the tip of the mountain was gone. All that was there was a massive opening that allowed the sunlight to illuminate the inside of the mountain.

As he walked closer to the city, he admired its construction. Some of the buildings, as they went up joined with the mountainside, as if the mountain itself made those dwellings. He couldn't tell if they were natural or made by hand. For several levels, the buildings stayed in the mountain like glorified caves, and then separated again to climb with the rest of the city. However, what he admired the most was not buildings—it was the inhabitants. Unlike human establishments, which consist of mostly the humans' likeness, the dragon city consisted of dragons of different sizes, colors, and breeds. Though very different from one another, they had one thing in common: they all seemed offended to see a human in their domain. So Jorn walked softly and stayed very close to his guide, almost hugging him. When they reached the base of the city, he noticed an odd design of stairs.

The stairs started at the center of the city, went up one level, and then stopped. A long landing went from one side of the city to the other, giving access to different rooms, buildings, and corridors that led deeper within the city.

At opposite ends of the landing, there was a stairway that gave two more access points to the next level. Every level appeared to be the same as the first, a landing that sat on the dwellings below it and provided a great thoroughfare for the buildings behind it. Jorn looked higher to see another stairway in the center of the city again. The pattern continued: one stairway in the middle, and then two stairs, one on either end. For more than forty levels, the pattern did not stop. Jorn thought to himself what it would be like to see the city from a dragon's point of view, flying into the hole at the top of the mountain. In his mind, he could picture the city looking like a big set of stairs, themselves, each landing being one of the steps. Thinking of steps, he brought himself back to focus on the stairs in front of him.

"What a strange stairway," he muttered.

"I will see you at the top, human. And don't stray," Jorn's guide said as he spread his wings and took flight, leaving a cloud of dust around Jorn and laughing as he went. Jorn now understood the meaning of the stairs. Most dragons had no need for stairs, so why have stairs? The dragons needed to give their friends who had no wings access to the metropolis and at the same time, make it hard for invaders to take over the city. Jorn was wondering why the dragon didn't simply fly him to the top.

As he looked around, he noticed the smirks on all the dragons' faces. It became clear to him that he was a form of amusement to them, someone to make climb all the way to the top. He set his left foot on the first step, took a deep breath, and began climbing the dragon city. Unfortunately, each step was like three steps of human stairs, which made climbing the stairs more difficult than it looked. Nevertheless, Jorn was determined to see this through, no matter the cost, although he had a feeling that his legs would disagree with that when he reached the top.

He climbed the stairway as fast as he could, and as he went, he was scrutinized and watched all the way up. It seemed like forever, but Jorn eventually reached the top. He turned to look back at where he had come from, amazed that he made it. As Jorn expected, his legs were sore and though he wanted to rest, the day wasn't over yet.

"Well, it's about time. I was afraid you would never make it," Jorn's purple- scaled guide said. He was leaning against the wall.

"I would have hated to disappoint you," Jorn replied, trying to catch his breath.

"Come along. There is no time to waste." The guide quickly turned with smugness and headed down a great corridor, which stuck out a way from the walls of the city. The passageway had straight walls and a rounded top. Jorn followed slowly, still a little nervous about this encounter. As he passed two massive doors that swung inward, he realized that this corridor was as big as the mountain opening he had walked through earlier. The only difference was that the great passage had carvings on it, up one side and down the other. He noticed that the carvings were of dragons, elves, dwarves, and men, in a design that depicted peaceful coexistence.

Jorn stopped and walked up to the wall, putting his hand on a carving of a man standing in front of a dragon. The man wasn't fighting the dragon but was simply standing with the dragon, overseeing symbols of plants and animals. Jorn ran his fingers across the carvings, feeling the intricate design, filling his face with a smile. He did not understand it; however, it gave him hope that dragons and men could live in peace. The longer he looked at the carvings on the wall, the more intrigued he became. The carvings seemed to be moving, as though they were infused with life or some form of magic that reached out to him. The only thing that would come to his mind was a sense of loss: how much had mankind missed out on by separating themselves from other races?

Before he could think of anything else, his guide hissed at him, so he turned and quickened his pace. He also began to notice that not only was the city wide, but it was deep within the mountain, and that there must be thousands of dwellings. As they reached the other end of the corridor, Jorn saw two more guards. The guards had the same armor as the ones outside; the only difference was that these ones had shiny green scales. The doors on this side were shut, so Jorn assumed that this room must be important. The massive doors were made of a reddish and green stone that had dragons carved on them.

"Open it," his guide said.

The guards turned and pushed on the doors, making them creak as they opened to reveal a massive room. Jorn followed his guide in. Shortly after, he recognized it to be a throne room, with a beautiful white marble floor and a black onyx ceiling. There were four guards in the throne room. Like the other guards, they had the same armor, but these ones were red-scaled. Two of the guards were on the other side of the throne room doors. Jorn stopped in the middle and looked to his right, to see the other two guards. This was a sight that confused him. He saw the guards in front of a single room that had a magical wall blocking it. The wall was more like a mist or silk that covered the entrance. As he peered through the mist, he saw the only thing occupying the room—a sword stood in the middle on a nicely carved stone. The sword was not in the stone; its tip just touched the stone.

On its own, the sword was standing there untouched, with nothing holding it up. There were strange markings on the blade, a language Jorn did not recognize. The writing seemed to appear and disappear as he looked at it. The hilt had an odd design—it was of a man and a woman standing back- to-back. Their arms were to their sides, and they had wings like bird wings that were spread out, shaping the cross-guard. However, the sword was not as big as it would be if it was made for dragons; rather, it looked more like it had been made for humans. Still, it had an ominous power about it that seemed as though humans could not wield it. Even though he was standing very far away, Jorn could tell it had otherworldly powers, as though it had a destiny of its own that could not be controlled by any mortal.

Trying not to look nosy, Jorn turned his attention back to the front of the room, where a single throne was sitting. The throne itself had a mystery that also confused Jorn. The throne was large enough to seat a dragon. It even had a special design on the back of the throne to accommodate what Jorn believed was a tale. It was the back rest that was a mystery. It was beautifully carved from silver and gold. The carving was of a man standing with a dragon behind him; the man was faceless. Jorn could not help but stand there with his mouth gaping in awe over everything that he had seen.

"Beautiful, is it not? You will see nothing like it anywhere else," a deep voice called from a corridor to the left.

Jorn turned to see who was speaking to him. To his amazement, he saw a large black-scaled dragon enter the room, towering at well above thirty feet. Walking on all fours, and with his wings wrapped around his back, the dragon seemed overpowering. He had two horns curving to the side and slightly to the back of his head, and they looked as though they were pearls. Jorn realized right away that this was the king, for all the other dragons bowed immediately as he entered the room, although he did not have a crown, breastplate, or jewelry that would single him out from the others. The dragon walked slowly and graciously over to the throne, unfolding his wings and wrapping his tail up behind his back, and sat on the throne. Even though some dragons could sit, Jorn could tell that this one did not fancy it because of his tail, even with the throne's added tail design.

"My name is Larzencarak," the mighty dragon said. "And who might you be, one so foolish to set foot here?"

"Forgive me, oh mighty Larzencarak," Jorn replied quickly as he respectfully bowed his head. He then took a moment to gather his wits, trying not to seem terrified even though he was. "I am called Jorn, and I have come here in search of your help. I'm sorry if my presence offends you."

"It does offend me, oh foolish Jorn! There has not been a human in these halls for a very long time! And why do the humans need our help?" Larzencarak leaned forward and glared down at Jorn. He then let a puff of smoke out of his nostrils to indicate his disgust with a human presence.

Jorn had taken months to prepare an elegant speech, but now in the actual presence of dragons, he couldn't recall any of his prepared words. Instead of trying to drag up his speech, he decided to go with his feelings and say whatever came to his mind. Later, when he looked back upon this day, he realized it wasn't the smartest decision, but it probably saved his life. "I am sure that you are aware of the evil that infests this earth," Jorn said as he took a few steps closer to the throne, even though his heart was beating fast. "My friends and I have done all that we can to stop it. However, there are still a great many things that are more powerful than us. Dragons are one of them, and surely you must know that some dragons have turned to the darkness. And we cannot hope to defeat them without you."

"So you hold us accountable for the darkness!" Larzencarak shouted.

"No, I do not hold you accountable. You cannot control every dragon's choice, just as I cannot control every human's choice. I am simply asking for your help to fight against the darkness." Jorn was now staring Larzencarak eye-to-eye, unwilling to back down, though the thought of being eaten by a dragon did not sit well in his stomach.

"So you want us to fight your battles for you, kill our own kind, and risk our lives for you. That is a bold thing to ask, human. You are, indeed, foolish. What you ask is impossible. I will never agree to such a thing," Larzencarak replied as he leaned down even farther, bringing his nose right to Jorn's face. But Jorn stood firm, even as Larzencarak breathed out through his nostrils, sending a disgusting and foul air through Jorn's hair.

"Larzencarak, is that the way we present ourselves to guests? You should know better." Another voice came from the corridor to the left.

Jorn turned to see another dragon emerge into the room. This one was unlike anything he had ever seen before. Its gray scales seemed almost as wrinkled as an old man's skin, and its color seemed faded. He had tentacles that came down from his chin like a beard, and he didn't have any horns. The dragon had only its front arms and no legs; his tail was long and dragged behind him like a snake. He did have wings, however, they seemed weak and broken; there were even a few holes through the skin of the wings. The dragon walked with his front arms and hands and looked like someone crawling through a room. Even though he walked on his hands, this gray-scaled dragon was nearly the same height as Larzencarak. Jorn realized that this dragon was very old, and from the looks on the faces of the dragons in the room, he was highly respected. Even though Jorn did not know the dragon, he too felt respect for him from the mere look of his body and sound of his voice.

As he came closer, Jorn's purple guide bowed very low and softly whispered, "Hello, Ancient."

The old dragon nodded in response and kept walking closer to the throne.

"Ærlonosanis, I have not invited you to join in this conversation with the human," Larzencarak responded, very agitated.

"Come, come now; since when have I ever listened to you?" the old dragon replied, letting out a small chuckle. "Don't forget that it was I who helped raise you."

"I have not forgotten that because you never let me forget it. Out of all the dragons, you're the only one who contradicts everything I say!"

"I do not, and besides, king or not, someone must balance you out, and who better than me." The old dragon chuckled again as he wrapped his tail up underneath him to perch himself up to sit next to the throne. "So who do we have here," he said as he patted Jorn on the back. "I am so old that only two remember my name. You can call me Ancient. For last time I looked, that's what I am."

"I am Jorn, Mighty Ancient," he replied respectfully as he bowed.

"My Jorn, mighty I am not. Just old. But thank you for the compliment," Ancient said, a huge grin on his face. "I see that you have already upset the king today. I give you credit for that."

"Ærlonosanis, this is a serious matter," Larzencarak yelled as he slammed his fist against the throne's armrest, clearly upset about being left out of a conversation that he started.

"Yes, it is a serious matter, and I think you should start treating it like one," Ancient snapped back at him. "This man's proposal does hold some weight, and you should at least think about it first before discarding it as a bad idea."

"I do not care if you liked his proposal. It is still my choice!"

Crossing his arms and leaning back, Ancient softly remarked, "Remember the mistakes of your mother, Larzencarak. I ask you not to make the same mistakes as she did."

Larzencarak stood up from his throne, angry at Ancient. "You are not to speak of my mother in the presence of an outsider!"

"You're right, Father," a third voice called from the left passageway.

Jorn quickly turned to see what else was coming through into the room. The voice was that of a female's, possibly a human, so he was eager to see who or what it was. He looked deep into the corridor until he saw the beginnings of a shape. At first, the shape was dark, and then it began to sparkle. For a while, he thought his eyes were playing tricks on him, and then he realized what he was seeing—a female dragon as large as Larzencarak; however, her scales were a ruby red, and they were so shiny that they reflected even the smallest shimmer of light. She was fit and strong, and her body seemed perfectly designed. She had a medium snout and twin pearl-colored horns at the back of her head, each horn had a golden band wrapped midway up. She walked gracefully, with her wings lifted just a bit off her back as if she was ready to fly. Green eyes sparkling like emeralds, she watched everyone as she entered the room.

She walked up to Jorn and sat on her hind legs. She looked down at him with a smile that filled her face. "We should leave Grandmother out of this," she began to say. "However, it does not mean that we should isolate any chance we have to make an alliance with humans. I have always known you to be grumpy, but never foolish. Wasn't it you who taught me that it was better to have more friends than enemies, especially in dark times like these?"

"I can't believe this! First, Ancient, and now my daughter disagrees with me," Larzencarak said as he sat back on the throne. "I am getting too old for this."

"Not old enough, my young friend," Ancient replied as he once again gave a small chuckle.

"Come, human, let the old ones speak by themselves, and I will show you the city," the female dragon remarked when she noticed that Jorn had not taken his eyes off her. "Do I offend you, human?" she asked, staring back at him.

"No, not at all. You're very beautiful—for a dragon, that is. Forgive me if my lingering eyes upset you." He took a couple of steps forward, his gaze not leaving her face. Taking a deeper look into her eyes, he said, "I have never seen dragons before this day, and out of all the marvels that I have seen, you are more overwhelming than anything else here," he remarked, bowing his head yet keeping his eyes on her.

"Careful, human, with the way you talk to my daughter," Larzencarak quickly said, glaring at Jorn.

"Oh, Father, calm down. It has been a while since I've received such a compliment. And for a human, it is rare to say such things as he did. He must hold me higher than the females of his own race. To me, that is a compliment I must take with honor and pride." She lowered her face down to Jorn's so she could see him eye-to-eye. "Thank you," she said. "I am known as Kirianadréth. And what might your name be?" she asked, grinning and showing her glittering, sharp white teeth.

Jorn looked at her and smiled. "I am called Jorn, Your Highness."

"Well, Jorn, let us go see the city together. There's plenty of time for you and Father to talk later." She rose and pointed to the passage she came from. "Furthermore, I would be honored to show you my home." Kirianadréth turned and began to walk back through the corridor, and Jorn followed without question, pausing only slightly to give a small bow toward Larzencarak and Ancient.

Larzencarak rose quickly from his throne, but Ancient grabbed his arm. "Let them go, Larzencarak. I believe she is safe enough. Besides, we must talk. There is much to discuss."

"There is nothing more to discuss, old friend!" Larzencarak muttered as he sat back down on the throne, eventually letting out an audible sigh.

"What is wrong, my king?" Ancient asked, holding back a grin. He had known Larzencarak too long to be fooled by anything the king did. Ancient knew the king was disturbed about something and that he was trying to hide it even though he was hiding it very poorly.

"I never thought a human would ever walk into my kingdom," Larzencarak stated, sounding ever so depressed. "Let alone walk out, following my only daughter."

"My king, there is more on your mind than your daughter and a human. You were never really good at hiding things from me, especially when they matter." The grin that Ancient had on his face faded when he turned his attention to a more solemn topic. "My old friend, that human's words did not fail to get your attention. You understood them and the weight within them. You yourself cannot ignore the truth when it stands in front of you. Larzencarak, we ourselves have tried to get rid of the darkness. However, with each passing generation, more have seemed to turn to hatred. This is not how we were created or what we were meant to be. You know that, and you also know that there has been too much bloodshed among our races. Perhaps your daughter is right. We could gain a lot by working with humans. The way I see it is that we have more to gain than we do to lose."

"I don't know," Larzencarak said as he turned away from Ancient, his face rippling with anguish as he thought about the choices before him. "There's a lot of hatred among our races. If we could unite, would it be worth it? The humans are so much like animals, unable to have any control."

"And the dragons who fight for the darkness are they any different?" Ancient's remark made Larzencarak turn back around to stare him in the face. "There are good humans and bad humans, just like every other creature on this earth. We must give them a chance for redemption. Please, Larzencarak, I have seen many things in my life, but never this. Let us choose something different."

Ancient waited a moment for Larzencarak's response. When he got nothing but silence, he changed his argument. "Look at it this way, my king: you have always had disdain for dragons that disobey the Creator. You have said to me many times that you are troubled by the dragons on the other side of the world—the ones who no longer remember that there is a Creator or that they have a king and merely act like animals. Did you not say that you wished you could do something about them?" Ancient paused a moment, straightening up and strengthening his tone of voice for the seriousness of what he meant to say next. "Well, what of the dragons on this side of the world? What of the dragons that you can do something about? Are you not the king? Are they not your responsibility? Do you not remember that even your sons have been banished for dark deeds and only your daughter remains loyal? Be angry with me if you wish, but these are matters you must answer to, sooner or later."

"Very well," Larzencarak hesitated to say as he stood up from his throne. "If you want an answer, then here it is: I will make the alliance with the humans. I will tend to my duties as a king and deal with my subjects who disobey the Creator. We will see how this goes. Just to let you know, I don't like where this is going. Something does not seem right, from the scouts that we sent out, have come reports of too many gatherings. This is more than just a simple local war; it seems like a flood or a tidal wave. If I'm right," Larzencarak said firmly leaving no room for discussion, "there will be a bloody war against good and evil, and we may not make it out the other side. You told my mother thousands of years ago that the Great War wasn't over, and no one believed you even when the great elven city of Lithlothrim disappeared. I look back and realize how foolish we were because it looks like you were right."

"You believed me, and you did what I told you to. Back then, it did not look like it would help us much, but now it makes a difference. Do you still know where all the messenger dragons are?"

"Yes, Ancient, I do; however, there are only twelve still alive. I'm not sure how much that will help us."

"It will help us more than you know; call them in. Let us start gathering our army."

Larzencarak let out an ominous sigh. "I think we're too late; we should have prepared long ago."

"I know, Larzencarak, I know. But we must do this for the sake of our inheritors. The Great War never ended; it would be good to finish it once and for all. Also, it would be nice to see it finished for the ones we love." Upon those words, they both looked off to the corridor, where Kirianadréth was leading Jorn off to see the city.

***

Kirianadréth and Jorn walked through many halls, all of them beautiful and inspiring to Jorn. Kirianadréth couldn't keep quiet and spoke to him on many subjects. She was like an excited child, wanting to tell him everything she knew. She divulged as much as she knew about the Creator and the dragons. Jorn acted in a similar way to Kirianadréth; he had a new liveliness to his step as if his eyes had just been opened and he was seeing everything for the first time. He was absorbing everything like a sponge—everything he heard, saw, and felt. Of course, he was grinning from ear to ear, and that only made Kirianadréth grin herself. Jorn couldn't stop his mind from racing with thoughts about what good things would come out of this alliance.

They eventually reached a balcony overlooking the entire city, and Jorn stared down in amazement. The city was in a bustle; dragons were walking or flying in and out. They were on every level of the city, like ants on the side of a hill. Kirianadréth walked up next to Jorn and looked down at the city herself. "This is one of my favorite places to go. Beautiful, isn't it?"

"Yes, it is very beautiful," Jorn replied, still amazed at what he was seeing. After a while, he walked closer to the ledge. He sat down and draped his legs over the edge.

Kirianadréth came up beside him and lay down, looking over the ledge with him. "You aren't scared of much, are you?" she asked.

"Besides the darkness that has covered the earth, not much."

Upon his response, Kirianadréth nudged his back with the tip of her tail. Losing his balance, Jorn quickly put his hands on the ledge to keep himself from falling off. He turned to look at her and saw a big grin on her face as she began to laugh. He rolled his eyes and glared back out at the city. He couldn't help but laugh himself.

When Kirianadréth finished laughing, she let out a small sigh and then began to make a few remarks. "I love my home so much I would hate to see anything happen to it. I always fear that the evil in this world would destroy it. So I'm always looking for new hope to cling to." She looked up through the hole in the mountain up at the sky.

Jorn looked up at her, wanting to say something that could comfort her. "I believe our two races can do great things together, even stop the evil," he said confidently. "That is, if your father agrees to help."

"He will. Ancient always has a way of talking him into almost anything," Kirianadréth said with a smirk, remembering all the times she sent Ancient to talk to her father about something she wanted, which she usually got, because of Ancient.

"I sure hope so. The humans could sure use your help," Jorn replied, keeping his voice sounding as positive as he could.

"We could use your help as well, Jorn."

As soon as Kirianadréth made that remark, Jorn realized that her tail was no longer close to her. It was now lying on the other side of him, barely brushing his leg. However, this did not bother him. He felt safe and secure. For once in both their lives, they felt a sense of peace. They continued to stare down at the city for hours, as if there was no evil lurking around. No words were exchanged between the both of them; there was just peace—a feeling that both of them had not felt in a long time— and they wanted it to last.

The End of the Great War

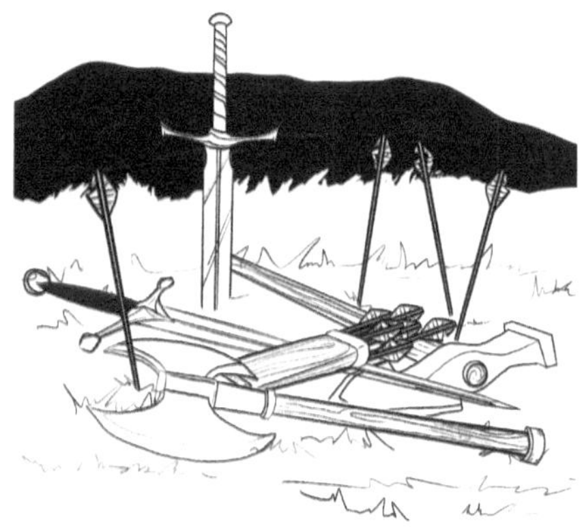

So the war started again. It was different from the first part of the Great War, the war that followed after the fall of man. This war had a sense of hope to it, that there might be a new beginning on the other side of it, with the unity between the two races. However, that hope was challenged greatly.

Technically, the Great War never ended. It merely went dormant, giving everyone, including evil, time to regroup. Jorn and Larzencarak joined their armies as quickly as they could. With every day that passed, more and more came to join their great army. Both leaders constantly worried over, whether the two sides would get along. Despite a few fights, ugly glances, and some unkind words, the army seemed as if it would hold.

Though Jorn and Larzencarak had the numbers and unity of their army, something began to worry them. News of their army spread not only to good but to evil as well. They thought that this would discourage the armies of darkness, but it did not have that effect. It had been known that some good races had joined together for a common enemy. Almost never did evil races join against a common enemy, and if they did, the alliance did not last long. But this time, it seemed as though the impossible had happened: the armies of darkness united and readied themselves for this war. This knowledge vexed Jorn and Larzencarak, for they did not know what united them or who led them. It was rumored that the Deceiver had resurfaced and taken command of the Dark Army, but that rumor was never verified. The lack of knowledge made them more determined to see their victory in this war, but it still made them uneasy.

They did not wait for the darkness to come to them; they marched forth upon the earth. At first, they were met with little resistance. But the farther they went from their homeland, the more they began to see the difficulty of the war. What they had hoped would last a few months dragged out for longer than five years. Even with their vast numbers, it seemed as though the war would never end, almost as if the earth itself betrayed them. So on the eve of the dragon's New Year, sometime before winter faded, all the high leaders in the Army of Light met in the war council room in the heart of the dragon city.

The room was massive, round, with one entrance and an enormous table in the middle, with maps sprawled out all over it. Daggers held the corners of the maps down to the table, corner to corner, like a puzzle. For no map was the same; they looked like a broken picture. The first column of maps was four straight up; second column to the right was only the top three. The final column was only one map, second from the top. Even though the maps were large for humans and average size for dragons, they were overwhelming nonetheless.

Each map by itself covered thousands of leagues within its descriptions, for they were created from the point of view of a dragon in the sky. The leaders of the army were staring at these maps, deciding the fate of the earth. The war council contained three dragons, four humans, two dwarves, and two elves—Larzencarak, Kirianadréth, Ancient, Jorn, and three of Jorn's captains. Also, the two dwarf kings Ronnar and Red Helm as well as the two elf kings Ravelle and Sinon. Since the table holding the maps was a dragon's table, everyone besides the dragons was standing on the table as they look at the maps.

"We eliminated the threat in this area," Jorn remarked as he pointed to the middle map of the second column. "The mountains gave them good cover and great defense; however, thanks to the dragons, they couldn't hold the defense. After three days, we pressed through to the other side, and now the mountain territory is all ours. However! The farther south or east we go, the armies against us keep getting stronger and more organized." Jorn pointed to the unknown areas on the table, where there were no maps. As the leader of his army, Jorn always spoke confidently to inspire the people around him. But what only Kirianadréth, Larzencarak, Ancient, and of course he himself knew was that they were overwhelmed by the amount of ground they were fighting over and desperately trying to keep out of their enemy's hands. His greatest concern was that they were spread too thin over the land.

"No!" Larzencarak yelled as he slammed one of his massive fists onto the table and whipped his tail. He shared Jorn's concerns, and their strong opposition did not help the matter.

"Calm yourself, Father," Kirianadréth replied. "Now is not the time for anger. We have more important things to do."

"I'm not angry. I am disappointed! Just for once, I would like to receive good news." Larzencarak took his fist off the table and placed it on his forehead. He turned away and began to stare at the wall. "Besides, there is something wrong here. I can feel it."

"What, do you mean, my king?" Ancient asked as he leaned against the table for support. It seemed as though he too was exhausted from the war and weary of its mysteries.

"Evil is not easily ruled," Larzencarak answered. "Whatever is leading them has done the impossible."

"I don't understand," said Red Helm, looking utterly perplexed.

"Evil is void of order. It has no control," Larzencarak said as he turned back around to face the council. "We have gone too far. Look at these maps. The dragons of my kingdom have traveled through half of these lands. Even as a young dragon, I traveled to some of them, and what I learned is that they are vast. I even spoke to dragons in this land." Larzencarak leaned back over the table and pointed to the bottom map of the first column. "The dragons barely knew who I was, let alone spoke in my own tongue. The farther away we go from our homeland, the more the customs and languages change. So if we cannot understand the languages of others, how can the armies of darkness?"

Before the others could respond, Larzencarak continued, turning back around and walking away from the table again, his mind a whirl of thoughts. "Whatever is leading them must have great powers to control armies of different races and languages. He or it must've traveled through our lands and other lands for thousands of years. No wonder their armies keep getting bigger. We gather from only our lands. When we lose good warriors, we have nothing to replace them with. Whatever this darkness is can replenish its ranks by traveling to a new land. We need to find a way to back them into a corner!"

"Fear has no language," Ancient spoke quickly. "Whatever it is, it must be using fear to drive these armies to fight us."

"It must be the Deceiver," one of the human captains shouted, sounding certain and a little scared.

"That has not been proven," Larzencarak replied sharply. Though he thought it himself, he was not willing to spread fear through the army. "We are discussing facts here."

"All right. So what do we do?" asked Jorn, becoming a little frustrated himself.

"We need more knowledge of the lands that we are going to be fighting in," Larzencarak said. "I have sent five dragons, each with a human, to seek out maps or any knowledge of the lands we're going to be moving into. They went out three weeks ago. I should be getting some news back soon, I hope."

Before anyone could say anything, another voice cut in. "Sooner than you think, my king!"

Everyone turned quickly to see Marahezron enter the room. He was Larzencarak's strongest warrior, leader of his armies, and loyalist subject, besides Ancient. Raised alongside Kirianadréth, Marahezron was usually in Larzencarak's presence before eventually taking his father's place as the head general of the dragon armies. Marahezron was the same size as Larzencarak. He had dark black scales on his back and shiny silver scales on his chest and belly. Marahezron was well built; you could see the muscles in every inch of his body. There were four silver horns on his head, one on each side and two on the top. Like a crown, they stood straight out.

Walking proudly, he showed that he was a warrior; even his tail was strong. It was always lifted, and never once did it touch the ground. The tip of his tail, when flexed, flattened itself and released four razor-sharp, curved spikes like ax blades on the sides. He had a rough expression, and if you did not know his loyalty to the Creator and his king, you would think him evil. Marahezron walked up to the table and set two new maps down. Taking some extra daggers that were on the table, he quickly plunged them into the corners of the maps. The maps were placed in the third column to the right, directly under the existing maps. "My king," Marahezron said. "I bring news—the location of the armies and where they will march."

"That is good news, but only two maps? Did I not send five dragons and five humans?" Larzencarak asked as he leaned over the table to look at the maps.

"Forgive me, my king," Marahezron replied. "Only one dragon has returned, and his human that rode with him may not survive the night. The others are rumored to be dead." He turned to Jorn and remarked, "I'm sorry, human. They were brave men."

"This is not the news I was hoping for," Larzencarak said, lowering his head in disappointment.

"It gets worse, my king." Marahezron pointed to the bottom map he had brought in. "Darkness has amassed an army in this territory—as great as our army, if not greater. They will march north." He pointed to the other map. "Then they will head to the mountains."

Larzencarak turned away from the table. "How are we to fight this darkness that never ends," he said, a feeling of hopelessness in his voice. The despair in his heart was worse; he felt as though everything was lost. "How could the Creator let the last five years count for nothing?"

Jorn walked toward Larzencarak and stood at the edge of the table, seeing this proud king seem so defeated. "We can win this," he encouraged the king, unwilling to let himself become discouraged.

"I suppose you have some revelation that will save us," Larzencarak sarcastically remarked.

"I do, my king," Marahezron interrupted. He pointed to the top of the new map and remarked, "This land is dead. A hard, dry earth covered with nothing but stones, as far as the eye can see."

"How will that help us?" Larzencarak sharply asked Marahezron, his mood not improving. It would take a lot more than hard, dry earth to make his day better.

"Let us meet them there, out in the open, so they can't hide anything. It might even the odds a bit, and if things go bad for us, we can retreat to the mountains that border that land. We can surprise them with a bold move if they follow us. They do not even know that the mountain passes have been taken by us." By the conviction in his voice, all knew that Marahezron believed his plan would not fail.

Larzencarak thought for a moment, and then let out a sigh as he leaned against the table. "We will be risking much," he said heavily. "We don't know what we will be up against."

"I know, my king. However, I believe we may not have a choice," Marahezron replied strongly. "Sooner or later, their armies will come to us, and we will have to meet them. It is better to fight them prepared and on our terms."

Ancient moved slowly around the table, stood next to Larzencarak, and put his hand on the king's shoulder. "As much as Marahezron and I like to disagree, for once, his words might have some wisdom."

Upon that remark, Marahezron glared at Ancient as though he had something to say in return.

Larzencarak put his hand on his scaly chin and thought for a moment. "If no one disagrees," he began to say, "we will move our armies, and with luck, we will prevail." A moment of silence passed, and Larzencarak looked at Jorn to see if he had anything to say.

Recognizing the look on Larzencarak's face, Jorn did not hesitate to speak. "I am with you to the end, my friend." The words came easily to his lips, but it made him think back to the first meeting with the king and how far they had come together.

With Jorn's words, Larzencarak smiled and turned to the others. "Then let us move our armies," he stated and then he moved to the door. The only one who did not move with Larzencarak was Kirianadréth. She stood still with a grin on her face, for it had been a long time since she had seen a smile on her father's face. It gave her comfort and some joy to know that it was a human who made him smile again.

A little while later, Larzencarak and Ancient were together in the king's chambers, and the mood surrounding them was heavy and dark. "Tell me you feel it Ancient," Larzencarak asked.

"Feel what my king," Ancient replied honestly, not wanting to have this conversation.

"Don't play the fool with me. You feel the pull of power. There's going to be a shift, isn't there?" Larzencarak waited a moment to see what Ancient might answer. When he did not answer, Larzencarak continued his train of thought. "It is rumored that whenever the world goes through a great change, a massive amount of power is pulled and moved. It is said that it is the Creator putting his plans in effect to stop the Deceiver. Others say it is when the Deceiver and the Creator fight over control of this world. Whether true or not, I know something is coming."

"You are right, my friend," Ancient replied with a sound of awe in his voice. "When change comes to this earth, there is a power in the air, and only the most powerful of magic users can sense it. I am one of them, and there are a few others. If you can feel this power, then that could only mean one thing,"

"Do not speak of it," Larzencarak snapped. "For now, keep this between us."

"As you wish, old friend, but this changes much."

"I know, when the time is right, I will tell one other."

***

It did not take long to move the armies, especially with the assistance of the dragons. Within twenty days, they had assembled on the other side of the mountains. The mountain chain was like a wall that went up to the heavens. In one location, it was split apart, as though something had driven a wedge through the mountains, revealing a single pass. They were so far from their own lands that they did not know what to call these mountains. However, the armies did not care. All they could do was stare at the dry, rocky desert on the other side, for tomorrow this was where they would meet the armies of darkness. As for now, they were camped at the foot of the mountains, with tension high among them. Most of the warriors stayed awake throughout the night, readying themselves for battle.

The ones that would sleep were in their tents. There was only one tent that was well lit late at night. In the middle of the encampment was an enormous tent, bigger than all the rest. This tent was not made for humans. Inside, Larzencarak, Marahezron, and Ancient were looking over a map of the area, and discussing tomorrow's plans.

"I have separated the armies into three groups," Marahezron said, pointing to the map. "Originally, I had planned for our army to attack the enemy directly. But now after seeing the field that we are to fight on, my plans have changed. For some strange and unknown reason, the desert forms a mist in the morning, which is gone by midday, but it will last long enough for my plans to work. One group on the left of the desert, one on the right, and one small group to guard the mountain pass. Since there is only one way through the mountain, there is no need to guard it heavily. We only need to use it for an escape if it ever comes to that. However, it will do us no good if they have more dragons than orcs." Marahezron looked at Larzencarak and then at Ancient, showing his concerns, and then continued, "The dark armies do not know that we have taken the mountain and that we are here. The element of surprise will be ours. When they reach the mountain, we will charge in from both sides hidden in the mist. They may have superior number, but I believe that with the element of surprise, we can even the odds."

"I may not like what we are up against; however, things could be worse," Larzencarak remarked. He walked across the tent to a wooden chair made for dragons and sat down. "Very well, prepare everything for tomorrow and bring me Jorn. Make sure he is by himself; this is a private conversation."

"He has been spending more time with Kirianadréth lately," Ancient added. "It is good to see her smile again, old friend."

"I don't see why you would let that human so close to your daughter, my king," Marahezron said, a little aggravated. He, of course, took careful consideration to hide his own feelings for Kirianadréth, away from the others.

"It is none of your business, Marahezron," Larzencarak snapped. "Just bring him to me."

"Dead or alive?" Marahezron remarked.

Larzencarak quickly glared at him and growled in response.

"Sorry, my king. I just had to ask," Marahezron justified himself and then turned and hurriedly left the tent to find Jorn.

Ancient spoke up. "You didn't answer his question. Why do you let them spend so much time together?"

"It is none of your business either, old friend," Larzencarak replied.

Ancient chuckled for a moment and then stated, "you were always better than your mother; that's why I like you." Then without another word spoken between them; Ancient left the tent so Larzencarak could speak to Jorn alone.

***

Across the camp, Jorn and Kirianadréth sat staring at the stars as they reminisced of old times. Kirianadréth's tail was wrapped around Jorn's back and brushed against his side.

"My sister was always the fighter in the family," Jorn was saying. "She left when I was young to fight in distant battles. She always wanted a name for herself, a name that people would remember. I was hoping, as great as this war is, that she would come back from wherever she is to fight in it. Every day I wake up thinking this might be the day that I can see her again."

"You will," Kirianadréth replied as she pulled her tail in closer and put her hand on his back. "If she is anything like you, you will see her again."

Jorn smiled at those words and leaned closer to her. In the years that they fought beside one another in battle, they had become almost inseparable. Their hearts came closer together, and they relied on each other's words to see them through this darkness.

"Jorn!" someone yelled behind them. They quickly turned to see Marahezron standing there, glaring hatefully at Jorn. "Larzencarak wants to see you," he snapped, giving no other greeting or well wishes.

"Very well," Jorn answered as he got up, unwilling to upset Marahezron. He had known Marahezron for years, and he had hoped that they would come to an understanding, as he had with Larzencarak. However, time seemed to have made things worse between them. If it were not for Larzencarak, Jorn was certain that Marahezron would have gotten rid of him long ago. He had a strange feeling that it had something to do with Kirianadréth, but he wasn't quite sure what it was.

"I will go with you, Jorn," Kirianadréth added as she got up and turned to follow them.

"No," Marahezron quickly replied. "Your father asked for only Jorn."

"Since when have I listened to you or my father?" she answered, growling at Marahezron.

"You will listen today, and I will make sure you do!" As he said those words, Marahezron stepped forward, showing his teeth, and glared at her.

Kirianadréth also stepped forward, preparing to fight. Jorn put his hand on her forearm, softly patting her shiny scales, and said, "I will be all right, Kirianadréth. Wait for me here, please." She looked down at him, glancing for a moment into his eyes. Then she backed up and sat down quietly. She was stubborn, but lately, Jorn had been able to talk her out of any bad mood.

"Good," Marahezron said as he too backed up. "Come, Jorn. The king is waiting." Marahezron turned and started walking back to the king's tent.

Jorn looked back at Kirianadréth and said, "I will be right back, I promise." Then he hurried to catch up with Marahezron.

As they walked through the encampment, Jorn noticed that Marahezron had a foul look on his face. "You have a problem with me, don't you?" he asked. For a moment, he was shocked that he would ask such a question, knowing the answer would be nothing pleasant.

"I thought that would be obvious, human," said Marahezron, puffing a black smoke out of his nostrils.

"Why, I have done nothing against you," Jorn asked. He was also confused at himself, wondering why he was continuing this conversation and why it mattered to him what Marahezron thought.

"You are human, and that is bad enough," Marahezron started. "Larzencarak should have killed you rather than sided with you."

"I'm sorry you feel that way," Jorn replied, knowing there was more to it than that.

"I'm not," Marahezron quickly responded. "You humans are not much better than dogs. You shouldn't even have the right to speak to Kirianadréth. You just talking with her is an insult to dragons."

"I didn't know you cared for her that much," Jorn said, wanting to see Marahezron's response and curious to see whether his intuition on the situation was correct.

"I care more than you know," Marahezron said, staring down at Jorn. "Sometimes I just question whether I'm on the right side or not."

"That's funny," Jorn said. "I never thought of you as a traitor." The moment the words were out of his mouth, he knew it was a mistake.

Suddenly Marahezron turned and grabbed him by the throat. His massive fingers easily wrapped around Jorn; it would have taken no effort for him to squeeze the life out of Jorn. "Listen, human," Marahezron snapped, "my thoughts, my emotions, and my life are my business." He pointed to Larzencarak's tent. "There is the king's tent, so go! I have things to do. Hopefully, he sees you for what you are and gets rid of you!"

Jorn pulled on Marahezron's fingers, gasping for air. "And what am I?" he gasped.

"You're human," Marahezron answered with disgust as he let Jorn go and then stomped away, almost knocking Jorn over with his tail. Jorn put his hand to his throat and rubbed it as he tried to take a deep breath. Jorn had thought that Marahezron disliked him, but now he realized that it was more a case of simple jealousy and pride.

Jorn walked in to Larzencarak's tent and found the dragon king sitting in his chair with his hand on his head, thinking. "You asked to see me," Jorn said respectfully. Of course, he said nothing of what Marahezron had just done; he did not want to trouble Larzencarak more than he already was.

"Yes, Jorn. Come in and have a seat. We need to talk." Larzencarak waited until Jorn had come all the way in and had sat down in a human's chair not far from him. "Well, Jorn, I have asked you here because I want to talk about you and my daughter."

"Not you too," Jorn said defensively, quickly getting up from his chair. "First, Marahezron, and now you. Why do people care that we spend time together!"

"Let me finish," Larzencarak jumped in. "I care, however, not for the same reason as Marahezron. What I'm going to tell you I have never told anyone before, except Ancient, but he doesn't matter."

Jorn sat back in his chair, now curious about what Larzencarak needed to say. "When I look at you and my daughter, I am reminded of myself. You see, when I was young, I had what some would call a pet. She was a human, and she was more than a pet to me. I called her friend and friend she was. You might say that I loved her." Larzencarak stopped for a moment to think of his fond memories of her, his face filling with such a joyous expression.

"So what happened to her?" Jorn asked to keep the conversation going.

"Well," Larzencarak continued, "my mother was a hardhearted ruler. When she found out about my feelings for the woman, she told me to get rid of her. And when I couldn't, my mother had the woman killed. The Creator punished her greatly, nothing ever seems to go right for my mother from that time on. Still, I never forgave my mother; and that day, my heart also became hard." Larzencarak paused for a moment, absorbing his own words as though he didn't want to believe them.

"I'm sorry to hear that," Jorn said with deep sympathy. "But, my king, what does that have to do with your daughter and me?"

"I see the way you two are together, and I know that you will take good care of her," Larzencarak replied.

"Why should I need to take care of her?" Jorn asked, curious about where Larzencarak was taking this conversation.

Larzencarak rose from his chair and walked to the tent's entrance. He slightly pulled back on the entrance cloth cover to see the stars, gazing up at them as if seeing something that no one else could. He let out a small sigh. "Jorn, some of the older dragons, and also the royal line, have been gifted with sight or something of that sort. We can sense when our time has come. Mine will end tomorrow."

"No!" Jorn yelled as he jumped up from his chair. "I will not let you die!" Of all the things he thought Larzencarak would say, that was the last thing he expected.

"You have no control over this matter. If I die, it is my time," Larzencarak argued.

"Then don't fight tomorrow," Jorn pleaded, trying to think of anything that could help him win this dispute.

"I will not send others to fight in my stead. Besides, I feel that if I do not fight, we will lose the battle. On the other hand, if I fight, I will die. It seems as if our victory is tied to my death," Larzencarak reasoned.

"There must be another way," replied Jorn, his face filled with such agony. Thinking back over how much they had gone through together, from enemies to respected friends, Jorn could barely contain the pain he was feeling at the mere thought of losing such a friend.

"Please, Jorn, respect my decision," Larzencarak asked as he turned to face his human friend. "In the time that I have known you, you have been a wise counsel and a good friend to me. You have given me hope in mankind again. As my friend, I ask a favor of you—take care of her. Don't tell my daughter about this either. I don't want her to worry about me. Promise me that you will do this." Larzencarak lightly placed his enormous dragon hand on Jorn's shoulder.

"I'm not sure if I can," Jorn muttered as tears ran down his face.

"You must, please, my friend, respect my wishes," said Larzencarak as he stared into Jorn's eyes.

"I swear, my king, my friend, I will do this for you," Jorn said as he stared deeply into Larzencarak's eyes.

"Excellent. Now good night, Jorn. We have a big day ahead of us." Larzencarak patted Jorn on the back and then turned to go sit in his chair.

Jorn slowly left the tent. Once outside, he wiped the tears from his eyes and let out a deep breath. As he headed back to Kirianadréth, he was trying to think of any reason why Larzencarak wanted to see him, so that Kirianadréth would not know the truth. He found her right where he had left her. When she saw him, she immediately began asking questions.

"What did my father want? Are you okay? Marahezron was such a troll, but the next time I see him I'll give him a piece of my mind."

Jorn finished walking up to her and sat down beside her. "I'm okay, and your father just wanted to go over tomorrow's plans and to make sure the humans were ready for this." Even though he said it with confidence, Jorn was hurting inside. He didn't like lying to her, but he told himself that it was for a good reason. Still, he was trying to keep all of his emotions from showing to Kirianadréth.

"Oh, okay, however, I'm still going to talk to my father about Marahezron's attitude."

"Do you know your dad once had a human pet?" Jorn said, desperate to change the subject.

"No, I didn't; what dragon told you that?"

"Your dad told me himself."

The look on Kirianadréth's face was both amusement and shock, which made it look quite comical. "Really, my father did. He has never told me anything like that. After tomorrow's battle, I'm going to have a talk with him."

"I bet he's got a lot of stories you don't know, him and Ancient both. When this war is over, you will have time to hear them." Jorn leaned against Kirianadréth, enjoying the warmth of her body. He looked up at the stars, hoping to find some type of guidance or revelation on what to do. However, what he had on his mind the most was that he would get no sleep that night worrying about his friend, and tomorrow was going to be a long day.

***

Tomorrow became today faster than anyone would have wanted. It was early morning; the sun was not up yet, and the armies were in place. Ancient had a small group entrenched on the mountain; the rest lay in wait in the desert. Looking down the mountain, you had one group on the right, led by Jorn and Larzencarak. On the left, the other group was led by Kirianadréth and Marahezron. Dragons, humans, dwarves, and elves were ready for battle; however, the tension among the army was very high. Not only was it a cold morning, but a thick, mysterious mist formed in the desert. You could not see two feet in front of you, and this made the army nervous.

No one understood how such a thick mist could form in the desert; it had the smell of magic. The leaders of the army knew the mist would form, but they didn't know it would be heavy and dark. It seemed the only calm ones there were Jorn and Larzencarak. They waited patiently for the return of a dragon scout. For hours, it seemed as though silence would consume them; even their breath was a disturbing noise. Finally, in the distance, they could hear the flapping of a dragon's wings. It wasn't long before a golden-scaled dragon landed quietly a few feet away from Jorn. The dragon came scurrying up to Larzencarak through the mist. He stood only a few feet taller than Jorn and was quite scrawny. He put his hands on his knees and bent over, trying to catch his breath.

"My king," the scout said, wheezing and gasping for air. "The mist goes on for a long distance, and it even reaches up to the clouds. My king, I do not believe this mist is natural. Something dark must've created it!"

"Calm yourself. What of the Dark Army?" Larzencarak asked.

"It comes this way – a massive army of all kinds of hideous creatures," the scout replied. "Because of the heavy mist, scouting was almost impossible; I nearly walked right into the Dark Army."

"What about dragons? Do they have any dragons?" Larzencarak urged, needing more details.

"Yes, my king, many dragons. But they do not fly, my lord. They walk with the army itself," the scout revealed.

"They can't see in the mist either," Jorn added.

"So it would seem," Larzencarak remarked. "The reason for this mist remains a mystery. However, we can use it to our advantage."

"I don't see how this mist will be an advantage to us," Jorn voiced his concern. "I have a feeling that this battle will become very confusing, very fast."

"Hush," Larzencarak said as he quickly put his whole hand over Jorn's face to silence him. "Listen," he said quietly.

Jorn looked as though he had gotten his head stuck in a hole as he pulled and tugged at Larzencarak's hand, trying to get free. His head almost made a popping sound when he pulled himself free from Larzencarak's grip. He glared at Larzencarak as if to make a remark, but then turned his attention to what he needed to be listening for.

For a moment, he couldn't hear a thing. Human hearing wasn't as good as dragons. Then slowly, he began to hear a slight rumble. Then, after awhile, not only could he hear it, but he could feel it. Jorn's stomach turned as he felt the very earth underneath him shake. He knew an army was approaching— and not a small army.

They all crouched down, peering through the mist, trying to see this massive army that was approaching. Their hearts beat fast from not knowing where the enemy might come from. It didn't take long for them to start seeing figures appearing through the mist. They couldn't see much because of the thickness of the mist; the figures seemed more like shadows.

Jorn and Larzencarak were trying to keep quiet, hoping the army would get farther into their midst. They were as still as they could be as they watched many creatures pass by; even the dragons held their breath as best as they could. After awhile, they picked themselves up just a bit in preparation to charge. They were hoping to get the army just a bit farther in. However, as they readied themselves, an orc that had strayed from its army came up and stood only a few feet from Jorn, who quickly stiffened his body, trying to keep quiet as he stared at the hideous beast.

The orc stood for a few minutes, not seeing Jorn, and then he caught wind of something that didn't smell right. He sniffed for a minute, trying to figure out the peculiar smell. It didn't take him long to recognize the human smell or to track it. The orc caught a glimpse of Jorn; however, before the orc could warn anyone, Jorn jumped to his feet. He drew his sword without making a sound and thrust it through the orc's throat. Jorn had hoped that he was quiet enough not to alarm the Dark Army, but that was not the case, as the orc let out a small, high-pitched squeal as he died. This caught the attention of two dragons and another orc. Larzencarak heard them stop in their tracks and turned to see what the noise was. He knew that now was the time to fight.

Larzencarak stood up, unfolded his wings, lifted his head back, and let out a mighty roar. Within a single moment, the entire army stood up and screamed for battle. As the Army of Light rushed in, the Dark Army screamed for battle itself. But because of the mist, there was no way to organize themselves. They could not see where the enemy was coming from. The warriors from both armies just ran straight ahead until they could see something to fight. Some dragons even took flight, but they didn't go very far. They either ran into each other or saw a shadowy figure that they chose to fight, not knowing that those were their own.

Most of the dragons from the Army of Light chose not to take flight; there was enough trouble on the ground. At first, it was more of a clatter in the midst. It was such a mess that the first to die were killed by their own army. From Jorn's point of view, the battle looked like a sea of shadows dancing. The only two that stood out were Jorn and Larzencarak. You could hear them screaming from miles away; their cries were fearless. They seemed unstoppable; they kept running through the mist, cutting down any enemy in their way.

Jorn stayed close to Larzencarak, unwilling to let him get out of his sight for a moment. As they fought side by side, they began to hear their army cry out. The cries were not filled with fear or doubt, much to their surprise. The army's cry was one of victory and ingenuity. It started with only a few men and dragons. The humans, elves, and dwarves began to cry out Jorn's name, and the dragons began to cry out Larzencarak's. Soon the entire army was crying out Jorn's and Larzencarak's names over and over.

The two quickly caught on to the fact that the army's cry was helping. Not only did it give the warriors courage, but it also helped them recognize each other in the mist. Those who did not cry back were the enemy. With that knowledge, the two pressed on, crying out each other's names. The cry itself had another effect: it began to strike fear in the hearts of the Dark Army. Some of the orcs and dragons began to scatter, trying to escape from the mist. A few of them made it to the mountain, only to be killed by Ancient and his group. The old dragon himself squeezed the life out of some of the dragons. As old as he was, he too did not want to miss out on all the fun. The battle was going well for the Army of Light, but Jorn had a bad feeling that something was poised to turn.

As Jorn continued to fight by Larzencarak's side, he heard Marahezron not far from them. Jorn took a moment to listen carefully, not liking what his ears were picking up. From the sound of it, Marahezron didn't seem to be doing well. For a moment, Jorn lost interest in protecting Larzencarak and quickly turned his focus to Marahezron. He left Larzencarak's side and headed out in what he thought was the right direction toward Marahezron. Jorn did not like Marahezron, but he could not let such a valuable ally fall to the enemy. As he got closer to the noise, he began to see two big shadows wrestling on the ground. From the shape of the shadows, he realized that Marahezron was pinned to the ground on his back while the other dragon was trying to get a clean bite at his neck. With no hesitation, Jorn started running toward a nearby rock that stood about eight feet tall. Without losing the momentum of his run, he quickly scaled the rock and then hurled himself into the air over Marahezron's attacker.

Marahezron's eyes filled with surprise when he saw Jorn's figure come falling out of the mist with a sword in hand. Jorn landed on the side of the enemy dragon's face as he plunged his sword directly into the dragon's eye. Quickly letting go of the sword, Jorn fell to the ground and rolled away. The dragon whipped his head back and roared in agony. Taking the opportunity, Marahezron hurriedly put his hind legs on the dragon's belly and pushed up. Flexing his tail to reveal its spikes, he thrust it into the dragon's chest. The dragon squealed and then fell over dead. Jorn walked up to the dead dragon and pulled his sword from its eye. As Jorn wiped some of the gunk from his sword, Marahezron picked himself up off the ground. The two locked eyes for a moment, and Jorn realized that Marahezron didn't understand why Jorn had saved his life. Marahezron did not say anything; however, Jorn knew that although Marahezron's pride was hurt, he was grateful.

Jorn suddenly realized that he had left Larzencarak and that he had no clue where he was. As fast as he could, he ran back in the direction he came from, hoping that Larzencarak was not far away. Marahezron didn't have to think twice; he followed Jorn, hoping to pay back his debt. Jorn was running frantically through the mist, not stopping for anything, not even to fight. As he ran by orcs, he cut them down with one swing as he continued running. He kept screaming Larzencarak's name, hoping to hear something back. He was becoming very worried until he heard a familiar sound. Jorn heard his own name called from a distance by a familiar voice.

He headed in the direction of the voice, with Marahezron following close behind him. He stopped suddenly as an orc went flying by him, thrown by the hand of a mighty dragon! Jorn turned to see Larzencarak's mighty figure emerge from the mist, standing tall and strong. Jorn peered into Larzencarak's eyes and smiled, and Larzencarak smiled back. For a moment, everything seemed to be all right, and Jorn relaxed. However, as he took his first step toward Larzencarak, he noticed a shadow growing darker and larger as it came closer to Larzencarak.

"No!" Jorn screamed as he reached out his hand to warn Larzencarak. But it was too late.

Larzencarak felt a sharp pain in his back, and then everything went numb. He looked down to see a jet-black tail piercing his chest like the tip of an ax. It seemed all too familiar to him, as though he personally knew it. As Jorn came running up, the dark figure did not linger long; it quickly retracted its tail from Larzencarak's body, twisted, and then took flight into the mist. Jorn yelled after this faceless and nameless evil as Larzencarak stood for a moment, holding his chest, and then collapsed. Jorn finally reached Larzencarak and quickly knelt by his head. Marahezron stood behind Jorn in shock, but he was silent. Across the field, they could hear the screams of Kirianadréth, for she could feel her father's pain.

"Jorn," Larzencarak began to speak.

"No, my friend, be still," Jorn replied, trying to keep Larzencarak from moving. "Ancient, come quick!" he screamed.

Ancient heard Jorn cry for help, and he did not ponder its reason. He knew that his friend, the king, was dying. He unfurled his old wings, and with all his might, he took flight. He did not get high off the ground, as his tail still dragged behind him, scraping against the earth. However, it was enough to send him hurling down the mountain toward where Jorn's screams were coming from.

"Jorn, listen to me." Larzencarak continued fidgeting about. Jorn stopped his obsessive worrying for a moment to stare into Larzencarak's eyes. "Keep your promise to me."

"I will, but there is no need. Ancient is on his way, and he will heal you," Jorn quickly answered as he drew closer to Larzencarak. He placed one hand on Larzencarak's cheek, and a small tear ran down his own face.

"My time has come, and you know this. I have lived a full life, yet there is much I still regret," Larzencarak remarked as he gasped for a breath of air. "Jorn, I have had many children. Kirianadréth is only the second oldest. However, she is the only one who has stayed with me while the others have turned to darkness." Larzencarak raised his hand and placed his finger against Jorn's cheek. His one finger was larger than Jorn's head, yet he touched Jorn gracefully. "If I had one wish, Jorn, it would be to have another son, and I would want him to be like you."

Upon hearing those words, Jorn pushed more firmly against Larzencarak's finger and grabbed his hand. The tears could not be held back.

"More than a friend you are to me, a son I consider you to be," Larzencarak said as his voice became raspy. "Love my daughter and help her become the great ruler that she was meant to be. Do this for me, my son." As the last word came out, Larzencarak's hand fell to the ground, with Jorn still holding on to it. His head slowly lowered down to the ground, but his eyes never left Jorn's, as though he was unwilling to let go.

Larzencarak, the great king of the dragons, was dead. Jorn stood up and let go of Larzencarak's hand. He backed away, his eyes never turning away. Kirianadréth came bounding up through the mist, screaming in agony. She came skidding to a halt and bent down to cradle her father's body. As she held his head in her lap, her wings folded over his body. She held him tight and then let out a mighty roar.

Jorn could not say a thing, so he took another step back. As he did, he bumped into Marahezron, but he did not turn around, for his eyes could not leave Larzencarak. Marahezron put a hand on Jorn's shoulder, and so did Ancient, who had finally reached this tragic site.

As they stood silent, the battle raged on around them. It was not long after that the Dark Army was defeated. The mist itself began to rise, and all those left could see the carnage. The earth itself was stained with blood; this desert would never have its color again. Those who were left gathered in the center, where the body of Larzencarak lay still. They stood there until sunset and mourned the loss of this great king. However, most of the eyes stayed upon Kirianadréth, who was still clutching her father's body and softly stroking his cheek with her hand.

***

Larzencarak's body was brought back to the dragon city. It was taken to the deepest catacombs beneath the city, where the other rulers were laid to rest. There was no great ceremony; there were just a few individuals who cared for him greatly. For the dragons never drew out the grieving for the dead; they understood that it was just another passing, and that the Creator had everything in his control. To them, the living were more important, and one could always remember the dead in their own time. To show this, there were no graves or tombs for the great kings and queens. In the depths of the city, there was a long great hall, with enormous shelves. Each shelf was carved out of solid stone and big enough to hold a dragon. Some shelves already had massive dragon statues on them.

Jorn was curious about what they did with the great kings and queens who came before. He watched as they placed Larzencarak on a shelf of his own, with his name carved underneath it. Then Ancient raised his arms high and said a few words in a language that even the dragons couldn't remember. Suddenly, the body of Larzencarak began to turn to stone, and in a single moment, he became as hard as the stone walls around him. Till the end of time, Larzencarak would lie there in stone form, looking as though he were peacefully sleeping.

Jorn's eyes widened with amazement and confusion. "I don't understand," he remarked to Ancient as quietly as he could, not wanting to disrupt the seriousness of the moment.

"Now he will be preserved for all time, and his memory will live on in us," Ancient replied.

"No, I mean, how is this possible?" Jorn quickly remarked, pointing at Larzencarak's body.

"You mean his body becoming stone? Well, there is a simple answer. You see, all dragons have the ability to turn to stone. It just takes some a long time to learn how. As for the dead, they cannot turn because they're dead." Ancient put his arm around Jorn and pointed to Larzencarak. "So I asked the Creator to turn this loyal servant to stone. With that gift, his stone body won't even crack thousands of years from now. He will be as you see him now."

"What a wonder and beautiful gift!" was all that Jorn could say to such knowledge.

"Now come, Jorn, we have much to prepare for. The days ahead are going to have great marvels of their own," Ancient commented as he turned to walk back to the heart of the city.

Jorn, however, did not get very far, for Marahezron was waiting for him. The dragon suddenly stepped out from around the corner, stopping Jorn in his tracks. Marahezron had a hard look on his face as he convinced Ancient to keep going and that he needed a private conversation with Jorn. Jorn, on the other hand, wanted Ancient to stay simply because he didn't want to deal with anything that Marahezron had to say. So he took a deep breath and prepared himself for whatever the dragon had on his mind.

"I apologize," Marahezron said quietly, almost inaudibly.

Jorn had nothing to say in return; he merely stood there with his mouth wide open in shock.

Marahezron was also having difficulty speaking. It was definitely apparent that he was having a hard time saying what he needed to say. "This is not easy for me to say, so if you would bear with me for a moment." Marahezron waited until he got a slight nod from Jorn. "I don't like humans and probably never will. Also, yes, I am jealous of your relationship with Kirianadréth. However, now I see that there's not much I can do about it. I would rather have her as a friend than an enemy, and if that means letting you two be together, then so be it."

Jorn opened his mouth to say something, but Marahezron cut him off. "Still, that's not why I'm here. I have a debt to repay more than you know. You saved my life after I had threatened yours. Even among the dragons, that is unheard of. In an odd way, you shamed my honor, and it didn't end there. Larzencarak was my king, and perhaps my closest friend. I would've loved to be called his son. Instead, he named you his son at his death. I could be mad at that. Instead, I see the truth in that. I see what my king saw. He looked at a man that was more of a dragon than even some of the dragons themselves. In the midst of danger, it was a man who tried to save my king." Marahezron's voice softened as he looked deep into Jorn's eyes. "I would not say this to any other human, but you have the heart of a dragon. And with it, I owe you my life and my respect. Live well and prosper, Jorn." With that, Marahezron nodded at Jorn and then turned and walked silently away.

All that Jorn could do was stand there in his own silence, watching Marahezron walk away. Many things were changing; things were even changing in the hearts of dragons. For some odd reason, that thought made Jorn smile.

***

Two days later, the city of the dragons was filled with excitement and bustle. Today was the crowning of the queen of the dragons. Another reason for excitement was that the Dark Army had disappeared; the war was over. However, Jorn and a few others were a little skeptical on the subject. They didn't think that the darkness would disappear that easily. They had an odd feeling that the battle wasn't quite over, and that someday, when least expected, the darkness would return. Not knowing how, when, and where, vexed them greatly.

Jorn and some of the other leaders wondered if it was a fair trade—Larzencarak for what they thought was a temporary victory. Nevertheless, they didn't want their opinions to ruin the joyous occasion. So today was a festive day, and many great guests arrived. There was an entourage of dwarves and elves. Many beings came for this great day. Though they came to celebrate this day with the queen, they also came to pay their respects to Jorn, the man who defeated the darkness. Anyone of great importance was packed into the throne room, which truly meant that they got it as full as they could, and anyone else was out of luck. The great doors to the throne room were left open, and the corridor itself was packed full. The other passageway leading to the throne room was left empty, for that was where Kirianadréth must enter from. Everyone was filled with excitement and anticipation for the crowning.

Jorn stood next to Ancient, curious about the proceedings. "So none of her siblings will challenge her for the throne?" he asked, very concerned and eager to get this coronation on its way.

"No, they will not," Ancient replied. "I doubt they even have the courage to enter the city, for they did not leave on good terms."

"What about anyone else? Can anyone challenge her?"

"No, that is not our law."

Jorn stared up at Ancient. "Once again, I am confused. You will have to explain."

Ancient took a deep, and calming breath. He admired Jorn for his wisdom and constant thirst for knowledge. Though Jorn's questions seemed never-ending, Ancient had a lot of patience for him, probably because the human reminded him of himself. "The crown must go to the next heir. The only way someone else could get it is to challenge and kill our ruler in this room. Don't ask me where that law came from. For some reason, this place is also the symbol of the ruler and so a challenge must be issued here."

"Won't the guards or others seek vengeance upon the killer?"

"No. Among dragons, our honor and loyalty are very high. No one will harm the killer, for they will be our new ruler. The only one who can challenge them is the royal line. If they do not, then the killer will become our ruler—however, without the blessing of the Creator.

"How does the Creator bless them? Does he bestow something upon them?"

"Yes, it is a wish. When the royal line is crowned, they are given one wish, within reason. Those who are not in the royal line are given nothing."

"Has anyone ever falsely claimed the throne before?"

"No. This city is well-defended from the dark dragons. It is rare that an evil one should even make it past the front entrance. It is my personal belief that we may never—"

"Here she comes," someone rudely interrupted.

"Forgive me, Jorn. I have a duty that needs attending to," Ancient said. "We will continue this conversation at another time, my dear friend." Ancient turned and walked quickly toward the throne.

Kirianadréth walked ever so slowly into the room, which erupted in cheers. She gave a soft smile but seemed as though she did not want to be there. When she reached the throne, she put her hand on the side of it. The cheers quieted when everyone realized that she hadn't sat down. She knew it was her duty; however, she couldn't help but dwell on the memories of her father. She stood still for a moment, and no one dared say a thing to her.

After a while, Ancient cleared his throat to get her to pay attention. She quickly snapped out of her thoughts and finally decided to sit down. She looked at Ancient and nodded to him that she was ready. He walked closer to the left side of the throne, holding a pillow that carried her father's crown. Larzencarak barely wore his crown, so earlier that day, Ancient had to have it dusted and polished just for the occasion.

The crown was a large golden wavy band with seven jewels evenly placed on it, with a large diamond as the front jewel. He lifted the crown as high as he could and spoke very loudly. "To all creatures from the heavens to the earth, I give you Kirianadréth, queen of all dragons!"

Ancient slowly placed the crown on her head in between the two mighty horns. The moment it touched her brow, the entire room filled with cheers again.

"Now, my dear," Ancient began, "you have but one wish, so make it a good one. One worthwhile, and you know that you cannot ask for your father back."

Kirianadréth nodded, and then rose from the throne and gave the old dragon a big hug. Then she turned to the crowd and called for Jorn to come forth. When he finally emerged from the crowd, she smiled and began to speak. "In my life, I have learned a lot from my father. However, none more than in his last few days, when his friend was this mighty man," she remarked as she pointed to Jorn. "I've learned from them that dragons and humans can live together in peace and that we need to. So in the memory of my father and for me, I will bridge the gap between the two races."

Upon hearing those words, the whole crowd began to whisper, curious as to what could possibly be her wish.

Kirianadréth raised her arms high and closed her eyes tightly. Very quietly, she began to mutter something. Suddenly, her whole body was bathed in white light. Everyone in the crowd had to turn away, for the light was blinding. For several minutes, the room glittered with light; no one could see a thing.

Finally, when the light faded, everyone turned back around to see what had become of their queen. In astonishment and amazement, everyone quickly began chattering about what was before them. Jorn himself could hardly believe his eyes upon the knowledge of her wish. Kirianadréth, as they knew her, was no more; what stood before them was a naked female human.

There was no comparison to her beauty. However, she retained a few characteristics of her old form. Her hair was ruby red like her old scales, and it even glittered in the light. Her body was fit and yet still feminine; her skin was fair and smooth like silk. And her eyes still gleamed like emeralds. Everyone stared at her beauty, and even Jorn's jaw dropped in amazement. Ancient quickly grabbed a cloak and covered her.

"Thank you," she said. "It's a little different, but I'll get used to it." Even though her body had transformed, her voice was still the same. The only difference that could be heard was an air of authority that seemed to come from her having been crowned queen. No one would question that the Creator had his hand in this. With his power, he changed her body yet left her with all the authority of the dragon queen.

"Why?" Jorn asked as he came within arm's reach of her. He did his best to steady himself, but his heart and lungs seemed not to be working correctly.

"I thought you would like this," Kirianadréth replied, confused by his question. "I wish to be human as long as you live."

"I do like it. However, won't you lose your throne?"

"No, my sweet Jorn. I may look human, but inside, I'm not. Inside still flows the blood of a dragon, and my people can still feel my power. I have lost nothing. If anything, I have gained something more." Kirianadréth looked deeply into his eyes, longing for him to respond.

Jorn stood for a moment, staring at her. His heart was fluttering and filled with joy until he could no longer contain it. He reached out, put his arms around her, and kissed her lips deeply. As her arms wrapped around him, his heart filled with the peace that he was longing for.

The crowd began to rejoice, for this was a historic day. The dragons roared, the elves sang, the humans cheered, and the dwarves laughed in excitement. Marahezron and Ancient stood side by side, watching Jorn and Kirianadréth continue to kiss and embrace. They both had a smile on their faces as if they shared the same joke. However, in their hearts, they were filled with contentment and excitement, for they both knew that out of these two, a great story and adventure would come.

***

Later that night, Ravelle and Red Helm were walking through the dragon city, enjoying the sights, when they came across something peculiar. They turned and began to head down the hall that led to Kirianadréth's room. At the door of the queen's room, they found three female human servants listening at the door and giggling.

"Very suspicious," Red Helm grumbled.

They both walked quietly towards the women. When they were right up behind them, Ravelle spoke softly. "And what are all of you up to?"

All three of the women servants jumped from being startled, but not one of them made a sound. One of them kept their ear towards the door and didn't turn around; as for the other two, they quickly turned to address those that had caught them.

"Forgive us, your majesties," one whispered.

"We were just making sure everything was okay," the other justified herself.

Ravelle smiled and leaned in to whisper, "is Jorn in there?"

Both servants nodded their heads excitedly and smiled.

"How is he doing?" Red Helm asked, excited to get some juicy dirt on his friend.

"Horrible from the sound of it," one servant replied.

"They've fallen off the bed twice," the other servant stated.

"Make that three times; they just did it again. Sounds like she hit her head on the floor this time," the servant whispered, with her ear to the door.

Both Ravelle and Red Helm winced at that comment.

"That's certainly not something for the storybooks," said Red Helm.

"Elves normally don't write those things in our storybooks, but I would be one to agree with you," Ravelle replied.

The servant to the left stepped forward and gave her opinion. "In my queen's defense, she has only been a human for several hours. So, she has no clue what she's doing and cannot be held responsible for this disaster. Master Jorn on the other hand, has no excuse for his lack of performance.

Ravelle feeling the need to come to Jorn's defense, gave his own opinion. "Jorn was a farmer and secluded for many years."

"Oh, come on, it should come natural to the lad," Red Helm stated, "he's letting all males down. It's an embarrassment to males of any race."

The servant with her ear to the door snapped her fingers, getting everyone's attention. "I think he figured it out."

"How can you tell?" asked Ravelle.

"They stopped squirming around, and her sound changed from grunting to moaning."

With that, all of them got close to the door and put their ears up against it. A moment later, there was a very rough cough and the clearing of one's throat. They all turned around to see Ancient glaring down at them.

"Oh my, look at the time, Ravelle," Red Helm said as he grabbed the elf's arm and hurriedly walked away, dragging Ravelle with him.

Ancient leaned down and stared at the three servants. "Not a word of this to anyone," Ancient growled. After he got a nod of understanding from each one of the servants, he calmly continued. "Now I believe you three have things to do elsewhere."

All three of them bowed and hurried away as fast as they could. Ancient continue to stand at the queen's door, and chuckle at the situation. "So, this is how it begins; there's going to be interesting days to come. The days of Kirianadréth, the human queen of the dragons."

An Expected Arrival and an Unexpected Departure

As with any great kingdom, there were times when you could sit back and listen to nature, as well as times when things seemed to be falling apart. Overall, Kirianadréth's reign was a quiet one. The only problem they seemed to have since the Dark Army disappeared was the threat of a few bands of orcs or goblins that came out of their hiding places from time to time to cause trouble. There were even a few dragons who caused some problems, but the lands maintained the peace.

Since the war was over, there had been no reason to maintain an enormous army, so a great portion of the army returned to their homes with tidings of victory and peace. Only one-eighth of the army remained with Jorn, unwilling to leave him. So on the outskirts of the dragons' kingdom, they created small farms for them to dwell. Yet they maintained a sense of alertness in case the Dark Army ever decided to return.

That, surprisingly, was not the most pressing thing on Jorn's mind. Within the sixth month of Kirianadréth's reign, the kingdom was excited with the news that their queen was with child. Needless to say, the first words out of Jorn's mouth when hearing that news were, "How did that happen?"

Even the dragons, who didn't know much about man's form of mating, found that comment very humorous. It didn't help that there was already an ongoing joke with the human women who served the queen. Kirianadréth enjoyed the presence of human servants, especially now that she was one. She loved the conversations with her female servants as they talked about everything, which the human males called gossip. Unfortunately, during one such conversation, she let slip that on their wedding night, when they were supposed to know one another intimately, there was a problem. Since Jorn was a virgin and Kirianadréth was new to being a human, there was much trial and error. They had spent most of the night in each other's arms laughing since they couldn't find the right position. The female servants found this information quite amusing. Several of the servants smiled and giggled, not willing to admit that they already knew some of the struggles Kirianadréth and Jorn had that night. Occasionally, the servants would make sarcastic remarks at Jorn that would make him blush. However, knowing the men in Jorn's army, the female servants kept the information only among themselves to save Jorn's reputation with his men.

Still, Jorn and Kirianadréth were happy about the news, but they weren't quite sure what to expect. Time flew by quickly, and soon the day of the baby's arrival came. The entire city was filled with joy and anticipation, just waiting for the good news. Kirianadréth and Jorn were also filled with anticipation, along with a little bit of fear. The baby came sooner than a normal human offspring would, and although they knew that it was only half-human, it still bothered them. Five months seemed a little too soon for a human. Nevertheless, they were as ready as they could be for whatever came their way.

Jorn was a little nervous that day; he wasn't quite sure what to do, so he had several women come in from the outer farms to help with this great burden. The women made Kirianadréth as comfortable as she could be, for no one could prepare her for the pain she was experiencing. Several times she wondered to herself why humans would do this more than once; it seemed so much easier to simply lay an egg.

Jorn was there with her, running his fingers through her hair and holding her hand. He continued to talk to her and look her in the face because he did not want to see the birth. Though he was a strong man, some sights had a tendency to make him just a little queasy. This became another ongoing joke with the female servants: Jorn could handle war but not childbirth.

Ancient was also in the room, for he was family to Kirianadréth, and she didn't mind. Dragons had no clue that birth was a private thing. On the other hand, he was hardly noticed; he just sat in the corner, and although he took up most of it, he was quiet, so no one paid him any mind. He just sat there, stooping, looking ever so diligently at the miracle of birth. He had never seen the birth of a human, so this was just one more thing that he would experience in his days. And he took it very seriously; he had no expression on his face even when the child started to come out. Kirianadréth's screams became louder; they could even be heard through the great halls of the city. As she continued to push, she gave several angry glances toward Jorn. Then she made the comment that she would get him back for this. The women in the room laughed as they continued to tend to her.

It wasn't long before the baby was out and screaming, as normal babies do. Kirianadréth relaxed when she heard the baby's screams, and Jorn was able to pry his hand from hers, shaking it to try to get some feeling back into it since she was squeezing it so hard. "Is the baby all right?" Kirianadréth asked the women as they were cleaning the baby.

"Yes, Queen, the baby is just fine," one woman answered. "You have a beautiful little boy. Even his eyes are open, which is rare for a baby just born." Then the woman exclaimed, "That's odd."

"What?" Kirianadréth quickly asked, thinking something was wrong with the child.

"Oh, nothing serious," the woman said, trying to keep Kirianadréth calm. "It's just his eyes. They're not human. His eyes are dragon eyes, and they keep changing color."

"Well, that makes perfect sense," Ancient finally spoke.

"What do you mean it makes perfect sense?" asked Jorn as everyone turned to look at Ancient, confused by his comment.

"Well, Jorn, you see, some dragons can change their color," Ancient began to explain with a silly expression on his face. "However, most of them take thousands of years to learn how to do it. Something odd must be causing the change in his eye color. It's probably his emotions, but when he gets older, he will learn to control his eye color. On the other hand, when he calms down, they will probably settle at the same color as his mother's eyes. At least I hope so. I like her eyes better than yours."

"Thank you, Ancient. I will take that as a compliment," said Kirianadréth, still breathing heavily.

The woman holding the baby chuckled as she handed him to Kirianadréth. "And that's not all," the woman stated. "Look at your baby's right shoulder, my queen."

Kirianadréth pulled back the cloth that covered her child's shoulder and saw a stunning sight. On the back of her son's shoulder was a small, round, red scale. "How peculiar. A single scale on his shoulder. I wonder why."

"Well, it makes complete sense to me," remarked Ancient once more, confusing everyone in the room with his random comments.

"Ancient, you can always find a reason for everything, whether it's true or not," Kirianadréth pointed out. She remembered when she was young that Ancient had often made sense out of things when others could not. "So tell us, what is the reason for this scale on his shoulder?"

"Well, it makes perfect sense, my dear Kirianadréth. He will carry the weight of his people on his shoulders. What better place to show that the people he carries are dragons?"

"That is absolutely ridiculous, but an interesting opinion," Kirianadréth said. She turned her eyes away from Ancient and back to her baby. She began to notice that he was still crying, and she couldn't figure out why. He wasn't hurt, and he was warmly wrapped in a blanket. She even tried feeding him after one of the women told her how, and still, he wouldn't stop screaming. Something else must be bothering him, she thought to herself.

***

Meanwhile, a long way down the corridor in another room sat Marahezron. He was sitting at a dragon-sized table, quietly staring down at a small dragon egg. Even though Marahezron was a great dragon warrior, this little egg meant a lot to him. Several months after Kirianadréth and Jorn came together after her crowning, Marahezron realized that he needed to move on with his life. He knew that his love for Kirianadréth was unrequited. If anything, she thought of him as a brother. Nevertheless, Marahezron never regretted his decision to move on. He found a lovely dragon who was a little younger than him to settle down with. She had laid an egg in hopes of starting a family; however, their hopes of a family were very quickly crushed.

One day, as she was walking in the countryside, as she always had, she was attacked by a band of orcs and was killed. She was one of the few casualties after the war ended. Marahezron, with the help of Jorn, hunted down and destroyed the band of orcs. Marahezron was devastated, so he poured all his hope into the egg. Others still wished the best for him, and when the egg did not hatch, they began to feel sorry for him. That did not destroy his hope, however, every spare moment he had, he continued to watch the egg. Month after month, he never gave up hope that he would have a family. So on that day, he continued to watch the egg vigilantly as he always had, yet that day was gifted with another arrival.

Marahezron heard the screams of the queen's baby and turned around to look at the door. He was hearing the screams very well because his door was slightly ajar. He stood up and turned, making sure his tail did not hit the egg, and went to shut the door. He was happy for Kirianadréth, though he did not want to hear the sound of a screaming baby. He was curious how humans could allow their offspring to emit such a sound. Still, he was sure that everyone was enjoying the arrival nonetheless.

The moment his hand touched the door, he heard a small crack. Quickly, he turned to look at the egg, worried that it had fallen to the floor. It was still safely sitting on the table, but now it had a small crack on the side. Marahezron ran over to the table, knocking his stool out of the way to look closely down at the egg. After a while, the egg cracked further along the side. Marahezron became very excited and could barely hold his breath. Suddenly, the sides exploded as two wings burst out. Marahezron was startled and jumped, knocking another stool over. He quickly gathered himself and looked back down at the table. He brought his face close to the table so he could see what emerged from the egg. To his delight, he saw an adorable baby dragon with dark red scales on its back and light red scales on its belly.

To him, the baby was perfect: its wings were well formed, and it had two legs and two arms. However, he couldn't say much for its head because there were still pieces of the egg covering it. The little dragon scampered across the table, trying to get the eggshell off its head. Then it ran into Marahezron's snout, breaking the rest of the egg. Marahezron couldn't help but laugh when he saw the baby was startled that it hit something.

A little dazed, it plopped down on its butt and shook its head. Looking at its head, Marahezron was pleased. The little dragon had a nicely shaped head with four small horns at the top, and its snout wasn't too long. The horns didn't look like they would grow much. Marahezron's heart and mind were filled with peace; he had finally fulfilled a piece of his life. He was a father, and he believed that nothing could take that away from him.

In time, the baby dragon rolled over onto its back and curled its tail up. As soon as the little dragon spotted its tail, it began to play with it, the way a kitten would play with a ball of string. When the baby dragon caught its tail, it quickly put it in its mouth and began chewing on it. Then the dragon pulled its tail out of its mouth and began wiggling it in front of its nose. Marahezron looked carefully at the tail, realizing that it wasn't a normal dragon's tail. At one moment, it looked to be rounded into a single point, and then it seemed to split into five separate tails.

Confused by this, Marahezron started tapping a finger on the table, trying to get the little dragon to use its tail. And sure enough, the baby dragon rolled back over and hunched its back up as though it were preparing to pounce. Whipping its tail around, the young dragon flexed its tail muscle, making the single rounded tip become a very sharp point. The little dragon then thrust down at Marahezron's finger, and he quickly removed it as the tip plunged into the table.

Marahezron thought for a second, and then, using both hands, he put down five of his fingers since his dragon hands had only four. He then tapped them softly. Quickly, the little dragon flexed again; this time its tail's tip opened up into five separate tails. All of them flexed into a point, and the little dragon once again thrust at Marahezron's fingers. And once again, Marahezron quickly removed them as the tails plunged into the table. Then he dangled his fingers up in the air, and the baby dragon responded to that, quickly turning its five-pointed tail into rounded tips and grabbing at Marahezron's fingers. It got a hold of one finger and quickly began to pull. Then Marahezron lifted the baby dragon in the air; it was kicking and squawking, unhappy with its present state. So Marahezron began to tickle its belly, and the baby dragon began to laugh. Marahezron's heart was filled with joy; he felt that his life was now complete. However, he knew that this little baby was going to be a bundle of trouble. His first dilemma was figuring out whether it was a male or female and what to name it.

* * *

Back in the queen's room, the baby was lying on the bed next to his mother, still crying loudly. They were beginning to worry; they couldn't figure out what was causing the baby so much pain. Suddenly there was a knock on the door, and Jorn answered. "Come in."

"I hope I'm not intruding," Marahezron said as he popped his head in around the door.

"No, not at all. We could probably use some company," Jorn answered.

Marahezron came out from behind the door and walked into the room, carrying his little dragon. He walked up to the bed, wagging his tail in excitement and pride. "I just wanted to show you my little daughter."

Kirianadréth quickly responded with a smile on her face, "That's wonderful, Marahezron. I was hoping the egg would hatch soon." Then very slowly, the smile on her face turned into a frown as she looked down at her son. "However, I don't mean to be rude, but we seem to have a problem."

"I can see that. Is there anything I can do?" Marahezron asked as his daughter quickly jumped down from his arms and landed on the bed. They all stopped and watched to see what the little dragon was going to do. Marahezron was ready to grab her in case she got a little rough with the baby. To everyone's amazement, she didn't do anything aggressive; she just scurried over to him and started sniffing. As she was sniffing him, the baby reached out his hand and grabbed her nose. She stared bright-eyed for a moment and then began to giggle. Then she lay down beside him, and wrapped her wing over him, and nestled her head right next to his. Suddenly, the baby stopped crying.

"Well, it looks like someone was just missing a friend," Ancient said. "Perhaps that's why your egg didn't hatch. It was waiting for an opportune moment. These two are destined for greatness."

"That's ridiculous. Things like that don't happen," Marahezron quickly replied. Yet even as he said it, he was afraid that it might be true. He didn't feel like holding a grudge against Jorn; however, he felt as though history was repeating itself. The person he cared about the most was being taken away from him by a human—or, in this case, a half-human, but it felt the same to him. He almost didn't know what to say or what to do.

"Never underestimate the greater powers, my old friend," Ancient added. "There are many things that are beyond us, and for a reason."

"Well, I choose not to believe them. Come, daughter, I have many things to do today, and they need to get their rest," Marahezron said as he reached for his daughter. To his surprise, she turned and snapped at him, as if she was protecting the boy. He quickly pulled back his hand, and she laid her head back down. Slowly, he began to go from surprise to anger.

"Calm down, Marahezron," Kirianadréth said. "Your daughter is safe here. If you have things to do, she'll still be here. And from the looks of things, I don't think she wants to leave. Also, my son is quiet, and I would like to enjoy this peace."

Marahezron hesitated for a moment, unwilling to give up his daughter; still, Kirianadréth was the only one he would trust with his daughter's care. "Very well, my queen. If it makes you happy." He turned and started to walk toward the door. His heart felt crushed at that moment. He cared for Kirianadréth and did not want to disagree with her. On the other hand, he did not like leaving his daughter with this boy. Even though the boy was only half human, he still looked human, and that was enough to make Marahezron uneasy. His excitement over finally having a family was lessened by knowing that this would probably cause problems down the road.

"Wait, Marahezron," Kirianadréth ordered. Marahezron stopped and turned to face her. "Did you give your daughter a name?" Kirianadréth asked.

"Yes, it's Soræniya," Marahezron replied. "I named her after her mother. And now, if you don't mind, I have things to do." He turned and walked out the door, leaving it open.

"Well, I think that's a beautiful name for a dragon girl," Kirianadréth said, looking around to see if anyone would argue with her. "I just wish I could find a name for my son. Unfortunately, nothing is coming to mind. What do you call a half-dragon and half-human child?"

"Certainly nothing, dragon. I can barely pronounce those words." Jorn voiced his opinion as he sat at the edge of the bed, staring at his family.

"I don't think a human name would be fitting for a royal dragon," Kirianadréth answered.

"He's only half dragon, remember that," said Jorn, getting a little aggravated.

"He is my son. I bore him, and I think I have the right to name him!"

"Please, will you two stop?" Ancient butted out, almost laughing. "He already has a name."

"He does? When did this happen?" Kirianadréth asked sarcastically, shooting Ancient a strange look, thinking that his comment was just another of his odd remarks.

"His name was given to him before he was ever born," Ancient said. "It will be a name that will travel with him wherever he goes. For he is the Dragon Child, and so is his name."

"No, wait," Kirianadréth said as she put her hand on Jorn's arm. "Dragon— that is his name. We shall call him Dragon."

"That makes sense," Jorn agreed. "We can't call him a human name in the dragon tongue, and we can't call him a dragon name in the human tongue. So it's better to call him Dragon, and we could say it in any tongue."

Ancient began to laugh and slowly walked toward the door. "You two are a funny thing. You always complicate everything. However, it will work. So I leave you two to rest, for you have one of the greatest burdens to ever carry. To raise a child who is from two worlds, and I believe he's going to be a handful, and so will his new friend." Ancient walked out the door, leaving them to stare at the most precious thing they had ever seen—and stare they did, all night long.

***

Several days came and went peacefully, and Dragon was quiet as long as Soræniya was there. Jorn and Kirianadréth didn't have to worry much about Dragon. However, early one morning, as Jorn was preparing to leave to visit the outer farms, Kirianadréth felt uneasy. She pleaded with him for a long time, trying to change his mind about going. "Please, Jorn, your son is only a few days old, and I have a bad feeling."

"Don't worry. Everything will be fine," Jorn said to calm her down so he could reason with her. "Besides, I've put this off for far too long, and now is a perfect opportunity to get it done. I just need to see how things are going—a few days out and a few days back. I won't be gone long, and you need to rest, so just relax. I'll be back before you know it."

"I just don't like you being gone for so long," Kirianadréth continued her argument. "I could have one of the dragons take you. It will be faster."

"No, I'm not much for flying." Jorn put his hand on the side of her face and rubbed her skin gently. "My mind is made up. I'm going, and I must be leaving soon if I'm to get back at an earlier date. Take care of the little one for me and let him know that I love him." Jorn embraced Kirianadréth tightly, almost unwilling to let go. He pulled back and kissed her gently, then turned to leave. Kirianadréth stood quietly, just watching and hoping she would see him again.

Jorn walked down the halls with his arm slightly stretched out, letting his hand brush against the walls. The beauty of this city had always amazed Jorn, and one of his favorite things was the carvings on the walls. Not all of the halls had carvings; only a few of the major ones and ones closer to the throne room. Still, he liked walking those halls, for they meant a lot to him. He felt as if there was magic in them, and at times he could swear some of the carvings moved. Some of the old dragons in the city said they were the history of dragons, just like the scrolls and tomes that Ancient had locked away in his library. Yet Jorn never found any of the dragons in the city staring at the carvings the way he did, except for Ancient. That old dragon was always an exception; at times, Jorn thought that Ancient had some human qualities in him. One moment he would be childlike, and the next he would speak with the wisdom of the ages. The one thing that Jorn knew for sure about Ancient was that the old dragon never did anything without a purpose or reason.

As Jorn finished that train of thought, he rounded a corner only to find Ancient standing in the corridor as if thinking about him magically summoned him. Jorn stifled a laugh, realizing that he should've expected the dragon to be here. "Good morning, Ancient," Jorn said as he walked up to the old dragon.

"Good morning, Jorn," Ancient replied as he turned around to greet the human. "Still planning on leaving to inspect those outlining villages?"

"I am; I figured this is the best time to get it done. Kirianadréth thinks it's a bad idea; she's got some type of feeling or premonition that something's going to go wrong. What do you think, Ancient?"

Ancient stared up at the ceiling and rubbed his chin for a long moment while making a hhhaaammmm sound. Eventually, he looked back down at Jorn and replied, "I smell change in the air."

Jorn sniffed a few times and responded, "I don't smell anything except for some stale air, but these halls usually have that smell."

"Forgive me, Jorn, it is the way dragons speak. It is not the smell in the air but a pull of magic. In times of great events that changed the course of the world, magic tends to pull towards the area where it happens. It is an effect that dragons and wizards of all kinds have never figured out why. We just know that change is coming, though we do not know what changes. Sometimes it is a good change, sometimes it is a bad change. What makes it interesting is that sometimes the magic will pull towards an area for years before something ever happens. That is why wise beings will never predict the future." Ancient laid a hand on Jorn's shoulder. "Unlike Kirianadréth, I cannot speak either good or ill in this matter. I could tell you to stay, but then something bad might happen to you here, though I doubt it. You could leave and nothing would happen at all. The pull of magic may not have anything to do with you."

Jorn nodded his head in understanding of Ancient's words. Then he paused and thought for a moment. "Why are you in this hall?" he asked, trying to put his thoughts into words. "When I saw you, I assumed you were waiting to talk to me about this very subject. Now it appears that we only had this conversation because I brought it up. As I think back, I realize your back was to me and you were facing the other direction as if you were waiting for someone else."

"That is why I like you Jorn," Ancient replied with a smile. "Not a lot of humans are as observant as you are. I am here because I'm waiting to meet an old friend of mine. Perhaps you have heard of the messenger dragons."

"I have heard only rumors; most believe them to be myths."

"My dear Jorn, they are not myths even though most of the dragons today believe they are; I assure you they are not. What have you heard about them?" Ancient couldn't help but have an amused look on his face.

Jorn thought for a moment, trying to gather all the rumors that he had heard over the years of the war. "Stories said they were small, able to fit in a man's cupped hands. It is also said that they are related to the historian fairies of legend, which means they're fast, extremely fast. The weirdest story of all is that they don't speak."

Ancient couldn't help but let out a small chuckle. "Well, some of that is right, let me correct the rest. What you got right was their size one could fit in your cupped hands. About being related to the historian fairies that is not true. Also, on a side note just to let you know the historian fairies are not legends, they are real. The reason why they were rumored to be related to the fairies is in fact when their wings beat you cannot see them as they are beating so fast. When they fly you cannot see them either. So you were right on that fact they are extremely fast. Now the last bit is a little hard to explain. It is rumored that they do not speak because they choose not to speak. They have the ability to speak if they want to, but they have a better form of communication. They have what the humans called mind speaking. They can project their very thoughts into other people's minds which is a faster way to speak. If they need to, they can even pass images. They can show you what they have seen as if you were looking through their eyes. It makes the passing of important messages fast and easier. Another reason why they were given the name messenger dragons. The name didn't bother them and down through the generations, their real name was forgotten. I have it written down in one of my scrolls because even I forgot it. It was one of those weird names, believe it or not, messenger dragons suit them better."

"That's amazing, and you say one is coming here," Jorn said, excited like a little child.

"Yes, I did, and it was perfect timing, it seems," Ancient replied as he turned Jorn to face down the hall. "Will you hold out your hands for my friend to rest upon while we speak?"

Jorn held out his hands, and cupped them together, and waited with anticipation. As if that is what the dragon was waiting for, a gust of wind blew down the hall. In a blink of his eyes, Jorn's hands held a dragon. It was a lot bigger than he expected, about the size of four of his hands. Still, it sat in his cupped hands, much lighter than he expected. At first, Jorn could not see the dragon's wings until the dragon slowed his wings to a stop. The dragon's wings had a very fine membrane that was almost see-through. The wings and the scales glittered and almost changed color with every reflection of light. To him, the messenger dragon looked like a miniature and more colorful version of Kirianadréth when she was a dragon.

The messenger dragon took one look at Jorn and Ancient, and the conversation began. Jorn had never experienced a conversation like this in his entire life, and he wasn't sure if he could ever describe it to anyone. His mind exploded with words, feelings, and images that made up the conversation. He was sure that if something like that had happened outside of his head, he wouldn't be able to follow along. Because it was happening in his head, his mind was able to understand it and take each word, feeling, and image as they came. At first, he was in awe and completely humbled by the fact that Ancient and the messenger dragon would allow him to be a part of this conversation. Then came the flood of information he had to sort through and understand. There were a lot of things Jorn missed in the conversation since he was human and did not understand a lot about dragons. To him, this is how the conversation went.

"It is good to see you old friend," the messenger dragon imparted.

"It is good to see you as well," Ancient replied. "I'm glad to see you survived the war."

"It depends on your meaning of the word survived. There are only two of us left, one old male and one old female. The chance of us carrying on our kind is very unlikely."

"I know the pain that you are feeling right now. There are many that do not exist now because of the first war. It saddens me to see you affected this way, especially since you served so faithfully. You didn't have to come to Larzencarak's call, but you and the others did. I wish there was a way to repay you, but I know there isn't. This war is not over yet. Many of the dragons are calling this the second war, but it is merely a continuation of the first. Like before, I do not think this war is over, it will start again, and you will be needed one last time. I ask that you and the one other hide yourselves, like you did before, and wait for the ruler to summon you."

"How I long for the days when we were numerous and did not need to hide ourselves. Nevertheless, I will do as you ask; I will not cease from serving the Creator. Perhaps in our exile, we will find a way to save our kind. I have a feeling that I will not see you again until the end of all things."

"I feel the same. I will see you again when the Creator makes everything new. Farewell, Moahdee."

"Farewell to you, Ærlonosanis."

With that, the conversation was over, and Jorn looked down to see his empty hands. He knew that he had missed a lot of the conversation since he had never communicated that way before. Nevertheless, he felt empty, like his hands, as if a significant part of the world had just disappeared. Without saying any words, Ancient began to walk away. However, Jorn felt that he had to say something in the wake of what had just happened. "What do you mean the war isn't over and that it will start again?" he asked, his voice shaking from the experience he had just gone through.

Ancient turned to look at Jorn with a solemn face. "It is not anything you need to worry about," Ancient replied. "The last break between wars was thousands of years. It is not anything you need to concern yourself with. Take care of your family and let the long-lived worry about what comes next." Without any more explanation, Ancient turned back and continued, leaving Jorn to sort through all that he had just witnessed.

Jorn took his time walking to the entrance of the mountain, letting his thoughts wander. For a simple man, he had gone through so much in his life and had seen more than what most humans would ever see. He thanked the Creator for allowing him to have such a life, and his thoughts were filled with the possibilities of what was to come. He walked through the mountain entrance and waved farewell to the two dragon guards on both sides of the entrance, and he received the farewell wave in return. Not far from the mountain entrance, two groups were preparing to leave. One of the groups was Jorn's men, and the other was a group of elves and dwarves. As he came closer, one of the servants ran up to him and bowed in respect.

"All the men and horses are ready to depart, my king," the servant said.

"Liam, how many times do I have to tell you to stop calling me that and to look me in the eyes," Jorn replied.

Liam slowly lifted his head to look at Jorn with a smirk on his face. "You're too nice, you know that. I don't think I will ever get used to a king that acts like a farmer."

"I would think after all these years you would be used to it already. Remember I didn't ask for a servant to wait on me hand and foot. The kings and generals of the army suggested I needed somebody and they sent me you. Now I'm not complaining; you have been a good companion and friend during the war. But you must stop bowing like that; it creeps me out."

"In that case, I should do it more often," Liam reported. The two of them chuckled and embraced in a hug. "You ready to go? I think you're as eager as I am to get there and get back."

Jorn clasped Liam's forearm and looked him right in the eyes. "Not this time, my old friend." From the look on Liam's face, Jorn could tell that he was thinking of a response, so Jorn continued. "I need you to stay here and help Kirianadréth if she needs anything."

"Yes, but couldn't you get someone else to do that, even one of the soldiers?" Liam stuttered out.

"Liam," Jorn said in a calming tone as he let go of Liam's arm. "I trust many in this place with a weapon, but I don't think I trust them with a child. I need you here."

Liam thought about it for a second, then nodded his head. "All right, I'll stay. Don't have too much fun without me."

"I won't, I promise. The only exciting part about this trip is seeing the forest as we ride through it. I'll see you when I get back." Jorn gave Liam a clap on the shoulder and continued to the horses. Liam held his head high as he walked back towards the mountain, yet his pace was slower than his normal walk.

Jorn was almost to his horse when he heard a familiar voice: "There's the new father!" Jorn turned around to see Red Helm and Ravelle coming from the group of elves and dwarves. All Jorn could do was shake his head while laughing and walk over to say farewell to these two.

"What did I tell you, lad?" Red Helm blurted out with the biggest grin on his face. "Making babies is a lot funner than having them. It will be a long time before you and Kirianadréth get a moment of quiet to try and make anymore."

"You're one to talk; you said you had over thirty-one children?" Jorn said in return.

Red Helm burst out laughing and almost tripped himself. "Well, what can I say? I always liked to hear my wife scream more than the babies."

"Barbarians, you are all barbarians," Ravelle stated, looking down his nose at both of them.

Jorn and Red Helm couldn't help but laugh at that. Then, a moment later, Ravelle joined in the laughter. "I don't know what I'm ever going to do with you two," Jorn stated. "You two are the most unlikely pair ever."

"What can I say? I like his long silver hair," Red Helm sarcastically remarked as he smacked Ravelle on the back. "If he gives me a chance, I'll braid it for him."

"If you give me a chance, I might be able to turn you into a civilized creature," Ravelle countered.

With that, they all burst out laughing again. It took a few moments before they could bring their laughter under control. Jorn looked at these two and realized he was honestly going to miss them. "So where are you two headed?"

"Well, with the war being over, we need to see to our people," Red Helm answered. "First, we'll stop off at my kingdom."

"If you can call a village and a mine shaft a kingdom," said Ravelle.

"You know it's bigger than that, you pointed-eared elf. It takes several days to go through my kingdom. Sorry, it's not as glamorous as Ronnar's Shieldholt."

"Hopefully it won't take too long, you stinky bearded dwarf."

"Long enough to get things in order; besides, you enjoy our ale and song."

"What do you mean get things in order?" Jorn interrupted.

"Well, my dear friend, I'm retiring as king," Red Helm stated. "I've been king long enough; I'm going to let my oldest son take the throne, and I can see some of the world before I die."

"Where will you go?" Jorn asked deeply concerned.

Ravelle smiled and answered, "the crazy dwarf is coming with me. He will come down to my city in the far south, there he will stay a while and enjoy elven hospitality. After a while, he's free to go anywhere he wants, but I wager he'll get fat and comfortable and live out the rest of his life with the elves."

"Fat and comfortable, yes, but I won't stay there forever. There's only so much elf I can take. Unless I find a short elf for a wife, then I might consider it."

"I doubt you'll find an elf to your liking; all of our women do not have facial hair."

"That's all right, I have enough hair for both of us."

With that said, Jorn stopped the conversation by reaching out and grasping Red Helm's forearm. "That is a conversation between you two on the road; farewell, my friends." Jorn then grasped Ravelle's forearm and said, "I hope in a few years you two will come up and visit; have a safe journey." Jorn took a lingering look at their faces, then turned and continued to his horse.

It didn't take long before they were all on their horses and waving goodbye at each other one last time. A few moments later, the two groups separated and went their ways. Jorn and his small group of soldiers rode out towards the outer farms. The further he rode into the forest, the more he reflected on the last few days. So much had happened he needed time to sort it all out, and a quiet ride through the forest was the perfect place to do it.

* * *

As the day wore on, Kirianadréth continued to walk the halls of the dragon city, still worried about Jorn. From time to time, she checked in on Dragon. He was either sleeping or up playing with Soræniya. He didn't feed as much as the human female servants said he would, which left her with time for other things. Kirianadréth could not help but move around the city; it made her feel a little better. After a while, she found herself in the great throne room, looking up at the great chair that was once her father's. It fit her better when she was a dragon, she thought to herself; nevertheless, it was still hers. She was queen and that burden still weighed heavily on her. She thought of all the possibilities of what the world would become and how her son would fit into that world. After long moments of pondering, she turned her thoughts to the old days and then went to sit in the chair.

Suddenly she felt a great pain in her heart, and she fell to her knees. Kirianadréth clutched at her chest and screamed.

Marahezron came bounding through the doors when he heard her screams. "My queen, are you all right?" Marahezron shouted with deep concern in his eyes and voice, trying to find out what happened.

Kirianadréth looked up and quickly replied with great pain in her voice. "Locate Jorn. He's in pain. Something terrible has happened to him!" She wasn't quite sure how she knew Jorn was in pain, but she guessed it had something to do with her wish, which must have connected them somehow. Still, it didn't matter how it happened to her; it was the fact that it happened that filled her with dread.

Marahezron did not need any more information. He quickly turned and ran out the door. After he was gone, Ancient entered the room to see if he could bring some comfort to Kirianadréth.

Marahezron flew as fast as he could. He had taken four other dragons with him. He knew the general direction that Jorn took, but he wasn't sure where to find him, so he needed as many eyes as he could have. However, as he was flying so fast, the other four could barely keep up. He didn't let his wings glide for a moment. His eyesight scoured the land as it rushed by below him, not leaving it for a moment. After a while, he spotted several horses in the distance, running around riderless. As he approached the horses, he found the rest of the group in a small opening in the forest.

Marahezron quickly landed, his feet making a thud upon hitting the ground. To his surprise, he saw that the group had been attacked by a band of orcs. He saw that most of the group seemed to have been killed quickly, and beside their corpses lay a few bodies of orcs and horses. He followed a trail of orc corpses deeper into the woods, away from the initial fight, till he found Jorn. He was lying with his back on the ground, with more than twenty slain orcs around him.

Marahezron moved in closer to examine the scene. Jorn himself was missing a leg, right below the knee, and his body had been pierced with many arrows. However, he was still alive, but barely enough to speak.

"You're late," Jorn remarked as he moaned in great pain.

"Be still. Try not to speak," Marahezron said as he bent down and put his hand underneath Jorn's head. Though his hands were massive, Marahezron was as gentle as he could be out of consideration for Jorn's fragile state.

"Looks like my time is up, my friend," Jorn said, still gasping for air and moaning in pain. On the threshold of death, Jorn could only think of things unsaid.

"No. You will be just fine. Ancient can heal you. I will take you to him. Just don't give up. We did not come this far to lose you now. I will not fail you as I did my king!"

"You did not fail me, good friend. This was beyond your hands. I'm sorry I won't be around to see our kids grow up together." Jorn lifted up a bloody hand and set it upon Marahezron's arm. He tried gathering all of his strength to speak, but blood started coming out of his mouth, making it harder for him to breathe without choking. "Promise me you will help raise my son, and that you will look after him. He will need guidance."

"I promise, friend. I will look after him. I will train him to be a good king like his grandfather, like his father. And if I have to, I will get Ancient to help." Marahezron looked down at Jorn to see him breathe his last. All he could do was stand there and hold Jorn's lifeless body. No words came to his mind, only the thought of failure. Jorn had once saved his life, and he had hoped to repay that debt. But now he could only repay the debt by keeping a promise to Jorn's son.

✳✳✳

Back at the dragon city, Kirianadréth lay on the throne room floor, still clutching her heart. The doors were shut, so no one could see her in pain. Her only company in the room were Ancient and four guards, who were watching her intently. For a moment, it seemed as though she might get better, and she even looked up at Ancient. But then suddenly she screamed in pain, and the room was filled with a bright light. Even as a light illuminated the room, they could still hear her screams—and these were not from physical pain but from the pain of the heart, the pain of loss. Then her screams became a mighty dragon roar, and as the light faded, they could see her magnificent form.

As beautiful as she was before she became human, she now lay there as the dragon queen of old. A mighty ruby-scaled dragon with her large wings open and draping across the floor. However, there was no pride or dignity in her bones; she simply lay on the floor, weeping and unwilling to get up. Ancient and the guards knew what had happened and were filled with grief—not only for the queen but also for the young child who would never know his father. Ancient himself worried about the upbringing of Dragon, for when the human servants of the queen would leave, Dragon would be the only human in the city. Raising him would be more difficult now than it was before, but nevertheless, they would raise him, no matter the cost.

As for Dragon, he was in his mother's chambers, on her bed. Soræniya was there with him, her wings wrapped around him, keeping him warm as he slept, not knowing what was going on. He had no idea that his whole life was changing around him, and that it was only the start of what would happen.

***

Later that evening, Marahezron returned to the city with the bodies to be laid to rest. He brought Jorn's body to Kirianadréth in the throne room. There he laid Jorn in Kirianadréth's arms and left the room as she began to weep over her beloved. Moments later, he found himself deep in the city, standing in front of Larzencarak's resting place.

"I'm sorry, my king, I failed again," Marahezron began to whisper to the stones with his head downcast.

"You did not fail," Ancient strongly replied as he came up beside Marahezron.

"I feel otherwise," Marahezron snapped back. "The ones that I swore to protect seemed to keep dying. If that is not failure, I do not know what is."

"There is more going on than you or I can ever understand. So tell me what you saw and what you heard."

Marahezron turned to face Ancient. "There was only one other human survivor, and he did not last long. Before he died, we were able to get some information out of him. This was not an accident; it was not a band of wild orcs stumbling on a group of traveling humans. Orcs appeared out of nowhere; the forest was not dense enough to hide easily. Which means it was a planned attack; they knew the route Jorn was taking, and they laid a trap." Marahezron put his hand up, stopping Ancient from replying. "Which means two things: either we have a spy in our midst, which I doubt, or dark magic was used. Either way, it does not look good, and I don't think this war is exactly over."

"Now, Marahezron, you're beginning to sound a little like me," Ancient sarcastically remarked. "I thought I was the only one who could speak doom and gloom. Is there anything else we should know?"

"Yes, before he died, the humans spoke of something he heard an orc say. He knew a little bit of the orc language from the war, and he caught bits and pieces being shouted in the fight. From what he could understand, the orcs were acting on orders from one called the Dark One." With that being said, there was a long moment of silence between the two of them until Marahezron got up the nerve to ask. "Could he mean the Deceiver?"

"I don't think so," Ancient finally said after taking another moment of silence to ponder the question. "That name could be attached to anyone with evil intent; it doesn't necessarily mean the Deceiver. On the other hand, we can't take this lightly; we must remain vigilant. The war seems to be changing; we do not know what form it will take. However, I have a feeling we will not be the ones fighting it. I believe that battle will be led by our prince. Our jobs now must be to train him and prepare him for what's to come. I would like to say we can go easy on him, but I don't think we can. I do not know what timeframe we have, so we must train him hard and fast."

"We," Marahezron remarked. "Why do, I have a feeling that I will do all the hard training and you will tell him bedtime stories?"

"Marahezron, teaching someone the difference between good and evil sometimes is harder than teaching them how to fight with the sword. You should know; I taught you when you were young."

"All I can remember is being bored during your lectures. However, if this child is anything like his two parents, this is going to be harder than you're making it sound."

"Yes, I know, but we have no choice; the fate of the world just might rest on his shoulders one day."

"That's what I'm afraid of; what type of being is he going to become?"

They both looked up at Larzencarak's stone form as if asking him for answers.

"I don't know," Ancient finally replied. "For once, I can honestly say I do not know. He is the Dragon Child, and I do not think this world is ready for him or him ready for this world. The Creator knows what he is doing so we will have to wait and see what the child will become."

Raising Dragon

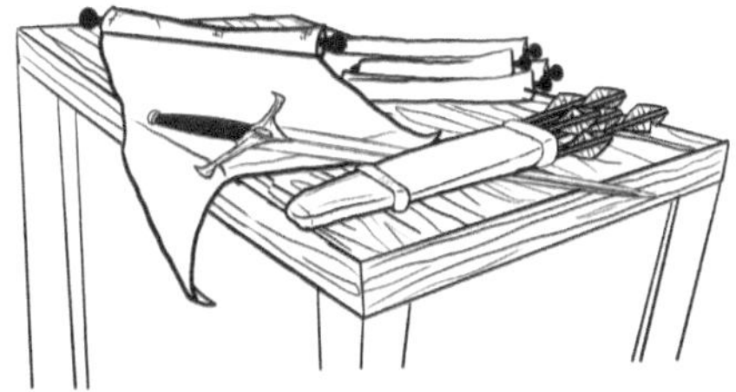

Time moved on steadily, and things returned to normal. Evil seemed to shrink back farther into the darkness, leaving no trace of its whereabouts. The elves and dwarves, as well as the other creatures, returned to their secluded homes, quickly becoming a myth. Even the dragons kept to themselves, never showing themselves to the younger races. Man, soon became the major race out in the open. They were finally able to increase their population across the earth, and because man rarely saw the other races, the truth quickly became a legend and was sometimes forgotten altogether. Only the settlements that dwelt near the dragon capital kept accurate accounts of the past and saw dragons and other races. The dragons also began to see the effects of the passing of time: the younger dragons within the capital showed little respect for the old ways.

Dragon, of course, grew as every child does. However, because he was half dragon, he grew quicker than human children, which was one of the things that made raising him a little harder. There was no way to measure where he was in his growth physically, or mentally. That and the fact that there were no humans in the dragon city, and Dragon himself had never seen a human. The humans who served his mother returned to their homes shortly after she returned to her dragon form. That did not affect him much; he loved being raised in the dragon city. He felt at home among the dragons, even though he knew he was different.

Sixteen years after his birth, Dragon grew into a stout young man. He did not look like a young man of sixteen; instead, he looked to be in his late twenties or early thirties. He was average in build—not too muscular, but not sloppy either. He stood about five feet, ten inches tall, and had short, reddish-blond hair. His hair did not grow long at all; it grew no longer than half an inch. He had no facial hair and had a light complexion. Though he seemed to be an average man, he was not. Dragon's strength and agility surpassed that of any normal human.

It was around the time of year that the humans called harvest time, when the weather was still fair, though it just seemed to rain a little bit more. Dragon liked to take walks in the forest near the dragon city. He loved the smell of the woods after a fresh rain. On one particular day, he walked far into the forest, not taking notice of how far he had wandered away from the dragon city. Taking deep breaths, he slowly absorbed every little thing that was happening in the forest. He let the forest life brush against him as he walked by, listening to the moisture drop off the leaves as well as hearing the birds and insects go through their daily lives. He stopped to take in the sight of an enormous tree when he heard some rustling in the bushes behind him. He slowly turned and peered at the bushes.

He planted his feet wide apart, preparing to move at the slightest sign of trouble. He stared at the bushes for a moment, and when all seemed safe, he began to turn back around. Then suddenly, a red dragon burst out from behind the bushes and snapped its jaws at Dragon. Quickly, Dragon rolled to the side and then bolted through the forest, with the red dragon right behind him. He ducked under branches and jumped over logs, moving as fast as he could with all the grace of an elf. He burst through the underbrush like it was nothing, doing everything he could to stay one step ahead of the red dragon. As he was running, he saw two trees standing close together, which helped him devise a plan. He stretched out his arms as he jumped through the trees. With his massive strength, he broke through the trees like sword through skin. The trees fell on each other, blocking the red dragon's path. He skidded to a halt and turned to see if the dragon was still following him. He stood still for a moment, waiting to see the dragon come into view. After a while, when the dragon didn't come out of the brush and trees, Dragon took a step back. He looked around worriedly. Something was not right.

With his second step back, he heard a noise above him. When he looked up, his eyes filled with fright. The red dragon jumped down upon him, its hind feet crushing Dragon's face down into the dirt. Dark red scales on its back and light red scales on its belly, the dragon stood at least four times taller than Dragon. With four short horns crowning its head and a unique five-tipped tail, the dragon sat upright, crossing its arms, and looking down at its prey. Feeling the pain of a massive beast standing on his back, Dragon muttered something underneath the dragon's foot that could barely be heard.

The red dragon began to laugh, and then with a look of delight, it put its hand up to its ear. "I'm sorry, I can't hear you," the red dragon said sarcastically in a feminine voice.

Dragon used as much strength as he could to push himself up just enough to be heard. "You win," he said, barely, as he was trying to keep from being crushed.

The red dragon stepped back and sat down, looking at Dragon. As he picked himself up off the ground and dusted himself off, he glared at the red dragon. "You've cheated, Sonya," he said, very aggravated.

"No, I didn't," she replied, smiling an innocent smile.

"I said you couldn't fly—that's what made this game fairer," Dragon remarked as he walked closer to her. "You keep winning because you keep cheating." He sounded aggravated, yet inside he found the whole thing amusing, as he usually did.

"I don't cheat," Soræniya commented as she turned her head, as though she were insulted by Dragon's words. She then quickly put her hand up in front of his face, indicating that he could talk to her hand.

"So you don't cheat. How do you explain getting behind me so fast?" Dragon sarcastically asked, ignoring her hand.

"I'm just too fast for you," Soræniya said. She smiled and lowered her face close to his.

"I still think you cheated," Dragon said as he put his hand on her nose and rubbed it, as he had always done since he had known her. Soræniya began to laugh, and so did Dragon. He knew she cheated, as she had done many times before, but he cared for her too much to argue. Besides, it was just a game—a game they had played ever since they were young. Soræniya, or Sonya, as Dragon called her, was very playful, like a young puppy. Dragon liked that aspect of her, for he was a lot like her. Kirianadréth, his mother, constantly tried to get him to be more serious since he was the prince of the dragons. She even made him attend long and grueling classes with two of her most trusted subjects, Ancient and Marahezron, Sonya's father. Still, in spite of everyone's efforts, Dragon had a tendency to daydream. He also had a tendency to disappear when no one was looking. That was when he and Sonya would take their walks together, away from all the bustle of the city.

Dragon walked over to a nearby fallen log and laid down on it, looking up at the sky. Soræniya came over and laid her head on the log next to Dragon's. Together, they stared up at the blue sky, enjoying the day and letting everything else that mattered slip away.

Dragon took a quick glance at Soræniya and began to think back to all they had gone through together. At first, he thought about her name and her nickname. She got the nickname Sonya from Dragon when he was young, since he couldn't say all the dragon names properly. So instead of saying Soræniya, he said Sonya, and she liked it, and so did some of the dragons in the city. To her father's dismay, many called her Sonya, which was an odd dragon name. However, Sonya was anything but odd; she happened to be among the most talented of the dragons.

For example, one of the greatest misconceptions that humans have about dragons is that they are too large and cumbersome to do anything delicate and intricate. The truth of the matter is that dragons have fine-tuned many arts, and one of them is carving. Even with massive hands, dragons are able to hold the smallest of tools and carve the most beautiful of things— more intricate than anything the dwarves can carve and more majestic than anything of the elves.

One of the best carvers in the city was Sonya. In fact, she had many talents, with the help of her five-tipped tail. She was declared to be the best at many things; however, a great majority of the dragons said that she had one problem—that at times she could not focus because she was too hyperactive and could not control herself. Of course, they blamed Dragon for her problem, saying that he taught her to do that. Dragon, unfortunately, was blamed for many things, whether he had a part in them or not. He, if anything, was the true oddity in the city, and he stood out more than he liked to. Still, Sonya was there with him from the time of their birth. She was, and still is, his closest friend—a shelter, a rock to lean upon. Though he wouldn't admit it, he wouldn't know what to do if she wasn't there. Sonya never judged him, or expected things out of him like the rest of the city did because he was the prince. Around her, he could be himself and just enjoy his time with her like a normal dragon.

"It's a wonderful morning," Dragon said, taking another deep breath. "It's always nice to be out after the rain."

"Especially when the sun is up," Sonya simply added.

"The sun!" loudly exclaimed Dragon as he sat up quickly. He rapidly scrutinized the position of the sun in the sky, trying to estimate the time of day. "It's midmorning. I'm late again!"

"Not again! My father is going to kill you if you miss another lesson!"

"I know," Dragon quickly replied as he jumped off the log. "Come on, let's hurry!"

Sonya got up and unfolded her wings, knocking over a few bushes. As she jumped in the air and began to get lift, she grabbed Dragon's arms and then took flight. As they rose higher than the treetops, they were able to see the mountain where the dragon city was. Without hesitation, Sonya began flapping her wings as fast as she could, gaining great speed toward the city.

The closer they came to the city, the more Dragon urged Sonya to move faster. By the time she reached the mountainside, she could barely breathe. However, without delay, she swooped into the opening at the top of the mountain and dove straight down. As for Dragon, he was very confident in her flying skills, so he was relaxed as she maneuvered into the city. She whipped past other dragons trying to enter the city through the mountaintop. Sonya's swift flight caused other dragons to swerve out of her way as well as shout a few curses in her direction. She didn't slow down until she reached mid-city, and then she opened her wings to glide over a walkway. When Sonya reached it, she dropped Dragon so she could land and catch her breath. The moment Dragon's feet touched solid ground, he bolted into a nearby passageway. The mid-city corridor was the largest in the entire city; the average dragons stood only one-fourth of the height of the corridor. Dragon himself was too small to be noticed in such a large space. He was running as fast as he could, ducking under feet, bellies, and jumping over tails. He was trying to reach the opposite end, where two massive doors stood and the passage tapered off to smaller halls. The massive doors lead to Marahezron's training room, where all the warriors in the city were trained, where Dragon was supposed to be earlier that day. Dragon wasn't absent-minded; he simply had different ideas than his mother about what was important.

Two-thirds of the way down the corridor, Dragon spotted something familiar— an enormous gray dragon that seemed to be slowing down the traffic in the passageway. Even with his wings wrapped tightly around himself, his back and head scraped the walls and the ceiling. The gray dragon happened to be coming Dragon's way and had spotted him.

"Young Prince Dragon, it's so good to see you again," the mighty dragon said in a voice so deep that it seemed to echo in the hall.

"Venor," Dragon called back. "I haven't seen you in weeks. Where have you been? And what are you doing in here? You can barely move!"

"Young prince, I'm sorry," Venor replied. "I'm too big to see any other place in the city, so I come here from time to time to say I at least saw some of the city. Most of the time, I'm visiting my brother. You remember me telling you about Ganez." Venor and his brother were dragon legends: for many years after their birth, they never stopped growing. It was rumored that Ganez was almost the size of a mountain, but no one had seen him for years. Venor had stopped growing, but he was big enough to be talked about. Dragon and Venor were great friends, because both of them were never truly accepted. One was too big, and the other was too small. Still, they accepted each other, and they enjoyed talking to each other.

"How is your brother?" Dragon asked, easily forgetting everything else on his mind.

"He's doing fine, or as well as a dragon his size could be doing," Venor replied, his deep voice drawing out the words.

Venor began to tell Dragon about how easy it was to visit his mother than his brother. Of course, Dragon listened to Venor as he smiled and laughed. That is, until Dragon heard a horn blow at the end of the hall. Quickly, he remembered what he was doing, and with a face full of shock, he asked Venor if he could help. What Dragon was asking for, they had done this several times before. The truth of it was that they had done it only twice before, out in the forest, and Sonya was there to catch Dragon.

Venor curled Dragon up in the tip of his tail. "Are you ready, young prince?"

"Yes," was all that Dragon answered as he gritted his teeth and hoped this was a good idea.

"Then here we go," Venor said as he picked Dragon up. Then he whipped half of his tail, and when it snapped, he let Dragon go. The force of Venor's tail sent Dragon flying across the corridor toward the large doors. Dragon sailed over all the other dragons with ease. Many of the dragons in the corridor stopped and watched their wingless, and probably witless, prince go sailing over their heads. As he came close to the doors, he put his feet out to prepare to stop against the doors. However, the moment he got close, one side suddenly opened. Dragon let out a yell as he hurled into the room, crashing against a table.

Marahezron stood by the door with his hand on it, looking down at Dragon. Then he looked up to see his daughter coming down the passage. He quickly shut the door and realized why Dragon was late. "This is the two hundredth and sixty-ninth time that you have been late," Marahezron noted, expressing his disappointment and frustration with Dragon. "What am I ever going to do with you? What is so much more important than these lessons?" Marahezron just wanted to find out why Dragon couldn't attend his class properly.

"I don't know. Anything else?" Dragon sarcastically remarked as he picked himself up off the table he landed on and broke.

"Watch your mouth, Dragon," Marahezron snapped. "Your mother wants you to learn as much as you can. Now I take care of teaching you how to fight, and only the Creator knows what Ancient teaches you." That, of course, was his usual remark about Ancient; Marahezron thought that defending oneself and others was the greatest skill one could learn.

"Ancient teaches me wisdom and knowledge, things you never grasped." Dragon gained a little bit of delight with every mocking thing he said. He and Marahezron never got along, and Dragon couldn't quite figure out why. Of course, a part of him didn't care one way or another. He had a few ideas, but he could never get Marahezron to admit anything. Dragon wasn't necessarily someone looking for trouble, but he did sometimes enjoy pressing his luck, especially with Marahezron.

"What did I say about your mouth? For that, I will be harder on you today," Marahezron said as he glared at Dragon. "I know you respect Ancient, but I wish you would respect me too. Knowing how to be a warrior is just as important—at least that's what I think. Your grandfather probably would agree with me if he were still alive." With his massive hand, Marahezron tossed Dragon a sword. "Now, with no more delay, let us begin."

As Dragon grasped the hilt of the sword, preparing to spar, he reminded himself once again that perhaps someday he should learn to keep his mouth shut. But not today.

***

For several hours, Marahezron and Dragon sparred. Marahezron used—only his tail and claws as he attacked Dragon. As for Dragon, Marahezron made him try everything, attempting to give him a wide range of fighting knowledge. He used a sword, then a spear, an ax, his hands and arms, and then back to a sword. Out of all the dragons in the city, other than his mother, Dragon was the only one who could keep up with Marahezron. The knowledge of that unfortunately gave Dragon a little bit of a hothead. Many of the dragons would have loved to be in Dragon's place and to be taught by Marahezron. However, Dragon would've wished to be anywhere but there, wandering the city or even traveling through the forest. As time wore on, they both became rigid and began to get on each other's nerves. Marahezron, as always, continued to make highly critical remarks. As for Dragon, he always replied sarcastically and made faces at Marahezron when the dragon had his back turned. Like most typical young males, Dragon continued to push Marahezron's patience and control to their limits.

Marahezron and Dragon circled the room several times, throwing aggressive glances at each other, preparing for the next attack. Then suddenly, Marahezron swung his tail horizontally at Dragon. As he did, Dragon back- flipped over the tail, landing on his feet and bringing his sword up to block. Marahezron quickly brought his tail back and clashed against the sword. Then he began whipping his tail around like a sword, and with every motion, Dragon's sword answered, blocking every move. Marahezron became more aggressive and started pushing Dragon back, and with every step back that Dragon took, Marahezron could see his frustration grow.

Finally, Dragon had been pushed back far enough; in a desperate move, he swung hard at the tail. Marahezron pulled his tail back, allowing Dragon to overswing, and when he did, Marahezron hit him in the chest with his tail. The force of the hit sent Dragon sailing back, landing on the ground.

Marahezron stood there, shaking his head in disappointment. "Pay attention and focus," he snarled, aggravated at Dragon. Of course, he was grateful for the break in the fight, which gave him time to catch his breath. Marahezron would never admit it, but Dragon was a fair match for him, even though he was half-human.

"I was," Dragon answered as he picked himself up and threw his sword down, showing his dislike for Marahezron's constant barrage of both physical and verbal attacks.

"You are just like your father, unruly and undisciplined," Marahezron commented.

"Since I didn't know my father, I'll take that as a compliment," Dragon replied, trying to keep his calm. Still, he noticed that his father was always a touchy subject with Marahezron, as it was with himself. Dragon realized he might regret it; nevertheless, he wasn't going to drop the argument this time.

"It wasn't a compliment," Marahezron snapped back. He glared at Dragon for a moment and then turned around, unwilling to see Dragon's smugness.

"You're just jealous," Dragon said, unwilling to let this conversation go. He had enough, and he was determined to get a straight answer from Marahezron. He just needed to push the right topic far enough to make Marahezron break. Even though Marahezron was staring at the wall, ignoring his comment, Dragon continued anyway. "I've heard what the other dragons say about you and my mother."

"You shouldn't listen to them. They know nothing," Marahezron finally responded.

"It's a funny thing what others say." The more Dragon spoke, the more his words became scornful and hard. "It must've been a mighty blow for a great warrior to have loved a great dragon like my mother, then for him to be passed over and lose her to a human."

"Watch your tongue, Dragon. Those are some bold words!" Marahezron's temper began to rise, and in order to control it, he took deep breaths and blew puffs of smoke out of his nostrils.

"What's the matter, Marahezron? Feeling a little guilty?"

Marahezron turned back around to look at Dragon. His face was filled with frustration. "There is no reason for me to feel guilty about anything," he said.

"It's a strange thing what the dragons say—that you were the only one there when my father died. It would be a lot easier to have my mother without my father in the way," Dragon speculated.

"You were not there," Marahezron started yelling at Dragon. "You did not see him die. I had great respect for your father and your mother! I would have never done such a thing, no matter how much I desired your mother!"

"So you did desire her!" Dragon stepped forward, encouraging this quarrel, determined to see it through.

"This conversation is over, Dragon!"

"Not to me, it isn't. I finally figured out why you are always so hard on me!" Dragon took a few more aggressive steps forward, staring at Marahezron, unwilling to back down. "It was a mighty blow to lose my mother to my father! But now you will lose your daughter to me! Haven't you noticed that she hasn't spent very much time with you?" Dragon watched as Marahezron's face filled with rage. "Truth is, she doesn't want to be around a coward and a traitor!"

Upon hearing those words, Marahezron had enough. He snapped his tail at Dragon, sending it speeding through the air like a spear. Which was exactly what Dragon expected. He quickly stepped aside as the tip was thrust at him. Acting quickly, Dragon wrapped his arms around the tail. Then he dug his hands underneath the scales and pulled tightly. When he did this, Marahezron's face filled with surprise and fear at the speed and agility with which Dragon responded, not to mention a move he had never seen Dragon do before. As Dragon pulled, Marahezron lost his balance and fell to his stomach, scratching and clawing at the walls and floor, trying to save himself from Dragon's aggressive move. He had trained Dragon for years and had never seen his full strength until now.

The truth was that half of Marahezron's mind was in shock, not knowing what to do, and the other half stayed focused on resisting Dragon's attack. However, this had no effect; when Dragon mustered all of his strength, he swung Marahezron around like a rope. The first time around, Marahezron's head scraped against the nearby wall, carving a niche into it. The second time around, he let go, sending Marahezron hurling toward the doors like a boulder.

Marahezron's head and wings smashed against one of the mighty doors, taking it right off the hinges. The door fell to the ground, with Marahezron crashing down on top of it. A little dazed and out of focus, Marahezron looked up, trying to get his bearings, only to see Ancient staring down at him with an enormous grin on his face. "I see your student is learning well," Ancient said with a slight chuckle. "Better than expected from one so small."

"If you have come for him," Marahezron replied as he got up, shaking the rubble from his wings and back, "you can take him. As a matter of fact, he is all yours! Permanently," Marahezron snapped and then stormed off with smoke literally coming out of his mouth, as though he was getting ready to throw fire. However, as much as he was angry with Dragon, he was somewhat prideful of being bested by him, for it was he who taught Dragon everything he knew.

Ancient peered into the room to see Dragon still standing firm with his fists clenched. However, his head was bowed in shame, unwilling to look Ancient in the eyes. "Dragon," Ancient said in a deep but calm voice as he motioned for Dragon to come forward. Slowly but surely, Dragon moseyed his way over to Ancient, still unwilling to look him in the eyes. Ancient looked down at him with a smile and commented, "Dragon, as much as I'd like to see one of Marahezron's students defeat him at his own game, I would ask that you would be nicer to the doors. They have stood here as long as I have." Both Ancient and Dragon looked down at the door in rubble and began to laugh.

"Forgive me, Ancient. It won't happen again," Dragon said remorsefully to Ancient as he finally looked up at him. For as long as he had known him, Ancient had always been able to make Dragon open up and speak his mind. Dragon felt safe around Ancient, even though he was considered to be the most powerful dragon in the entire city. Marahezron, the greatest warrior in the city, would not take on Ancient. No one ever said why, but there was something about Ancient's demeanor that said there was more to him than just looks.

"There's nothing to forgive, Dragon," Ancient replied as he pointed to the door. I myself have broken many things in my days. As a matter of fact, me and a few others made quite a mess of the throne room in our earlier years." They both laughed together, and then Ancient put one arm on Dragon's back and pointed down the corridor. "Now it is my turn to teach you things. Come, Dragon, we have much to discuss," said Ancient.

As they made their way through the city, Ancient began to inquire about the reason for the fight. "Marahezron will take several days to calm down. You had him so mad that his lungs were fuming with smoke. I give it about a week, and then you'll be back, fighting with him again," Ancient said.

"No, I don't want to go back to him," responded Dragon with no hesitation, showing his aggravation on the subject.

"All right, Dragon, what started this?" Ancient asked in a calm yet firm voice.

"He treats me like I'm human!"

Ancient put his hand on his head and shook his head in sheer amazement at their foolishness. "Dragon, I am not one to agree with Marahezron. However, you are half human, whether you like it or not." No sooner did the words come out of Ancient's mouth than Dragon quickly snarled, giving Ancient a dirty look. "Now that's enough," Ancient quickly snapped back. "You can treat Marahezron with that disrespect, but you will not treat me that way."

Dragon, feeling ashamed of his behavior, quickly responded by lowering his head and apologizing. "I'm sorry, Ancient. I have been a little on edge lately."

Ancient let out a small sigh, acknowledging Dragon's hard position in the city, feeling a bit sympathetic for him. "Then I apologize as well. I could not imagine the hardships that you go through being what you are. A dragon that is half human, being raised in the city that is filled with nothing but full-blooded dragons. I also understand that some of them even have a disdain for humans. However, I would like you to know that you are a blessing to many."

Dragon shook his head slowly. "I don't see it, and I don't believe it." He knew Ancient meant well, but still, he felt as though there was a hole in his heart. "How could I be any type of blessing for the drag-ons?"

Ancient stopped and looked down at Dragon, wanting to answer the question. Then again, there was no easy answer to that question. "Come with me," was all that he could say. He then turned and con-tinued walking down the hall, with Dragon quickly following him.

For a while, they walked together with no words exchanged. Dragon periodically looked up at Ancient, patiently waiting for him to speak. Still, no words came out of his mouth, so they continued on deeper into the city till they reached the gardens, which were mag-nificent and made to look like the gardens of old where the dragons once dwelt with the Creator. They were tended daily so that nothing would look out of place. There were some plants that could not be found anywhere else in the world. Mist seemed to hover at the base of all the plants, and light peered into the room. The light itself was brought down from the great opening in the mountain. It traveled down through the city, in specially designed holes that opened up in the gardens. The lighting then bounced off of reflective shields, which sent the light over the plants. Deep within the roots of the city and the mountain, this paradise glittered with light as if it were midday.

The gardens were a place of rest and relaxation for all dragons. However, Dragon himself felt that the outdoors was a better place for him. Even though the gardens were large and beautiful, they were still within the city, giving him the feel of a prison. Nevertheless, he had great respect for Ancient, and he followed him anywhere he wanted to go.

There were only four entrances to the gardens, evenly spaced throughout the cavern, as well as four sets of stairs leading down into them. Ancient carefully walked down, and since he only had his front appendages, he looked like someone crawling down the stairs. With his tail trailing behind him, he reached the bottom and sat at the base of a beautiful marble fountain that was carved in the shape of a tree. The water came out of the top of the tree then ran down the leaves like rain and filled a beautiful silver pool. He flipped his tail over the side of the pool and dipped it into the water. He put his hand out and let the water from the fountain fall onto it. Ancient took a moment to wait for Dragon to settle himself down onto the ground. "I do not understand why you hate humans so much," Ancient said with such curiosity. "You have never seen a human. If anything, you should be proud to be a human. Your father was a great man, and many dragons loved him."

"So everyone keeps telling me," Dragon responded, a little annoyed. "I never knew my father. It's a little hard to grow up underneath the shadow of a man I never knew."

"I know. It's a shame you didn't know him. Perhaps if you did, you would have a different opinion of humans."

"I don't think so. Humans deserve no respect from us. From the stories I've heard, they destroy everything they touch," Dragon said. "They are no better than the beasts of the earth!"

"I do not think that is what is bothering you, so why don't you tell me what is truly on your mind." Ancient was always able to read Dragon's facial expressions, no matter how hard he tried to deceive him.

Dragon hesitated for a moment, and then he looked at Ancient with clarity. "The dragons are saying that my mother was human at one point in time. If that were so, then why am I not human? Would it not be better if I was one or the other?" As Dragon continued talking, he became more aggravated with the whole subject. "I prefer to be a dragon, but being half a dragon is no fun at all. Everyone says I'm meant for greatness, but how can I be great if I'm stuck in a human body!"

Ancient quickly took his hand, cupping it full of water, and threw it at Dragon. As the water flew toward Dragon, he covered his face with his arms. The water hit him, drenching him completely. Dragon uncovered his face and glared at Ancient, who was now leaning back and laughing. "Cool down, Dragon," Ancient said, still laughing.

"Dragon, let me share something with you, which may perhaps give you a little more enlightenment in your life." Ancient leaned forward to talk to Dragon more closely. "Dragon, let me share with you what the humans call the realm of magic. Now magic is a poor word for such a great thing. You see, magic is the essence of what the Creator put into effect, or as other dragons call it, the essence of creation. You see, the Creator formed everything you see before you, and in everything he put an order. He created a balance between everything. There is nothing on this earth that does not have a purpose. The unseen force that keeps that balance or purpose is what the humans call magic."

Dragon crossed his arms and rolled his eyes. "So what does this have to do with me?" He respected Ancient and what he had to say, knowing it was important; still, he always had a hard time listening to Ancient's long answers.

"I'm getting to that. Be patient," Ancient quickly replied, remembering Dragon's short attention span. "You see, there are gifted beings that could tap into magic. A few of these beings are dragons, elves, dwarves, and humans. And what they all have in common is a choice. What most beings do not understand is that their choices have consequences. Even if they do not see them at first, they will see them at the end. For those who use what the Creator has put in motion for wrongdoings will pay a terrible price, especially if it is not the will of the Creator. No matter how powerful anyone may become, they still must answer to the Creator."

"I still don't see how this applies to me," Dragon said as he rubbed his hand across his forehead, confused about what Ancient was talking about. Though Dragon enjoyed talking with Ancient, the old dragon definitely had the gift of rambling on.

Ancient glared down at Dragon, annoyed by his comment. "Let me finish," he said. "You see, Dragon, I have heard about other halfbreeds." The moment Ancient mentioned that, Dragon began to pay attention. So Ancient continued, "I have never seen them, but the rumor is that they exist. Great dragons and wizards have tried to harness the power of both races. Every attempt has ended badly for various reasons. One reason is that the half-breed is overwhelmed with power and destroys everything in its path. The other reason is that the half-breed is deformed. The Creator does not smile down on those half-breeds because they were created by dark magic."

"So you're saying he smiles down upon me?" Dragon cut in, anxious to find out where Ancient was going with this. "One thing though: if the other half-breeds ended up bad, how did I come about?

"That is a very good question. I can see the wheels turning in your head. You were always a bright boy. You see, the others ended up the way they were because it was not meant to be. How humans mate and dragons mate is extremely different—as different as fire and ice. It is impossible to make a half-breed between dragons and humans. However, that never discourages evil people from trying to attempt it. Your mother and your father loved each other and obeyed the Creator. So he granted her the ability to be with your father by making her human. How else do you think they were able to mate? Now don't ask me how it's done. You're too young to know that."

To Dragon's shock, he could've sworn that Ancient blushed after that comment. As for him, he was somewhat discouraged because no one would talk to him about the mating of humans, which always vexed him.

"However," Ancient continued, clearing his throat, "I believe he did it for another reason as well. I do not think she was entirely human, because if she was, she could not have continued to rule the dragon empire. So by that act, the Creator allowed your birth. And now, before me stands the one and only, for the lack of a better word. A perfect half-breed." Ancient put his hand on Dragon's back and looked him in the eyes. "What better way to unite two old rivals—not through a union but through flesh. There was only so much that your mother and father's love could do. Your birth united the races in a way we could not dream possible. I believe you were born to bring peace between the races."

Dragon sat with his head lowered, contemplating what Ancient had said. For a moment, he felt foolish that he had not seen it that way. All this time he had been looking for a purpose, and he sat questioning whether Ancient was right or not. You could see it in his eyes that his mind was racing with many thoughts. He still did not think well of mankind, so instead, he focused on great deeds and making a name for himself.

"Come on, Dragon, we will talk about your thoughts as we walk," Ancient said as he got up from the fountain. "Perhaps on the way, we will meet up with Soræniya." Ancient looked at Dragon and saw an odd look on his face. "That's right. You call her by her human name, Sonya. I keep forgetting that you have a hard time pronouncing dragon words. That is why the dragons have three languages—one for the dragons, one for the magical creatures, and one for the humans."

As Dragon stood up, Ancient flicked his tail, splashing more water on Dragon. Shaking the water off, Dragon looked at Ancient with a smirk. Ancient laughed and then began to walk back up the stairs.

Dragon paused for a moment as a thought entered his head. "Ancient," Dragon called up to his mentor.

Ancient stopped moving and turned around to look at Dragon. "Yes, young prince."

"I just thought of something," Dragon stated.

Ancient chuckled and couldn't help but remark back. "That does happen from time to time."

"Very funny, Ancient; however I'm being serious."

"All right, young prince, what thought do you have?"

"Why don't you teach me magic?" Dragon waited a moment for Ancient to respond, but when he didn't, Dragon continued his train of thought. "You said magic is a part of this world, and you said I would do great things. So if I'm going to do great things, it would be wise for me to learn magic. It is rumored that you are the greatest with magic, so why don't you speak about it more?"

Ancient let out a long sigh as if he was waiting for that question for a long time. "Dragon, like all things, there is a time and a place to learn. Just like sword fighting, you don't hand a baby a sword; you wait until they are ready."

"Am I ready," Dragon eagerly asked.

"Unfortunately, not," Ancient replied watching Dragon as his words hit home. It was as if life simply drained out of Dragon upon hearing those words. So Ancient continued trying to find ways to encourage him. "The truth of the matter is that it is not up to me. The Creator himself has ordained when and how you will learn magic. I do know this, you have much more to go through in life before you learn magic, and it will not be taught by me."

For a long moment, Dragon was silent as he contemplated Ancient's words. It made him sad that he would not be learning magic anytime soon and that his favorite mentor would not teach him. Then his imagination started to roam, trying to figure out the possibilities of when and who would teach him magic. To bring himself back into focus, he decided to change the subject; he would ponder these things later. "I lied to you before about Marahezron," Dragon said a little hesitantly, knowing that he needed to tell Ancient but not quite sure how to bring up the conversation. "I started the fight with Marahezron. Some of the younger dragons said he used to like my mother and that he wanted my father dead."

"Ah, so that's how that fight got started," Ancient stated with a smile on his face.

"I know I shouldn't have started the fight, but I need to know. I am tired of everyone in the city thinking I'm too young to know the truth."

"Dragon, some truths must be earned, and not with age. Others, it is never your place to learn the truth because it belongs to someone. However, I will tell you what you're missing." Ancient gave Dragon a very serious look, basically telling him not to interrupt. "You will one day have to deal with this as a king. You will have subjects that will come to you with two different stories. It is your job to listen to both and distinguish the truth within. That is a mark of a wise king to take two half-truths and turn them into one full truth. The problem which you are suffering from is the fact that you do not have the whole story. It is true that Marahezron had feelings toward your mother and that at first, he hated your father. But time changes many things in people's lives. Your father saved Marahezron's life and Marahezron took that act very seriously. He was forever in your father's debt and as the days went by, he became friends with your father and let go of his feelings toward your mother. Another thing that you are missing is that Marahezron feels as if he has failed. His chief role is to protect the royal family and he personally blames himself for the death of Larzencarak your grandfather. It is called survivors guilt, there was nothing he could have done to prevent your grandfather's death, but Marahezron constantly questions whether or not there was something he could have done. Your father's death did not help, Marahezron blames himself for that as well. He fears that everyone he cares about will be taken from him. Perhaps that is why he is so hard on you because he fears that he will fail you." Ancient paused for a moment looking into Dragon's eyes to see if his words had soaked in at all. "Now we will not speak any further of this today. I want you to think upon it, and perhaps you and Marahezron can come to an understanding. Now I have many other things to teach you before you lose interest in my words." With that, the conversation was done, and Ancient had turned and started up the stairs into the city's corridors.

Dragon followed quietly, trying to organize his thoughts. He was used to this when it came to his time with Ancient. There were days when their conversations were simple and well-constructed, and then there were days when Dragon had a headache from absorbing too much of Ancient's information. That's why Dragon liked walking in the forest, it gave him time to unravel his thoughts. As for today, he had several more hours with Ancient, and his head already felt full.

Dragon and Ancient talked about many things as they walked back through the city. They talked about serious conversations and odd conversations- anything that entered Dragon's mind. Occasionally, when Ancient would start off on one of his long explanations, Dragon would quickly lose interest. He would let his mind wander, and as he did, his eyes would also wander. Several times he almost tripped over Ancient's tail, so in order to steady himself as he daydreamed, he stretched out his arm and let his hand brush against the walls as he walked. Dragon enjoyed feeling the magnificent carvings underneath his fingers. He felt that it brought him closer to his dragon heritage, even though he could only read a portion of the writings on the walls.

Ancient had not yet finished teaching him the rest of the ancient language. As they walked through the hall to the throne room, their conversations could be heard.

"So why can't I cry?" Dragon asked. "There are some days I am just dying to cry, yet no tears come out."

"Well, Dragon," Ancient began to answer, "that is because most dragons cannot cry, so you are probably a lot like them. Perhaps your body has a place for tears, but your body does not produce them. Who knows, Dragon, maybe when you need them the most, they will be there."

They finally reached the throne room, and as they entered, Dragon's eye caught the haze of the barrier that guarded the sword. He stopped dead and turned to look at it. He felt drawn to it for some reason; he always did. Even in his youth, he couldn't explain the strange pull of the sword.

Ancient noticed that Dragon had stopped. "Come on, Dragon, don't linger." He motioned to Dragon to keep moving.

"I have asked you for years, and you have never given me a straight answer," Dragon said. "So I'll ask you one more time: what is the story about the sword?" Dragon wasn't one for giving orders; still, there was a tone of determination in his voice.

Ancient let out a small sigh and then turned around to face Dragon. Today seemed to be a day for questions and answers. Ancient had been confronted for the last time and finally decided that perhaps Dragon should know. "Very well. If you must know, then I will tell you, but you probably won't believe me. That sword is a powerful weapon against the darkness. It is rumored that it is not made from any material of this earth."

"Then where was it made?" Dragon asked. He was not going to let Ancient leave this conversation hanging, as he had done with several over the years.

"It was made in the heavens by the hand of the Creator himself. Of course, these are only rumors. No one knows for sure."

"Why is it here?"

"It is believed, that is the sword that drove man out of the garden. It is the sword of truth, and it was entrusted to us for safekeeping, but no one knows for what exact reason. All that is known is that it was made to aid man. However, man cannot handle it. It would consume them. Since man had fallen into darkness and the sword destroys darkness, the two could not be together. So it was given to the king of the dragons to keep until the time it was needed again. So the only dragons who could touch it were of the royal line. That is why it is protected by the barrier, so the dragons or man cannot get to it. Not to protect it from them, but to protect them from the sword."

"So I can pass through the barrier and touch it," Dragon quickly asked, showing the curiosity of his youth.

"No, not until your mother passes you the throne. If you tried to pass through the barrier while your mother is still alive, you'd be turned to ash."

"So does it have a name? Something magnificent like darkness destroyer, or something similar in the ancient tongue? Something awesome like Thrimfall the powerful."

Ancient smacked his forehead, irritated by the very name. "Thrimfall was a stupid weapon for a foolish elven king. I can't believe out of all the stories you younglings remember, you remember the dumbest of them all. Larzencarak was right the younger generation is going to get us killed."

"It's not my fault all the other stories were boring. You still didn't answer my question, does the sword have a name?"

"Yes, it is rightfully named Truth."

"That's kind of a silly name for a sword. It must not be that powerful," Dragon said with a smirk.

"On the contrary, the sword is very powerful. It is said that the sword could never be broken and that it can even look into the souls of any being. Other than the Creator, that sword is the only other thing on earth that has been given the power to judge. If it is asked to judge, it could wipe out an entire city."

"I doubt that. Now you are just telling stories, and you said Thrimfall was a bad story."

"In that case, let's keep moving then," said Ancient as he turned and continued into the throne room.

Dragon stood for a moment, still staring at the sword. Then he began to move away slowly, his gaze remaining on the sword for a few more moments. When he finally broke off his gaze upon the sword, he realized that his mother was in the room, sitting comfortably on her throne. This knowledge made him quicken his pace a bit, for it had been a while since he had seen his mother. He understood that running a kingdom was a lot of work; there were times he wouldn't see her for weeks, yet he never complained. He cherished every moment with her and did everything he could to make her proud.

As he got closer, he realized that she wasn't alone. Hovering very closely to her head was a small fairy, who was only about four inches tall. Dragon had never seen a fairy, but from the stories he had heard, he assumed that this must be one. She was quite beautiful for a fairy, he thought to himself. Her skin was somewhat pale, yet it seemed very smooth. She had a very thin figure and dark brown hair, almost black. She wore a very thin fabric, almost revealing but not quite, and it seemed to fit to her body like a second skin. Plus, her wings flickered like silver and gold as they moved so rapidly that it almost appeared as though she had none at all.

To Dragon, she was a beautiful sight; she had an aura of light around her as though she were a star that had fallen to earth. When he got a little closer, he realized that her eyes were light green. On the other hand, they peered like daggers at everything she looked at. The more he studied her, the more curious he became about what her personality was like. He didn't want to seem too curious, so he walked slowly up to his mother and bowed respectfully.

"Hello, Mother. It's good to see you," Dragon said as humbly as he could.

"Now, Dragon, stop showing off your manners," Kirianadréth remarked with a little giggle. "You might as well be yourself in front of this guest. By the way, I missed you too. I'm glad you came this way. I want you to meet someone." Pointing to the fairy left of her, Kirianadréth introduced the two. "This is Tilly. She is a historian, or, as the humans call it, a legend keeper."

Dragon turned to the fairy and smiled. "Hello, it is nice to meet you," he said respectfully. Oddly enough, the fairy said nothing in return. She just stayed there glaring at him, almost as if she was disgusted by his very presence. Dragon found this rather rude, but he didn't say anything, thinking it was just their way. "Mother"—Dragon looked to his mother like an excited child— "I was hoping later today we can go flying together."

"No," Kirianadréth responded quickly, without even thinking the request through. It wasn't until she saw the sad and disappointed look on her son's face that she felt the need to explain herself. "Dragon, there are so many things I need to do today, and some important things just came to my attention. Perhaps tomorrow we could spend time together."

"All right, as you wish," Dragon replied, respecting his mother's wishes even though he didn't like it. "Tomorrow you will say the same thing," he added quietly, muttering the words to himself, making sure that no one else heard it. Even though Dragon didn't want to admit it, especially to himself, not seeing his mother lately was starting to depress him.

"Dragon, will you do me a favor," his mother asked, trying to keep his spirit up.

With no hesitation Dragon answered, "Yes."

"Tilly and I are having a very serious, private conversation. I would appreciate it if you would give us a moment alone. Also, unfortunately, I need Ancient as well. So if it is all right with him, I would like to release you from your lesson early today." Kirianadréth turned to Ancient to see what his remark would be, but instead of any remark, he simply bowed. "That's good," she continued. "I'm pretty sure that Soræniya is just a room away. She never stays too far away from you," Kirianadréth said with a smile.

"Thank you, Mother. And thank you, Ancient," said Dragon. "Tilly, I hope we meet again sometime." Dragon quickly turned and ran out of the room, not aware that Tilly was still glaring in his direction, and also that Ancient now had a look of worry on his face.

Dragon ran down the corridor from the throne room, looking for Sonya. He quickly stopped a little way back from the first corner that he came upon. He stared at it intently, getting a strange feeling that someone was on the other side. He smiled and then continued running to the corner. As he approached the corner, he jumped forward, hitting the ground, and slid past the corner. As Dragon's body quickly slid past the corner, a massive dragon hand came slamming down, trying to catch him. Dragon quickly jumped back up to his feet and turned to see Sonya with her back to the wall and a smile on her face.

"Haw, you missed me!" Dragon yelled. He quickly turned and ran down the passageway, laughing as he went. Sonya leaped into pursuit, laughing herself as she chased him down the halls. In and out of the halls they chased each other through the dragon city. Dragon reached the bottom steps of the city and stopped dead in his tracks, staring out at the dragons below. Sonya quickly halted behind him, curious as to the reason why he stopped. Then she noticed what he was staring at and rolled her eyes at his foolishness.

Dragon had caught a glimpse of Rhyisara—a rare dragon, but one of the most beautiful. She stood tall and straight, with shiny silvery scales on her belly. However, she had no scales on her back at all. On her wings and back, she had silver feathers that glittered in the light. For a long time, Dragon was captivated by her and wanted to say something. Even though he was the prince, Dragon always had a hard time getting the females to so much as give him a passing glance, let alone talk to him at all. The situation always made him feel out of place, especially when he tried to find status with the male dragons in the city. When she came closer to the stairs, Dragon ran down to greet her. Mustering what courage he could, he smiled. "Hi, Rhyisara, how have you been?"

Rhyisara stopped suddenly and stared down at Dragon as if she was looking down at an insect. Her face filled with disgust at the very sight of him. She didn't say a word; she just continued walking as if nothing happened. The pain was easily visible in Dragon's eyes; his heart felt like it was pierced by a weapon. For a moment, he just wanted to run and hide. A moment later, his heart filled with rage as he thought about her arrogance. As much as he desired her, he wanted to lash back at the way he was treated. However, his earlier fight with Marahezron quickly came to mind, which didn't help the situation.

"What's the matter? Did your mother mate with too many birds? That's why she didn't teach you any manners?" Dragon snapped.

Rhyisara quickly turned, ruffled her feathers, and barked back, "How dare you speak to me that way, half-breed. You have no right to treat me that way!"

"And you have no right to treat me like I am nothing," Dragon responded.

"But you are nothing. Look at you—you are nothing but a human," Rhyisara yelled as she turned back around and kept walking.

"I am more than you'll ever be," Dragon answered, unwilling to let this fight go. "At least I know who my father is. At least I am part of a royal line. You can't even trace your family back to a lizard!"

Rhyisara turned her head and let out a roar, and quickened her pace to get as far away from Dragon as she could.

Sonya came walking down the stairs with a smile on her face and stood next to Dragon. As they started to walk away together, she couldn't help but ask, "So are you over her yet?"

Dragon looked at her with a smirk on his face. "Maybe, maybe not. Why is it important to you?" Dragon responded.

Sonya gave a small chuckle and innocently grinned, as if she didn't want to answer the question.

They had walked only a few steps farther when they heard laughter behind them. They both turned around to see three young dragons laughing as they were coming toward them. All three looked to be around the age of four or five years old, yet they were half the size of Sonya. The leader of the pack was a black dragon. He wasn't much to look at; he looked to be more bones and horns than scales and muscle. Still, it was enough to be intimidating. As for the other two dragons, one had red scales, and the other one had green. They were plain and simple dragons, yet they had a look of trouble in their eyes.

"What's so funny?" asked Dragon. He took on a defensive stance and tightened his body, thinking that something wasn't right and that this wouldn't end well. Dragon knew these three younglings very well. He had dealt with them several times before. They always liked making trouble for Dragon, as if that was their whole goal in life. Dragon was always curious as to why their parents had never dealt with them.

"You, that's what's funny," the black dragon said as they all stopped only a few feet from Dragon and Sonya. "You are quite brave, half-breed," the black dragon continued. "Not only for making us put up with your filth by living here, but also by thinking you have the right to speak to one so glamorous as Rhyisara."

Sonya quickly snapped back at the dragon, "Watch it, hatchling. You're speaking to your king!" As long as she lived, Sonya always defended Dragon, as if she were taking up her father's role.

"King," the black dragon said. "He will never be my king. My father and I would never serve him!"

As Sonya growled at the young one, Dragon crossed his arms and let out a small chuckle. "From what I hear, your father served nothing but darkness, so that makes you the son of a traitor!

No sooner had Dragon said those words than the black dragon became enraged. He quickly snapped at Dragon, attempting to bite down on him. Dragon, expecting this, quickly moved to the side, letting the dragon bite nothing but air. In the same quick motion, he grabbed the horns on the top of the dragon's head, and with a strong pull, he flipped the dragon in the air and slammed him on his back. He continued to hold the dragon down by the horns, wrenching the head from side to side.

Unfortunately, Dragon wasn't paying too much attention to the other two dragons who decided to join in. As one leaped for him, Sonya caught the red dragon by biting him on the neck and stepping on his tail, but she wasn't able to catch the other one, who continued toward Dragon.

Dragon quickly let go of the pack leader and turned his attention to the green dragon coming toward him. He swung up with his fist, hitting the dragon in the lower jaw and sending him flying back and skidding across the ground. At that moment, he turned back around, only to see that the black dragon had gotten back up. Dragon pulled back and then jumped toward the dragon. In mid-jump, a tail slapped against his chest, sending him falling to the ground. He hit the ground with a loud thud, and the air was knocked out of him. When Dragon finally caught his wind and stood back up to look around, he saw that the fight was over. Much to his dismay, he saw that several of the elders who witnessed the fight had joined in to stop it. Some of them had the young ones gripped by the throat, and two were holding Sonya by the arms. As Dragon turned to look at the black dragon, he realized what had happened. Marahezron was standing with his foot on the dragon's back, pressing him to the ground.

"What started this?" Marahezron demanded.

Dragon swiftly pointed to the black dragon under Marahezron's foot. "He called me a half-breed."

At that moment, Ancient, apparently done with his conference with the queen, emerged from the crowd, very upset. He pushed past everyone and came right up to the black dragon, stopping only inches from him to stare down at him. "Young one, your father would be very disappointed in you. He has nothing but respect for Dragon! Whatever inspired you to say such a thing?"

The black dragon pointed to Dragon as best as he could under Marahezron's foot and remarked, "He called my father a traitor!"

Marahezron and Ancient both glared at Dragon, and then they motioned for the elders to take out the three young ones. When the elders were gone with the young ones to take them back to their parents for discipline, Ancient began to speak to Dragon. "Why would you say such a thing?"

"He called me a half-breed first. I only responded," Dragon defended himself. He began to feel that no matter what he did to please everyone, he would still always get into trouble.

"It doesn't matter who started it. You are older and supposed to be wiser," added Marahezron, clearly still holding some resentment for Dragon for his earlier incident.

"Perhaps if both of you give me some room to breathe, I can learn something," Dragon said.

Marahezron answered, seeming very annoyed, "That is no way to talk to us!"

"Why don't you leave me alone? You're not my father!"

Ancient stepped forward to add something to the argument but was quickly cut off by Dragon. "You're not my father either!"

Ancient put his hand on Dragon's shoulder, urging him to come along quietly. "We need to talk."

"No," Dragon said as he pushed Ancient's hand off his shoulder and took a few steps toward the mountain tunnel. "I cannot do anything right, especially when I'm treated like a human and a child!" Dragon had enough of being told what to do, to live, and even how to think. He just wanted to feel the wind in his hair, the ground underneath his feet, and the sound of life around him. He wanted to escape the title of being prince, a prince of younger dragons that didn't even respect him. At that moment, he wanted just a mother, a father, and a simple life, no matter how trivial it might seem.

Marahezron started to walk toward Dragon to catch him, but then suddenly fell over. He looked up in time to see Dragon run out of the city and then looked back to see what had happened. To his surprise, his own daughter had her tail wrapped around his legs. Marahezron's face burned with rage at the thought of his daughter's betrayal.

Ancient quickly put his hand on Sonya's arm and pulled her back. "Now is not the time for this," he said to Marahezron. "We have bigger issues to deal with. You must go find Kirianadréth. Dragons' training is not going the way we had hoped. We cannot afford to lose him this way."

Marahezron got up and quickly ran into the city to go find Kirianadréth. Ancient looked down at Sonya, disappointed by her actions. Although he had nothing to say to her, he understood her reasons for doing what she did, for he too felt a form of loyalty and love for Dragon; at the same time, he worried for him. But right now, he knew that the only one who could get through to Dragon was his mother.

5

The Pain of Loss

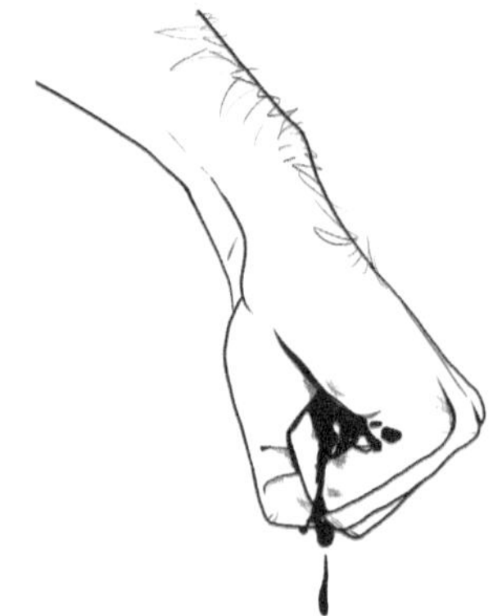

Kirianadréth sat on her throne, thinking about where her son might be, while she awaited the return of the two dragons that she sent out to look for him. When they came back empty-handed, she began to get very worried about her son. Many things crossed her mind as to what could possibly have happened to him. However, she also thought about whether she had been a good mother. She took in the fact that she had been busy lately, but she never thought for once that it bothered him so much. She knew Dragon needed a father figure, and she thought that Marahezron and Ancient could fill that void. Apparently not.

Kirianadréth laid her beautiful dragon head in her hands when she came to the knowledge of something else that troubled her deeply. When she questioned herself of why she didn't spend time with her son, the oddest thing came to her mind. She concluded that she could not bear the sight of her son, merely because he reminded her of his father so much and how much she missed him. Kirianadréth could neither agree nor disagree with that thought, but one way or another, it bothered her. When her worry began to overwhelm her, she thought of a place that Dragon mentioned several times. If he had to go anywhere, it would be there. It would be a good place to relax, think, and hide. Kirianadréth told everyone to wait behind, that this was a matter that she and her son had to deal with by themselves. So without hesitation, she flew out of the city and deep into the forest.

On the far side of the forest, there was a beautiful waterfall that overlooked a valley. It was so tall that you could barely see the bottom; on the other hand, it gave you a beautiful view of the sunset.

Kirianadréth landed not far from the edge. Lo and behold, there was Dragon sitting at the edge. His legs were draped over the rock side, and he was close enough that he could reach out his hand and dip it in the water. Though the water was running fast, it seemed smoother and peaceful until it fell over the edge.

Dragon sat there quietly staring out over the valley and watching the sunset. Kirianadréth walked only a few steps forward, and then Dragon spoke. "Hello, Mother, I'm not in the mood to talk."

Her face lit up with a smile. "How did you know it was me?"

"There are only two people who would know where I would go. Considering what happened today, it's not that hard to guess which one. I just expected you to find me earlier."

Kirianadréth let out a small laugh. "I'm sorry to disappoint you."

"It's all right. You've been doing that a lot lately," Dragon replied solemnly. He didn't turn around to look at his mother or acknowledge her. He simply sat still.

Her son's words cut her deeply, yet Kirianadréth couldn't deny them. She walked slowly up beside him and sat down to look over the falls with him. "Son, we need to talk, whether you want to or not."

"There's been a lot of that going around as well," Dragon sarcastically replied. He was still mad, yet he didn't know exactly where to direct his anger.

"Dragon, you don't know how hard it is to be a ruler of a kingdom, or what I'm going through," Kirianadréth said, hoping her son would understand.

Dragon turned his head and glared at his mother. "How hard it is for you, what you are going through," he coldly repeated her words as he became aggravated. "Are you that ashamed of me? Do you not care for me at all?" Because he had heard those excuses before, he wasn't quite sure what to think or believe.

"No, I'm not ashamed of you. Why would you say such a thing?" responded Kirianadréth as her face took on a look of shock.

"Because you ignore me and never spend time with me," Dragon said, his voice sounding as though he was going to cry. "You put me in the hands of dragons that aren't even my family. I want to be raised by you, not others. It seems like the only way I can see you is to get in trouble. What is wrong with me, Mother?"

Kirianadréth gently put her hand on his shoulder to calm him down. "It's not you, son. It's me. I'm not as strong as I used to be, and I'm not talking about my body. I am still one of the only ones in the city that can defeat Marahezron. However, I heard today that someone gave him a good beating," she said as she looked down at him with a smile.

Dragon, on the other hand, was not amused by her attempt at humor, so she continued to explain herself. "After your father's death, the only thing that could keep me going was you, and you look so much like him."

"You're blaming your problems on me, so it is my fault!"

"No," she quickly answered. "You remind me of what mattered so much to us. We fought to bring peace to this earth, and I will guarantee that it remains. So I worked very hard every day to maintain the peace that we won. However, sometimes it's a little bit more than I can handle, so my time is occupied a lot. I think it was easier to fight orcs than it is to keep the peace between humans, elves, dwarves, and dragons." Kirianadréth rubbed her finger against the side of Dragon's face and looked him in the eyes. "I think about you every day, and how you are the most important thing in my life and in the kingdom. So I couldn't leave you with just anyone. I gave you to the only two individuals that were worthy to train you. If you were not important to me you wouldn't be trained at all."

"That would make me happy," Dragon said. "I never asked to be trained, and it's not like I need to be. What do you want me to be, as great as my father? I can never be that great, and why would I be like a man who deserted his son?"

"He didn't desert you," Kirianadréth said. "He did everything in his power to come back to us. That is one thing you do not understand about humans. They have a will and a heart that dragons could never understand. That is their power. Humans have overcome unbelievable odds for the things and people they love. He survived the greatest war this world has ever seen. And nothing short of that could have stopped him, so don't you ever speak disrespectfully about your father again!" Kirianadréth looked as if she was going to cry thinking once again about how strong her love for Jorn was.

Dragon sat there and lowered his head, somewhat ashamed that he had upset his mother. In his heart, he was mad at his father, yet he missed him. He just didn't want to reveal it to anyone, but he had a feeling that his mother knew.

Kirianadréth wrapped her arm around Dragon, pulling him close to her. "I know things have been very distant between us, we cannot fall apart now, son. I'm sorry that I let the kingdom take precedence over you. I didn't realize how much it would affect you. From now on, I will find time to spend with you."

Dragon looked up at her and smiled. "It would help. However, it won't solve the problem, Mother." Dragon looked back out across the valley, almost as if he was looking for answers. "Whether you believe it or not, Mother, I'll never be at peace. I do not know the human race. I could never live with them. Also, I could never have the respect of the dragon race. Some of them may respect me, but most of them don't even know how to speak to me." Dragon looked down to the ground, overwhelmed by mental agony. "Maybe something like this might have worked between two closer races, like the humans and the elves. The dragons and humans are too far from each other; there is no under-standing between them. How could you and my father have ever given birth to something like me?" Dragon flicked at the water, trying to keep his mind off the very comment he uttered.

Kirianadréth rubbed her fingernail across his head, a gesture that calmed him down when he was younger. She nuzzled her head next to his and tried to find the words to encourage him. "How could we not have something as perfect as you?" she began. "Your father's and my love transcended even our own races and brought us together. What better way to show that love than to give birth to you. Perhaps you're right—there will be those that will never understand, and some that will even hate you. Don't let their ignorance destroy our family and everything else your father and I worked so hard to build." She hesi-tated for a moment to gather her thoughts. "Personally, my son, I be-lieve that you will have a great impact on the future of both dragons and humans. You will live a life that will shadow any of the deeds your ancestors have done."

Dragon finally gave in, wrapped his arms around her snout and gave a big squeeze. She lifted her head up, picking him up off the ground and setting him on top of her nose. As he sat on her snout, he stared into her eyes.

She smiled and then began talking, which bounced him about on her snout while she talked. "So does this mean you're done having an attitude?"

"Maybe," he replied as he tried to hang on as best as he could.

She sat him back down on the ground and stared him in the eyes. "Let's try to forgive each other," she said. "It's better if we make the best of the time we have."

"Well," he replied, "we've got some time right now, and there's no one around to bother us." Dragon's eyes opened wide as he stared at his mother, hoping this time she would accept his request for time.

"All right, what do you have in mind? As long as it doesn't take too much time. I should be back in the city before the sun sets completely," Kirianadréth replied, making sure her son understood the boundaries of time.

Dragon thought for a moment, and then his face lit up with a smile. He was good at thinking of things to do, especially crazy and dangerous things that his mother most likely wouldn't approve of. He motioned for Kirianadréth to come closer, and when she did, he whispered something in her ear. As he did, her face filled with fear, and she quickly answered. "No, I will not allow it. It is too dangerous!"

"Come on, Mother. Sonya and I do it all the time," Dragon begged. Then he realized he admitted something that he should have kept to himself. Dragon gritted his teeth, hoping that his mother would overlook that comment.

Unfortunately, she did catch his remark and didn't like it at all. "If I knew you did that before, I would have never let you out of the city!" Kirianadréth turned to head back to the city, unwilling to play along. Her tail and wings were lifted just a bit to show that she was somewhat ruffled over the conversation. She thought to herself that perhaps from now on, she should send a chaperone out with Dragon and Sonya, just to make sure they didn't do anything foolish like what he just suggested. Then she quickly dismissed the idea, realizing that he already had too many restraints within the city, and that his only freedom was out of it.

"Mother, won't you ever trust me?" Dragon urged. "I trust you, and I know everything will be all right. I know I'm young and a little unruly, but if I do not live life, then how will I learn?"

Kirianadréth stopped in her tracks and turned to look at him. From the look on her face, you could tell that she wanted to spend time with Dragon, yet she feared what he had in mind. He was young, yet he was right. If Dragon was to be king someday, he would need to learn how to be one, and sheltering him would not help. Still, there was a big difference between learning to be king and doing childless acts of adventure. She thought for a moment, uncertain of what to choose. Then finally, she agreed, nodding her head. This was time with her son, and they needed time.

"Yes," he screamed as he ran up and hugged her arm. "This is going to be fun. Of course, it would be a lot easier if you and Father had given me wings," he said. Then he let go and turned toward the falls. "I love you, Mother," he said as he quickly glanced up at her. Then, without another word, he darted off toward the falls, picking up great speed as he went. When he reached the end of the falls, he jumped, pushing himself out over the falls. With his arms stretched out wide, he hovered over the falls for a moment, watching everything below him with a rush of excitement. When his momentum stopped, he began to plummet down.

Kirianadréth stood with her body shaking and her claws gripping the ground she stood upon. Though she was overwhelmed by Dragon's stupidity, she focused on counting quietly as best as she could. Then suddenly, she screamed out the number ten and jumped into action. She lunged without delay off of the falls, folding her wings up so she could gain more speed. Like a spear, Kirianadréth's body sped down in the direction of her son. In the distance, she could see her son falling fast. She tightened her body, pushing to catch up with him. Then with a single motion of her head, her body whipped behind the water and out of sight.

As Dragon continued to fall, he did not do anything to attempt to save himself. He left his arms and legs open wide, as if he was trying to catch the wind. There was no look of fear on his face, only the biggest grin. As he got closer to the bottom, a dark figure appeared in the water behind him. Just before he hit the rocks at the bottom, wings opened up, and Kirianadréth came bursting out from behind the falls. She flew directly underneath Dragon, catching him on her back. Soaring only a few inches over the rocks at the bottom, she disturbed the falls mist with the gust off her wings. As she picked up speed and gained more height, you could hear Dragon yelling in excitement for miles.

"That was amazing!" Dragon screamed, throwing his arms up in complete exhilaration.

"No, it wasn't!" Kirianadréth answered loudly. "You made my heart almost stop! That is the first and last time I'd ever do that!" Even though she did not want to admit it to Dragon, she too felt alive, as though her youth had come back within the length of the jump. It made her remember all the crazy things that she and Jorn used to do.

"Come on, Mother, don't stop now. Go higher!" Dragon urged, his heart still racing with longing for more excitement.

"All right, but hold on." She opened her wings wider to give them longer strides. In no time at all, both of them were flying on top of the clouds. Dragon's and Kirianadréth's heads barely appeared above the clouds as their bodies were hidden in the white billows, as though they were swimming in water. There they hovered for a while as they stared together at the sun's beauty. Then she turned down and began to slowly descend back to the ground. She found a nice hill in the middle of the forest, and once her feet touched the ground, Dragon jumped from her back. Then he turned and gave her a big hug, as much as he could since his arms wouldn't go all the way around her arm.

"Thank you, Mother. It has been a long time since we've been able to spend any time together."

"I know," she replied. "But what time we do spend together, I cherish it very much."

"So do I," Dragon said as he gave her another big hug and then looked up at her. "Mother, promise me that you will always be with me.

Kirianadréth looked down at her son with a face full of surprise; she wanted so desperately to say yes. On the other hand, something in her heart told her that things might change very soon. She couldn't leave him without saying something, so she looked him deep in the eyes and answered him the best way she could. "My beloved son, I will be with you always. I promise."

Her words were enough to bring a big smile to his face. At that moment, he heard a branch break behind him. He turned to see Sonya hiding behind a few bushes. Obviously, she wasn't trying too hard not to be seen since the bushes covered only half of her body. She must have seen them flying low to land and hurried to meet them. Dragon looked at his mother as if he were going to beg for some more time to play.

"It's getting late, Dragon," she said, encouraging him to come home. However, the more she looked at his big begging eyes, the more she wanted to give him some time to play. She realized that he had been through a lot that day, so she believed a little time couldn't hurt. "All right, but don't stay out too late." She gently rubbed his cheek with her finger as she looked into his eyes with love and concern.

Dragon returned her loving gaze for a moment, and then turned and stuck his tongue out at Sonya. Then he quickly ran off into the woods. Sonya sprung out of the bushes in hot pursuit. Kirianadréth almost laughed when she saw Sonya come bounding out of the bushes. Like a puppy, she scurried across the hills after Dragon with her tongue slightly out of her mouth. Kirianadréth watched as they disappeared into the woods and then turned to head back to the city. Mid turn, she stopped to stare at a distant hill. Quickly, she rubbed her eyes and tried to focus on what she saw.

In confusion, she scanned the hillside with her excellent dragon sight, and what she thought she saw wasn't there anymore. Kirianadréth could have sworn that she saw two figures that looked like dragons. She told herself that perhaps she was seeing things and that she needed to go get some rest. However, as she walked away, she couldn't shake the feeling that something was wrong. Her body then began to get a chill, which told her something bad was going to happen. She quickened her pace by taking flight and hurried back to the city. She couldn't quite figure it out; she felt as though she recognized this feeling as if she had it once before. Kirianadréth knew that Dragon was safe with Sonya and that he would return to the city soon. So, she desperately went in search of Ancient and Marahezron to discuss this feeling and her concerns.

***

Dragon and Sonya spent the rest of the day coming back from their fun in the woods, almost through the tunnels in the mountain. Suddenly Dragon's chest began to hurt as though someone had shoved a knife through it. He grabbed his chest and fell to his knees in pain; somehow, he knew in his heart what had happened.

A great roar erupted across the city that sounded like Kirianadréth. Then all the other dragons in the city roared and rushed toward the throne room. As for Dragon, he picked himself up and also ran up the city toward the throne room. He wasn't sure what was going on, but he knew he had to reach his mother. Unfortunately, because he was the smallest, he kept getting pushed around and stepped over; he could barely keep up. Finally, he got closer to the top of the city, to the corridor to the throne room, yet he was still several levels down. He could see that the guards had run inside and shut the doors, which stopped the stampede of dragons. Dragon couldn't blame the guards; it was one of the things they were trained to do. If there was ever a panicked rush to the throne room, they were to close the doors regardless of what was happening. As for himself, Dragon stopped and looked at the passageway that protruded out a bit from the city walls. The only way to get in through the crowd and the doors was to go through the walls, he thought to himself. The other passageway to the throne room was deep within the city and would take too long to get to it. Then his eyes widened with enlightenment as he turned to see a dragon not far from him that he recognized.

"Venor!" he screamed as he pointed toward the wall of the corridor. He knew this was a very risky maneuver, but he had to reach his mother quickly.

Venor looked at Dragon and nodded, knowing exactly what Dragon had in mind. He wrapped his tail quickly around Dragon like he did earlier that day. However, this time, he used the full force of his tail and part of his body weight as he hurled Dragon up in the air. Dragon went sailing over all the dragons and structures in his path as he flew toward the wall. He flexed his whole body to make it as hard as he could before he hit the wall. His shoulder and part of his back smashed directly into the side of the passage wall, shattering the very structure and sending him crumbling with the wall into the passageway.

Swiftly, he picked himself up out of the rubble to look around, ignoring the pain in his side. He turned to see the two guards holding the doors with all their strength, keeping back the stampede. Then he turned to look down the corridor to see the other two guards closing the doors to the throne room. Without hesitation, Dragon darted down the hall to reach the throne room. The closer he got to the chamber, the harder the dragons would push to close the doors. With little time left, he pushed himself into the air, sending him sailing sideways through the doors as they slammed shut.

Dragon hit the ground, rolling and skidding to a stop on the marble floor. Then he picked himself up, ignoring his pain again to desperately look around for his mother. Even though the throne room was large, he spotted her immediately. His face filled with horror, and his breath became shallow as he looked upon the tragedy that befell his mother. "No!" he cried as he ran over to her. She was lying with her head on the ground and a hole in her chest, her blood leaking onto the white marble floor. Dragon walked up to her head and kneeled down beside it, taking his hand and softly stroking her face. "Mother," he whispered, hoping that she was still alive.

"Son," a small and weak voice answered. Kirianadréth slowly opened her eyes and turned her head to look at her son. She tried talking to him, but as it was, she could barely breathe.

"Everything is going to be all right, Mother," Dragon said, staring her in the eye. Even though he said it, he wanted more than anything to believe it was true. His world was falling apart around him as his nightmares became a reality.

Kirianadréth managed the strength to pull her hand up and put it against his face. "I love you, son," she said, trying to push the words out. "I will always be with you." Those were the last words she could push out. Her breathing stopped, and her eyes closed for the last time.

Dragon quickly grabbed her hand, holding on to it as he cried out, "No, Mother, don't leave me!" Then he buried his face into her cheek and began to weep.

Because Dragon was paying too much attention to the loss of his mother, he didn't notice any other beings in the room. Across the room, dancing around the dragon throne, was a small, pale green dragon. In his hands, he held Kirianadréth's crown as he danced about and cried out in excitement. "It's all mine! The entire kingdom is all mine!"

At that moment, Marahezron and Ancient entered the room from the other corridor. Amid the confusion, they ascertained what happened, and Marahezron became enraged. He spotted the pale green dragon across the room and roared in anger as he moved to confront the dragon. Unfortunately, Ancient stopped him by wrapping his tail around him several times and grabbing him by the arms. "Let me go!" Marahezron yelled at Ancient. "Let me avenge my queen!"

"No, it is not your place," Ancient calmly answered.

Then from across the room came a laugh, for the pale green dragon had heard Marahezron's anger. "Now look at that," the dragon said sarcastically with an eerie and raspy voice. "A student being held back by his master. What's the matter, not brave enough to fight me alone?"

Upon hearing those words, Marahezron squirmed, trying to get free of Ancient's grip. "Let me go! I will tear him apart!"

"Like I said, it is not your place," Ancient reminded him. "He has taken the crown. Only the royal line can challenge him."

"That's right, coward," the pale dragon hissed. "I rule all of you now, and I see no royal line to challenge me. I heard from far away that she has no dragon heir. That means none of you could ever challenge me!"

Ancient whispered into Marahezron's ear, "Dragon is our only hope. He must fight for the responsibility of his kingship. His right was challenged by the spilling of blood."

"He is not ready," Marahezron whispered back. "I know that dragon—he is an assassin. Sithalanos is his name, and he is the darkest assassin ever known. Dragon is not ready to fight one as skilled as he is."

Marahezron was not wrong; assassin dragons were some of the worst dragons ever. They were said to be gifted with strange abilities, which allowed them, no matter how small they were, to take down some of the strongest and biggest dragons. Because of their profession, none of them were good; they all served the dark powers that fed chaos. Sithalanos was the most mysterious of all assassin dragons. Many dragons knew of him but knew nothing of importance about him. Marahezron, out of all the dragons, knew the most, for he had spent many years attempting to hunt this mysterious assassin. That was why seeing Sithalanos now upset him the most. He concluded that if he had killed the assassin years before, his beloved queen would still be alive.

"Nevertheless, we must trust Dragon," Ancient remarked, trying to keep Marahezron out of this situation. Ancient and Marahezron both glanced over to see Dragon still clinging to his mother.

Unfortunately, Sithalanos caught their gaze and realized what they were looking at. He glared down at Dragon and hissed. "What a disgusting creature. I can't even imagine dragons keeping them as pets." He motioned for the guards. "Kill this animal!"

Dragon finally lifted his head to pay attention to what was going on. Everyone in the room could see his pain, for a tear of blood was running down his face. The blood was not from his mother; because he couldn't weep tears, his body gave the only thing it had. He stood up and glared at Sithalanos with a rage that he had never known. It felt as though a dark cloud had come over his mind and he couldn't calm himself. He was filled with rage, but there was something deeper inside him—a madness that he could not explain and almost could not control. It took all of his concentration to push the madness back and focus on his anger.

However, Dragon knew that sooner or later, he would have to deal with this madness whatever it was. In the meantime, he had anger at the forefront of his mind, and he was going to deal with that at the moment. His body grew hard like a stone, and he had a strength that he never felt before. Dragon's eyes slowly began to change color till they reached a dark red. Dragon threw his hands straight back, lifted his head high, and then let out a mighty roar. The sound of his roar echoed and filled the entire throne room. Sithalanos jumped back, and everyone else stood in awe. Even Marahezron and Ancient had never heard Dragon make such a sound. It was not the yell of a man; it was the mighty bellow of a dragon. When the sound subsided, Dragon went back to glaring at Sithalanos with a look of vengeance in his eyes.

"I can't believe it," Sithalanos said in utter shock. "I have heard the rumors of Kirianadréth's half-breed abomination, but I could never believe it." He then turned to speak to the guards as he pointed at Dragon. "Kill him. Now!"

The guards hesitated for a moment, looking at each other and wondering what they should do. However, they both knew no matter how much they cared for Dragon, they must obey their traditions. Sithalanos had the crown, and until Dragon defended his kingship, they were bound by oath. So they slowly but steadily walked over to Dragon, looking down at him with their eyes filled with sorrow. "Sorry, my prince," one of the guards said as they raised their spears.

Dragon stood still, intently watching the guards, waiting for them to move. Before anything else happened, Dragon saw the guards wink and smirk. The guards plunged their spears down into the marble at Dragon's feet.

"Whoops, I missed," one guard said as he let go of the spear and stepped aside, leaving the spear standing straight up out of the marble.

"That little one is faster than I thought," the other guard said as he also let go of the spear and stepped aside.

"Awww," Sithalanos screamed in outrage over the guards' poor attempt to kill Dragon. "It seems that I will have to do everything myself!" He dropped Kirianadréth's crown and ran toward Dragon.

Dragon grabbed one of the guard's spears and prepared to defend himself. The first few seconds of the battle were a blur. Sithalanos came in fast, snapping with his jaws, then followed it up by whipping his tail like a spear. Dragon had to work hard to keep Sithalanos at bay, for the assassin dragon was fast and agile. For a while, Dragon was able to keep his distance by using the spear to block every attack. However, with every attack, his spear got smaller and smaller, until it was the length of his forearm. At that point, he abandoned the spear and decided to try his luck with his hands. Sithalanos, seeing a chance to dispatch the human, came in closer; he turned and thrust his tail at the human.

Dragon with his fast reflexes, moved to the side, dodging the tail. He grabbed a hold of Sithalanos's tail and attempted to pull. The tail slid out of Dragon's hands with ease, and Dragon let out a scream. He looked down at his hands to see that they were shredded and bleeding as though he had rubbed them against hundreds of sharp objects. Then he took a closer look at Sithalanos's scales and realized what was wrong. Now he understood why assassin dragons were feared, no matter their size.

Sithalanos had a rare scale design; each scale had several scales of its own but pointed in the opposite direction. Dragon had heard that assassins' scales were as hard as diamonds and razor-sharp. So he had no way to get a hold of Sithalanos without getting cut. Plus, assassins' tails were pointed like spears, so that they were able to pierce even the hardest of dragon scales. His face began to show a little fear as he hurriedly tried to figure out how he could fight. At that moment, Sithalanos saw his face and attacked, hoping to end this quickly. Dragon swiftly ducked and rolled to the side as Sithalanos's tail went whipping by.

Getting back onto his feet as fast as he could, Dragon grabbed the other spear the guards left and set it straight up. He was hoping to block Sithalanos's tail, but as the tail came back, it cut the spear in half. Dragon stood there, looking at the two halves, desperately trying to think of something to do. Before he could come up with anything, Sithalanos hit him across the chest with his tail, sending him flying back across the room.

Dragon hit the floor and skidded toward the sword alcove on the other side of the throne room. Surprisingly enough, he slid through the barrier and smacked against the stone that held the sword. Sitting up, Dragon shook his head, looked at his chest and saw that it had been cut from one side to the other. Then he lifted his head to look for Sithalanos and was shocked to find the sword's magical barrier. Turning to look up at the sword, an idea popped into his head. Even though he knew all the warnings that Ancient told him about the mighty and mysterious sword, it seemed to be his only hope. What better way to defeat an assassin than through something stronger than him. Dragon only hoped that the stories about the sword were true, because if it was a plain sword, it wouldn't stop Sithalanos.

He got up and stood with his foot against the stone. Dragon reached for the sword. When his head was only a few inches away from it, a magical energy erupted from it like lightning. It burst out at Dragon, burning his hand, making him step back for a moment. Oddly enough, the lightning only made him more determined, so he stepped back in, this time using both hands.

Dragon ignored the pain from being hit by the lightning and grabbed the sword and pulled with all his might. As he held on to the hilt of the sword, the lightning seemed to crawl up his arms like snakes, until it reached his back. Then it gripped the single scale on Dragon's shoulder. The sword began making a screaming noise, and the nice human-designed handle began to melt like hot wax. Then it began to reform itself into the shape of a dragon. With its wings as the cross-guard, it led into the dragon's neck, which was the grip, and then for the pommel, it became a dragon's head, which seemed to twist and turn and make all sorts of dragon noises. When the handle finished re-shaping itself, it let go and came off the stone.

Dragon stood there for a moment, glancing at the beauty of the blade. The blade itself seemed to be made of shiny steel, yet it was al-most transparent like a diamond. The handle was nicely formed into a black dragon. As he held it, he could feel the power of the sword pulsing through his veins. Even though he needed it, Dragon feared the sword at that moment. He realized that the sword was alive, and somehow it had reached into his consciousness and felt his rage, inten-sifying it as well as rejecting the rage. Realizing the power that he held in his hands, Dragon grinned and turned to look at Sithalanos, who was standing patiently on the other side of the barrier in the middle of the room.

Dragon could hear Sithalanos mocking him and urging him to come out from under the protective cover of the barrier. Dragon slowly walked out from behind the magic barrier as if he was walking through a waterfall. With the sword held low in his right hand and to his side, he walked into the middle of the room to face Sithalanos. There they stood, staring at each other for a moment, until Sithalanos caught a glimpse of the sword. Then he began to laugh loudly and tried to explain something to Dragon.

"Little fool, you think you could defeat me with a sword. No sword has ever pierced my body. My scales have cut swords in half. I will enjoy killing you."

"Come and get me, then," Dragon growled, putting all his faith in Ancient's stories about the magical sword. The odd thing was that more faith Dragon put in the sword, the more the sword's magic seemed to reassure him that all would be well. So with this reassurance, he was able to calm down and focus on what needed to be done. With his cut hand, he gripped the hilt tighter, making the blood squeeze through his fingers.

Sithalanos smiled and then thrust out his tail, planning to pierce the half- breed's chest. Once again, Dragon moved to the side, but this time he swung the sword up and over with both hands, bringing it down upon Sithalanos's tail. Far from what Sithalanos expected, the sword sliced through his tail like it was cutting through water. Sithalanos let out a howl as he quickly grabbed his tail in pain. Dragon backed up to get ready for the next attack, allowing Sithalanos to soak in what had happened.

It wasn't very long before Sithalanos became enraged over the loss of his tail. So he turned and lunged at Dragon. At the same time, Dragon jumped back, letting Sithalanos fly above him. For a moment, they were both in midair, moving horizontally together until Sithalanos grabbed Dragon by the arms and landed on him, making a tremendous thud when they hit the floor. Their bodies lay still on the ground; no one quite knew what had happened.

Sonya now entered the room from the other corridor. Instead of fighting her way through the stampede, she went all the way through the city to enter the throne room from the other side. She stood near her father, frantically looking around for Dragon. When she saw his body entangled with the assassin's, she feared the worst.

"No!" she cried out as she collapsed to the ground, weeping. Her wings draped on the floor; she had no strength to lift them. Then she heard some rustling near the bodies, so she stopped weeping to look. As the assassin's body began to move, the entire room held its breath. They were all relieved to see Dragon crawling out from underneath Sithalanos's body. Ancient finally let go of Marahezron, now that everything was finished. Sonya began to walk toward Dragon, but then her father grabbed her by the arm. He shook his head no, urging her that this was not the time to speak to Dragon. She saw the look of solemnness in his eyes, something that she had never seen before, so she obeyed him, even though she didn't want to. However, she understood that Dragon's thoughts for now were on his mother.

Dragon stood next to Sithalanos's dead body, still holding the sword Truth in his hand. He realized for a moment how lucky he was that he had Truth pointed in the right direction when Sithalanos landed on him. Truth pierced Sithalanos chest and sank into his heart, killing him instantly.

Dragon took a moment to look at the blade, and to his surprise, he saw the dragons' blood dripping off the blade. Not a single drop of blood stayed on the blade; it ran off like water off a duck's back. It seemed almost as if no evil could stain the blade. He decided to drop the sword, and as he did, the black dragon handle turned bright white. No one saw the handle turn white as it hit the floor, for all their eyes were on Dragon.

As Dragon's rage subsided, his eyes turned back to green, which everyone saw. Dragon then looked down at himself to realize that his clothes and his skin were shredded and bloody from touching Sithalanos's scales. However, the pain that he had sustained physically didn't compare to what was in his heart. Dragon turned and slowly walked to his mother, with all eyes in the room on him.

As he got closer to her body, he felt his feet getting warm, and something squished between his toes. He stopped and looked down to see that his mother's blood had now covered more of the white marble floor. Her blood was so hot that against the cold floor, steam rose from it. Most dragon blood is very hot; normally, it would scald the flesh of a human. Yet even though it was burning Dragon, he continued to walk forward. He walked up to his mother and sat down beside her. It didn't bother him at all to be sitting in her blood; he just wanted to be close to her. He took her arm and pulled it over him and then wrapped it around his stomach with her hand close to his side. Laying his head against her side, he closed his eyes and proceeded to rest in his mother's arm.

Ancient and Marahezron knew how much pain he was in, so they cleared the throne room of anyone, including Sonya. They wanted to give him some time to grieve. Sonya stayed right outside the doors and didn't go far. A little way down the corridor Marahezron and Ancient spoke in hushed tones.

"I just realized a few things," Marahezron said as quietly as he could sense he had such a deep voice. "My daughter entered through the other entrance, but no one else in the city did. I was expecting the throne room to be packed with onlookers."

"Normally you would be right," Ancient replied. "However, when I grabbed a hold of you I also uttered a spell. I have cast the spell only twice in my lifetime and it seemed appropriate for this situation."

"What did you do?

"Every being inside the mountain saw through my eyes, except the ones in the throne room. It stopped everyone right where they were, and it also stopped outside interference in the fight."

"That was quick thinking. It also helps that we don't have to relay the story of what happened a hundred times or more."

"It's served another purpose my friend. Today the dragons saw not a prince but a king fight for them and his crown. I doubt even the young dragons will question him and his right to rule now."

"You saw what happened," Marahezron stated even quieter than before. "He passed through the barrier."

"Yes, I saw," Ancient replied, matching Marahezron's conspiratorial tone.

"What does it mean, Ancient?"

"Well, for starters, it means that Dragon was recognized by the Creator as the next ruler regardless of Sithalanos having the crown. So, I do not believe we need to hold a coronation."

"What of his one wish, as rulers, shouldn't he have one?"

"I think he unwittingly used it when he grabbed the sword. I believe deep down that the sword was meant for him. A human-sized sword with great power entrusted to the royal line of dragons was a peculiar circumstance until Dragon was born. It was only a matter of time, but he still had to give up two important things. The first was his mother, making him king, and the second was a powerful wish. Those two powerful sacrifices have linked him to that sword in ways that we will never understand."

"I still don't understand what all of this means," Marahezron said, a little frustrated.

"It means that the age of dragons has come to an end and the old world will never be the same. We will discuss more of this later. I have things to do. I believe you also have things to attend to. Good luck."

With the conversation over, the two of them went their separate ways. Ancient went to prepare for Kirianadréth's burial as well as a few other things. Marahezron went to keep order in the city. There was not much said in the city that night; the dragons were quiet in their mourning. For today they had lost one of the greatest rulers they had ever had. This loss would devastate them for years. As for Dragon, some believed he would never recover from this loss.

6

The Vision and a Quest

That night and the next day, no one entered the throne room, and Dragon never came out. Toward the night of the next day, Ancient came to Sonya and told her to take Dragon to his room. At first, she was hesitant, but she eventually agreed with him. She slowly opened the doors and entered the chamber. She crept along quietly, hoping to make no noise at all. It did not take long before she found Dragon; he was still in his mother's arms. "Dragon," Sonya called out to him. "It is time to go; let me take you to your room."

For a moment, there was no movement, almost as if he were as dead as his mother. Then slowly, he stirred, moved his mother's arm, and got up. He slowly walked toward Sonya, in no hurry to leave his mother. He was almost out of the puddle of his mother's blood when something pierced his foot. Even though it hurt, he made no sound at all. He simply lifted his foot to see what it was.

Jabbing into his foot was a two-inch broken scale from his mother. It probably shattered when Sithalanos's tail pierced Kirianadréth's chest. The scale was almost shaped like a pentagon, and its red ruby brilliance still shown brightly, even though it was now covered in blood from two beings— his mother's and now his. Dragon gently covered his fingers over it and held it tightly. He continued to walk over to Sonya, keeping the scale close to his heart. When he reached her, he collapsed into her arms in exhaustion.

Without saying a word, Sonya picked Dragon up and carried him to his room. She held him in her arms like a mother would. Once there, she cleaned off all the blood and bandaged his wounds. She laid him down on his bed, and then she lay down at the foot of his bed. It wasn't long before he fell asleep, still holding his mother's scale tightly.

* * *

"Dragon," he heard a familiar voice call his name. Slowly, he opened his eyes to look around. He was startled to realize that he wasn't in his room; he had no clue where he was. All he could see was mist all around him, and he noticed that he was standing. He took a moment to think and then realized that this might be a dream.

"This has to be a dream!" Dragon exclaimed, trying to reassure himself that he was not going mad.

"Yes, it is a dream," the voice answered, mysteriously echoing through the mist.

"So this isn't real?" Dragon curiously asked, almost as a statement, reassuring himself.

"Yes. It is real, my son." The mist parted to Dragon's right, revealing his mother.

Without hesitation, Dragon quickly ran up to her and warmly embraced her. "Mother, you're alive!" he cried out.

"I'm sorry, my son, but I'm very much dead."

Dragon stepped back with a disappointed and confused look on his face. "I don't understand, Mother. You said this is real."

Kirianadréth looked down at him to explain. "You are dreaming. However, this dream is not made by chance. I am here in this place for you, and the only way you can be here is to dream."

"I still don't understand, Mother." It was one thing to expect a dream about his mother, but this was torture to him.

"The Creator made this place specifically for you."

Dragon then became quickly aggravated. "Why, is it because he feels guilty for stealing you from me?" Even in this dream world, Dragon's face still showed red with his growing anger. In his youth, he constantly heard about the Creator from everyone in the dragon city. He heard and understood all the tales of the mighty Creator but wasn't sure if he believed them or not. Unlike the dragons, he never felt the presence of the Creator or heard his voice, even though they told him he was always there. What aggravated Dragon the most was that now the Creator wanted to be involved in his life after he had lost his father and his mother.

Kirianadréth simply ignored Dragon's remark. "He made this place for you, to help you on your journey."

"What journey?" Dragon asked as he began to get frustrated with his mother's responses. "What are you talking about?"

"Let me show you. There is much you need to see." Kirianadréth's dragon body began to melt away into the mist. When most of her body was gone, what was left began to reform into something else.

Dragon stared in amazement as a female human with a stunning figure appeared in a white gown. "Mother, is that you?" He had heard that his mother was beautiful as a human, but he never imagined that she could be this stunning.

"Yes, my son, this is the human body that I once had before your father died." She gracefully walked over to Dragon and put her hand on his shoulder. "Like I said, son, there is much you need to see and understand. One of the things you must come to grips with is that I am dead. I am dead to your world, which is fleeting, yet I live in the eternal world of the Creator. It is his gift to me for serving him, and it is my wish that you do the same. For in the Creator's hands, there is no death and no pain—only peace and tranquility. The Creator's world is beyond any imagination and beyond any comprehension. This place set aside for you is at the edge of his realm so that a selected few may help you when you need them. That is why I am here, to guide you on what to do next."

Kirianadréth took her hand off his shoulder, waving it at the mist, and then, surprisingly, the mist began to float away. All Dragon could see was sky, no land. He looked down at his feet but couldn't see anything because the mist still covered the ground. Then she waved her hand again, and the mist at Dragon's feet pulled back. He jumped in surprise at what he saw. There beneath his feet was no land, only water. When the mist fully disappeared, he looked out to see all that was around him. His eyes widened even further with the knowledge that there was no land. It didn't matter which direction he looked. There was nothing but an endless body of water.

"What is this, Mother?" he asked, breathing heavily.

"This is the future," Kirianadréth simply replied, keeping her tone calm.

"Stop talking in ways I do not understand. Tell me everything that is going on and why you are showing this to me."

She pointed out across the water to a small speck in the distance. Dragon's line of sight followed where she was pointing. He glared very hard to see what he was looking at. After a while, he realized that he was looking at a ship. From the look of it, and the distance between them, he concluded that the ship was enormous.

"What race could have built a ship of that size, and for what reason?" Dragon asked, fearing the answer.

"A small group of humans built it."

"For what purpose would they have to build a ship of that size?" Even though Dragon could see the reason for the ship all around him, he needed straight answers.

"They built it in response to the Creator's command."

Dragon turned to look at his mother, seeming more confused than he was before. "What is going on?"

"Long ago, the humans fell from grace with the Creator, and it has long bothered him. There are some human civilizations that become better over the generations. However, the majority of them get worse over the years. The Creator has decided to give mankind a second chance to sit by his side."

"Mankind doesn't deserve to sit by the Creator," Dragon snapped with some of that dragon superiority he had learned in the dragon city. "They don't even deserve to be in the presence of dragons! What's that got to do with the ship and all the water?"

"Listen carefully, my son. In order for humans to have a fair chance at redemption, the old world must die. The humans cannot redeem themselves. The Creator knows this; they do not have the strength within themselves. So as the Creator prepares their redemption, they still need to choose him, to serve the Creator. That in and of itself is a hard thing to do, and the old world will only cause more problems. The Deceiver has shattered the world with the war and has created hundreds of creatures to do his bidding. He has even infested the hearts of humans, so all the humans tainted by evil must die."

Dragon stepped back as his face filled with shock over such an outrageous comment. "What about all the magical creatures?"

"All the magical creatures have already begun to fade. By the time this event happens, magical creatures that serve the Creator will be gone."

"The dragons will never just lie down and die for the humans! The Creator has no right to take our world from us! I will not allow this to happen, not for the Creator and not for you! Why should I listen to a mother who promised her son she would always be with him and then left him all alone?"

"Silence!" Kirianadréth screamed, the sound of her voice echoing.

Dragon backed up and stared angrily at her. When Kirianadréth was satisfied that he would not speak out again, she began to try to explain things to him. "I am sorry that you feel that way. I have not left you. No matter how angry you are at this moment, I need you to be still and listen. The dragons are the only ones that could survive the Creator's flood. All of the old worlds will be washed away, and the elves, dwarves, and even orcs, will disappear. Whether you like it or not, dragons will disappear as well. You do not know them as well as you think you do. Some of them that are loyal to the Creator will fade. When they hear his call, they are to turn into stone and wait for the day that the Creator sets foot upon the earth again. For the ones that don't and turn their heart away from the Creator, they will be destroyed. In this moment of trials and tribulations for the humans, they cannot be touched by the ancient world."

"So the ancient world will just disappear," Dragon stated, thinking of the thousands of dragons, elves, and dwarves that had done mighty deeds in their days and now would never be remembered. Dragon pondered how a Creator could destroy what he claimed to love.

Kirianadréth, understanding her son's thoughts, tried to think of a way to make him comprehend what was going on. She knew he only thought of things from a mortal point of view, and she needed him to understand that there was more than what was before his eyes. That there was a beautiful plan in the works that she had only a glimpse of, yet the Creator knew the end of it. "Dragon, all is not lost. The Creator has set aside a place for all those that he loves and the ones who love him back. As for those that who turned their backs on him, the Creator will destroy them."

"Good luck with that," Dragon said, showing his complete lack of faith in the Creator's powers. "Evil will not simply disappear and let men rule the earth, especially the dragons that are filled with darkness, who will do anything to destroy the humans."

"That is why the Creator has called you here. Your journey, or quest, if you will, is to seek out the dragons that will not fade. You are to give them a choice to fade or to die, and if they will not fade, you are to kill them."

"No, I will not do that," Dragon argued, completely shocked by that request. "Even if I would, it is an impossible task. It would take thousands of years to search them all out. Why doesn't the Creator just destroy them himself?"

"Because it is not in his plan," Kirianadréth simply replied, trying to explain the unexplainable when she herself didn't know all of the Creator's plans.

"That is no answer," Dragon retorted, realizing he was not going to get a straight answer. "So what is his plan?" Dragon asked, rubbing his hand down his face, showing his clear frustration.

"No one knows the Creator's plan until the end, when all is revealed."

"Great," Dragon stated, feeling as though he was in the middle of some game that the Creator was playing. "So when is this flood supposed to happen?"

"That depends on you. When you have found and dealt with the last dragon, the Creator will continue with his plan. Also, do not worry about how long it will take. Because of your dragon and human blood, you will not age like a normal dragon or human. You have perhaps only a few more years left to age, and then you'll stop. You may be immortal to age, son. However, be careful. You can still die by other means."

"That does not make everything better. I will not spend hundreds, if not thousands, of years of my life hunting my own kind. You can tell the Creator I will not do this for him, and I will not do this for the humans."

When he finished arguing this point, his mother didn't look surprised. She waved her hand, and the mist rolled back in under his feet and swarmed around them. It also covered her human form and turned her back into her dragon self. "My son, if you do not do this, you will never see me or anyone else you have loved ever again." Kirianadréth's voice was firm and deep as she confronted her son. "The Creator built this place so that I might assist you on your journey. The scale you hold in your hand binds us."

Dragon looked down to see that he was holding his mother's scale, and that it was glowing ominously. He didn't quite understand it, but for some reason, it calmed him.

"That scale holds both yours and my blood. It is the link that will bring you to me here in this place. Through it I can speak to you and help guide you. Also, listen to the sword Truth. It too will guide you and help you on your way." She brushed her hand across his cheek as the mist started to carry her away. "Good-bye, my son. I love you, and I will always be with you."

"No, Mother, don't leave me again!" Dragon screamed as he reached out for her. The mist came in and smothered him, cutting him off from her. Even though he couldn't see her, he continued to scream out to her.

Dragon awoke and sat straight up in his bed, screaming, "Mother, no!"

Sonya jumped to her feet and ran over to the side of the bed. She wrapped her arm and part of her wing around Dragon, pulling him close and doing her best to comfort him. He was sweating and breathing rapidly as he mumbled something about his mother.

At the same time, Ancient was right outside of Dragon's room when he heard the scream. He decided to enter the room. He stared at Sonya, holding Dragon tightly, and knew immediately what had happened. This was the day he had feared for many years, and now it had come. In his heart, he felt the pull of the Creator and a sense that destiny was about to be fulfilled.

****

Even though Dragon didn't get much sleep that night, he was up early the next day. He found himself in the tombs of his ancestors. There in the depths of the city, he stared at his mother. Earlier that night, when Ancient passed by Dragon's room, he had just come back from laying Kirianadréth to rest. As with her father, she had been turned to stone. The only thing that made her memorial different from all the others was the statue of Jorn standing beside her. After his death, his ashes were put in an urn and placed in the middle of a statue carved in his likeness. There, it stood alone for many years until Kirianadréth could join him.

Finally, after many years, the memorial was complete. The two whose love transcended their races, were together again. Their statue remains, staring down at Dragon, sending him their love. All he could do in return was to stare back, but love was not what he was feeling. His heart was filled with anger, fear, and loneliness. No matter how hard he tried, he couldn't keep those things out. For a good portion of the day, he stood alone in the tombs.

As the day grew closer to its middle, Ancient finally went in search of him. He approached Dragon slowly, knowing that he wanted to be left alone. He stood behind Dragon silently for a moment, paying his respects to the dead. Even though he didn't want to break the silence, he needed to talk to Dragon. "My king."

"No, Ancient," Dragon interrupted him, anticipating his conversation.

Ancient stood there, perplexed at Dragon's quick reply. "How do you know what I was going to talk to you about?"

Dragon turned to face his teacher. "I know what you're going to say because I know you. You are the oldest and wisest dragon in the city, and out of everyone else, you are the only one in tune with the Creator's voice. You usually know something before anyone else does, and I'm positive that you are feeling the Creator's pull right now." Dragon seriously stared at Ancient, as though he wanted him to attempt to deny it.

"You might be right on that subject," replied Ancient, hoping not to aggravate the situation.

"I won't do it, Ancient," Dragon stated as he went and sat down by his parents' memorial.

"You must do this," Ancient urged. "You have no choice in this."

"Oh yes, I do, and I will not obey the Creator—that is, if he even exists. My rule and the dragon race will not end."

Ancient began to look a little worried. "So what are you going to do?"

"Well, I will not take the throne yet, if that's what you mean. I need a little time by myself, and perhaps my mother's idea of a journey isn't so bad. I was thinking I'd leave for a little while, go see the world beyond the forest." Dragon was hoping that by getting away for a while, he would avoid the great responsibility put before him. As childish as that thought was, it was the only thing he could think of at the time.

"How long will you be gone?"

"Who knows. I don't think I will be gone for too long. Maybe twenty days at the most. I just want to see what's out there. Perhaps I might get a new perspective on life. Besides, I'll be leaving you and Marahezron in charge while I'm gone, so that means I have to come back. I can't leave Marahezron in charge for too long. It will go to his head." Dragon and Ancient both chuckled. "Come, Ancient, go get Marahezron and meet me at the city entrance. I will go get my things. I won't be long." Dragon got up and Ancient stood there and watched him walk back to his room.

"It's a shame that you have no idea how wrong you are," Ancient whispered to himself. "One usually meets his destiny when he does everything to avoid it." He then looked at Kirianadréth's and Jorn's statues as if they would nod and agree with him. As Ancient glared into their stony eyes, he wondered if they were paying attention and hoped that they would look after their beloved son.

As for Dragon, he reached his chambers and started packing his things into his traveling bag. Unsure what to take, he simply packed some clothes and nothing else. He didn't think he would be gone too long, so he didn't see the need for anything else. Yet as he held his traveling bag, he was conflicted in his mind and heart. He put his bag down and sat on his bed to think this through. Part of him wanted to go, but the other half didn't. He realized that he was scared of what was beyond the forest and over the hills. The dragon city was his home. Though it had fallen apart, it was all he knew.

Dragon reached for his mother's scale, which he had laid on his bed earlier that day when he went to see her tomb. The moment he touched the scale, it began to glow slightly, unfortunately reminding him of things he would rather forget. Still, it reminded him that he needed to do something. The bad thing was that the only thing that came to his mind was to simply run away. That thought actually gave Dragon an idea: he would go and hide in the farthest part of the forest. Dragon wouldn't actually leave home, but he would be away from everything for the time being. Gripping his mother's scale tightly, he concluded that was the best thing for him to do. Dragon grabbed his bag and headed for the door, thinking that he should probably keep this idea to himself for the moment.

***

By the city entrance, Sonya was standing around, waiting for Dragon. At the same time, Marahezron was arguing with her about her decision.

"Soræniya, I do not agree with this," he yelled at her.

"Father, it doesn't matter what you want. I'm going!" Sonya did her best not to look her father in the eyes.

"You will not disobey me!" Marahezron began to reach for Sonya but felt a familiar hand grab his shoulder. He turned to see Ancient with a smile on his face.

"May I say something?" Ancient said, wanting to desperately join the argument.

"No," Marahezron replied without hesitation.

"In my opinion, I think you have a few issues we need to discuss," Ancient continued anyway, watching Marahezron roll his eyes. "Personally, my old friend, you and Dragon have a lot more in common than you think. The two of you are afraid of loss because you've lost so much already. First, you lost Larzencarak, Soræniya's mother, then Jorn, and then Kirianadréth. Now you're afraid you're going to lose Soræniya." Ancient did his best to calm Marahezron as well as attempt to appeal to his wisdom.

"Your words are not helping to calm my anger. Besides, that has nothing to do with it. The Creator has commanded that she fade. She is to obey him. If she doesn't, that would reflect badly upon me."

"Now, I think you know nothing about yourself. You cannot try to fool me like that. I know you care for your daughter, but you and I both know she was meant for greater things. Also, that Dragon and her were meant to be together for this journey. No matter how much you want to deny it, the fact that they were drawn to each other from birth proves my point."

Marahezron began to get really aggravated with Ancient. "It is not only about my daughter. I do not approve of Dragon going at all. I know that Dragon and I have not gotten along as best as we could, but I still care for him as if he were my own son. He is not ready for this journey. I fear for his life."

"The Creator thinks he is ready. Perhaps we need to trust him instead."

"What if the Creator is wrong and we lose both of them?" The fear that Marahezron felt began to show on his face, which was something that rarely happened.

Ancient, put his arm around Marahezron to comfort him. "I know the fear is in your heart, but we must put our trust in the Creator. Let them go. It is the only thing we can do."

Marahezron lowered his head and nodded in agreement with Ancient. Then he reached out and took his daughter into his arms, with his wings drooping in sadness. He held her as tight as he could without hurting her. He kissed her on the cheek and then looked her in the face, giving her his blessing.

"We're only going to be gone for a short time," Dragon remarked as he came walking up to them from the city steps. "The way you two are acting, you make it seem like we're leaving forever." He walked up to Marahezron, pointing his finger at him. "Now don't make a mess of my city while I'm gone."

As Dragon turned to walk away, Marahezron quickly spoke to him. "Dragon, I know things between us have been rather unfriendly lately. Perhaps I was too hard on you. I apologize, and I do care about you." Even though Marahezron would not admit it, that was the hardest thing he ever had to do; he was never fond of apologizing to anyone. Still, he knew he had to make amends with Dragon before he left on this journey, and only a fool would leave things broken.

Dragon looked him straight in the eye and saw his sincerity. "I know. Perhaps I didn't make things easy for you as well. I take back the last words I spoke to you. You are a brave and honorable dragon and I'm honored to have you in my life. Maybe when I get back, we can work on talking a little more, and fighting less." Then Dragon did something that shocked the other three; he stepped forward and hugged Marahezron.

Even though Marahezron was a little confused, he returned the hug, then he looked into Dragon's eyes and nodded his head in agreement. "Yes, talk more, fight less," he replied. He then turned to take one last look at his daughter. At the same time, Ancient handed Dragon something long and wrapped in cloth.

"What is this?" Dragon asked, giving Ancient a strange look.

Ancient smiled, let out a small chuckle, and then replied, "It's Truth."

"I don't think I'll be needing a sword, but it's always nice to have one." Dragon kept his face blank, not wanting Ancient to see his mind—that he was thinking of hiding in the forest. Dragon draped Truth over his back with his bag, leaving its cloth cover carefully wrapped around it, and then looked up to see Ancient holding something else. It looked very similar to the bag that he had on his back already, but there was something a little different about it. "All right, what is this?"

"It is something special that I made for your trip," Ancient replied with a smug grin on his face.

"I already have a traveling bag," Dragon stated, not wanting to hurt Ancient's feelings.

"This one is very different than the one that you have; as a matter of fact, it might be the only one of its kind."

Dragon had a strange feeling that magic was involved and a long explanation was coming. So he took a deep breath and rolled his eyes. "All right, what makes this traveling bag different?"

Ancient smiled as if he was waiting for such a response. "I'm glad you asked Dragon. This traveling pack is very special indeed. I first got the idea during the first war. We needed to move lots of supplies with less dragon power; we didn't have very many dragons to spare for transporting supplies. The sad thing is I didn't get to start working on my idea until three thousand years ago. I finally completed it a month before your father died; it was meant for him. I have been waiting for the right time to give it to you."

"Three thousand years to make a traveling pack is a little eccentric Ancient."

"For a normal traveling pack, yes; however, this is not a normal traveling pack. I magically enlarged the space within the traveling pack so it could hold more supplies. Believe it or not, that's a lot harder than some people think. Most people think wizards and magicians can do almost anything, but that's not true; there are some things that are beyond our control. Time and space are two things that are beyond anyone's control; only the Creator has that power. So, it was very hard to expand the inside of the traveling pack without expending the outside."

Dragon looked at the traveling pack, a little concerned and trying to understand what Ancient was saying. "So what you are saying is, you used dark magic to make this thing?"

"Not quite, but I came very close to crossing some lines. In honesty, I bent rules, I didn't break them. That's exactly what I did with the magic. I could not create new space inside the bag, but I could bend the space that was already inside. That's why it took so many thousands of years to figure out how to do it. It's not easy trying to figure out how far to magically bend space without breaking it. Also, the bag continued to break every time I tried, so I had to find a way to reinforce the bag at the same time stretch the boundaries of the inside."

"So exactly how big is the inside of the bag?" Dragon asked as he poked the traveling bag, thinking it would pop like a bubble.

"Well, the center of the bag can hold about fifty days of both clothes and food supplies."

"That's enormous; good luck trying to find something in there."

"Yes, that is why before I expanded it magically, I added some inside pockets to help organize things. You have two on the back, two on the front, and one on each side. The pockets are expanded as well but not as large as the main pouch of the pack."

Dragon was still unwilling to take the traveling pack from Ancient's hand. "So how long is this magic supposed to last?"

Ancient chuckled like he usually did when Dragon noticed something that others didn't catch. "You're right, the magic will not last. It's like blowing a bubble; without constant pressure, it will deflate. With the amount of power that I put into the bag, it should last about ten thousand years, then the space inside should reduce back to its normal size. Unless you can find a way to reinflate it, however, I doubt that.

As for the traveling pack itself, it's practically indestructible. I had to make it that way to hold the pressure that was within it. Just do me a favor and don't put it in harm's way and test my magical skills."

"All right," Dragon replied as he finally took the traveling pack from Ancient's hand. He still wasn't quite sure about it, but since it was a gift for his father, he wasn't going to disappoint Ancient by saying no. He took his traveling pack off and didn't unpack it; he simply stuffed it into the new pack. Dragon figured he'd look at it later; he was eager to get on his way. He slung it back on his shoulder next to truth hoping that the two magical items wouldn't have a problem with each other. He looked up at Ancient again, only to see him holding two more items that were in the shape of a foot. "What are those?"

"I'm not sure what the humans call them, but they are meant for your feet on long journeys. These were your father's. He made them and never had a chance to wear them. So I thought, what better parting gift to give you for a long journey than something for your feet." As Ancient handed them down to Dragon, he noticed something dangling around Dragon's neck, hidden by his shirt. Ancient stared at it intently until he figured out what it was. Dragon had taken a small piece of rope and fastened it to his mother's scale.

Dragon sat down for a moment, carefully taking Ancient's gift, and attempting to figure out how to put them on his feet. Even though it appeared very apparent how they were supposed to go on his feet, he realized it was a lot harder than it looked. When Dragon eventually got them on and snug against his feet, he looked back up to see whether Ancient was laughing. Immediately, he noticed Ancient's gaze upon the scale and tried to defend himself. "I just wanted to take a piece of her with me." He then stood up and dusted himself off.

Ancient patted Dragon on the back. "Then you take all of us with you." He bent down and gave Dragon a hug. "Good-bye, young one. May the Creator be with you."

Dragon ignored that last comment and turned to head out of the city. He began walking to the entrance, with Sonya close behind him.

They both stopped and turned for one last look at what was their home. After taking in all they could of the beautiful city, they turned and left.

Ancient and Marahezron closely watched the two they loved the most walk through the mountain entrance. "It's a shame we couldn't tell him. There is so much he doesn't know. I will miss them both," Marahezron commented.

"Yes, it is," replied Ancient. "However, I have a feeling that they will miss us more." Ancient turned to look at Marahezron. "Good-bye, my old friend. Until the day we wake again."

"The same to you, old friend. I couldn't go through this without you by my side."

With those words, they lay down side by side together and looked down the tunnel. Within moments, their bodies began to change, starting at their tails and working its way up their bodies. It seemed as though their bodies were hardening into stone. Finally, it enveloped their heads, and all that was left of their figures were solid stone statues. The statues' stone eyes were still peering down the tunnel as though waiting for someone to return.

＊＊＊

Dragon and Sonya were almost out of the tunnel. They were not paying attention to anything that was happening behind them. Pretty soon, they stepped out of the darkness and into the sunlight. They gazed around, taking in the beauty of the day, thinking that nothing could possibly go wrong. So they continued on out from the mouth of the tunnel and headed into the forest. Dragon, however, was somewhat curious about what happened to the guards at the tunnel entrance. They were not there.

What Dragon didn't notice was that the moment he set foot out of the tunnel, something began to happen. It seemed as though the rocks and the pebbles on the ground came alive. First, it started deep within the tunnel; then the rocks began moving, rolling toward the entrance. Then, when Dragon got farther away from the entrance, the rocks from outside began moving toward the entrance. There were even rocks coming down from the mountainside. They all herded toward the entrance— first the big rocks, then the smaller rocks. The bigger rocks settled firmly in place, with the smaller rocks filling in between. The rocks packed themselves so tight that they began to look just like the mountainside. Working on the outer rim of the entrance first, the rocks slowly moved toward the center.

Dragon got a slight chill up his back and decided to look back one last time at the mountain. When he turned, his face filled with fear at the knowledge that the entrance was half blocked.

"No!" he screamed as he dropped his stuff and took off running back toward the entrance. He was running as fast as his legs could carry him. Dragon could see in the distance that the rocks themselves were beginning to pick up their pace. He pushed himself as hard as he could, seeing only a tiny hole left in the entrance. As the last pebble slid into place, Dragon's body slammed against the rock wall. Besides a massive booming sound, nothing happened; the wall was unscathed. He stepped back to look as his mind whirled with the thought that he might not be able to get back in, that even with all his strength he could not scratch the barrier.

"No, no, no," Dragon continued to scream as he hurled himself at the wall. He turned to Sonya and pointed at the top of the mountain. Without a word, she took flight as quickly as she could to reach the entrance at the top of the mountain, while Dragon began scratching at the wall, since his attempt to slam into it achieved nothing. For a long while, he continued to do everything in his power to break down the wall. He stopped his onslaught on the wall when he saw Sonya come flying back down. "Well, what did you find?"

"Nothing," she said, trying to catch her breath. "The entrance on top of the mountain is completely sealed as well. I cannot see any way to get through it. I tried."

Dragon became enraged, and he turned back to the wall, pounding his fists against it and screaming to the sky. "You expect me to serve you when you willingly take everything from me! You are not my Creator. I swear on my mother's blood that I will never serve you!" Dragon gave up on the assault on the wall, knowing that there was no hope of getting inside. At that moment, his mind was a whirlwind of thoughts; he wasn't sure what emotion to have. He was filled with rage, but at the same time he was overcome with sadness over the loss of his home and everything he held dear. He put his hands against the wall and lowered his head as he continued to scream and cry. His chest hurt, his head hurt, and he couldn't seem to get control over himself. For a moment it seemed as if his rage and grief would send him into madness.

However, while Dragon may have lost everything else, he was not ready to lose himself. He applied every mental discipline that Ancient taught him and pushed the madness back. When the struggle finally ended, Dragon was exhausted. He turned and leaned his back against the wall, letting himself slide down to rest on his bottom. He laid his head down on his hands and began to weep. At that moment, he could not imagine anything worse than being separated from the beings whom he loved; even being separated from the stone statues of his parents made him feel alone and abandoned.

Sonya so desperately wanted to say something but realized that this was once again a moment where silence was best. She lay down only a few feet from him and decided to wait on him. Unfortunately, she didn't realize that waiting would take a very long time. The day had gone into the night and then crept back into morning. Sonya finally decided that she needed to confront him.

"Dragon, I can't imagine what pain you're going through," she began, carefully seeking out the right words as she got up from the ground. "Sitting here waiting for a sign of hope or a sign of revenge will not help the situation. As much as you love this land, we must move on." Sonya stood still, looking at Dragon for any response.

"You're right," he said, getting up and dusting himself off. "If I am to seek vengeance, it will not be here."

"That's not exactly the attitude I was hoping for," Sonya replied openly, with an odd look on her face.

"Everything in my life, everything that I have ever known, has been taken from me. I will not let this go lightly. This will be a day I will remember. And I will remember everything the Creator has done to me!"

"I'm still here," Sonya said trying to add a little optimism to the situation.

Dragon, being so consumed by rage, heard her comment but ignored it. He took a deep breath and then slowly began walking away from the mountain, picking up his things as he went. This time, he did not look behind him, and neither did Sonya. However, she stopped suddenly, thinking she had clearly heard a voice. She looked around but didn't see anyone, not to mention that Dragon kept on walking, so he didn't hear anyone. Suddenly a gust of wind blew by Sonya and in the wind, she heard the voice again.

"Look after Dragon. Be a shelter for him until he is ready to return to me." The voice whispered in Sonya's ear as it blew by.

Sonya couldn't tell who it was that was speaking to her, but the power that she felt from the voice made her believe it was either Kirianadréth or the Creator. She didn't bother trying to figure out who was speaking to her, she simply answered with a whisper. "I will," she said and meant it with all her heart. Sonya trotted after Dragon, more determined to watch after him than ever before. At the same time, she was excited and had a feeling that the journey was going to be one full of adventure. When she caught up with Dragon, she stayed only a few feet behind him. They both made their way through the forest and out into the world, leaving behind everything they knew.

***

For days, Dragon and Sonya continued to travel south. First, they squeezed out of the forest that surrounded the old dragon empire. On the way out, they snuck by the human villages that were loyal to his father. He was curious about what humans were like, yet at the time, he did not desire to deal with anyone, for the pain of his loss was still too close to his heart. Dragon had a hard time contemplating everything that was running through his mind. His thoughts continued to be a whirlwind upon his mother, father, friends, and his city long gone. When he focused on the humans, he became enraged over the fact that they were the ones to be saved. His anger, however, peaked when he thought of the Creator—the one who caused everything. He wasn't sure if he believed in such a being, or whether he should. Why believe in someone that you could not see yet took everything from you? he thought. In an effort to control his anger, he simply pushed everything out of his mind. He merely focused on each day and every step away from his home. It seemed as though the simple things were easier to deal with, and that made everything better for the time being.

They made their way out across beautiful plains, which eventually turned into rocky hillsides and then a desert. Continuing on, they crossed over mountains and back down into a valley. Dragon was so intent on keeping his mind closed that he didn't count how many days they traveled. He only noticed the distance when he could no longer recognize the types of trees, bushes, and animals they saw.

Sonya was the one who really kept time for her own sake as well as Dragon's. However, she never told him that they had traveled for more than three months, because she didn't know what would upset him. The entire time they traveled together, Dragon kept to himself, and Sonya had a hard time trying to make conversation with him. She constantly ran the thought through her mind of how to talk to someone who had lost so much. How do you speak to someone who lost their father when they were young, their mother when they were older, and eventually their entire home? Still, she did her best to make his life easy. Each and every night, Sonya would make a fire, which was easy since she could breathe it. Then she would go hunting for food, leaving him to think by himself. When she would return with her catch, she would cook dinner for him, which wasn't easy since she wasn't too good at skinning an animal. But she made up for it with her cooking. She herself enjoyed the cooked meal; unlike many dragons who favored raw meat, Sonya enjoyed the taste of cooked meat, perhaps because she spent so much time around Dragon. She, however, did notice that with each passing day, Dragon would open himself up a little bit more to her, which gave her hope for the future.

The landscapes that they crossed were vast; it took them a long time to make it from one to another. With every step of the way, Dragon became angrier with the Creator. At least every other day, he would see a strange rock formation that had a dragon-like shape. Inside them, he could feel the essence of what was once a dragon. Knowing that the dragons were a touch away but that he could not embrace them enraged Dragon. The more stone dragons that he recognized, the more he wanted to get far away from his home. But for now, he wanted to find a place where he could rest and forget all that had happened.

From a valley, they entered into another forest, which stretched as far as the eye could see. They weren't far into the forest when night fell, and they decided to camp. Sonya found a nice hill that overlooked a good portion of the forest. Dragon, on the other hand, didn't care about much; he just wanted to rest. So Sonya started a fire and then quickly went hunting, as she usually did.

While Dragon waited for Sonya to return, he sat down with his back to a tree. He tried listening to the sounds of the forest in an attempt to relax himself. But for some reason today he was agitated more than usual and couldn't focus. Dragon looked down at his legs to see that his pants were full of holes. Then he realized that he had been so consumed by rage, grief, and the need to get away that he hadn't stopped to pay attention to the small things. He took his tattered clothes off and threw them into the bushes. He then went to a nearby stream and washed himself, for the first time since he had left his home. After he cleaned himself up to what he thought would be his mother's standards he went back to the fire to dry off and get some new clothes. Dragon sat down next to the fire and pulled his pack close. He took a moment before he opened the pack because it had things from home, so he had to take a deep breath and prepare himself before he opened it.

When he opened the pack, he remembered that this was the magical traveling pack. He reached in and pulled out his original backpack. He then opened his pack, and got out some fresh clothes, and got dressed. He sat back down and was almost content to wait there till Sonya got back. However, curiosity got the better of him again, and he was bored.

Dragon reached over and pulled Ancient's traveling pack to him. First, he reached into what Ancient called the main pouch. He was surprised when his arm reached all the way in the pack. Being told by somebody that you have a magical traveling pack is one thing; realizing it for yourself is another. He felt around in the bag amazed at the amount of stuff inside the pack. On one side, he felt clothes individually wrapped, which made him sigh in relief and then chuckle. Ancient really did think of everything. Trying to pick loose clothes out of a traveling pack was a pain by itself; trying to do it out of a magical traveling pack would be a nightmare. However, Ancient thought ahead and bundled each pair of clothes together so it was easier to just reach in and grab one. There were ten bundles of clothes for Dragon.

Dragon then reached to the other side of the traveling pack and felt smaller cloth bundles. He pulled one out to examine it. The bundle was the size of his two hands put together. He neatly opened it to find dried meat and a type of flatbread. He knew from the smell of them that they were made by the dragons, which means they would probably last for years. Dragon really didn't need food since Sonya and him were good hunters. However, it was nice to know that he had a second option if hunting went badly. He tied the food back up and put it back in the pack, then counted the food bundles in the pack. It was hard because he didn't want to pull them out of the traveling pack, but Dragon estimated over a hundred food bundles.

When Dragon was done messing with those, he decided to look at the inside pockets of the travel pack. Four of the pockets were empty, and the two that were full had scrolls in them. Dragon pulled a few of the scrolls out to look at them. They were Ancient's scrolls in the dragon language and the ancient language. It appears as if Ancient wanted Dragon to continue his learning and thought that might be of some use. Dragon put the scrolls back into their pockets, knowing that he would look at them someday but not anytime soon.

He then emptied the rest of his traveling pack and put the contents into one of the pockets inside the magical traveling pack. Dragon then threw his traveling pack with his ruined clothes. He then went and sat with his back against a tree again and began to mutter to himself.

"Ancient, you think of everything, don't you," Dragon said as he let out a harrumph. "You and Marahezron are bastards. The two of you knew what was going to happen and you said nothing. If I ever see you two again, I will break your tales and your wings." Dragon went silent and stared at the fire, waiting for Sonya to return.

When she got back, they both filled their bellies, thinking that to-morrow would be a long day. When they finished eating, they decided that perhaps it would be a good time to get some rest. Sonya found a nice spot to lay down. Like she had done every night since they left their home, she opened her wing and let the end touch the ground. Dragon then came over and lay down on the end of her wing. She then curled him up into her wing and tucked him close to her. As she did that, it began to rain slightly, so she made sure he was tucked com-fortably under the cover of her wing. The rain did not bother her too much, so it wasn't long before the two of them were sound asleep.

Dragon awoke in the middle of the night, feeling a little uneasy. He looked out from the covering of Sonya's wing to see that it was still raining. As he did, something else caught his eye—a faint light in the distance. He rubbed his eyes and then took another look, trying to focus on what he was looking at. It wasn't any form of fire, he thought, that made him more curious. So he carefully wiggled out of Sonya's wing and walked quietly away from her.

The rain was cool yet heavy, and within a few seconds, he was completely wet. Dragon stood at the side of the hill overlooking the forest, letting the rain drench him completely. The rain did not bother him at all; to him, it seemed like cool refreshment. He let it relax him as if it was washing away everything that had happened to him. For a moment, he had forgotten why he got up from the cover of Sonya's wing.

Dragon took a deep breath of the refreshing forest air and the smell of rain, thinking for a moment that he had finally found peace. Then, very abruptly, it was gone, and reality came crashing back to him. Sixteen, he thought. He was only sixteen years old, and life was unfair. He might look older, but he was still very young. Dragons were younglings till they turned one hundred, and humans were considered young even in their thirties. As for Dragon, he was considered very young in both accounts. He once believed that he would live many years before any responsibility was thrown at him. He thought that he would be in his fifties when his mother would ask him to take on a more prominent role in the kingdom. In between those years, he would have all the time in the world to be a young dragon and get into all the mischief that he could. However, that was not how things turned out. As prideful as he was, Dragon was willing to admit, if only to himself, that he was still too young. Dragon was only sixteen and was the king of the dragons, cut off from his home, sent on a quest that he did not believe in, and separated from everyone that he loved but one. He wasn't ready for this, and deep in his heart, he wanted to cry out for the injustice that had been done to him.

Eventually, he came back to himself and spotted the light again, noticing that it was coming in his direction. The light didn't seem as if it was carried, more like it was floating. It was moving gracefully through the air, making slight turns here and there. It wasn't long before it was close enough for Dragon to recognize it.

The fairy Tilly came flying up to Dragon, stopping only two feet from his face. The rain didn't seem to affect her; it disappeared the moment it touched her light. She stared at him silently for a moment, giving his eyes time to adjust. During the day, she was easily seen; however, at night or in darkness, when she chose to be visible, her body glowed brightly. Her light illuminated Dragon's face and most of his body, making him very visible in the dark night. "Greetings, Dragon," she finally said. "I have come to give you my condolences on the loss of your mother."

Dragon simply stared at her with no expression on his face. "Thank you for your concern, but I need no pity. Is that the only reason you would come to see me?" He then crossed his arms, clearly troubled by the memory of his most recent loss, as well as wondering why it took Tilly so long to come give her condolences.

Tilly hesitated for a moment and then simply replied, "No."

"So why have you left your charge to find me? Even though I have heard that your race of fairies has unbelievable speed, that you could almost be in two places at one time, it still makes me wonder why you need to speak with me."

Tilly began moving around a bit, and Dragon could see that she was trying to choose her words carefully. "I have a new charge," she stated, almost as if it hurt her to say it.

"Why a new charge? What happened to your last one?" Dragon thought for a moment and then quickly came to an odd conclusion. "Was my mother your last charge?"

"No, she wasn't, but she did have one of us. When I went to see her, I got to meet your mother's and father's fairy. Before your mother had time to speak with me, her fairy told me your parent's entire story. I have to admit, it was quite impressive. They were worthy to have one of us."

"So who was your last charge?"

"He died thousands of years ago. I have been waiting all that time for a new one." Once again, her words seemed painful, as if she didn't want to say them at all.

"If you had to wait thousands of years, your new charge must be important."

Tilly looked Dragon straight in the eye. "My new charge is you." There was no mistaking the scorn in her voice.

Dragon threw his head back and laughed out loud. "It is just like the Creator to assume that I will do something for him." He raised his hand and fluffed Tilly away. "I have no need of you."

"Why, you dirty—"

"What?" Dragon interrupted, glaring at her. "Dirty what? Go on and say it!"

"Why, you dirty half-breed, have you no clue what an honor it is to have one of us!" Tilly held back behind her lips a few more rude comments; her face was flushed with anger, clearly visible even at this time of night.

Dragon smirked. "No, I don't. Why don't you go ahead and tell me everything that is on your mind, little speck."

Tilly became aggravated even more and then began spouting off. "If you want to know what is on my mind, then fine, I will tell you! I was the very first historian created, and I was given the very first charge. Even though he died thousands of years ago, I felt important. Perhaps I might have gotten arrogant and felt better than all the others. However, I couldn't be arrogant for long. I have been waiting years for a new charge. I saw other fairies' charges come and go and never understood why I didn't have another one." Even as she was hovering in the air, she waved her arms in frantic motions as she continued to rant and rave. "I made myself believe that it was because the Creator was waiting to give me someone special. I thought it might be someone as mighty as a dragon or as intelligent as an elf. After waiting so many years, I was excited to finally get a charge. Then I found out that my charge was nothing but you!"

"You say that as if I am not worthy enough to deserve you," Dragon said.

"You're not," Tilly said. "Sonya is more deserving than you are! You are nothing! I can't believe the Creator gave you to me!"

"So why don't you ignore his command and leave me alone?"

"Because I am not like you. I cannot disobey what the Creator has put in motion. My very existence rests upon my obedience to him. Whether I like you or not, I am your historian. So I hope for my sake that you will die quickly so I may be free of you!"

Dragon took a step closer, getting nose-to-nose with Tilly. "Listen here, fairy. I do not care what you think of me, but I will tell you what I will do! I will live every day and not satisfy you by dying! I will survive thousands of years just to torment you! Then I will drive you so mad that you will beg the Creator to end your existence!"

Tilly backed up with a look of utmost hatred on her face. "This is not over, half-breed!" Then with a spark of light, she disappeared, leaving Dragon in the darkness.

Dragon, however, was not amused or amazed. "You may have vanished, fairy, but I still know you are there. From this day forth, I will live to torment you." He continued to stand in the rain, staring out at the hillsides. Their conversation seemed to harden his heart even worse. All he could do was stand and stare at the darkness of night, waiting for the first touch of dawn. No epiphany came to him, his life seemed more confusing than ever.

As dawn approached, the first touch of light did not warm Dragon. The rain that was still falling felt warmer than the light. He was wondering what the Creator was going to throw at him next. One way or another, he was determined to live on. He was stubborn that way.

7

Two Encounters

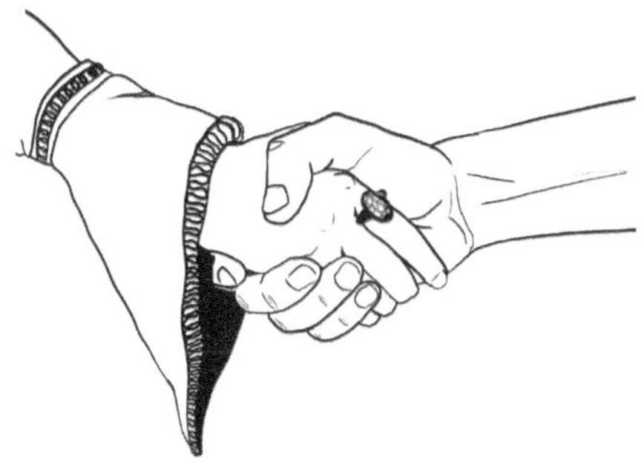

Dragon and Sonya set out early the next morning, although Dragon didn't get much sleep the night before. The rain had stopped several hours after dawn, but the smell of the renewal that it had caused hung in the air. Though it had a calming effect, in his mind, Dragon was still upset over the conversation between him and Tilly. Nevertheless, he went through most of the day doing his best to keep his mind off it. He did not tell Sonya about their conversation; he thought it best that he keep it to himself. Throughout the day, as they walked through the forest, Dragon did his best to keep up a simple conversation with Sonya. However, she could see that something was bothering him. She gave him his space for a while, hoping he would open up and say something, but when it appeared that he wouldn't, she decided to intervene. To keep his spirits up, she would tell jokes and play games – anything she could do to get him to smile. Sonya was determined; she could not bear to see Dragon so depressed.

After they had walked through the forest for most of the day, she resorted to jumping out of bushes to scare him. But with every attempt she made, Dragon kept a straight face. Getting aggravated at her own failed attempts to make him smile, Sonya quickly came up with another idea. "Catch me," she yelled at Dragon as she darted off into the forest. As she got farther in, she could see Dragon intently watching her every step. Suddenly she stopped, sticking her nose up in the air and sniffing around. Sonya had caught a whiff of a strange scent; it intrigued her, so she went to find out what it was. Like a dog, she went sniffing around the forest, and Dragon slowly followed her, wondering what she was doing. It wasn't long before she came upon a dead animal lying in the middle of a small clearing. She approached it and bent down like a puppy, ever so curious about what it was.

"Wait, I have a bad feeling about this," Dragon screamed after her. From the tip of his nose down to his feet, his whole body was tingling with the strange sensation that something was wrong. He could see Sonya in the distance, but he was still too far away to do any good.

Sure enough, the moment she went to touch the animal, something happened. A huge net came crashing down over her, startling her at the very sight of it. Then, before she had any time to react, dozens of creatures came bursting out of the bushes and out from behind trees. These two- legged creatures carried ropes and threw them over her. While some of them quickly grabbed at the ends of the ropes and wrestled to keep her down, the others tied the ends to the trees. Before Sonya knew it, she was pinned to the ground with no way to escape. She couldn't see much underneath the net, but she heard a lot of yelling and cheering.

As Dragon saw this in the distance, he quickened his pace. He had already lost everything of value in his life; he could not lose her. When he got a little bit closer, he realized that the creatures looked like him, so he quickly assumed that these must be humans. Even though Ancient told him never to judge or assume anything, upon seeing them, Dragon quickly formed a heated opinion about the two-legged creatures. He skidded to a stop only a few feet from them.

"Let her go," he snapped. The moment he spoke those words, the humans' attention turned from Sonya to him. They stood still, looking at him with faces filled with confusion. Dragon took that short moment to study them quickly. He realized that they weren't warriors; they had no helmets or armor, and only a few of them had swords. Most of them were carrying strange items that looked more suited for the purpose of farming. All of them wore similar garb—tattered, worn, and dusty—and none of them appeared to be wealthy. They didn't answer him, so he thought that they couldn't understand him. He listened to them babble for a moment, then adjusted his language accordingly. Ancient taught him how to learn languages quickly and to speak them. He believed that if one could speak the dragon language, one could speak any language. "Let her go," Dragon repeated in a different dialect, drawing out the words to show he was serious.

This time, he got a different response. It seemed as though they could understand him. The looks on their faces seemed to be more of understanding, yet they still didn't want to comply. Then one of the humans began to laugh as he walked toward Dragon. He was only a few feet taller than Dragon; however, from the looks of him, he was well-built and strong. The man was scruffy-looking and looked hard, as if he had suffered much in his life; still, his attitude reeked of overconfidence.

"Let her go," the strange man said, mimicking Dragon. "We have no intention of letting it go. This dragon has been killing our herds for far too long, and we mean to get rid of it."

"I don't know what you're talking about," Dragon said, his mood not improving with this human's comment. "I assure you we have never been here before. You are making a terrible mistake."

"Mistake? I don't make mistakes. I am Bragnaugh. I don't know why this dragon means so much to you. Perhaps it is your pet. In that case, be grateful that we don't punish you for the things that it has done. Now get out of my sight before I kill you too!" The man waved his sword at Dragon, indicating that he would use it if this odd person continued to defend this dragon.

Dragon, however, stood firm, unwilling to move. "I will not say it again. Let her go!" Dragon didn't want to fight, but he was willing to protect Sonya. At that moment, all the thoughts of Ancient's wisdom and Marahezron's fighting knowledge came to him. The only thing that dominated those thoughts was the thought of losing Sonya, and that thought alone made him clench his fists.

Bragnaugh was confused, not understanding why someone would give their life for a dragon. "That's it. You've asked for more trouble than you can handle. You should've left when you had the chance." He took the sword in his hand, raised it high above his head, and brought it down toward Dragon.

Dragon was in no mood for long confrontations, so he raised his hand to stop the sword. The sword's swing came to an abrupt stop, down into the palm of his hand. Dragon closed his fingers around the sword, holding it tightly so Bragnaugh couldn't move it. On the other hand, there was no need. Bragnaugh and the other humans stood with their mouths open in astonishment. They couldn't understand why the sword did not slice through Dragon's hand.

Dragon looked up at his hand to see that it was bleeding a little. Steam was rising from his hand, caused by his hot blood touching the cold metal. He then looked back at Sonya, seeing her body pinned to the ground. He became enraged and decided to punish the man. While holding the sword in his right hand, he brought up his left hand. He clenched it into a fist and brought it across, striking the sword in the middle. The blade broke in half with a shattering ring, leaving one piece in Dragon's right hand. He then brought his right hand back down, still holding the broken sword. Without hesitation, he thrust it through Bragnaugh's chest.

Bragnaugh stood there for a moment, still holding his half of the broken sword. He briefly looked down to see the other half shoved into his chest. It wasn't long before his body stiffened, and he fell to the ground dead. Even though the sound of his body hitting the ground wasn't loud, it seemed to echo around and was heard by every onlooker. That one sound had an ominous effect on the other men, which gave Dragon a little bit more control over the situation.

Dragon stepped forward, placed one foot on Bragnaugh's dead body, and roared at the other humans. They all rapidly let go of the ropes and jumped back, startled by his roar. "I am called Dragon. I am the king of all dragons," he started to say. "I mean you no harm. However, if you do not release her now, you will suffer the same fate as your friend!"

Not even waiting for Dragon to say anything else, the humans quickly scurried around Sonya, untying her ropes and cutting pieces of the net. She quickly got up and threw the net off. She let out a puff of smoke and growled at some of the humans. Needless to say, that terrified them even more, thinking that they were going to be her next meal. One of the humans came running up to Dragon, falling to his knees and lowering his face to the ground, begging for mercy.

"King of the dragons, I beg you not to harm us. We are a peaceful village."

"I doubt that," Dragon said, staring down at the pitiful man. Because of what had recently happened, Dragon's distaste for the human race strengthened, and he even considered striking them all down right then and there if it weren't for Ancient constantly teaching him that he never had the right to judge and to never assume anything. Remembering and heeding Ancient's advice, Dragon took a deep breath to calm his emotions. "However, I will consider not harming you. Take us back to your village and give us something to eat. And then you'll tell me how a village of peace turns into a village of dragon hunters."

Dragon still wasn't keen on the idea of visiting a human village; nevertheless, he realized he could not avoid them forever, especially after what just happened. On the other hand, he thought that the more he knew about humans, the better it would help him avoid them.

"Yes, good king. We will do this for you. Come with us. Our village does not have much, but what we do have, we will give it to you." The terrified man got up and began to lead Dragon to his village.

"Wait, aren't you forgetting something?" Dragon asked as he pointed at Bragnaugh. "Don't you want to give him a proper burial?"

The men turned to quickly answer Dragon. "No, King, his body should stay there and rot. He is the main reason most of the trouble began."

Dragon was somewhat taken back by the man's attitude toward one of his fellow villagers; still, he let it go, knowing he would get answers sooner or later. So Dragon kicked Bragnaugh's body over, not necessarily out of rudeness, but more in the fact of an odd respect for the dead, so no birds might pick at his face. Even though animals would ravage the body, it just made sense to Dragon to show some respect. Eventually, he began to follow the humans to their village. Sonya came bounding up to him, hyperactive yet curious. "Are you, all right? How's your hand? How did you do that?" she rambled on.

"Yes, I'm all right. What about you?"

"I'm fine," she replied as she unfurled her wings and looked at them. "Not a scratch, but I can't say that about you. How did you know the sword wouldn't cut you?"

"I didn't. I just hoped that it wouldn't. Your father always said that my skin was tough like dragon scales. I thought for a moment that he might be right. I'm glad that he was. Nevertheless, it does sting a bit," he said as he poked at the cut on his hand.

Sonya then had a look of surprise on her face and took a deep breath. "Dragon, you killed a man. What was it like, and how do you feel about it?"

Dragon stopped for a moment and looked down at his hands. "Marahezron taught me everything that I needed to know about being a warrior. I learned well how to protect the ones I love. He even told me that death is something the warrior has to live with. However, all of his training could never have prepared me for this." The look on his face was distant as he tried to focus on everything he was feeling. He could barely describe his emotions to himself, let alone to Sonya.

"Are you, all right?" Sonya asked as she bumped her snout against his head, hoping to bring him back from wherever his thoughts had taken him.

"No, I don't think I'll ever be all right inside. My hands feel cold, and I have shivers that go up my back. I know that humans and dragons kill all the time, but I cannot see why. I understand killing to protect the ones you love, though it still seems like a heartless act. To take responsibility and power over someone's life is not something that should ever be taken lightly. I could almost feel his life leave his body." Dragon looked back at Bragnaugh's body. "For a moment, his eyes gazed into mine, as if he were holding on to any form of life. It is a feeling that I will never forget, and I do not long to feel it again."

Dragon and Sonya continued on, following the humans to the village. "There is much I have to learn out in the world," Dragon continued. "Judging from my first encounter with humans, I do not like what is before me. And I have a feeling that the lessons I will learn will be just as great and just as painful." He clenched his fist, attempting to stop the bleeding in his palm as well as strengthen his control over his mind to focus on the task ahead.

After a short time of Dragon and Sonya following the villagers, they found themselves in a strange place. For what was supposed to be the villagers' home was definitely less than what Dragon expected. From the stories that he had learned from his mother, he was hoping for at least a village with a wall or fence around it. Or well-constructed dwellings built by great craftsmen. Instead, he looked out upon a village that was definitely underdeveloped. They emerged from the forest and faced out upon a small clearing that seemed to be a marsh. What appeared to be homes looked more like tents with grass thrown on top of them. The animals in the village roamed freely among the humans, leaving quite a mess in their path. Dragon's eyes widened when he saw the rest of the villagers, mainly the women and children. It seemed as though the animals cleaned themselves better than the humans. Dragon was definitely disappointed; he was hoping for his first encounter with the humans to be more dignified.

"Come this way, great king," their guide urged him to follow.

Dragon merged slowly into the village, cautious of everything around him. He definitely paid attention to the awestruck faces of the villagers, as well as a few audible gasps and muttered words. At the same time, he walked carefully, keeping track of his feet, making sure he stepped on grass and not mud or animal waste, which was a lot harder than it seemed.

Sonya, on the other hand, quickly pranced through the village like the other animals without a care in her mind. Her head was quickly turning left and right, curious of everything that was going on. Several times, she splashed in the puddles and giggled like a little child enjoying making a mess. The women and children seemed to have disappeared when they saw Sonya, perhaps thinking she was going to destroy the village.

They were eventually led to a small dwelling and then asked to sit at what appeared to be a table, although it seemed more like a tree stump, with smaller stumps as chairs. The guide quickly ran inside the dwelling to grab some food, as the other villagers scattered throughout the village to tell everyone what they had seen. Then the guide came back out and gave Dragon and Sonya what looked to be dry old bread.

"Thank you for the gesture. I'm not hungry," Sonya said politely as she handed the bread over to Dragon.

Dragon smiled at her, knowing that she wasn't completely truthful. She might not have been hungry for the bread, but Sonya was eyeing a few of the animals running around in the village. However, that did not deter Dragon from tearing into the bread, for he had acquired an appetite after his new lessons on life and death. He tore off big chunks of bread and stuffed them into his mouth. "So tell me, villager," Dragon muttered with a full mouth. "You owe me an explanation—how peaceful villagers came to be dragon hunters."

"Forgive me, King. You're absolutely right," the villager said as he pulled up a stump and sat down. "To tell you the truth, there's not much to say about our village. We live out here, free from anyone's rule. We like to live life our way. We are so far removed that no one bothers us. Even the orcs pay us no mind. It may not be easy to live out here, but this is the way we like it. However, there are times when there's not much to do. That is where Bragnaugh had trouble. He always dreamed of great things. He fancied himself a great warrior, but instead, he caused more problems."

"It seems to be accurate enough," Dragon said as he shoved more bread into his mouth.

"Yes, but you never knew him, King. Doesn't matter what it was—could've been the smallest of problems, but to him, it was a chance for adventure. He always exaggerated everything and always got the villagers stirred up. No one knew quite how he did it, but he always got everyone angry enough to do something. That's how this whole thing started. Some of our livestock went missing. I believe that it might have been a wild animal. Perhaps they even wandered off." The villager waved his arms excitedly, indicating the gravity of the situation.

"No one knows what happened, but to Bragnaugh, it was another chance to make things go his way. Believe it or not, he decided to pick on dragons. I don't know why. We've never seen a dragon. I don't even think they even live in this area. Our luck, we stumbled on the only dragon traveling through this land." The guide then got off the stump and knelt beside Dragon. "Dragon King, please forgive us. We never thought we'd catch a dragon. Honestly, we meant her no harm. The only trouble in our village was Bragnaugh, and now that he's gone, we can go back to our lives. Please do not punish us for his mistake!"

"Do not worry," Dragon replied, patting the man on the back. "One death is sufficient for today, and we will be on our way soon. I do not believe that you will ever see us again, so you can go back to your peace." That was his answer, but it was not what he was thinking. Dragon believed that all those who went out with Bragnaugh wanted some form of adventure too. Because if they didn't believe they would catch a dragon, then why did they leave the village? In the end, Dragon believed that they just needed to get out of the village for a time, like he would leave his city for the woods sometimes. He would never admit it, but for a moment, he had some sympathy for these villagers.

"Thank you. You are a good king," the man said as he got up and then stared out into the village. "Oh no!" the man then exclaimed.

Dragon and Sonya quickly looked out to see what he was worried about. To their confusion, they saw an old man hurrying through the village with a young woman trailing behind him. The old man didn't look to be in the best of health or cleanliness, yet he seemed eager to see Dragon.

"Forgive me, Dragon King," their guide said, very annoyed. "Perhaps there is one more person that causes trouble around here." The man picked up a rock and threw it at the old man, nearly hitting him. "Go away, you old fool. We need no trouble here. We have had enough trouble today!"

Dragon sat there, confused but silent, as he watched the old man continue to come closer.

The man finally reached Dragon and kneeled at his feet. "I hear you are the great dragon king who killed Bragnaugh," the old man finally spoke, slightly out of breath.

"I am, and what is it to you?" Dragon coldly replied. He never thought of himself as an arrogant and superior ruler, yet he was somewhat enjoying all the attention he was getting.

"Careful, King. You might regret this conversation," their guide added.

"I am called Rowan," the old man continued, paying no attention to the words of the other villager. "Bragnaugh's death means much to me, for I owed him much, but I had not the means to pay him. I was certain that when he returned, he would take everything that I have."

"Which isn't much," the guide added sarcastically.

"By killing him, you have released me from that debt, so now I owe you my life."

"You owe me nothing," Dragon swiftly answered, unwilling to be involved in this village any more than he already was.

"Oh, great Dragon King, it would be an honor for me to give you my greatest possession. So I hand over to you my daughter. Do with her as you please," the old man rambled and then darted off back into the village.

The old man was so quick that Dragon didn't have the time to respond. Of course, he wasn't sure how to respond in the first place. He didn't know what had taken place. He looked back at the guide, confused and longing for answers. The guide saw Dragon's confused look and then began to explain everything.

"Well, Dragon King, looks like you got yourself a mate—or, in other languages, a wife."

"What?" Dragon snapped as he stood up, begging for answers. Sonya herself had a very agitated look on her face and growled quietly.

"Let me explain a little more," the guide said as he urged Dragon to sit down. "Let's start from the beginning. Rowan is the closest thing this village has to a fool. He wasn't always like this. At one time, he had a lovely wife and five daughters. However, when his wife disappeared and left him, no one knows why or where, that's when he fell apart. He stopped providing for his family and lived off of others, almost like a village beggar. He lost everything. He even gave his daughters away to provide for himself. The only thing that he couldn't foresee was that his youngest was a lot like her mother. She was very free-spirited. She had been handed out to six men already. Unfortunately, none of them could tame her, and eventually, she ended up back with her father. She is so bad that no one will even take her as payment for anything anymore. If I were you, I'd pay her no mind and leave the village."

"Good advice," Dragon said. "I think that's exactly what we need to do. We have endured enough trouble here today."

"Good-bye, Dragon King. Have a safe journey," the guide replied as he shook Dragon's hand before going back into his dwelling.

Dragon then turned to leave the village. When he spotted the young woman, however, Dragon stared at her appearance for a moment. She seemed to be the cleanest person in the village. Although her clothing was tattered and torn, there wasn't a single speck of dirt on her skin. She was light-skinned like Dragon and about the same height. She wasn't fat; her body seemed to be in good shape, almost as though she had done a lot of hard labor. She definitely didn't carry herself like a woman; she seemed to act more manly. In spite of her personality trait, one could certainly tell she was a woman, with her beautiful face, blue eyes, and long, dark blonde hair.

After staring for a moment, Dragon turned and quickly walked away, seeming very eager to leave the village. However, without hesitation, the young woman followed after him. "Please, sir, I must speak with you," the young woman yelled.

"I do not have the time, and I have no need of you," Dragon retorted.

As soon as he responded, the young girl attempted to continue; on the other hand, it was quite difficult because Sonya was in the way. The young girl noticed that the female dragon didn't take a liking to her and that she was in between her and Dragon, doing everything she could to make it hard for her to speak to him. "I know, but I need your help!"

Dragon stopped abruptly and turned back to her. "Why do you need my help? Have I not helped your father enough?"

She stumbled to find the next words as if she didn't want to upset him. "I'm pretty sure you've been told enough about my father and me. But I am not like him, and I do not want to stay here."

"Then why don't you just leave?" Dragon said.

"I would leave if I could. You see, the next village is days from here. I would not make the journey alone. I would not last a day in the woods."

Dragon walked closer to her to talk to her face-to-face. The moment he got close, she lowered her face, unwilling to look him in the eye. "So what you are saying is you need us to protect you through the forest."

The young girl stood still and simply nodded her head in compliance, continuing to look down.

"And when we get to this village, you will leave us and find your own way," Dragon continued to inquire.

"Yes," she finally answered after a moment of silence.

"What is your name?"

"Yolana," she quickly answered.

"Well then, Yolana, you have my word. We will take you to the next village." Dragon began to turn and walk away, and then he turned back to add one more thing. "Try not to bother us too much. Dragons are easily annoyed."

Yolana smiled softly and lifted her head to look Dragon in the eye for the very first time. She didn't need to gather anything, so there was no long wait. The three of them set off toward the forest. Most of the village members stopped what they were doing for a moment to see the three travelers disappear into the trees. There was no long goodbye, no weeping. This meeting was trivial to the villagers, so they went back to work as if nothing had ever interrupted their lives. However, for Yolana, her life was just beginning. As for Dragon, the only thing he could say after his first human encounter was, "Sonya, go wash your hands and feet. You stepped on something."

***

The three of them walked for most of the day, and toward nightfall, they found a place to camp. Dragon and Sonya slept as they normally do, while Yolana slept uncomfortably across the camp. She felt like a nuisance to the two and didn't want to upset them in any way. It was a restless night for her, but she looked forward to the morning, which would bring a whole new day.

When she awoke in the morning, she was tired yet eager to begin the day, for this was the first day she had not woken up in her village. She brushed her eyes and then looked around the camp to see what was going on. It appeared that Dragon and Sonya had woken up earlier, and Sonya had gone hunting. She had caught and prepared a deer for them to eat. Yolana didn't need to ask how they started the fire or cooked the deer. She took one look at Sonya with fresh smoke coming out of her nostrils and understood why traveling with dragons was a good choice. She sat down, not far from Dragon, as Sonya handed her some meat. Dragon himself seemed not to be holding any standards of elegance; he was digging into the meat like a wild animal. So Yolana felt at peace and decided to eat. With her first bite, she stopped and looked at the well-cooked deer meat. She realized that Sonya was an excellent cook and knew exactly what she was doing when she prepared the deer. Yet Yolana felt a little out of place when she realized that Sonya had handed her an uncooked piece of meat. She didn't want to say anything to insult Sonya's cooking or to insinuate anything, so she did her best to stomach the meat. However, when Sonya wasn't looking, Yolana did grab some cooked meat to offset the sick feeling in her stomach.

"Well, that was delicious and most fulfilling," said Dragon as he got up. "I'm going to take a look at our path ahead. You two finish eating and get ready. We'll leave shortly." Dragon took another chunk of meat and stumbled off into the forest as he ate.

The moment Dragon was out of sight, Yolana started feeling a lot more awkward being alone with Sonya. After a few moments of silence, she looked up to say something. When she looked up, her face was filled with fear, and she leapt out of the way. Sonya's tail came smashing down right where Yolana was sitting, and Yolana picked herself up and turned to see Sonya coming after her. She jumped behind a tree as Sonya's jaws snapped right behind her. Then she darted off into the forest, leaving only her screaming behind. She ran off in the opposite direction that Dragon was going. She didn't care; she simply wanted to get away.

It wasn't long before she fell into a stream. She quickly got up, pulled her wet hair out of her face, and turned around to see if Sonya was right on her tail. When Yolana saw nothing, she slowly began to back up into the middle of the stream, looking in all directions, waiting for Sonya to appear.

Suddenly, Sonya came from above, landing on Yolana and pushing her down into the stream. Sonya stood with one foot on Yolana, holding her under the water, attempting to frighten her. She had an evil smirk on her face as she slapped her wings against the water. She seemed to get enjoyment out of watching Yolana struggle for air.

"Enough, Sonya. Let her up!" Dragon yelled from the bank.

Sonya was startled at Dragon's quick reappearance; she jumped off of Yolana. Then she backed up, looking embarrassed. Yolana came bursting out of the water, gasping for air. "She had dirt on her from the village. I was just helping her wash it off," Sonya stated and then grinned innocently.

"Are you all right?" asked Dragon.

Yolana nodded her head, letting Dragon know that she was all right, even though she seemed a little confused and out of breath.

"You must excuse Sonya. She plays a little rough. She's not used to humans," Dragon explained. Then he turned to his dragon friend. "Sonya, I think you owe her an apology."

"I'm sorry," Sonya said, looking as innocent as she could.

"Good, that's better. Now, come on you two, let's move on." Dragon turned and walked back off into the forest. He had a feeling that there was more to this incident than what Sonya said. There was no blood spilled, so he let it go. He remembered Ancient and Marahezron agreeing on only a few subjects, and females were one of them. They both told Dragon never to get involved with two females and their disagreements; the fact that both of his mentors said it made Dragon pay attention and want to heed it.

Yolana walked dripping wet to the shore and turned to face Sonya. At the same time, Sonya also walked toward the shore and walked right up to Yolana, almost touching noses with her as she stared down at her. Yolana, on the other hand, did not seem afraid.

"All right, let's get one thing straight," Yolana started to say. "I may not know much about the outside world, but I'm not a fool. I know you were not playing around with me. I don't know exactly why you feel as if you have to get rid of me. I will let you know, right here and now, whatever life you have with Dragon, I am not here to come between you two. I was hoping all three of us could be friends. However, it seems like we need to work on that. And I may only be human, but don't you ever do that again!" Yolana then turned around and firmly walked off into the forest after Dragon. She took a slow and deep breath, realizing that she had just snapped at a dragon. Her eyes opened wide with the understanding of what she had just done and how foolish she was. Yolana needed a dragon to help her through the forest, yet she seemed to have picked a fight with a dragon herself. She recognized that she was definitely hot-tempered and free-spirited like her mother. Though she needed to watch her step, Yolana definitely didn't belong in her village.

Sonya, with a childish grin on her face, stood for a moment, watching Yolana storm off into the forest. In her mind, she was thinking of all the fun things she could do to Yolana when Dragon wasn't looking. Then she cheerfully pranced after them, looking forward to the next few days.

***

The village that they were seeking was a lot farther away than they expected. Instead of a few days, it took them a total of nine to reach it. The journey itself wasn't easy, and there was a lot of tension between Sonya and Yolana. However, Yolana dealt with it as best as she could. She stayed as close as she could to Dragon to avoid Sonya. The most trouble she had was nine days of uncooked meat. Even though her stomach wasn't settling too well, she was happy to reach the village.

When they got closer to the village, Dragon started begging Sonya to stay hidden. Of course, she complained and argued about the reason why Yolana could go to the village and she couldn't. Then Dragon became quite stern and firm with her. "This village seems bigger, more like a town, and we don't want the same incident as we had in the last village. I will let you know when it is safe."

Dragon himself didn't like the idea of leaving her behind, but he didn't want any reason to stay there longer than he had to. He wanted to arrive, drop Yolana off, and continue with his travels. The thought of continuing to avoid human settlements pleased him greatly.

"All right," Sonya replied. "But I still don't like it!" She fluffed her wings and blew smoke out of her nostrils, indicating she was not happy at all.

So Sonya hid in the forest while Dragon and Yolana approached the settlement. As they came out of the forest and looked upon the town, they became intrigued, especially Dragon, because this community seemed more up to his expectations. The entire town was surrounded by a massive wall that stood higher than four average men. The wall looked like it was made of a bunch of trees that were just tied together, although there was no crack that you could peer through. The only entrance they could see was a big gate that opened inward. Dragon was smiling when he saw the wall, but when he entered through the gate, he was really surprised at what he saw. As he expected, the houses were well-built and well-crafted; they seemed to be made of wood and stone.

As they looked deeper into the town, Dragon could see some slight differences. The houses near the wall seemed small and designed simpler; the farther in they got toward the center, the more the houses seemed more elegantly designed and larger. This confused Dragon, even though it was an interesting sight to see. He admitted to Yolana his confusion and desired an explanation. Yolana, understanding his confusion, took a small moment to explain to Dragon the difference between the wealthy and the poor.

After she was done, Dragon was still confused, as he believed that all men should be equals. Then Yolana explained to Dragon that some men worked for their wealth and deserved it, and others did not, gaining it by destroying others. This, in return, perplexed Dragon even more; he couldn't seem to grasp the reasons for the things that men would do. He thought for a moment that all the wisdom he learned from Ancient was not in the race of men. But that didn't stop them from looking around, and even though Yolana knew more about the human world than Dragon did, she was just as intrigued as he was.

"This place is interesting," Dragon exclaimed. "I notice that there are some humans here with different skin colors."

"Yes, some colonies are like that," Yolana answered.

"Amazing. For a while, I thought humans only had my skin color. I wonder why," Dragon began to say and then was stopped by a strange sight. He saw in the distance an extremely dark, almost-black-skinned man lying on the ground, surrounded by four other men of the same color. Even from a distance, Dragon could tell that they seemed to be beating him. He quickened his pace to find out what was going on.

"No," Yolana urged him not to get involved, realizing that this was not a good sign.

Dragon paid her no mind, for this seemed more important. As Dragon approached, he could hear one of the men yelling at the man on the ground.

"I've had enough of your insolence. You will pay for this!" the man said as he raised his hand high, holding a whip with many thongs.

Dragon got there just in time, as the man's hand was in midstrike. Dragon caught the man's hand, stopping the whip. He wasn't sure why he did it or why he cared at all. He just felt that the whole situation was wrong. Ancient and Marahezron told him that as king and a man of strength, it was his responsibility to look after the innocent and the weak.

The man turned around quickly, enraged that someone would dare stop him. "Who are you, and what business do you have interrupting me!"

"I am called Dragon, for I'm the king of all dragons," Dragon snapped back. "What gives you the right to beat a defenseless man?"

The man began to laugh loudly, and so did the others. "The king of dragons! More like a madman! And I have every right to do whatever I want to this man. He is my slave!"

Dragon took a few quick seconds to evaluate the situation, realizing he didn't know what was going on. The man who was beating what he called his slave was definitely wealthy, Dragon observed. He was dressed in silky fabric that was made of many-colored threads and glittered against the sunlight. His hair was long and well-combed, and he had gold piercings and rings. The other three men were simple, wearing armor that was made of leather, yet they bore no sword; they had clubs instead. Still, no matter how much he looked those men over, Dragon still had the gut feeling that something was wrong with them harming the man on the ground. "I don't know what a slave is.

However, I do know that no one has the right to beat a defenseless man!"

"You don't know your own business, fool. When I'm done with him, I will start on you next!" The man turned around to take another swing at the man on the ground.

Angry over the arrogance of this man, Dragon threw his hands back and roared at him. The sound that echoed out of Dragon's mouth nearly knocked the men over. Unfortunately, it had a greater effect on the other people in the town. They scattered: mothers ran to grab their children, and the men grabbed whatever weapons they could. As for the four men Dragon was dealing with, they stepped back in terror, confused and unsure as to what they were looking at. Dragon, however, continued to stand there, growling, enjoying the terrified look on their faces.

"Excuse me, King," a voice called out from the side. Dragon took a step back to see who was speaking. "I don't mean to interrupt, but I couldn't help but overhear the conversation." The man who had spoken seemed simple; he was well-dressed but not overbearing. He seemed very close to the same height and build as Dragon, and even had the same skin color. "I am Krandal," the man introduced himself. Then he came up, stood beside Dragon and proceeded to speak to the other men. "I agree with the king here. You should let this man go."

The arrogant man stepped forward, a little aggravated by this suggestion. "How dare you propose such a thing. You know my power in this town. I am Asanon Darrowman. I must teach this slave a lesson or face losing credibility."

"I'm sorry, Asanon. I believe you've already lost your reputation today," Krandal continued. "If this is truly the king of the dragons, do you really want to risk offending him? Do you think we could go to war with the dragons, a town like us?"

Asanon thought for a moment, almost unwilling to comply. It wasn't until he stared deeply into Dragon's eyes, realizing that this was definitely no man, that he quickly concluded that he was outmatched, and there was no way to win this argument, so he relented. "Fine, have him," Asanon snarled. "But this is not over between us, Krandal!" Asanon fixed his hair and clothes, which seemed to have been ruffled by Dragon's roar, and then motioned to his men to leave. They stormed off in a huff, pushing people out of their way.

"Thank you for your help," said Dragon, looking at this new acquaintance. He never liked to admit that he needed help; still, he couldn't deny that if this Krandal didn't show up when he did, things could have been worse.

"No, thank you for not attacking the town," Krandal replied.

"I don't understand what you mean." Dragon gave Krandal a strange look, startled by the very comment. He always thought himself fierce, but he never thought that people would be terrified by his look.

"Well, I believe you are the king of the dragons. For one, no human sounds like you—the roar, I mean. And two, you had a little help convincing me." Krandal pointed to the wall surrounding the town.

Dragon turned to see what Krandal was pointing at, only to see Sonya peering over the top of the wall. Her tail was sticking up and wagging in excitement over all the new things she was seeing. Dragon put his head in his hand and shook it, slightly embarrassed by Sonya.

"She's harmless; trust me," he reassured Krandal.

"That's good to know. Welcome to our small town of Falistoran."

Dragon and Krandal turned back around to look at the man they had just saved. He was no longer lying on the ground; he was now bowing at Dragon's feet. Dragon took a few steps back, confused by this behavior.

"Get up, Phanis," Krandal remarked.

"You know this man?" inquired Dragon, becoming more confused about the very behavior of mankind.

"Of course I do. He is the most sought-after slave in this community. That is why Asanon was unwilling to let him go at first." Krandal turned to the slave. "Now get up, Phanis. Everything will be all right."

The man began to get up off the ground, showing his true likeness to Dragon. For a moment, Dragon was amazed at his stature. The man stood at least seven feet tall, and his muscles were strong and well-built. He had no facial hair or hair on his head, and his clothes were very tattered. Even though he stood strong and still, he seemed very quiet and shy. His head was bowed, and he wouldn't look anyone in the eye.

"Well, Dragon King, what do you want to do with him?" Krandal couldn't help but say that with a smirk on his face.

"I don't understand the question," Dragon said.

"You freed him from Asanon, so he is now yours, to follow you wherever you go."

"No, no," Dragon began to rant and rave. "I am not taking him with me. I have enough trouble of my own." Dragon quickly turned and pointed at Yolana. "I am here to leave this young female in your town, not to pick up someone else!"

"That would not be wise," Krandal replied swiftly in low tones.

"Why not? This is a human settlement. She should be safe here," Dragon responded in similar tones, not quite sure why.

Krandal looked over at Phanis and said, "Go spend time with your mother and prepare to leave."

Phanis bowed slightly and then left them to converse with his mother. Then Krandal threw his arm around Dragon and talked lightly to him. "Come with me. Eat in my home tonight, and I will explain everything."

Dragon thought for a moment and then agreed willingly. The more information he could learn about mankind, the better off he would be, Dragon reasoned. He turned around and whistled for Sonya to come into the town. Without hesitation, she bounded through the gate and down the streets of the town. Needless to say, on her way, she gave a lot of the residents the fright of their lives. If it wasn't for Krandal raising his hands and telling everyone that all was well, there could have been a serious incident. She skidded to a halt when she reached Dragon.

Marveling at her for a moment, Krandal couldn't help but smile, and then he led them to his home for some food and conversation. This pleased Yolana, for she was looking forward to some good cooking for once.

***

Later that day, as the sun began to set, they found themselves enjoying Krandal's hospitality. Krandal's dwelling was one of the largest in the town and located close to the center. Sonya sat outside with a couple of Krandal's slaves; they had given her an entire ox to eat. As for the slaves, they had plenty of meat to eat themselves, and they enjoyed conversing and eating with Sonya. As for Dragon and Yolana, they were inside Krandal's dwelling, enjoying a feast of their own. The house was well-designed with interlaid wood and stone; there were even several levels of the dwelling large enough to accommodate many families. In the center of the home, there was a nice-sized open fire pit, and circling it was a nicely carved seat. Yolana sat and ate her food slowly, enjoying every morsel of well-cooked meat. Dragon, on the other hand, ate very quickly and with no manners at all, although he looked up from time to time to see if Krandal would start the conversation he was waiting for.

After a while, Krandal sat down with his own food and began to explain himself. "Dragon, I can see how someone can be easily bothered by someone else. But I tell you, this is not a town to leave your friend."

"I'm going to need a little bit more explanation than that," Dragon said with a mouthful of meat.

"I am happy to explain," Krandal continued. "Dragon, Falistoran has some strange laws, but we do abide by them. One of the strange laws is that people that are born here cannot become slaves, unless born by a slave. However, outsiders, if they can be captured, can become slaves. Most men do not become slaves. Women, on the other hand, are easily made into slaves if they are by themselves. I know for a fact if she stays here, she will become a slave."

"Why can't I just leave her with you? You seem like you could take care of her." Dragon wasn't trying to be rude to Yolana; still, he wanted to continue traveling with Sonya alone.

"I would if I could. However, Asanon will say I have no claim to her, and before I know it, she'll be missing." Krandal pointed to the open door. "Asanon lives only two homes away, and it causes much trouble for me and my own."

Dragon grabbed another piece of meat and began gnawing on it. "All right, tell me what exactly it is between you two," he asked, still shoving meat into his mouth.

Krandal stopped eating and set his plate off to the side. He then stared Dragon in the eye, knowing that much more needed to be explained. "You see, I do not believe in slavery. When I came to this town as a young boy with my father, we agreed that we would do everything in our power to stop slavery. However, in Falistoran, it is a lot harder than it seems, as you can tell. My father did a better job of it than I have. I happen to be very cowardly. I'm not strong and powerful like you. I can't take on the whole community by myself. So I do my best with whatever courage I do have. Whenever I can, I buy as many slaves as I can."

"What good does that do?" Dragon asked, a little aggravated at the whole subject itself. He always thought of humans as being animals, but this subject seemed to prove his point.

"Well, to me, they're not slaves. I give them their freedom and anything they may need. Most of them don't leave because they have nowhere to go."

"What if you die? What happens to them?" asked Yolana, finally joining in the conversation. She didn't sound upset, even though half the conversation was about getting rid of her.

"Good question," Krandal answered. "One of the great things my father did was he got the town to implement a law. According to the law, if an owner dies, then the slaves are free unless they were sold publicly before the owner's death."

"That was nice," Yolana replied.

"Yes, that seems nice," Dragon agreed as he spat out a fat chunk of meat into the fire. "Unfortunately, that doesn't explain why you want me to take this freed slave, Phanis."

Krandal took a few more bites of food and then began to discuss Phanis. "When he was born, Phanis wasn't much, but the more he grew, the more valuable he became. It wasn't long before he became the most sought-after slave in the town, and of course, Asanon got his hands on him. Although, Asanon was no fool. He bought his mother as well. As long as he had Phanis's mother, he had control over Phanis— until about a year ago, when I tricked Asanon into selling me Phanis's mother, and it wasn't easy or cheap."

"And I bet that gave him another reason to dislike you," Dragon said.

"Yes, it did. It made him very angry, especially when he started losing control over Phanis. That's why he was trying to punish him, so the other slaves wouldn't get any ideas. Unfortunately, now that he lost Phanis to you, he has suffered a great disgrace. That is where the problem lies."

"I don't understand. You still aren't making sense to me," said Dragon. He began to think that mankind's only talent was to make things worse than they needed to be.

"Dragon, the problem is if Phanis stays here, he will be a constant disgrace for Asanon. Because you freed Phanis, Asanon can't buy him back or take him back. The only way for Asanon to be at ease is to kill Phanis, this I am sure of." Krandal quickly knelt in front of Dragon. "Great Dragon King, I know you don't want any more trouble traveling with you. Nevertheless, I am begging you. Do not leave him here to die. His mother will be fine. It is him that I worry about. Besides, you have looked at him. Does he look like a man who deserves this life?"

Dragon sat back for a moment, thinking about what Krandal said. Also, it impressed Dragon that a wealthy man would beg for a slave's life. Though he wouldn't admit it, this brought a little hope to Dragon that mankind wasn't all bad. He waited for a little bit with a small smirk on his face and then answered when it looked as if Krandal was going to beg again. "All right, I will take him with me."

"Thank you. You have no idea how much that means to me," Krandal shouted as he got up and shook Dragon's hand firmly.

"Is there any other place where I could take him and leave both him and Yolana safely?" Dragon quickly shot Yolana a look to remind her that she was also to be left behind when they found the place.

Krandal rubbed his chin for a moment and then replied, "I know of many places, but I am sure of only one city's location. If you go south, you should run into one of the largest settlements that I've heard of. You can leave them there safely."

"Thank you, Krandal. That does help."

"Phanis's mother was right about you," Krandal stated, excited about the whole situation.

Dragon looked immensely confused by that statement. "Now you make no sense. How can she be right when she doesn't even know me?"

"Forgive me, Dragon; I did not mean to confuse you." Krandal sat back down next to his plate and began to pick at his food again. "Phanis's mother is known around here as a seer."

"What does she see?" Yolana asked, once again trying to join the conversation but not knowing quite what to say.

"There are times when she sees much of the future," Krandal answered. "And there are times when she sees nothing at all. It's always different."

"So what did she see about me?" Dragon asked.

"She didn't see much of who you were. She saw only that someone was coming for Phanis. At first, I took that as a bad sign, but as time went on, she reassured me that whoever it would be was good." Krandal got up and motioned to another side of his home. "You will probably see her tomorrow when you come to take Phanis. For now, let me show you to a room where you may sleep for the night."

"Oh, that will be wonderful," Yolana said as she jumped up and quickly followed Krandal. As for Dragon, he followed slowly, in no hurry to sleep for the night. For tomorrow he would have another unwanted human traveling with him.

Krandal led them to a small room with two furry mats laid on the ground for sleeping. Once they were both in the room, Krandal bid them good night and went off to his own room. Yolana quickly jumped down onto one of the mats, as if this were a wealthy life for her. She had spent too many years sleeping in mud huts or among the trees; tonight, she would sleep well. Dragon, on the other hand, seemed a little disappointed and said that he would rather sleep outside with Sonya. That, in and of itself, proved to be a little difficult. When Dragon looked out to see what Sonya was doing, he realized that she was already asleep on her side, with several of Krandal's servants sleeping against her. Even though he was not too happy, he didn't want to wake her, so he went back to the room and decided to get what sleep he could. He thought that Krandal's gesture was nice. Nevertheless, he longed for a real bed fit for a dragon king.

****

When Dragon awoke the next morning, being cheerful was far from his mind. His back and neck ached from the odd sleeping arrangements. As strong as he was, he seemed to be no match for the common floor. Nevertheless, he woke Yolana, who was in a deep sleep, and then made his way through the home to the entrance, interested to see what the new day had brought. That, and he was unwilling to admit that he had missed sleeping in Sonya's comfortable wing, and he wondered what she was doing. Once outside, it didn't take long for his eyes to adjust to the light. Quickly, he realized that the city was already in a bustle and that Sonya was waiting for him quietly.

"Aw, I see you are awake," said Krandal as he came out of the house from behind Dragon. "Are you still planning on leaving today? Will you at least stay for breakfast?"

"It is a good idea that we leave," Dragon quickly replied. "We have caused enough trouble already. It is better that we not linger in this town. We need no breakfast. We should be fine on our own." Dragon didn't want to admit that he was hungry and breakfast would be nice. Still, he just wanted to get as far away from the town as he could, thinking that he might find some wild berries or something else in the woods that would feed him for the day.

"Well then, if that's settled, I will take you to Phanis's home so you can take him with you. That is, if you haven't changed your mind."

Dragon looked Krandal firmly in the eye. "I'm a dragon of my word. I will take him with me." With that said, Krandal led the way through Falistoran with Dragon, Yolana, and Sonya following closely.

The company finally reached the outer parts of the town, farthest away from the entrance gate. The houses here seemed very small, almost like single-room dwellings. Even though Dragon did not know much about mankind slavery, he realized that these dwellings were meant for them. On the other hand, he could also tell the difference between Krandal's servants and Asanon's slaves. It sickened Dragon to see that Asanon's slaves were barely alive, and once again, he couldn't understand the cruelty and brutality of mankind.

The slaves' dwellings were barely standing and didn't provide much shelter from the elements. They had nothing to cook or clean with; they didn't even have anything to eat. As a matter of fact, most of the slaves were nothing but skin and bones - hardly what you would call people at all. As for Krandal's servants, the man spoke true; they were well cared for. The dwellings were well-built and would hold up against the weather. As for the servants, they were clothed and fed as people should be. Some of them even took on a few of Krandal's characteristics, in that they too did what they could to help the slaves nearby. Dragon began to appreciate the work that Krandal was doing, no matter how small the deeds were.

"Here we are," Krandal said as he pointed to a particular dwelling. "You better wait here. I'll go in and see if he's ready."

Dragon nodded in compliance with Krandal's wishes and stood still while he went inside. The moment he was gone, Dragon took a few steps closer and leaned against the wall of the dwelling. He wasn't much for eavesdropping; on the other hand, since this involved him, he deemed it necessary. He didn't have to strain to hear anything; his dragon hearing picked up everything perfectly. Inside, he could hear that Krandal was silent; the only conversation going on was between Phanis and his mother.

"Mother, I will say it again," Phanis began. "I do not wish to leave you. Who will protect you when I am gone? What am I going to do? All of my life, I've never been far from your side."

"Stop your worrying, my son. Krandal will protect me." They both looked at Krandal, who nodded in agreement. "You see, everything will be fine. There is no need to worry. As for what you're going to do, I will tell you what you're going to do. You are going to go with this one called Dragon."

"Why, Mother? It makes no sense for me to leave you."

"No, it doesn't, when it comes to love of family. However, when it comes to destiny, it makes all the sense in the world. Wouldn't you agree, Dragon? Come in here so I can see you. It is not nice to overhear a conversation."

For a moment, Dragon was startled that the woman knew that he was listening, and he hesitated to move. Then, after a moment, he eased his way in through the doorway to see Phanis's mother. At first glance, he was surprised; she looked nothing like her son. She, on the other hand, was a little shorter than Dragon and very skinny. Yet Dragon could not deny that he saw wisdom and knowledge in her face;

it reminded him of Ancient. So he spoke no words and had no strong posture; he simply waited for her to speak.

She walked slowly up to Dragon, placed both of her hands on the side of his head, and stared into his eyes. "I have waited a long time to see this face—so much like your father's, yet you have a small hint of your mother's. It's probably your eyes. You have a great destiny unfolding before you. Don't destroy it with your blind and hateful eyes."

"I don't understand," Dragon replied respectfully. She was confusing, yet he knew that she was indeed gifted in many ways.

"No, you wouldn't understand right now," she said as she softly patted the side of his face and turned around to speak to her son. "You have a part to play in his destiny, and many people will suffer if you do not help look after this boy."

Dragon got a little flustered at her remark. "I am not a boy. I am a grown dragon!"

Phanis's mother turned back around to Dragon, aggravated herself. "Sixteen years is hardly anything for a man or a dragon. You are still young, and you have much to learn. I'm afraid you will have to learn some things too quickly, and very soon, I might add! So there is no more time to waste. You must go, and go now!" She began pushing them out of her home. For Phanis, she gave him one last big hug and then pushed him outside.

Dragon turned and peered back in at the old woman one last time, seeking answers. "Tell me what you know about my future, since it is so important," he calmly demanded.

The old woman peered deeply into Dragon's eyes, her face mirroring a serious yet concerned look. Once again, she softly placed her hand on the side of his face. "My dear Dragon, what I know is for my eyes only, for it is my burden to bear. Now go." She gave him a final shove out of her house.

Once outside, Dragon was upset and more determined to leave this town. He took one step and then realized that something was amiss. He noticed that Sonya wasn't where he left her, so he went to ask

Yolana where she might be. When he found Yolana, she was standing with a few slaves, laughing. He quickly demanded to know what was going on and what was so funny.

"You might have trouble getting Sonya to leave Falistoran," was all that Yolana said while laughing.

Dragon quickly understood what she meant, he spotted Sonya not far in the distance. He could see her frantically running around the buildings. She was chasing a small, dark-skinned boy around the age of ten. The boy, however, wasn't frightened; instead, he was laughing as he was running. This went on for several minutes, then suddenly it changed. The boy turned and began to chase Sonya, who herself was laughing hysterically as she was running from the small boy. When the boy started to get tired, Sonya dropped to the ground and let the boy catch her. When he did, he began to tickle her belly, and she laughed loudly.

Even though Dragon thought it was a cute sight to watch, he was eager to leave the town. He began to walk away and then whistled at Sonya. She quickly jumped up and patted the boy on the head, to say good-bye, and then ran to catch up with Dragon. On their way through the town, the only one who seemed to drag their feet was Phanis. As much as he knew he had to go, he did not wish to leave. Though he lived his life in slavery, this was his home. Nevertheless, he followed behind the others, keeping his head slightly bowed. When they reached the gate to the town, Dragon said good- bye to Krandal and grasped his forearm firmly in a farewell manner.

"Hopefully, the next settlement you arrive at will be less eventful," Krandal said sarcastically.

"Yes, I agree. My first two encounters with human colonies didn't go exactly the way I expected. Perhaps it is the way I greet people. I think I need to work on a greeting."

"Perhaps you're right, but you will have to test that in the next place you go. I suggest you leave the term dragon king out of your greeting. It might make things easier."

Dragon could say no more; he simply smiled lightly and then turned and left the town. Yolana and Phanis followed right behind him after saying their own farewells to Krandal. A warm hug from Yolana and a firm handshake from Phanis, and then they were on their way. Krandal once again reassured Phanis that he would protect his mother with his life. As for Sonya, she stood for a moment, waving good-bye to all the town dwellers. Then she proceeded to walk backward, still waving farewell.

* * *

On the first day with Phanis as a new traveling companion, things went a little slow. Dragon was beginning to be very annoyed with Phanis. He always walked behind the group and never kept up, and he didn't say a single word the entire day, in spite of the numerous attempts by the others to get him to talk. It wasn't until later that night that Dragon felt it was time to talk to Phanis. They had stopped in a nice clearing in the forest, and as always, Sonya prepared a nice fire and a meal. Dragon didn't have to worry too much about Yolana; ever since they had left the town, she and Sonya had been talking. It seemed as though Sonya realized that Yolana's life was very close to the slaves' lives in the town, and she felt a little bit of pity for her and remorse for the way she treated her. As for Dragon, he was sitting down on a fallen log, thinking of how to speak to Phanis.

"Phanis, come here and get some food," Dragon called to him, thinking it was the perfect way to engage the man in a conversation.

Phanis came around from the other side of the fire, where he had been sitting by himself. Without hesitation, he walked up to the meat that was sitting by the fire and grabbed some. Then surprisingly, he brought it to Dragon. This enraged Dragon, and he stood up and smacked the food out of Phanis's hands. Immediately, Phanis fell to his knees at Dragon's feet, which only made Dragon angrier, and he went over to the fire and grabbed a fresh piece of meat. "Stand up," he snapped at Phanis. When Phanis finally stood up, he wouldn't look Dragon in the face, and this only made Dragon more determined. He knew that Phanis had lived the life of a slave, but he didn't need to live it anymore. Of course, Phanis wouldn't look Dragon in the face until Dragon told him to. Dragon wanted to make sure that he had Phanis's complete attention when he slapped the piece of meat into his hand.

"This is for you to eat," Dragon snapped.

"I don't understand," Phanis said as he stood there with a confused look on his face.

"Great. Now you're starting to sound like me," Dragon sarcastically remarked. "You are a free man. You're not my slave. You do not have to do anything that anyone tells you to anymore."

"It is all I know," Phanis replied, sounding as if he was going to cry.

"Phanis, I know it is not easy to change something that you have done for a long time. However, this is something you must change for yourself and for your mother's wishes." Dragon stared Phanis deeply in the eye. "Would your mother put her hands on the face of any master?"

"No," Phanis quickly replied.

"Then that should show you that I am no master. I am a king of dragons and not of men. I took you from that town for your own safety." Dragon put his hand on Phanis's arm, led him to the log, and sat him down beside him. "From this day forward, you must do what you feel is right for you. And if you ever follow someone else's command ever again, let it be that one. As long as you are with me, you will be free." Dragon sat back and watched Phanis run those thoughts in his head a few times. Then he slowly began to eat the meat that Dragon had given him. "Good," Dragon said as he patted Phanis on the back. "You have much more to learn about being free." Dragon could tell that even though Phanis wasn't used to this treatment, he enjoyed it very much. That in and of itself, put a smile on Dragon's face.

The next several weeks were very amusing for Dragon to see everyone in his company open up to one another. Each day seemed pleasant, and each night seemed entertaining. Sonya and Yolana grew closer, and Phanis began to do more things without hesitation, including speaking and looking at others. This began to ease Dragon's mind and made him think less of his troubles. He and Sonya even began telling stories each night, about how Dragon would always do something to upset Sonya's father. The more that they traveled together each day, the more like a family they became, which didn't seem to bother Dragon. As long as the day was uneventful, he was all right, although he was concerned about what his next encounter would be like.

8

The Gift in Tragedy

The company of four traveled for many days, with no clear direction. At least once every other day, Dragon would change the course of their direction randomly. It seemed as though he didn't care where they were going as long as they were always on the move. This, of course, didn't bother the others because they were content with Dragon being peaceful. It seemed with each passing day, Dragon began to open up more to his company. Only occasionally did he get grumpy, the reason for this his company knew nothing of. Little did they know of Tilly and her existence; Dragon kept it to himself. He only got agitated when he saw a twinkle in the trees, knowing it to be her—a constant reminder of his quest, something he longed to forget.

Dragon and his company traveled mostly in the southern direction; their main purpose was to find another place that was safe to leave Phanis and Yolana. Yet Dragon was in no hurry; he would not say it, but he was beginning to enjoy their company. Like many long journeys, the landscape changed around them several times, from forests to rolling hills and back to forests. It seemed like it would be an uneventful journey, yet Dragon remembered that this was what it felt like just before he met Yolana. And believe it or not, the bizarre decided to happen again—but this time with an unexpected outcome.

One day, as they were walking through a forest, their path was suddenly obstructed. The forest abruptly ended in a marsh—a very unpleasant- looking marsh. They could see only a few bushes and a little bit of land, but mostly it was water for as far as the eye could see. The water was not deep, about four feet at most. If anything, they would have to worry about sinking into the mud. Dragon, however, could see far in the distance more trees, which he took for the other side of the marsh, but to be sure, he sent Sonya to scout things out. She took off, and Dragon expected her to be back very quickly; instead, she took longer than normal, which made Dragon very curious. When she eventually landed, she had a bewildered look on her face, which made Dragon even more curious.

"Well, what did you find?" Dragon asked in his usual manner.

Sonya opened her mouth to speak, but nothing came out. She was thinking too hard on how to relay what she had seen. "You won't believe this," she finally blurted out. "This marsh is nearly endless."

"How is that? There are trees right over there," Dragon said as he pointed to the trees he could see in the distance.

"Well, first I flew over it, and when I couldn't get a good look at everything, I changed my position. I flew higher so I could get a direct view of everything. The marsh is so big it would take us six whole days of steady march to cross, if we found firm land."

"Then what's that?" Dragon asked, now confused as to what he was seeing in the distance.

"That's the interesting thing," Sonya started again, very excited about this part. "The marsh is almost a perfect circle, and in the dead center is an island. Not just any island; it has a thick forest on it. Also, it's not small either. Out of the six-day journey across the marsh, the island would take up two of those days." Dragon was about to say something when Sonya interrupted him for a change. "And there's one more thing: Upon coming down from my high flight above the marsh, I found something on the east side. A narrow path above the water level that travels from the island all the way across the marsh into the forest. It is only wide enough for one of me. I don't know what it's used for, but it looks like animals cross it."

"I don't know," Phanis said. "Something doesn't feel right about this whole marsh. Why don't we just go around it and take our time? I'm in no hurry."

"I agree with Phanis," Yolana put in her opinion.

As for Dragon, he was not listening. He was standing at the edge of the marsh, looking across at what was supposed to be the island. He couldn't quite say why, but he felt drawn to the island, as if something of interest was out there and that he needed to see it. He wondered for a moment if this was some trick of the Creator trying to get him to do what he didn't want to do. That thought he dismissed, realizing that it was something from the island giving him this feeling, not from the Creator. "Let's go," was all he said. Dragon then turned to look at his companions, only to realize that was not what they wanted to hear.

"Are you crazy?" Yolana mocked. "Didn't you hear what Phanis said? He thinks it's a bad idea, and I am inclined to agree with them."

Dragon, for some reason, did not want a long, drawn-out argument on the subject. "Look, you can either go with me or stay here. The choice is yours. As for me, I am going out there no matter what anyone says." He then shot Sonya a serious look, making sure she understood that this was not up for discussion.

"Well, I'm not staying here by myself," Yolana huffed.

When Sonya eventually nodded her agreement to this idea, Dragon began to work on figuring out how to get across the marsh. "Well, Sonya, I think it's time for you to earn your keep," he said mockingly.

"What?" Sonya snapped back. "As if hunting dinner every night and cooking isn't good enough, now you expect more! Males!" she exclaimed.

"Come on," Dragon said in an almost begging manner. "You could get us over there before the sun sets today and without getting our feet wet."

Even though she was somewhat ruffled by his earlier comment, she thought this through. After a moment, she replied, sounding almost hesitant, "All right."

With her reply, Dragon quickly jumped on her back and held on tight. She then opened her wings and began flapping them, getting a little lift off the ground. When she was hovering just nicely, she reached out with her hands and grasped Phanis and Yolana underneath their arms. With a tight grip, she took off, moving swiftly over the marsh yet gaining no height. Phanis's and Yolana's feet hovered only a few feet above the marsh. Dragon was used to Sonya's speed, but the others had to cover their faces with their arms, unable to breathe because of the buffeting winds.

As Dragon predicted, the flight to the island was very short and took almost no time at all. Sonya set Phanis and Yolana down on the edge of the island, while Dragon jumped off her back, landing not far from the others. Before Sonya could land properly, Yolana lost her balance and fell into a small mud puddle. Dragon turned to see what happened, only to find Yolana's face splattered with mud.

Dragon let out a slight chuckle. He was not trying to be rude; rather, he just found it somewhat humorous. "Well, a little mud didn't hurt anyone," he commented. "Try to keep your feet underneath you," he added with a small chuckle again.

Yolana picked herself up and shook off some of the mud as Sonya came up to her and whispered in her ear. By this time, Dragon had turned around and was looking at the forest on the island, which was thick with trees but not as much underbrush. The moment he took one step toward the forest, he got hit in the back of the head with a big mud ball. He turned quickly, only to see Sonya whistling innocently, the tip of her tail covered in mud. Instead of getting mad, he grinned and began to reach into a mud puddle near him. Before he could grab any mud and throw it back, he got his head hit again, but this time from a different direction. Dragon looked around, only to see Yolana standing with fresh mud on her hands and a grin on her face.

"Well, a little mud didn't hurt anyone," Yolana mocked, trying hard not to laugh.

Dragon, of course, smiled again and then rapidly grabbed some mud and flung it at Yolana, hitting her in the middle of the chest. He then swiftly ducked as a mud ball from Sonya came flying over his head. He darted toward the trees. As Sonya began to make another mud ball to throw at Dragon, she got hit on the side of the head. She shook off the mud and turned her head to see Phanis laughing as he ran toward the trees.

"This is war! Males against females!" Sonya roared at the official start of the battle.

Of course, in Dragon's mind, Sonya cheated as usual. She was standing in the middle of a mud puddle, which was a good source to supply mud balls, and she motioned for Yolana to join her. Yolana stood in between Sonya's front arms and right next to her head. Their only protection was Sonya's wings, which she unfurled in front of them as a barrier. With one quick motion, Sonya could drop them, allowing Yolana to fire mud balls. Then she would raise them again, shielding them from Dragon's and Phanis's mud balls. At the same time, Sonya would fling giant balls of mud with her tail up and over her back like a catapult. As a matter of fact, one of Sonya's mud balls hit a tree and actually knocked it over, somewhat indicating this was a serious mud fight, with much laughter coming from Yolana.

Dragon and Phanis didn't have the protection of Sonya's wings, so they had to do the best they could behind the trees. Phanis especially hoped that the trees he was hiding behind would hold up against the bombardment from Sonya. As for Dragon, he was faring a little better; he was able to stay out in the open a little longer than Phanis, which allowed him to fire more shots. Because of his dragon attributes, he was doing back flips, front flips, and even ducking to avoid almost every shot that came at him while at the same time returning shots, hoping to catch the females with their defenses down.

Needless to say, Dragon and Phanis were losing, and they needed to do something soon. "Phanis!" Dragon shouted, getting his fellow male's attention. "We need to take them down before things get worse! I won't lose to two females! I'll take Sonya out. You take Yolana!"

"Aye, King!" Phanis shouted back, showing his support for Dragon's idea. "To victory!" The moment Phanis said that one of Sonya's massive mud balls hit the tree he was hiding behind, making it shake and almost tear out of the ground. Phanis, of course, was hoping that Dragon knew what he was doing.

Thinking the time was right, Dragon jumped out from behind his tree with two mud balls in hand and began to run with great speed toward Sonya. He timed his mud ball throws well enough to keep Sonya's shield up. When he got within a few paces of her, she lowered her wings to give Yolana time to throw, and that was their downfall. Dragon leaped over Sonya's lower wings, startling Yolana as he rushed past her. He hit Sonya in the chest, right below her throat, with such force that it knocked her back, throwing her and him down into the mud, with Dragon on her chest.

With Sonya down, Yolana was left wide open, and that was when Phanis stepped out from behind a tree and threw two shots. The first one struck Yolana in the shoulder, the second on the side of her head, knocking her flat on her back in the mud. Before she could get up and throw anything back, Phanis was standing right above her with another mud ball in his hand, daring her to try something. Yolana and Phanis could hardly contain their laughter, even as they were covered in mud. As for Dragon, he was standing on Sonya's chest, letting out a victory roar. He then jumped down and walked over to Phanis, grasping his forearm and giving him a slight pat on the back.

"We work well as a team," Dragon stated, extremely proud of the outcome of this fight. He had won against Sonya, which rarely happened.

"Yes, we did," Phanis replied, proud of the outcome as well.

It was a strange feeling Dragon had as he stood there next to Phanis, covered in mud from their fight. They had worked well as a team, he had to admit that. Sonya and Yolana eventually picked themselves up out of the mud and joined the other two. The four of them stood there for a moment, each looking at the other in their muddy state. They finally remembered where they were and how mysterious the island was. Oddly enough, the mud fight had calmed everyone's nerves, so that the forest island now seemed less strange. "I think we need to get cleaned up," Yolana stated.

"Yes, but not out here. This is only mud and marsh. Maybe there's fresh water farther into the island," Dragon said as he began to walk toward the shelter of the trees. The other three followed Dragon without hesitation, and as night began to fall, the company faded into the forest, looking for fresh water and a place to camp.

* * *

Dragon, Yolana, and Phanis made their way through the forest with no problem. As for Sonya, because the forest was so thick, she had to squeeze her way through, trying her best not to knock over any of the trees. They weren't too far from the edge of the island when they stumbled across a small stream. It was there that they cleaned themselves of all the mud.

"The stream must flow right into the marsh," Dragon commented. "That means there must be a spring somewhere in the middle of the island. I think that would be a good place to camp." No one else said anything in reply; they just nodded in agreement. "Sonya, are you, all right? Do you think you can make it through the forest?"

"I'll be fine. Just keep going. I'll be right behind you," Sonya replied, giving her voice a tone of confidence. However, Dragon wasn't too sure as he looked at her. She was trying to get her wing unstuck from two trees. She was stubborn, all right; still, she was willing to go on, and so was the rest of the company.

And that was exactly what they did. Dragon led the way, with the others following, Sonya doing her best to keep up. Dragon decided to follow the stream and seek out its source, which didn't prove to be too hard. As they came upon the very center of the island, they found a great pile of rocks looking as if they were thrust out of the earth. The company could see the spring of water coming up out of the top of the pile of rocks and flowing down some before turning into the stream that headed out toward the marsh. The company could also see that the great pile of rocks had some caves in it that looked big enough to house dragons, but no one was home, which made everyone feel at ease.

"We'll make camp here," Dragon stated, hoping that it would be an uneventful evening. It didn't take long for Sonya to grab some wood and make a fire. As for food, she said she would go hunting a little later. She was tired from the mud fight as well as squeezing herself through the forest. She wanted a little time to rest. That didn't bother Dragon or the others, for they were tired as well, and a nap would suit them well. Unfortunately, even though Dragon was tired, he couldn't rest his eyes or his body. The place was peaceful, but something about it made him uneasy. He had the oddest feeling that he was not alone and that something was watching him.

***

Several hours later, Dragon was startled by the soft crack of a branch. He looked out away from the fire into the darkness to see big, glowing eyes staring directly at him. He was just about to rouse the others when he noticed they weren't the only set of eyes around. The company was surrounded by at least fourteen different sets of eyes, all glowing at them. Whatever the creatures were, their eyes weren't glowing by themselves; it was merely the reflection of the firelight in their eyes. Dragon thought for a moment and realized that perhaps subtlety and a clear head other than fighting would help them in the situation.

"Sonya, Phanis, Yolana, wake up and don't move," Dragon said slowly, yet loud enough to be heard. At the same time, he didn't move.

To Dragon's relief, the others awoke slowly and quietly. As for him, he stood up slowly and took a few steps forward, confronting the mysterious eyes in front of him. At the same time, the creature in the shadows decided to step forward. When it left the darkness of the trees and stepped into the firelight, Dragon's jaw dropped in amazement. What stood before him was a beautiful white wolf, but not any ordinary wolf. It was huge—larger than a normal wolf. It stood taller than Phanis when all its paws were on the ground. Dragon was hoping that this was the only abnormal wolf, but he was proven wrong quickly. As the other wolves came into the firelight, he could see that they were all giant wolves. However, most of them were gray, whereas the one in front of Dragon was white. Though the wolf looked fierce and powerful, it also had a beauty that Dragon could not explain. As the firelight flickered, its white fur coat would shimmer like silver, which gave it a very alluring look. Dragon could not help but take a few more steps forward to stare deeply into the eyes of this magnificent wolf.

Greetings, Dragon Child, a beautiful and feminine voice said in Dragon's mind.

Dragon was startled and somewhat confused; he looked at his companions to see if they said anything. When he realized that they had not spoken, he turned back to look at the wolf facing him. As he stared the wolf in the eyes, he had a sinking feeling that the voice in his head came from the wolf. Strange thoughts began to whirl in his head; finally, he decided to try to communicate with these wolves. To the shock of his companions, he stepped forward and spoke out loud to the white wolf in front of him."Did you speak to me? Do you understand me?" Dragon asked, hoping he wasn't going mad or that the wolves would not take this the wrong way.

Yes, it is I who spoke to you, and I do understand you, Dragon Child, the voice whispered again in his head.

"So this is how you speak," Dragon said.

"Dragon," Yolana spoke up as best as she could. "The wolves aren't speaking." She took a step closer to Sonya, still a little startled that she was surrounded by wolves. It didn't help that she thought Dragon was going mad by talking with wolves.

Humans cannot hear us, the voice echoed. *However, dragons can.*

On hearing that, Dragon turned to Sonya to see if she could hear anything. Surprisingly, she nodded, indicating to him that she could hear what they were saying. After she reassured Dragon that he was not mad, she lowered her head and began to speak to Yolana, calming her down and letting her know what was going on. Phanis leaned over to listen to their conversation, also curious of what was going on; still, he stayed silent, patiently awaiting the outcome.

Once Dragon understood the communication between dragons and the wolves, he decided to move on to other questions. "How do you know that I'm a dragon?"

The white wolf came closer, getting right up to Dragon, and took a big sniff of him. *First, because I can smell that you are a dragon and that you can hear me is proof of that. Second, because the Creator told me who you were and that we were to not harm you.*

"Great. Not him again," Dragon said as he turned away from the wolf, getting very aggravated. "Can't I go anywhere without him interfering in my life?"

Do not speak ill of the Creator in this place, the wolf snapped back. *This is our sanctuary. We keep our borders well, and intruders do not live. The Creator has stated that you are not to be harmed and that we are to see you safely on your way.*

Dragon may not have liked the fact that the Creator was involved, but he was not going to get into an argument with the wolves.

For now, you're alive and safe in our domain—that is what should matter to you, young Dragon Child. The white wolf turned her head and barked a command to another. Shortly after that, a light gray wolf came into the firelight, carrying a deer in his mouth like a cat would a mouse. The wolf dropped the deer and then went back into the shadows of the trees. *We have provided you with food. Eat it as you will.*

Dragon was about to say thank you when he heard a squeal coming from Yolana. He turned around to see what was happening and found a humorous sight. Yolana was standing stiff, somewhat frightened, as a wolf licked her face. Of course, with the size of the wolf and his tongue, it looked quite humorous as one lick covered her face. Dragon wasn't sure whether to laugh or go over there and help her. However, it turned out he didn't need to, after a couple of licks, the wolf lay down in front of her, possibly wanting to enjoy some of the warmth of the fire. Dragon couldn't tell. Yolana decided to sit down next to the wolf as she wiped the slobber off her face. She then began to stroke the wolf's fur, indicating that they had now become good friends. As for Phanis, he sat next to Sonya.

"Looks like we're getting along just fine," Dragon said somewhat sarcastically.

You must forgive my mate. He does not greet humans often, the white wolf stated.

"He's your mate?" Dragon inquired carefully, not wanting to overstep his bounds.

Yes, we are the leaders of this pack. He is called Mischief, because that is what he has been getting into since he was a pup, and not much has changed.

Dragon thought he heard a small laugh inside of his head; he wasn't sure if wolves could laugh. "So what do they call you?"

I am called Silver Snow for my unique coat, which has not been seen for a long time. The last time a wolf carried this coat was in the gardens when the Creator walked among us. After she said that, Silver Snow said the conversation was over and walked back into the shadows.

Dragon stood there for a moment, unable to take his eyes off where Silver Snow disappeared into the shadows. He had recognized the tone of voice and that last statement she said—there was pain in that voice. He didn't know why, but he had a feeling that it had something to do with mankind.

* * *

Once again, Sonya ended up cooking, and no one argued whether she was a good cook. It helped when you could control fire within your lungs. Phanis continued to stay close to her throughout the cooking and eating. Yolana, oddly enough, had become good friends with Mischief and ate her food while she sat next to him, practically leaning against him. Though his fur was rough, Yolana thought he was comfortable nonetheless. As for Dragon, he sat outside of the firelight, up toward the top of the rock pile, and he had eaten nothing at all, for he had other things on his mind. Where he sat on top of the rock pile was a large overhang, like a spear thrusting out of the rocks. Dragon sat at the tip with his legs draping over, looking up at the stars, when he heard a sound behind him. It wasn't hard for Dragon to identify Phanis's footsteps as he came up the stone pile and stopped right beside him.

"I brought you some food. You need to eat something," Phanis said as he handed some food to Dragon and sat down beside him. Dragon, of course, accepted food and welcomed the interruption to his thoughts. "Much on your mind?" Phanis asked, not wanting the silence to draw on.

Dragon took a bite of the meat and shrugged. "I'm all right," was all he could respond with.

Phanis took a deep breath, trying to tread carefully in this conversation. Most people wouldn't even bring this conversation up, but he felt that he had a unique perspective on it. "You know, tragedy is a gift," Phanis stated, thinking the direct approach was probably better.

Dragon immediately stopped moving, with a piece of meat just inches from his mouth. He slowly turned to look at Phanis and raised one eyebrow, almost as if he was not sure what he was looking at. "What?" was all that he could utter.

"Look, Dragon, I know this is not a conversation you want to have with anyone, but I believe I have a different view on this." As Phanis spoke, Dragon resumed eating, pretending not to listen. However, Phanis knew that he was listening, so he continued. "I know losing your mother and your kingdom wasn't something easy to take, and it should not be forgotten. I know whom you blame, and in your life, I would blame him too." Phanis paused for a moment, looking up at the stars, gathering his thoughts on what to say next. "The only problem you have with this is you're looking at it from only one side. There is good and bad in everything that happens to everyone. For example, through your tragedy, Yolana and I are free. If your mother and your kingdom were still here, then Yolana would probably still be at her village, and I would still be a slave. Through your tragedy, you have traveled far and met us. We have even found this place and seen these wolves. Isn't that unique in and of itself?" Phanis paused again, wondering if Dragon would say anything, and when he didn't, Phanis continued.

"Earlier today, in the mud fight, I saw you smile and have fun, which I have never seen you do before. It made me think about tragedy and the two sides that it causes, and I came to a conclusion." Phanis risked putting a hand on Dragon's back. "Tragedy is a gift that lets us know what we took for granted when we should have enjoyed them when we had them. The Creator hasn't taken everything from you. Sonya, Yolana, and I are still here. Don't forget that." With that, Phanis stood up and walked away, feeling as if he had said all that he could.

Phanis had gotten only a few steps away when Dragon finally spoke. "Phanis." Of course, Phanis stopped, but he didn't turn around. He merely stood there, letting Dragon have the time to put his words together. "For a human, you're pretty wise," was all that Dragon said. He didn't need to say more, and Phanis didn't need to hear more. To Phanis, this was a compliment and a reassurance that his words had sunk in. As for Dragon, it was a powerful statement. He didn't like humans, yet he admitted the worth of this one. The thought that there were some humans that deserved to live and have a chance for redemption was an odd thought to Dragon, but he could not deny that if anyone deserved this chance, Phanis did.

Dragon continued to sit there, silently pondering his thoughts. Phanis's words were both good and bad. They had much wisdom, but they did not ease the confusion in Dragon's mind. There was a constant battle between him, the Creator, dragons, and humans, and it was not something easily sorted out.

***

Several hours passed, and Dragon could still be found sitting at the edge of the rock pile, staring at the stars and contemplating his thoughts. He heard another sound behind him, but this time it was not Phanis. He didn't need to turn his head to see who it was; the sound of her paws on the rock gave her away. Silver Snow appeared beside him, her beautiful coat shimmering in the moonlight. She lay down beside him, letting her silky fur brush against his skin. She looked out into the forest as if she had deep thoughts of her own.

Though Dragon wasn't sure about the facial expressions of wolves, he was pretty sure he understood that look, almost very similar to his own. Oddly enough, he decided to take a page out of Phanis's book and decided that talking to her was probably the best thing to do.

"Silver Snow, tell me the truth about this place and about you, please." He didn't have much finesse when it came to talking with others, especially females, but he thought this was a good way to begin.

There was a long, drawn-out silence before Silver Snow said anything at all. *It's not something I like to speak of.*

"Please," Dragon asked again as he put his hand on her paw and stroked it gently.

Silver Snow turned her head and looked at Dragon's face, and what she saw there was not sympathy but empathy. *Very well,* she acknowledged, making her voice echo in Dragon's mind. She turned her face back out into the forest, looking upon her domain. *We are descendants of the wolves who lived in the gardens and walked with the Creator. There is great anger between us and man because man is the reason why we are not there. We did not disobey the Creator, so why are we made to suffer? However, our greater hatred is reserved for the Deceiver, who has taken wolves and twisted them into evil. However, Deceiver or man, it doesn't matter—we are now a dying race.*

"How is that possible? There are many of you here." Dragon intervened with his thoughts on the matter.

It is true that there are a lot of us—a total of fifty-nine—but not as many as there were. It is a strange thing that is happening to us. With every generation, there are fewer of us. We give birth to a whelp of six, and only one is a Great Wolf. The rest that are born are normal wolves. They leave our pack to join packs of their own kind. Over the last hundred years, our pack has dwindled to half of what it was. Most of us believe it is because the Creator's power that was in the gardens is slowly leaving this world and us. Turning what was unique and special into ordinary animals with nothing but instinct— no wisdom or understanding of the things that were. There are days when it seems as if there is no hope for us at all.

"I'm sorry" was all Dragon could say.

It is not your fault, Dragon Child, Silver Snow responded as she brushed her head against his. *One of the reasons I became the leader of the pack was my fur. The last time a fur coat like this was seen was in the gardens, so the wolves believed that I was an omen that great things were coming. But now I'm not so sure, as we dwindle as a race of great wolves. The only reassuring thing is that we can still hear the Creator's voice, and he gives us comfort. I know that would not be much to you, but to us, it means a lot. He brought us to this refuge that we have kept hidden. Orcs, men, elves, and dwarves— none enter this place and live.*

"It's hard to believe that you remain hidden all these years."

The marsh helps to keep us hidden, even the wild tribes of men think a marsh is a bad omen. However, we were found once by your mother during her war. I recognize her smell on you.

"Figures that my mother would be the one to find you. So, what did she do?"

She heard our story, decided to leave us alone, and kept us hidden. She even threw a few orc corpses into the marsh to help dissuade other beings' curiosity. She knew how important it was for us to stay secluded. For not only are we a sanctuary for wolves, but there is also a race of forest fairies that live here for the same reason.

Upon hearing the word fairy, Dragon twitched, remembering his dislike of Tilly, even though he understood that they were a different type of fairy. Nevertheless, the thought of fairies being all around him gave him a shiver up the spine.

Silver Snow continued to speak, not realizing Dragon's reaction to the word fairy. *You will see them tonight, and it is a beautiful sight that no one but us wolves have seen. So in a way, you were honored by being allowed to see this place and the beings that dwell here. As for me, I'm glad to have you here. It is nice to have someone to talk to who understands what I'm going through.*

"What do you mean?" Dragon commented, not sure where she was going with this.

I heard the call from the Creator about how all the dragons must fade. It must not be easy for you or for me to watch our people fade, while the humans thrive.

"There's not much we can do about it," Dragon said, somewhat frustrated. "The choice has been taken away from us, and I don't know what the Creator is doing or why!"

I understand your frustration, Dragon Child, but we must have faith in the Creator. We are not given the understanding of what is to come, but we must have faith that it will work out for the good of all. Having faith in the Creator is not easy, but falling into darkness would not serve us. Not only are we to have faith in the Creator, we must have faith in one another as well. Silver Snow nudged her head against Dragon's again. *And I have faith in you, Dragon Child, that you will do what is necessary to save your kind and mine. However, I give you this warning: You may not like the Creator right now, but do not turn your back on him. It is not wise.*

After Dragon nodded in understanding, Silver Snow stood up and looked up to the sky. *It is almost time. You will like this,* she said, not indicating what she was talking about. At the same time, all the other great wolves that could be seen in the firelight stood up. Dragon sensed that even the wolves hidden in the darkness did the same. The company of travelers did nothing; they stayed where they were, merely observing what was going on.

After a brief moment of silence, Dragon noticed something that he hadn't realized before. The moon was right above them, and it was a full moon. Oddly enough, it was the largest Dragon had ever seen the moon. He thought that maybe it was the presence of the wolves that made it seem bigger than it normally was. Also, its light was brighter than he remembered it. Silver Snow's fur shimmered with its brilliance, more than it did with the firelight, making her a true silver wolf. Dragon stood up and took a couple of steps back, not out of fright but out of curiosity, wanting to get a better look at what was going to happen. Starting with Silver Snow, the wolves began to howl at the moon. Dragon had heard wolves howl at the moon before, but never before did it sound like music. These giant wolves were perfect musicians in the animal world. However, it didn't stop there; Dragon began to hear something else.

A beautiful hum began to sound everywhere, as if thousands of small people were singing. Suddenly, Dragon realized it was thousands of small people singing. In a heartbeat, fairies appeared out of nowhere, filling the empty spaces of the forest. Dragon remembered that Silver Snow mentioned that this was a sanctuary for forest fairies. However, something was odd; forest fairies never showed themselves, and if they did, they did not emit any light. Still, somehow, these forest fairies did; perhaps it was the magic of the place intertwined with the wolves and the fairies. Dragon didn't know why, and he didn't care. At that moment, the forest looked as if the stars had come down from the heavens and had filled the forest with music and light. Between the music of the fairies and the howling of the wolves, the forest came alive. Dragon could not see it with his eyes, but he could feel it in his dragon senses. This was worship to the Creator in its purest form. Dragon had seen similar worship amongst the dragons in his city, but he had never seen it in such a setting.

He might have been angry at the Creator; however, he could not turn away from this beauty. A warm breeze seemed to wrap around him, not only relaxing his body, but it also seemed to relax his heart and the heaviness that was on it. As for the others in the company, they would look back upon this moment and describe it very similarly to what Dragon described it as.

While Dragon was enjoying the beauty that he knew he would never see again, something strange caught his eye—a star among the woods that stood out. One of the fairies in the distance with a different light than the others, not to mention it was trying to hide behind a branch. Dragon didn't need to be up close to remember that light. It was Tilly, and he knew it for certain. There was a part of Dragon that still hated her, yet being among these fairies, he began to look at her in a different light. Dragon wasn't quite sure why all of a sudden, he thought of her differently; perhaps it was the fairies, wolves, or the place. One way or another, he did. What shocked him more than that was the fact that he compared her to himself. For the rest of his life, he never understood why, but for some reason, he did.

Dragon realized that they had a lot in common that he never understood before. He wanted to be with his people but was forced to be somewhere else, and so was she. He was asked to do a quest that he did not like, as she was asked to take charge of something she did not like. No matter what they did, the Creator was at the center of their lives, directing and guiding them or manipulating them, as Dragon looked at it. They also had in common the sense of being alone, having people around them but no one who understood what they were going through. After all those things that he thought they had in common, Dragon had a strange feeling. He could not yet forgive her for her words, but for some strange reason, he felt pity for her. He thought that it must be the place and that when he left, he would go back to his usual dislike of her. But for the time being, he could not deny that he pitied her.

After a moment, he changed that thought. It was not pity that he felt, but understanding. Dragon understood her. As Dragon's life unfolded, he decided to throw his anger at the Creator. As for Tilly, as her life unfolded in a very similar way to Dragon's, she decided to throw her anger at Dragon. For some odd reason, Dragon understood her reasoning, and even odder still, he accepted it. He was not accepting her or her presence in his life; he was merely accepting her reason for hating him.

Deciding to change his thoughts before he thought of anything else just as crazy, Dragon brought his mind and eyes back to the beautiful events around him. Though he had to admit this was a strange place, all night he had been surrounded by wisdom, knowledge, and understanding. As much as those things made him uncomfortable, they oddly made him comfortable, reminding him of his mother, Ancient, and even Marahezron. The wolves howled and the fairy's music lasted a little more than an hour, and then it slowly subsided, with the fairies disappearing back into the woods and the wolves going silent. The company had no words to say; in a way, they didn't know what to say. With things done, there seemed to be peace in the forest, as well as in the hearts of all who witnessed the event. With the night halfway spent, the company merely decided that it was time to get some sleep, for tomorrow they would continue as they did every day.

As much as they enjoyed this place, there was no reason for them to stay. Yolana lay against Mischief as Phanis lay next to Sonya. As for Dragon, he stayed up on the great rock pile with Silver Snow. She lay down close to the overhang, and Dragon sat beside her and leaned his body against her, feeling the silkiness of her fur. It didn't take long for him to fall asleep, for he felt safe and comfortable, and he had peace in his mind and heart this evening, something he had not had in a long time. Before he passed out completely, his dragon ears picked up only a few sounds. He could hear in the distance that the wolves in the forest were still awake and keeping guard. Then he could hear the sound of the company and the wolves near the firelight, breathing in their sleep. Finally, his ears picked up the sound of the spring of water that came up from the great rock pile and flowed down its side and out to the marsh. This place was truly a sanctuary.

***

As the sun rose above the treetops, the company slowly awoke. All of them felt refreshed, not only in body but also in mind and spirit. This place really did have an effect on those who stayed here. Dragon and Yolana were somewhat perplexed for the wolves that they were sleeping against weren't there. Dragon thought they were really talented wolves when they could leave without waking him. As he stood up, he saw a glitter among the trees, and with a careful glance, he saw Silver Snow in the distance. He jumped down from the rock pile, gathered his things, and motioned for the others to follow. They made their way through the forest to where Silver Snow was waiting for them. When they reached her, more wolves came in and surrounded them.

It is time for you to leave, Silver Snow said, sounding sorrowful. *We will escort you to the border of our sanctuary.*

Dragon and the others said nothing in return, for they knew that this was a solemn moment; they merely nodded in understanding. With their understanding, Silver Snow turned and headed toward the edge of the island. Dragon and the company followed, with the wolves still surrounding them. The wolves surrounding them didn't seem to be watching them or protecting them; it seemed more as though they were honor guards showing respect to a king and his entourage. As much as Dragon liked the thought, it also saddened him, for it meant that he was leaving and that he would never see this place again or these wolves.

They continued in this manner through the forest till they reached the edge of the island. Then, with Silver Snow in front, they crossed the narrow land bridge in single file. When they reached the other side, they reformed their procession's formation. They walked about two miles from the marsh and stopped in a small clearing in the woods, and it was here that they needed to say farewell. No words were said, yet the wolves suddenly stopped indicating that they would go no farther. This was their hunting ground, but not their sanctuary. The company turned around and faced the great wolves. Sonya bowed in respect, making her comments in her mind between herself and the wolves. Dragon never knew what she said or what they said in return to her. Phanis merely mimicked Sonya and bowed in respect. He never heard their thoughts; he was just happy that he wasn't eaten by them. Yolana, likewise, did not hear the wolves, but oddly, she developed a friendship with Mischief. She walked up to him and, standing on her tippy toes, threw her arms around his neck and buried her face into his fur. When she was done and let go, he gave her a good lick across the face, indicating that he too would miss her. Dragon was the one who felt the greatest hurt in this parting, for he had developed a bond with Silver Snow, or an understanding, if you will.

Nevertheless, it was as if he were leaving another one of his family members behind, and the memory of his last parting with Ancient and Marahezron came to his mind. He slowly walked up to her, reached up and gently grabbed her fur underneath her jaw, and brought her head down. When her head was lowered to his, he let go and began to slowly stroke the fur on the sides of her head while he placed his forehead against hers. He closed his eyes as his face began to feel the silkiness of her silvery fur.

Be at peace, Dragon Child, her beautiful feminine voice echoed in his mind. *I know you are angry, but do not lose faith in the Creator's plan. We neither know nor see all, but all will work for good. Do not grieve for us. We had our time, and when the world is renewed through the Creator's redemption, you will see me again, as long as you don't forget me.*

Dragon pressed his head harder against hers. "I will never forget you." He then pulled his head back and kissed her forehead. "Goodbye, Silver Snow. May the Creator's light be with you." Dragon wasn't quite sure why he said it; it just seemed like the right thing to say to her at that time.

Before he stepped back, Silver Snow gave his head one last nudge with her nose. *Farewell, Dragon Child. May the Creator bring you peace.* With that, she turned and led her pack back into their sanctuary.

Dragon and the others stood silent for a long moment, staring at the wolves slowly disappearing back into the woods. Silver Snow was the last to disappear, mainly because her fur coat was very distinguishable in the sunlight. At his last glimpse of her, Dragon let out a sigh. It was time to move on, he thought, but he had not the words to voice it. He merely turned around and walked off in the opposite direction, holding on to the memory of the night before and all the things that had happened. As for the others in his company, they too dwelt upon the memory of last night as they followed Dragon.

A little time later, the group returned to their usual cheerful traveling ways—all except for Dragon. He wasn't depressed. He just had a lot on his mind, as he usually did, but this time, he dwelt upon Silver Snow and her words. He also wondered what the Creator had in store for him, especially since Dragon was angry at him. One way or another, Dragon admitted that since he left his home, he had been very closed-minded, and that was not how his mother, Ancient, or Marahezron taught him to be. He concluded that he needed to pay attention to the things around him. Whether or not he would be good at them was another matter. In the meantime, he merely focused on putting one foot in front of the other. Before the sun would set that day, he and the company with him would travel a good distance and get closer to whatever the Creator had in store for them.

Tyrilcrysalith

It had been over a month since the group left Falistoran and several days since they left the wolf sanctuary. They had even left one forest, crossed over some plains, and entered another forest. Dragon realized this forest wasn't as dense as the other, so it should be easier to cross. They had been walking in the forest for half a day when something happened. Dragon stopped suddenly, beckoning the others to stop and be quiet as he listened intently. Yolana and Phanis could not hear a thing. Sonya, on the other hand, also heard something. After a moment of standing still, Dragon motioned for them to follow him quietly. Each one of them, including Sonya, moved stealthily through the forest, following an unknown sound.

Soon even Yolana and Phanis began to hear the sound, but it did not do any good. To all of them, it was an unknown sound; however, the closer they got, the more ideas they concluded about the unknown sound. The echo of metal upon metal, raised voices, and the sound of wild animals produced the thoughts of a battle. Still, they could not be certain until they saw whatever it was for themselves. They crept up a hill that overlooked a small clearing. Sonya stayed behind so that she couldn't give away their position with her enormous body. When the other three glanced over the top of the hill, their eyes beheld a strange sight.

Down in the clearing, they came upon a gruesome and bloody sight. The clearing was littered with bodies, mostly humans and some other creatures, unknown to the company. As they continued to stare, they realized that not all were dead. At the far end of the clearing, three humans had been tied to trees, and they were surrounded by thirty creatures. In light of what they saw, they slowly backed up to assess the scene and decide what to do.

"What is going on?" Yolana asked.

"I don't know," Phanis answered promptly, also keeping a low voice. "Looks like a band of orcs attacked a group of humans. Now they intend to eat the survivors of the battle."

"Those are orcs; are you sure?" Yolana asked.

"I think so. Dragon, are those orcs?" Phanis asked as he and Yolana turned to look at Dragon for answers.

Dragon slowly shrugged his shoulders, admitting he had no clue. Then he crept forward again to take another look at the creatures. As he peered at them, he quickly concluded that they weren't much to look at. From his knowledge of what most creatures should look like from everything Ancient taught him, he knew that they weren't dwarves or elves. On the other hand, he had never seen dwarves or elves, so to him, it was still a mystery. Yet he concluded that they looked like warped and twisted elves; some of them had skin that was a pale gray, while others had a color that looked like mud. They wore no great armor or wielded great weapons. Some had axes and others scimitars, yet all their weapons looked rusted and old blackened metal, just like their armor. They didn't seem to be well organized; it almost looked like they were a pack of wild animals. Yet they spoke to one another in raspy voices, which let Dragon know that they had a little bit of understanding. Still, the bodies gave the impression that they had been lurking in dark places for many years and that sense and reason had left them. Dragon then shrank back again to speak with the others.

"Well, what do you think?" Phanis inquired.

"I'm not quite sure. I believe them to be orcs," Dragon replied, still a little unsure of his decision. "From what I learned from Ancient, they don't seem like trolls or goblins. They're not big enough. And they're not dwarves or elves. The only thing I can conclude is that they must be orcs."

"I thought goblins were smaller than orcs," Yolana stated.

"I don't think it matters whether they're orcs, goblins, and what size they are. So what are we going to do?" continued Phanis.

"I don't know. I've never been in a situation like this." Dragon's face was blank as he tried to think of what Marahezron or Ancient would do in this situation.

"Well, we have to do something," Yolana added. "We can't let those animals hurt humans."

"It's not as simple as it looks," Dragon replied. "You see, Ancient told me that some orcs are good, and we don't know how this fight started. We could be helping the wrong side."

"Yolana is right. We have to do something," Phanis added, disgusted at the thought that orcs could be good.

"Fine, you two stay here, and Sonya and I will go down and see whether they're good or not." Without delay, Dragon began to take everything that he was carrying off so that it wouldn't get in the way.

Among these items was the sword Truth, which was still wrapped in the cloth that Ancient carefully put around it. Dragon had forgotten about it; even now, he paid it no mind. Phanis, on the other hand, heard the sword make a small noise when Dragon put it down. Even though it sounded like metal clashing together, Phanis swore that it sounded like the sword was moaning, as if it were eager to fight. Still, Dragon left it behind and went down the hill to speak to Sonya. After a moment of collaboration, they were ready to introduce themselves.

Dragon was still somewhat hesitant; he had dealt death out once before, and it did not sit well with him, and he was not eager to put himself in a place where he might have to do it again. Nevertheless, he felt an odd pull toward the situation, as if he needed to do something. So he buried what feelings he had and pulled his emotions together to deal with the situation as he needed to, running Ancient's and Marahezron's training through his mind.

* * *

Dragon walked by himself over the hill and down into the center of the clearing. "Pardon me, orcs. I don't mean to interrupt," Dragon blurted out.

All the orcs quickly turned in response and began to hiss and growl. They looked at Dragon, confused about where he came from yet eager to have some more fun. "Look, more food for us to feast upon," one of the orcs said in a raspy voice.

Dragon got a small smirk on his face, amused at the orcs. It was surprisingly easy to understand their language and to speak it back at them "You will not feast upon my flesh. I'm a lot stronger than you think," he said proudly.

The orcs began to laugh among themselves at Dragon's comment. "You must be a fool," the same orc spoke again.

"There are over thirty of us and only one of you," another orc commented with a deep and garbled voice. "What could you possibly do to us?"

Dragon crossed his arms and stood firm with a small smirk on his face. "Well, I was here to ascertain whether you were pleasant or not. Now that I see your motives, I guess I will have to deal with you accordingly."

The orcs began to clatter their weapons against their armor and make war shouts that sounded like deathly screams. While some of the orcs continued their barrage of noise, one charged at Dragon. Using his scimitar, he attempted to cut Dragon's head off. Dragon, thinking quickly, leaned back, allowing the scimitar to miss, almost nicking his nose. With one fluent move, Dragon reached down and grabbed the orc by the ankle. Then he picked up the orc and flung him over his head, smacking him down on a nearby rock. The strength of the blow split open the orc's skull and killed him immediately. This action, unfortunately, enraged the orcs, and they began to charge at him wildly.

Dragon gave a quick whistle, and Sonya flew over the hill. She landed with her back feet, crushing two orcs, and then she let out a roar and began to chase the remaining orcs. Some were startled and ran for their lives, while others continued to fight. Sonya, however, thought it was fun and began to chase the orcs that were scattering, while the ones willing to fight continued to charge at Dragon. Dragon was not frightened; he took the dead orc, whose ankle was still in his hand, and began to fight back. He used the dead orc like a club and began to swing it madly around, beating orcs from left to right, smashing them with the weight of one of their own.

When Dragon was done beating the last orc that was attacking him, he dropped its dead body and looked up to find Sonya. She was across the clearing, finishing off the rest of the orcs that had scattered. She was jumping from orc to orc like a child would jump from rock to rock. She would crush one with her foot and then leap to the next one using her wings, only to guarantee she would land correctly, smashing the orc underfoot. Dragon watched for a moment, smiling, while Sonya continued to play. When she was done, she came over to speak to him to see how he had fared with his orcs. "Are you all right?" she asked, sounding concerned.

"Yes, I'm fine; there's not even a scratch on me," he replied. "It's funny; I would have thought from all the stories that Ancient told that the orcs would've been a more formidable foe."

"Actually, I was more concerned about your feelings," Sonya added, looking deep into his face. "The last time you killed, you didn't feel too good. How are you handling this?"

Dragon found it very amusing that Sonya would think about his feelings more than his physical body. Still, he did appreciate her concern. He was not fond of death. "I seem all right. This time the feeling is different. Perhaps for the human, I was more connected, because they're supposed to have enlightenment. With the orcs it seemed different, almost like killing an animal in the forest. They acted wild, almost as if they had no heart and no soul. Even though they could talk, it was as if they were filled with only darkness. Even Silver Snow and her wolves were more enlightened and seem to have more of a soul than the orcs. On the other hand, death is still nothing to enjoy, and I do not take this lightly."

* * *

While Dragon and Sonya were talking, they paid no attention to the three men tied to the trees. In the course of the battle, the largest of the men loosened his ropes enough to get free. He thought that now would be a good time to act since the two were not paying attention. He grabbed a nearby orc scimitar and rushed toward Dragon.

Hearing him coming from a distance, Dragon turned and knocked the scimitar away with his arm. Then he punched the man in the chest, knocking him down and sending him skidding across the clearing to the feet of his friends. The man then got up, a little dazed yet still determined to hold his ground.

"That's enough," one of the other men cried out. Without hesitation, the man backed up and found something to cut the ropes for his friends. Once cut free, the three of them gathered together and slowly walked toward Dragon. They stopped only a few feet from Dragon and Sonya so they would not provoke a fight. Dragon, on the other hand, stood still and quiet with his hands made into fists, ready to fight at a moment's notice. The one who spoke earlier seemed to be the leader, so Dragon fixed his eyes on him.

"Greetings, and many thanks for your help," the leader eventually spoke. He was a well-aged man who had lived at least forty-five years. He stood about six feet tall and was well built, not overpowering, yet he looked as if he could hold his own. His dark brown hair was down to his shoulder and was a little curly, although it did match his well-rounded face. The man seemed peaceful to Dragon; his face gave off the look of someone who was filled with wisdom and knowledge yet would still seek adventure. The clothes that he wore were tattered from battle, but they seemed almost kingly.

"Is this how you greet all who help you?" Dragon asked as he pointed to the man who attacked him. He didn't want to start a fight; however, he did want answers.

"I apologize for that. He was simply trying to protect us. It seemed as if you were trying to steal the orcs' food, which happened to be us. I believe the dragon frightened us as much as the orcs did."

"Who are you, and where are you from?" Dragon snapped, still a little flustered. The man apologized for his friend, but Dragon still felt as though he needed more recompense for being attacked.

"I am called Brenath, and I am captain of the guard from the city of Tyrilcrysalith."

"Tyrilcrysalith. I've never heard of that city."

"It happens to be one of the greatest cities in the whole world," Brenath exclaimed proudly.

"I doubt that," Dragon replied, remembering the beauty of his own home.

"Well then, you will have to see it for yourself," Brenath calmly responded.

"That's a good idea," Sonya interrupted excitedly.

Brenath let out a small laugh in response to Sonya as he studied her. He then brought his attention back to Dragon, wanting some answers himself. "If I may inquire, who might you be?"

"My name is Dragon, and I'm the king of all dragons," Dragon arrogantly replied. Then he quickly shut his mouth, remembering Krandal's words, that he should not mention being the king of dragons. He rolled his eyes at his own foolishness, realizing he spoke too quickly.

Brenath looked at him for a moment, scrutinizing every bit of him. At first, Brenath wasn't sure whether to believe him or not, until he got a glimpse of Dragon's eyes and realized that they were not human. "A half-breed," Brenath exclaimed in awe. "I have heard that many have tried to magically combine the two races, but I've never heard of it being successfully done. If you don't mind me asking, how was this done?"

"I was born this way, from a combination of my parents' love and an ancient magic older than any elf, dwarf, or wizard." Dragon crossed his arms, aggravated— not at the question but at the fact that he had to acknowledge the Creator's existence.

"I see no reason to disbelieve you," Brenath continued. "There is much that I do not understand in the world of magic, but this I do understand—that anything is possible. Here you stand before me as proof of that." Brenath marveled for a moment and then turned his attention to Sonya. "And who might you be?"

Sonya quickly lowered her body to the ground and put her head right in front of Brenath. "I am called Soræniya. You can call me Sonya for short."

"In that case, I will call you Sonya," Brenath said as he ran his hand across the top of her snout. As he did, she gave out a chuckle, and then pulled her head back and smiled at him. Turning back to his two companions, he began to introduce them. "This is my second in command, Cromwin," Brenath explained as he pointed to the man who attacked Dragon.

Dragon finally took the time to get a good look at this man. Unlike Brenath, he was almost seven feet tall, and every muscle on his body was well built. It was as if he was bred for a single purpose—to wage war. Even though he was about the same age as Brenath, he looked as if he was more weathered. His face showed strength and anger more than anything, with several scars laid upon his face. One scar ran down his right side from his eye, and another ran up his left cheek. His hair was dark brown and short as if someone had taken a sharp edge and cut straight across the top of his head. Cromwin did not wear as much armor as his two companions, probably because it slowed him down too much. Dragon noticed that Cromwin didn't say much other than an occasional grunt directed at Dragon.

"Why doesn't he say anything to me?" Dragon inquired.

"That is because he cannot speak," Brenath answered and began to explain. "Cromwin had many enemies over the years. One had the privilege of taking his tongue. Though he cannot speak, he still makes an excellent captain of the guards. One can usually understand what he's thinking just by the look on his face and the gestures he makes with his hands."

"That's very interesting. What about your other friend? Can he speak?" Dragon turned and looked at the other man standing beside Brenath. This man definitely seemed different from the other two, in more than just looks. He was a little shorter than Brenath, yet he carried himself the same way; even his hair seemed a little modeled after Brenath except for the color, which was light brown. Also, he was a lot younger, either in his late twenties or early thirties. Dragon could tell by looking at him that he was eager and courageous, but not wise. The man definitely looked for approval from the other two, and he seemed especially close to Brenath. Dragon noticed a certain bond between the two.

"Yes, I can," the third man interrupted. "I am Tobin. Brenath is my brother. I am also third in command of the guards in Tyrilcrysalith."

Dragon stood for a moment, looking at Tobin, as the young man filled himself with pride. "Tobin, I have a question for you then," Dragon said, willing to put the young man to the test. "If you three are the captains of this city, Tyrilcrysalith, then why are you out here?"

Tobin looked at Brenath, seeking his approval to answer this question. Once Brenath nodded, Tobin proceeded to answer. "Tyrilcrysalith may not rule the surrounding lands. However, we do help with their defense. Lately, we've heard of a large band of orcs roaming openly through the lands. We were sent out to find them and to stop them from doing harm to some of the smaller villages. Unfortunately, they found us first."

"It seemed as if they knew we were coming for them," Brenath cut in. "They laid the perfect trap for us. We had no chance. I'm glad you came along."

"It was the least I could do," Dragon replied.

"Thank you. At least let me repay you in some way," Brenath urged. "Please come with us to Tyrilcrysalith. It would be an honor to show you our city. And while you are there, I guarantee you wonderful food and good rest. It is the least we can do. I would also greatly appreciate it if you could accompany us there for protection. There are only three left of our great company, and we would very much like to make it home."

Dragon thought for a moment of all the different choices that he had. He wasn't too eager to be in another human dwelling, yet this was a big city different from the villages he had seen before. Also, he wasn't too eager to continue his quest, so lingering there wasn't a bad idea. It would also give him a chance to see new things that he hadn't seen before. That idea put a smile on his face, and he agreed to go with Brenath to see Tyrilcrysalith. Dragon reached forward and shook Brenath's forearm in agreement, promising that they would make a safe journey home.

"It's settled, then. We will travel to Tyrilcrysalith," Brenath said. "However, it's going to be slow going, without the use of our horses."

"Horses? What are they, and what happened to them?" Dragon asked.

"Horses are the beasts that humans ride. They make our journey faster than walking," explained Brenath. "Every man with us had one until the orcs attacked. Then they ran into the forest."

"Then that's no problem at all. Sonya will bring them back for you." Dragon looked at Sonya, and without hesitation, she took flight over the forest in search of the horses. It didn't dawn on either one of them that they had never seen a horse before. So Sonya was simply looking for something that was new to her.

While Sonya was gone, the three humans gathered their weapons and their belongings together and then waited for her to come back with news of their horses. While they waited, Dragon took the time to bring Yolana and Phanis down from the hill and introduce them to the other three. They took a brief moment to get to know one another and discuss the places that they were from. It seemed a little embarrassing for Yolana when Brenath told her they knew nothing about her village. On the other hand, they did know about Falistoran, especially Cromwin, since some of his enemies were there.

As the wait for Sonya to return with the horses lasted longer than expected, the group made use of the time to do what was needed. While they were talking, they thought of the dead lying around them, especially Brenath, who felt the need to deal with his fallen friends. For it was Brenath who suggested that something, no matter how little, should be done for the fallen humans. They were too far away from the city for the bodies to be returned, so they discussed several options that were available to them until they all finally decided on burning the dead so that no animals could devour the bodies. In that way, they would be honored as heroes of Tyrilcrysalith. The majority of the time was spent separating the humans from the orcs' corpses; as for the orcs, they were simply thrown off to the side. Dragon was the strongest, so that task fell to him, and he did not object. Like a child throwing branches, he grabbed the orcs and threw them into a pile. The human corpses, on the other hand, were neatly laid in a row so that they could be set ablaze by the only real source of fire they had, which was Sonya. After that was done, the company continued to wait patiently for Sonya to return. Yolana, however, took it upon herself to go and gather flowers that she could find in the forest and lay one on the chest of every fallen warrior. Brenath and the other two appreciated that sentiment and told her so.

After a while, they heard a noise and turned to look into the forest, only to see a bunch of animals come running into the clearing with Sonya right behind them. Dragon took a brief moment to marvel at the four-legged creatures. To Dragon they seemed like a normal beast, but they were certainly big enough to carry a human. Each one of them had an object strapped to their back that looked to aid humans in riding these beasts. "Those are horses?" Dragon asked.

"Yes, they are. Are you ready to learn how to ride one?" asked Brenath.

"I'm not sure. I will give it a try," Dragon replied, curious and anxious as ever.

Since there were plenty of horses to go around, they all picked one and jumped on it. Dragon, on the other hand, took his time, not quite sure how to get on a horse. After a while of scrutinizing what Brenath called a saddle, he finally got onto a horse and was ready to ride. Tobin had just finished roping the extra horses together for the return journey to Tyrilcrysalith. Dragon and the others would have all taken off if it weren't for Sonya, who seemed to be a little confused. She was frantically looking around at all the horses as if she were trying to pick one.

"What's the matter?" Brenath asked, finding her actions quite humorous.

"Which one do I get to ride?" Sonya asked back.

"None, I'm afraid. I do not think there is a horse that could carry you," Brenath answered, holding back a laugh.

Disturbed by this news, Sonya sat back and crossed her arms in disappointment. Her face looked as if she was pouting, and then she let out a small puff of smoke from her nostrils. "It's not fair. Dragon gets to ride on my back and now the back of a horse! I want to know what it's like to ride on something!"

Tobin rode up beside her. "If I may say, Sonya, you are far too great and beautiful a creature to lower yourself to riding on an animal."

"I thank you, Tobin," Sonya said, cheering up a bit. "Finally, someone finds me beautiful," she sarcastically remarked as she made a face at Dragon. Before she departed, she was briefly asked to do the honor of lighting the fire for the fallen. Without seeing any reason not to, she took a great puff of air and let out a long burst of flame that did exactly what it was intended to do. When she extinguished the fire from her mouth, the line of fallen heroes was well lit and would continue to burn for a long while. Then she took off in flight, letting them know that she would be nearby all the way.

When she was out of hearing range, Dragon rode over to Tobin. "Nice work," he said. "I think you just made a new friend." Dragon then gave him a pat on the back. "I should warn you, though. There are some days when she's quite cranky. Good luck with trying to calm her down then."

"I thought what he said was rather nice," Yolana commented.

Realizing that his sarcastic comment had failed, Dragon urged everyone that it was time to move out. Of course, since he had never ridden a horse, he allowed Brenath to lead the group. Yet he stayed very close to him so they could talk. Dragon was always curious about new things, and it seemed as if Brenath was the right person to talk to.

* * *

The group rode the horses throughout the rest of that day and most of the night. They stopped only for short periods of time to rest the horses and give them water. While riding, they kept the horses at a nice fast pace so they would get to their destination in good time. Only occasionally did they slow the horses to walk to give them time to catch their breath and to allow brief conversations between the traveling companions. While riding next to Brenath, Dragon took each opportunity to strike a conversation with him, for he wanted to learn as much as he could before entering a mighty city. Since he made several mistakes in his first two encounters, he didn't want to make one in a great city. At the same time, Brenath had a few questions of his own, and he asked them as eagerly as Dragon asked his. Most of the conversations, however, were not inspired by wisdom. They seemed to be of simple curiosity.

The group eventually brought their horses to a walk near the ocean and continued south along the shore. As the forest faded away, they came out upon a great expanse of plain land that stretched as far as the eye could see, like the ocean alongside it. The plains were common; however, the ocean, of course, pleased Dragon since he had never seen an ocean before, and he marveled at the beautiful sight of endless waters. He would've stared at it forever if it weren't for Brenath's desire for more answers to his questions. This was the last chance for Brenath to ask Dragon a question; he knew once they reached the city, Dragon would have more questions than he would. Speaking loud enough to drag Dragon's attention away from the endless water, Brenath asked his question. "You said, when you first met humans, you couldn't understand them. How did you learn our language so quickly?"

"Well," Dragon began, "it's a lot harder to explain than you'd think, so I'll start at the beginning. Dragons have three forms of speech: the dragon tongue, the ancient tongue, and the modern tongue. The dragon tongue is the most difficult and misunderstood language of the dragons. When heard by others, it is misconstrued as the cry of an animal. To you, the dragon tongue would sound like a dragon roar or a dragon cry. However, to the dragons, it is speaking in a form of a song; every sound is perfectly pitched and placed."

"That's amazing," Brenath said. "If they have such a beautiful language, then why choose two others?"

"The problem with the dragon tongue is that even the elves cannot understand it. I myself have learned only a portion of the language. Being born with a human tongue hinders me from speaking the entire language. So a long time ago, when the dragons decided to get involved with the younger races, they devised what is known as the ancient tongue. That is more refined like the elves' speech. Dwarves can even understand it."

"What about the modern tongue? Why did they develop that?" Brenath asked. He turned his eyes away from Dragon and looked at his horse, keeping his observation to himself. He had an odd feeling that man was the reason for the modern tongue, and perhaps the only reason for it. Brenath wasn't quite sure how to feel about that - whether to be honored or insulted.

"Unfortunately, humans couldn't learn either language, so the modern tongue is a dragon's way of saying, 'we learned your language.'"

Brenath let out a huge laugh, finding that comment more humorous than insulting. "That is all fascinating, Dragon, but it still doesn't explain how you could learn our language. I am almost sure if you follow the rising of the sun, you will come to an inhabited place of humans that do not speak my language. How will you understand them?"

"You have a very valid point, Brenath," Dragon continued. "There are other human settlements that have other languages, elves, and dwarves the same. However, it matters not. The dragon tongue is more than just making sounds. It is also in this hearing of sounds. Every sound out of the mouth has a meaning and a purpose, and young dragons are taught to listen as well as speak. All I need to do is just listen to whatever language for a moment, and in a while, it becomes clear to me as if I'd known it all my life. I can say that if it wasn't for my trying to learn the dragon tongue, I would not have this ability. On the other hand, I am kind of slow at it. Dragons are much faster at learning languages than I am."

"That explains how you were able to communicate with the orcs. That is a wonderful gift. I wish that I had it," Brenath exclaimed, staring off into the distance. "Tyrilcrysalith sometimes has newcomers from far places. It is almost impossible to understand them. Everything would be so much easier if we were able to understand languages like you can."

"Sometimes I don't think it's a gift. It would be easier to ignore the things around you if you couldn't understand them," Dragon replied, also staring into the distance.

"So if you have three languages, do you have three names?" asked Brenath. He had a smirk on his face to let Dragon know that he wasn't expecting a serious answer.

Dragon smiled and chuckled and returned to the question. "Believe it or not, we do. Take Sonya, for example. You could not pronounce or even say her dragon name, so it is shortened into an ancient tongue. Soræniya is what we call her in ancient tongue, and we simply shorten it even more for the modern tongue. So in the end, all you're left with is the simple name Sonya. I think it suits her just fine."

"I couldn't agree with you more," Brenath quickly replied. For a moment, he had a smile on his face, which then turned to curiosity. "Dragon, would you humor me and call Sonya by her dragon name if you could?"

Dragon was silent for a moment and thought about it. Eventually, he realized there was no harm in it and wouldn't mind humoring a new travel companion. He leaned his head back and took a deep breath. Then he began to let out a small hissing sound, which at first confused Brenath, who was looking for something stupendous. Next, Dragon began to let out a high- pitched bellow that seemed to echo around them. As he held on to the note, the sound seemed as if two people had begun to cry out. Out of Dragon's mouth now came a low-pitched bellow at the same time as the other. Both bellows went up and down, and then Dragon ended it with an abrupt bark, which shook the very rocks on the ground as well as startled their horses.

At the end of that, Dragon turned to Brenath to see if he approved, only to see that he had a look of awe on his face. Brenath did not have much to say; he simply smiled and then nodded forward saying, that they should keep going and pick up the pace. Dragon had to steady himself on his horse since he was shifted after he startled the horse, and he still wasn't quite used to riding one yet. Nevertheless, once he had steadied himself, he picked up the pace to stay right with Brenath so that if he had a question, he could have it answered if need be.

* * *

As they continued on, the shore along which they were traveling began to change. The land began to rise from the shore, above the water, into a vertical cliff face. The farther they went, the more the ocean dropped, which gave Dragon an interesting sight he had never seen. As he rode alongside the cliff, he enjoyed watching the waves beat against the sides of the rock walls. After a while, his attention was drawn to something else in the distance. Even though it was a good distance off, it wasn't hard to spot. Whatever it was, even though it looked small, he knew it was quite big in reality.

"What is that?" Dragon yelled out to Brenath.

"That is Tyrilcrysalith," Brenath yelled back with excitement.

"Your city is a rock," Dragon continued, a little disappointed.

"Not at all, Dragon. We are still a good distance off. Don't worry. The closer we get, the more you will see its greatness. I promise you, you won't be disappointed."

Dragon trusted Brenath and continued on, eager to see what the city actually looked like. However, the closer he got, the more confused and intrigued he became. What appeared to be a small rock in the distance began to grow to a great height. Dragon finally realized what he was looking at — it was a mountain of great standing. It was not a simple hill or a mound of dirt in the middle of these great plains leading away from the ocean cliffs. It was indeed a great mountain that towered high, yet it did not sit firmly on the earth. As they approached, Dragon realized that half of the mountain sat on the ocean and the other half on the land, and the cliffs rode right up to the side of the mountain. This was strange to Dragon; never had he seen a mountain in the middle of plains, let alone on the side of the ocean. It was as if this mountain was meant to be the divide between the two. Dragon could also see that the top of the mountain was cut flat and something twinkling and sparkling in the sunlight. The company of riders rode up to the side of the mountain that loomed over the ocean cliff face. There they all stared up at the vastness of the mountainside, and for a moment, Dragon was breathless.

"You have much to explain to me, Brenath," Dragon finally spoke. "This is not what I imagined when you spoke of your city."

"I will explain everything as we go," Brenath replied with a smile on his face. Ever since he was young, he always enjoyed showing off his city. "The reason for that is it would be too hard to explain to you all at once. For example, the cliff face goes right up to the mountainside, and it is the same on the other side except for our beautiful waterfall. Water comes from inland and flows out to the ocean. Nevertheless, the cliff face stops invaders from reaching the harbor on the ocean side, unless they come by boats."

"I see no harbor," Dragon commented, frustrated by the whole confusing situation. But he said no more, giving Brenath a chance to explain. For Dragon himself lived in a city in the heart of a mountain and knew how confusing it was to explain such things.

"You can't from here, but you will see everything once we reach the inside of the city. Now come with me around to the gates." Brenath turned from the cliff face and headed around the side of the mountain, pointing upward, hinting to the others to look at the mountainside. "Dragon, look up and tell me what you see."

Dragon did as Brenath asked and beheld the mountainside. It seemed to go straight up, and the sides were sharp and rugged, almost impossible to climb. As he looked farther up, he could see large, open cracks and holes in the mountainside. He turned and asked Brenath, "What are in those cracks in the mountainside?"

"Those cracks and holes go all the way into the city. Right now, there are sentinels in those cracks, and they are excellent marksmen with the bow."

"I thought you said this was a peaceful city."

"It is, but there's no reason not to be prepared, and if we were not peaceful, you would have been shot already." With that said, Brenath spurred his horse to quicken its pace and hurried to the gates.

When the company had reached close to the center of this half of the mountain, they beheld two massive gates. At first, Dragon was shocked at the size of the gates; they were big enough for a dragon twice the size of Sonya. Dragon never thought that a human city would need gates of that size. Both were made of some type of metal that had a rough look to it, almost the same color as the mountainside. When the gates were closed, they blended very well with the mountainside; only up close could anyone tell the difference.

The group gathered their horses near and marveled at the gate for a moment, waiting for Sonya to arrive. It didn't take long for her to get there; she flew in over the plains, heading straight for the gate. As she came closer, she glided closely over the ground and landed softly behind the group facing the gates. With her there, Brenath waved his arm to signal to the watchers, and the gates slowly opened inward. What was before them was a long tunnel into the mountain, and the group slowly entered.

"Brenath, why did they let us in so easily without knowing our names and our business?" Dragon inquired. At the same time, he was carefully keeping an eye on his surroundings, wondering if they would be able to get out of the city if they needed to.

"Because I was there," Brenath simply replied.

"That doesn't explain much. We could have threatened you with your life to let us in. Also, we happen to have a dragon traveling with us. Wouldn't that bother the denizens of your city?"

"Dragon, people's names here go far. Everyone, including the simple folk, knows that I would die before I betray my city." Though Brenath stated that with pride to Dragon, he had a humble appearance. "Not to mention we have had dealings with dragons before, though it has been many years."

Dragon nodded in acknowledgment and in understanding, then looked forward to the light at the end of the tunnel. However, the closer they got to the other end, he had a strange feeling that he would be asking a lot more questions.

When the company finally came out of the tunnel, all of them were awe- stricken, except for the three who had come from Tyrilcrysalith. The entire company dismounted, and Brenath called some guards to take the horses to the stables to be settled. Dragon took a few steps forward, staring out at the wonder that stood before him. He realized that the tunnel came out directly in the middle of the city, and he looked down at what was to be the lower part of the city.

He was amazed because most cities' lower half rarely looked as beautiful as this did. He was looking out over hundreds of houses that were carved straight from marble and silver. From where he stood, he could not see any plain metal or wood in these constructions. After staring at the houses for a moment, he then looked down at the boulevard he was standing on and realized that even the street was laid with beautiful marble bricks. The thoroughfare itself was well designed and ran around on both sides of the lower half of the city down to the harbor, with smaller walkways weaving between the buildings. Dragon then turned his eyes to the harbor, which was an eye-opener in and of itself. The ocean came right into the mountain and up to the base of the city. There were only three large docks that thrust out into the water, so large or small ships could tie up. The docks themselves were designed out of marble and beautifully carved wood, perhaps the only wood Dragon could see in the city.

Brenath tapped Dragon on the shoulder, eager to speak to him and show him something. "Look," he said as he pointed to the harbor. "There on the mountain peninsulas on either side of the harbor opening. High above the water are our mountain walkways and our ocean sentry. We have several catapults up there and many rows of archers that defend us from enemies approaching from the ocean. I hear from old stories that many ships lie sunken out there, belonging to ones who tried to take this place."

"That is most impressive," Dragon replied, still staring out at all the new things.

"You think that's impressive, come with me to the upper city to meet the queen. You haven't seen everything yet." Brenath gave Dragon a slight tug on his arm, urging him to keep going to see more of the city.

Dragon agreed and turned from the beautiful sight before him to see what was behind him. The moment he turned all the way around, his jaw dropped in amazement, and for a moment, his breath stopped. Dragon now understood what Brenath meant about the greatness of his city, and he looked up at a sight that he had never dreamed of. The entire mountain was hollowed out, and the upper part of the city had buildings carved directly from precious stones. The upper city was divided into three sections. The lower-section buildings were carved from ruby, and the middle section was carved from emerald. If that was not enough to amaze Dragon, the highest part of the city was overwhelming.

There, at the back of the mountain, five towers loomed up into the air, carved straight from diamond. The towers looked perfect as they stood straight and tall, side by side. They seemed to almost be connected because they were so flush against one another and had many windows going up them. The center spire was the tallest, with the adjacent towers equally shorter and the two outer towers shorter yet again. He now understood what glittered at him from the outside of the mountain, for the center tower was the only thing that stood higher than the mountain. Dragon could not turn his eyes from the sight. It was as if all the gems in the world had gathered together to build this city. Brenath had to grab Dragon's arm and drag him away from the site, for he was unwilling to leave it. The pathway that led down also forked and went upward on both sides around the upper city, with smaller walkways in between the gemmed buildings.

As Dragon followed Brenath, he twisted his head from side to side, looking at every single intricate design of the buildings. Sonya, on the other hand, followed carelessly, wagging her tail back and forth and fluffing her wings. Her tail accidentally smacked against one of the buildings, and Dragon turned, aggravated at her. He began to correct her on being more careful, and Brenath interrupted.

"It's quite all right, Dragon. She did no harm." Brenath interceded for Sonya. "I do not think she could do much damage to the city. Observe." Brenath drew his blade and sliced at the side of one of the ruby buildings. His blade did not break the gem, but it made a very visible gash. He then sheathed his sword and pointed at the building for Dragon to see his meaning.

Without hesitation, Dragon bent over to look closely at the gash in the building, and to his surprise, it began to disappear. It looked as if the ruby grew back right before his eyes, and not long after, there was no evidence that there was ever a mark. This sight intrigued and confused Dragon more than ever about the city. "I don't understand," Dragon said, turning to Brenath for answers. "What I have just seen would seem impossible. How is this done?"

"I seem to have given you more questions than answers," Brenath replied, laughing out loud. "I apologize for this. Unfortunately, I won't answer them. It is better that the queen answer them for you. Besides, she is better at telling stories than I am."

Dragon, still unsatisfied with that answer, asked another quick question. "What about the lower city? Does it do this marvelous work as well?"

"No, I'm afraid. From old stories, it seems that the lower city was built long after the upper city was. Come along," Brenath urged the company. "We have much more to discuss, and the queen will answer everything." So the group continued to follow Brenath up into the upper city. Sonya, however, was walking more carefully than she was before—not out of fear of hurting the buildings, but not wanting to be corrected by Dragon.

The company followed Brenath up the walkway and into a beautiful courtyard, which lay in between the emerald buildings and the diamond towers. In the center of the courtyard was a beautiful mountain-shaped fountain, where water flowed up from a spring and came out of a diamond in the center. The water then flowed down over emeralds and rubies into a marble base that held the glittering water. Dragon could see that the water flowed nowhere else, so he assumed that it went back underground and down to the harbor. As the group walked by it, they admired the fountain for its symbolic tie to the city.

As they rounded the fountain and headed away, Dragon bumped into something. He immediately looked down to see what it was, and to his surprise, he realized that it was not something but someone that he had bumped into. The being was stout and stood about four feet tall, with long red hair and a red beard, which was forked and braided down to the middle of its chest. "Watch where you're going!" the individual said, quite aggravated with Dragon.

Dragon noticed that the being had two small axes by its waist and one large, decoratively designed battle ax hanging on its back. It also had gauntlets and a helmet that looked to be of dwarfish design. So Dragon immediately made the assumption that this must be a dwarf, and he did not wish to offend him. "I apologize, sir," Dragon said, wanting to calm the situation. Instead, his words had a different effect than he expected.

"Sir, sir!" the dwarf yelled, extremely upset at those words. The dwarf immediately cupped his arms underneath his chest and puffed it up for Dragon to see something. "Do these look like something that a male would have?"

Confused, Dragon looked down at the dwarf's chest to see a substantial amount of cleavage. Puzzled for a moment, he then realized that he was looking at breasts. This dwarf was a female. Immediately, a look of shock broke on his face, and he tried to correct this mistake. "Ma'am, ma'am!" In response to this, the female dwarf simply rolled her eyes and went off in a huff, pushing Dragon out of the way. Dragon, still wanting to make amends, called after her, "But I've never seen a dwarf before!" As she continued to walk away, Dragon turned to Brenath, seeking support in this moment of grievous mistake.

Brenath shook his head and gave Dragon a smirk. "Don't worry about it," he encouraged Dragon. "She's been here for several months, and I hear from everyone that she's like that. She's not very talkative. No one knows anything about her past or her lineage. However, it's no secret why she's here. She's looking for some type of adventure. So far, nothing has come through this city that has intrigued her." Brenath put his arm on Dragon's back and urged him once again to keep going. "It's all right. She'll get over it."

Dragon and the company turned away from the fountain and headed toward the doorway to the towers. As they faced the center tower, where the entrance was, Dragon beheld something he thought was peculiar. The entrance had no door; it was simply an open archway. Then he thought back and realized that there were only a few doorways that had doors. Most of the city had open archways, as if the people themselves didn't care for doors. He thought to himself that this city must be definitely peaceful and trustworthy. Nevertheless, they entered the archway and headed into the towers. Sonya herself entered the towers, for the archway was large enough for a dragon of her size.

Once inside, Dragon beheld more wonders and sights that continued to baffle him. The first thing he noticed was that the walls were pale, like uncut diamonds, yet they still had a nice shine. This baffled him since he thought that they were carved halls. They would have the same glitter and shine as the outside of the towers. Yet he speculated that it would get quite annoying looking at your reflection all the time, so he simply accepted this. Still, he could not ignore one thing, and that was the fact that every hall and doorway in the tower was large enough for Sonya to move without lowering her head. It seemed odd to him that a human city would be big enough for dragons. Since he had asked so many questions before, he thought it was better to just keep silent until he came before the queen. Unfortunately, he had a little trouble doing that. "So will I have a chance to meet the king?"

"There is no king at this time," Brenath explained. "The last king and queen died a while back, leaving only their daughter to rule in their absence. I might add she's doing a wonderful job for one so young. You see, she was only eleven when she took the throne, and now she is twenty, soon to be twenty-one in a few months."

"A young child asked to take the throne unexpectedly. That must have been hard for her," Dragon said, thinking of his own recent rise to the throne and all the responsibility forced on him.

"Brenath!" an unexpected voice yelled through the halls.

Dragon looked up to see a man quickly walking down a flight of stairs to the right, coming from another tower. The man was overly dressed, with many rings on his fingers and trinkets of gold around his neck. The clothes he wore were richly colored silks that hung loosely upon his body. His long straight hair was dark black and draped down his shoulders. Not a single strand of his hair was out of place. Dragon could see that this man was of some importance and coveted his looks highly. The man was not strong like a soldier but skinny like the dignitary, who did not work at all.

Brenath stopped suddenly and flashed a look of aggravation toward this man; it appeared as though he did not want to deal with him.

"What do you want now, Malic?" Brenath asked the man, very agitated.

"I thought you would never betray our city. When I heard that you let a dragon in, I could not believe it!" The man reached the bottom of the stairs and walked right up to Brenath. "And here I see you in the very heart of the city with a dragon. What do you have to say for yourself!"

Dragon quickly assessed the situation, looking at all their faces. Brenath, Cromwin, and Tobin seemed to have disdain for this man. Yet at the same time, they gave him what respect they could, keeping their characters clean. On the other hand, the man facing them seemed to have a great deal of arrogance.

"I have nothing to say to you," Brenath finally replied. "I will vouch for all of their characters before the queen. The dragon called Sonya is with this being, and he saved our lives."

The man quickly turned his attention to Dragon. "Who are you?"

"My name is Dragon, and who might you be?" Dragon replied, calmly hoping this talk would not end badly.

"I am Malic Wilarchon, great wizard and adviser to the queen," the man replied, taking a very arrogant posture and almost looking down on Dragon.

The moment Dragon heard the word wizard, he began to dislike the man even more, referring back to the words that Ancient spoke to him about wizards. When he was young, Ancient told him that one of the best ways to discern a good wizard from a bad wizard was that good wizards were normally not concerned about their appearances. Though Dragon could not judge the man only on his appearance, it did seem to correspond with his attitude.

"You do not look like a wizard or any magical being that possesses the ability to control dragons," Malic continued. "How do you control this beast?"

Dragon, a little offended by Malic referring to Sonya as a beast, replied, "I do not control her. She is a friend, and she travels with me willingly, for I am the king of the dragons."

Malic began to laugh and mock Dragon's words. "King of the dragons, I doubt that. No human could control such beasts! Even if they could, what human in their right mind would want to be king of such foul creatures?"

"Watch your tongue, Malic!" Brenath snapped. The last thing Brenath needed was for Dragon and Malic to get into a fight before he introduced Dragon to the queen. So, he took it upon himself to be Dragon's advocate, for he was used to getting into fights with Malic. "Not only is he the king of the dragons, he is a dragon himself."

Malic stepped back in shock and took a good look at Dragon, only to realize that what Brenath had said was true. "A half-breed," Malic exclaimed. "Only the darkest of magic could breed such an abomination! You have brought doom upon us, Brenath. Kill it before it destroys the city!"

Dragon was now deeply offended, so he took a step forward, growling at the wizard. Then suddenly, another voice cried out, "That is enough, Malic!" Dragon turned to look at the stairway to the left, only to see another beautiful sight. A young woman about twenty years of age came gracefully walking down the stairs. She was slender and just a little taller than Dragon, and she wore a white gown that sparkled. Her complexion was light and fair; and she had golden blonde hair that was straight and hung long down her back. On the top of her head, she wore a beautiful crown made of silver and diamonds, yet it was not an overpowering crown; it seemed to fit her body size perfectly. Dragon gazed deeply into her rich blue eyes, and there he seemed captivated.

When she reached the bottom of the stairs, the three captains bowed, and so did the wizard, Yolana, Phanis, and Sonya. Dragon, on the other hand, could not turn his gaze away.

Malic, still bowing, turned and snapped at Dragon. "Bow before the queen!"

"I am the king of the dragons. I bow to no one," Dragon firmly responded as he crossed his arms and stood still at the same time, not taking his eyes off the queen, but he did put a smile on his face.

"Would you bow for a lady?" the queen asked nicely.

Dragon, of course, still captivated by her look, thought about it for a moment and then concluded that it couldn't hurt to be respectful to a woman. His bow wasn't something spectacular; he slowly bent over yet kept his eyes on her.

"Thank you. You are very nice and courteous," the queen replied, giving her own slight bow in respect to the dragon king.

"Please spend a day with him. You'll change your mind," Sonya sarcastically remarked as she rolled her eyes. Upon hearing that comment, everyone chuckled except for Malic and Dragon, who did not find it funny at all.

"I heard that dragons are majestic creatures," the queen said to Dragon. "I also heard that they are both wise and knowledgeable, and that they should be respected. Is that not true, Dragon King?"

"It is, my lady," Dragon replied respectfully, hoping to redeem himself from Sonya's comment.

"Then I expect you to be peaceful in my city," she said as she also glanced over at Malic.

"My queen, you do not know dragons like I do," Malic defended himself. "They are vicious creatures. They follow no law or form of peace."

"Yet it was you who spoke the first harsh words, not him. This is my city, and he has done no wrong in it. Also, Brenath has spoken for his character, and I trust Brenath's instincts. They have served us well in the past. So with that said, Malic, you are to be courteous to our guests." The queen's eyes did not leave Malic until he reassured her that he would obey her commands. Then she walked over to Dragon to properly meet him. "So Dragon is your name?"

"Yes, but how did you know?" Dragon replied, quite intrigued by her.

"I heard the whole conversation. Words seem to echo in these halls very well. By the way, I am Crysaia, queen of Tyrilcrysalith, and I welcome you to my city. As with most visitors, I'm pretty sure you have many questions about Tyrilcrysalith. I will be glad to answer them over dinner. Would you and your companions love to join me for dinner?"

Dragon had no hesitation in his reply. "We would love to join you."

"Good, that is wonderful. Brenath will prepare some rooms for you so you can wash and clean yourself from your long journey. Then I will see you later this evening."

"I look forward to it," Dragon replied, giving a slight bow, this one being a proper bow and more respectful than his first.

Crysaia took her leave of the room, and as she did, Dragon's eyes never turned from her. Of course, this did not have a good effect on some of his companions. Phanis turned to look at Sonya and Yolana, only to see that they had agitated looks on their faces as they watched Crysaia and Dragon. Phanis took a few steps away, unwilling to get in the middle of this situation. At this time, Malic stormed off in the opposite direction, clearly showing his frustration. Once gone, Cromwin walked up to Dragon and gave him a strong pat on the back.

Dragon, now confused at this new event, turned back to Brenath for answers. "I thought Cromwin didn't like me."

"Oh, he didn't," Brenath added. "However, Cromwin despises no one more than Malic. Since you made enemies with Malic, Cromwin has found a new respect for you. I think you now have a lifelong friend," Brenath said and began to chuckle. "I'll have Tobin show you to your rooms. I must tell the queen all that happened on our journey." Brenath's face then darkened with sadness. "After that, I must go to each family of the fallen and tell them of their loss." A moment of silence hung in the room, and then Brenath gave Dragon a nod that all would be well. With one more look at the company, Brenath turned and left to do what was his job to do. So with nothing better to do, Dragon and his company followed Tobin up the stairs into the towers of Tyrilcrysalith. There in their gracious rooms, they would find some peace and relaxation until it was time to dine with the queen.

10

A Queen's Courtesy

Tobin showed Dragon and his companions to their rooms, and there they cleaned up and rested for many hours. Sonya and Yolana were shown to one room, while Dragon and Phanis were shown to another. Dragon enjoyed a few moments of peace and quiet in the room; still, he was amazed by the accommodations. The room was definitely made for visitors; it was wide and had a very high ceiling. It was circular, and there were five beds scattered around. The beds themselves were not small in size; three people could rest on one bed alone. Dragon lay on his bed and looked up at the ceiling, calculating how many dragons he could fit in here roughly the size of Sonya. He got as far as ten.

Just before it was time for them to meet the queen for dinner, Sonya came to visit Dragon. She burst into the room unannounced, eager to see what their room looked like. "This is wonderful," she said, turning in circles, looking at everything about her. "Although it does look a little like ours, except my bed is bigger and in the center of the room."

Of course, what she was referring to was that in the last hour, the servants of the towers had brought more than a hundred pillows and thrown them in the middle of her room for her to lie upon. "It's so nice to have a bed again. It's been a while since I've slept on a bed." Sonya rolled on her back and lay with her head only a foot from Dragon. "Can we stay here for a while?" she said, looking up at him. "At least we could get a few nights of good rest."

"Now, Sonya, you know that you could sleep pretty much anywhere," Dragon replied, patting her chin. "You don't need a bed to rest upon. However, you might be right. It would be nice to get a couple nights of good sleep. I will think about it." Dragon then looked her deeply in the eye, attempting to be serious. "But don't get too comfortable. This isn't home."

Knowing that Dragon's comment was an attempt to bring back the memory of home, she lifted her tail up and over and softly stroked the side of his face. "Dragon, I know you miss home, and I know that this place could never replace it. But promise me this while you are here: that you will have a good time. You need it more than any of us, and I want to see a smile on your face."

"I can't promise you anything," Dragon replied as he laid his head upon her cheek. "I will do what I can."

At that moment, Yolana and Tobin entered the room, announcing that it was time to dine. Tobin, of course, was continuing in his brother's stead by escorting them through the towers. Brenath had left his duties to inform the queen as to what was going on outside their city. At first, the group didn't move, for they were set back by the very look of Yolana. Not only had she cleaned up for supper, but she had a brand-new look. Yolana had on a beautiful gown, and her hair was nicely combed and braided. She told the group that the queen was generous enough to give her new traveling clothes as well as the gray gown that she was wearing. It took a moment for the company to say anything, but once they did, they complimented her greatly on her gown and her beauty. Then, from there, they followed Tobin to the dining hall for supper.

＊

The dining hall was a great rectangular room with lots of tables and chairs. As they walked down the center, they could see hundreds of carved, elongated silver tables and chairs on either side. As they walked farther, they could see, at the other end of the hall, a larger table set apart in the middle. Chairs were set all around it, and sitting at the left end was Queen Crysaia. To her left, with his back to the wall, was Malic, and to her right sat Brenath. For the moment, no one sat next to Malic; Cromwin, on the other hand, was sitting next to Brenath. The rest of the chairs were empty, which did not bother Dragon. Something in his mind told him that he would not like to be here in this great dining hall full of people.

Also, he was looking forward to having many of his questions answered, and it seemed it would be easier with less people to interrupt. Still, he was uneasy that Malic was invited; he didn't know what it was, but something about this man unnerved him. Yet Dragon greeted everyone with respect, and the queen requested him to sit and eat.

"I have requested a private dinner tonight to make you feel more at ease," the queen said, gesturing with her arms to indicate that they were to sit. "Brenath suggested that you would probably prefer this setting."

"I appreciate the gesture. It does make things easier," Dragon responded.

Tobin sat beside Cromwin, and Yolana followed and sat beside him. Phanis, on the other hand, walked around the table and tried to sit down beside Malic, only to find out that it upset Malic. Unfortunately, Malic did not think it was right for a slave to sit next to him. Of course, he was rudely interrupted by Phanis, who told him that he was no slave and would sit where he pleased. So he sat one chair down from Malic, if only to keep from hitting him.

Dragon, of course, sat three chairs away from Malic, right beside Phanis, perhaps for the same reason as Phanis did. Then, when it came time for Sonya to be seated, she walked down to the other end of the table. She politely picked up the chair and set it off to the side, and then she sat down. Even though she was a good four chairs away from everybody, her height gave her an advantage over everyone else.

Now that everyone was seated, the servants came out from the side doors bearing great trays of various foods. They quietly filled the tables with food and drinks and then left the room. The entire table waited for the queen to grab the first piece of food, and when she did, they all filled their plates with whatever they desired. As for Sonya, she had several full trays of freshly cooked meat before her. As the company started eating, conversations started around the table, especially between Dragon and Queen Crysaia.

"Queen Crysaia, I must say your city is quite breathtaking," Dragon said. Still, he kept the thought to himself that his home was greater than this city.

"Thank you. It is, indeed. By the way, just call me Crysaia," the queen replied, trying to make this as amiable as she could.

Dragon, of course, nodded respectfully and then continued, "I must ask: how was this place built? I'm guessing that magic had to be responsible for most of its construction, but still, that must've seemed like an impossible feat."

"I'm sorry to disappoint you, Dragon. We did not build this city, nor did any of our ancestors."

"This is absurd. The more I stay here, the more confused I get," Dragon said as he began to gorge himself. Of course, Sonya didn't take a liking to this, so she pulled her tail around the side of the table and smacked Dragon on the back of the head. When he turned to look at her, she was shaking her head in disapproval of his eating habits before the queen. So in fear of getting hit again, he began to eat a little bit more elegantly.

"I'm sorry to confuse you, Dragon. Let me tell you the whole story to clarify everything," Crysaia continued. "This city has been here long before man ever had understanding. This city was founded in mankind's earliest years, when we as a race first came to understand order, knowledge, and wisdom. The first rulers to ever govern man stumbled on it; they were the fourteen king brothers and their queens. They found the place with its gates wide open and its halls abandoned, so they put it to good use. At first, they were always afraid that the original owners would come back and claim it. Their fear was great because no known race built this city, and they didn't know why they abandoned it. Still, in their absence, the kings decided to put their knowledge of the city to good use."

"This is all, indeed, fascinating. It seems you know just as much about the city as I do. I was hoping you would at least have some answers for me," Dragon said, beginning to get a little aggravated. "What did you mean by putting the knowledge to good use?"

"Have you ever heard of the city of Atlantis?" Crysaia asked as she saw Malic roll his eyes at the mention of the name.

"Yes, once or twice. Ancient, my old mentor, mentioned it to me when I was young." Dragon's curiosity was once again sparked by the mere mention of Atlantis.

"Atlantis is Tyrilcrysalith's younger sister. The thirteen younger kings set out with the knowledge derived from this city and built Atlantis on the other side of the world. They built it to be a beacon and a light unto the world, where wisdom and knowledge would rule and protect all."

"Why build another city?" Sonya asked, hoping to beat Dragon to the question. She knew he was curious, but she didn't want to be left out of the conversation.

"Is it not better to have two lights instead of one?"

"The kings feared that if whoever built this place took it back, then the knowledge found here would be lost to humans," Brenath interjected.

Crysaia took a deep breath and continued ignoring Brenath's comment. "My ancestor, the oldest of the fourteen brothers, stayed here over several hundred generations ago. He stayed here to protect the knowledge that was left here in this city. The others left because they knew the city that they would build would be so great that it would need more than one to govern it. Even though Atlantis is much larger than Tyrilcrysalith, not a soul there speaks poorly of this city. We are not forgotten either. Many of the various races come from all over the earth to see the writings on the walls."

"My queen, you speak too much!" Malic interrupted, very upset.

"What written walls?" Dragon inquired now that Malic seemed disturbed by the very mention of them.

"It's quite all right, Malic. Many strangers already know about the walls," Crysaia reassured him. "You see, Dragon, if you continue to go downstairs in any part of the towers, they will all lead to one point. The downward stairs of the five towers eventually converge in one room, with only one stairway leading down. If you choose to go down the stairs, at the bottom you will find yourself deep within the earth, almost a mountain's height below the level of the sea."

Dragon leaned forward, intrigued by her words. "What is down there?"

"A long hallway as far as the eye can see, with writings on both sides. It was left here by the ones before, and from down there came some of the knowledge that helped build Atlantis. The rest of the knowledge came from looking at the city itself."

"What type of writings?" Even though Dragon's questions were serious, he couldn't help but sound like a child with never-ending questions.

"I'm sorry, Dragon, I cannot describe them. I will have to show them to you tomorrow."

"I believe that will upset Malic," Dragon sarcastically remarked as he looked toward Malic.

Malic waited a moment before replying, choosing his words carefully. "I'm sorry you feel that way about me," he said. "I agree that when we first met, perhaps my words were unjust. However, I only look out for the welfare of the city and the people within it. Brenath and Queen Crysaia have not seen the things that I have as a wizard, and they do not understand the dangers that are outside these walls."

As Malic made a poor attempt to excuse his behavior, Brenath leaned back in his chair and rolled his eyes. "Yes, Malic, we all know how brave you are behind these walls. However, next time, it would be wise to use less haughty words in speaking to a race that is greater than ours. If he was hostile toward us, he would've already done something. Besides, it makes no sense to deny him the right to see the walls when we have given every other race the right to see them."

"Very well. Perhaps you are right," Malic replied, a little uneasy. He then sat back in his chair, showing his dislike for the whole situation. On the other hand, he was unwilling to give up the chance to turn the situation around. "So, Dragon, Brenath told everyone that you're passing through and that you have some journeys ahead of you."

"That is true," Dragon replied, uncertain of where Malic was taking this conversation.

"So why would the king of the dragons leave his city and go on such a journey?" Malic tapped his fingers on the table and grinned greatly at the thought of the possible answers.

"I had to leave," Dragon replied simply, unwilling to give Malic more information.

"You had to leave. That seems odd," Malic continued, reveling in the chance to get back at Dragon. "To me, the only time that the king should have to leave his city is if he betrays it."

Malic's words immediately upset Sonya, and she decided to get involved in this conversation. She slammed her fist on the table, and with her other hand, she pointed at Malic. "Now that's enough! Dragon loved his people and would never have betrayed them! That is why he is here, to save his people! If you say one more thing about my friend and king, you will deal with me!" Sonya eventually calmed down, brought her arm back down, and then apologized to Crysaia for the mark she left on the table.

Crysaia, of course, reassured her that no harm had been done and then asked Malic to keep quiet. Yet his question did make her curious of Dragon's situation. "I may not agree with Malic's choice of words; however, Dragon, he does have a point. I would like to have peace of mind. Would you please tell me why you had to leave your city?"

Dragon sat forward, putting his elbows on the table, cupping his hands together, and resting his chin on his hands. For a moment, he sat there, thinking whether or not he should tell his secret. Then, after a while, he deemed it safe and no harm would ever come of it. "The Creator told me to."

"The Creator—who is that? Is he some form of a god?" asked Crysaia, now curious about Dragon's story.

"A god, what is that?" inquired Dragon.

"A god is an all-powerful and all-knowing being," Malic quickly answered. "Every race has a god or more, and there are even gods for many different things."

"Then no, he is not a god—he is the Creator," Dragon replied in a sterner voice. "He put the stars in the sky and made every grain of sand in the seas. The old dragons used to call him the father of the heavens, who even made the mothers of the earth."

"There is more than one. This is fascinating," said Crysaia, beginning to get excited and eager for more information.

Malic sat there and began to get frustrated with every word that Dragon said. "Well, I never heard of this Creator!"

"The greatest of wizards knew of him, or they knew of the force that created the heavens. They called it by many names, but they knew of the thing that gave them the very magic they were using, and they respected it. It doesn't matter what you call it. It is there, and only the darkest of wizards or the lowest of wizards never recognized it."

Sitting back in his seat, Malic was somewhat insulted by that. For whatever reason, whether it was because he had nothing to say in return or he didn't want to speak to Dragon, Malic kept his mouth shut.

"So why did the Creator want you to leave your home?" Crysaia asked, wanting to hear the rest of the story.

"The Creator has a love for mankind, and I do not understand why. Of course, mankind has fallen out of favor with the Creator through their deeds. So the Creator will test mankind for the right to sit by his side. In order to do this, the world of magic must fade. Over the course of thousands of years, mankind will see the ancient world fade, from wizards to elves— even the dwarves will diminish in time."

Several of those at the table looked shocked, almost willing to cry, especially Crysaia. "I am deeply troubled and saddened by this news," she said.

"The sadness is all mine, Queen. For I was sent out from my city to seek out the dragons across the earth and tell them to fade. If they choose not to, then I must kill them." Dragon's voice hung on the last two words, almost as if he was unwilling to say them or think of them. "Though, in all honesty, I have not yet taken it upon myself to obey the Creator. I was forced out of my home, and I lost everyone that I loved. All for a foolish quest that I'm not sure I believe in."

For a long moment, everyone at the table went quiet. No one knew what to say. "I can understand your hesitation," Crysaia responded. She was able to relate to being in authority and being asked to do some things you didn't agree with. Wanting to change the subject, she turned to what she believed was a safe subject. "So, Dragon, how did you come by that name?"

Dragon, of course, was grateful for the change in topic and was very willing to answer that question. "You can blame my name on my parents, as most children can. My father did not like the idea of calling me a dragon name, since humans can't speak the dragon language. As my mother didn't think it was appropriate for the king of dragons to be called by a human name, they settled on calling me Dragon so that all tongues could say my name."

"That's like calling a man, a horse or a dog," Malic interrupted.

"Well, I am not a horse or a dog. I am a dragon!" Dragon said, gritting his teeth as he crushed with one hand the metal goblet he was drinking from. Then, feeling a little abashed at what he did, he gently set the crushed goblet down and grabbed another one.

"I believe that your name fits you well." Crysaia smiled, trying not to laugh, for she found the story amusing. Before she could say anything else, a servant entered the room and spoke softly into the queen's ear. Crysaia nodded at the servant and then turned back to speak to Dragon. "If you loved the city during the day, Dragon, you will love what happens each and every night. Also, your timing couldn't be better. We have a custom here in Tyrilcrysalith. Every ten days, we have a celebration—a celebration of life and good fortune, especially since the city is richly blessed. We have never truly seen hard times. We are blessed in wealth and an abundance of food, for the lands around the city could supply enough food for eight cities of this size. There will be feasting, and much singing and dancing. It would be an honor if you could join us, and perhaps it might lighten your heart before you rejoin your quest."

Dragon replied that he would stay for the celebration, and the queen was overjoyed. She then announced that she must take her leave to prepare for the celebration. Though she looked elegant enough, she preferred something more casual, so that if she chose to dance, she could. Then she turned and left the room, leaving all the others to continue eating or talking, whichever they chose. Of course, without her there, the room seemed a little bit tenser. Most of the tension was between Malic and everyone else, and he did feel the pressure.

Malic got up, deciding that he did not wish to be in the room with such high tension and high numbers against him. However, as he began to leave, he could not hold his tongue any longer and had to have one last word. "Dragons, such a civilized race, and here their king is sent out to kill his own kind. How ironic." Malic then turned away from the table and headed down the hall toward the door that everyone had entered.

Dragon, on the other hand, was unwilling to let Malic have the last word. He took a big bite of the meat that he was holding in his hand and then spat it out toward Malic. With his perfect aim, the piece of meat flew more than forty feet and smacked Malic in the back of the head.

Malic, aggravated by this, turned quickly and yelled back. "You half- breed!" Then he turned his attention toward Brenath, looking for some reaction. "Brenath, you are the captain of the guards. Do something!"

Brenath leaned back in his chair, looking at Malic and trying so hard not to laugh. "I would, but I can't spit as far as Dragon."

Malic's anger grew, and his face turned red. "You are all barbarians, and why the queen puts up with you, I will never know!" He then turned and stormed off in a fit of rage, leaving everyone else in the room to burst out in laughter.

After Malic had finally left the room, Cromwin got up, grabbed a pitcher from one of the servants, and went and filled Dragon's goblet. Then he patted Dragon on the back, showing his approval of yet another disgrace to Malic.

"So tell me, Brenath why does the queen, keep him around if he is so disliked?" Dragon asked, puzzled by the very situation.

"It is not an easy answer, Dragon," replied Brenath, also puzzled by the situation. He took a quiet moment of thought as he swirled the liquid in his goblet and focused on it as if that helped him think over the situation. "She was eleven years old when she took the kingdom after her mother and her father died. It was hard for her to even comprehend how to rule a city. However, what she did know was that she needed help, and she believed the more help, the better. By most standards, that form of reasoning would be a wise action, though it requires people of good standing. I served her father well, so she kept me close. For all intents and purposes, you might say I finished raising her. On the other hand, she believes I'm good only for combat—that is why she keeps Malic around. She understands that the world outside these walls is filled with magical creatures, so by her reasoning, she needs one wise in magic. Unfortunately, she didn't succeed in that."

"I understand that. Malic is no great wizard. He is more of a fool," Dragon said, thinking about the difference between Malic and his beloved mentor, Ancient. "Why do you dislike him so much?"

"Unknown to Crysaia, Malic arrived in the city the day her mother and her father died unexpectedly. I suspected that he might have had something to do with it, but I could never prove it. Within days, he became acquainted with the new queen and graciously offered his services. Of course, her needing all the help she could get, she agreed, and I've been dealing with him ever since. Still, we will not let him walk freely through the city. There are several of us that keep an eye on him at all times. He may have pulled the wool over her eyes, but not ours. One of these days, I will avenge the death of Crysaia's parents, who were my beloved friends." With that said, Brenath downed the rest of his drink, as if that could wash away the thought of Malic.

"I do not doubt that day will come," Dragon said as he grabbed another plate of food, as if the whole conversation had made him hungry.

"It is just so hard to catch him. Unlike you, who show your colors, he is like the wind that changes with each passing day. We can never figure out what he will do or say next. I know more about you than I do about him." Brenath sat silent for a moment, discouraged about the whole thing, and then he put a smile on his face and decided to move on.

"Come, my new friends. Let me take you to the throne room, and from there, we will wait for the queen and the celebration." The whole company got up and rose quietly, except for Sonya, who actually knocked over a few chairs with her tail. When she finished picking them back up, the whole company followed Brenath to the throne room.

* * *

Crysaia was in her room, just finishing putting on her gown for the evening celebration, when she heard a strange noise that sounded like the flapping of small wings. She quickly looked around the room, expecting to see a small bird or something like it. When she didn't see anything at all, she stood still and began to be concerned. It wasn't easy for something to go amiss in her room, where everything was perfectly placed and the walls themselves were made of diamond. She cautiously took a couple of steps forward, continuing to look around.

Suddenly, out of the corner of her eye, she saw something sparkle near the window. Turning to see what it was, she saw something small on the ledge. The closer Crysaia got to the window, the more she could see of the small being. Only a few steps away, she could see that the creature was a fairy. Crysaia then knelt down by the window to look at the fairy face-to-face, even though it was no bigger than her hand.

"Greetings, Queen Crysaia," the fairy said. "I am called Tilly. I am a legend keeper."

"I remember you," Crysaia replied, her face filling up with warmth and joy. "When I was a young girl,—six, I believe—you visited my parents."

"Yes, that is when we first met. I came for your grandfather's fairy. She was not given a new charge right away, so she lingered for a while with your family until I came for her. Your mother and your father were good people. I'm sorry for your loss."

"I thank you for your words, but why are you here?" Crysaia asked, thinking it had something to do with Dragon.

Tilly didn't want to answer that question, so she lowered her head, attempting to avoid it. Crysaia, on the other hand, watched her motions carefully, and quickly put two and two together.

"You're here with Dragon. You are Dragon's legend keeper," Crysaia said excitedly.

"It's not like I want to be here," Tilly snapped.

"You don't like being Dragon's keeper. Why?" Once again, Tilly refused to answer questions, so Crysaia decided to push the issue. "Very well, why are you talking to me, then? I thought historians were not supposed to get involved; doesn't this break the rules?"

Tilly looked up at the queen, almost in tears. "Long ago, when I didn't receive my charge, your mother was kind to me. With her soft voice, she spoke to me, and she gave me hope. I am so frustrated. I need someone to speak to, and I wish she was here."

"That makes two of us. However, since she is not here, I will do the best that I can. So tell me everything that is bothering you."

Even though Crysaia was putting up a brave front to help Tilly, silently she wanted to cry upon the mere mention and memory of her mother.

Feeling a little bit comforted, Tilly began to pace back and forth on the ledge and began to speak of her problems. "I was the first legend keeper ever. I was given the greatest charge. When he died I waited for thousands of years, before I was given another. At that time, the other fairies began to say that I did something wrong, and I began to believe them. At most, a fairy waited a hundred years without a charge, not a thousand. When I was finally given a charge, I thought it was someone great—only to find out it was a punishment after all. What could he possibly do in his lifetime besides wander about? The Creator himself kicked Dragon out of the dragon city. The boy has no obligation to the quest."

Once Tilly was done rambling and had taken a moment to stand still, Crysaia answered as softly as she could, "Tilly, to me, it sounds as if you're looking at this the wrong way."

"What's that supposed to mean?" Tilly's wings began to flutter really fast, and even change color to match her temper.

"If you will listen for a moment, I'll explain." Crysaia waited a moment for the fairy to calm down and then continued. "I believe that Dragon is a great gift to you, and that is why you waited thousands of years. The Creator couldn't give such a great charge to the other fairies, which is why he gave them all the lesser charges. Also, he needed you to be ready for such an undertaking, so he made sure you had all the rest you could."

"What could he do that would possibly be great?" Tilly asked, almost as if she were asking herself.

"I think you are being too hard on Dragon, thinking of only your own problems. Dragon has been sent out, away from everything that he loves, perhaps never to see them again. He is to find his race and tell them to fade, and if they don't, he himself must kill them. So either way, as he walks along this journey, he will be alone." Crysaia wanted to say more in Dragon's defense, but she couldn't because her face and her voice welled up with sorrow just thinking about his hardships.

Tilly sat down, her face filled with shock. The things she never understood finally became clear. "I didn't think of it in that way; I was too busy feeling sorry for myself. I have made a grievous error in treating him so badly."

"All is not lost, Tilly. There is still time to make amends."

"I wouldn't know where to start," Tilly replied, looking up at Crysaia for some kind of answer.

Crysaia could not help but look down at Tilly and smile. "Neither do I, but I will help." Crysaia stood up and motioned for Tilly to come along. "I have an idea."

Without hesitation, Tilly jumped up and quickly flew to Crysaia's shoulder, where she sat down, letting Crysaia carry her away. As they were leaving the room, Tilly flickered her wings, and her body quickly glittered and then disappeared. Yet you could still hear her talking to Crysaia as they went up to the throne room.

***

The company of Dragon was up in the throne room, waiting for the celebration and the queen. Though they waited for a long time, they were not bored. They were amused by the sights they saw. The throne room was quite large, with a very high ceiling and four great pillars that loomed up. The shape of the room was square, and so was the position of the pillars. The pillars themselves created a nice divide for an outer court and inner court to the throne room. There were two entrances on either side of the room, and a great archway opened out onto a balcony facing west toward the sea. On the east side of the room, there was a dais with two diamond-carved thrones facing the balcony. One of the thrones was set back as though it were waiting for someone to eventually fill it. The other was set forward and centered on the dais. Dragon was especially amazed by the beauty of this room and asked Brenath if they were at the top of the center tower.

The only reply that Brenath could give was. "Certainly not. We are very close to the top. Outside each entrance is another set of stairs leading up to the watchtower. Right above the throne room rests the watchtower, whose windows open on all six sides, allowing the guards to see a great distance in every direction. In the middle of the watchtower, there was a set of spiral stairs going up to the last room of the tower. There on the pinnacle of the tower, rests a great horn.

I'm sorry to say that it is believed to be a dragon horn. Nevertheless, no other horn could do what this one can. If it is blown in times of danger, the sound that echoes forth from it could be heard at great distances in any direction. Some from the town of Falistoran said that they had heard the horn of Tyrilcrysalith. Whether or not that's true, we'll probably never know."

Though Dragon did not like the fact that the horn might have been a dragon's, he was intrigued, nonetheless. He then stood out on the balcony, looking down upon the great city of Tyrilcrysalith, still in awe of its beauty. Dragon couldn't help but compare any place to his home. Still, Tyrilcrysalith was great enough to make him feel at ease.

Finally, after a few brief conversations, Queen Crysaia entered the throne room and walked out onto the balcony. "Oh, good. All of you are here. It is almost time," Crysaia announced.

"Almost time for what?" Dragon asked. At the same time, he was trying not to stare at the queen, for she had on a silver-colored dress that was loose for dancing. Still, it did not diminish her beauty.

"You are about to see another beauty of Tyrilcrysalith. Look out upon the city, and you'll understand what I mean in a moment."

The entire company looked over the balcony wall down toward the city and out over the sea, waiting in anticipation. However, the marvel did not take long to show itself. As the sun began to set, something beautiful began to happen. When the sun touched the top of the water, it began to magnify its brilliance. It seemed as if the light of the sun was being funneled across the water and into the harbor, and once the light hit the city, the city itself began to shine.

The gemmed buildings began to be illuminated, as if a fire had been lit in the middle of them, and they put forth a light of their own. The city became a brilliant flash of different colors that lit up high into the sky. As Dragon continued to watch, he was amazed, for when the sun disappeared, the brilliance of the city did not. The city continued to shine as brightly as it did when the sun first hit it. As much as Dragon loved his city, he had never seen such a marvel.

After sunset, music began to rise from the courtyard to the balcony. The celebration had begun. The whole company was quite taken over by the music, and their bodies seemed as though they wanted to move whether they wanted them to or not. The one taken over the most by the music was Sonya, whose great body could not contain the urge. She swayed from side to side and wagged her tail impulsively as she looked over the balcony and down at the people dancing in the courtyard and through the streets. She then looked at Dragon, pouting and longing to join the crowd.

Dragon walked up beside her and brushed his hand gently against her cheek. Then he gave her a nice, warm hug. He then nodded in compliance to her wishes, and she sprang up and leaped off the balcony. Sonya let her body plummet along the towers down toward the courtyard. Just before she reached the bottom, she unfurled her wings and slowed her descent. Still, people got out of the way quickly, and she landed on the ground with a nice thud.

The people of Tyrilcrysalith were very accepting of all races, so they didn't run, but they didn't move either. They were waiting to see what she was going to do. Seeing their reaction, Sonya left her wings open, while slowly folding them back. She then lifted her head high up in the air and began to sing. The melody that came out of her mouth was magnificent, and it echoed throughout the city. The melody seemed to amplify the music of the city, and together they made such a symphony. In only a few moments, the people were dancing again. As the music continued to play, some found themselves dancing around and beneath Sonya. As for herself, Sonya enjoyed singing and dancing with the people; her heart was as free as a dragon should be.

***

Back up on the balcony, the entire company looked down, watching Sonya enjoy herself. Then Tobin offered to take the group down to enjoy the celebration. Dragon refused. The others, on the other hand, liked the idea and went off with him. Crysaia then nodded to Brenath and Cromwin, saying that she would like a moment alone. Not even asking why, the two left quietly and respectfully. She then stood next to Dragon on the balcony, gracefully leaning on the edge of the wall that was looking out over her city.

"You have some wonderful friends," Crysaia said, trying her best to start a conversation.

"Yes, you could say that," Dragon replied, relishing the chance to talk to Crysaia. He wasn't quite sure what it was about her, but he enjoyed her company. "My old teacher and mentor used to tell me that a person's wealth is better counted by friends and not riches. Being one as young as myself, I haven't found out whether or not that's true."

"I'm sure it is, Dragon, and I'm also sure that you will need as many friends as you can on this journey of yours." Crysaia spoke as carefully as she could, trying to purposefully direct the conversation.

"I doubt that. I was hoping to leave the two here and move on with only Sonya," Dragon said, a little agitated, thinking about all the trouble that he had been through so far.

"I'm sorry to hear that because I found someone who would love to help you," Crysaia mumbled, almost as if she dreaded saying it.

"Now who in this city would you find who would want to take up with me?"

At that moment, Tilly reappeared on Crysaia's shoulder. And then she jumped down to the ledge, standing right in front of Dragon.

Startled by this, Dragon turned to Crysaia with a face filled with betrayal. Crysaia saw the look on his face and quickly interceded to defend Tilly. "Now, Dragon, just listen to her!"

"What, more dark things to say that you didn't say the last time?" Dragon snapped.

"I was wrong!" Tilly snapped back.

"What was that?" Dragon asked, now more confused than ever. The last thing he expected from her after their last encounter was an apology.

"I was wrong. I thought I was being punished by being given an ordinary individual. I did not know of your abilities or the great trials that lie ahead of you."

"I wish I was ordinary, so I wouldn't have to take part in any of this!" Dragon leaned closer to Tilly, glaring at her. "I was driven from my city to do the Creator's bidding, and he even has you watching over me! The worst part of it all is that I didn't want this, and he never asked me. Therefore, I will never do what he tells me to, so I don't need you!" Dragon glanced over at Crysaia to see her reaction to his comment.

Crysaia showed no disregard for his comment; she merely moved closer to him and laid her hand gently upon his back, rubbing it lightly. Then she interceded again. "Dragon, you are looking at this the wrong way, just like Tilly was."

Dragon was strangely calmed by the very touch of Crysaia's hand. The moment she touched his back, his body seemed to relax and calm itself. He began to feel drawn toward Crysaia, and he would have believed her right away if it weren't for his stubborn streak. "What do you mean?"

"Simply this: Tilly should be one of your greatest friends and allies. Her very life depends on obeying the Creator's wishes. Believe it or not, she is more trapped than you are. You at least have the opportunity to refuse. She does not, so that makes her more of an ally than you know."

Dragon stood for a moment, silent, knowing that what Crysaia said was true, even though he didn't want to believe it. He then leaned forward to look at Tilly face-to-face. "Perhaps we were both too harsh on each other. I will befriend you. However, this does not mean that I will do the Creator's bidding."

Tilly nodded in understanding and then turned and nodded at Crysaia, thanking her for her help. Then, in a flash of light, she disappeared, leaving the two alone on the balcony. The two stood silently beside each other, staring out over the city for a long time.

Then eventually, Crysaia broke the silence. "So you won't obey the Creator?" She waited a moment for Dragon to respond. When he remained silent, she continued. "I don't blame you. There are days I don't even want to be queen. Especially when you know there is a great darkness before you."

Intrigued by that comment, Dragon finally broke his silence. "What do you mean by that?"

"Dragon, I will tell you a secret," she began as her face took on a sad look. "There was a prophecy given to my grandfather a hundred years ago when he was young. Ever since it was spoken, it has troubled the royalty of this city. It was prophesied that the two great cities would someday disappear by a great tragedy. It is said that Atlantis would be swallowed by the sea and disappear forever. Atlantis would never be found, but it would be remembered across the earth. For Tyril-crysalith, it is to be destroyed by a great upheaval of the land. Its gems would be scattered across the earth, for others to fight over. As for the memory of this place, unlike Atlantis, we are to be forgotten forever."

Crysaia paused for a moment, taking a deep breath and absorbing the harshness of her own words. "The kings and queens of Atlantis do not believe this prophecy. However, in my heart, I know it to be true." She turned to look at Dragon, her eyes filled with tears. "My greatest fear is that this will happen during my rule, that somehow I will be the cause of this!" She then turned from him and leaned back against the balcony wall.

As Crysaia's right hand lay on the balcony wall, Dragon put his hand upon hers and held it gently. He then looked her in the face with all sincerity he felt and spoke his mind. "I am no seer, nor do I know much about my own future, but I will tell you this: I believe this great misfortune will not happen during your reign as queen. It will be left for your great descendants to deal with."

"How can you be so certain?" Crysaia asked, looking into Dragon's eyes for some sign of hope.

"I just know this; trust me," Dragon replied as he gently wiped a tear from her cheek.

With that said, the two looked back down toward the courtyard, where all the celebration was going on. As they continued to watch the others dance, there was a peace that came over them both. They had confided in each other about their troubles and found support in their time of darkness. They stood still together, holding each other's hands and for once, not worrying about what tomorrow might bring.

Later on, that night, as the festivities ended, Sonya and Yolana went to their own room to sleep, eager for tomorrow. Phanis went to his room as well, and the moment his head lay upon the pillow, he was out and dreaming of wonderful things.

As for Dragon, he stayed up many hours later than all the rest. He sat perched on the windowsill like a bird of prey, with his feet tucked up underneath him and his arms hanging to his side. Many thoughts went through his head, and half of them were on Crysaia. He took a deep breath, and another thought came to mind. "Sixteen," he whispered to the night air. "How much have I endured? What more magnificent things will I see in my lifetime? Good or bad, I have encountered more than I ever expected, and what will tomorrow bring?" Dragon was conflicted inside. A part of him was eager for tomorrow to see Crysaia and speak with her more. But the other half of him feared tomorrow and what the Creator might have in store for him. After a while of running those thoughts around in his head, Dragon eventually went to bed with a heavy heart, and as he slept, his dreams were filled with both good and bad.

11

Morning Brings Death

The group rose early that morning, just as the sun was beginning to rise. After a good night of fun and fine rest, they awoke very refreshed. They had a filling meal with the queen in the dining hall, the same one where they ate the night before. The only difference was that in the morning, there were a lot more people in the room. Dragon still had to watch his table manners, afraid that Sonya might smack him again if he tried to eat as he normally did. When the company had filled their stomachs to their heart's desires, they rose and then accompanied the queen down to the secret walls.

There, deep beneath the city, they found themselves at the end of a set of stairs, looking down an enormous hall. It led east away from the sea; the end was as far as one could see. The hall was perfectly square, thirty feet on each side, which made Dragon believe at first perhaps that the dwarves built it. When he examined the walls, he was more perplexed: they were a mixture of gray and white, like marble, yet they were as hard as a diamond. Strangely, the hall held its own light, like the gym buildings of the city, looking as bright as day. The ceiling and the wall to the left were white, and the floor and the wall to the right were gray.

It didn't help ease his confusion when Crysaia told him that they didn't know what the material was. As they walked down the great hall, Dragon then learned that it had not been built by dwarves. Every thirty feet on the side walls were pillars that went up to the ceiling, and in between the pillars were writings carved into the walls. At first, the writings were simple—the first four languages of the humans and then those of the other races.

The next to be written were the eight known languages of dwarves, followed by the twelve known languages of the elves. In between each race, there were six or more walls of what appeared to be the same type of language but were unknown. When the company looked to the right to see the other wall, they only became more puzzled. On the gray walls, it seemed as though the same language had been written down, but only backward or twisted, making them unreadable. So the group didn't bother with the gray wall; they merely looked toward the white wall. Dragon walked over to one of the white walls that contained a form of dwarven script. He placed his fingers on the writing, tracing it as he read.

"Can you read the dwarf language?" Crysaia asked. "We had many dwarf scholars and historians translate this wall, but it is one of the unknown languages. A dwarf historian thought it must be one of the original dwarven languages lost at the beginning of time."

"Because of the dragon language, I can read pretty much anything," Dragon responded. "This wall speaks of how to build pillars as tall as fifty feet in height. The pillars will not weather or fall in a thousand-year period. They will also produce light so that when two or more stand within a hundred feet of one another, it will create a barrier through which dark creatures cannot pass." Dragon stepped back and looked at Crysaia. "Is this some of the knowledge that was used to build Atlantis?"

"Yes," Crysaia replied. "The walls that could be translated were used in the building of Atlantis. However, some of the walls are great words of wisdom and not building instructions."

Dragon thought of that for a moment as he looked at the gray walls. "Those must be the opposite—how to undo what has been done," he thought out loud.

"Probably, but no one has been able to read those walls, at least no one that we know of," Crysaia said.

"I bet the Deceiver can," Sonya muttered.

Eventually, they continued farther down the hall. After they had passed the ninety-seventh wall segment, there were no more recognizable languages; nevertheless, the group kept going.

Finally, they reached the end of the hall after passing a hundred and seventy-two wall segments. The last wall was far from being the least, and Crysaia explained its greatness.

"Many of these walls have been examined by different races, including the high elves—or light elves as some will say. They not only looked at their own languages, but they tried to translate all the others. Even the dwarves did their best to translate the walls. So far, only seven of the unrecognizable languages on the walls have been translated. Still, many every year continue to try to translate the rest. All we know is that from the stairs leading in, the walls began to speak of times long ago and great deeds that were done. Farther in, they reveal even more—magic, knowledge, and wisdom beyond understanding. As you know, some of the knowledge helped to build the city of

Atlantis. It was believed that if someone could read all the walls, they would be all powerful. That is why we guard the city very carefully."

Crysaia then pointed to the gray walls to the right with a look of dread on her face. "We believe that these are an evil version of what you see. As you said, an opposite. If darkness took the city and knew how to read these walls, good would forever be driven from all lands. However, the wall we fear the most is this one."

Crysaia finally showed the group the last wall, which stood in between both sides at the end of the hall. The wall was neither white nor gray; it seemed to be more transparent, and it held no reflection. The entire company seemed to be awestricken by it.

"Why do you fear it so much?" Phanis asked out of simple curiosity.

"Touch it and you'll understand," Crysaia replied, urging the group to do so.

The entire company did as she asked and reached forward to touch the wall. As they did, the writings on the walls seemed to sink farther away, and as they pulled back, the writings returned. The company was quite taken aback by the walls' reaction to their presence. Dragon, however, was intrigued by the wall for a whole different reason. He was the only one in the company who actually dared to physically touch the wall. As he stood there with his hands against the wall, his face filled with both wonder and pain.

"This is more wondrous than you know," Dragon commented, sounding as if he wanted to cry. "The last wall to my left is old, indeed. It is the oldest language of the dragons, said to come from the time when the dragons walked in the gardens with the Creator. My old mentor, Ancient, was the last dragon alive that could read only a partial of it. The writings before me are older still. I have seen them before. Deep within the city of the dragons, there is a great cornerstone with these writings upon it. No one could read them. It was rumored that the Creator himself wrote them." Dragon then placed his forehead against the wall as though it would bring him closer to the home he had loved so much.

Sonya and the others gave Dragon his moment of peace; they all stepped back and started looking at the other walls, discussing their ideas of what they might mean. Crysaia was the only one who stayed. Her heart went out to Dragon, and she longed to comfort him. She took a step forward and placed her right hand on the wall and her left on Dragon's right hand. This was the first time in all her life that she ever dared to touch that particular wall. Dragon slowly lifted his head and looked at her, his face still showing sorrow. He noticed her hand on his, and he didn't pull away, for it gave him comfort and peace, though his thoughts were still heavy with the knowledge of his great quest.

"It's not fair," Dragon said, feeling the urge to scream. "I have been sent out from my city to give mankind a chance for redemption. From what I've seen so far, I wonder if it's worth it? I wonder over, the course of thousands of years, what will mankind become?"

Crysaia stared Dragon deep in the eyes, understanding only a portion of the pain that he was going through. Still, she felt the need to encourage him no matter what. "I'm not sure if this will help or not, but I will tell you what my father told me. When I was young, he told me that there is darkness deep within the heart of man. That everyone sooner or later will have to choose whether to starve the darkness out or feed it and let it grow. He said right now you don't see very much evil, because we are even with it—there is as much good as there is bad in the lands. However, there will come a day hundreds of thousands of years from now when good is greatly outnumbered, almost to the point of annihilation. Still, evil will not win as long as there are people pure of heart and song."

"Indeed, I will say your father was a wise man, but that does not help me. For that is what I fear the most—that mankind will take this chance for redemption and breed a new evil. With none of the ancient races to help guide them or control them, they will become like a flood that will cover the earth in blood."

Dragon looked at Crysaia, agitated. He knew she was trying to help, but he did not see her point. "Let me ask you this: why should I continue my quest? Why should I tell the dragons to fade when mankind needs them more than they know?"

"Perhaps it is because mankind needs to choose its own fate." Crysaia now turned toward Dragon, still holding his hand, and placed her other hand on his cheek. "Perhaps you are not meant to do this for mankind but for people who deserve it. Don't trust in mankind. Put your trust in individuals. Mankind may be filled with evil, but the people in this city are not. Are they not worth it? Or what about me? Am I not worth it?"

Dragon took a step back, shocked by her remark and the truth within it. He stood staring at her, unwilling to answer her question. This was the first time in his life that he had ever been conflicted between the two races. He suddenly realized that he had begun to have feelings for her that he didn't understand and that he was unwilling to harm her with his words.

Crysaia was somewhat hurt by his silence, yet she could understand his reason for it. She simply respected him and turned back to the great wall. "So it seems as though our cities have a connection after all," she replied, trying to find a way to keep the conversation going. "Perhaps you were meant—"

Crysaia's words were suddenly drowned out by the sound of a horn. The sound that echoed down the hall seemed as though someone had blown a horn just a few feet from them. The whole group turned around quickly, both startled and confused.

"What is that?" Dragon demanded to know.

Crysaia replied quickly with a look of fear on her face, "That is the horn of Tyrilcrysalith. The city is in peril!"

Without hesitation, the entire group acted quickly. Sonya bent down and demanded that everyone climb up on her back; the journey back would be too slow on human feet. So as quickly as they could, Crysaia and Yolana climbed onto Sonya's back with the help of Phanis, who scurried up after them. Dragon, on the other hand, decided to run beside Sonya. Without further delay, they ran down the hall and back up the stairs to see what had befallen the city.

***

Brenath, Cromwin, and Tobin stood with several other guards in the watchtower at the top of Tyrilcrysalith. As the great horn blew above them, Brenath stood still, looking out toward the east. In his hand, he held a hollow branch, and it had two diamonds of different sizes, one on either end. This device allowed him to see at a great distance off, like an elf's eyes. When Brenath looked through the device, his face went as pale as the mountain snow.

It was shortly after the fourth time the horn blew that the company and the queen entered the watchtower. Some of the company looked over and down at the city to see the people running quickly to the towers for safety. Dragon and Crysaia looked toward Brenath for answers as to what was going on.

"Dragons, my queen. Lots of dragons coming from the east!" exclaimed Brenath.

"It's impossible!" Dragon responded quickly and stepped back in shock. The last thing he remembered about dragons was that all of them should fade. So it troubled him why the dragons were awake, even though he longed to see more dragons.

Brenath handed Dragon the seeing device and pointed to the east. "Look for yourself. I count at least seventeen."

Dragon having no need for the device, handed it back, stepped toward the edge, and looked out. His dragon eyes were keen, and he could see farther than any elf. He lifted his hand to shade his eyes from the sun, and as he did, he saw what looked like dark clouds moving closer in the distance. "You were right. There are dragons coming," he verified. "However, you're wrong. There are not seventeen but only sixteen of them. There are a few that are bigger than Sonya. The rest are her size or smaller."

"It doesn't matter how many or how big they are. We have been betrayed!" a voice shouted behind them.

Everyone in the watchtower turned to see Malic standing there with a grim look on his face. "The king of the dragons had spied out our defenses, and now he has sent for his army. He has betrayed our hospitality. Kill him!" Malic shouted to the guards.

Dragon immediately took a defensive stance and growled at the guards. The guards themselves looked to Queen Crysaia to see if she would give such an order. For a small moment, no one did or said anything. Eventually, Brenath stepped in between Dragon and the guards, pleading to the queen.

"My queen, I believe Malic is wrong. I've seen Dragon and Sonya in battle. I believe if they wanted to take the city, they could do it by themselves. I may have only known Dragon for a short time, but I trust him. Perhaps the dragons are friendly?"

"I can't believe you're going to listen to these lies," Malic continued to plead his case.

Crysaia was both scared and confused, and she didn't know whom to trust. She looked into Dragon's eyes, looking for some trace of hope and truth. "What do you say, Dragon King?" Crysaia said regally, offering Dragon a chance to plead his case.

Dragon relaxed from his defensive stance and stared back at the queen. For a moment, he stood silent, not knowing how to respond, for he himself was conflicted inside. He drew upon the thoughts of Ancient and his wisdom, which helped him make his decision. "I do not know these dragons; however, since I am the king, I will take responsibility for their actions. I will command them to fade. If they do so, they are good. On the other hand, if they disobey my command, I will know they are evil. So I will do everything in my power to help defend this city."

Crysaia took a deep breath and nodded. "I accept your decision in this matter."

"What!" Malic said. "I can't believe you are going to do this!"

"Malic!" Dragon quickly shouted at him. "If you have any magic other than hiding, I suggest you use it."

Malic, of course, took this as an insult and stormed off down the stairs and back into the city. Dragon then turned to Brenath to give him a few commands. "Get everyone that needs protecting into a safe place. Right now, your archers are your best defense. Have them aim for the eyes, not the scales. Also, if they get a chance, tell them to fire down the dragon's throat. Let us hope they are peaceful. If they are not, wait for my signal."

"How will I know your signal?" Brenath asked, halfway turning to the stairs, ready to bolt into action.

"You will know when you see it and hear it. Now go. Everyone except Sonya and I must leave the watchtower."

Everyone began to leave the tower and head back down the stairs. Before Phanis left, Dragon quickly grabbed his arm and whispered to him, "You and Yolana stay close to the queen. I do not trust the wizard." Phanis nodded in compliance and then left the tower in search of the queen. Soon Sonya and Dragon stood alone, staring out toward the east, watching a cloud of dragons move closer to the city.

"Dragon, I'm worried," Sonya said. "We've never gone up against dragons in a real battle before. Are you sure we can do this?" Even though dragons' facial expressions were different from those of the humans, anyone could tell the look of fear on Sonya's face.

"I'm pretty sure we can," Dragon responded confidently. "I believe your father trained us well—at least better than they probably were." Dragon smirked as he pointed out at the oncoming dragons.

Sonya gently put her finger on the side of Dragon's face, turning it so she could look him in the eye. "I think what I meant was, are we ready to kill our own kind? What if the humans provoked them and we're defending the wrong side?"

Dragon stood for a moment, looking at her, showing in his eyes that he too felt the same way. He then pushed past those feelings and answered as best as he could. "I do not believe the people in this city could provoke them. This is a peaceful city. I may not want to harm my own kind, but the people here need protection. Also, Ancient and your father taught us to defend the innocent, even from dragons."

Sonya nodded in understanding and agreement. Then they both looked out again at the coming storm that they now had to face. Dragon took a step forward and let out a high-pitched bellow, commanding the dragons to fade. Immediately after, he could see from far away a fire spark come hurtling out of a dragon's mouth.

Dragon and Sonya stood still as the ball of fire came toward them, striking just below the watchtower. It hit the side of the tower with a deafening explosion, yet it only left the side of the diamond tower merely scorched. Then Dragon shook his head in disappointment. "This is not what I was looking forward to. We must see to the defense of the city."

"At least we have one thing in our favor," Sonya commented, a slight smirk on her face.

"What's that?" Dragon demanded to know, curious about how she could find something humorous in a time like this.

"They have a terrible aim," she sarcastically remarked as she looked over at the scorched wall.

Dragon gave a quick chuckle at her remark and then took a serious stance and reached for his sword, Truth. Earlier that morning, he had decided to wear it for some odd reason. He couldn't explain it, but something within the deep recesses of his mind told him that he would need it. At first, he thought of merely impressing the queen, but the longer he wore it, the more he thought he looked very kingly with it on. And now, at this dark hour, he was grateful that he listened to his instinct. He pulled it off from around his back and then drew it from its sheath, and as he did, it sparked like the sun.

He quickly turned away from the bright flash, and when it subsided, he looked back at the sword. Truth stood in his hand, gleaming bright and strong. The handle was still a white dragon with its wings opened wide, and the eyes glittered emerald-like Dragon's. As Dragon looked at it, the sword rang as though it were eager for battle. Smiling, Dragon gripped Truth tightly and glared out at the oncoming foes.

"Let us show evil how the good fight!" yelled Dragon, ever so sure of himself. He and Sonya let out a roar and then rushed to the edge of the tower. They both jumped simultaneously over the ledge and out into the open air. In mid-jump, Sonya flew beneath Dragon, catching him on her back. Losing no time or momentum, they flew quickly toward the dragons.

Dragon rode close to Sonya's back, quickly trying to formulate a battle strategy. His eyes widened with a sudden thought, and he tapped Sonya on the side three times. She turned her head and glared at him, wondering if this was, in fact, what he wanted to do. Dragon nodded, reassuring her that this would work. She turned her head back around and headed toward the dragons with increasing speed.

It wasn't long before several of the dragons sent fireballs hurling at the two of them. Sonya quickly weaved through the fireballs, missing every single one. And then they were right in front of the dragons.

Dragon patted Sonya one more time and then stood up. Using the wind, he slid right down her back to the tip of her tail. Sonya quickly wrapped her tail around Dragon and launched him over her back and at the dragons. She then turned right and did a quick somersault in the air, piercing one of the dragons right through the chest with her tail. After the dragon made a quick squeal and died in midair, she jumped to the next closest dragon. Rolling up and over its wings and landing on its back, she bit deep into the dragon's neck. At the same time, she used her hind legs and kicked the dragon's wings, breaking them and sending the dragon plummeting down. Sonya then looked frantically around her for the next dragon to fight.

While Sonya flew off, Dragon was hurled headfirst straight toward a group of dragons. He let his body hang back as he held Truth aloft with both hands. To the dragons, this look seemed inviting, and one flew in close to take a bite. However, the speed at which Dragon was hurled was surprisingly fast, and the dragon missed, biting down right above him. Truth, on the other hand, did not miss; the mighty sword hit the dragon's lower jaw and sliced down his body as if it were cutting through water. The dragon made horrible noises as his chest and belly were sliced open, and then it curled up and fell. Dragon, of course, was still hurling through the group of dragons when suddenly he hit the side of a dragon's neck. He quickly grabbed one of the scales and held on tightly. Then he pulled himself up to the back of the dragon's neck, still holding tightly on to the scales.

As the dragon shook his head back and forth, trying to free himself of Dragon, Dragon raised his sword high and thrust it through the back of the dragon's head. This dragon made no noise; it simply stiffened and began to plummet. Quickly responding, Dragon stood up and, using the dead dragon's body as a foothold, launched himself high into the air. Soaring high, he passed by another dragon; and as he did, he quickly cut off its wing. However, his momentum did not stop there. He went higher yet and smacked into the belly of another dragon. With his left hand, Dragon gripped tightly to a belly scale, and with the other hand, he plunged Truth into the belly. He hung on to the dragon's belly, desperately clinging for his life. Though the dragon felt the pain of the sword and was not happy, he began to claw and kick at Dragon. He even tried to use his tail to knock Dragon off him.

Nevertheless, Dragon did his best to fight off the assault and cling to the dragon's belly. After a while, he looked down and realized that they were now flying over the city and that several dragons had landed within the city. He knew that somehow, he needed to get down to the city safely. So when the dragon bent his head down to take a look at the pest clinging to his belly, Dragon moved. He pulled Truth out, and with his best aim possible, he flung the sword at the dragon's head.

Truth struck the dragon through the neck and into its head, killing it instantly.

As the dragon began to fall, Dragon clung desperately with both hands to its belly. Then he realized that perhaps this was not one of his best ideas. The dragon twisted and turned, continuing to plummet, and all that Dragon could see was a blur. He knew that this probably would not end well. Still, he pushed himself away from the dragon. As His body flung away rapidly, it suddenly smacked into something. He felt a painful sting on his back, and then he was surrounded by water.

***

Brenath, Cromwin, and Tobin stood upon the parapet that surrounded the inside of the mountain walls. There were three levels of these protective walkways, which came out from the towers and around the mountain all the way to the peninsula guard towers. The three captains stood on the north side, with hundreds of archers following their every lead.

With the first whoosh of dragons overhead, a burst of fire fell into the city, and everyone leaped back into the cracks within the mountainside. Starting with Brenath, yelling ensued from leader to leader as they hoped to gain control over the archers and their fears. The dragons were terrifying; they made a high-pitched whine the closer they got and brought a gust of wind when they passed over. Not to mention, they let out bursts of fire in all directions, striking whatever humans they saw. Brenath organized the archers to fire just before or just after the dragons passed. Needless to say, it had no effect; it merely bounced off the scales. The archers couldn't get a good aim on the eyes or the throat, as Dragon had told them to. Brenath began to feel a little overwhelmed, unable to do anything even though he had superior numbers.

After a group of dragons had passed, Brenath and Tobin stuck their heads out from the crack that led into the mountain hiding place.

They looked around, desperately trying to think of something they could do. The two of them also glared up at the sky, hoping to find Dragon and Sonya, their only real hope in this battle. Brenath immediately caught sight of an enormous dragon plummeting toward the lower city. As he looked closer, he could see something small push itself off from the dragon's body and crash into the bay. "Dragon," Brenath muttered to himself, thinking that he had lost one of his greatest assets and a new friend.

"Brenath," Tobin yelled as he grabbed his brother by the shoulder and pointed up to the sky. Looking in the direction of the upper city, the two of them could see a familiar red dragon furiously fighting three smaller dragons. Like a bunch of vultures over a dead piece of meat, they swarmed around Sonya. It wasn't long before they had forced her down into the city, gripping and biting at every limb she had. "Sonya!" Tobin yelled furiously as he ran out from the crack and wildly shot an arrow at the dragons, hurting his friend.

At that same moment, Brenath could hear a high-pitched whine growing louder. Without hesitating, he yelled at Tobin to come back within the confines of the mountain's shelter. Unfortunately, it was too late. A burst of fire struck the mountainside, shaking everything around Brenath. "Tobin!" Brenath yelled after his little brother, thinking he had lost the last member of his family. He fell to his knees, clenching his fist and roaring in anger at his failure to protect his little brother. That all abruptly stopped when Brenath heard a familiar voice call back, letting his brother know he was all right. Brenath couldn't hear much from the noise of fire outside his fortification, but what he could hear brought him to his feet quickly.

Tobin had notified him that he was stuck with fire on either side and could not get to any shelter. Brenath immediately began thinking of ways to reach his brother. Then he heard a high-pitched whine. This sound, however, didn't sound like it did previously. It sounded as though it was coming directly toward him, as if it were coming for something specific. Thinking only of his brother, Brenath bolted to the entrance of his shelter and drew his bow. He leaped from the entrance of the crack in the mountainside, and in midair, he caught a glimpse of something flying toward his brother. He released his arrow. Brenath's bold attempt was not meant to kill the dragon; it was merely to distract him, hoping it would give his brother a chance to get away. To his and Tobin's shock, the arrow struck the dragon right in the eye, making him stop and howl in pain. The moment the dragon opened his mouth and bellowed out, Cromwin emerged from another crack in the mountainside and shot an arrow right down the dragon's throat. Gasping as he choked on his own blood, the dragon fell toward the city and landed on an emerald building's top. Fortunately, this building top spiraled up into a nice spike that pierced the dragon when he fell upon it.

Gasping for air and his face filled with shock that he had survived on the mere luck of his brother and his friend, Tobin finally made his way past the fire to help his brother to his feet, who was equally shocked at their triumph. Only glances could be exchanged at that moment, and when they tried to speak words, they were in trouble again. Another dragon had seen what happened and approached, hovering low over the city and glaring at them. Before they fully knew what was happening, the dragon had opened his mouth as wide as he could, and the gleam of flames began to rise from his throat. However, before the dragon could get the fire out of his mouth, hundreds of archers, who swore their allegiance to Tyrilcrysalith and the captains, materialized out of their hiding places. Their bows were drawn full length, and their eyes glared with hope and determination. With the twang of bowstrings, the arrows were hurled into the dragon's eyes and down his throat, dropping him to the city in a scream of death. The mountainside erupted with the cheers of victory, and hope scattered throughout all the soldiers. Brenath and Tobin, realizing that they were lucky on both counts, moved back into the mountainside with all the other archers, hoping that this would be over soon.

***

Dragon was slightly disorientated when he fell into the bay, yet he gathered what sense he could and swam to the surface. When his head surfaced, his eyes were blurred, and his head rang with pain. After a few moments, his vision cleared, and the ringing went away. He realized that he wasn't that far from the docks. Also, neither was the dragon that he killed, which was lying with its back on a building and its head on the walkway with the sword still in it. Dragon quickly swam ashore and got out of the water. He was still slightly disoriented, and the pain in his back was great. Nevertheless, he moved along as fast as he could, right to the dragon's head, and pulled Truth out.

Dragon looked up into the city, only to see more disaster. However, what caught his eye first was a large dragon chasing something small through the buildings. After a moment, he realized that the small being was the female dwarf that he had insulted the day before. Knowing that her odds were slim, Dragon picked up what speed he could to render assistance. As Dragon ran to help her, he could see her skill at work. The female dwarf ducked and dodged around the dragon and between the buildings, evading his bite. Occasionally, she'd take a swing with her ax, knocking the dragon's head away, simply to avoid being eaten. It wasn't long before the dragon knocked her off her feet with his tail and sent her ax flying away. The dragon then had her pinned to the ground, getting ready to eat her.

Dragon came running up. He jumped and kicked his feet against the side of a building, springing up and over the top of the dragon's head. He then came down fast, thrusting the sword through the dragon's eye, right into its brain. The dragon rolled over with a wail and then died, its body still twitching. Dragon pulled out Truth and then kicked the dragon's head in disgust. He walked over to pick up the dwarf's ax and hand it to her.

"Are you all right?" Dragon asked, hoping that now she would think better of him than she did the day before.

The female dwarf quickly got up, walked over to Dragon, and took the ax from his hands aggressively. She then violently pushed him and began to yell. "How dare you! That dragon was mine to kill!"

Dragon knew little of dwarves and their ways; still, her reaction seemed peculiar even for dwarves. He finally got tired of her attitude and yelled back, "I just saved your life!"

"I'll tell you what you just did: you just stole my great kill and the honor that went with it!" The dwarf continued to rant and rave and even spat at Dragon's feet.

Dragon took a step forward to make a rude reply when, suddenly, he heard a familiar roar. Without hesitating, he quickly turned and bolted up into the city, leaving the female dwarf behind. He ran up and into the middle of the ruby buildings, only to find Sonya pinned to the ground by three smaller dragons half her size. Even though the dragons were smaller, they were very muscular and had many horns protruding from their heads and backs; even their tails were sharpened like spears. All three seem to be related, and they had the same dark-green scale. Two held Sonya down with their arms, legs, and tails, while the third was standing on top of her chest, with his long tail raised like a scorpion over his back.

As the third dragon raised his tail high to pierce her chest, his eyes gleamed, and he grinned. For that instant, Dragon stood there, horrified, knowing that he needed to do something quick. So without thinking, he hurled Truth as hard as he could at the dragon standing on top of Sonya. To Dragon's surprise, his aim wasn't that bad. Truth struck the dragon right in the chest, piercing its heart. The dragon quickly keeled off of Sonya and fell to the ground, dead.

At that instant, one of the other dragons looked up, growing angry. It then let go of Sonya and sprinted toward Dragon in an attempt at vengeance. This gave Sonya a chance to bring one arm and her tail up to begin wrestling with the last dragon.

As for Dragon, he stood staring at the oncoming assault of a vicious dragon without a weapon in hand. He knew that he definitely had to rely on his non-weapon training. He stood still for a moment, and as the dragon attempted to bite down at him, he quickly jumped to the side. However, he didn't move fast enough. One of the dragon's long horns from its head cut Dragon's forearm. In spite of the pain, Dragon brought his fist up and pounded the dragon's head into the ground. From there, he reached for the dragon's horns in an attempt to use them as leverage. Then suddenly, he was knocked away by the dragon's tail.

Once Dragon landed on the ground, he tried to pick himself up as fast as he could, but the green-scaled adversary was surprisingly fast. The dragon slammed him back down to the ground with his tail, and then he quickly pinned Dragon down with his hands. As the green dragon bent down to bite him, Dragon's heart froze, for he thought that this might be the end. Just as the dragon's mouth was only a few inches from his face, Dragon saw an ax fly right over his head. The ax went right into the dragon's mouth and lodged itself deep within its throat. The dragon jumped back, choking on its own blood and slowly breathing its last breath.

Even though he was in a lot of pain, Dragon quickly picked himself up and looked behind him. He saw the female dwarf standing there, stout, with a big smile on her face. Then she began to laugh as she came closer.

"Don't think I will let you get out of owing me a dragon," the female dwarf said sarcastically.

"You've just killed a dragon, isn't that enough?" Even though the dwarf had just saved his life, Dragon really didn't want to deal with her. She was more trouble than she was worth, he thought to himself.

"That one doesn't count. It was smaller than the one I had before," the dwarf continued. Even though the battle was still raging around them, she was unwilling to let this matter drop.

Dragon rolled his eyes in annoyance and then walked off to see how Sonya was faring. To his delight, she was doing very well and had just killed a dragon. She was standing on the dead body with a wing in her mouth and her tail through its head. He was overjoyed and congratulated her on her victory. He then walked over to the dead dragon that held Truth still in its chest and pulled his sword out.

As he did, he looked at the blade and watched the blood melt off of it, leaving no stain. The blade itself was still shining brightly, and it had no notches or scratches on it. Dragon grinned and realized that he had a great marvel in his hands. Then, together with Sonya, they decided they should go and finish off the rest of the dragons. Just before they took off, Dragon looked back at the one that attacked him. He saw the female dwarf climbing into its mouth to fetch her ax. All he could do was smile for a moment, admiring her fearless attitude—or was it stubbornness? He couldn't tell.

So Dragon and Sonya went and finished off the dragons one by one; as luck would have it, the only dragons left were small. This time they worked more closely as a team, and although they were still outnumbered, they were in no serious danger. Before the sun had reached the highest point in the sky, the battle was over. The city archers claimed three, and Sonya and Dragon took the rest, except for one, which was promptly claimed by the female dwarf. There were only a few casualties among the humans, and the upper city seemed to be healing itself just fine. Most of the damage occurred in the lower city, which didn't have the ability to heal itself. A lot of the buildings were crushed, mainly by dragons falling on top of them. Of course, Dragon and Sonya lent a hand to the city by dragging the dead bodies out into the sea.

By late afternoon, all the dragons had been cleared from the city. Then Dragon and Sonya found Brenath, who was overjoyed to see them. After a few moments of sharing their enthusiasm for surviving this battle, they went to speak to the queen. Making their way through the city, they went back up into the towers to the throne room, where they found Crysaia quietly sitting on her throne. Phanis and Yolana were standing on either side of the throne, doing what Dragon had asked them to do. There were only a few other guards in the room.

Unfortunately, as Dragon and the other two came into the room, so did Malic. They all stood before Crysaia to discuss the current event.

"Thanks to my magic, I have protected the city," boasted Malic.

"Enough of your foolishness," Brenath quickly replied. "While you were hiding in your room, we were out fighting. Anyone with an eye to see knows that Dragon and Sonya saved the city!"

"Saved the city! I doubt that, for they are the ones that brought the trouble here!" Malic shot a distasteful look toward Dragon, almost begging for a conflict.

"Explain your words!" Crysaia demanded.

Malic rubbed his chin, thinking of malicious explanations for the queen. "We have lived peacefully for years. Is it not strange that the day after the king of the dragons arrives in our city, we are attacked by them?"

As Dragon began to snarl at Malic, Brenath stepped in again to keep things calm as best as he could. "Now, Malic, we do not know where those dragons came from or who sent them. It might be mere chance that brought them here at the same time. But what I know is this: if it wasn't for Dragon being here, we wouldn't still be here now."

"I agree with Brenath," Crysaia commented as she rose from her throne, eager to move about the company while she discussed things. "So for the time being, Malic, I ask that you keep your opinions to yourself."

Malic nodded respectfully and let her continue.

"However, Brenath, what concerns me is that the dragons did come. I would like to know why or who commanded them to."

"That is a good question, My queen. The problem is, I do not think we will ever be able to answer it," Brenath said.

Dragon, exhausted from the ordeal earlier, walked over to the empty throne behind the queen's and sat down. Before he had time to rest his head, Malic became enraged, and the rest of the company stared at him in awe. Brenath had a small smirk on his face, thinking that Dragon fit that chair quite perfectly, whether it was disrespectful or not.

"Dragon, out of that throne, you animal," Malic snapped.

Dragon sat there for a moment, glaring at Malic, wondering if he wanted to respond or not. "I am tired and completely worn out, and I do not see any other place to sit."

"I don't care how tired you are. No one deserves to sit on that throne, especially you!" Malic's face turned red; he was completely disgusted by Dragon.

Dragon, having had enough of Malic's attitude, rose from the throne and stepped forward, enraged. "I just saved this city, and I killed my own kind to do it! If anything, I deserve to sit anywhere I like!"

Malic stood quiet for a moment, debating with himself whether or not he should continue this argument. Seeing the need to point out one more detail, he couldn't keep quiet. "Just as I thought, only an animal would kill its own kind."

Dragon stood stunned by those words, unable to do or say anything, except wear a look of pain on his face. However, his companions were not stunned. Phanis stepped forward to do something, but he never got the chance. Yolana stormed in front of Phanis and slapped Malic across the face.

Malic stumbled back, his face turning beet red with anger and pain. He thought he could deal with almost anything, even being slapped by a slave, but being slapped by a female was more than he could handle, and the fact that he could do nothing in return enraged him even more. He quickly turned, grabbed his robes tightly, and stormed out of the throne room.

As for Dragon, he moseyed on over to one of the dais pillars and leaned against it, thinking that sitting caused too much trouble.

Crysaia, on the other hand, was standing in shock, unsure of what to do or say. As a queen, she was completely unprepared for a day like this. Brenath, seeing the look on Crysaia's face, escorted her back to her throne so she could sit and gather her thoughts. Even though she was distraught, she tried to resume the conversation they had earlier. "I wish we knew what was going on. I wish we knew where the dragons came from."

Brenath, standing beside her, could only answer as he did earlier. "I'm sorry, my queen. There were no survivors for us to interrogate. I do not think we will be able to answer that question." Brenath left out the fact that if there was a survivor, he didn't know how to question a dragon.

As Dragon listened to their conversation, an idea popped into his head when he looked at Phanis. "I have an idea," Dragon said, waiting for permission to speak further. After Crysaia nodded toward him, he began to unfold his thoughts. "I'm not sure if it will help or not, but there's a chance. In the town of Falistoran, Phanis's mother is a seer. She might be able to tell you where the dragons came from or who sent them."

"That's true," Phanis added. "She sees more than most. She spoke of Dragon coming to my village years before he appeared." Phanis, of course, liked the idea, hoping to see his mother one more time.

Crysaia thought for a moment and then concluded that it was the best option they had. So she commanded Brenath to take a small group and go to Falistoran to seek this seer. Then she asked a favor of Dragon—if he could accompany the group to the town, and from there, he could go his own way. Of course, Dragon agreed respectfully, seeming as though he couldn't say no to her. He turned to leave the throne room, wanting to clean up from the battle. That's when someone shouted at him.

Looking toward the door, Dragon saw the female dwarf entering the throne room.

"You ain't leaving without me," the female dwarf snapped.

"You have nothing to do with me and my company. Leave me alone!" Dragon shouted back, wondering if there was any way to get rid of this nuisance. He had a hard and emotional day, so he was in no mood to deal with her.

The dwarf walked up to Dragon and shoved her mighty ax toward Dragon's throat. "You have no choice in the matter. You owe me a great kill! And I will follow you whether you like it or not, and the only way you can stop me is if you take that sword of yours and kill me!" The dwarf glared up at Dragon, almost begging him to start something.

Dragon himself was very tempted to reach for his sword, but he stopped when he heard Sonya giggling. He turned, aggravated, only to see her cupping her mouth with her hands, trying very hard not to laugh. Dragon then turned back to the dwarf, his face still looking serious as ever. "I do not think this is funny. Nevertheless, I admire your spirit. Travel with me if you like, and I will see how long you last."

"Wonderful. We will have another traveling companion," Yolana commented.

"You and Phanis are not coming with me!" Dragon blurted out. "I brought you here safely, and this is where I will leave you!" Dragon wasn't trying to be mean; he merely stated a fact; but because of his aggravation with the dwarf, his words came out sharp. As they traveled together, they became close; however, Dragon never said that when they reached a city, they would continue with him.

"What are we supposed to do?" Yolana asked, looking as though she wanted to cry.

"I do not care. Work for the queen if you like," Dragon said as he stormed out of the room, longing for some peace and quiet. Dragon understood what Crysaia was feeling-like there was too much going on and he needed to clear his mind.

Sonya, who was laughing at first, now had a serious look on her face as she looked down at her two companions. She admitted to herself that they were troublesome, yet she had grown accustomed to their company. "I will talk with him," she said to the two, doing her best to encourage them. Then she too left the throne room in search of Dragon.

***

Sunset came and lit the city as night fell, though the city wasn't as bright tonight as it was the night before. Dragon thought it was because the city was too busy healing itself. He found himself walking by the outer walls, near the bay, and looking out over the water. He stood there alone for quite a while, until Sonya finally found him.

"Dragon, I need to talk to you about Phanis and Yolana," she stated as she stood a few feet back, not wanting to upset him.

"There's nothing to talk about," Dragon replied softly, almost as if he didn't want to speak at all.

Sonya came up and lay down beside him, so her head was on the same level as his. "It's a mistake to leave those two here. Believe it or not, they're a little like us. They're free-spirited. To leave them here in servitude to the queen would be no better than leaving them in the other two villages. There is nothing wrong with letting them travel with us. I think you are afraid of befriending anyone that is not a dragon. I think you're afraid it will make you less of a dragon. I know you don't like your human half, but that doesn't mean you have to dislike them."

Dragon didn't move or say anything; he simply stood there, soaking in her words. After the silence seemed as though it was choking them, he responded, "Fine, they can travel with us." He then quickly turned and pointed at her, making sure she was listening. "You will look after them. I will not be their nursemaid."

"What's a nursemaid?" Sonya asked, trying to remember where she heard that word before.

"I'm not quite sure," Dragon responded with a smirk on his face. "Mother said I had them when I was young. I think they're supposed to look after someone."

Sonya smiled and nodded in understanding, then began to get up. As she did, a heavy net fell over her, weighted down by large chunks of marble. When Sonya collapsed back to the ground, men began to come out of nowhere. They jumped from the wall and from buildings, landing on top of her. She let out a mighty roar in her defense. One of the men shot an arrow at Dragon, hitting him in the chest and knocking him back. Lucky for him, his skin was a lot harder than the men anticipated, and the arrow tip sank only halfway in.

Some of the men even started running toward Dragon, wielding swords and axes. This only enraged Dragon as he pulled the arrow from his chest and roared at the men. In his rage, he forgot that Truth was at his side; instead, he began beating at the men with his bare hands. They began to swing violently at him with their weapons, but he dodged each and every blow. Dragon began grabbing the men and ripping their limbs from their bodies. He even took their heads and smashed them against the walls and buildings. One man he hit so hard that his fist went through the man's body. It wasn't long before the fight was over, and Dragon stood over the bodies of the men, dripping in blood.

It wasn't until shortly after that Brenath, Cromwin, and a group of guards came around the corner. They stood still for a moment, in shock at what they saw, and then they slowly went over and helped Dragon cut Sonya loose. They were slow with their movements, not wanting to aggravate Dragon when he was in his rage. They didn't want him to mistake them as a threat.

Once the net had been pulled off of Sonya, Dragon brushed his hand across her cheek. "Are you all right?" he asked, deeply concerned.

"Yes, I think so, though my back is sore from the men jumping on it." Sonya shook her back and ruffled her wings, making sure everything was okay.

Brenath walked over to one of the dead men and kicked him over to see his face. "These are Malic's servers!" Brenath then spits on him, disgusted by the very sight of the man.

"I don't see how anyone would serve that coward," said Dragon as his eyes turned red with anger.

"Some men only follow riches, and they'll do anything if they're paid," Brenath replied.

"Sonya, go back to your room and get some rest. I will stay here with Brenath."

Sonya seemed to be in too much pain to argue, so she got up and began to head back to the towers. Brenath sent Cromwin and a few of the guards with her to escort her back to her room. When she was out of sight, Dragon bolted off in the opposite direction into the city. Brenath was not idle; he quickly darted off after Dragon. Rapidly weaving through the city, Dragon used his keen sense of smell. He had picked up the scent of something that he did not like, yet it was something he was after.

Halfway back up to the towers, he had caught up with Malic, who was moving as quickly as he could. However, Dragon was too fast for Malic. He sped up and pounced on Malic. As Malic fell to the ground, he let out an annoying squeal for help. Dragon instantly picked him up by his throat and slammed him against a wall. Malic was pulling and tugging on Dragon's hands, doing everything he could to keep from being strangled. He looked back down the walkway to see Brenath coming up behind them.

Malic did the best he could to speak with the breath he had. "Brenath, do something. You are supposed to protect the people of the city!"

Brenath, catching his breath from trying to keep up with Dragon, leaned against the wall only a few feet away and crossed his arms. "I am," he replied, showing his true dislike for Malic. He then stared at Dragon, waiting to see what was going to happen next.

Dragon, seeing that Brenath would not interfere, gripped Malic's throat tighter, so he couldn't speak at all. He then drew in closer till his nose almost touched Malic's. "Listen here, you worm. I do not care what plans you have for this city. My company and I have no part in this place. So if you ever try to harm any of my company again, I will squeeze the life out of you." Dragon didn't wait for any response from

Malic; he simply threw him aside like garbage and then walked away. As he was heading back up to the towers, his eyes still burning red, Brenath followed him.

"You could've killed him!" Brenath yelled after Dragon. "I wouldn't have stopped you! It would be one less problem for me!" Out of respect for the queen, Brenath would never admit openly that he hoped every day would be Malic's last.

"He is not my problem," Dragon shouted back. What little respect he had gained for mankind had once again been lost, and he wanted nothing to do with them.

"Then what exactly is your problem?" Brenath knew that the question would probably upset Dragon, but he had a feeling that something else was bothering him— perhaps something deeper than mankind.

Dragon swiftly turned around and glared at Brenath. "The Creator is my chief problem, and shortly followed by mankind!" He then stepped back around and continued storming off. "I'm going to bed, and so should you. We are leaving tomorrow, and I will wait for no one!"

Brenath stood still, watching Dragon stomp his way back into the towers like a child throwing a fit. He couldn't help but feel some form of pity for Dragon. For all his greatness, Dragon's heart seemed to be drowning in grief. Brenath knew that sooner or later, Dragon would have to come face-to-face with whatever it was that was burning inside him. Also, Brenath knew that when that day came, it would not be a pretty sight. Brenath turned his eyes to the sky and began to speak out loud.

"I knew deep in my heart that trouble was coming, and I prayed to you, Great Creator, for guidance and help. But this was not what I was expecting. I hope and have faith that you know what you are doing. If you ask me though, it is like throwing a log into a fire when I would prefer water." After that, Brenath turned his eyes back to his surroundings, mentally reassuring himself that things would be okay.

Eventually, he turned and walked back down into the city to help clean up Malic's mess. Needless to say, he had hoped that Malic might have been one of the fatalities. Still, he realized that life wasn't perfect, and that one day he would have to deal with Malic again.

***

Dragon came storming into his room, completely enraged. He walked to the nearest bed and picked it up like it was weightless. He was just about to toss it across the room to relieve his aggravation when he heard Phanis roll over in his bed only a few feet away. Dragon, realizing that this was not wise or polite, slowly set the bed back down. He then continued storming over to his bed and sitting angrily on the end of it, breathing heavily and clenching his fists. After a while of sitting still, he finally brought himself under control. He then looked up to the ceiling and began to mutter to himself and to the Creator. "I don't understand you; I don't think any creature on this earth understands you. You've ruined my life, and you're making it worse every day." Dragon then gritted his teeth and held his breath for a moment as though he were building up to blow fire out of his mouth. He then took one final glance up at the ceiling and uttered, "I hate you."

Dragon waited for a moment, hoping that his words would bring down the wrath of the Creator and end his life right then and there. Needless to say, it didn't happen. Still enraged, he crawled into his bed and lay down. As he tried to force himself to sleep, the only thoughts that went through his head were of what tomorrow would bring. Also, what the Creator had in store for him next.

12

Troubled Lands

Dragon awoke early before the sun appeared. He had a very restless night; his dreams were filled with terror. He could not shake off the feeling that he had betrayed his race the day before. No matter how many times he justified his actions to himself, he retained the guilt. That by itself made him eager enough to leave the city as soon as he could.

He woke Phanis and then went to rouse the females. He found Sonya awake, sitting quietly in the middle of the room. It appeared to Dragon that he wasn't the only one who was troubled by their actions. He did not say anything about his feelings or his troubled night; he simply notified her that they needed to move out quickly, and then he turned and left the room.

When Dragon was gone, Sonya proceeded to wake Yolana and get her ready to leave. Yolana quickly got up, and the first thing she did was put on her new tunic. She was extremely proud that morning because her new clothes were very nice. They were a lovely color of light brown and green. As they prepared to gather their things, both of them wondered where the female dwarf was, as she didn't stay in their room. They also wondered if she was actually going to come along like she said she would. They gathered everything and met Dragon and Phanis out in the hall, and together, they started down the stairs of the towers.

Yolana noticed when she was walking down the stairs that Phanis also had on new clothes as well as a sword. His clothes weren't as nice as hers; they were simple and one shade of brown. Probably because he still wasn't used to being a free man and wouldn't accept anything more than that. Nevertheless, they smiled at each other, acknowledging the fact that life was good and that their lives were taking a new turn.

It wasn't long before they were walking down the entrance tunnel to the city. On the way, they bumped into only a few people. Most of the city was quiet. Dragon was hoping that he wouldn't have to wait long for Brenath and his men. Fortunately, to his delight, Brenath, Cromwin, and a host of twenty men were outside the mountain entrance, preparing the horses and supplies for their journey.

"Good morning, Dragon," Brenath cheerfully exclaimed. "We were just getting things ready, and then we were going to wait for you, for whenever you and your company would be ready. It's nice to see you up this early. We will be able to cut some time off our travel. Are you feeling well enough to get under way?"

Dragon took a moment to answer because he was attempting to stop himself from yawning. "My feeling is as well as one would expect this early in the morning, but we are ready to travel. I agree with you.

The sooner we leave, the better." Dragon looked about everywhere, looking for someone in particular. "Where is the female dwarf? Has she cowardly backed out of our little adventure?"

"My name is Voraha, and I'm not a coward!" a hidden voice cried out.

Dragon looked wildly about, confused. He heard the voice, but he couldn't see her. "I know your voice, but where are you hiding, dwarf?"

A soldier on horseback rode closer to Dragon. Staring directly at the warrior, Dragon could see no dwarf about him. Then the rider turned to the side and revealed that Voraha was sitting right behind him on horseback, like a child behind a parent.

Dragon let out a small chuckle at the sight of this proud dwarf sitting behind the soldier. "Good. I'm glad you're not a coward," said Dragon, trying to find words that would not aggravate her. "Now that everyone is here, we should get underway. I'm surprised that Malic is not here to see us off. I thought at least he would approve of us leaving."

"I'm sure if he were here, he would do just that," Brenath replied, almost laughing at Dragon's remark. "He woke just before you and left as quickly as he could. He notified us that as we went north, he would go south, in an attempt to help us solve this mystery. I'm sure that last night had nothing to do with it," he said sarcastically, letting out a small chuckle. "It's probably better that way. It keeps him out of our hair. If you ask me, I think he's just hiding from you." Brenath jumped onto his horse's back and then rode over and handed Dragon the reins to his horse. "Did you say farewell to the queen?"

Slightly confused as to why Brenath would ask that question, Dragon inquired back. "No, why should it matter?"

"Nothing personal. It just seemed as if you two were getting along rather well. Since you may not return to this city, I just thought you might want to say a lasting good-bye."

"I appreciate your thought, Brenath. And you're right, I am fond of Crysaia. That is why I must leave without saying good-bye, because if I see her one more time, I may not want to leave this place." After that being said, Dragon quickly jumped onto horseback and turned to Sonya. "Are you ready to fly?"

Sonya sat by the entrance once again, staring at the horses, a little depressed. "I still think I should get a chance to ride a horse."

"I still think you are too great for such a beast," a voice said to her.

Sonya looked down to see Tobin standing beside her. "Why are you not on a horse. Are you not coming with us?"

"Not this time," Tobin said as he patted the side of her hind leg. "Besides, someone needs to stay behind and take care of the city while you're gone. I hope you come back before you continue your journey."

"I'm afraid not, Tobin. I don't think I will ever see you again. So this is farewell. Take care of yourself," Sonya said, a little saddened by the thought. She bent down and nudged his head with her snout, attempting to say good-bye, the only way she knew how.

"Look out after my brother, would you?" Tobin whispered to her as he rubbed his hand on her cheek, saying good-bye in his own way.

Sonya nodded, and then turned and began to walk out into the fields. Dragon and the others were now all on horseback, waving farewell and turning to leave. As they did, Brenath turned to speak to Dragon. "I have a strange feeling about this journey."

"You're not the only one with that feeling," Dragon replied. He turned his head slightly to look back at the entrance as they slowly made their way to the north. Before he turned his head back, he saw something glitter in midair. It hung for a moment and then quickly sped off to the south. The only thing that came to Dragon's mind was Tilly, and then he wondered why she would be going south. He thought for a moment and then figured that perhaps his journey to the north was going to be uneventful. He also concluded that she was probably going to check on Malic and see what he was up to. One way or another, it didn't matter. She was gone, and he had a company underway. So he turned his head back around and continued on with the rest of the company as they made their way through the fields. The horses were walking; there was no need to ride hard that early in the morning. Sonya, on the other hand, was running and jumping through the fields like an oversized rabbit or puppy, happy to be on the move again.

****

He was an inexperienced wizard, Malic thought to himself as he dismounted from his horse and began to climb up a charred mountainside. It had been nineteen years since his master's unexpected death and the appearance of his new master. Malic always felt uneasy in the presence of his new master; there was an unmistakable difference between his two masters. His old master always wanted him to grow and become a strong individual; his new master seemed to be holding him back, giving him only enough to survive. The only thing that Malic's masters had in common was that they were drawn to power, and they brought Malic with them. That was exactly what brought Malic to this place at this time. Years before, his new master had sent him to Tyrilcrysalith to gain control of the city. He barely got rid of Crysaia's parents, and the fact that he had been there for years and had not gotten any closer to taking the city had never sat well with his new master.

Until recently, his present master had formulated a plan that seemed unstoppable. He would draw out the captains from the city and kill them in the wild with his orcs, so that the city would have fewer leaders in this attack. Next, he would send his dragons to destroy the humans, and when all were dead, Malic would take charge. Malic realized that it didn't go the way it was supposed to and that he had to notify his master. That was what brought him there; everything had gone wrong and had become confusing.

Malic needed advice on what to do next. It wasn't my fault, Malic thought. It wasn't his or his master's fault that a half-breed claiming to be the king of the dragons would unexpectedly arrive the day before his master's plan would be put into effect.

Deep within the southeast of these lands, Malic stood with a torch in hand at the entrance of a massive cave toward the top of a mountain. The outside of the mountain looked beaten and charred with ash, and the inside didn't look too inviting either. He took one careful step at a time; he wasn't moving very fast because his knees were shaking. He dreaded the very sight of the place, yet he still inched his way in, out of the light of the sun. The moment he was completely consumed by darkness, he saw something move in the distance. He immediately froze and lowered his head. "Master, I bring bad tidings," he said, stuttering in fear.

"The winds have already brought me bad tidings," a deep and ominous voice reverberated off of the cave walls. "You have failed me yet again!"

"Master, it was not my fault." Malic began to defend himself. "The unexpected happened. I had no control over the events that unfolded!"

"The unexpected," the voice erupting in anger. "The only unexpected thing should've been the downfall of Tyrilcrysalith! First, I entrusted you to take it over yourself so no damage would befall the city. You failed me, so I had to resort to sending my dragons!"

"I needed more time," begged Malic as he fell to his knees.

"You had years. My patience is not endless. If I was not busy with other things, I would have terminated you long ago. I'm surprised I gave you the time you had, and now everything has gone amiss. My dragons are dead, and I am no closer to controlling the city! Tell me exactly what happened!"

Malic hesitated for a moment, wanting to choose his words carefully. "You would have controlled the city if it weren't for the king of the dragons arriving the day before."

"You lie!" the voice yelled. "There is no king of the dragons. The last to have the throne was a queen, and I know that she is dead."

"Nevertheless, Master, a half-breed arrived and said he was the king of the dragons. He is very convincing, and a dragon followed him also. It was the two of them together that destroyed all your dragons." Sweat glistened on Malic's face as he barely contained his fear. "They also killed the men you gave me to take the city."

The voice in the darkness became agitated, and its owner began to move around. "A half-breed. What races?

"Half human and half dragon," Malic said, knowing this news would probably upset his master more. He was beginning to reason that the more answers he gave, the closer to death he came. He even pondered whether he should answer anything else or just keep quiet.

Sure enough, the voice began to bellow. "It is impossible! I have heard of many dark wizards attempting to blend the races, but it has never been done with success. You must've been misled by a wizard who appears to be greater than you." After saying that, the agitated voice began to take shape. Its size filled the massive cave entrance. However, there was a strange power about it; the shape seemed to be darker than even the gloom of the cave. As it moved closer to Malic, the torch's flame in Malic's hand shed no light on the figure. It seemed as if the light itself shrugged away in terror. "I will accept no excuses. If you fail me again, you will die. You will help me take the city!"

Malic's whole body began to tremble in fear for his life. "Master, why don't you simply send more dragons? The half-breed is no longer there."

"Because I have no more, you fool! Dragons are scarce, especially ones that are dedicated to evil deeds." The dark figure suddenly grew silent, intrigued and confused by Malic's words. "What do you mean the half-breed is no longer there? Where has he gone, and why?"

"After the battle, everyone wondered why the dragons attacked and where they came from. So they traveled to the north as we speak to the town of Falistoran. They hope to find a seer that will tell them what they need to know. That is the other bad news that I bring." Malic bowed even lower, fearing that this news would cause his death.

"So this half-breed wishes to involve himself in things that are not his concern. Very well, I will deal with this problem myself. As for you, my servant Malic, return to Tyrilcrysalith and finish what you started."

"Can you not take the city, as mighty as you are?" Malic suddenly gasped, realizing what he said, and the weight of it.

"Perhaps, but why risk myself when I have whelps like you that will do it for me? Now stop quivering and do my bidding," the figure commanded as it threw something out of the shadows. The object hit the ground and rolled to a stop only a foot from Malic. "Here, this will help you to do my bidding since you are not powerful enough."

Malic cautiously crawled forward to pick up the object. When he did, he realized what it was. His dark master had thrown him a scepter—only three feet long and beautifully decorated. Its long handle was a bar of gold and a bar of silver woven around each other. The scepter's base was a diamond spike, and the top was crowned with four golden dragon wings folded outward. In between the dragon's wings were an emerald that seemed to glow yet held no light.

"What is this?" Malic asked, fearing the answer.

"It is a magical object that holds more power than you can imagine. It will help you take over the city when the time is right."

"Where did it come from?" Malic questioned, completely mesmerized by it.

The dark figure barked, "Do not ask so many questions! However, if you must know, before I found you quivering at my kingdom's gates, you were a starving wizard's apprentice. I obtained it from your master. I am the reason he is dead."

"I never knew he had it. How did he obtain it?"

"I gave it to him to do my bidding. Unfortunately, it only took two days before he decided to betray me. I disposed of him and took it back, and now I give it to you. Hopefully, you will prove worthier than your master was. Do not underestimate its power. It has passed through many wizards' hands, but it has always been mine to give.

Furthermore, where it came from is not your concern. I have gathered many things throughout my years that would help me obtain my goal as ruler of the earth. So stop asking useless questions and simply do what I asked. When my army is ready, you will help them to take the city."

"Exactly how do you want me to assist your army?"

"I do not care. That I leave up to you, as long as they take the city! However, with my dragons gone, it will take a while for me to gather an army large enough to take the city. Meanwhile, you will wait patiently until the time is right for you to act. This will be your last chance to prove your worth to me. Make sure you do not fail me. Now go!" The dark figure began to retreat back into the darkness, leaving Malic to his own devices.

Malic was still unwilling to raise his head; he stayed bent over and slowly retreated. Like a poor, pitiful animal, he crawled out of the cave and headed back to his horse. He wasn't quite sure what he was going to do, but he knew that he could not waste any time. So he headed north as quickly as he could.

* * *

The two companies of Dragon and Brenath traveled for days and were nearing the end of their travel to Falistoran. The journey back to Falistoran was a lot shorter than the journey away from it, Dragon admitted; of course, he did not have horses at the time until he met Brenath. Dragon also made sure that he steered both companies away from the wolf sanctuary. With the help of Sonya as his eyes in the sky, they kept the sanctuary a secret as a favor to Silver Snow. The traveling party had stopped and rested for the night in a clearing about half a day's journey south of the town. Before the sun rose the next day, they had started again. All were on horseback, slowly moving through the forest.

Sonya, on the other hand, was still in the clearing, scratching her back against a tree and bending it over by her weight. Earlier in the night, she didn't realize that she had slept on an anthill. When she was done scratching the ants out from underneath her scales, she caught up with the others. After rejoining the group, Sonya realized that Dragon was riding by himself far to the right. She thought to herself that he probably wanted to be alone, so she gave him his space.

As for Dragon, he did want his space, and he was enjoying the quiet of the forest. He was wondering to himself how long it had been since he had a quiet day. Everything was quite tranquil until he heard a noise in the tree right next to him. He quickly looked up to a branch just above his head, only to see Tilly perched on the branch, looking down at him.

"Well, where have you been?" Dragon sarcastically asked. Because of their history, he didn't want to openly admit that he was happy to see her.

"I cannot tell you that," she responded, seeming all mysterious.

Dragon was somewhat taken aback and silenced by that comment for a moment. But he decided to keep the conversation going. "Have you been keeping an eye on Malic?"

Tilly did not say anything in response. She simply smirked. A slight breeze came up, making her grab tightly onto the tree branch. Yet she still maintained a serious gaze aimed at Dragon.

"I thought as much," said Dragon, trying to keep the conversation calm. Even though they had recently become allies, Dragon realized that the tension was still high between them. "Believe it or not, your grin gave it away. So are you going to tell me what he's been up to since I have a feeling he might be a part of this?"

Tilly's grin quickly faded; she knew that this conversation was not going to end well. "I cannot tell you."

"Tilly, you told me you were willing to help." One could hear Dragon doing his best to hold back his anger. "How are you going to help me if you don't tell me what I need to know?"

"I do want to help, with all my heart. Unfortunately, on my way back to you, I was stopped by the Creator. He reminded me that my place is to observe and that I could not interfere in any way. Furthermore, if I interfered with so much as a word, my existence would be in jeopardy."

Dragon turned his head away as he burned with anger. Once again, he felt as though the Creator was getting in the way and controlling his life. He took a moment to calm down, then looked back to say something to Tilly, but she was gone and nowhere to be seen. Dragon, however, had a feeling that she was simply invisible and still sitting on the branch. He glared at it intently and then spoke. "I know that this is not your fault. Still, if you will not help me, then don't bother to show yourself to me." Dragon then spurred his horse off in the direction of the others, leaving the branch empty and silent.

Dragon rejoined the group, angry and frustrated, yet he hid it well. He spent a good portion of the morning just muttering to himself. They weren't far from Falistoran when the company suddenly stopped and began to sniff the air.

"Smells like smoke," Brenath commented. "It has a strange odor to it. I can't recognize it. Look ahead," he said, pointing to the trees in front of them that were surrounded by a cloud of thick smoke.

Dragon and Sonya were as still as they could be, their faces filled with concern. Then Dragon suddenly leaped from his horse and ran toward Sonya while yelling at Brenath. "That smell is burnt flesh. Something is wrong!" Dragon then leaped onto Sonya's back, and they quickly flew off above the trees.

Brenath and the others spurred their horses in hot pursuit, diving right into the smoke that was weaving its way through the trees. As for Sonya and Dragon, they were above the smoke, speeding toward Falistoran. It wasn't long before they saw the ruins and dove down toward the city. Sonya landed with a thud in what was supposed to be the center of the town. Dragon jumped down from Sonya's back, and they both stood together staring at the burning wreckage. To their shock, the whole town had been destroyed, and only a few buildings were still burning. Everything else was ash and rubble, and no survivors were yet to be seen. Dragon and Sonya stood still for a long time, just looking at the horror, almost unable to absorb the truth of this tragedy.

It wasn't long before everyone else arrived at what was once Falistoran. They rode into the middle, where Sonya and Dragon were standing. Brenath and the soldiers sat back on their horses and watched in dismay. As for Yolana and Phanis, they jumped down from their horses and ran in opposite directions. Phanis ran to search for his mother, and Yolana went to search for Krandal. In the panic, Sonya herself went off in search of someone familiar. After a while, some of the soldiers began to search for any survivors. Dragon, Voraha, Brenath, and Cromwin stayed together where they were, just staring out at the devastation.

* * *

Yolana ran through the debris and heavy smoke in her frantic search for Krandal. She might not have known him long, but she thought she knew him well, enough to be concerned. Coughing and spitting the taste of smoke and ash out of her mouth, she finally reached Krandal's dwelling, or what was left of it. As great of a building as it was, the entire thing had been burned to the ground; even the stones that were a part of the building seemed to have melted. The only thing that Yolana could do was stand there, completely horrified.

After a short moment, she did her best to search what was left of the building for Krandal. When she found no traces of him, she began to get disheartened. Then suddenly, she remembered something and quickly ran into the smoke. She was running to Phanis's mother's home; the only other place she could think of where Krandal might be. However, it was there that evil and despair gripped her tighter.

When she arrived, the sight that greeted her was worse than she could imagine. At first, she could only see Phanis standing still in front of a pile of rubble, looking down. When she came up beside him, she understood what had frozen him. There among the pile of rubble were two bodies, barely recognizable. The remains were mostly bone, with only a few bits of flesh and cloth that were their clothes. Even though the bodies had been decimated, there was no denying who they were.

After a long moment of silence, Phanis could no longer contain himself. He fell to his knees, and as he reached out to touch his mother's foot, he burst into tears. The only thing Yolana could do was place her hand on his shoulder and weep with him. Even though they were filled with sorrow, they had an odd sense of fulfillment as they looked at the bodies. Phanis's mother's body was lying in Krandal's arms, as though he were still protecting her even after her death. The bodies made Phanis think of Krandal's promise to him and the fact that he kept it at the last moment. That made him think of his own promise to his mother, and it made him question whether or not he would keep it.

While Yolana and Phanis continued to mourn, Sonya was wildly focused on her own search. On the other side of the city, she was frantically scurrying around the piles of buildings. She used every sense that she could to find what she was looking for: her eyes, ears, and even her powerful sense of smell. She was in such a rush that she could barely make heads or tails out of anything. In some places, the smoke got so bad that she turned around and became very flustered. That didn't make things better, because she ended up looking like a puppy chasing its tail.

Eventually, she caught the scent of something important and darted off after it. She came to a pile of what was an enormous building burned down. Sonya circled the building, sniffing carefully, making sure she had the right scent. After she determined it was what she was looking for, she moved quickly. Sonya was a dragon, so the little remaining fire that was still burning was not a problem. She reached in with her strong hands and arms, getting a firm grip on the building. With a massive heave, she threw the building to the side. Once done, she moved in on the rest of the rubble, gradually and carefully, like a cat, until she found what she was looking for.

***

Everyone had a look of concern and confusion on their faces, Brenath especially. He seemed overwhelmed by everything that was happening, and it didn't get any better when the soldiers returned with no news of survivors. The devastation was so great that only a few bodies could be found. The rest seemed to have been burned to ash.

"What could have done this?" asked Brenath, sounding as though he was in great pain.

"Perhaps it was, the dragons that attacked us," one of the soldiers commented.

"No, this was not them," Dragon quickly answered. "Those dragons came from the east, and besides, this was done recently. I'd say this happened last night or early this morning. The fires are still burning, and the smell of death is fresh."

"It may not have been those dragons, but this looks like a dragon's work to me!" one soldier said, getting very angry at Dragon for defending the dark dragons.

"You are the king of the dragons. It's your responsibility to do something," another soldier remarked.

"My responsibility," replied Dragon, getting angry himself. "Who are you to tell me my responsibilities? I told your queen that I would escort you here safely, and that I have done. I have nothing more to do with you and your people. I have done enough by turning on my own kind in defending your city!" Dragon then stepped forward, going face-to-face with the soldier. "I'm still not sure if that was a justified deed, protecting your pathetic race. I believe humans are a sickness upon the land, and you only help to confirm my belief. I am sorry for what has happened here. However, protecting the humans is not one of my responsibilities!" Dragon then turned to Brenath and glared at him, daring him to say anything in defense of the humans.

Before Brenath had a chance to answer, a massive thud shook the ground, and all of them turned to see what it was. To their surprise, Sonya was standing straight up, and she was holding something in her arms as though she was carrying a baby. The look on her face terrified them, including Dragon. He had never seen a look like that on her. As they stood still, she stomped closer toward Dragon, which did not look good for him. She stopped right before him and glared down at him, still holding something that they couldn't identify.

"You're wrong!" she yelled at Dragon. "It is your responsibility, whether you like it or not. When you became king of the dragons, you took responsibility for their actions, good or bad. This devastation is too unique to misplace. This was done by a dragon."

Sonya then leaned down to show them what she had in her arms. They were shocked and dismayed to see the remains of a small boy, whom Dragon identified as the boy Sonya played with while they were in town. The boy was barely recognizable. One side of his body had been burned down to the bone, and the other side was badly scorched. His body was still smoldering from the fire, and the smell made some of the soldiers back up. Sonya was so angry that she shoved the body toward Dragon, putting it right below his face.

Dragon turned his head away, unwilling to recognize this tragedy. Sonya, however, kept the body there, right below Dragon's face, making sure he knew her rage.

"This is what one of your dragons has done," she continued. "And it is your responsibility to punish them. And if you won't, I will!" She then pulled the boy's body back close to her heart and stormed off, not saying another word. As Sonya left, the soldiers, including Brenath, Cromwin, and Voraha turned and walked away to continue searching for any signs of life, leaving Dragon to stand alone in his shame.

***

That day was hard for everyone, for there were no survivors. Only a few bodies had been found, and most of them looked the same as the boy. Phanis could identify a few of them—his mother, for one, Krandal, and even Asanon. The soldiers buried what was left of their bodies in the middle of town— except for Krandal, the boy, and Phanis's mother. They were taken to a small hill right outside of town, where they were buried, with large mounds of rocks piled above their graves. Phanis, Yolana, and Sonya stood before the graves and grieved for their loss. As for Dragon, he stood at the base of the hill, staring endlessly at Sonya.

His body was stiff as though it had been frozen, and the irises of his eyes were light blue as if tears were forming behind them. He could almost understand their pain, for he himself was hurting. For the first time since Dragon had left his home, he felt truly alone. In their youth, Dragon and Sonya disagreed on many things, but they were never angry with each other. This time, Sonya yelled at him, shamed him before the humans, dishonored him, and eventually left him. At that moment, Dragon felt completely torn apart from her, and he knew that she was furious with him. The very thought of Sonya leaving him sent a chill up his back. What hurt him even more was that he knew that she was right. It was his responsibility, and he needed to do something, whether he liked the humans or not. For a long time, he wrestled with his pride—whether or not he should admit to the others that he was wrong. So Dragon simply stayed in the distance and watched everything that went on.

"I wish you were here, Mother." Dragon began to speak to the air around him, hoping that it would answer him. "What would you do in my stead? What would you do, wise Ancient, or you mighty Marahezron, or even you, Father? What would any of you do at this moment?" Dragon grabbed his mother's scale and held it tight, still hoping that someone would answer him. After a brief moment of silence, he continued to speak to the air.

"I know that you would all say that Sonya is right, and that a dragon did this, and that it is my responsibility as king to deal with the problem." Dragon's voice became hard as he pushed out what he said next. "It's not fair. I didn't ask for any of this. I was not ready to be king or to have the responsibility that came with it. I was not ready to leave my home and wander the world. I also was not ready to face death. I only killed when I hunted for food. Since I left home, I have shed the blood of orcs, men, and even dragons. If that is the responsibility that comes from being king, then I do not want to be king."

Dragon went silent for a moment to see if his last words would be answered. After no answer came, he took a deep breath and let go of his mother's scale. Concluding what he should do, Dragon spoke one final thing to the air. "Since none of you will advise me, I have decided to see this through. Though I was not ready for such things, I was taught to never run from what needs to be done. I do not like the burden of the responsibility of this, but there is no one else strong enough to take it up. Besides, there's nowhere for me to go right now."

After a while, the three at the graves returned to the group to discuss what would happen next.

"So where will you go from here, Brenath?" Phanis asked. "Will you return to Tyrilcrysalith?"

"I see no other course," replied Brenath. "The queen must be notified of what transpired here. On the other hand, I wish we could find out what is going on and why our lands are suddenly troubled."

Cromwin put his hand on Brenath's shoulder to get his attention and gave a few hand signals. Then he pointed to the east. He then stared at Brenath, giving him an unsettling look.

"Are you trying to suggest what I think you are?" Brenath asked. He shivered at the mere thought of what Cromwin was suggesting. Cromwin nodded quickly and then pointed again to the east.

"What is that supposed to mean?" Voraha finally spoke up.

"What Cromwin is suggesting is somewhat unsettling," Brenath quickly responded. "Many of the guards in Tyrilcrysalith enjoyed listening to stories of distant lands from travelers that came through. One of the stories that holds some weight—because of the many different people that have spoken of it—is a rumor of two witches who live on the other side of the gray mountains to the east. It is said that they have the power to see what is beyond all sight."

"What's so unsettling about that?" asked Sonya, joining the conversation as well.

"It is also rumored that these witches are dark, powerful, and nearly unstoppable," Brenath continued. "It is said that some of the great wizards, for good, have lost their lives to these witches."

Voraha stepped forward and slammed the handle of her ax into the ground. "So when do we go to look for them?"

"I admire your courage, Voraha. However, we are not going to look for them. As much as I want to find out who caused this tragedy, it is too dangerous. Even if we find them, we'll probably not leave their presence alive."

"Then I will go," Dragon blurted out as he stepped into the middle of their circle. "Sonya was right. As king, it is my responsibility to seek out the dragon responsible for this disaster. If seeking the witches is the only way to learn who did this, then that is my curse. I do not expect anyone to go with me."

Brenath stepped closer and glared at Dragon, to see if he was really sincere about seeking the witches. After a moment of staring into his eyes, Brenath knew there was no changing Dragon's mind. "If your intent is to seek the witches, then me and my man will go with you." Brenath was terrified at the thought of seeking the witches; however, the thought of Dragon leading them gave him hope that they might survive the foolish search for answers.

"Don't forget about me," Voraha stepped up, waving her ax over her head.

"I will go with you too," Phanis stated. "I have a score to settle with the beasts that killed my mother."

"Don't leave us behind." said Yolana as she stood next to Sonya.

Dragon took a moment and looked around at all the people who had vowed to go with him. As he did, he felt a sense of purpose and direction, something he had felt he was missing. "So now that we're all in agreement, what is the next stage of our journey?" he asked Brenath.

"We must go from here and head toward the gray mountains, and then we must reach the other side." Brenath answered very quickly, feeling sure in his direction.

"Is there some pass that we can cross, and will it be easy to manage?" Dragon was trying not to spoil the enthusiasm of the moment, but it was a question he needed to ask.

Brenath shot Dragon a serious look as he realized that he too did not want to spoil the moment. Nevertheless, he needed to give a truthful answer. "No, Dragon, the gray mountains have no pass. No one has ever gone over them."

"So do we go around them?" Dragon continued, rolling his eyes in frustration.

"We could, but that would take lots of months. The swiftest way to get to the other side of the gray mountains is to go through the dwarfish realm of Shieldholt."

"Will the dwarves allow that?"

"Are you saying dwarves are not hospitable?" Voraha snapped at Dragon as she grabbed the hilt of her ax.

"He didn't mean anything by that, Voraha. It was a simple question," Brenath quickly responded to calm her down. "And yes, Dragon, the dwarves will allow that. The dwarves of Shieldholt are prideful like any dwarves, but their halls are not hidden. They love travelers and guests as long as they are respectful. I've never heard of the dwarves turning anyone away."

"Well, let's hope they don't turn us away," said Dragon. "Voraha, I assume that Shieldholt is your home."

"It is not," Voraha grunted. "My home is much farther away, and I have never been to Shieldholt."

"Then we better get moving. I have a feeling this will be a long journey."

With that said, the group prepared to leave once again and head in a different direction, toward the gray mountains. Before they departed, Brenath ordered two men back to Tyrilcrysalith to inform the queen of their intentions. As for everyone else, once they were ready and on horseback, they rode off toward the east, leaving behind only a trail of dust. Their hearts were heavy, and their minds were filled with many thoughts. Still, they continued, knowing there was no turning back. This journey had to be completed.

Sonya was the only one who stopped for a moment and turned to look back at the devastation of Falistoran. She mostly gazed at the three graves on the hill. The longer she looked at them, the more she was filled with the pain of loss and the need for justice. After a while, she turned back around and continued on with the group. However, for the rest of that day, she did not fly. She walked behind the group with her head bowed. Her thoughts were filled with the memory of a small boy who played with a dragon.

13

Wild Tribe

Dragon and the company traveled east for a week in the direction of the gray mountains. The journey was relatively easy; it was the weight of their hearts that made things difficult. For a long time, their thoughts dwelt upon the people of Falistoran and the tragedy that befell them. The knowledge of what happened was a heavy burden and a pain for them to bear. Not much was said or spoken, even around the campfire at night. It wasn't until the third day when people started talking again, but no one suffered from the pain more than Sonya. She seemed unable to deal with it at all and took everything very personal. Phanis, on the other hand, seemed to be dealing with this tragedy very well, for some reason. He mostly dwelt upon the last words of his mother, telling him to look after Dragon. Her request helped him drown out his grief and gave him purpose, though it did not take away his thirst for justice. Still, he had stayed by Dragon's side ever since they had left his home, which gave them time to get to know each other a little better. As for Yolana, she spent time with Voraha, attempting to get to know the dwarf. Instead, it turned out to be Voraha trying to strengthen Yolana, saying that all women should be warrior women. No matter what, the company stayed together and supported one another through this difficult time.

The journey to the gray mountains was mostly uneventful until the ninth day. They were just beginning to see the shape of mountains appearing in the distance. However, that wasn't what the company was looking at that day. Brenath had dispatched a scout to go ahead of them to make sure the way was safe. The scout had come back in quite a hurry. He rode directly up to Brenath and Dragon.

"What did you find?" Brenath called out, not wanting to waste time.

"Trouble, my captain," the scout replied, trying to catch his breath even though his horse did all the heavy work. "One of the wild tribes is headed this way."

"Is there any way to slip past them?"

"No, sir, I think a scout spotted us first because they were headed directly toward us."

"Great," Brenath growled. "Do you know what tribe?"

"I'm not certain, but it looks to be the Wolf Tribe."

"As long as it's not the Stag Tribe, we might make it through this with little trouble," Brenath muttered. He then turned to Dragon and began to explain things because of the look of confusion on his face. "Around these parts, there are several groups of humans that travel the wilds. They don't have a home; their home is where they camp. Most people call them the wandering tribes."

"Are they hostile?" Dragon asked.

"Not really," Brenath replied, trying to think of the best way to explain this. "They are primitive people with their own beliefs and rules. Like I said, they travel about in groups; the largest group is about a thousand and the smallest is two hundred. They mostly keep to themselves and stay far away from settled places. They're harmless unless they're provoked and then a fierce enemy. They are one of the reasons why a wall was around Falistoran. It is rumored that even the orcs leave them alone, but I've never found out if that was true."

"So what does it mean that they are headed towards us?"

"I don't know, something's not right. I don't expect any trouble; we've had some dealings with them. Cromwin is friends with several of the tribes, so that works in our favor." Brenath then waved for Sonya to join the conversation. He waited until she came close before he continued. "I need a big favor from you, Sonya, and you're probably not going to like it. I need you to leave the party and fly ahead to the gray mountains."

"What?" Dragon asked, completely perplexed. "If there's a possible problem ahead of us the last thing we should get rid of is one of our strong warriors."

"I know this is a strange request, but just trust me. I don't know if there's a problem with the tribe, but the last thing I wanted to do is make a problem with the tribe. I do not think they will see us as a threat, there's no reason for them to attack us. However, if we have a dragon in our midst, then we become a threat. Not to mention she would be considered a good food source for them. If she's with us, it would be like us giving up a food offering to them."

Dragon and Sonya looked at each other as they thought this through and then silently agreed that it was the best idea. They both nodded in agreement to Brenath's idea.

"Okay good," Brenath stated. "You two won't regret this I promise. Sonya fly to the gray mountains and wait for us at the door to the dwarven city, you can't miss it."

The whole company watched as Sonya took flight and headed to the gray mountains. Dragon trusted Brenath, but he was still a little nervous about letting Sonya go. Even though the two of them haven't talked much over the last week, they were still in each other's company. Having her fly off was like losing a part of himself, and he felt a little out of sorts. Nevertheless, he tried to ease his concern by focusing on what was ahead of them. Dragon stayed close to Brenath so he could follow his lead since he had never dealt with the wandering tribes.

Brenath kept everyone on their horses and moving forward at a steady yet slow pace. He wanted the tribe to come to him, because he didn't want his company to look hostile.

It didn't take long for the wandering tribe to appear in the distance as a cloud of dust. Dragon, of course, with his eyes, could make out the approaching tribe before everyone else. He told Brenath that they were on horseback, and it looked to be about two hundred.

"That's just the hunting party," Brenath stated. "If we're in their company long enough, we'll see the rest of the tribe come up behind them. If two hundred are in the hunting party, then there's at least the same amount guarding the rest of the tribe. So we are probably looking at a tribe well over six hundred, too big to be the Wolf Tribe. This is not good."

The company came to a halt and stood still and quiet, waiting for the tribe to reach them, and it didn't take long. With the thunder of hooves and clouds of dust, the tribe surrounded the company with a massive procession. As the dust began to settle, Brenath counted the tribe's hunting party, only to find that Dragon wasn't that far off his count. Two hundred and nine was Brenath's count, which didn't make him feel any better about their odds. When he noticed their body paint and their wardrobe, he got a sick feeling in his stomach. He leaned over to Dragon and whispered, "the Bear Tribe, this is not good."

"I thought you were worried about the Stag Tribe," Dragon whispered back.

"The Stag Tribe is the most hostile, tribe; however, the Bear Tribe is stronger in battle. Most of the time they're peaceful, but when they're riled up they're trouble and it looks like something riled them up. I almost regret sending Sonya away."

"You want me to try to call her back; she might hear me."

"No, that will cause more trouble. We still have a chance of getting out of this; Cromwin is our best bet."

"Is this one of the tribes he is friends with?"

"No, unfortunately, but there's still a chance he could communicate and secure our safe passage." Brenath then motioned for everyone to dismount, showing that they were not a threat to the tribe. Brenath and Cromwin identified the tribal leaders and stepped away from the company to begin negotiations.

Dragon, on the other hand, was fascinated by the wandering tribe, and he looked at them up and down. Like Brenath said, they were primitive but not stupid; they were well organized. Dragon even looked at their horses and was amazed. They didn't have the beautiful, shiny saddles and gear like the horses from Tyrilcrysalith, but they had their own design that seemed to work really well. As for the tribe members, they weren't much different. They had simple animal skin cloths around their waist, and they showed off their bare chests. The body paint that they used seemed to cover their exposed skin. Dragon couldn't tell if some of it was permanent or if some of it was just today's addition to their dress. Nevertheless, the paint had intricate designs, showing that these people were also artists. Each design on each body probably had a story and a meaning behind it. It was one of the ways Dragon was able to identify the hunting party chief or possibly the tribe's chief. In addition to the intricate body paint, the leader had more feathers, animal claws, and teeth in his wardrobe. Next to the chief was what Dragon assumed was the tribe's wise one, or shaman, as he remembered what Ancient used to call them. He certainly wasn't a wizard, but he wasn't someone to mess with either. He had an entire bare skull over his head with lots of feathers and other trinkets. Dragon couldn't tell, but some of the trinkets look like fingers or ears, possibly from orcs. He could barely see the shaman's face inside the skull, which made it more mysterious and ominous. Dragon tried to keep his eyes downcast as much as he could. He didn't want to cause any trouble for Brenath and Cromwin as they tried to secure their safe passage.

Cromwin began to sign to the chief, with Brenath standing a few feet behind him. The chief, in response, began to sign back and speak as he signed. Cromwin and Brenath knew it was a delicate situation. No one knew the Bear Tribe's language, so they could only rely on Cromwin's hand language. However, it wasn't a sure form of communication. Cromwin's hand language was similar to the wandering tribes, but it wasn't accurate. Even Dragon could tell that Cromwin and the chief were having a hard time communicating.

So Dragon decided it was time to put his skills to use. He listened carefully to the chief as he spoke and signed. After several minutes of listening to the chief, his skill with the dragon language unlocked the secret to the Bear Tribe's language. Dragon then began to understand what the chief was saying and believed that he could speak the language back. He walked up beside Brenath to offer his assistance. Without thinking, Dragon responded to the chief in his own language.

"No!" Brenath shouted, trying to stop Dragon, but it was too late.

The hunting party immediately erupted with conversation, everyone talking to his neighbor. There was so much noise that Dragon couldn't follow what was being said.

"What are you doing?" Brenath snapped at Dragon.

"I was just trying to help; Cromwin's hand gestures were getting us nowhere.

"Well, you didn't help; in fact, you made things worse. You spoke in their language; even the other tribes don't speak the Bear Tribe's language. They probably think you're a spy or something crazy; these are superstitious people. Keep your mouth shut; hopefully, we can fix this." Brenath then nodded to Cromwin to continue and to do his best to fix the situation.

Cromwin turned back around to face, the chief knowing there was only one way out of the situation. He made a single hand gesture, and the entire uproar of speaking tribesmen fell silent.

The chief, sitting on his horse, leaned forward and spoke one word to Cromwin to verify his hand gesture. "Kodoc." He then turned and began to converse with the shaman.

"What does that mean?" Dragon asked Brenath. "I can't quite translate that one."

"That's an intertribal word; all the tribes know it. It's barely used, but it is used when the tribes have dealings with each other. I don't know why Cromwin used it; he must think it's our only way out of this."

"What does it mean?" Dragon growled, trying to grasp the situation.

"Cromwin challenges them."

"He challenged them!"

"Well, not all of them; he challenged their strongest warrior. It's a way to deal with a dispute between the tribes. The two strongest warriors face off in a fight. Basically, the Challenger is betting everything he has that he will win. In other words, he's fighting for his freedom or ability to leave unharmed when the other tribe has reason to harm him or his people."

"So basically, he just admitted that we're guilty of something and he wants to leave with our lives intact. Just great; I wish Sonya was here."

"Well, he wouldn't have to invoke that tradition if you would have kept your mouth shut."

At that moment, the chief was done conversing with the shaman and shouted, "Kodoc!"

With that, the entire hunting party dismounted and pulled their horses to the outside of their circle, creating an enormous circle of bodies. Some of the tribe's men even came in and took the horses from the company and led them out of the circle.

Brenath motioned to his men that everything was okay and to back up and join the circle of men. At that time, Yolana, Phanis, and Voraha came up to the others to discuss what was going on.

"I knew you'd get us in trouble," Voraha said as she gave Dragon a quick jab with her elbow. "Just point to the one you want me to kill, and we'll start the fight."

"No," Brenath quickly replied, "we're not going to fight, or at least not all of us."

"Where's the fun in that?" Yolana sarcastically remarked.

"Cromwin has bought a chance. He's going to fight for our freedom."

Yolana looked around at the surrounding tribe and said, "doesn't look like much of a chance."

"It's one of the only chances we've got," Brenath replied.

"What happens if he loses?" asked Phanis.

"Then technically we become the tribe's property and then we'll have to fight our way free. But let's hope it doesn't come to that. Get with the others and stand ready."

The other three went back to the rest of the company, while Brenath and Dragon stood with Cromwin for a moment. They were just about ready to leave when the shaman spoke. The three of them turned to face the shaman, confused about what was going on. The shaman was standing next to the chief, pointing at Dragon and speaking loudly.

"Dragon, what did he say?" Brenath asked, very concerned. He didn't know what was happening, and he didn't like having to use someone else to listen and speak. He trusted Dragon but this could go wrong quickly.

"I'm still not used to their language; it's very primitive. However, I think he said something about his mother and then something about choosing a worthy opponent."

Cromwin started making frantic hand gestures to Brenath clearly concerned about something. At the same time, the chief stepped away from the shaman and barked a command as he pointed at Dragon.

"This is not good," Brenath snarled.

"What's this mean?" Dragon asked, feeling completely left out of this conversation.

"We have a problem. Cromwin forgot about a certain part of the challenge, mostly because it's never been used before even among the tribes. Part of the Kodoc challenge is the acceptance from the other tribe; however, there's an add-on to that acceptance. If the accepting tribe believes that their honor is challenged as well, they have the right to pick a more formidable foe. It has something to do with if you can fight, fight the strongest. If you ask me, it sounds childish, but it's their custom."

"So what does that mean for me?" Dragon asked, still confused about the whole situation.

"It means you have to fight him instead of Cromwin." Brenath put a hand on Dragon's shoulder and stared into his eyes to make sure he was paying attention. "This is more serious than it looks. I think the shaman knows something is different about you. It's rumored that they can see into the spirit realm. Whether that's true or not, I don't know, but there's a reason he picked you. So be careful out there. No matter what, we must win; just don't kill the chief. Also, don't make a fool out of him either; if you take away his honor, it would be just like you killed him." With that said, Brenath gave Dragon a slap on the back, then Cromwin and him ran to join the others.

"Don't I get a say in this?" Dragon muttered as he watched the two of them run away. He turned around to face the chief and continued muttering to himself. "I wish Sonya was here; I'd feel better with her watching my back. I should have left with her."

At this point, Dragon and the tribe's chief were fifteen feet from each other in the middle of an enormous circle of people. As the chief stared Dragon down, Dragon took the time to look around and get a good look at the tribe's hunting party. Dragon now understood Brenath's concern about the Bear Tribe. All the men were six and a half feet or taller, and they were extremely muscular. He noticed that they had stone axes and spears. Such weapons would normally not do much against an army of soldiers bearing shields and swords. However, in the hands of such strong and tall men, they were people you didn't want to mess with. Dragon then began to understand that if he messed up this fight, that's what he would be fighting against to get everyone out of there.

He brought his attention back to the chief. Looking at the man, Dragon could clearly understand why he was the chief. He was among the tallest in the tribe and the most muscular. Dragon could tell that those weren't the only qualities that made him a good chief. From the look on the chief's face, Dragon realized that he was planning his attack, which meant the chief was more than just muscle. The chief then began to circle to Dragon's right. Dragon matched his movement as he tried to think of how to win a fight without making his opponent look weak. By the time they made one complete circle Dragon still had not come up with a way of how to fight this fight. The only thing he could come up with was to play it out blow by blow. Which was a good thing because at that time the chief attacked.

The chief came in fast and yelled as he swung his fists at Dragon's face. Dragon being shorter and faster, was easily able to dodge each swing. He could tell by the ninth time he dodged that the chief was starting to become enraged. By the eleventh dodge, Dragon glanced back at Brenath only to see a look with the meaning we're dead on his face. Dragon then decided that perhaps the chief should get a few punches in.

So Dragon gritted his teeth and prepared for the oncoming pain. The chief swung with his right fist, hitting Dragon directly in the face and knocking him a few steps back. The chief stepped forward again and swung with his left fist, hitting Dragon again in the face, sending him back a few more steps. Dragon was expecting another punch, but it didn't come. This time the chief decided to use his foot; he brought his right foot up and kicked Dragon in the chest, sending him flying back and landing on the ground.

For a moment, Dragon admitted that this human was very strong and a worthy opponent. But when Dragon's back hit the ground, his opinion changed very quickly. Marahezron and Ancient agreed on two things when it came to Dragon, they said he had two weaknesses. The first was that he got mad way too quick. The second is that when he got mad, he did not think things through. They told him it was one of the things he needed to get control over; otherwise, it would cause some serious problems for him in the future. Needless to say, Dragon got mad.

Dragon lay on his back for a few seconds as his temper built. The only thought going through his head was that I am the king of the dragons, and I will not be beaten down. With that, he quickly jumped back up to his feet searching for the chief. He was only a few feet away running forward with his fist raised for another punch. Dragon had enough and decided to end it right then and there. He ducked underneath the chief's swing and stepped in with his own punch. Dragon's fist hit the chief's chest with a loud smack, sending the chief flying back and skidding to the edge of the circle. Dragon then stepped forward and roared in frustration; his dragon roar echoed around them.

Dragon was so busy being mad that he didn't realize what mistake he made. Nor did he realize that his company reached for their weapons, preparing for a fight. As for the Bear Tribe's hunting party, they stood still, holding their weapons at the ready. Then a few of them began to speak a word that was picked up and carried by the rest of the hunting party. In under a minute, the entire hunting party was screaming the word "gul'daw!"

"What are they saying?" Brenath yelled, trying to get an idea of what to do next.

Dragon listened to the echoing chant for a minute before he answered. "Demon, I think they're calling me a demon."

"Well, they're not wrong," Voraha yelled back.

"This is not what I was looking for," Brenath Snapped.

Before any fighting broke out, the shaman stepped forward and yelled one word. With that, the entire hunting party went silent and lowered their weapons. He then walked over to the chief and helped him to his feet. After that, the shaman and the chief started walking towards Dragon.

Dragon wasn't sure what was going on, but he was doing his best to keep himself under control. The tribe had lowered their weapons, and he wanted them to keep it that way. He grimaced as he looked at the chief. Dragon could already see bruising in the middle of the chief 's chest. He thought to himself that there were probably some broken ribs in there as well. The two approached Dragon unthreateningly; as a matter of fact, the chief was grinning. Dragon still had a hard time looking at the shaman's face inside the bear's skull.

The shaman walked up to Dragon, and put a hand on his shoulders, and then began to speak to the tribe. Before Brenath or anyone else could ask, Dragon immediately translated. "This is the one who I dreamt of. When the dark shadow covered the south and threatened our way of life. We and several other tribes traveled north in search of safer lands. On our travels, I dreamt that our path would cross a dragon trapped in a man's body. I dreamt that he would free our lands of the shadow and that one day we could return to the south. My dreams were not false; even his eyes and his strength prove that my dreams are true. Tonight, we will feast with this warrior, and tomorrow we will send him on his way with our blessing." With that, the shaman and the chief patted Dragon on the back and walked away as if something like this happened every day.

The company then came up and surrounded Dragon, some of them excited for the turn of events and others frustrated at him.

"You are one crazy halfbreed," Voraha stated.

"You were lucky the Creator favors you," Brenath snapped.

"Leave him out of this," Dragon barked back.

"I wish I could, but that was too much of a coincidence. The odds that we would cross paths with a wild tribe at the same time their shaman has a dream about you. If the Creator isn't watching over you, someone else is. Just do me a favor next time, try not to get us killed." Brenath then turned and told his men to gather the horses and start unpacking the supplies.

"What are we doing? Aren't we leaving?" Dragon asked.

"No, it appears we were invited to dinner, and you do not refuse a wild tribe's hospitality. So for right now, I suggest we take a breather and wait."

With that, everybody seemed to scatter to see to their own needs and their horse's needs, and to wait on whatever the tribe had planned. Dragon on the other hand, was still somewhat frustrated over the whole fight situation, and the fact that it did seem like the Creator had his hand in his life once again. So he went off to find his horse and sulk by himself.

***

So as the day moved on, the company got to watch the hunting party as they worked on clearing the area. They were very thorough as they moved through and cleaned an area then marked things with stakes to indicate where something should go, and then moved on to the next area. It wasn't until the end of the day that the rest of the tribe met up with the hunting party. Just as Brenath had expected, it was an enormous tribe. As the tribe began to set up their tents, Dragon could hear the hunting party begin to explain to all the others what had happened earlier that day. Dragon very quickly got used to being pointed at by the tribes' members. Nevertheless, Dragon sat back and enjoyed watching the tribe set up camp and began preparing for a feast. Dragon also got time to observe the females of the tribe. They were tall, like the men; not one of them was below six feet. They were also muscular and very fit, some of the women were doing things that Dragon was pretty sure that Brenath's man couldn't do. Their clothes were simple animal hides like the men's, yet the women not only covered the waist but also went up around the neck. Even though the animal hides covered a good portion of the women they still revealed a little too much. Dragon realized that these people were very simple, and they didn't care what other people thought of them or how they looked. In a way that made Dragon relax a bit, thinking that he didn't have to worry about his table manners around this group of people.

As the sun went down, the feast started. In the middle of the camp was an enormous bonfire, and that is where most of the feast took place. Everyone in the company was made to drink, eat, and dance. Since they were outnumbered and surrounded, no one said no, even Voraha, who cursed and muttered foul things as she danced. Dragon found that to be one of the most amusing things of the evening, and he also learned a few new dwarven words that night.

Several hours later, the shaman made everyone pause so he could bless Dragon. He said a few strange words and sprinkled some dust and then some water on Dragon. After that, he told them that they could continue to feast or go wherever they wanted. It was no surprise that the entire company decided to leave the feast to get some peace and quiet. Voraha and Yolana went to sleep, as well as most of Brenath's men. For the rest of them, they found themselves around a small fire at the edge of the camp. Brenath, two of his men, Cromwin, Phanis, and Dragon, talked as the night wore on. The talks were light and humorous, but everyone could tell that Dragon was not used to talking in a group or on human subjects.

"I will never forget Voraha trying to dance," Brenath said as the others laughed.

"By the end, she looked like she was going to kill somebody," Phanis replied.

"I can't believe the number of women that tried to dance with Dragon," one of Brenath's men stated.

"I'm surprised they didn't drag him off to their tents," the other man said.

"Why would they do that?" Dragon asked seriously.

"Because the wild women like strong men," the first man replied. "Not to mention you defeated their chief; they were all over you. I'm surprised you didn't take one."

"Where would I take one?" asked Dragon as he raised an eyebrow.

"You know, to have some fun."

"What fun would we have?"

The man looked at Brenath, completely perplexed. "Is he serious?"

Brenath and Phanis burst out laughing, even Cromwin began to choke on his drink. "It's refreshing to have you around, Dragon," Brenath stated as he tried to get his laughter under control. "I think we forget that you are only sixteen; you look a lot older than you actually are. I doubt you experienced much of the human aspect of life in the dragon city."

"I didn't experience anything human in the dragon city."

"Your innocence is extremely refreshing."

"I wouldn't say it's innocence I think it's more ignorance," Phanis sarcastically mocked.

"Thanks, Phanis; who needs enemies when I have a friend like you," Dragon quipped back. Dragon leaned back, looking up at the stars, and let out a sigh. "I think my problem is that I didn't learn anything about humans when I was younger. Now that I'm out in the world, the more I learn, the more confused I get."

"I think that's all of us, Dragon; the human race is very confusing even to itself," said Brenath.

"The whole story of mankind confuses me," said one of the men. "Take the story of its beginning: how one man and one woman were supposed to make all of mankind."

"That never made sense to me either. I've seen a village that was made up of close relatives, and they had been doing it for generations. I'll tell you what, there was something really wrong with that village," the other man said.

"I think humans have that story wrong," Dragon commented. "My mentor Ancient told me something different. He said the Creator first created man like he did the rest of the animals and filled the world full of them. It wasn't until later that the Creator changed things. Ancient called it breathing the breath of life into them; basically, it was giving mankind a soul and spirit or knowledge and wisdom. Humans were aware of the Creator and communicated with him or something like that. I never paid attention to many of the old stories. Ancient did say that after the fall of man the enlightened humans spread out in the world amongst the animal ones. Which basically gives us the human race that we have now, full of both good and evil things."

"Well, leave it up to Dragon to ruin an evening," one of the men said. "This conversation has gotten too serious for me."

Brenath stood up and looked at the group. "Well, that's all right, we should go to sleep anyways. We will get an early start tomorrow if the tribe doesn't hold things up."

Brenath, his two men, and Cromwin left the campfire to go get some sleep, leaving Dragon with Phanis. There was a long moment of silence between the two as they just listened to the sound of the fire. Dragon wasn't sure what to say to Phanis; this was the first time they had a chance to talk alone since leaving Falistoran. Nevertheless, Dragon felt as if the silence was not what needed to be between Phanis and himself.

"Are you okay?" was all that Dragon could come up with to start the conversation.

Phanis sat for a long moment, staying silent as he stared into the fire as if he would find answers among the flames. Eventually, he let out a deep breath and asked Dragon, "Does the pain ever go away?"

Dragon knew what Phanis meant. He knew how it felt to lose a mother and how to blame yourself for not being there to protect her. Dragon knew that Phanis was thinking the exact same thing he was about his mother. That if he was there, he could've found a way to save her. Dragon knew Phanis's pain all too well.

"No," Dragon muttered. "I don't know. Ancient would say that grieving over time would get better. That the memory of them would still be there but the pain attached to it would become numb in time. Especially if you love the memory of them, you move on for their sake. But I'm not sure if any of that is true. It's been months since I lost my mother, and the pain is still deep. Like a fresh wound it burns when I think of her, and I don't know if it will ever go away. Part of me doesn't want the pain to go away, because if it does it means she's really gone."

"If you are trying to reassure me that everything is going to be okay, I think you failed."

"Sorry, I was never really good at wise things to say, that was always my mentor. I honestly don't know what to say or if anything I say could make you feel better. But I will tell you this, we will find who did that to your mother and we will make them pay with their life."

Phanis nodded at Dragon in agreement and then they both went back to staring at the fire for a while. When the silence got to be too much again, Dragon tried to start another conversation, this time he took a different approach.

"So, what are you going to do with your life?" Dragon asked.

"Well, for starters I'm going to do what my mother asked me to do. I'm going to follow you and keep an eye on you. Because, you need someone to look after you." Both Phanis and Dragon smile at that comment. "Then after I've seen some of the world, I'm going to find a wife and settle down. We will have a couple of children together. I will spend my last years telling stories to my grandchildren about the king of the dragons, who constantly got us into a lot of trouble."

Dragon couldn't help but laugh at that comment. "Sounds like a fun future."

"What are you going to do Dragon?"

"I don't know," Dragon replied as he looked up at the sky, thinking about the infinite possibilities that could happen in his life. "I have no idea what's in store for me. I think that's what worries me. I don't know if I will ever be able to settle down or if I'll find anyone. And if I do, will they be a dragon or human?"

"You could end up settling down with a dwarf or an elf," Phanis sarcastically replied.

"As long as it's not an orc, goblin, or troll I think I'll be fine."

"You will make it through this world; besides you have friends to help you on the way. I don't think any of us will let you settle down with a troll."

They both laughed for a moment and then stared at each other. They didn't need to speak to understand one another. They both knew that this world had so many unknown possibilities in it, yet they would face it together as friends.

＊＊＊

The next morning the company rose refreshed and ready to continue. They were happy that the entire tribe was not up and sending them on their way. There was only a total of sixty-three tribe members saying their farewells. Brenath did notice that forty-nine of them were women, trying to get their last look at the great warrior who defeated their chief. Brenath also realized that the men in his company would make jokes about Dragon for weeks to come. Nevertheless, they were all on their horses and ready to go, except for Dragon who was talking to the chief and the shaman. After they were done talking, Dragon and the chief clasped forearms in farewell. As for the shaman, he sprinkled more dust on Dragon's head. Dragon did his best not to seem disrespectful to the shaman, but the moment he turned his back, Dragon shook his head. He then came over to the company and mounted his horse, ready to leave as well.

Brenath, however, road up to Dragon curious of their conversation. "What were you talking with them about?"

Before Dragon answered, he shook a little bit more of the dust off his head. "I think that was bone dust; I don't want to know where the bones came from and what it was. The shaman and the chief wanted to bless me again and wish me luck for the battles ahead. They really believe I have a hand in what's coming and that I'm going to cure their lands."

"That's it?"

"Not really, I also took the time to ask them a couple of questions. I was hoping to get some more information out of them, to see if they knew anything. The chief only said they lost a lot of hunters this year. The shaman kept saying something about the darkness covering the land. I tried asking him more about the darkness hoping to get a direct answer. However, he said that him and another tribes' shaman was never able to figure out what it was. He then said that the darkness was clouded in shadow and that the spirits were silent, whatever that means."

"So, what do you think it means?" asked Brenath, a little concerned.

"If anything, it means we should be worried. There is something out there strong enough to destroy Falistoran and scare several wild tribes out of their territory. It means we need answers and quick. I know you're hesitant about the witches, but if they are the only ones that can tell us what's going on, we need to get to them as soon as possible."

Brenath couldn't argue with that statement, even though he didn't like the idea of looking for these witches. Nevertheless, they set out with haste for the gray mountains. Within a few moments, they could not see anything of the wild tribe's encampment. Knowing that the tribe was behind them, the company relaxed, except for Brenath and Dragon. They were still concerned, for they knew that something of greater danger lay ahead of them, and they were not eager to face it.

14

Shieldholt

After leaving the Bear Tribe, Dragon and the company continued to travel east for another week. Even though they could see the gray mountains, it still took a while to reach them. Eventually, they were finally standing at the feet of the gray mountains, and Dragon was amazed. He finally understood why these were called the gray mountains. There was a significant difference between the color of the ground and the mountainsides, which was a dark gray with no other color. It was as if gray spears had been thrust through the brown earth and up into the sky and then crowned with white. As he stood staring up at them, he also realized why no one could pass over the mountains.

Other than their base, which were difficult enough to cross by themselves, the mountainsides were sloped very sharply, almost vertically, and rugged.

Snow also covered half of the mountains, which made it even more difficult for anyone to find a pass over them. Dragon thought to himself that if it was only Sonya and him, they could fly over the mountains. Of course, thinking of all the others, he couldn't ask her to fly them over one by one. So he concluded to himself that going under was the best choice. He then looked over at Brenath and nodded, silently confirming their course. From there, they turned south in search of the doors to the dwarfish city of Shieldholt. Dragon was doing his best to contain his enthusiasm. He didn't care much for human cities, but a dwarven city was something he longed to see.

They traveled south for half a day until they finally stood before the doors. Dragon heard that the dwarves were secretive, so at first sight of the doors, he was quite taken back. The doors of the dwarfish city were massive and carved directly from the mountainside. There were also large steps leading up to the doors and two great pillars on either side. There at the base of the steps, the company found Sonya lying on the ground, sleeping. Dragon, of course, didn't hesitate the moment he saw her. He rode his horse directly up to Sonya, jumping off in mid-stride. When he landed, he ran up and hugged her neck.

Sonya was not startled by Dragon or the company; she merely opened her eyes and commented. "It's about time you get here; I have been worried sick."

"Well, we would've been here sooner, but we had some trouble," said Brenath as he rode up to Sonya. "Dragon almost got us killed with the wild tribe."

"Sounds about right; he always gets into trouble when I'm not around," Sonya sarcastically replied.

Dragon couldn't help but laugh as he patted Sonya on the side of her neck. "Thanks, I missed you too. I seem to get into trouble whether you are around me or not. But to tell you the truth if I get into trouble, I prefer to have you by my side."

"I would agree with that," Brenath stated. "While we're on the subject of trouble, Sonya, have you had any communication with the dwarves while you waited in front of the doors?"

"No, I have not seen a single dwarf in the entire time I've been here. And no one has come in or out of those doors."

"That's strange; I thought they would've sent somebody out to talk to you and question why you were sleeping on their doorstep. The dwarves of Shieldholt may go many years without seeing visitors, but they do keep an eye on their doors very well. I'm pretty sure they were keeping an eye on you and now know that we are here."

"So why don't we go introduce ourselves?" said Dragon.

Now that Sonya rejoined the company, they all turned their eyes up to the doors to the dwarven city of Shieldholt. The doors and the pillars were both richly carved with dwarfish writings and emblems. Everyone was chiefly struck by the mere size of the doors. Especially when they reached the doors and saw that Sonya, fully upright, stood only at half of the doors' height. This seemed to only make everyone more interested in what could possibly be on the inside of the mountains. There were no dwarves visible to let them in, or any visible way to call for the dwarves.

"How does one enter this supposedly great dwarfish city?" Dragon sarcastically asked.

Brenath stepped forward to answer Dragon in an attempt to keep him in a good mood so that he would not upset the dwarves. "I believe one simply knocks, and the dwarves will eventually answer."

"Voraha, are you not a dwarf? How is this done?" Dragon asked, continuing to be sarcastic.

"Dwarves are not as boring as humans," Voraha snapped at Dragon. "No two dwarven cities are the same!"

With a smirk on his face, Dragon took his fist and knocked on the great doors. Immediately, the doors rang as if Dragon had struck metal against metal. The sound emanated from the doors and enveloped the mountainside. Everyone in the company jumped back and covered their ears as the sound strengthened. Then, when the sound had slowly diminished, they all uncovered their ears and stood astonished once again at the doors. There was no doubt in any of their minds that their knocking had been heard. If the sound covered the mountainside, it must've drowned the inside of the dwarfish city.

"I'd hate to be inside the mountain when a hailstorm hits," said Dragon.

"I think the doors are magic; they must only do that when someone knocks," Brenath replied.

They all stood back and waited patiently, certain that the dwarves were quickly on their way to see who knocked on their doors. However, after a while, when no one answered the doors, Dragon began to fidget, getting very impatient. Everyone else, on the other hand, was very content to wait a little longer. Thinking that the dwarves were a little rude not answering the door, Dragon motioned to Sonya for help. She hesitated for a moment and then stepped forward to give him a hand in pushing on the doors.

"Dragon, I do not think it is a good idea to walk in unannounced to a dwarf city," Brenath suggested with a look of worry on his face, thinking that Dragon might cause some unwanted trouble again.

Voraha quickly spoke up and agreed with Brenath. "It is unwise to upset dwarves. It is also unwise to intrude upon their halls."

"I understand your concern," Dragon replied as he continued to push. "Still, time is of the essence, and I do not appreciate sitting on the doorstep. Besides, they wouldn't want to keep such an honored guest waiting outside."

"You'd be surprised what dwarves want," Voraha muttered to herself, thinking that Dragon was more arrogant than the dwarves themselves.

After a lot of pushing and grunting, the great dwarfish doors finally gave way and opened into the halls of Shieldholt. Dragon, of course, immediately walked in, as if he were expected. The others took a moment or two and then slowly followed after him. They left all their horses at the foot of the mountain, taking only their weapons and the bare essentials, as they did not know what they would find inside. Once they had stepped under the cover of the mountain, they got a good look at the inside. They seemed to be standing in what appeared to be a large cave. The only thing that stood out on the walls of the cave were torches lit and burning bright. At the far end of the cave, they saw stairs leading up into the mountain. Once again, Dragon took off without hesitation toward the stairs, with the others slowly trailing behind him.

"Dragon, I don't think this is a good idea," Brenath once again verbalized his concern. "Opening the door is one thing, but trespassing will certainly get us into trouble with the dwarves!"

"Don't worry, Brenath. I'm the king of the dragons. Everything will be fine." Dragon waved his hand back at Brenath, dismissing the whole thing.

Dragon's words, of course, did not comfort Brenath; instead, they seemed to aggravate him even more. He knew time was important; the sooner they figured out what was going on, the better. However, if Dragon got them killed in the process, it wouldn't do any good for Tyrilcrysalith. He thought that Dragon was getting a little too far ahead of himself, as well as getting too big of a head on his shoulders. Brenath appreciated Dragon taking responsibility for being king of the dragons, but he didn't think that responsibility should come with arrogance.

Dragon was nearly at the foot of the stairs when an ax came flying out of the shadows and embedded itself on the floor right at his feet. Immediately, everyone stopped and prepared themselves for a fight. At the same time, hundreds of dwarves came out of the shadows and surrounded the company. A good majority of them crowded around Sonya. All the dwarves were heavily shielded with armor and helmets. Some wielded great axes and swords, while others had dwarfish bows bent and ready to fire. As for the company, they merely had their hands on their weapons, hoping that they could talk their way through this. The only one sure of himself was Dragon, who was standing still, looking down at the ax at his feet.

"You got a lot of nerve opening our doors and invading our city," a stern voice cried out from the shadows.

Eventually, the voice that spoke exited the shadows and walked right up to Dragon. He was a dwarf of great stature; he was almost as tall as Dragon, which was unusual for a dwarf. Still, he was a dwarf, and Dragon was not afraid of him. Although Dragon would admit he was very impressive for a dwarf, with his muscles seeming to bulge right out of his armor. He had long red hair both on his head and his face; his beard was braided into two long braids down to his stomach. Dragon could tell right off that this was one of the leaders of the band of dwarves. However, Dragon noticed that this dwarf was quite young in the face, and that he probably acquired his leadership by his mere strength. After a moment of staring at each other, the dwarf reached down and pulled his ax out of the ground and held it up to Dragon.

"Now who are you?" the dwarf demanded. "And why have you trespassed here?"

Dragon did not move; he simply stared back at the dwarf and answered, "We are simply trying to get to the other side of the mountain, peaceably if possible. I'm sorry that you think we are trespassing, but no one answered the door when we knocked."

"We are not your servants," the dwarf said, becoming aggravated with Dragon and pressing his ax to Dragon's throat. "Our doors are not meant to be open to anyone, and our halls are not meant to be used by every traveler that comes this way! What makes you think you have a right to pass through our mountain?" The dwarf glared and breathed heavily at Dragon as if smoke would come out of his nostrils.

"Because I am the king of the dragons," snapped Dragon, stepping forward and puffing up his chest in a challenging motion toward the dwarf while the dwarf's ax was still pressed against his throat.

Immediately upon hearing those words, the entire group of dwarves broke out in fits of laughter. This only aggravated Dragon, making him take a defensive stance. He looked angrily at the dwarf standing before him, and then he let out a roar. Dragon's loud bellow knocked the dwarf off his feet and landed him flat on his back. As for all the other dwarves, they all jumped back and gripped their weapons tightly, a look of shock on their faces. They all stared at Dragon, not sure what they were dealing with.

Brenath came forward and grabbed Dragon by the arm. "Dragon, this is not helping us!"

"I will not be laughed at," Dragon yelled back. "I am Dragon, son of Kirianadréth, and I am the king of the dragons!" Though Dragon was far from his kingdom, he knew his lineage and clung to it desperately. He also felt that he was too important to be laughed at by a dwarf.

By this time, the mighty dwarf had picked himself back up and held his ax firmly in both hands. "I don't care who you are. You will pay for that," he said, preparing to charge.

"That's enough, Timbor," another voice shouted from the shadows.

Immediately, the angry dwarf stopped, lowered his ax, and waited for the other voice to appear. Sure enough, out of the shadows, a dwarf walked calmly and confidently toward Dragon. He was an older dwarf compared to all the rest, yet he was still strong. The other dwarves showed him great respect and lowered their weapons as he walked by. Dragon could almost see wisdom and courage written into the lines of his face; even his armor showed age along with fortitude.

The dwarf had long silver hair, both in the front and the back. The back of his hair was braided in one long braid down to his knees, and his beard was full down to his stomach, with two long braids from his mustache. In his hand, he held a mighty war hammer that seemed large enough to strike two men with one blow. When the dwarf reached Dragon, he set the hammer down and leaned on the handle, like it was a resting pole. He then stared at Dragon intently, not saying a word, merely sizing him up. Dragon, of course, took the time to do the exact same thing, wondering if this dwarf would be nice enough to let them through the mountain.

After a while of passing glances at one another, the dwarf finally spoke. "You must forgive young Timbor. He is very eager to earn a name as a warrior, and he is not used to dealing with outsiders."

"That is plain to see," Dragon was quick to reply. As he did, he got another glance from Brenath, who was not happy with Dragon's reply. Even though he was unwilling to, Dragon understood Brenath's concerns and changed his tone when he spoke to the dwarf. "I am called Dragon. Who might you be?"

"I am Drognen Hammerstriker, leader of Shieldholt's armies. And that is Timbor Rocksmasher, captain of the west gate—and the youngest captain we have ever had, I might add."

Drognen walked up beside Dragon and put a hand on his back, welcoming him. "Welcome to the dwarven city of Shieldholt. What can I do for you and your company?"

"We simply want passage through your city to the other side of the mountains— that is, if it will not be too much trouble."

"No trouble at all, Dragon. But first, you must meet our king." Drognen waved for the dwarves to make way and signaled for Timbor to lead the way. "Come, Timbor, show our guests to the throne room, where I'm sure the king will be anxious to meet them."

"I thank you, Drognen. You're quite a courteous dwarf," Dragon remarked. "What are we to do with our horses that are outside? Can they come with us?"

Drognen waved his hand to several dwarves and then motioned at the great doors. "No, Dragon, the horses will stay here at the gate inside the mountain. Do not worry. They will be well cared for while we go see the king."

With Drognen's reassurance that their horses would be cared for, the company was now ready to move on.

Timbor, on the other hand, was muttering quietly to himself and thinking that they were more trouble than they were worth. Still, he waved to them to follow and showed them the way, not willing to disobey Drognen's command.

Dragon turned to look at his group to see how they were all faring, only to see concern on all of their faces. It was all too obvious that they were worried that Dragon was going to get them into trouble even though they were safe for the moment. Seeing that look on their faces, Dragon simply turned back around without saying a word and followed Drognen and Timbor into the dwarven city.

***

Dragon and the company traveled with the dwarves deep inside the mountain, and their eyes widened with wonder at what they had been witnessing ever since they left the entrance. The impressive entrance seemed small in comparison to everything else. They passed through many great caverns, and occasionally they had to cross over bridges that overlooked great fissures as far as the eye could see. It wasn't long before Dragon looked back at Sonya and became aware of something that had never crossed his mind before.

He watched her as they passed through many of the different halls of the dwarven city. Some of the halls were small, and she walked through them by simply lowering her head. Other halls were so massive that even she could barely see the ceiling. Although their path had led them through ways that were easy for her, Dragon could see she was concerned. She turned her head side to side, paying attention to all the doorways only big enough for humans, which headed in all different directions throughout the mountain. As Dragon watched her concern, he realized that he had never considered that she might not be able to make it through the mountain. Then it dawned on him that he had never considered her size before. She had always been by his side, and they never really traveled anywhere that had a size limit. Still, he felt horrible that he had never really considered her size or feelings before. The only thought that came to his mind was that he was too self-centered.

As quickly as he could, he pushed the thought out of his mind. Now was not the time to work on his friendship with Sonya. So instead, he turned his mind and attention to the architecture of the dwarven city, since he did not know much about dwarfs.

As they walked into a massive cavern, Dragon turned his eyes to the lanterns on the walls and pillars. At first, the lanterns were small and illuminated only a small portion of the cavern. The farther they went in, the bigger the lanterns got. The cavern was enormous; however, it was well–lit. Toward the center of the cavern, the lanterns were no longer hanging from the pillars; instead, they were built right into the middle of the pillars, with fires that stood higher than two men together. This made Dragon pause for a moment and take a closer look at the architecture of the pillars themselves. He could barely see the ceiling, yet the pillars and the carvings on them went all the way up.

At first, Dragon couldn't understand why dwarves would live in such great halls. The only thought that came to his mind was that perhaps they were overcompensating for their size, or maybe they were just too arrogant. Nevertheless, he had to give them credit for the work they did. Some of the halls were natural caverns, while others had been carved completely out by the dwarves. However, the closer he looked at the intricate design on the pillars, the more he realized what was behind the dwarven cities. It was a sense of pride and honor, not arrogance. The love of true skill and art. With every tap and chip of rock, this whole mountain became a thing of beauty. No wonder some dwarves hoarded it like treasure, and others wanted to show it to outsiders. Dragon began to finally understand the true nature of dwarves— to bring the light into the darkness—and that in and of itself was a skill worthy of respect.

***

The company followed Timbor, Drognen, and a few other dwarves to Shieldholt's throne room. Once again, they all stood in amazement, looking at what was supposed to be the heart of the city. It was a massive room that had six large pillars lining a path down the center, with a high ceiling above. On the other side of the pillars, toward the walls, there were hundreds of chairs and benches surrounding long wooden tables. Not to mention, the entire place was packed full of dwarves, all curiously looking at the incoming travelers. The dwarves were used to travelers; still, they enjoyed staring and muttering about anyone who passed through Shieldholt. Although no traveler had ever had an entrance as startling as Sonya's. The moment she poked her head in through the door, all the dwarves rose with a great clatter and reached for their weapons.

No dwarf moved toward her, however; they simply stood silent, gripping their weapons, waiting to see what she would do. As for the company, they stopped where they were and turned to wait for her to enter the room. To everyone, it looked as if a dog was trying to go down a gopher hole. She pushed, pulled, and squeezed herself through the small door, at least small for her size. Dragon could tell by the look on her face that she was not having a good day, especially since she almost got stuck twice. Eventually, she, squeezed herself in and rejoined the company. She walked carefully and quietly, noticing that all the dwarves were still stiff and watching her.

When they reached the other side of the room, they stood at the base of twelve large steps leading up to a dais. On the dais, there was a large gold and silver throne where the king dwarf sat. He almost looked like a child sitting in an adult's chair. Still, he sat tall and proud on his throne. Dragon could tell that the king was a lot older than Drognen. He had definitely seen too many winters. However, he was still venerable, as though every passing day added to his strengths. The king wore no armor, yet his garments were kingly. Upon his head sat a golden crown tipped with different jewels of the earth. His hair was white, and his beard was full on the front with two braids on either side, held together by silver rings equally spaced on the braids. Leaning against his throne was a magnificent sword at his left hand and a mighty ax by his right.

Dragon noticed that the king did not stir on his throne or say anything as they stood below him. This made him a little uneasy and set him on edge.

"My great king," Timbor finally spoke, "these are trespassers from your west gate." Timbor then turned to the company to introduce the king. "You stand before Ronnar Shieldbreaker, king of Shieldholt. If you wish to pass through this city, you must beg permission from him."

King Ronnar leaned forward, looked down at the company and finally spoke with an old, deep voice. "Trespassers, what might your names be?"

Before Dragon had a chance to reply, Timbor quickly answered for him. "This one calls himself Dragon, and he claims to be the king of the dragons."

Immediately upon those words, the entire room erupted in laughter, except for Dragon, his companions, Drognen and King Ronnar.

Dragon crossed his arms and rolled his eyes, once again irritated by this display. Before he had a chance to explain, he was interrupted again—this time by Drognen. Quickly, stepping forward, Drognen bellowed over all the laughter. "This is Dragon, son of Kirianadréth!"

All at once, the entire room went dead silent upon the mention of Dragon's mother's name. Now the company was really on edge, for they wondered what could have silenced so many dwarves. All the attention in the room quickly turned to King Ronnar, who slowly rose from his throne. He steadily walked down the steps, stood only a foot from Dragon and stared deeply into his eyes.

Dragon, of course, had a firm grip on Truth's hilt at his side, not quite sure what was going to happen. Ronnar and Dragon stared at each other, taking a long moment to scrutinize each other. After what seemed to be hours of silence, Ronnar finally moved. He stepped forward, threw his arms around Dragon and gave him a tight squeeze.

At first, Dragon thought the king was trying to squash him to death. And then he realized that this was a form of dwarfish hug. As Ronnar continued to hug Dragon, all the dwarves in the room burst into cheers. Dragon, on the other hand, still had a firm grip on Truth, not sure what to think even as the king continued embracing him.

Once King Ronnar let go of Dragon and backed up, he realized Dragon demanded answers from the mere look on his face. "You are definitely, without a doubt, Jorn's son," Ronnar stated.

Dragon was so confused, he could barely speak at all. "What do you mean?"

"You have the look of your father. However, you have your mother's eyes. Although when someone says that about the eyes they are generally being kind, I, on the other hand, mean it. You literally have your mother's eyes. It's not every day you see a human with dragon eyes."

"How do you know my mother and my father?" Dragon asked.

Ronnar stepped forward and gave Dragon a pat on the arm. "I'm glad you asked, my boy. However, it is a long story," he declared. "I will tell you the tale as fast as I can, but you must forgive me if I ramble a bit."

After Dragon nodded respectfully, Ronnar began to reveal his story. "All the dwarves in Shieldholt know well the names of Kirianadréth and Jorn— all except Timbor and a few of the younger dwarves, who have not yet heard the story. Those two names are held in high respect in this city because we owe them our lives. It was back way before you were born, toward the end of the last Great War that covered the earth. We were living peacefully in our mountain and ignoring anything that happened on the outside world when suddenly, out of nowhere, an army of goblins and trolls invaded Shieldholt.

"In an effort to defend ourselves, the women and children went deep within the mountains' bowels while us men stood our ground. Eventually, we were forced outside the west gate and down to the foot of the mountain, where we were met by an army of goblins in the fields. There at the foot of our own mountain, we faced our extinction, cut off from our women and children, with no escape. Still, we were ready to fight to the last dwarf to defend our mountain, and we wouldn't have survived if it wasn't for your parents."

Ronnar then began to move with his arms, doing his best to make the story more exciting. "We heard trumpets sound over the hills, and as we watched, Jorn's army marched over the hills toward us. At first, we weren't sure what to expect. Nevertheless, we decided to be hopeful and believed that the army was there to aid us. We were just about prepared for the onslaught of the goblins when we heard a roar from up above. All the dwarves looked up to see dragons flying down from the mountaintop, led by your mother, of course. We were certain that they were with the goblins, so we cried out in desperation and cursed the goblins. Needless to say, we were all surprised when the dragons smote down the goblins on the mountainside. Then like great worms, they weaved their way into the mountain, devouring all in their path. As for the army of goblins in the fields, when we turned back around, Jorn and his army had enveloped them. Of course, realizing that we were liberated, we quickly rejoined the fight and did our fair share of fighting. However, no matter how prideful we dwarves are, no one here can say that we do not owe our lives to Jorn and Kirianadréth."

Ronnar put his hand on Dragon's back and drew him closer. "There is no way we could ever repay your mother and father except with our lives. And that is exactly what we did. Some of us joined your father and mother in the war. Drognen and I were even there at your mother's crowning, and might I say, your mother was an extremely beautiful woman, just as she was a dragon. After the war, we returned home. Still, we offered them our allegiance, to help them if they ever needed it. We had heard rumors of your birth. Unfortunately, they were drowned by the realization of your father's death. We mourned greatly over his loss, for he was a great man, and we respected him. You are a lot like him in many ways."

"So I keep hearing," Dragon stated as he slowly pulled away from the king.

"It is a shame you had to live your life without him. If anyone deserved to know him, it would be you."

Dragon had his own issues with his father's death, and he didn't want to bring them up in front of the king, so he did his best to take it as a compliment. "Thank you for your kind words, King Ronnar, and for the tale of your meeting my mother and father."

Before Dragon could say anything else, King Ronnar stepped away and walked toward Sonya. "Let me see," muttered Ronnar, scrutinizing Sonya. "You must be Marahezron's offspring."

Sonya quickly lowered her head, all excited. "Yes, that's right. How did you know?"

"I knew your father and your mother before she passed away." Ronnar gave her a small pat on the lower jaw. "Believe it or not, you resemble the two of them perfectly, if they were one dragon. I wish I would've known who you were earlier when they brought me news of the dragon sleeping on our doorstep. I would've brought you in and showed you our hospitality earlier. We thought you were a wild dragon, my apologies."

"It's okay, your Majesty; I enjoy the outdoors," Sonya reassured him.

"At least I see you have taken up your father's responsibility by watching over your prince, like Marahezron watching over Kirianadréth."

Ronnar then quickly turned his attention to Voraha and very carefully studied the ax that she held. "As for you, you must be a daughter of Brajan from Tivendel."

"How do you know that?" Voraha snapped back, sounding all defensive.

"Easy, young one. I mean you no ill will. I know you from the ax that you bear. It was your father's. I recognize it because I was there when it was made and given to him." Ronnar kept a steady gaze on Voraha to see what her reaction would be.

"What do you know about my father and his ax?" Voraha demanded.

Ronnar answered in a calm and slow voice. "When I was a young dwarf with fresh hair on my face, I traveled with my cousin to Tivendel. That is where I met your father. I even fought by his side in many battles and earned his respect. As for any information on the ax, that I cannot help you with. It was a gift of special magnificence and power that must be well cared for. If your father did not tell you anything about the ax, then I cannot tell you anything. I'm surprised that he actually let you take it so far from home." Ronnar noticed with those words that the look on her face changed drastically, which gave him a desire to make a few inquiries. "Your father isn't dead, is he?"

"No, he is not dead. He is well and living out his long years in peace." Voraha quickly defended herself.

"Since he is alive, that leaves me to assume that you took it from him without his permission." Ronnar began to laugh out loud, somehow amused by the whole situation. "I applaud you for your actions. To do what you did takes great courage, with a little bit of mischievousness. You are welcome in my halls, Voraha, daughter of Brajan. And don't worry, I won't tell your father where you are."

Ronnar then turned back to speak to Dragon again like a child with a very short attention span. "Which reminds me, how is your mother? We have often sent requests for her to come join us for a celebration, and then again, she was always too busy to come and meet us. I assume that is why you are here, to take your mother's place and visit us."

Dragon, of course, did not answer him right away. He simply stood silent, thinking back to the loss of his mother. He did as best as he could to push it out of his mind until that moment when he was forced to confront it. Then, after carefully choosing his words, he informed King Ronnar of what had transpired. "I'm afraid I bring bad tidings, King. My mother is dead."

Understanding Dragon's words all too clear, the entire room of dwarves fell silent in shock. Some dwarves even fell to their knees as though they were burdened heavily. King Ronnar himself stumbled back in shock over this depressing news. "How did she die?"

"She was murdered by an assassin dragon in her own throne room," Dragon answered promptly.

King Ronnar then began to stomp his feet and yell like a child throwing a fit. "An assassin murdered our beloved Kirianadréth! Must we go on a hunt and skin this beast alive?"

"No, my King Ronnar!" Dragon yelled back, trying to calm him and hold him at bay. "I avenged my mother, and I myself took the very life of the beast!"

In reply to Dragon's boast, all the dwarves raised their weapons and gave a victory shout, in salute to Dragon. Ronnar had to take a moment, for his face was beet red, and he had to catch his breath from his ranting. "I will never understand why anyone would want to hurt someone as sweet as your mother." Ronnar then took his hands and clasped them to Dragon's arms and stared him deep in the eyes. "Now I understand why you call yourself king of the dragons. My blessings go out to you. What can I do for you, Dragon?"

"My company and I would like passage to the other side of the mountain."

"Then passage through Shieldholt is granted to you, as long as the mountain stands. Though I must ask, would you and your company join us for a feast? It is our way to say good-bye to those that have passed, if it doesn't offend you."

Dragon thought about the king's request for a moment, and it put a smile on his face. He was sure that the company needed a good rest and food. Yet he felt strangely at peace, here within the mountain among the dwarves. Something about the city of Shieldholt reminded him of home, and he felt a strange connection to King Ronnar, almost as though he were family. After he considered everything, he informed the king that they would be staying for the feast, which made many of the dwarves quite happy.

"That's wonderful!" Ronnar shouted. "Tonight, we feast to the memory of your mother and father, and to you for gracing us with your presence. Then tomorrow we will give you supplies and lead you to the east gate, and there we will discuss your path." Ronnar then motioned for Drognen and Timbor to come hither. "While we prepare for the feast, Drognen and Timbor will take you to wash and clean yourselves from your journey. Then, when ready, we will meet in the dining hall of my fathers, and there, Dragon, we will have more to talk about."

When Ronnar motioned for them to leave, he quickly noticed the depressed look on Sonya's face concerning the entrance and the fact that she had to squeeze through it again. Getting a queer thought in his mind, Ronnar indicated that he needed to speak to her, so she lowered her head, and they conversed about his thought. "My dear, I've been meaning to make that entrance a lot bigger. Do you think you can help me with that?" Ronnar suggested, and then gave Sonya a wink and a pat on the arm.

For a moment, Sonya stood confounded until she finally realized what he was meaning. Then she bolted off to the door and slammed right into the wall above it. As Sonya broke through the wall it burst into hundreds of pieces, and it all fell to the ground like raindrops. After some of the dust settled, everyone could see that her act definitely opened the doorway by three times its size. Of course, the company and Dragon were shocked and overwhelmed by her actions, thinking that this would cause great trouble with the dwarves. However, that was not the reaction that the dwarves had. All of them were hysterically laughing, especially King Ronnar. Laughter or not, Dragon gave Sonya a distasteful look, and they all quickly left the room to go wash, especially since now they had a rain of rock dust fall upon them. Needless to say, even though Dragon was embarrassed by Sonya, she walked behind them with her head held high and wagging her tail, very proud of herself.

* * *

The entire company was led north in the mountain yet deeper into the city bowels. There, they found themselves standing in a massive room that was the source of Shieldholt's water supply. Once again, they stood in awe at the beauty of the inside of this particular mountain. On the far wall facing the entrance, high in the room, a natural mountain spring flowed out. The beautiful water that glittered like silver fell into a large natural basin like a small lake held with rocks from the mountain. Dragon could see that from there, the dwarves filled barrels of water to be delivered throughout the city. The water then flowed out of the basin in two directions, filling up two more big basins of the same size right below it. These basins were right next to each other yet divided by a twelve-foot wall of rock. Dragon could see that these basins were meant for the washing of clothes and of persons. Dragon also noticed that the rock wall between them made a perfect barrier for one side for the women and the other for the men, and since no one there was of tall stance, it gave them their privacy.

The water from these basins flowed out and back into one stream, which went down a tunnel right underneath the entrance to the room. Dragon was extremely amazed by the beauty of this place, but though he wanted to give the dwarves credit for its design, he noticed that the only thing that was made by dwarven hands was the entrance. It was as if the mountain itself favored the dwarves and built them this water structure, and no one could say that this was not a beautiful marvel of nature.

After a while of staring, Drognen urged the company to continue, but in separate groups, the females to the right and the males to the left. As the males rounded the walkway to their side, Dragon could see some male dwarves already bathing. He saw that even dwarves among themselves had different opinions about bathing. Some of them jumped in without hesitation while others were being dragged in by friends as they kicked and screamed, and that, of course, made Dragon chuckle. As they prepared to bathe themselves, they took off their weapons and laid them off to the side.

Dragon took the time to carefully wrap up Truth in the cloth that Ancient sent with it and then set it with the others. Then some dwarves, who were meant to aid them with anything they needed, took their clothes from them to be shaken out but not washed. With nothing else to do but to stand there and get cold, the company decided to get into the water, which, surprisingly, was a lot warmer than they expected. One of the older dwarfs bathing in the pool saw the confused look on their faces and decided to inform them about the water temperature—that the water flowing into the first basin was ice cold, giving them perfect drinking water. Somehow, as the water flowed over the basin into the other two pools, it warmed itself, and no dwarf knew how. Everyone in the mountain considered it as one of the acts of magic that no one would ever understand, and they didn't want someone's foolish curiosity to ruin the gift of the mountain. Even though Dragon and the others didn't understand it completely, they decided there was no harm, so they continued deeper into the pool.

There in the water, the company of men washed, talked, and laughed—all except for Dragon, who was sitting a little off to the side. He had much to think about. His life wasn't going to become any less complicated anytime soon. Of course, at the same time, he was carefully watching the other men. In his life living with dragons, he had never seen another naked male, and he was curious if he was truly built like a proper human. Still, he didn't make it too obvious that he was looking at them. He didn't want to upset them or confuse them in any way. Just before he was done convincing himself that he was built properly, his attention was quickly diverted by a large splash.

One of the men had been suddenly hit by a barrel-sized amount of water that came from above. All the men quickly looked up to see

Sonya peering over the wall. It had never occurred to them that she was the only one tall enough to do so. In seeing a man drenched in water, Sonya began to chuckle. She then lapped up the water falling from the top basin in her mouth and leaned over the wall again. She took a moment to carefully choose her target, and then with a big puff of her cheeks, she spat it out, knocking over one of the men with a sudden burst of water. Now the game was on. She lapped up more water, and the men laughed while they waited to dodge her next shot. Some of the dwarves sitting on the sidelines cheered with every hit she made. Other dwarves felt inclined to join the fun, and they jumped into the water kicking, thrashing, and laughing as they went. Of course, the dwarves were a little easier to target than the men, simply because they couldn't get out of the way as fast. Still, they enjoyed the game nonetheless.

Dragon was the only one not participating in the game; he still sat off to the side quietly. However, he did enjoy watching this peaceful pool become a storm for every man for himself while vast gobs of water came raining down upon them. Dragon had to admit that since they had left Falistoran, this was the first time that Sonya truly came alive. To him, it was as if an old friend had come back, and it brought him great comfort and joy. For a long time, he sat in the shallows of the pool and simply watched Sonya enjoy herself in her typical ridiculous fashion.

After a while, Drognen announced that it was time for the feast, so everyone got out of the water, even Sonya, who sent a few parting shots of water at the men. They all dried themselves as best as they could and dressed for the feast. As they were leaving the water hall, Dragon noticed that all the dwarves were quite polite to everyone but Voraha. Some of the responses she was getting from the other dwarves were quite rude, which confused Dragon. He didn't know much about dwarfish culture or about Voraha, which made him determined to find out sooner or later. Nevertheless, they followed Drognen back through the city to the banquet hall.

The company entered a room similar to the throne room, with a dais on the opposite side from the entrance. There were no massive pillars in this room to get in the way. It was stacked full of long tables and chairs; there was even one long table set on the dais for the king and his honored guests. There were two smaller entrances, one on either side of the dais, and from there, their food and drink entered and left the room at a quick pace. The company noticed that the dwarves had already started feasting without them; still, the dwarves lifted their glasses and gave a mighty shout as the travelers entered the room. The dwarves gave an even mightier shout when Sonya entered the room, simply because she could fit through this door with no problem.

The travelers were greatly welcomed, cheered and escorted down to the dais, where they sat beside the king, facing the rest of the room. There was no particular seating, just whoever could grab a chair first, except for the chair to the left of the king, which was saved for Dragon. The dragon king felt honored to sit by Ronnar's side, and at the same time, he was pleased because he had much to discuss with the king. However, at first, there was no talking between the two; there was only time for eating. The entire company followed the example of the dwarves; forgetting their manners just a bit, they began to ravage the food. Unlike humans, dwarves have no manners for eating; the only rule they had was to eat until they were full. If you were unhappy, you were to drink until you were merry. If, by then you still weren't having a good time, the dwarves would simply throw you out.

Sonya sat by the entrance to the left of the king and feasted well. She even took it upon herself to occasionally snatch up a tray of food as it entered the room, which scared the servants from time to time, making some of the other dwarves laugh. The entire company had a grand time; none of them, including Dragon, had ever seen such a feast. There were all types of meat piled high on trays, as well as different assortments of fruits, some of which the company had never seen. They even took to drinking the fine ale and beer that the dwarves had, all except for Dragon and Sonya, who didn't fancy the taste. They enjoyed the crisp, clear spring water of the mountain.

As Dragon sat beside King Ronnar and feasted, he noticed a dwarf that filled his mug with fresh water. It was a female dwarf, much different than Voraha. She was young, with long blonde hair and no facial hair at all. She wasn't built like a warrior; she looked more refined, almost human-like. Dragon noticed that when she filled the king's cup, Ronnar gave her a kiss on the forehead, which gave Dragon a curious question to start a conversation with.

"Is she your wife?" Dragon softly asked, hoping not to say the wrong thing.

Ronnar immediately began to laugh out loud. "No, my dear boy! She is Felewa, the youngest of my daughters, as well as the youngest of all my children."

"Why doesn't she have any hair?" asked Dragon, motioning to the face.

"That is because she is young," Ronnar replied, still laughing.

"When do young dwarves get their hair?" Dragon continued as he couldn't help but show his innocent curiosity.

"It depends on the young dwarf. Some bloom early at the age of ten, others as late as seventeen. You must give her time. She is only fourteen. Soon her hair will grow, and she will be the fairest in the city, especially with her rare blonde hair."

"Forgive me, Ronnar, if this offends you. I think she is fair now."

Ronnar began to chuckle again. "Thank you, Dragon. That is a compliment, but you have much to learn about the dwarven people."

"That is definitely true, King Ronnar. I hope to learn much from you. So how many children do you have?" Dragon asked, becoming more curious after every word Ronnar spoke.

"I have many children, since I have many wives. I think perhaps even in my old age. I might have forgotten one or two. Still, I have many sons and daughters. Felewa is my youngest, yet she is my first wife's only child. Which brings a strange thought to my mind. How would you like to marry my daughter?"

Upon those words, Dragon immediately spat out the water that he had been drinking, which made Ronnar laugh heartily. Dragon simply looked at Ronnar, speechless and stunned.

"I know this comes as a surprise to you," Ronnar continued. "Still, it wouldn't be a bad arrangement. I could never replace your mother or father. However, I would be honored to have you as a son. Besides, I've been looking for a good male for my daughter, not to mention our laws here are quite odd. If you marry my daughter, you will become my first wife's son. Therefore, you will inherit the throne. Believe it or not, no dwarf or child of mine would disagree with that, because you are of fine lineage. Not to mention we would be the only dwarven city with a dragon king." Some of the other dwarves sitting at the table, who happened to be brothers and sons of King Ronnar, lifted their mugs of ale in salute to the idea.

Dragon still had a stunned look on his face as he tried to carefully answer King Ronnar. "I am honored by your request, King Ronnar," he spoke as delicately as he could. "However, I must decline at this present moment. I have much to do, but I promise you that I will think about it. I must say it is not a bad idea. Shieldholt is welcoming, and you would make an excellent father."

"That's wonderful, my boy," Ronnar shouted as he smacked Dragon on the back and threw another piece of meat on his plate. "Come, daughter, fill Dragon's cup again and let him have another look at you."

Felewa slid in between Dragon and her father to fill the cup, her face red from blushing. Dragon also had a slight blush on his face when he looked at her; still, he gave her a small smile. This interaction between the two only made Ronnar laugh louder. He gave them a small moment and then, with his hand, motioned for her to leave so that he and Dragon could talk. After she stepped back and out of the way, Ronnar started in with a long-desired conversation. "So, Dragon, there are some things I've been meaning to ask, if that doesn't bother you."

"Not at all, King Ronnar. There are things I would like to ask you as well," Dragon replied, taking an enormous bite out of the meat on his plate.

"That's wonderful," Ronnar stated, getting all excited. "We dwarves are filled with rumors of other races but rarely ever get a chance to see if they are true. For example, I may have known your mother, but in all that time, I never truly learned about dragons. Your mother was a kind and wonderful dragon and seemed to be of great standing, as well as the dragons of her city. However, that does not fit the rumors we heard about dragons. It is said that dragons are vicious and love to steal and hoard precious metals like gold and silver."

Dragon smiled at that comment and raised his voice to speak, since his mouth was still full of food. It seemed as if Dragon's natural manners were well welcomed here with the dwarves. "I cannot say that is not true, King. Just like every race, there are ones that do evil deeds, and that would be those dragons. The reason why that rumor is widely spread is because good dragons normally keep to themselves. So when one sees a dragon, unfortunately, it happens to be an evil dragon."

"That is fascinating," King Ronnar said, encouraging Dragon to continue.

With a fresh bite of meat in his mouth, Dragon went on with similar subjects. "I believe that dragons are misrepresented everywhere. With different lands comes different cultures. No matter how different dragons are from one another, everyone seems to think they're exactly the same. Dragons of one-color breed only that color, and their temperaments are all the same. Somehow, we are believed to be some mindless animal. Do we look like animals to you, King?" Dragon asked, motioning to Sonya, not realizing that she had just swallowed a whole tray of food.

That tickled the king, making him laugh greatly once again. "You need not tell me, Dragon," Ronnar said, giving Dragon a reassuring pat on the back. "I have walked through your city. I know the splendor and true nature of dragons."

Ronnar's words gave Dragon some peace of mind and a much-needed moment of silence. Unfortunately, the silence did not last long; Dragon's sense of curiosity spurred him to ask a question. "King Ronnar, can you tell me about dwarves?"

"What would you like to know, my boy?" Ronnar asked as he too took a big bite of meat.

"Well, you at least have heard of dragons. I, on the other hand, have heard very little, almost nothing, about dwarves, so anything would help." Dragon tried not to sound desperate for information, but it came out in his voice anyway.

"Then I will do my best to help you, as long as I do not bore you." Ronnar finished chewing the meat in his mouth and took a good drink of ale before he started his long tale of dwarves. "I wish, my boy, that I could tell you that all dwarves are the same. Unfortunately, they're not. You are lucky that you met reputable dwarves on your first meeting," Ronnar said as he motioned out to the other dwarves in the room. Following Ronnar's hand, Dragon looked out at that feasting hall of dwarves to see them laughing, eating, and occasionally falling out of their chairs from too much drink.

"Dwarves are different between each city, even to the very language that we speak. There are great dwarven cities within the mountains, where they mine for precious ores, and dwarven cities within the forest that loved to farm. I have seen dwarves that are stout and grim, built for battle, with beards down into their knees. I have also seen dwarves that are barely three feet tall, skinny as a beanpole, and with no facial hair at all. We have heard rumors of cities of dwarves that are vicious and even hate other dwarves, and then there are cities as welcoming as we are. There are dwarves that are honorable and trustworthy. There are also dwarves that would betray you for mere food. My dear boy, if you're looking for something in particular, I'm afraid you're out of luck. Unless the information is about Shieldholt dwarves then I could tell you much. If it deals with other dwarven cities, then it gets quite confusing. We dwarves have cities that are ruled by males, others ruled by females."

"This is all wonderful information, King," Dragon said. "I am enjoying it immensely and am thankful for it, though your words just now reminded me and encouraged me to ask a question." Dragon respectfully waited until Ronnar nodded his head in approval. "Why are the dwarves in your city so rude to Voraha, who is a member of my company?"

Ronnar immediately became aggravated and rose from his seat. "That is uncalled for. I wish I would have known about this sooner! Drognen, why is this so?" Ronnar shouted, motioning for him to come forward and account for these actions.

Unfortunately, before Drognen could get out of his chair, Timbor stood and gave an answer of his own. "It is because she is a thief and dishonored her father by taking his weapon!" He then gave a sharp look at Voraha, urging her to try anything that would start a fight. Instead, she simply strode up with a blank expression on her face and walked with her ax in hand right past Sonya and out of the room. Her action pleased Timbor, and he gave a slight chuckle.

Ronnar, on the other hand, did not find this amusing, and in a quick reaction, he grabbed his cup and threw it at Timbor, which, with perfect aim, hit Timbor right smack on the forehead. Dragon could tell from the expression on Timbor's face that this was not the first time his foolish words had received this response.

"Timbor Rocksmasher!" Ronnar bellowed down at him. "How dare you, insult my guests in my city! You do not know her father, nor do you know her, and from where I am sitting, she has more honor than you do! She is to be treated with the same respect that is shown to Dragon!"

Timbor quietly sat back down and angrily grabbed his mug and began to drink from it, all frustrated. Dragon, on the other hand, sat quietly by Ronnar, both stunned and confused. When Ronnar finally sat back down, Dragon began to inquire about what just happened. "May I ask what that was all about?"

"Forgive me, Dragon. That will not happen again. Voraha will be treated with respect. It seems that I have forgotten that some dwarves do not hold women in high esteem as I do. You see, some dwarven cities like Shieldholt allow females to bear weapons to protect themselves. I must admit that some of my wives are fiercer than some of the men here. However, in a city like Tivendel, where Voraha was from, women were not allowed to touch a weapon, even in last defense. By taking her father's weapon, she has shamed her family's name. I, on the other hand, hold her with respect. I was there when her father received that ax, and I know much that she does not, and I understand why she took it. As for the rest of the story, I'm afraid you must ask her yourself." Ronnar then motioned with his hand for Dragon to go off and speak with Voraha.

Dragon, already filled with much curiosity, wasn't hesitant to get up and go after her. Just before he left the room, he patted Sonya on the side and told her that everything was okay and she could enjoy herself. Through the door, he rounded a corner, and there he found Voraha sitting partway down on some steps. She was quietly holding her father's ax in her hands, looking at it intently. Dragon was uncertain for a moment, for he wasn't too good at speaking to people. Still, he knew that he needed some answers, so with a deep breath, he walked down the steps and sat down beside her.

"Voraha," Dragon started to say, trying to find the right words. "If you wish to travel with me, I need to know who you are and why you are here. I cannot have any uncertainties traveling with me. I need to know whom I can trust." Though the meaning of his words was firm, Dragon said them as calmly as he could.

After a moment of silence, Voraha slowly handed her ax to Dragon, which gave him his first opportunity to really examine its design. In his hands, he carefully held the ax, looking at every intricate part and appreciating each design. First, he studied the ruby knob at the end of the ax that was fitted well in the handle. The ruby was polished and well rounded with a slight glow. He then studied the long ax haft, which was sturdy metal tightly wrapped in leather, which, oddly, was as white as snow. Finally, he studied the ax's head, which made him smile in amazement. The entire ax seemed to be made out of some form of strong metal, yet it looked like silver, especially on the head. The medal went up into a nice spike, and just below the spike, the metal fanned out into the two large blades of the battle ax. The spike was just an inch above the top of both blades, making it a deadly weapon if used properly. The most interesting feature was the carvings on each blade. Etched into one blade looked to be elfish writing, and on the other blade dwarfish writing. It was also duplicated on the other side. Dragon could not read the writings on the blades, and neither could Voraha.

"The ax has been used by my father for many years, but has never needed sharpening," Voraha said. "It was made by the elves and given to my father when he was very young. It was said that they gave it to him as a gift for helping in some great war of theirs. It seems that Ronnar knows more about that time than I do."

"Yes, that seems true. However, Ronnar is not the issue," Dragon said, trying to get her to divulge more information.

"I was my father's firstborn," Voraha continued, almost unwilling to talk. "He was proud to have a daughter, and he still had many chances to have a son. It wasn't until I got older that things began to change between us, and he began to pull away from me. It was because he sired no sons, only daughters, and in our city, that is a dishonor. No one knew why, however, he seemed to blame me since I was his firstborn. At first, I was angry with myself for dishonoring my father, and then I realized all I needed to do was to prove myself, to become greater than all the dwarves in Tivendel. Then my father, Brajan, could lift his head again with no shame."

"Now I understand," Dragon replied, comforting her. "So you took his magic ax, so it seems, and set out to make a name for yourself in order to honor your father. That is why you need some great kill, like a dragon perhaps."

"Yes, I need something to prove that I'm greater than the males." Voraha clenched her fists as though she were disgusted by the very thought of males.

Dragon thought for a moment and then stood up, handing her back her father's ax. "I will make this bond with you. You can come with me on my travels, and I promise you that someday you will have your great kill."

"I will accept this bond only if you will add one thing," Voraha said, rising herself to face Dragon.

"If it is within reason, I will consider it."

Voraha gripped her father's ax and held it in front of her as though it would seal the bond. "If I should die on my travels with you, I want you to promise that you will take my tale and my ax back to my father."

"Very well, I promise you that I will," Dragon replied, extending his arm. With a smile underneath her red beard, they clapped forearms, sealing the promise.

Immediately after, Dragon heard Sonya roar from the other room, he and Voraha darted off back to the feasting hall as fast as they could. When they burst back into the room, they could see Sonya wildly thrashing about in the middle of the room, with hundreds of dwarves attacking her.

Dragon took a firm grip on Truth and started to lend a hand. Suddenly, he was stopped by the voice of the king. Turning to look at Ronnar, Dragon was surprised to find him laughing in his seat. "What is the meaning of this?" Dragon shouted.

"Come sit down, Dragon. Everything is fine," Ronnar responded, still laughing wildly.

Dragon walked over to the king and pointed to the disturbance. "You call this fine!"

"It's a friendly fight, Dragon," explained Ronnar. "You see, Timbor got so drunk that he boasted that he could defeat a dragon. In response to that boast, Sonya challenged him to prove it. When the fight started, the others joined in, not willing to miss a chance to fight with a dragon. Come sit down beside me and enjoy. This should be interesting."

Dragon and Voraha sat down beside King Ronnar and watched the brawl that took up the entire room. All the dwarves looked like an army of ants as they tried to overpower Sonya. She, in return, repelled them with her wings and the five tips of her tail. Sonya also used her body, moving it around and knocking the dwarves over as they came at her. To the onlookers, it was quite a humorous sight. For hours, dwarves swarmed up to her and were knocked clear across the room. Unwilling to quit or admit defeat, they picked themselves back up and came back. Nothing changed until Sonya noticed that some of the dwarves were too drunk or too tired to continue. So she started to give way to their attacks, even though she still had enough energy to keep this going all night. Dragon and Ronnar seemed to be the only ones who had realized that she was giving in, and they grinned at her and at each other. It wasn't long before she was down and the dwarves were shouting in victory, surprisingly, with Timbor standing on top of her, waving his arms with success. With the room completely thrashed, everyone simply sat on the ground, gathered and filled their cups, and drank to the health of Sonya.

"This was the most excitement I've had in years," spoke Ronnar as he rose from the table. "I believe it is time for sleep. Tomorrow we will wake, eat, and then I take you to the east gate. Drognen will show you to your room where you may sleep for the night. As for me, I'll bid you good night." With that, he left the room quietly, leaving them in the capable hands of Drognen.

Since most of them were quite exhausted, they didn't hesitate to follow Drognen. Even Dragon followed, simply to see the accommodations and to see if they were good enough for him to stay the night away from Sonya. When they reached their rooms, they were surprised at the size of the dwarven beds. They were big enough for two people of normal height. Everyone found their way to their beds quite easily—all except for Dragon who felt the need to return to the feasting hall. Before Dragon could leave the room, Brenath grabbed his arm, wishing to have a quick word with him. This conversation looked quite humorous since Brenath was drunk from much feasting and was steadied by Phanis's hand, who was also drunk.

"Dragon," Brenath started to say, slurring his words, "you and the king get along just fine, so I let you do the talking for the whole company, including my men. But don't forget in your conversation with the king that we are on a mission for the queen and for Tyrilcrysss, Tyrilcrysss, for home. Earlier today, you almost got us into trouble. Don't do it again."

Dragon grabbed the other side of Brenath and helped Phanis take him to a bed to sleep. "Don't worry, friend. I won't let you down," Dragon replied as he laid Brenath on a bed. After that, Phanis stumbled to a bed of his own to sleep. As for Dragon, he eventually made his way back to the feasting hall.

By the time he returned to the hall, all the feasting was over. Most of the dwarves were either knocked out from the fight or had passed out from drinking. Sonya herself was asleep in the middle of the floor, with piles of dwarves around her. The only ones awake in the room were a few servants and Felewa, cleaning what they could, especially the king's table. Dragon's eye caught Felewa's, and he gave her a gentle smile and bid her good night as he walked toward Sonya. Dragon stopped halfway to Sonya and stared at her. He smiled, seeing her asleep with the dwarves sleeping around her. Dragon couldn't help but think fondly of her and her joyful heart.

"You love her, don't you?" a voice spoke next to him.

Dragon turned to see Felewa next to him with a smile on her face. "Yes, I do," Dragon responded, thinking it through. "She is all I have.

She has been with me from birth. It is not the love that you think. She is a part of me. Like my arms and legs, she makes me be what I am."

"I like what you are," Felewa said, blushing a bit.

Dragon smiled at her for a minute, and then his face turned solemn. "I wish I could say the same."

Felewa understood what he meant. The fact that he was from two races was not easy on him. Deciding to change the subject to something more desirable, Felewa asked a simple question, though she had her reasons. "Do you like Shieldholt?"

"I like Shieldholt very much. It reminds me of my home." Dragon went silent for a moment as he looked off into the distance as if he was seeing something long gone. He then looked at Felewa with a very serious face. "Felewa, I did not tell your father, and I ask you not to." Felewa nodded in agreement, so he continued. "The Creator has told the dragons to fade. In so doing, my kingdom is lost forever. I can never go home. If your father heard that, he would never let me leave as a way of taking care of me."

"You can stay here and marry me. I will make you a fine wife." Felewa said, sounding very eager for it. "I would even shave my beard for you, whenever it comes in."

"Why for me?"

"Father always said I was a strange dwarf—a lot like him when he went on his adventures. That's why he likes me more than his other children. He says I think for myself. And he's right. I don't think the same as the other dwarves, especially the females." Felewa paused for a moment, thinking of her next words as she blushed a bit. "You are an honorable man from a great lineage, and to me and my odd way of thinking, you are better than a dwarf man. I would have an adventurous life as your wife."

Dragon smiled at her and enjoyed her words. He couldn't help but think of the possibilities in his mind, thinking of all that his life would entail. Still, he had to admit the reality of it. "I'm sorry, Felewa," Dragon began softly. "I cannot do that to you. In the beginning, it would be wondrous, and we would enjoy each other's company. However, as time moves on, things would change. When the weight of my life begins to bear me down, you would spend every waking moment trying to make me happy with nothing in return." Dragon placed his hand on her cheek. "And I could not do that to you."

Felewa's reaction to Dragon's words was not what he expected. She stood on her toes, and with her hands, she reached up and gently grabbed Dragon's face. Bringing his face down to hers, Felewa softly kissed him on the lips. As she let him go, she blushed more than she had all night. "No matter how hard it would be on me, I still think I would make you a good wife." With that said, Felewa turned and went back to her work, leaving Dragon to think things over.

For Dragon, he continued to walk toward Sonya with a smirk on his face. As he did, he noticed that Felewa was keeping a close eye on him, studying him intently. He let out a small chuckle as he thought back to the king's proposal. Still, it was a nice gesture. When he reached Sonya, he realized he was not ready for sleep. Dragon had too many thoughts running through his head and needed to sort them out. Since the servants were still cleaning up, he thought it was a perfect time to go for a walk. It would give him a chance to sort through the thoughts in his head and see more wonders of the city. He knew Sonya would still be there when he was ready to sleep. He carefully wrapped Truth back up in the cloth that Ancient put around it. Then he set it and his pack next to Sonya, so he could explore unburdened. With that, Dragon walked out the door of the feasting hall and into the vast realm of Shieldholt.

15

The Hall of Kings

After leaving the feasting hall, Dragon wandered the city of Shieldholt. None of the dwarves he met as he wandered stopped him or asked what he was doing; they simply nodded in respect. He rather enjoyed having time all to himself. As he walked through Shieldholt, his mind seemed to wander as well, which was something he hadn't done in a long time. It was nice being able to relax and not focus on all the horrible things weighing him down.

He enjoyed seeing the sights of Shieldholt. He went from hall to hall, exploring as much as he could. Dragon never opened any doors if he passed by one because he didn't know what was on the other side and didn't want to intrude on someone's private chambers. At one point, Dragon laid down on one of the bridges spanning over a giant crevasse, and he stared down into the emptiness. As the night wore on, Dragon did notice a strange but magnificent change in Shieldholt. When he first entered, during the day, lanterns with fire lit the city. However, at night, the city was lit by a strange new light. The fire lanterns were put out, and the city began to glow in certain areas. Right above each lantern was a stone on the wall that glowed a bright blue. Even the giant pillars that once held massive fires had a section above the fire pit that now glowed. Some areas of the city glowed a dim blue while others glowed so brightly that it looked like daylight. Dragon couldn't tell if this was natural dwarven ingenuity or magic. He added it to the list of things he was going to ask Ronnar. Nevertheless, the change of light didn't stop him from exploring, it encouraged him to go further.

At one point, Dragon found himself in a massive forge larger than the town of Falistoran. This he really enjoyed since there were some dwarves still at work. Dragon could tell that the forge was not fully manned, and he could only imagine what it looked like during the day. He went to each work area that was being used, watched each dwarf for a moment, and then moved on to the next. Dragon saw one dwarf making a sword. He found another dwarf finishing a battle ax by putting gems on its haft. One of his favorite things he found was a dwarf cutting newly found diamonds. After an hour of watching the dwarves in the forge, Dragon realized he should get back to Sonya and get some sleep.

He was almost to the forge entrance when Dragon noticed an old dwarf struggling with his project. Stopping, he took a moment to observe the dwarf. Dragon could tell that this dwarf was old, even by dwarf standards. He had a large piece of metal glowing red, fresh from the fire on the anvil. The dwarf was having trouble holding it with the tongs and hammering it. Dragon wanted to help, but he knew it wasn't that simple. He wasn't the best judge of character, but Dragon had a pretty good idea about this dwarf's personality. He had seen many old dragons share the same characteristics back in his own city. They poured their lives into their work, and it was their passion. However, when their bodies can no longer withstand the work, they become lost because their work defines them. If you try to help them, they usually lash out to guard their pride. Dragon watched the old dwarf struggle for a few moments longer until he came up with a way to both help the dwarf and save his pride.

Dragon walked over to the work area. "Excuse me, master crafter," Dragon said as humbly as he could.

The old dwarf paused for a moment and looked at Dragon with a little bit of frustration on his face.

"I'm sorry to bother you," Dragon continued. "Do you think you can teach me to work metal? I have heard of the craft but never done it or seen it." Inwardly, Dragon acknowledges that the last bit was a lie; he had seen dragons in his city work metal, but he never paid attention to it.

The old dwarf paused for a moment and set his hammer down. He looked Dragon up and down several times before he responded with a smile on his face. "I know who you are, son of Kirianadréth, and it would be an honor for this old dwarf to teach you, his craft." He waved for Dragon to come closer. "I'm not quite sure what it's going to be yet; I was just beginning to get the metal moldable. I hold the tongs, you come over here and take the hammer."

Dragon did as the old dwarf told him to; he walked over and picked up the hammer in his right hand. He then walked closer to the anvil, with the dwarf to his left holding the tongs that were clamped firmly on the glowing metal.

"It's fitting that the first time you work metal you should be holding my great-grandfather's hammer. It forged many great things for Shieldholt; let's see what the dragon king can make. Now bring the hammer up and strike the mental."

Dragon once again did what he was told, he raised the hammer level with his head and brought it down as hard as he could. Dragon put so much force behind the hammer that when it hit the glowing metal, sparks flew. "That was strange," Dragon muttered. "The hammer and my hand came to an abrupt stop like I expected it to. However, it felt as if the other metal moved and absorbed the strength that I put into it."

"Now you're starting to feel the lure of our craft, the ability to make something bend to your will. To take something plain and ugly and turn it into something magnificent. Now bring your stance in a bit; this is not a battle; you don't need to flail around. Focus your strength into your arm and bring the hammer down. This might look simple, but you need to focus on the metal and your hammer. Keep going until I tell you to stop."

Even though Dragon first started this to help the old dwarf, he felt committed now. Also, he had a strange feeling when the hammer hit the glowing metal. It was an odd feeling he couldn't quite place, and he wanted to feel it again. So, Dragon lifted the hammer, but this time he didn't lift it as high as he did the first time. He focused more strength into his arm and aimed his blow. When Dragon brought the hammer down, the sound was almost deafening, and sparks flew even higher. He definitely felt the glowing metal give a little when the hammer struck it, and he still had that strange feeling as well. Nevertheless, he kept going, just as the old dwarf told him to. With each strike, more sparks flew, and Dragon began to lose himself in the task. He stared at the glowing metal and focused on the sparks when they flew. Pretty soon even the sound of the hammer strike began to fade as he became numb to it, though he could still feel the power when the two metals collided. He had been hammering for a short period of time, but to his body and his mind, it felt like hours. Eventually, he let his eyes completely drift off into the sparks as they flew, and his mind wandered. With every strike of the hammer, he felt as if his heart had stopped. The only thing that came to his mind was how precious life was—that within a heartbeat, something that you love could be taken away from you.

The hammer fell, sparks flew, and as Dragon looked into the sparks, the image of his mother flashed in his mind, vivid and very real, as if she were right before him. Hammer strike, Ancient flashed before him. Hammer strike, Marahezron stood there. Hammer strike, Sonya appeared in a flash. Hammer strike: Yolana appeared; strike, Phanis; strike, Voraha; strike, Brenath; strike, Crysaia; strike, Ronnar!

"Stop," the old dwarf yelled as he reached up and grabbed Dragon's right hand.

Dragon shook his head, pulling himself out of his daze. "What happened?" was all that he could ask.

"A miracle," the old dwarf muttered as he pointed to the metal.

Dragon looked down at the metal that he was hammering, and to his surprise, it was no longer glowing red from the heat of the fire; it was glowing in a brilliant blue, almost a white shine. "I don't understand; what's going on?"

The old dwarf leaned in and whispered as if his voice would ruin what just happened. "You infused the metal with magic."

Dragon looked confused. "I don't think I did that," he said, lowering his voice to a whisper like the dwarf. "Why do you look so amazed? Isn't this a dwarf city, and don't dwarves make magical things?"

"You don't understand lad. We used to make magical things thousands of years ago. Unfortunately, since there was no war or need for magical items, over the generations we lost the knowledge to make such things. In the war that we joined with your father and mother, we were only able to offer warriors. The last magical thing made in Shieldholt was by my great- grandfather. Now don't think that we are worthless, we can still craft magical things. There's a difference between making something magical and crafting something magical. If the magic is already in the metal or jewel, then we can shape it into something that can use the magic. However, we can no longer put magic into something. I heard a rumor that one of the smiths in

Tivendel still has that skill, but we don't know if it's true. That's why we're excited about the new metal we just found deep in the mines; it is rich with magic."

"That's good for Shieldholt; you can start crafting magical items. Maybe this metal is of the same stuff, and you didn't know it." Dragon still didn't believe he was the cause of magic.

"I'm a dwarf; I know the difference between metals," the old dwarf replied, raising his voice back to normal. "What you just did, no living dwarf in Shieldholt has seen; we've only heard about it and what our ancestors used to make. I have to go tell the others."

With that, the old dwarf hobbled away further into the forge to notify the other smiths. Dragon believed that now was a good time to get back to Sonya. So, he slipped out of the forge as quickly and quietly as he could, and he hoped that Ronnar wouldn't learn of this until after he left Shieldholt.

***

Dragon however, didn't hurry back to Sonya; he took his time and explored on his way back. He thought it was a good idea to take a different route on his return. He was happy that he did because he saw many different sites that he hadn't seen the first time. He was about halfway back to the feasting hall when something caught his eye. It was an entrance to a tunnel big enough for three humans to walk side-by-side but not big enough for Sonya. It wasn't the size of the tunnel that caught his eye, but the entrance itself. There were dwarven carvings all over the entrance, and they glowed. They didn't glow like the illuminating stones of the city the words themselves glowed like they were written with magic. Dragon oddly felt pulled into the tunnel, and since there was no door saying stay out, he made his way in.

Once inside the tunnel, Dragon could tell that it wasn't long; he could see the other side about sixty feet away. What made the tunnel more interesting than its entrance was the fact that there were carvings all the way through the tunnel. For a moment, Dragon forgot he was in Shieldholt because the tunnel reminded him so much of home. He placed his hand on the wall like he did in the dragon city and walked, letting his hand brush against the carvings. A moment later, he was in the next room, and his eyes widened with surprise. He knew what he saw would be hard to explain to the others, for it was magnificent. The room he entered was certainly unique; he noticed it was a perfect square, on the sides at least. It was a stairway and a statue room at the same time. The hole in the middle going up and down the mountain was two hundred feet across. What Dragon was standing on was a walkway that was one hundred feet from the hole to the wall. To his right was a stairway the same width as the landing that led down to the next landing. On the next landing below the stairway leading down was on the far wall. On his landing, the stairway leading up was also on the far wall. Once again, Dragon admired how perfectly square the room was, with stairways leading down or up to the next landing. He thought for a moment that it would be a nice way to lose track of time. If he put his hand on the wall and turned right, he would continue to walk for hours just following the walls as he spiraled down into the mountain, or he could use his left hand and go up the mountain. Dragon had to admit he liked the design; he had seen spiral staircases before even in Tyrilcrysalith. However, he had never seen one in the shape of a square, especially with an enormous hole in the middle. He also enjoyed some of the other things that made the room unique. On every level, there were illuminating stones above the stairs, which gave enough light to see everything as if it were daylight. Dragon completely understood the reason for so much light. On each landing, there was an enormous statue carved into the wall that stood over sixty feet tall. Another thing that made the square rooms design unique was from each landing you could see the statue below and part of the statue above. Dragon also noticed that each landing, had a tunnel on either side. So, this room could be accessed from every level of the dwarven city. Dragon never thought that he would admire a room with stairs as much as he did this room.

Eventually, he turned his attention to the statue on his landing. The statue was so intricately designed that he could see wrinkles on the old dwarf's face. The dwarves must've taken years to carve the statue, especially since they took great care to make it look like a real being made of stone. Even the clothes that the dwarf was wearing were well carved from stone; Dragon could tell they were wealthy clothes for a dwarf. What told Dragon about the position of this dwarf was the crown on his head. He realized that this room was a memorial to the kings of Shieldholt. After realizing that Dragon had an interesting thought, he was curious if Ronnar's statue had been made yet. Since he didn't feel like climbing upstairs, he decided going down would be easier. With each landing, he showed his respect and took a moment to look up at the king's statue. Dragon really admired the workmanship on each statue; it was as if he were looking at the real kings, just a lot taller.

After twenty-one levels, Dragon finally stopped at what he called the bottom of the room. He believed it was the bottom because the landing below him had no statue, and he could barely make out the ground below. From what Dragon could see, there were a lot of tools down there as if the dwarves were continuing to dig it out, making more landings and stairs. Dragon turned around to pay attention to the statue. At first glance, it looked very similar to Ronnar, but Dragon could tell that he was not the current king of Shieldholt. However, this statue did have a different feel than all the others above it. The other statues had faces that were either emotionless or smiling; Dragon even saw one that had a smirk. This statue had a very sorrowful face almost frowning. Even the statue's body seemed weak in some odd way, as if it were depressed. Dragon couldn't help but feel sorry for the king. Then it brought up other emotions that Dragon did not expect the statue to invoke. Sadness flooded into Dragon's heart as he remembered looking up at the statues of his mother and father. The memory alone almost brought Dragon to his knees if it weren't for the voice that spoke.

"You're looking at my father."

Dragon turned to his right to see Ronnar emerging from the tunnel. At that point, Dragon's emotions went wild; he wasn't sure if he wanted to cry or be happy. Still, he wasn't going to collapse in front of Ronnar, so he pulled himself together. "Your father," said Dragon as he looked back up at the statue, taking a deep breath to steady himself.

Ronnar walked up and stood next to Dragon staring at the statue. "Yes, that was my father; he died long ago. Now he stands here in the hall of kings."

"Hall," said Dragon, a little confused by the choice of word.

"That's exactly what I said when I was a young dwarf. The last time I remember, a hall was a long passage, not a hole in the ground. However, that's what the first king decided to call this chamber, and they never changed the name."

"The statues are magnificent; it's an excellent way to remember them. Where are the bodies? Are they in another chamber? Because I'm pretty sure dwarves are not turned into stone like dragons are."

"No, we're not turned into stone, although some dwarves may not mind the idea. I know your meaning behind this question; I saw your grandfather's memorial. It was strange to touch the stone statue knowing it was once his real body. To answer your question, their bodies are right here underneath the statue of their likeness. We placed the body underneath the statue and then sealed it, then we wrote their deeds on the seal."

Dragon almost berated himself for not seeing this deal earlier because he was too busy looking at the faces of the statues. Down below the feet of every statue were carvings that described the name and the deeds of each dwarf. "That's amazing workmanship; I can't tell that part of the wall was removed and then replaced."

"That's the idea; that helps them rest in peace. Also, if Shieldholt ever fell to enemies, their graves would not be robbed, especially since some of them were buried with magical items and powerful weapons."

"Where is your statue? I thought they would've started carving it," Dragon asked as he pointed to the next level.

"They do it after the king is dead. It seems to be bad luck to build your memorial before your are dead. The third king of Shieldholt did that; one day he got the idea to start building his statue. He said he wanted to see his face among the hall of kings. A month after it was finished, he died."

"How did he die?"

"He fell down the longest stairway in Shieldholt. It's rumored he was mean to his wife, and she pushed him. That's another reason why male dwarves respect the females here in Shieldholt."

Both Ronnar and Dragon laughed for a long moment, letting the sound of their laughter echo through the chamber. Then they went silent for an even longer moment, staring at the statue as if it were a link between the two of them.

"So, you couldn't sleep," stated Ronnar, breaking the silence.

"No, I've got too much on my mind," Dragon replied.

"You're a lot like your father. He was always worried about so many things."

"That's one of the problems on my mind," Dragon snapped as he finally turned away from the statue. "Everyone keeps telling me I'm so much like my father and that bothers me. I'm so conflicted inside when it comes to him. At one moment I love him, miss him, and wish he were here. At other moments I hate him for leaving me even though I know it wasn't his fault. It's so frustrating when everyone expects me to be like him when I don't even know him. It seemed like my entire life everyone pushed me to be something great when I'm not.

Ronnar came up and placed a hand on Dragon's shoulder turning him back around. "Do you want to know how I found you here?"

Dragon had a confused look on his face, but he was silent which is exactly what Ronnar wanted. In order to help Dragon, Ronnar needed him to listen.

"When I can't sleep, this is where I come, to remind myself of what I've overcome." Ronnar pointed up at his father, giving Dragon something to focus on. "My father's statue is the only one that has a depressing look because that's how all the people of the city came to know him. He did many great deeds in his life, and they're written at his feet, but his face tells a different story. He was never proud or happy, and that's because of me."

Dragon then turned and faced Ronnar, giving him his undivided attention. "Why?" was all that he could say.

"Because to my father, I was the future of Shieldholt and I never lived up to his standard. It never mattered how many things I did it was never good enough. It was as if he wanted me to surpass all the deeds of every king in this hall. It got so bad that one year I left Shieldholt and wandered on a quest of discovery. That's how I met Voraha's father in Tivendel. I spent many years there and even helped them with a war. I sympathize with Voraha, I spent over thirty years away from my home making a name for myself. I did hundreds of amazing things, but they meant nothing to him when I returned. Still to this day I do not know why he was like that, or why he found no worth in his own son. If it wasn't for the people of Shieldholt I would've fallen into a dark place. My father may not have seen my worth, but the people did and they showed their love for their prince. They even wrote songs about the deeds that I have done, and they sang them at feasts. I think in a way that made my father even grumpier than he was before. Nevertheless, the people of Shieldholt helped me to learn something very important."

Ronnar stepped forward and clasped Dragon's shoulders excitedly, as if he were going to reveal a secret that no one on Earth knew. "Your life is not defined by your victories or your defeats, it's defined by your choices. Even if you lose a battle, if you fought for the right purpose then you have reason to hold your head up high. Most of the kings above us didn't die of old age they died in battle. They died protecting the people that they loved. When they weren't fighting in battles, they were too busy loving life and spending it with the people around them. I know you feel like you're living in your parents' shadow and that you must live up to some measure of them, but you don't have to. We're not our ancestors and we were never meant to be. I became a great king when I stopped trying to be like my father and started to act like myself. You will always have a part of your parents in you but that does not mean you have to become them. The moment you were born you were meant to be you, no one else and you must find your own way in this life."

"I don't know what I'm supposed to be," said Dragon, his voice cracking with the emotional pain. Even though he couldn't shed a single tear, Ronnar heard his suffering.

"And you probably won't for many years, I was well over a hundred years before I found who I truly was. You have to make many mistakes and learn from them for you to truly find who you are. Until then that's what your parents are for, to guide you. You knew who your father was, and you knew your mother, what they taught you is supposed to hold you over till you find who you are. If you're lucky, you'll even have a good group of friends to help guide each other. However, I'll give you a warning if you get a bad group of friends, you could really mess up your life. I experienced that once on my journeys outside of Shieldholt. I wish I could tell you things get easy, but I'd be lying. You have to fight to find yourself. The biggest battles in your life won't be outside, they'll be inside. The battle in your heart and soul between what's right and wrong and the choices you make."

"I'm scared of making the wrong choice," Dragon admitted.

"So it should be, anyone with wisdom should be wary of making the wrong choice. Just don't let it stop you from moving forward, especially after you do make a wrong choice. Always pick yourself up and keep going no matter what. That is what made your parents so great. They made lots of mistakes, but it never stopped them. In the end, I don't think anyone remembers the mistakes. And I'll tell you something else, you were not one of their mistakes. From where I'm standing, I think they'd be extremely proud of you."

Dragon couldn't help himself; he came in and hugged Ronnar. "Thank you."

Ronnar gave him a good squeeze in return. He knew Dragon looked like a man, yet he also knew Dragon was still young and had much to learn. "Do you want to know something interesting?"

"Sure," Dragon replied, pulling back from his hug.

"We almost made a statue of your mother and father somewhere here in the city, but we never did."

"Why didn't you?" asked Dragon with a smirk on his face. He enjoyed talking with Ronnar because the king had such a youthful personality.

"Because a lot of the people in the city believed a statue of a human and a dragon would be out of place amongst the dwarven architecture. So instead, we wrote down everything they did for us and what they meant to us in the records, which are kept in the hall of records. Do you want to know something else?"

"Sure, why not?"

"During the time of the fourth king a prophecy was given to Shieldholt. It foreshadowed that when the hall of kings reaches its end, Shieldholt will end as well."

"What's it all mean?"

"Well, the end of Shieldholt is obvious, no city lasts forever. About the rest of the prophecy, we're not quite sure but we have some ideas. With each king, we dig deeper into the earth. One of these days we might break open into a chasm. Or with a dwarven lock, we might dig straight into hell and release a demon to destroy us all. I look at it as the older this city gets the closer we get to our end. I think that's why my father stopped digging at my landing. He probably believed that I was the king to bring Shieldholt down. So, when I became king, I dug down several levels just to prove him wrong. Too bad he wasn't alive at the time I would've loved to see the look on his face. After that, I stopped digging because I didn't want to press my luck. The kings after me can decide when to dig and how far to go."

"That is very interesting and somewhat depressing at the same time," replied Dragon.

"Well then, I have something that might cheer us up. Why don't we go to the training room and have a fight?"

"Have a fight; you want to fight with me?"

"Yes, I assume Marahezron trained you; I want to see how well his training went."

"Marahezron did train me, mother wouldn't let anyone else."

"I don't blame her; only the best for her son and prince. So, what do you say?"

"Sounds like fun; I've never fought a dwarf."

"Good, you'll enjoy this. And when we're done we'll both be tired enough to get some sleep."

Ronnar turned and left the hall of kings, with Dragon following right behind him. As Ronnar led him through the city to the training room, Dragon began to question what he got himself into. He reminded himself that he needed to start thinking things through just a little bit more thorough.

＊

Dragon and Ronnar finally reached the training room and Dragon was intrigued by its design. It reminded him a little of how Marahezron's training room was designed. It was a circular room in design, with weapons and armor lining the walls, leaving the center of the room for the training. The room wasn't very big compared to other training rooms; Dragon realized this room was for personal one-on-one training. The training circle could hold four sets of training combatants without bumping into one another. If they added more than that, then it would be a lot harder to train someone without hitting someone else by accident. Dragon assumed there must be other rooms for training armies.

Dragon walked to the center of the room and inspected the weapons and armor while Ronnar got ready. Ronnar put on some light chainmail and a pair of boots and gauntlets that looked a little too fancy for a fight.

"Are you ready lad?" asked Ronnar smiling a little too much.

Dragon was a little nervous and hesitant now that he had time to think it through. "I'm not sure if this is a good idea."

"What's the matter, afraid to fight an old dwarf?" Ronnar mocked.

"It's not that," Dragon replied, thinking of the best way to describe the situation. "The problem isn't your age; it's who you are. I don't think the dwarves of Shieldholt would take kindly to me hurting their king."

"Well, don't worry about that. You see the two guards at the door; they will tell everybody it was a fair fight. Besides, I'm known for doing things like this, and I think that's one of the reasons why my people like me so much."

"Okay, I'm just concerned about you getting hurt."

"I understand your concern; just don't hold anything back. Your mother didn't when she fought me."

"Wait, what? You fought my mother? How bad did you lose?"

Ronnar grabbed a good-size battle ax and walked toward the center of the room. "Who said I lost, boy."

Dragon looked at the battle ax in Ronnar's hand and realized this fight wasn't exactly what he expected. "Wait, shouldn't you use a wooden one for training?"

"Wood weapons are for children. I doubt Marahezron trained you with wood weapons. Besides, if you know it won't kill you, then you won't fight as hard. I want this fight to be real; I want to see how good you are."

"Wait, I don't have a weapon," Dragon said, trying to find a way to get out of this. Dragon wasn't too concerned for himself. He just knew that if he truly fought, then Ronnar might actually get hurt.

"You should've grabbed one before you entered the center," Ronnar countered as he swung his ax at Dragon's neck.

Dragon leaned back just in time as the ax came sweeping across. He then jumped back when Ronnar reversed his swing and brought it back across. Dragon landed with a smirk on his face. Even though he thought this fight was a bad idea, his heart was pumping fast, and he had an odd feeling he was going to enjoy it.

Dragon ran back in and committed himself to this fight. He was fast, and used that against Ronnar. He dodged twelve of Ronnar's swings before he made his move. On the next swing, Dragon somersaulted over Ronnar and landed right behind him. When Ronnar turned to catch Dragon, he stepped in and grabbed the ax haft stopping the swing. Dragon was just about to ask Ronnar what he was going to do now, but he never got the chance. Before Dragon could utter a word Ronnar punched him in the chest. The punch was more than what Dragon expected; it sent him flying back and slamming against the wall. He fell to the floor, clutching his chest in pain. That punch reminded him of when Marahezron would get a strike in with his tail.

Ronnar, setting his battle ax down and stepping forward, clapped his hands together. A sound like thunder issued from his hands that shook the armor and weapons around the room. Ronnar then picked his ax back up and began to laugh. "Do you like those?" Ronnar asked, still chuckling. "I got them when I was in Tivendel with Voraha's father. They were made during the war with the giants; they give me the strength of a dragon."

"I thought dwarves fought with honor," Dragon muttered as he looked up at Ronnar. He could see a large red jewel glowing on the back of each gauntlet.

"That's what people say when they want to make themselves feel better for losing. I am fighting you with honor. I'm not using any tricks to entrap you or stop you from fighting back. I have no one hiding to stab you in the back when you're not looking. It is still one-on-one, you against me. Still, I'm not foolish enough to enter a fight without leveling the playing field. This just gives you a harder challenge to see if you're worthy of winning."

Dragon picked himself up with a smile on his face. "All right, you want to fight with a dragon; you've got one."

Dragon came back in fast hoping to put an end to the fight as quickly as possible, but Ronnar was ready. The dwarf dodged several of Dragon's punches and then came back with several of his own. Dragon was trying to get a punch in, but it was a lot harder than he realized. Ronnar was coming at him with both the ax and fist, so Dragon had to dodge both. At one point, he nearly got hit in the face with Ronnar's fist only to be caught by the ax that grazed his upper arm. Trying to get close to Ronnar was extremely hard, so Dragon tried something new. He ran in fast, slid underneath Ronnar's ax swing and came up inside the dwarf's defenses. Which was extremely hard since the dwarf was short to the ground anyways; nevertheless, it wasn't what Ronnar expected. Dragon could see the shock on the dwarf's face when he grabbed Ronnar's wrists and held his hands up to put an end to the fight. Once again, before Dragon could say anything, Ronnar brought his foot up and kicked Dragon. He went flying back and hit the wall again, collapsing to the ground. Dragon peered up to see what he had missed before. He realized there was a glowing red stone on each of Ronnar's boots.

"Oh, did I forget to mention those?" said Ronnar as he began to laugh.

Dragon picked himself up again. "Okay, let's finish this," Dragon growled. He did a quick calculation of what it would take to bring Ronnar down. He knew he couldn't fight the boots or the gauntlets without risking getting hit. So he decided to take out the ax. Once again, Dragon came running in fast, aiming for the ax. Ronnar swung the ax across in front of him, trying to keep Dragon back, but that's what Dragon was hoping for. He jumped up into the air, making his body go into a horizontal spin. For a brief moment in time, Dragon was spinning parallel right above the ax. He used the momentum of his spin combined with the strength of his punch and he brought his fist down on the head of the battle ax. The force of his punch made the metal of the ax head shatter. That, of course, made Ronnar lose his balance, and he stumbled. Dragons still in the air saw his opening. When he landed, he quickly stepped in and hit Ronnar in the chest, sending the king of Shieldholt sailing back. Dragon tried not to hit the king too hard; still, he made Ronnar fly across the room and land on his back next to the wall. The two guards that stood next to the door ran to help their king. At first, Dragon thought they were coming for him, but they merely ran to either side of their king to offer assistance.

Dragon couldn't help but chuckle as he watched Ronnar try to pick himself up. "Did you really beat my mother?" asked Dragon as he walked up to the king.

Ronnar finally, with the help of the two guards, got up from the ground. He couldn't help but smile as he rubbed his chest where Dragon landed his blow. "No," the king admitted sheepishly. "I didn't win against your mother; she was too good for me. It appears her son is a lot like her. I'm going to remember this fight for a long time." Ronnar smiled and rubbed his chest again.

"Did I hurt you?" Dragon asked, hoping he didn't overdo it.

"No, I'm fine. The chainmail I have is enchanted; it took most of the damage. Still, I'm going to have some bruises for a while, well-earned though."

"The boots and gauntlets – does every dwarf in Tivendel have those? If so, I might avoid visiting that place." Dragon was serious about the question, but he laughed and played it off as if he was just curious.

"No, unfortunately. There were only three sets made during Tivendel's war with the giants. One set was given to an elf, and the other was given to the king of Tivendel. How I acquired mine is a story for another time. Now that we're properly bruised, I think we will sleep just fine."

Dragon thought that last comment was just the king's way of getting out of the conversation and ignoring the fact that he lost the fight. He began to understand why the dwarves of Shieldholt loved their king. Ronnar had a wild spirit to him, but he was an honorable king. "Thanks, thank you for everything," Dragon started to say, trying to find words for his emotions. "This night has meant a lot to me, and I will never forget it or you."

Ronnar walked up and gave Dragon a hug and a pat on the back. "You're going to be fine lad. You have a stubborn streak, and this world won't be able to take you down easily. Now go get some sleep; you have a journey ahead of you tomorrow."

With that, Dragon gave Ronnar another quick hug and then left the training room. On the way back to the dining hall, Dragon's thoughts were still filled with many things. However, his heart wasn't as heavy as it had been earlier that day. He took Ronnar's words to heart and really enjoyed his time with the king.

When Dragon finally made his way into the dining hall, his eyes fell on a bizarre site. The people who had been cleaning the room earlier were gone, and they did their job well. The tables and chairs were picked up, cleaned, and put into place. All the mess on the floor was cleaned up, and the dining hall was almost spotless. The odd thing was that all the sleeping dwarves were still there. Floor was still littered with sleeping and drunk dwarves. Dragon could tell that some of them had been moved so the tables and chairs could be put back. It was very comical to see dwarves sleeping all over a clean dining hall. Dragon could tell that this wasn't the first time something like this had happened in Shieldholt.

Sonya was still in the middle, with tons of dwarves sleeping around her. Dragon couldn't help but chuckle as he walked over to her. He had several thoughts of what it would be like to live in Shieldholt and what it would mean for him and Sonya. He moved her hand and gently kicked a drunken dwarf away from her so that he would have a place to lie. With careful attention, he sat down and leaned back upon her neck, trying not to wake her up. Feeling her body next to his had a comforting effect, and even with some noise in the room—mainly the dwarves snoring loudly—he fell asleep quite easily. That night, his dreams were quite peaceful, filled with dwarves singing, laughing, and feasting.

16

The Mountain

Dragon and Sonya awoke to the noise of dwarves moving about the room. Wiping the sleep from his eyes, Dragon could see that most of the dwarves had already started eating their breakfast, as well as Ronnar, who was sitting up at his table, waving for them to join him. Dragon and Sonya were both hungry and didn't hesitate to join in the meal. After a while, their other companions also joined them. Everyone ate merrily and talked about the excitement they had last night. As they enjoyed the company of the dwarves, the day moved on steadily, and soon their stomachs were full, and their hearts were also full with the pleasures of the dwarves. Then Ronnar took them to

Shieldholt's stores and gave them whatever supplies and tools they needed, and led them to the east gate. Since the mountain on the east side was too treacherous, they left their horses in Shieldholt for safe-keeping. It was also a way of guaranteeing that Ronnar would see them again. There at the east gate, they once again stepped out into the sun-light that gleamed from around the clouds.

Standing on the steps of the mountain, Ronnar was unwilling to say good- bye. "We did not speak of it last night. However, I'm curious. Where are you headed?" asked Ronnar, attempting to keep Dragon there a little while longer.

"My company and I are seeking two witches that are supposedly on this side of the gray mountains," Dragon responded openly, keeping nothing a secret in the sunlight.

Hearing Dragon's reply, King Ronnar and several of the dwarves gasped in shock. "If I would have known that last night, I would never have led you so easily to the east gate," Ronnar exclaimed. "Why do you seek those evil beings?"

"We must seek them. Trouble threatens the lands around Tyril-crysalith, and they seem to be the only ones that can give us news of who threatens those lands."

"I wish I had an answer for you so that you need not go to them," Ronnar responded, feeling the need to discourage them from going. For Ronnar had grown fond of Dragon in the time they spent together.

"We thank you for your concern, King Ronnar, but this must be done," Brenath spoke up.

Ronnar looked at them, realizing there was no way to persuade them to do otherwise. "Very well, I will help guide you. We here at Shieldholt know of them and the atrocities that they commit. Villages to the south and farther east of here have been tormented by them for years." Ronnar then began pointing with his hands, giving them specific directions. "You must go north, till the mountains turn east. Then you must go through a swamp that is cursed by their powers. None have ever come out alive. If you survive your way through the swamp, there is only one pass up the mountain to their dark hiding place." Ronnar then turned to Dragon and put his hand on Dragon's arm. "I would much rather prefer you stay here and marry my daughter," Ronnar stated, sounding concerned. "I would hate to lose you to those horrid creatures, especially after I found out that you can make magical items."

"I'm pretty sure I didn't do that; I don't know anything about magic," Dragon replied.

"Oh, you did that," Ronnar said with a laugh upon seeing Dragon's face. He had the look of someone who had just done a terrible taboo. "It's all right, lad; it did a lot of good. You thought I wouldn't find out, but the smiths came and found me right after I left the fight last night. I heard, the whole story and I even got to see your handiwork." Ronnar gave Dragon a good pat on the back. "You did a lot more than you expected. First, you helped the old smith. We've been trying to help him for years, but because he's too prideful, no one's been able to help. You, however, found a way to offer help and save his pride at the same time. More than that, you changed his fate."

"How in the dragon's domain did I do that?"

"Being a dwarven smith is a hard thing; you constantly better yourself to make that one perfect thing. After you achieve making that item, there is not much more you can do to better yourself. So, you can relax and enjoy the rest of your life. For the old smith he never achieved that item, until now. You put magic into the metal, but it was his project, so he will take credit for the crafting of that item. Without meaning to, you helped the old smith get the relaxation and rest that he needed for a long time."

"I'm glad I could help. But I still don't think that I put magic into the metal."

"You did, but we're not quite sure how you did. You used one of the old hammers; we think that might have helped. We don't know much about the old crafting ways and how they put magic into items. But we do know that some of the old hammers were magical themselves. I believe there's a connection between you and the hammer that might've contributed to the making of that magical metal."

"I know so little about magic," Dragon said, lowering his head in shame.

"Don't worry Dragon, I believe someday you will learn more than any of us here. Give it time lad."

"So what's going to be done with the metal?" Dragon asked honestly interested.

"Some of the smiths wanted to give me something, but I declined. I already have magical items; I don't need another. So, the old smith decided he was going to make it into a battle ax for the next king."

"I assume the whole of Shieldholt knows; what do they think about it?"

"They are honored to be able to present a magical weapon to the next king. About the knowledge that it was you who helped make it, they say it's a good omen. They say Shieldholt is blessed and that good times are coming and that the king of the dragons is a friend worth having. I happen to agree with them, and I'd love to have you as a son."

"Once again, I thank you for that generous offer." Dragon then put both his hands on Ronnar's shoulders and stared him deeply in the eyes. "I must be honest. Shieldholt has been the closest thing to home since I started wandering. I would love nothing more than to stay here with you and feast well into the night. However, I must keep going, and I'm afraid that I will never see your halls again, though I do hope."

Dragon did not think that his words would mean much to the king, but Ronnar's face was wet with tears. In a sudden surge of emotion, Ronnar once again embraced Dragon tightly, saying his goodbye. "Farewell, my boy. The time you have spent with us has been a blessing and an honor to my city. You are too much like your father not to stay in one place when things need to be done. May the blessings of dwarves, dragons, and men go with you and shelter you from any evil."

Dragon respectfully bowed to King Ronnar and to Felewa, who was standing at her father's side. He then took Felewa's hand and kissed it in farewell, which made her blush and her father smile. With that, he turned with the company and began their descent down the steps and to the north. Suddenly realizing that Sonya had fallen behind, they stopped for a moment and waited for her. It wasn't long before she exited the darkness of the mountain halls, being escorted by Timbor into the light. They were both laughing out loud, enjoying the last of their time together. Timbor had a bandage over his head and a piece of a chair nestled underneath his arm, helping him walk. Though his appearance looked terrible from the night before, considering his excitement with Sonya, Timbor was quite fine, and he had a newfound respect for her. Knowing that the others were waiting for her, Sonya bent down and said a quick good-bye. In response Timbor patted her side and said his own odd farewell. "Well, you overgrown red bird, travel safe. And if you ever need another dwarf to fight with, don't hesitate to come back."

Sonya nodded in agreement, and then darted off down the mountain to join the others. With two hops and a jump, she rejoined the group, and they started off once again. This time, they had a little bit more knowledge of where they were going. However, once again, their hearts were filled with a dark gloom. One of the soldiers mentioned that the way would be difficult, especially since they had left their horses inside the mountain. Another soldier justified their actions, telling them that they left the horses because they didn't know whether they could go through the mountain or not. Brenath, of course, quieted all discussions as quickly as he could, reassuring them that everything would be fine. Dragon, on the other hand, said nothing at all. He merely trotted off into the distance. The others, unwilling to be separated, quickly followed and stayed right behind him. Dragon desired greatly to turn back and look at Shieldholt; however, he was unwilling to complicate things, so he merely kept his head straight and continued walking. Although he did know that Ronnar and Felewa were still watching him leave, away from their care and toward danger. That knowledge gave him odd feelings: a feeling of comfort that someone behind him cared and would miss him, as well as a feeling of fear for what lay before him, for he was far from home.

***

Their way north was not easy as they had hoped. They stuck to the mountainside because the base was more rugged, and when it wasn't rugged, the trees and underbrush were too thick to pass through. To make the journey on the mountainside more enjoyable, Sonya took it upon herself to occupy them. Starting from below, she would jump over them to the higher ground with a series of somersaults and twists, and then jump back over them down to the lower ground, using different aerial motions. She did this for hours, keeping everyone, including herself, amused and their minds from their worries. That is, until they reached the top of the mountain chain on this side of the gray mountains, turned east, and were eventually stopped by a new issue. Dragon and company stood on the mountainside, staring down at what Ronnar described as the swamp that was cursed, and from the look of it, it fit the description. Any stable path that could be trodden upon went down and disappeared underneath the murky water. It looked as though the water had been sitting there for hundreds of years, and nothing grew upon it but slime and gunk. Out of the water stood hundreds upon hundreds of tall, gnarled trees, looking like deathly hands so interwoven that you couldn't see through them. Not to mention there were lots of lichen hanging from the dead trees like spiderwebs or long dwarfish beards, giving the swamp a definite creepy and uninviting look.

Everyone, including Dragon, stood for a long moment, unwilling to venture in, uncertain of just how cursed this swamp really was. "Well, Dragon King, after you," Brenath sarcastically proposed. "After all, you are the leader of our company."

Dragon glared at Brenath, showing his dislike for Brenath's choice of words, even though he knew he was the logical choice to go first since he was the most likely to survive out of the company. Nevertheless, he bit his tongue and slowly made his way down to the swamp. However, Cromwin's laugh, did not ease his aggravation. With his first step into the murky water, Dragon made ripples that seemed to go as far as the eye could see. That reaction sent a shiver up Dragon's spine; he was certain that if anything lived in the swamp, they would know that trespassers were coming. Still, Dragon buried his concerns and slid the rest of the way into the slimy water, which made him cringe at the very feel of it.

One by one, with Dragon in the lead, they made their way into the water. It wasn't being in the water that bothered them, though it was disgusting to the touch; it was the mere fact that they could not see anything below the water. Dragon commanded everyone to walk and step carefully, thinking of several different things that could harm them. Then, realizing that Sonya couldn't make her way through the swamp, he waved for her to take flight and to keep an eye out for trouble. So without hesitation, she opened her wings, and with a gust of wind on the company's necks, she was gone. As for everyone else, they trudged and pushed through the horrid swamp, with all the supplies encumbering their backs. Lucky for the company, as they traveled on, the water never went above their chests. The driest out of the bunch was Voraha, since she was astride the back of Phanis, who was keeping her from getting lost or drowning. After a while, everyone began to be jealous of Voraha, especially Dragon, who missed being on Sonya's back as they flew to their destinations.

Their going through the swamp was very slow, and after night fell even slower. Sonya took up a perch on the mountainside, keeping a close eye on them as much as she could through the treetops and listening for Dragon's cry for help, if he so needed it. As for the company in the swamp, even though they couldn't see through the trees in front of them, they could see up through the trees. They were thankful for the full moon, giving them the only real light they had. Everyone in the company was on edge, and their hearts and minds were filled with fear. Dragon himself, who had lived his entire life with dragons, had never before felt such dread. Even when he was fighting the dragons in Tyrilcrysalith, with his heart racing and his mind a whirlwind of thoughts, he had never truly feared for his life, until now. Dragon had placed himself a little ahead of the group, doing everything he could to stay alert for trouble. He had never fully understood all of his dragon gifts; even in the swamp, he was learning new senses. His dragon eyes peered deep into the swamp as his ears picked up hundreds of sounds that did not make him feel any better. There was something else that made him uneasy, a feeling that he could not quite explain. Something was telling him that danger was near. The only thing that made sense to him was that his dragon half was picking up dark magic, perhaps from the witches, or something the witches had empowered. Nevertheless, whatever it was, he knew it was coming closer, and that it was strong.

"Look over there, in the water!" one of the soldiers shouted as he pointed far off to the side.

Everyone immediately froze and turned their heads to look at what the soldier had seen. Unfortunately, the only thing that could be seen was the stirring of some water, as if something had swam by. Not knowing what had stirred the water began to bother the company greatly. Brenath and Cromwin, as well as some of the other guards, were not foolish; they drew their swords quickly as they stared down at the water. Dragon, on the other hand, didn't move. He simply stood still and quiet, just listening.

After a long moment of silence, the company finally began to slowly inch their way toward Dragon. However, as they began to move, they heard a strange noise. At first, no one could make it out, and then, as it grew louder, it sounded as though thousands of people were whispering all at once. No one in the company knew where it was coming from; the noise was penetrating everywhere. It eventually began to affect their minds, making it hard to concentrate or focus on anything. Everyone brought their hands up to their ears, trying any way possible to muffle the noise. Dragon, however, stood there gritting his teeth, dealing with the noise as best as he could. Just when things seemed as though they couldn't get any worse, a gigantic snake burst out of the water. Rising high into the air, it turned over and then came down, swallowing a soldier whole. In one fluid move, the snake disappeared underneath the water, leaving the entire company in shock. The snake was enormous, Dragon thought to himself. From what he could see, it was nearly the same size as Sonya.

"Cathurax," Brenath yelled as he quickly tried to move everyone back.

"Cathurax," Dragon yelled back curiously. "What are those?"

"In short, they're giant serpents with magical powers. Defend yourself!"

In spite of Brenath's warning, Dragon merely stood there, dumbfounded and uncertain of what to do. Brenath, on the other hand, pushed everyone back to a tree, and there the company formed a circle around it, giving themselves a better chance for defense. When Dragon finally came to himself, he looked up to call for Sonya's help, only to see that she had already seen the commotion from the mountainside and was on her way. Sonya didn't attempt to land carefully; she tightened all of her muscles and crashed through the trees. She sent branches and water hurling in all directions as she landed directly upon a snake that she had seen from above. With the giant snake firmly in her grip, she bit down hard right behind its head and then gave a firm pull on its tail, ripping the snake's head right off.

Unfortunately, Sonya didn't anticipate how many more snakes there were or how fast they were. Before the dead snake's head touched the water, another one burst out of the water, speeding toward her side. With her wing, Sonya knocked the snake's head back, deflecting its bite; and then, using her tail flexed into one mighty tip, she pierced the snake through the throat. Once again, before the snake could drop dead in the water, another one attacked, and then, another and another. Before she knew it, Sonya had been surrounded by at least seven snakes that were the same size as her. She was jumping and thrashing about, using everything—from her wings to her tail, as well as her teeth, feet, and hands—to keep the snakes at bay. She even utilized the trees around her, smashing herself with the snakes against them; however, the more she struggled, the more they coiled around her.

Dragon, who was watching all the commotion that happened so suddenly, finally decided that it was time to join in. He reached down to grab Truth and pull it out of its sheath. Before he could get Truth so much as an inch out of its sheath, he heard a familiar voice behind him.

"Dragon, come to me," the voice demanded in a whisper.

As Dragon turned to see who it was, the world around him began to change. First, the trees melted away into clouds, and the water became solid as stone. Standing only a few feet from him was a very familiar figure. Dragon's face was filled with both pain and joy as he stared deeply into the emerald eyes of his mother. She was standing in her human form, with arms stretched out, and immediately Dragon accepted this, thinking it was a vision like he had before and thinking she had come to aid him.

"Be still. I am here for you," his mother softly whispered.

Dragon simply stood there, lowering his hands away from his sword and staring into his mother's eyes as she slowly moved closer to embrace him. Everything that was racing in his mind, everything that mattered in these recent days, seemed to melt away at the mere thought of holding his mother.

****

Brenath, Cromwin, and the others surrounding the tree did the best they could to defend themselves against the giant snakes. Even

Voraha, who was now sitting on a branch where Phanis had put her in order to fight, had taken out a snake's eye with a swipe of her ax as it made for her. Phanis also had a fair share of attacks; in one such attack, he took the snake's tongue clean off. As for Yolana, she didn't know how to fully fight yet, so she was hiding behind one of the soldiers. Things were getting pretty intense and hopeless when Brenath looked over in search of Dragon. Spotting him in the distance only brought more fear and hopelessness to him. He almost choked when he saw Dragon standing with his sword still in its sheath, staring into the eyes of a mighty serpent slowly bearing down on him. Brenath was greatly perplexed, not knowing what could have caused Dragon to go still.

"Sonya!" Brenath yelled, begging for whatever help he could get. Quickly realizing that she was overwhelmed herself, Brenath and several of the soldiers made a move away from the tree in an attempt to help Dragon. Suddenly, their plans were thwarted by a snake smacking into them, knocking them back. The same snake came up rapidly and took a firm bite into the side of the soldier who was standing in front of Yolana. Immediately, the soldier dropped his sword, yelling in pain, and then turned, reaching for Yolana's hand, frightened of being pulled away. Yolana did not pause; she grabbed the soldier's hand as quickly as she could, and when she did, she realized there was no motion in his grip. The serpent's poison had worked quickly in his body, turning him stiff as a log. Yolana could still see in his eyes the fear of knowing certain death as he was pulled away from her grip and into the water. Even though that moment was very disturbing to Yolana, it was quickly interrupted by the sight of another serpent coming toward her.

Fortunately, before it sunk its teeth into her, Brenath and Cromwin jumped upon the snake's head, stabbing wildly with their swords. At that time, all the snakes were currently occupied, and the others were too far way to do anything at all. Yolana looked over at

Dragon. Rapidly reliving the moment of losing that soldier, she mustered what courage she could and reached her hand into the water.

***

Dragon was still staring into his mother's eyes, overjoyed that she was there. He did not question anything, nor did he pay attention to anything. It did not occur to him that his mother's scale that was around his neck was not glowing like it did before. It also did not occur to him that his legs were stuck in the ground as though he were standing in water. He merely stared at his mother, waiting for her embrace.

When Dragon's mother reached him, she stood ever so tall over him and then slowly bent down to give him a kiss on the forehead. Unexpectedly, she stopped an inch from his head and threw herself back, giving out a bloodcurdling scream. Immediately, the world around Dragon returned to normal, and he was standing once again in the swamp, though, to his shock, he was looking up at the two fangs of a mighty serpent only inches from his head. He noticed that it wasn't moving, mainly because it had a sword going up through its throat into its head. He looked down to see dark green serpent blood dripping from the hilt of the sword and running down the arms of a very frightened and shocked young woman.

Yolana's body was shaking with the mere knowledge of her actions. Previously, she did not organize her thoughts when she reached into the water, grabbed the dead soldier's sword and hurried over to save Dragon. Now that the serpent was dead by her actions, she had a good moment to think, and she was very shocked at herself. Dragon, however, gave her a look of appreciation and nodded his head in approval. Yolana let go of the sword and let the dead snake sink into the water as Dragon came up and laid a hand on her shoulder, doing his best to comfort her.

Unfortunately for them, the fight was not quite over. Before Dragon could say anything, another snake came up from the water to bite Yolana. Dragon, already aggravated that a serpent had messed with his mind, was not idle. He pushed Yolana aside and jumped into the serpent's mouth, using his feet to hold down its bottom jaw and his hands to grip the two fangs, holding open the upper jaw. With a loud grunt and tremendous strength, Dragon ripped the two fangs out of the serpent's mouth and jumped up as its mouth slammed shut. When Dragon came back down, he thrust the serpent's fangs deep into its eyes, killing it instantly with its own poison.

Splashing back into the water, Dragon stood firm and was quite eager to finish this fight. As another snake came closer, he reached for Truth and pulled it from its sheath. Dragon pulled on Truth so quickly that its tip struck a nearby tree. In doing so, it rang as though it had struck metal. However, instead of the ring fading, it grew and intensified. All Dragon could do was hold on to the sword as it vibrated and emanated the sound. The company was lucky the sound was more than it seemed; it affected the serpents greatly. All around them, the giant magical snakes hissed and squealed as they thrashed about violently as if their bodies were being tormented. The farther the snakes got, the less the sword emanated the sound, and it didn't stop until the water itself stopped stirring.

Dragon could not help but stare down at Truth once again, amazed at its abilities. Carefully and respectfully, he sheathed the sword and took a look at what damage had been done. Oddly enough, his first attention was not turned toward Sonya but to Yolana, who was standing nearby, still traumatized.

"Are you okay?" Dragon asked sincerely, concerned about her well-being.

Yolana took a moment to form her words and attempted to stop herself from shaking. "I don't know," she replied, with tears in her eyes. "I didn't know when I decided to come with you that this would happen. I have never been in any real danger in my entire life. I have also never needed to take the life of any creature, even in my village."

Dragon put both hands on her shoulders, doing his best to keep her together. "I cannot say that you will forget this or that it will ever go away. Although I will say that you did the right thing, and I'm grateful and forever in your debt. I know that Voraha was helping to teach you how to fight, but no one can teach you how to deal with death. Just be grateful that your first kill is a vicious and vile creature and not a human. Believe it or not, it does make a difference." Dragon then put a hand on her cheek and nodded at her, seeking a response. Though she couldn't give a verbal response, Yolana did nod in return, showing that she understood.

By that time, Brenath and the survivors had gathered together and made their way toward Dragon. Slowly turning his attention away from Yolana, Dragon commented to Brenath, "You were right. Those were magical serpents. I wonder why they didn't attack me the way they did everyone else."

"Perhaps they thought you were the biggest threat," Brenath quickly responded. "They didn't know Sonya was watching on the mountainside, and you were the strongest out of all of us. They may be serpents, but their magic allows them to see more than just flesh. They probably saw your strength and knew you would be harder to kill, so it was better to entrap you. Although I do not know exactly what their powers are."

"They read your desires and then turn them against you," Dragon responded, thinking back to the image of his mother.

"That's probably what that confusing noise was, them reaching into our minds searching for our weakness," Brenath concluded.

"I may be the strongest, but I am still vulnerable to magic," Dragon said, being a little harsh on himself. Living his entire life with the dragons, and even being taught how to fight by Marahezron, had given him a sense of superiority, thinking himself almost invincible. This one incident had taken his delusions of himself and shattered them to reality. It was not easy for him to accept, and it even sent a chill up his spine. Quickly taking his mind off that thought, he turned to Yolana, giving her credit for her actions. "I would be dead right now if it were not for Yolana's heroic actions." After seeing her take a step back, not willing to take credit for anything, Dragon turned his attention to other serious matters. "Is everyone else okay?" he asked Brenath.

"I'm afraid we lost six of my men. Everyone else seemed to have survived," Brenath answered with the sound of anguish in his voice. He had lived many years without losing a single soldier, but this year was disturbing to him. He lost his company when he first met Dragon; he lost several in the defense of Tyrilcrysalith; and now in the swamp, he lost six more. He couldn't help but think how many more he would lose before this whole thing was over.

"I'm sorry for your loss," Dragon replied as sincerely as he could.

"I think our quest folly. It would be mad to continue," Brenath voiced his concern. "We may not make it out of the swamp, and even if we do, we still must find the witches. There's a good chance that none of us will return from their presence alive, and if any of us do, we could not make it back through the swamp."

"I do not think the swamp will be an issue from here on out," commented Dragon as he pointed to Truth. "As for the witches, leave them to me," he said with confidence. Dragon did not say it, thinking he could handle them, especially after what just happened. He said it merely to give strength to Brenath and to stop fear from spreading.

"From how you handled the snakes, I somewhat doubt that," Brenath replied with some skepticism.

Dragon shot a serious glare at Brenath, realizing he had a point, but Dragon was unwilling to give up this quest. "I told you back in Falistoran that this is something I must do," he said. "You came of your own free will. Do as you please." With that said, Dragon did not wait for a response. He moseyed on over to check on Sonya. As he did, the company slowly followed after him, wanting to stay as close as they could to him and his sword. When Dragon reached her, he was taken aback for a moment at the sheer ferocity of her wounds. "Soræniya, are you okay?"

"You haven't called me that in a long time. You must really be worried," Sonya replied in a whisper, her voice filled with exhaustion and pain. She was lying down in the water with her back against a tree for support as she tried to regain what strength she could. Dragon, on the other hand, did not respond to her but he merely stared at her, seeking a serious response. "I'll be fine," she finally replied to his question. "My scales were a lot tougher than the snakes anticipated. The only place they could get a firm bite was on my wings." She then shook her body to indicate that it was hard to move, especially her wings. This did not reassure Dragon that she was okay in any way.

Seeing the look on his face, she continued to try to find ways to keep him calm. "I'm stronger than I look, Dragon. My blood burns hot, making it difficult for their venom to affect me. I will get better. In the meantime, I won't be able to fly for a couple of days."

Dragon leaned his head against Sonya's snout and softly stroked her cheek. "Be more careful next time," he said.

"I must say the same for you. It didn't look like you were doing any better," Sonya stated, giving him a small nudge with her snout.

"True. Perhaps next time we should both be careful. In the meantime, let's get you out of this swamp." Dragon turned back around to indicate to the company that it was time to keep moving. Then he noticed someone of significance was missing. "Where's Voraha?" he shouted as he motioned to the perch she had been sitting on, indicating that she must have been knocked off during the battle.

"I'm right here, you overgrown blackguards!" a voice yelled off in the distance.

The entire company looked to see if it was indeed who they hoped it was, and lo and behold! In the distance, they could see coming slowly and steadily toward them an ax head as well as a helmeted dwarf head, bobbing in the water. Nothing else of her could be seen, which, to the company, made quite an amusing sight. They did their best to keep quiet; nevertheless, they burst out laughing as soon as she reached them, looking like just a head floating on the water.

"Very funny," she sharply replied to their humor. "If you're finished laughing, can someone give me a hand?"

Even though he was still trying to suppress a smile on his face, Phanis kindly walked over, picked her up, and once again set her upon his back. Now that the company had fully regrouped, they pressed on once more. This time they moved slower than before, as they had to make a way for Sonya, cutting and hacking at the dead trees. Even Voraha on Phanis's back did the best she could, trying to reach all the tall branches.

Just as the sun was rising, they took their last step in water, and the company was overjoyed to finally see stone underneath their feet again, especially Voraha. Though everyone was tired and wanted to rest, they decided that it was better that they kept going, mainly because climbing a mountain at night was very hazardous. Not to mention that everyone was very intent on putting more distance between them and the swamp. They did, however, take a short break to catch their breath and cook what small rations they had for breakfast. They also took the time to go through their supplies to see what they had lost in the fight with the serpents. Mostly, everything they carried was just wet from being dropped in the water. Their food supplies, on the other hand, were still dry because of the way the dwarves had tightly packed them.

"I just thought of something," one of the soldiers said as he picked at his breakfast. "We went through the swamp because we couldn't find a path on the mountainside. So why didn't we just go south and around the swamp? I know it would've taken longer because we don't know exactly how big the swamp is, but it would've been safer."

No one answered the soldier; silence merely hung in the air except the sound of people eating their breakfast. Brenath and Dragon both looked at each other with the same expression on their faces. They didn't need to say a word, yet they understood each other. Neither one of them had thought of that idea; it didn't even occur to them to walk around the swamp. Sure, Dragon was in a hurry but even he would've added days to his journey to save lives. Both of them shook their heads knowing that it was no good trying to ponder what might have been. What was done was done and they had to shoulder the burden and move on.

Once done eating, they gathered together and started up the mountainside. Yet Dragon felt uneasy as they traveled, for there were some things that did not seem right. For the mountains on this side of the swamp were very rugged and almost impossible to travel upon. The only thing that made their travel easy was a path leading from the swamp up into the mountains. It was wide enough for four people to walk side by side comfortably, and that made Dragon quite curious.

"I thought witches hid themselves," he stated to Brenath. "But this path seems to lead right to them."

"The quicker we reach them, the quicker they can kill us," Brenath answered in a sinister way. "I don't think they fear anything."

Dragon nodded in understanding and then reassured himself that this had to be done, whether it was easy or not. Pressing on, he looked up at the mountains where the path disappeared into them. The mountains were vast, and they could not see the peaks as they loomed high above the clouds. Snow covered most of the mountains, confirming to Dragon that their troubles were not over yet.

* * *

The path went ever so steadily up, and the company made very good time during the day. By the time that nightfall had come again, they had risen above the clouds. They were so high that the air itself was hard to breathe. The company had some fur clothes to help them on their way; still, it was not enough. They had begun to feel the painful effect of the cold, all except for Dragon and Sonya. Their dragon blood ran so hot that even a snowflake melted upon them. Unfortunately, the cold was the least of their problems; a storm with heavy winds came up and battered against them. The company would have been blown clear off the mountain if it were not for Sonya. Even though she couldn't fly, her legs were very sturdy; she went before the company, using her body and wings to shelter them from the wind. However, no matter what, they were still partly assaulted, and things were going poorly for them.

"We cannot take the wind or cold much longer," shouted Brenath. "We must find some way to shelter ourselves!"

"Around the next bend should prove to be less wind," Dragon replied, thinking of anything he could do to help save the company. He pushed in front of Sonya, letting the full force of the wind and storm strike him. He stood with all his strength far in front of them, like a statue standing on the snow. Though his surroundings were harsh, he did his best to use all his dragon senses, especially his eyes, to find a place that would protect his company. Reassuring himself that he was correct on the location of the shelter, he turned back to inform Brenath, "We must keep moving!"

At that moment, Dragon heard a strange sound coming from above. As he looked up, his eyes filled with terror when he saw an avalanche of snow coming down upon them. "Look out!" he shouted, but too late. The great wave of snow hit them and knocked the entire company off the side of the mountain, sending them hurling down what looked to be an endless abyss between mountainsides.

Dragon, knowing that Sonya could not fly yet, was faced with a hopeless situation. So in a moment of fear and desperation, he let out a mighty roar.

Suddenly, as they passed through a wisp of clouds, the company and the snow falling with them came to an abrupt stop. They didn't know what they hit; they were only grateful they were still alive. Even though the snow had knocked them off the mountain, they were appreciative that it helped to cushion their landing, giving them only minor bumps and bruises. Though it took a moment for them to get to their feet, they eventually realized that what they landed on was not rock but something white like snow. Dragon could swear that he saw scales, which did not help his confusion. Then eventually, the wind stopped, and the clouds were blown away to reveal something that none of them would ever forget.

The company was standing in the hands of a colossal dragon with snow-white scales. The dragon was not clinging to the mountains; it was one of the mountains. It had come out of its hibernation rock form and unfolded its wings around the other mountains, blocking the wind and snow but allowing the moonlight to reflect off its scales. The massive dragon had caught the company in its hand and was holding them steady as it looked down at them, looming taller than the mountains.

The company looked up at the dragon in utter shock; it was easily as big as two mountains, and that was without its wings. Sonya wasn't even one-fourth of the size of its fingernail. Three of the soldiers wet themselves in complete fear, turning the snow beneath them yellow. Dragon was the only one who was excited. Though he had never met this dragon, he knew him well.

"Ganez!" he shouted.

"You know this dragon," Brenath demanded answers, terrified himself.

"No. However I was friends with his brother, Vevor."

Ganez lowered his head to speak, and as he did, everyone shrank back into the snow, attempting to hide. Dragon, however, stood tall and firm, not afraid but more relieved. When Ganez spoke, though, he was speaking in a whisper. His voice was deep as it resonated and shook the mountainsides. "Welcome, my king, Dragon."

"You know of me?" Dragon asked ever so curiously. "We have never met before."

"I first learned of you from Vevor when we last spoke several years ago. However, you were only a prince at the time. I have learned more recent things from the Creator."

"You speak to the Creator? How is this done?" Dragon wasn't interested in hearing about the Creator; still, he was curious about how Ganez could speak to the Creator in his rock form.

"When dragons enter into their frozen state, they enter into a place of communion with the Creator," Ganez slowly explained. "From him, I have learned of the recent departure of your mother and the fading of the dragons, as well as the quest that you are upon. Why have you summoned me?"

"I summoned you. How did I do that?" Dragon asked as curiosity swelled within his eyes.

Ganez let out a small chuckle and grinned. "Ancient didn't tell you about your gifts as a king. Just like him to tell you what you only need for the moment. My king, you have the right to summon us back from stone."

Dragon immediately had a look of delight on his face. "I could bring my home back."

As quickly as Dragon had the look of delight, Ganez took it away. "I'm sorry, my king, that is not how it works. You can bring us back to assist you, only for a short period of time, and then we must return to stone."

"What good does that do me?" Dragon shouted at Ganez, frustrated by his words. Ganez, in response, looked down at the mountain floor and nodded. Realizing that Ganez had saved their lives, Dragon lowered his head, ashamed by his very words.

"I must ask, my king—what are you doing up here?" Ganez was not used to asking a king for his business; nevertheless, he was deeply concerned for Dragon's well-being.

"I am seeking two witches," Dragon replied, thankful that the conversation topic had changed.

Even though Ganez was a big dragon, everyone could see the overly concerned look on his face. "I will take you to the entrance of their home. However, I must warn you, my king: they have magic against dragons. I have met them once, when I was younger and half the dragon I am today. They were powerful and nearly defeated me. Fortunately, I was too big even then for their magic to work right. I beg you to be careful, my king."

"I thank you for your concern, as well as the information about the witches. I will be careful."

With that said, Ganez covered them with his other hand, so no one would fall, and took them to where they needed to be. He set them down about half a mile from the entrance to the witches' domain, which was at the peak of the highest mountaintop. Since it was night, Ganez used his wing and covered them to give them some shelter. He also reached down to the swamp and pulled up some dead trees to give them some firewood. The company split the wood, and Sonya lit it easily, giving them a nice fire and a well-needed thawing. There at the top of the mountain, they huddled around the fire, regaining what warmth they had lost, with Ganez keeping a watchful eye over them. Dragon had even begged Ganez to stay awake for several days to ensure their safe return to the foot of the mountain. Though he was eager to sleep again, Ganez agreed to at least two days, which gave Dragon some peace of mind.

As the night wore on, everyone slept except for Brenath, Phanis, and Dragon, who were sitting around the fire discussing many things. They had many funny stories to tell, as well as emotional moments in their lives to share. The longer they talked, the more Dragon felt torn inside. He had long felt that humans did not deserve the respect of a dragon. Not to mention, ever since his quest started, Dragon had felt as though the sacrifice of the dragons was in vain. The humans did not deserve the right to have redemption, especially after all the things they had done to others and themselves. Now oddly enough, Dragon was enjoying their company and sharing intimate things with them.

He was especially becoming close with Phanis and could not think of a day without his friend there. This was indeed odd to Dragon, but he was determined to enjoy himself in their company.

"I have to say Dragon is the brave one," Brenath spoke out.

"How so?" Dragon questioned him.

"Most men have trouble dealing with one female in their life. You have three, not to mention of different races. I do not envy your shoes. I'm surprised they haven't killed each other or you yet."

Dragon let out a small chuckle at this interesting comment. "Believe it or not, there are four females. I have a fairy that follows me as well. She shows herself from time to time."

"Then you are definitely a brave one," Brenath said as he and Phanis began to laugh. "I'm surprised that Sonya hasn't killed the other three."

"What's that supposed to mean?" responded Dragon, sounding completely confused. He fidgeted as he sat, trying to think of ways to defend Sonya no matter what was brought against her. Then he relaxed, remembering that this was a friendly conversation.

"Don't tell me that you haven't noticed her feelings toward you," Brenath commented, completely amused by Dragon's unawareness of Sonya's feelings. He then quieted down, thinking that perhaps this was not the right friendship to get in the middle of.

"What feelings?" Dragon was going to say more but then stopped himself, thinking back to Sonya's actions and realizing that there was some truth in Brenath's words.

Phanis actually didn't want to be the one to tell him, but since Brenath was looking to leaving the matter alone, he felt the need to inform him. "Dragon, everyone could tell by the way she looks at you. She cares for you more than a friend."

"I never noticed," Dragon replied, completely surprised. "She's like a sister to me. We've been together since birth. It never occurred to me that she could ever have those kinds of feelings toward me. Perhaps I've been too occupied to notice. On the other hand, it does explain a lot, especially her reactions to Yolana when they first met," stated Dragon, a little eager to change the subject.

"Like I said, you're the brave one," Brenath sarcastically reiterated as he rejoined the conversation upon seeing Dragon's reaction.

"May I be honest?" Dragon asked. "I must say, I think you two are the brave ones. I've lived my entire life with dragons and took great pride in my dragon half. I contributed all my strengths to my dragon half. I could not think of any strength in the human half, though Ancient always told me I had some. All my life, I had wanted to discard my human half. It is hard to be a part of both worlds. There for a while, I've thought it would be better if I went one way or the other. The two of you are made of strong will and mind, and you overcome so much. Looking at both of your lives, living without dragon abilities, I do not think I could've survived as a human. There is so much in me I take for granted."

Phanis patted Dragon on the back in an attempt to reassure him. "Don't worry, that's part of your human side," Phanis remarked. They all looked at each other seriously for a moment and then burst out laughing. "Listen, Dragon, I understand how it feels not to belong, but don't start questioning yourself now. You are who you are. There is a reason why you are who you are. Not to mention we wouldn't have made it this far without you being here."

Dragon looked at Phanis with gratitude in his eyes for his words. His life was filled with anger and pain, and each day brought new issues to his heart. Still, he felt a little at ease with his new friends, thinking if they stayed with him, he could accomplish and survive anything. At that time, Brenath rose, announcing that he was going to get some sleep. He took a few steps away from the fire, wrapped himself into his blankets, and went to sleep. As for Dragon, he sat there staring into the fire with more thoughts on his mind.

Phanis noticed the look on his face and decided to interrupt his thoughts. "All right, what's on your mind?" Phanis asked, almost like a father would his son.

Dragon's eyes lifted to meet Phanis's eyes, his face heavy with his thoughts. "The death of Brenath's men. I can't help but feel responsible."

"I would worry if you didn't," Phanis replied as he grabbed a branch and poked at the fire. "We are each other's keepers, and if men would take responsibility for each other, darkness would not stand."

"Why don't they?"

"Do you like feeling responsible for those men?"

"No, I don't. It's a heavy burden."

"That's why it's easier to take care of yourself. That's why mankind as a whole will fail. However, individual people will still make a difference. Take Brenath, for example. He does what he does because he cares. Or take the king of the dragons, who saved a slave when it was none of his business and he could have walked away. You take responsibility even when it hurts because someone must." Phanis smiled at the thought of what he was to say next. "It makes you human." He took a moment to let Dragon think it through, and then he added his final thought on the matter. "The only thing you need to make sure is to not let it get you down. Let the burden reassure you that you are doing what's right."

"Ancient always told me to do what is right, not what is smart," Dragon stated, reassuring Phanis that he understood.

"That sounded like my mother."

"I said it before: you are a wise human."

"I try," Phanis replied with a smirk on his face. "Just think, you are stuck with me." Phanis couldn't help but laugh as he got up. He bid Dragon good night as he grabbed his blankets and wrapped himself for a night of sleep.

As for Dragon, he got up and went his separate way to get what sleep he could, for tomorrow was going to be a busy and trying day. Dragon walked over to Sonya to sleep with her, as he had always done. However, as he looked into her wing, he saw Yolana sleeping soundly. She was curled up in Sonya's wing with some fur, trying to stay warm.

Dragon was a little aggravated that she took his spot, but he kept silent. He went around to the other wing, only to find Voraha curled up in that one. For a moment, he stood flushing with anger and then calmed down, realizing that perhaps they needed it more. Sonya was awake and looked at him, gesturing that he needed to be quiet so that he wouldn't wake them. He nodded in compliance and laid down by Sonya's neck, cuddling with her there.

As he got comfortable, he gave her a quick glance and whispered at her. "When you first met Yolana, you didn't try to drown her out of jealousy, did you?"

The only response he got from her was a big grin, indicating that she was innocent. In return, he gave her a smile and a pat on the side, reassuring her that there were no hard feelings. Before they closed their eyes, they gave each other one last glance. They didn't need to say a single word to the other; they knew what each other was thinking. Much in their lives was changing, and they needed to change with it. However, they still knew that they would always be together, no matter what.

17

Two Witches

Dragon awoke to the sound of voices chattering only a few feet from him. Though he was tired and didn't get much sleep, he got up anyway and roused Sonya. She took a little bit longer to get to her feet as she carefully woke Yolana and Voraha out of her wings. When Dragon was done wiping the sleep from his eyes, he took a good look at his surroundings. Ganez had lowered his wings, revealing them to their elements. The morning sun was rising quickly; still, the morning air was cool and thin. The sky was clear and blue, with no clouds above them, but there were many clouds below them. The mountain peak where they were standing was like an island in a sea of clouds, with only a few other islands jetting out. With every movement that Ganez took, he made waves in the clouds. It was truly a sight beyond sights, something Dragon would remember and cherish.

Unfortunately, the beautiful moment was quickly interrupted by the chattering voices getting louder.

Dragon walked over to the group consisting of Brenath, Cromwin, Phanis, and two soldiers, who were all talking loudly and very troublingly. They were all talking and pointing to the ground, which gave Dragon concern, not knowing quite what they were pointing at. He nudged his way in as calmly as he could, only to stare down at footprints in the snow. "What's going on?" Dragon asked Brenath.

"Two of my men are gone," he replied forebodingly.

"Did they run away in fear?" Dragon responded, trying to think of the best scenario.

"I wish I could say that," Brenath replied, pointing to the direction that the footprints were going. "However, I fear the worst." Brenath motioned to his men to grab their gear and follow as he and Cromwin made their way up toward the witches' lair.

Dragon stood for a moment, confused, staring at the direction of the footprints. Things began to come together in his mind when he saw the footprints steadily go up the rest of the mountainside and enter a cave, which was supposed to be the witches' home. Dragon immediately gathered his things together and ran to catch up with Brenath, so that he might ask him some questions. "What does this mean?" Dragon shouted after Brenath, running as he strapped Truth to his side.

"It means that they were taken," Brenath shouted back, fastening his own sword to his side.

"How is that done? Their captors left no footprints in the snow, and the soldiers left no blood behind."

"Witches don't often leave footprints. Also, the men weren't killed. They were probably lured inside." Brenath kept his answers short, even though he knew Dragon desired as many answers as he could. He was more concerned about his two soldiers that were lost instead of answering the ongoing barrage of questions.

Brenath's words did not help Dragon feel any better; Dragon began to think he underestimated the witches' powers, and that worried him. What worried him more was that he felt as if Brenath was not telling him everything he knew. Dragon quickened his pace to reach Brenath, and when he did, he grabbed him by the front of his shirt and pressed him against the wall of the mountain, right before the entrance to the witches' lair.

"Something isn't right. You're not telling me everything," Dragon shouted. "Before we set foot in their domain, I want to know everything, you know!"

"It is just myth," Brenath replied, urging Dragon to let go of his shirt and the conversation.

"Some myths are truths. Now, tell me everything," Dragon said firmly as he stared strongly into Brenath's eyes letting the man know that he would not back down.

"Very well, I'll tell you what I know," answered Brenath as he pushed Dragon's hands down to give him more room to relax. "For thousands of years, there were rumors that witches lived in these mountains, and they terrorized villages hundreds of leagues away. No one knew how many there were or what powers they had. Until one man escaped their grasp, or was let go. Since he was old, everyone was certain he couldn't have escaped on his own; leading to the belief, that the witches let him go specifically so that he would spread the knowledge of them. Even though some witches are evil, they like anyone else do not like rumors that are not true. When my grandfather was young, the old man spread the knowledge of the witches, creating more fear upon the knowledge of their existence. My grandfather believed that's why they let the old man go, to spread fear and to straighten up the rumors at the same time. Unfortunately, after two generations, the knowledge of the witches has returned to rumor and myth."

Brenath paused for a moment to see if Dragon had anything to say or questions to ask. When he saw the look of boredom and frustration on Dragon's face, he realized that this was not quite the information that Dragon was looking for. So quickly redirecting the conversation to the witches themselves, he continued, "As for the witches themselves, there are supposedly two—a mother and a daughter. They are each other's opposites; one's weakness is the others strength, making them almost invincible. No one knows if their power is endless, however, as Ganez commented, they are powerful. Also, no one really ever comes to them. They leave the mountain and hunt for people down in the valleys."

"How do they capture the people, and what do they do with them?" asked Dragon, now interested in what Brenath had to say.

"It is said that the daughter does the hunting; if the mother comes along, that is only to protect her daughter. They say her daughter is very beautiful and endowed with many powers to entice her victims. Once in her grasp, she could make them do anything she desired, including die. Then they would take the people back to their domain and devour them, gaining power from their victims."

"That sounds horrifying," responded Dragon with a look of disgust on his face.

"More than you know, the daughter picks at the victim first. Rumors say that she sleeps with her victims."

"When has sleeping with someone ever harmed anyone?" Dragon interrupted.

One of the soldiers leaned over to whisper to Dragon, hoping not to add to his embarrassment. "The witch mates with them."

Dragon's eyes immediately widened with surprise. He always considered himself a grown dragon; however, no one in his life had ever discussed matters like these. For the first time in a long time, he felt very young. "Does she breed for offspring purposes?"

"No," Brenath replied, knowing Dragon's need to ask such a question. "It is said, she breeds out of pleasure. When she hits her peak of sensual gratification, she begins to suck the life out of her victim, leaving nothing but flesh and bones."

"Do all females do that?" asked Dragon, sounding concerned.

"I don't know. You could ask my wife," a soldier sarcastically remarked.

"Quiet," Brenath quickly snapped, indicating the seriousness of the moment. "Females do not do that; she does it because she is evilly empowered. The witches gain more power by sucking the life out of others; it is said that they have even brought great wizards to their death."

"What of the mother?" Dragon demanded, a little uneasy about the answer he would get.

"She, on the other hand," Brenath continued, sounding more sinister than before. "She is rumored to be hideous, not needing to lure anyone in. She feeds off of her daughter's leftovers, devouring the flesh."

"No wonder no one comes to see them. They don't sound inviting at all," Dragon stated, sounding sarcastic and serious at the same time.

"In spite of all the darkness that is in them, if there is a good trait, it is in their site. When asked, they can see the past, present, and future; at least that is what is rumored. I wish there was more that I could tell you. As I said, a lot of it is myth and rumor."

Dragon nodded in response, knowing that Brenath could say no more. Then he took a look at the opening of what was the witches' lair. It was a fair-sized cave opening, large enough for Sonya to squeeze into if she needed to. Like the witches, it too had an uninviting look; the light itself seemed to creep out of it, unwilling to venture in. Dragon turned back to Brenath with a smile on his face; his heart was filled with both fear and adventure. "Let us go then, and find out what is myth and what is truth."

Brenath could not help but let a smile show as well. "You are either brave or foolish, or perhaps both. Nevertheless, I couldn't agree with you more." Brenath had his soldiers fashion some torches from the dead swamp trees, given to them by Ganez. Then, after Sonya lit them with a burst of fire from her mouth, they all slowly made their way into the witches' domain, only to leave Ganez, peering into the opening, wondering if they would ever come out again.

***

As the company made their way through the dark cavern, they continually tripped and stubbed their feet on protruding rocks from the floor. Though they had light from the torches, it was not enough to see everything. The torches' fire continued to flicker as if the fires were afraid to be there themselves. On several occasions, Sonya had to relight the torches. With every step, the company grew steadily in fear, including Dragon, although instead of focusing on his fear, Dragon was doing his best to pay attention to his dragon senses, which were going crazy. The cavern seemed to echo anything, from their very steps to the whispers out of their mouths. Even the shadows began to move, which made Voraha terrified, and she had lived most of her life inside a mountain. Frightened or not, they steadily made their way until they came to a wide spot in the cavern with a smooth floor. Dragon immediately grabbed Brenath, suddenly stopping him with his foot midstride over the smooth floor.

"What is it?" Brenath asked, too terrified to move.

"The ground is moving," Dragon replied, pointing to the smooth surfaced floor and pulling Brenath back a few steps.

Brenath took a torch and looked down at the ground, only to see a solid, smooth rock floor. "It is just rock. What is wrong with you?"

"It may be just rock to you, in the form of a mirage for human eyes. As for me and my dragon eyes, I see the floor move like black water with ripples."

Thinking that this was nothing but a waste of time, Brenath threw his torch out toward the floor to prove Dragon wrong. The torch landed on the floor, unfortunately with the sound of a splash. Then the company watched as the floor reached up, like watery hands, and dragged the torch down in what looked to be black tar, putting out the flame. Everyone stood in shock, uncertain of what to say. Dragon didn't want to sound arrogant by saying, "I told you so." Instead, he just stood there silently, with a smirk of confidence. Brenath, on the other hand, felt inclined to say something. "You were right. So what now? How do we get across?"

Dragon thought for a moment, then took a torch himself and threw it as far as he could. Fortunately, his torch went twice the length as Brenath's torch did and landed firmly on the other side. With a little light on the other side, Dragon was able to see where the ripples stopped and the firm ground was. "I'm not sure exactly how to measure that," he stated. "I'd say it's at least seven Sonya lengths apart."

"Too far to jump," Phanis commented.

"Rope. Give me what rope we have," demanded Dragon, developing a queer idea in his mind.

Everyone quickly began searching themselves for what rope they had, and in a moment, Dragon had five good, strong ropes lying on the ground. Voraha was all excited, recognizing that those ropes were given to them by Ronnar as they left Shieldholt. "Good, dwarfish rope!" she exclaimed. "There's nothing better to be used inside a mountain."

Dragon quickly nodded in agreement, knowing that it was no use arguing with her on that subject. He then tied the ropes together, making sure they were firm and wouldn't come apart. Eventually, tying one end to a jagged rock high on the side wall, he then tied the other end to his waist.

"There's no way humanly possible you could make it to the other side," said Brenath, catching on to Dragon's idea. "The walls go straight up on either side, with barely anything to hold on to."

Dragon looked at Brenath with a hint of stubbornness. "No way humanly possible, but you forget I'm a dragon."

"Only half dragon," Brenath insisted on reminding him.

Dragon gave Brenath a sharp glare and then proceeded to walk to the wall at the edge of the deathly ground. With a strong jump, he leaped halfway up the cavern wall and grabbed firmly onto it. Brenath was right; there wasn't much for Dragon to hold on to, just a few uneven surfaces. Still, he clung with all his might, digging his nails into anything he could to get a grip on. Slowly, he began to inch his way to the other side, like a spider sidestepping across a wall, as the entire company waited in suspense wondering if he'd make it or not.

Dragon was fortunate enough to make it halfway across, and then he began to lose his grip. He was scratching and clawing at the wall, trying to hold on to anything. Timely for him, he got one hand to grip, which stopped him from falling, but he knew his grip would not last long. He turned his head and shouted to Sonya for help, telling her to throw a large stone. Instantly, without any question, she used her tail and picked up a boulder twice the size of Dragon. With a firm flick of her tail, she hurled the rock in his direction, not knowing quite what he was going to do.

Dragon had it in his mind that he was going to drop on to the rock and use it to propel him to the other side. Thinking that nothing could go wrong, Dragon, with what little grip he had, put his legs against the wall and pushed off as the rock came closer. Unfortunately, Dragon had done this too late, so instead of him landing on the boulder, it smacked right into him. When they collided, the large stone shattered into hundreds of pieces, and it sent Dragon hurling back head over heels. Lucky for him, though very painful, he landed on his back with his feet only an inch from the deadly ground. When the ringing in his ears stopped, he slowly raised his head to look around. Even though he was a good distance away from the others, he could see the delight on their faces that he was still alive. Then, shortly after, the entire company began laughing hysterically at Dragon's display, especially his landing. Dragon picked himself up and dusted himself off, trying to ignore their laughter. He then untied the rope from his waist and tied it to another rock on the other side, so the company could cross safely.

As they started across one by one, Dragon looked over at Sonya, who was still chuckling. "I should've let you throw me across instead," he acknowledged. "It would've been easier, and less painful." He put one hand on the back of his head, rubbing gently and feeling the bruise, while the other hand wiped a little bit of blood dripping from his nose. Even though he wouldn't admit it to the others, Dragon realized that he was a hasty person. If he had just stopped and thought about it, he could have avoided the whole mess.

Once everyone, except Sonya, had made it across, Dragon noticed that there was a problem. Sonya couldn't come across on the rope, and the ceiling was too low for her to jump or fly across. Feeling a little discouraged since he wanted her by his side, he quickly came up with another idea. "Sonya, why don't you go back out and fly around to see if there's another way in?" Dragon shouted.

Lowering her head and frowning in disappointment, she nodded in agreement and turned, heading back out. Everyone felt bad for Sonya, especially when they watched her walk away with her tail dragging on the ground. No one could say that they weren't a little bit worried for themselves, since Sonya leaving decreased their chance of survival. Nevertheless, when she was out of sight, they all turned and followed Dragon deeper into the witch's cavern.

✳✳✳

The farther the company went, the more the dark tunnel would twist and turn. They had just rounded a sharp corner that was overlooking a straight stretch in the cavern when Dragon stopped. He raised his hand, motioning for the company to also stand still. Because of their incident with the magic floor, none of them argued the point. They simply came closer together to avoid any problems. Dragon, on the other hand, was standing in front of them, staring into the blackness of the tunnel. Once again, his dragon senses were going crazy, and he couldn't figure out why. Even his sword, Truth, hanging at his side, felt heavy, as if it didn't want to go any farther. There in the silence of the cave, he mulled it over in his head for a moment till he finally figured it out. These witches were not foolish and would not let people simply walk into their domain. Like the trap that was behind them, the way ahead was like a spider's web, filled with more than just things that could kill you but alarms that would alert the witches to their presence. Upon knowing that, Dragon also knew they couldn't go any farther. But where else could they go?

Dragon took a step forward, attempting to get a closer look at what was in front of them, and if there was a way they could get by. Then suddenly, Truth began to burn Dragon's side as if it were on fire. He quickly jumped and turned around, startled by the sudden heat. As the rest of the company stared at him, confused about what had happened, Dragon stared past them at a strange sight that he had never noticed before. There on the wall of the cavern, hidden almost out of sight, was a hole. Even in the gloom of the dark tunnel, Dragon could tell that the hole went a good way back, and it was just large enough for someone of Phanis's or Cromwin's size to crawl through.

As Brenath was trying to talk to Dragon about what was wrong, Dragon was paying no attention to him; Brenath's words seemed to be drowned out by Dragon's thoughts. Even though the hole was interesting enough, Dragon was trying to figure out why Truth burned him. Dragon was putting all of his intelligence into quickly figuring out what was going on. Assuming that Truth was a magical sword that had a mind of its own, he began to work out possible ideas. While Brenath continued to chatter at him, Dragon slowly turned left and then right. Immediately, Truth reacted. When turned either way, it began to burn, but when he stared directly at the hole, it did not do anything at all. Immediately, Dragon figured it out: Truth, like him, knew the way ahead was safeguarded by the witches, so Truth found an alternate route that they could pass undiscovered. Dragon had to admit, for a sword, Truth was pretty smart.

Just before Brenath could start another onslaught of questions, this time wondering why Dragon was ignoring him. Dragon finally responded by grabbing Brenath's arm, pointing to the hole in the wall, and began describing his most recent revelation. This time, as he said it out loud to Brenath, he finally began to fully realize how much he truly underestimated his sword. At the same time, Brenath was grasping the idea of what Dragon wanted to do, and he didn't like it at all.

"No, no." Brenath started to disagree completely. "I don't care if the way ahead is safeguarded. We at least know there's a chance we might make it through it. If we go into that small hole, there's a greater chance we may not come back out. We might get stuck. It could be a trap, and we might come out into a pit, not to mention our torches are having enough trouble staying lit as they are. I guarantee you: we go into that hole, they will go out." Brenath strongly stood in opposition of Dragon and pointed to Dragon's sword. "Are you going to trust our fate to that piece of metal?"

Dragon stood silent for a moment, thinking carefully on what he would say. Even though he didn't want to bring any conflict between him and Brenath, Dragon knew his answer. "Yes," Dragon said firmly and confidently. "It saved our lives in the swamp; I think it can do the same here."

Brenath was unable to respond to that. He knew Dragon was right, even though he didn't like or agree with the idea of going into the hole. As for the rest of Brenath's men, including Cromwin, they too didn't agree with Dragon's idea. Nevertheless, Dragon, paying no attention, walked over to the wall and scurried up and into the small hole, disappearing out of sight.

With Dragon gone, the company began to mutter among themselves, worried about the possibilities of what might happen. Phanis was the first one to take the initiative to follow Dragon; tightly gripping a torch, he crawled up into the hole and disappeared also. He was swiftly followed by Voraha, and then Yolana, mainly because she had to help push Voraha high enough to get into the hole. Once the two of them were gone, the rest of the company stood in shock, mainly because a young woman was braver than they were. Realizing that it was foolish to stand there with their mouths gaping open, they mustered their courage and eventually, one by one, scurried into the hole and out of sight, with Cromwin bringing up the rear.

As Brenath feared, several of the torches went out as they crawled through the long, confining tunnel. If that wasn't bad, the air was stale and very thin, making all of them lightheaded. When Dragon finally emerged on the other side, he crawled out onto what seemed to be a ledge overhanging a dark abyss. Before he did anything else, he helped everyone as they came out of the hole. As Cromwin finally emerged, they all huddled on the ledge, facing a new dilemma. The moment it was fully exposed to the new area, the last torch finally burned out, leaving the company in complete darkness. The only thing that could be heard was Brenath telling Dragon his mind. "I told you this was a bad idea," he hissed. "Now what are we supposed to do? We have nothing to relight the torches with, unless you can breathe fire."

Dragon was just about to reply with something snappy when he heard a small ring. He quickly acknowledged the fact that it came from his sword, so without thinking twice, he drew Truth from its sheath. Immediately, everyone could see a pale light emanating from the sword, and not just the blade but the dragon hilt as well. Everyone stood in amazement as the pale light began to increase, letting their eyes adjust as it eventually became an overpowering brilliance. The light of the sword did not hurt their eyes, but it was penetrating; it seemed to seek out the darkness and push it away in every corner it could be found. Dragon stood holding Truth aloft with one hand, letting its light show everything around them.

"All right," Brenath spoke, breaking the silence. "From this day forth, I will trust your sword." The declaration was mainly for himself, but Brenath didn't care if other people heard it.

Before anything else could be said, Yolana let out a gasp that drew everyone's attention. At that moment, as Dragon looked at what frightened Yolana, he regretted the power of his sword. He didn't realize that when you shine the light of Truth upon something, it exposes everything. As much as Dragon wanted to take it back, he could not withdraw the brilliance of the sword. When the company looked over the ledge into what they thought was an abyss, their hearts went cold. Right below them was a pit filled with thousands upon thousands of remains. As horrifying a sight as it was, none of them could pull their eyes away. It was a pit of bones for thousands of humans, elves, and dwarves. The only thing that allowed them to distinguish between the bones were the articles of clothes that were thrown in the pit with their bones. What shocked them the most was the state of the bones. They had been picked clean of flesh; not even a speck on any of them. What made it worse was that there were teeth marks all over the remains, especially the skulls. The company was terrified by the knowledge that no animal could ever clean remains that well. Something dark and evil had done this and had lived too long.

Dragon himself was horrified, especially when his eyes caught a skeleton remains that was fresh. Not because it had any meat on it, but because it was dripping with drool. To occupy his thoughts, Dragon wondered if Ancient or Marahezron had ever seen anything like this during the Great War. Before he could think of anything else, something caught Dragon's eye. To their right there was a larger passage, a lot easier to manage than the one they came through. Dragon quickly urged everyone to move away from this dreadful place, and without arguing they all edged their way to the other passage, keeping their eyes on the walls. The only one who ever dared another look was Dragon; he wanted to make sure he remembered what evil was like. He also remembered that it was Truth that exposed what evil had done and where it hid. At that moment, Dragon had a newfound yet odd respect for the mighty sword. Dragon turned back, and with Truth lighting the way, he led them into the passage to continue their search for the witches.

***

Truth and Dragon safely led the company away from the horrid pit. The only good thing about their path was that there were no safeguards from the witches. When the company got farther along, they began to hear some noises in the distance, which made them soften their steps. The closer they got to the noise, they began to see firelight. As the firelight got brighter Truth began to dim as if it didn't want to give away their position. When there was enough light from the other source, Truth went out completely, and Dragon sheathed it as quietly as he could. After a short while, they crept into a large room, with torches hanging on the walls all around. There was a small natural opening in the ceiling, allowing a little sunlight to enter the room. They stayed as low as they could, hoping to see the witches before the witches saw them. The room was almost impossible to navigate through; it had stone steps, tables, shelves, and even half walls three or four feet high, dividing the room into different sections. It appeared as though this room was the center of all their activity, and activity they found. Dragon and Brenath spotted some movement on the far side, so they crept up to a wall, crouching low, and peered over, only to be partially blocked by another wall further away. However, that did not bother them; for what they saw, they were happy not to see all of it. There behind the far wall was one of the missing soldiers; all that could be seen of him were his chest, arms, and head. He was sitting quietly with a blank expression on his face, while the noise was coming from a beautiful human woman sitting right in front of him. She had her arms around him, with her fingernails digging into his back and while his blood ran down his back, he made no sound at all. The woman, on the other hand, was making lots of noise, even moaning, but not in pain. She was moaning in pleasure.

Those that could peer over the wall without being seen looked upon this sight with much confusion. As the woman's moans got louder, something began to happen to the soldier. First, the color and texture of the skin began to fade, leaving him pale and dry. Then his body began to shrivel, as if the very fluids in his body were being drawn out. In the end, they both let out piercing cries—one in agony, one in pleasure. Those that dared to look were horrified at the remains of the soldier; what was left could not be recognized. As for the woman, she got up with her body resonating, almost glowing, making her look younger and more beautiful. She walked around the one wall, giving the onlookers a better view of her, especially Dragon.

Dragon did notice immediately that she was completely naked, and he took a moment to observe her carefully. She was a fair-skinned woman, with white hair like snow, which came down to the bottom of her back. The human body always intrigued him, especially the differences between males and females. Even though he was no expert on the physical look of the human body, he could tell that she was well–built and endowed in all the right areas. Still, he had never seen a naked female before; all his judgments were based on all the other women he had encountered who happened to be clothed. When Dragon looked at the other men in his company, he realized that his judgments about her were correct from the expressions on their faces.

Dragon realized how easy it was for her to entice and capture men. Add a little magic, and it would be no struggle for her. He also noticed how comfortable she was and how easily she flaunted herself. Especially when she draped a robe over herself. It was a thin fabric that glittered like diamonds yet showed every intricate part of her body, almost as if she wasn't wearing anything at all. Dragon cocked his head to one side, taking one more good look before he had to do anything. "So that's what a naked human female looks like," he muttered quietly.

"I know. It's terrible. There's not a single bit of hair on her face or her body," Voraha responded as she peered over the wall right next to Dragon. "It's just not right," she continued, a disgusted look on her face.

As the woman started to walk away in the opposite direction, Dragon knew that he had better do something now rather than later.

So he quickly stood and walked over to the opening in the wall as he called out to the witch. She immediately turned, startled by his presence, and then got a mischievous look on her face. She simply stood there still and firm not intimidated or bothered by Dragon at all. Knowing that things were not quite right, Dragon motioned for the others to stand. Slowly and surely, they rose into sight. Seeing the others only made the witch's face grow more mischievous.

"Mother," the woman called to the other side of the room, where nothing could be seen. "The others are here. They came willingly into our home." Though she was a witch, her voice was very sweet sounding, almost calming.

"That's wonderful for us, but unfortunate for them," another voice echoed back from the shadows. This new voice was not like the beautiful witch's voice. It sounded more hideous and coarse. "They probably came looking for their friends—only to find their deaths. Daughter, keep them occupied. Control them."

The daughter witch turned back to the company with a devilish smile. "As you wish, Mother," she sinisterly replied. She then raised her arms in a welcoming gesture and began her magic. A mysterious breeze crept up around her and the others as her body began to be illuminated with a strange light. Within that strange light, her body's beauty seemed to grow, while in all of their ears, they could hear a slight humming, almost singing. With that, everyone except for Dragon and Voraha ducked back down behind the wall.

"Don't look at her!" Brenath shouted a warning at Dragon.

As no surprise to anyone, Dragon did not heed Brenath's warning. He simply stood there, staring at her. No one was truly worried about Voraha, because they could see the expression on her face. She still had a disgusted look on her face as she continued to watch what she thought was a hideous woman with no facial hair.

The witch's light illuminating from her body seemed to reach down toward Dragon like a pair of hands. "Come to me," she spoke seductively. When Dragon did nothing at all, she repeated herself once again. When he crossed his arms and spread his legs into a firm stance, she stepped back in awe. As she did, all the magic she was conjuring stopped instantly, and the room faded back to normal. Dragon could tell from the look on her face that she had never been rejected before, so in response, he smirked.

"Mother, this one is immune to my powers," the daughter said as if she had been insulted.

"He must be blessed by a wizard," the mother hissed back. "Or he is a wizard himself. Let me have a look at him." Everyone could hear the footsteps of someone approaching. From the sound of the steps, it sounded as if her body was deformed. Eventually, out of the shadow, she came, shuffling her way toward her daughter. As everyone peered over the wall to see what this witch looked like, they were horrified. Even Dragon was disgusted. Her very flesh looked as if it had been burned, and her arms and legs were twisted. She had a wooden staff to lean upon, that looked very similar to her own body. In one hand, she was carrying the remains of a human foot that looked like it had been gnawed on by an animal. She stood next to her daughter, staring down at Dragon as he stared back up to her. It was hard for Dragon to look her in the eye since she had none. Her eye sockets were empty; however, it didn't look as if her eyes were ripped out, just that they were never there. Even though she had no eyes, she moved her head to every noise in the room as if she saw everything. She particularly glared at Dragon, as if there was something she could not place. She then stuck her nose up in the air and began to sniff.

"I smell thirteen human males," she began to utter. "One human female, as well as one female dwarf," she continued and then pointed to Dragon. "And then there is this. He is no wizard. He is a half-breed."

"A half-breed! Is he part elf?" her daughter exclaimed, getting quite excited.

"No, my daughter," the mother hissed. "He is part dragon."

"Dragon," her daughter gasped as she stepped back in amazement. "He's perfect." She uttered those words as if she greatly desired him.

"Yes, he is, and we will gain much strength from feeding off of him."

Dragon took a step forward, irritated by their idle chatter. "I am Dragon, son of Kirianadréth. Who are you?"

"I am Shandra," the young woman stated. "And this is my mother, Breea."

"Yes, what can we do for you, Dragon son of Kirianadréth?" Breea hissed as she licked her lips at the thought of a tasteful half-breed.

"It is rumored that you can give us answers to our questions," Dragon remarked, trying to keep everything calm.

"That is true," answered Breea. "When I choose, I can see much; I can even tell you much about your ancestors. Unfortunately, there's no point in telling you about your future. It ends soon." The old witch took a step down toward Dragon as he reached for his sword.

Suddenly and unexpectedly, the ceiling to the right of them shattered and came crumbling down. With it came Sonya. Falling to the ground, she let out a quick roar and snapped her jaw at the witches. She had been watching and hearing everything through the small opening at the top of the room. Fearing that Dragon was in serious danger, she used her wings and tail to break in. On Sonya's unexpected arrival, Shandra fell back; as for her mother, she stood firm, yet very enraged.

"A dragon!" Breea shouted as she threw back her hand, lighting it with sudden green fire. She then drove her hand forward, letting go of a fireball made of the same green flame. Dragon, without hesitation, pulled his sword and leaped in front of Sonya to block the witches' shot. He landed as he brought his sword down to meet the fireball. When the two collided, a burst of blue and green energy sparked and then subsided into the sword. Truth had absorbed the witch's magic, leaving no trace on the blade. The sword then let out a brilliant flash of light, like lightning. Everyone in the room turned their heads quickly, blinded by the light, except for Breea, who was shrieking as she fell to the floor, as if the light had burned her. "Keep it away," moaned Breea as she kicked the floor. "Keep that abominable thing away!"

Dragon had one hand on Sonya's snout, keeping her at bay, while the other hand held aloft his sword. Dragon had no intentions of hurting anyone; still, he was going to use this to his advantage. "Tell me what I want to know, and we will leave you in peace," Dragon said firmly yet calmly.

"Very well," Breea responded as she coiled back from the sword. Though Truth had not emitted any other light, she moved as if it were still burning her. She carefully leaned against a nearby wall and lifted herself up. Breea turned her head upward and then side to side as if she were looking for something. Then, when her face had a blank expression, she spoke. "Ask me your question, false king."

All the questions in Dragon's mind were put on hold after hearing that. "What do you mean false king?" he inquired.

Breea's facial expression didn't change; she merely answered, "You are not the king of the dragons."

"Yes, I am," Dragon snapped back.

"Are you? Did they crown you king? Did those close to you tell you everything? This was a plan by the Creator to get you out of your city so he could crown one who was all dragon and not a half-breed."

Dragon felt his anger rising, and he had to get control of it. Ancient had told him about witches like this. They spoke the truth, yet they merged it with lies. The hard part was distinguishing which part was true and which part was a lie. Dragon knew it would take him a while to find out which one was which, so he moved his mind to other things. "What troubles the land around Tyrilcrysalith?" Dragon asked without any hesitation, putting all his mind on that.

"Your blood," Breea responded quickly, almost as if she anticipated his question.

"What?" a soldier quickly spoke out. "Does that mean Malic was right about Dragon?"

Brenath, seeing an aggravated look on Dragon's face, pushed the soldier back behind the others. "Quiet," he snapped, indicating his own dislike for the soldier's choice of words.

"What do you mean, witch?" Dragon continued to question her, but now it was a little bit more personal than before. It was one thing to make him doubt himself as well as other things, but it was another to blame him for all the trouble.

"The problem is closer to your heart than you understand. If you truly seek answers, go south. Follow the gray mountains to the end, where they become a ring of death. In the center of that ring, you will find everything that you are looking for and more."

"Is that all you have for me?" inquired Dragon.

"No, son of Kirianadréth," Breea hissed back. "There you will have to make a choice—one choice of the many to come. Choices that will break you and scar you. I do not think you will survive."

"We will see," Dragon boldly replied. He then sheathed Truth and turned to walk away. "I thank you for your time, and as I promised we leave in peace." Even though they didn't get direct answers from her, Dragon was pretty sure that what they got was all they were going to get.

After Truth had been sheathed, Breea regained her full height and composure. "Hear me well child of the dead," Breea yelled. "You have no idea what is before you! If you survive this upcoming trial, you only unleash greater perils! You have no clue what hides in the shadows that even darkness fears it! You will unleash a title wave of death and destruction everywhere you go!" Breea glared hatefully at Dragon's back and lowered her voice muttering quietly to herself. "But none of that matters; no one leaves my domain alive." Then, behind the wall, where no one could see, her hand lit with flame again. When she thought no one was looking, she hissed and launched a fireball at Dragon.

Dragon, walking away slowly, heard something coming toward him. Without thinking, he immediately drew his sword and turned to face whatever it was. He swung Truth horizontally, once again clashing with a fireball and sending sparks in all directions. This time, instead of diminishing the power of the fireball, the sword sent it hurling back at the witch. Breea's face filled with fear at the sudden enlightenment of her mistake and imminent death. The old woman could not get out of the way, and the fireball struck her, knocking her back as it burned a hole through her body. When the majority of the fireball's energy dissipated, the body fell to the floor with a thud, lifeless.

"Mother!" Shandra screamed in horror as she ran over to Breea's lifeless form. Dragon, holding the sword firm, looked at Shandra's reaction, and it gave him a momentary flash of seeing his mother die. When he came back to himself, he felt heaviness in his heart, and he motioned for everyone to leave as he sheathed the sword.

Shandra, weeping over her mother's dead body, heard everyone begin to shuffle away. That very sound filled her mind with rage, and she desired vengeance. Like her mother's magic, she lit both her hands with a green flame and leaped after Dragon. However, unlike her mother, she didn't throw anything at Dragon; she had her hands outstretched, reaching for his neck, and bore down upon him.

Dragon turned just in time to catch her forearms, stopping her dead with her hands only an inch from his neck. He could see that her face was filled with a burning rage that he knew all too well. She was screaming and struggling wildly, trying to do anything to get him. Dragon pulled her arms up and apart, and then using his forehead, he smacked her in the face, knocking her unconscious. When Shandra's body went limp, the flames subsided from her hands, and then Dragon let go, dropping her to the floor. He stood there for a moment, simply staring at her, feeling an odd sense of pity for her, and then he turned and walked away.

One of the soldiers ran up with his sword to kill her, but Dragon shouted for him to stop. Brenath, confused, walked up to Dragon in an attempt to reason with him. "Why don't you kill her?" he asked.

"There is no need to," Dragon replied, sounding sincerely concerned about her well-being.

"There is no need to," responded Brenath, becoming agitated. "She tried to kill you, and if that is not a good-enough reason. She is one of the most dangerous witches that have ever troubled these lands. What about my two soldiers that she killed? What about the thousands of remains in that horrid pit that she is responsible for? Is that not a good-enough reason? It would be a blessing to be rid of her."

Dragon stood convicted by Brenath's words; he knew that Brenath was right. The witch didn't deserve to live, but something stopped him. Perhaps it was the way that Shandra cried mother that struck something deep within Dragon's heart, reminding him of his own life. Whatever it was, Dragon was steadfast in his decision. "I will not kill her, and neither will anyone in this company."

Brenath got nose-to-nose with Dragon, determined to win this argument. "When she wakes, she will seek her vengeance upon us!"

Dragon slowly and firmly pushed Brenath back. "Fear not, my friend. She will not seek vengeance on any of you. It is my name she knows, and by my hand, brought her mother's death. If she seeks vengeance, she will come after me. That makes her my concern, and as of today, no harm will come to her. She has already lost a mother."

"A mother that was a wicked and vicious witch," one of the soldiers commented.

"A mother, nonetheless. I will not take her life. That is my final decision." Dragon gripped Truth's hilt firmly, and where everyone could see as if he was daring someone to challenge him.

"Then let me say this," Brenath spoke, still aggravated at Dragon. "You're making one of the biggest mistakes in your life."

"Perhaps," Dragon replied, looking down at the witch and wondering if she would come back to haunt him. "Let's go. We have much to do."

As Dragon motioned for Sonya to leave, the company grabbed new torches from the witch's cavern and headed down a different tunnel than the one they entered. Shaking her head in disappointment over the whole situation, Sonya leaped back out of the hole she had made and took flight. For a moment, Dragon stood, taking one last look at what had happened. He said he would leave in peace, but now he wasn't so sure if he had kept his word. As he followed the company through the cavern, he continued to wonder if there was something he could have done to avoid all that trouble.

***

After the death of Breea all the magic in the tunnels seemed to disappear allowing Dragon and the others to leave with no problems occurring. The company made it safely outside, where they were wonderfully greeted by Ganez, who was happy to see them alive again, especially Dragon. Sonya was also there, patiently waiting for them. While some of the soldiers went to rest back in the camp they had made, the others plotted. Brenath, Cromwin, Phanis, Yolana, Voraha, as well as Dragon and Sonya, stood in a circle discussing their next actions. As usual, Dragon took the lead in making most of the comments. It wasn't long before his mind was made up, and no one could make any deviation from his plan, even though some tried.

"Brenath, take your men as well as Yolana and go back to Tyrilcrysalith," Dragon commanded. "I will have Ganez take you by his hand and set you at the doors of Shieldholt before he fades back into a mountain. So you can avoid the swamp. From there, Ronnar should give you safe passage through the mountain, and your way back to your city should be easy. I will take with me Sonya, Phanis, and Voraha. We will go south and see what we could find and then meet back at Tyrilcrysalith."

Brenath had no objections to this plan, seeing the need to regroup back in his city. However, Yolana did. She was, in fact, very upset at Dragon, feeling as if she was being left behind. As she was starting to argue, Dragon cupped her cheeks with his hands, calming her down.

"Yolana," he spoke softly to her, "I will not leave you there. I will come back for you. Besides, we have a long way to fly, and Sonya cannot carry four for that long of a distance. Not knowing quite what we will find, I need ones that can fight. I know you were very brave to come along with us, and even braver in the swamp. Still, I do not think you are ready for this." Dragon then looked at her with a pleading face. "Please go with Brenath, where I know you will be safe."

Yolana stared at Dragon for a moment, shocked and surprised that he cared that much about her. She then lowered her head, still not satisfied with the whole idea, yet she nodded in compliance to Dragon's wishes.

As they all said their good-byes, Dragon went to speak to Ganez. He waved, getting the magnificent dragon's attention, and then waited for Ganez to bring his massive head lower so they could speak. "Ganez, I have a favor to ask of you."

"If it is within reason, my king I might comply," Ganez replied as quietly as he could so his voice wouldn't echo off the mountains.

"I have to go south to seek more answers. Can you take the remainder of my party and safely set them at the doors of Shieldholt?"

"Before I return to stone, I will do as you ask."

"Thank you, Ganez," replied Dragon. He started to turn around and then stopped. A thought and a question came to his mind that he wanted an answer to. "Ganez, may I ask you a personal question?"

Ganez looked up to the stars, contemplating whether he should allow such a question. Eventually, he looked back down at Dragon and nodded.

"Why didn't you fight in the war? In the dragon city when they would speak of you they mentioned you were never in the war."

"I had a feeling that was going to be your question," said Ganez, looking back up at the stars. "I was asked to join in the fight by Larzencarak himself. He was extremely disappointed when I told him no. Even the Dark Army came looking for me, but I made sure they never found me. My heart is too soft for war, and I love life too much. It seemed better for me to commune with the Creator and contemplate the meaning of life. And what better place to do those two things than high upon the mountain where one can see the stars. When you want to know how small you really are in the course of things, just look up."

Dragon was slightly shocked by Ganez's answer; it wasn't what he was expecting. "Because of your size and strength, you could have saved so many lives."

"Yes, I could have," Ganez replied, looking back down at Dragon. "However, I could have destroyed so many other things. That choice will forever be my burden and my guilt to bear. You will face similar things in your life, my king. Sonya told me what you did in the cave, how you saved the daughter witch. Though others will disagree with me, I believe you made the right choice, and I believe you will make an excellent king. Nevertheless, right choices still come with consequences, and those will be your burdens to bear. Farewell, my king."

With that, Dragon returned to the others, letting them know that Ganez would help them to safety. As everyone went to gather their stuff, Dragon thought about what Ganez said. He couldn't blame the dragon for wanting to get away from the chaos of the world and stare at the beauty of the stars. There was a part of him that wished he could do the exact same thing and just disappear.

When all were ready, Dragon, Phanis, and Voraha climbed up on Sonya's back. While Brenath, Cromwin, Yolana, and the remainder of the soldiers climbed onto Ganez's hand. With one more passing glance to Brenath, Dragon shouted, "Tell King Ronnar, as well as Queen Crysaia, that I am alive and well for the time being." Receiving a nod and a farewell gesture, Dragon turned back around to Sonya. Patting her on the side, he gave her what encouragement he could about their journey. She then stood on the edge of the mountain and unfurled her wings. She seemed to have fully healed from the injuries she acquired in the swamp. With Dragon in front, Phanis behind, and Voraha in the middle, they all held on tightly, preparing for a long flight. With a wiggle of her tail, Sonya shot off the mountainside, flying high and fast, disappearing quickly into the distance.

As for the others, Ganez did as he promised and set them at the east gate of Shieldholt. Then, slowly yet loudly, he took his place back among the mountains. With an enormous smile, Ganez once again became a rock. For a short time, Brenath and his company watched the mighty dragon in admiration. Then eventually, they entered Shieldholt; and as they were welcomed back by the dwarves, they wondered if they would ever see the other four again.

18

The Next Challenge

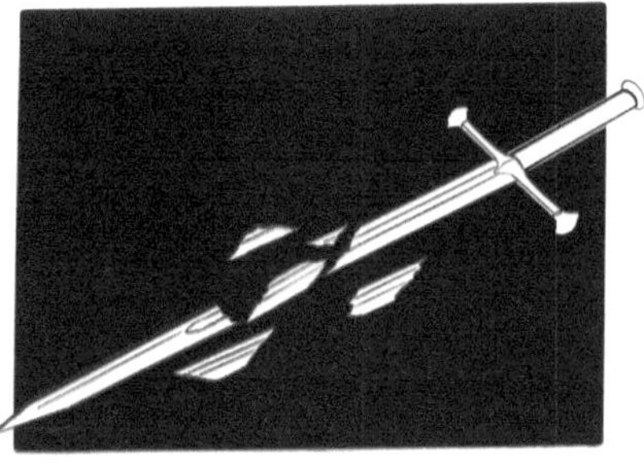

As Brenath, accompanied by Yolana and his soldiers, returned to Tyrilcrysalith, Dragon, Voraha, and Phanis, astride the back of Sonya, flew south. Even though they were flying, the way south was long and hard. Though Phanis and Voraha were warmly dressed, the high winds assaulted their bodies, freezing the warmth out of them and making their teeth chatter. Dragon, on the other hand, was warm and enjoying himself immensely as they followed the mountaintops. The other two had never ridden on a dragon's back before, so every flap of Sonya's wings and turn she made jolted their already-throbbing bodies. For three days, they traveled south, with an occasional stop to rest and eat. Phanis and Voraha cherished those moments when they could stretch their legs and relax their aching bodies. They appreciated fresh food in their stomachs since every time they stopped to rest, one of them would throw up what they had eaten during the last stop. That would always make Dragon laugh and constantly remind him that dragons were the only ones with the stomachs to fly.

On the last leg of the journey, Phanis and Voraha had forgotten all about their aches and pains and nauseated stomachs. Instead, their minds were filled with a sudden sense of dread. In the distance, all four of them could see dark clouds rising from the ground like smoke or ash. Not knowing what was before them, Dragon urged Sonya to stay out of sight. So with everyone holding on tight, she made a quick flick of her tail and a snap of her wings and flew straight up into higher clouds. Immersed in the clouds, Sonya stayed at their base with a thin layer between them and everything below, yet the clouds were thick enough to keep them hidden.

Dragon and Sonya could see everything quite well with their eyes, whereas Phanis and Voraha could only see passing shapes. As they reached the end of the gray mountains, Dragon now began to understand the witch Breea's description of the mountains. She called the end of the mountains a ring of death, and that was a poor description of what met their eyes. At the end of the gray mountains, instead of fading back into the lowlands, the mountain chain turned eastward. There they stretched far, eventually coming back and making an almost-perfect ring of mountains. Dragon could also understand why Breea chose the word death. Inside the mountain ring, there were several great fissures in the earth, sending up great clouds of ash and smoke, as well as letting loose rivers of fire. As for the ring of mountains themselves, they did not look like the gray mountains; instead, they were charred black and covered with ash and soot inside and out. On the other hand, they were still high mountains, though they could not keep snow on their peaks.

It wasn't long before Dragon and Sonya spotted movement within the ring of mountains. At first, they thought the ground was moving, until they realized it was something else. Orcs: thousands of orcs stood filling the inside of the mountain ring, wherever there was safe ground. Not only were the orcs on the inside of the mountain ring, but there were also some on the outside. Armies of orcs marched from all directions to join the ones within the mountain ring. Orc sentries stood all around the mountain ring, guarding this domain from any direction. There was only one entrance in or out of the mountains, where the gray mountains met the ring of death—an enormous crack at the base leading in. There, the armies of orcs marched in while others stood and watched, guarding the entrance. From their height, Dragon and Sonya could not get an accurate count of how many orcs there were; however, what they did count was over a hundred thousand orcs. They made several passes above the ring of mountains, to see all that they could. Knowing that nothing could be done since it was day and they would be spotted easily, the four of them flew off to wait till nightfall.

Sonya took them back to the gray mountains, and there on a ledge they perched. They were far enough away not to be noticed, yet they could still see most of the ring of death. As they settled down to wait for nightfall, Sonya and Dragon began to describe what they had seen to Phanis and Voraha.

"There were a hundred thousand orcs within the ring and hundreds more arriving," Dragon exclaimed. "Most of them were armed and ready for battle. The ones that weren't are being armed."

"What are they doing there?" asked Phanis, concerned for more than just his life alone and thinking back to Falistoran.

"Looks like they are gathering and preparing for battle," Sonya answered.

"Perhaps they mean to attack Tyrilcrysalith," added Voraha. "Orcs know better than to attack dwarves."

"Whatever they mean to do, it is not good," Dragon continued. "Far on the south side, there is a cave on the highest peak. It is well guarded from the foot of the mountain to the cave opening itself. It is my belief that whoever is controlling and leading these orcs dwells within that cave."

"Why does evil always lurk in caves?" Voraha sarcastically remarked.

"I wonder what we will find in there," Phanis asked as he got a shiver up his spine upon that very thought.

Dragon gave Phanis a reassuring glance as he put his hand on Phanis's shoulder. "I'm not sure what we will find in there, however, I'm certain that it is dangerous. You and Voraha do not have to follow me, if you do not wish to."

Phanis gave Dragon a sharp glare in return. "My mother said you have a destiny and that I would be a part of it. I will not leave your side."

"Well, you're not leaving me behind," Voraha interrupted as she shook her ax in her hand. "I'm going with you too, no matter how dangerous it is. I think we need to go and pick a fight."

Sonya and Dragon couldn't help but laugh as well as admire the courage of their two companions. So together, the four of them sat and leaned against the mountainside, waiting for night to fall. As they waited, they talked of many things and shared humorously about things of their past, making the time go by faster.

When the conversations paused for a moment, Dragon took the time to think of something that was pressing on the back of his mind. Your blood, the witch said to him. What could it possibly mean? Why his blood? What could his blood possibly do to cause so much devastation? The only conclusion that he could come to was that it was some type of hidden meaning that would reveal itself when he found it. Still, he couldn't understand what would cause dragons to turn evil or draw so many orcs to battle. Whatever it was, it worried Dragon, especially since he had to face it.

***

When night finally fell, they prepared themselves to leave. Still, they waited for several hours until the bright moon went behind some clouds. As darkness fell completely around the mountains, Sonya, with the three holding tightly onto her back, took flight as quietly as she could. Sonya stayed low and close to the mountainside, gliding as much as she could, so the sound of her wings would not draw any attention. Like a black shadow, she passed by all sentinels, unseen and unheard. Lucky for them, as the moon came out from behind the clouds, Sonya had reached the south side of the ring of mountains. She landed halfway up the mountainside, below the highest peak, and from there, they quietly clambered up and around into the ring of mountains. There they stealthily lurked, looking at the enormous cave entrance, which had a natural long, jagged ledge that overlooked the mountainside. On that ledge stood two orc guards: below them on the mountainside were all the rest, at least twenty. Dragon was not in the mood to harm anything; still, he could not let the two guards alert the others, and there was no way to get by them without being seen. As they slowly made their way down to the ledge, Dragon was hoping he could find another way to get by the guards. Looking at them from behind, Sonya claimed the left guard, making Dragon deal with the right guard.

The left guard was startled when something wrapped around his neck and in front of his mouth, pulling him back. Sonya had used two tips of her tail and wrapped them around the orc's neck, then wrapped another around his mouth, stopping him from crying out. Then, using the last two tips of her tail, she flexed them into points and shoved them through his back, piercing his chest. The right guard turned when he heard some noise, only to be grabbed from behind.

Since Dragon had no tail and he wasn't yet fully accustomed to using a sword, though he thought of it, he wrapped his arm around the orc's head, covering the mouth and making sure he too could not cry out. Then, while he twisted his arm, Dragon strongly kicked the orc's legs out from underneath him, making his body drop and his neck snap. As both Sonya and Dragon lowered the bodies quietly to the ground, they heard someone running behind them. In astonishment, they saw a third orc guard running out from the cave entrance. Fortunately, before he could so much as utter a word, his head was lopped off by a dwarfish ax. As the head and body collapsed to the ground, Voraha quietly chuckled and smiled at her certain victory. After they waited a moment to make sure all was quiet and there were no more surprises, they slowly ventured into the cave.

***

As the four of them entered the cave, they marveled at its size a dragon seven times the size of Sonya could enter without a problem. The same dread that filled their hearts when they entered the witches' cavern filled them now. This cave was dark, uninviting, and it had the smell of death. The smell was so horrid that both Voraha and Phanis almost vomited. They had to take a moment to catch their breath, and then they both picked up unlit torches from the dead orcs' supplies at the mouth of the cave. Not knowing what they would run into, they watched their steps carefully. As they entered into the dark shadow of the cave, Dragon's heavy heart was lifted slightly when he saw a twinkle of light in the distance. He immediately recognized the light as Tilly, and it gave him a little peace of mind to know that she was there diligently watching him. The farther they went, the more dismal it seemed, even though Dragon and Sonya could see perfectly in the dark. Phanis and Voraha could not. Since they had no idea what was there, they did not want to give away their position by lighting the torches. So Phanis and Voraha carefully listened for the steps of Sonya and Dragon and stayed right in between them. The farther they went, the more they realized that this cave opened up into deeper caverns.

Since they had several options for a direction, they took a moment to choose. Unfortunately, their choice was interrupted by a deep, ominous voice speaking out from the center cavern.

"Who is trespassing in my home? You do not smell like my orcs," the mysterious voice roughly spoke.

Since they have been discovered, there is no need for further darkness. Sonya sparked a fire in her chest and lit the two torches as Voraha and Phanis held them up. Then, very quickly, they all backed up and prepared themselves for conflict as they waited to see what would emerge from the cavern.

"Something does not sound or smell right," the voice bellowed out. Slowly, the voice's shadow emerged from the cavern and towered over the four trespassers. Eventually, the figure appeared from its shadowy hiding place and into the torches' light. All four of them stood in fear, looking up at the figure as it loomed above them. It was a dragon that stood three times the height of Sonya, and as it opened its wings, the dragon seemed to fill the cavern. Its scales were large and jet black; some of them seemed to reflect, while others seemed to devour the light of the torches.

The dragon's head was massive, with four large gray horns thrusting back from the top of its head, as well as two enormous gray horns coming out from the side of its head, curving and thrusting forward down toward the sides of its mouth like two spears constantly guarding its head. Its teeth were sharp and jagged, and protruding out of its mouth in all directions. The dragon glared down at them with eyes that gleamed red like fire. All four of them observed that the dragon had short fat spikes, like horns running down its back all the way to its tail, as well as claws at the tip of its wings. As for the tip of its tail, it looked like an oversized dwarfish ax made of black scales. The dragon's forearms were massive and muscular, just like its hind legs. Its' clawed hands looked very similar to its feet, unlike Sonya, where there was a significant difference between her hands and feet.

The black dragon looked down at the four trespassers with disgust; still, he recognized a dragon in his midst. He immediately ignored the other three and focused everything on Sonya. "A dragon," he snarled. "Have you come to serve me, and are these your offerings to me?" the dragon asked as he pointed to the others and licked his lips. "You are young. Nevertheless, I can use you."

"She is not here to serve you, and neither are we," Dragon shouted up at the black mammoth of a dragon, interrupting him. Even though Dragon's fear was great, he knew never to show it, especially to a dragon.

The black dragon hissed at the very words uttered by the human. "Who are you, and what right do you have to speak to me that way, insect?"

"I am called Dragon, and I am the king of the dragons!"

Dragon was interrupted himself by the laughter of the black dragon. "You are not the king of the dragons," he bellowed. "The last ruler was a female dragon, and she is now dead. I doubt that she would hand over her rule to a human."

Dragon took a step forward, taking a firm stance and a stronger tone. "I am Dragon, son of Kirianadréth and grandson of Larzencarak, and I am the king of the dragons! And it is you who has no right to speak to me that way!" Dragon had a feeling that what he said would not help the situation; still, he did not want to show any weakness before this dragon.

The enormous black dragon went silent, yet everyone could see his face was in shock. He slowly bent down closer to get a better look at this so-called king of the dragons. He got only close enough to look into Dragon's eyes, when he realized that they were not human. He stepped back. "It can't be," the black dragon muttered in shock as he put a hand on the wall of the cavern as if he were going to faint. He then began to talk wildly to himself. "I had heard rumors that she had given birth to such a thing, but I never thought it possible. I never thought she would disgrace her body and her throne. Obviously, I did not know her as well as I thought." He regained his composure and turned back to face Dragon. "What do you want, Dragon King?"

Dragon could tell by the sound of his voice that the dragon was not being respectful but was more frustrated with the thought. Nevertheless, Dragon calmly continued with his objective. "It is believed that you might be responsible for the things troubling the lands around the city of Tyrilcrysalith."

"You are right; I am the one responsible," the black dragon said condescendingly, not trying to hide his pride in the very act.

Dragon was somewhat taken aback by the fact that he admitted to it openly. "Very well," Dragon continued, trying to keep things short and simple. "As your king, I command you to stop, as well as fade away to stone as the Creator commanded."

"So not only are you the king of the dragons, now you are the herald of the Creator," the dragon ironically remarked. "Let me tell you something, boy; I will not obey the Creator, and I will not obey you! You have much to learn, dear nephew."

Dragon took a step back, almost falling in utter shock. "What did you call me?" The words of the witch flashed quickly in the back of his mind regarding his blood.

"What, your mother never told you that you had an uncle? I am Zyrmazonus, son of Larzencarak, and older brother to Kirianadréth!"

"You lie," Dragon snapped back. "My mother never mentioned anything about having siblings, and neither did Ancient!"

"It appears that my dear sister, as well as Ancient, kept many things from you. It doesn't surprise me, since my father commanded them never to speak my name again!" Zyrmazonus slammed his massive hand on the ground at the very mention of his father.

"I wonder why that was," Sonya softly interrupted. She had never heard of him either, but she wasn't too quick to dismiss what he said. However, she believed that if Ancient didn't say anything, it was because there was a good reason behind it.

Zyrmazonus quickly turned his head to her and snapped. "You want to know why, Marahezron's offspring? Yes, I recognize his scent on you now. I couldn't place it at first, but all is coming back to me." He then turned his head back to Dragon to reveal even more. "My father disowned me and banished me. He had Marahezron as well as some others throw me from the kingdom. All because I refused to listen and obey the Creator. I believed the dragons deserved to rule over mankind. So once again, I will tell you that I will not obey the Creator's call to fade."

"What about your king telling you to stop attacking the lands?" Sonya boldly questioned him as she stood firmly by Dragon's side.

"As I said before, I will not obey him, for Dragon is not the king." Zyrmazonus lowered his head to speak more closely to Dragon. "I am the oldest sibling; the throne belongs to me before it is idly passed down to a half breed. Fortunately, you need not fear, Dragon. As my nephew, I can use you. In my future empire, you can sit at my right hand, be my ambassador to my minions and slaves. Since you look like them, you will have an easier time speaking to humans than I will."

"That day will never come," Dragon strongly replied, unwilling to relinquish his throne.

"Oh, Dragon, your eyes are saying more than you are," Zyrmazonus said, his tone becoming more sinister. "Is it not better to be my right hand than the servant of the Creator? Tell me, you lived your whole life with dragons. What did you say when they turned to stone? What praises did you sing to the Creator, when he took your home and everyone you loved, for the sake of humans? How did you feel when dragons faded so humans could thrive?" Zyrmazonus's tone of voice began to grow, becoming more aggravated and violent. "You know as well as I do, that they do not deserve any of this! If any deserve the blessings of the Creator, it is the dragons, the mightiest of his creations! Humans are nothing but filth. They do not deserve to live!"

To those words, Dragon had no reply at all; he simply stood there, his face in an emotionless gaze. He heard and understood Zyrmazonus's words all too well, what was worse is that Dragon could not disagree with him.

"Join me," said Zyrmazonus compellingly. "Together we will awaken the dragons and rebuild this world to suit us."

"Ganez told me that the dragons could only stay awake for a short time," replied Dragon completely confused and trying to sort everything out.

"What does he know of the power given to the king of the dragon? If you trust me, we will take back what is ours." Zyrmazonus scratched his claws on the ground as if he were imagining, scratching away the human infestation of his kingdom.

Sonya stood there and watched Dragon contemplate his options. The fact that he was simply considering Zyrmazonus's offer aggravated her beyond control. She quickly stepped forward between them, cutting off Dragon's view of his uncle, and loudly voiced her opinion. "The dragons will only obey the true king, and that is not you. Dragon will never disobey the Creator!"

Zyrmazonus, enraged by Sonya's insolence, grabbed her by the throat and slammed her body against the wall. Using his other arm and his full body weight to keep her pinned, he tightly squeezed her throat. "Silence, you whelp! I am king!"

"Zyrmazonus!" Dragon yelled as he steadied his feet and clenched his hands into fists.

Zyrmazonus turned around to see Dragon glaring at him, his eyes changing from emerald green to dark blue. "You almost had me convinced on joining you. It is true I am not fond of the Creator at this moment. However, your first and only mistake was touching her. Soræniya is the only family I have left, and you will not harm her. Let her go!" Dragon then reached down, gripping Truth and pulling it from its sheath. Strangely enough, there was no brilliant flash like before, which confused Dragon; the sword simply glowed like a pale light.

When Zyrmazonus began to laugh, it only worried Dragon more. Taking Sonya with a firm grip, Zyrmazonus smashed her face down onto the ground and sat upon her, making sure she could not move. Then, with a malicious look on his face, Zyrmazonus turned back to torment Dragon. "I see you have Truth with you."

"You know this sword?" questioned Dragon, completely caught off guard.

"Yes, I would recognize that sword's power and scent in any form that it took. It's too bad that it will do you no good against me," Zyrmazonus mocked.

"Why won't it? It has killed many dragons before," Dragon quickly replied, attempting to stay positive.

"I'm assuming that Ancient never told you everything about that sword." Seeing a worried look on Dragon's face only reassured Zyrmazonus's assumption, making him chuckle. "Just like Ancient not to tell you everything, only just what he thinks you need to know. Well, let me tell you the true secrets of that sword. The reason why the dragons could not and would not hold the sword is that it is connected directly to the Creator. That sword may be the most powerful thing on earth, but it does the bidding of the Creator. It gives you what you need, not what you want according to the Creator's design. One day it would destroy a city; the next it wouldn't even cut a tree. You cannot control it. Besides, I challenge your right to the throne. It will not get involved in our dispute." Zyrmazonus took a moment and glared at Dragon, letting his words sink in, and then added one more thing, "Not to mention your heart is divided. You don't know whom to serve—me or the Creator. That creates a division that Truth does not like."

Dragon stood silent for a moment, thinking of what he could do; then, surprisingly, his mind was filled with memories of Ancient as well as Marahezron, and eventually, he got several ideas. With an enormous grin on his face and a gleam in his eyes, he sarcastically barked back at Zyrmazonus. "Perhaps the true reason the dragons and you wouldn't hold the sword is that it would tell the truth, revealing you to be nothing more than an animal! Besides, with or without its powers, it still is a sword, and I can still use it against you!" Dragon gave Truth a quick twirl and then held it firm as he stood on his toes, preparing for anything.

Letting out a vicious roar, Zyrmazonus, with his jaws open wide, lunged down at Dragon. Immediately jumping high and back, Dragon cleared Zyrmazonus's jaws as they snapped shut. Then, as he came down, Dragon held his sword high above his head and brought it down on his uncle's nose, right between his nostrils. Truth, however, did not cut through Zyrmazonus's thick scales; still, from the ferocity of Dragon's strike, it left him bruised and dazed. Taking that single moment to act, Sonya rolled over, using her four limbs as well as her tail she pushed as hard as she could against Zyrmazonus's stomach. With a tremendous heave, she hurled him across the cavern, smacking him against the far wall.

Dragon ran over to Sonya, hoping she was okay. He grabbed her face and stared into her eyes, deeply concerned.

"I'm all right, Dragon," Sonya muttered, seeing the level of his worry.

"Can you move? We've got to get out of here," Dragon said. He then began pulling on her arm, trying to get her to her feet.

Before Sonya or Dragon could move so much as an inch, they heard heavy, thundering footsteps running up behind them. They quickly diverted their gaze to see Zyrmazonus charging fast. At the same time, Phanis and Voraha stepped back and far out of the way, for they couldn't do anything to help; it was like ants watching giants fight.

Meanwhile, Sonya, attempting to protect Dragon, smacked him away with her wing just before Zyrmazonus landed on her. He held her down with his hands and snapped his jaws at her like a dog eating a piece of meat. The only thing that prevented him from biting her was that her tail was still free, and every time he lowered his head to bite, she would stab at it with her tail's full force. Dragon had picked himself back up and saw Zyrmazonus desperately trying to sink his teeth into Sonya. He had lost Truth when Sonya had knocked him away, so he had to think of something quickly. So without hesitating or properly thinking it through, Dragon ran over and grabbed Zyrmazonus's tail. Firmly placing his feet and gripping onto black scales, Dragon pulled with all his might. Though he had done something similar to Marahezron, it never occurred to him that he might be taking on more than he could handle.

Zyrmazonus, however, paid no attention to Dragon as he continued to get a firm bite on Sonya. Dragon began to grunt and growl while he gritted his teeth, pulling as hard as he could. Even though it seemed impossible, Dragon's stubbornness stopped him from quitting. The blood vessels in his neck and head began to rise; the vessels in his arms also began to bulge, and some of them even burst, leaving dark bruises.

Eventually, Dragon had enough force behind his pull, and he slung Zyrmazonus onto his back near the cave entrance. Although Sonya was free to get up, Dragon realized the mistake he had made. Zyrmazonus was now lying at the entrance, cutting off their escape. Improvising quickly, he pointed up and yelled to Sonya. A little out of breath and dazed from Zyrmazonus's thrashing. Sonya still understood what Dragon was saying. She took a deep breath, filling her lungs, and then with a spark of fire, she let loose a huge fireball. It hurled toward the ceiling above the entrance, and with a massive explosion upon impact, it brought down enormous rocks on top of Zyrmazonus.

Once the dust settled, all they could see of him was a hand, a horn, and one eye glaring at them. Dragon motioned for Phanis and Voraha to get on Sonya's back as he went to find Truth. Still glowing, Truth lay only a few feet from Zyrmazonus. As Dragon picked it up and sheathed it, he glared into Zyrmazonus's eye. With a sarcastic smile and a humorous wave, he turned and ran to join the others. Aggravated by Dragon, Zyrmazonus began to kick and scratch, digging himself out of the pile of rocks. Knowing that they could not get by him and out the entrance, with the three on her back, Sonya darted off down the left cavern. While she moved quickly, the other three kept their heads down so they wouldn't get knocked off her back. Like a serpent, she moved fast and stealthily through the caverns, searching for another way out. With surprising speed, she whipped around corners and down into other tunnels, widening the space between them and Zyrmazonus. The only noise that could be heard was that of her nose sniffing for fresh air. And eventually, she came across a scent that wasn't so foul.

They came around a corner, only to see a glimmer of moonlight peering through a side wall. Sonya immediately stopped and let the other three off in order to examine it closely. Seeing that it was a small crack and a possible way out, they all began to quietly yet quickly mutter to one another.

"The wall is very thin. I could possibly break through it," said Sonya, starting the very hurried conversation.

"That's no good. All that noise will bring Dragon's uncle upon us," Voraha voiced her concern. "If he followed us into the tunnel, can't we double back and escape through the front entrance?"

"Were you watching where we were going, because I was in too much of a hurry to count the tunnels," Sonya said, pointing to the tunnel they had come from with a face of aggravation.

"One thing is for sure; we must escape to fight another day. We must find a way to bring Zyrmazonus down on our terms," Phanis added. "I do not think we will find anything to aid us in the tunnels behind us. We need to look at what's before us."

"He is right," Dragon stated as he turned to face the tunnel behind them. "Sonya, make an opening for us. I will keep Zyrmazonus occupied in the meantime. He will be on to us in no time. He can probably smell us."

Phanis stepped in front of Dragon, stopping him with his hand held out right in front of Dragon. "If Zyrmazonus is coming too quickly, why is it you that has to occupy him?"

"Because I am one of the strongest," Dragon retorted, smacking Phanis's hand away. "Besides, it is me he wants more than all of you."

Phanis continued to argue, unwilling to let Dragon sacrifice himself so quickly. "You and Sonya are the only ones that can stop him. Therefore, you two must escape in order to find a way to stop him. I am the least valuable. I will go and stop him."

Dragon immediately grabbed Phanis's arm, stopping him from moving, and looked deeply at him. "Phanis, you have a full life ahead of you. You do not need to sacrifice yourself for me. My blood will never run as red as yours. If any is to be spilled today, it will be mine."

Phanis's eyes widened with surprise. Then he firmly grasped Dragon's forearms with both hands. Looking down at this proud dragon, Phanis felt such love of friendship. Looking into Dragon's eyes, he could see fear—not the fear of death or the fear of pain, but the fear of loss. "So the truth finally comes out," Phanis remarked with a smirk on his face. "As much as you hate and despise mankind, you abhor your very existence."

"It was always better if I was born one way or the other," snapped Dragon, raising his voice a little too far. "I could never blend in on either side. At least you have a place."

"Shhh, quiet," Voraha said, urging them to keep their voices down.

"Dragon, my mother said you have a destiny, and there is a reason why you were put in between those two races. It is not a curse, it's a blessing, and I am honored to be a part of it. My mother said I would be, and that many would suffer if I didn't look after you. This is my fulfillment of yours and my destiny." Phanis thought back to what his mother had given up to bring him to this place, and that thought gave him courage to do what was necessary.

The two of them were momentarily distracted by the sound of large footsteps running through the caverns. Since the footsteps echoed, they knew that he was still a good distance off, but coming quickly. Phanis looked back at Dragon with a heart-filled stare. "Good-bye, dear friend, my brother; don't hate me for this," Phanis said softly and earnestly. He then looked up at Sonya and yelled for her to take Dragon. With one quick, fluid movement and no hesitation, Sonya wrapped her tail around Dragon and grabbed his shoulders with her hands. Realizing what was happening, Dragon gripped Phanis's arms tighter, no longer caring if his voice carried, and he began to yell. Sonya pulled with all her might, hoping that Dragon would not rip Phanis's arms off. Voraha herself got into the wrestle by standing right in between Dragon and Phanis pushing against Dragon. Eventually, Dragon lost his grip on Phanis's arms, and he was pulled back, slowly and irresistibly as he kicked and thrashed. As they forcefully pulled Dragon back to their one hope of exit, he constantly and repeatedly screamed no and Phanis.

Phanis took one last good look at Dragon as he was being pulled away. He then drew his sword, that he so cherished ever since receiving it in Tyrilcrysalith. Gripping his sword firmly and a torch in the other hand, he turned and ran down the tunnel as the free man that he was, yelling a mighty battle cry. The farther away Phanis's cries got the louder Dragon would yell for him. However, nothing affected them more, when they heard a dragon roar and Phanis was silenced. All at once, they stopped breathing. They even stopped moving. Voraha laid her head against Dragon's chest as Dragon still had his arms outstretched towards the tunnel where he had last seen Phanis. Even though her heart was heavy with the loss of such a great friend, Sonya knew that she needed to move quickly, so his sacrifice was not in vain. Wrapping her wings around the other two, she quickly picked them up and bolted to the wall. With the full force of her body, she crashed against the small crack. With a thundering noise, the cavern wall shattered, making an exit for them to escape. Unfortunately, the wall gave away too easily, throwing Sonya out with the shattered rubble. Since there was no ledge for her to get a grip on and steady herself, not to mention her wings were bruised from the breaking of the wall, as well as safely holding the other two, her body merely plummeted down with the mountain fragments.

Sonya's body hit the mountain floor with a massive thud, throwing Dragon and Voraha from her grip. As they lay scattered on the mountainside, bruised and unconscious, great piles of dust and debris from the mountainside settled on them like ash, making their bodies disappear from sight. As the rubble continued to settle on them, Zyrmazonus thrust his head out through the hole in the mountainside. He immediately looked down to see nothing but rubble, so he rapidly glared up at the sky. Seeing only clouds, he quickly assumed that they must have escaped, which only aggravated him.

After a long moment of Zyrmazonus carefully searching the sky, two orc soldiers came up beside him and peered out through the hole. "Who were they, my Lord?" one orc asked reverently.

"Scum!" Zyrmazonus snapped, still filled with rage. "A matter of tainted blood–that needs to be dealt with sooner or later!"

"What do we do now?" asked the other orc, sounding as if he was terrified to ask anything at all considering what ill temper his master was in.

"Continue mustering all the orcs and arming them. Once ready, you will march as soon as possible to the city of Tyrilcrysalith. When you arrive, destroy every living thing!"

"What of the intruders? What will we do if we find them at the city?" the first orc spoke again.

"Do not worry about them. If they return to the city my servant there will deal with them. My time for power and glory has come, and nothing will stand in my way." With that, Zyrmazonus turned and went back into his domain, trying to think of anything that would keep his mind off this unexpected visit. As for the orcs, they peered out of the hole one more time, and then they too scurried off back inside.

As dawn began to rise, Dragon slowly stirred awake. After his eyes fully opened, he picked himself up without seeing whether he was hurt or damaged anywhere. It was as if he felt no physical pain at all. The only pain he was feeling was in his head. There was not much fight in Dragon's wounded state, and with shock of losing Phanis, he gave into despair. It felt as though someone had poured ice-cold water over his head. His head was filled with a blur of thoughts and emotions. Dragon wanted to scream and cry out, but he was so broken that he couldn't. The only thing that kept flashing through his mind were thoughts of all the people he had lost ever since he was born. He first thought of his father and then his mother, continuing on to all the people in his city that he left behind, then eventually ending with the recent thoughts of Phanis.

The only thing that he could conclude from all of this is that everyone that he cared about was either killed or hurt. In that moment, he was filled with a rage that he could not understand, and in the silence of his mind, he cursed the Creator. Pulling together what logic he could, he finally decided that it was better for all that he loved if he simply left and disappeared. If he wasn't there, they wouldn't get hurt, he thought. Dragon finally understood why the mighty dragon Ganez was so reluctant to fight at all. Thinking back on Ganez's words, they began to have a new meaning to Dragon. It didn't matter what side he fought on; he would destroy life and leave suffering behind him.

So at that moment, Dragon made a choice. He would look back and regret that choice, but at the time, it seemed the only way to keep Sonya safe. Dragon began to walk away; he never checked on Sonya or Voraha to see if they were okay. He merely thought that they would be fine if he was far from them. Traveling southwest, he never looked back, and before the sun had reached its height, Dragon was out of sight.

19

Death Still Hurts

The great city of Tyrilcrysalith was in no way quiet upon the surprising return of Sonya and Voraha, but without Dragon or Phanis. The whole city was filled with talk, for no one knew quite what had happened. Sonya was housed in the largest rooms of the tower, where her wounds were greatly attended to. She was lying down as the tower healers did their best to soothe her wounds and bandage them. Though they had never tended to a dragon before and their medicine was not designed for anyone beyond humans, what they were doing seemed to be working.

Sonya, on the other hand, was making a great deal of noise even though her body had stopped hurting from the wounds she received. She was moaning and weeping like a mother who had lost her child. Cromwin and some of the guards had to leave the room because they were so annoyed by all the fuss. Yolana, Crysaia, Brenath, and Tobin were in the room with her, doing their best to calm her down. As for Voraha, she was in another room being tended to as well, though her wounds were not as severe.

"I don't know where he is," Sonya cried. "When I awoke, I couldn't find him. I searched as much as I could of the mountainside! I thought he might have gone back inside to look for Phanis, but that would have been death for him! If I had stayed, they might have found us, so I took Voraha and came back! As I flew, I was hoping that I would see him walking this way! Did I abandon him? Did I leave him there all alone?"

Crysaia approached and began stroking Sonya's snout right above her nostrils. "You did the right thing, Sonya. Don't be so hard on yourself."

"Where's Dragon?" Sonya wailed like a child.

As Sonya cried out again in another burst of emotion, Brenath had other things to attend to. He gently placed his hand on Crysaia's shoulder and quietly spoke into her ear that they needed to talk. With that, they gave their respect to Sonya and exited the room, leaving Tobin to guard it. For a while, Tobin had to stand outside of the room because his ears could not stand Sonya's wailing. After what seemed to be ages, the noise stopped, and all that could be heard was quiet whimpering and the sniffing of her nose. Finally, after the room returned to a tolerable noise level, Tobin reentered the room to give what support he could. Once in the room, he realized that he would have to give his support at some other time, for it seemed as if Yolana had everything under control. She was sitting on the ground with Sonya's enormous head lying beside her lap. Yolana spoke, whispering in Sonya's ears as she softly stroked the side of her cheek. All Tobin could do was lean against the entrance and watch Yolana tame Sonya's frantic emotions.

"Everything will be all right," Yolana calmly whispered to Sonya. "Dragon is strong and stubborn. He's alive, and I know it. We will see him again, and when we do, we'll give him an earful. Until then, I am here, and I will not leave your side." Even though Yolana was silently grieving for her beloved friend Phanis, she knew that Sonya needed her just as much as she needed Sonya at this painful moment. Only together could they make it through this.

* * *

As Yolana continued to calm Sonya, Brenath and Crysaia walked to the throne room, while Brenath spoke his mind. "I'm surprised Sonya returned as fast as she did, especially as battered as she was."

"Yes, I agree. She is very strong-willed," replied Crysaia, sounding a little distracted as though her thoughts were on something else.

"I feel almost guilty that our return was easier," Brenath openly admitted. "As a matter of fact, this morning when I described our journey to you, it seemed to take longer than our return journey itself."

"You exaggerate much, Brenath," Crysaia interrupted, noticing that he was a little uneasy. She had known him all her life, and he was never an exaggerator. "This is a sign to me that you have something on your mind. Please speak whatever it is."

Brenath took a moment, choosing his words, and took a deep breath. "My queen, trouble is coming. I can feel it in my bones and with every breath I take. I'm not sure what it is, or when it will come. I just feel that I need to prepare the city."

"That's absurd. We are quite safe here, and even Malic predicts that we are safe now." Even though Crysaia spoke the words and wanted to believe them, she had to admit that she was beginning to feel a little uneasy herself.

Brenath quickly stepped ahead of Crysaia; turning to face her, he stopped Crysaia in her tracks and caught her full attention. "Queen, I respect you, but I do not agree with you," Brenath said with sharp tones. "You are wise to have more than one council. However, today I beg you to listen to me. Even if it costs me my life or my position in your kingdom, I will disobey you. I feel as if it is better to be wrong and have the city safe than to be right and lose the city."

After a long silence, with Crysaia looking deeply into Brenath's concerned eyes, she finally nodded in agreement. "Make the city safe," Crysaia replied warily. "Bring whatever provisions you need inside and store them, and arm whatever men you need. Since Malic will disagree, I will keep him at bay. You protect the city."

Brenath bowed in respect and then turned to walk away. Before he got so much as two feet away, he was stopped by Crysaia's voice. Hearing his name called out, he turned back around and looked at her face, which wore the expression of someone who was overwhelmed by everything that was happening. "Yes, my queen?" he respectfully inquired.

"I respect your honesty and your loyalty to me and this city." Crysaia then got a funny look on her face. "However, you need to work on your manners. I think you picked up a few bad habits from Dragon," she sarcastically added.

Brenath had an enormous smirk on his face and then nodded once again, agreeing with her comment. He then turned and left to start the preparations for securing the city, leaving Crysaia to her own thoughts. There in the emptiness of the hall, she let her graceful posture fall as she slumped with her back against the wall. She wasn't quite sure what to do or whom to trust. Even though she had a rough childhood, she had never felt so alone before. Now in the silence of the hall, she felt as if the world was falling around her, and her eyes filled with tears. In her mind, like Sonya, she cried out for Dragon, desperately needing him to be by her side. Crysaia realized at that moment that even though she had known him for a short time, she relied on him.

***

After leaving Sonya and Voraha unconscious on the mountainside, Dragon walked for two days without sleep or food, still trapped in his mental rage and confusion. When he thought of the words of the witch and his uncle, it only added to his confusion and rage. *His blood* was the words that constantly repeated themselves in his mind, and the endless possibilities of what they meant and what they could become. It wasn't until the dawn of the third day that he stopped and rested in a field of tall grass that hid him even when he was standing. He sat among the grasses and brushed his hand gently against them, making their tall tops move. Though it seemed as if his confusion was beginning to lift, his anger toward the Creator did not subside. Still, he did what he could to keep his mind off of anyone or anything. After the sun had moved a quarter of the way into the sky, he got up and continued traveling south.

When he eventually wandered out of the tall grass, he came upon another sight. Dragon was standing on a hill that led down to an enormous lake. As he looked to the left, he saw a tall mountain with its roots going down into the lake. It startled him for a moment because it had a cloud rising up from the middle of it, reminding him momentarily of the ring of death. He quickly calmed himself, realizing that it was only an old single mountain still open to the fire below. He eventually looked to the right of the lake, and he saw a fair-sized town. Even from a distance, he could tell that it was well-constructed and filled with a large number of humans. The town had great docks leading out into the lake, which was filled with many fishing boats.

Farther to the right of the town, there were vast, lush farmlands, and they were filled with a large assortment of growing foods. For a while, Dragon was quite hesitant and merely stared at the town. Then, eventually realizing that he couldn't avoid places forever, he moseyed on down toward the town.

As he slowly approached the town, Dragon realized that there were no gates, fences, or guards protecting the town. It seemed as though the town and the people were very open and welcoming to strangers. Still, he kept his head lowered just a bit, so people could see his face, but not enough to look him directly in the eyes. At first, he wondered why the town was not more defensive and had at least a wall. Then, the farther he went, he got a good look at the people and understood why. The men of the town were very tall and strong, and the women, even though they were very beautiful, were also muscular themselves. The entire town seemed to be built of fishermen, hunters, and farmers—not a single weak person in the lot of them. Dragon moved slowly through the town, being as respectful as he could. The last thing he wanted was to start any trouble. He eventually found himself in an unusually large marketplace, with many shops and tables lining the outside, and a bustle of people in the middle.

He carefully made his way through the crowd, paying attention to everything around him. He was amazed at the variety of things this town had. He saw shop owners that carried fruits, while some carried vegetables, others carried meats, and some carried fish. Some shops had trinkets of all different kinds, and other shops had clothes. He even found some craftsmen of metal as well as wood. He thought to himself that if he were a human living there, anything he wanted could be found at this marketplace, including things he didn't want to find. When the crowd got a little too thick for his comfort, Dragon backed into a corner next to a shop that had a single table with a lady sitting at it proclaiming that she could read people's futures. He hid there for a moment, out of people's way, almost content on staying there permanently, when the strange lady noticed him.

"Aww . . . a newcomer, do you wish to know your future?" the lady asked as she grabbed Dragon's hand and began to look at it.

It appeared as though she was going to tell him his future, whether or not he wanted to know. Dragon turned his head away so she couldn't see his eyes. The woman was staring at Dragon's hand, preparing to tell him about his future, when she glanced at his sword. Truth's white dragon head turned and stared back at her. If that wasn't startling enough, it then snapped its jaw in warning, indicating to her that she was out of place and had no real power. The woman was so startled by this that she merely sat back down in shock, unable to scream or say anything. Dragon of course, didn't see anything as his head was turned, but when he noticed something was wrong, he didn't hesitate. He simply moved back into the crowd as quickly as he could.

In time, Dragon found himself standing in front of a market table that was filled with an assortment of jewelry apparently made for women. There he stopped for a moment, trying to avoid the major groups of people like he did before. It wasn't long before he heard a woman talk to him from behind a table. She was trying to greet him, and he merely kept his head low, avoiding any eye contact. He was now thinking that coming into the town was a bad idea. Since he gave no response, the woman walked out from behind the table to speak to him.

"Greetings. How are you today?" she said very warmly. "I haven't seen you before. Is there anything I can do for you?"

"No, thank you. I'm fine," Dragon quickly replied. He then took a brief moment to carefully look her over. She was quite beautiful, with a trim and fit body, long curly brown hair, and hazel eyes.

As she continued to have a conversation with Dragon, she slowly nudged her body along the table toward him. "Is there something wrong?" she said, gesturing to his lowered head. "Is there nothing that you like?" She then slowly leaned back against the table, pushing out her chest, attempting to be seductive. Dragon forgot for a moment why he had lowered his head and brought it up just enough for her to see his eyes. Seeing his eyes, she gasped and jumped back, knocking some of the jewelry off the table. "What are you?" she screeched.

Realizing that he had made a mistake and that he couldn't take it back, Dragon lifted his head all the way, staring her directly in the eyes. Unfortunately, before he could say anything, a hand slapped down on his shoulder and turned him around forcefully. Standing before Dragon was a very tall and burly man, staring him down. Somewhat like the woman, the man was startled a bit by Dragon's eyes. Still, the man maintained an upright and threatening posture toward Dragon.

"What are you, and what business do you have with my daughter?" the man said in a deep and aggravated voice. "We are a peaceful town, but we do not like odd outsiders that bring trouble." The man then gave a sharp jab at Dragon's shoulder, indicating his dislike of him.

Dragon stepped forward, indicating that he was not afraid in any way of this man. "What I am and what I'm doing is no business of yours," Dragon replied. "And I most certainly have no business with your daughter!"

As Dragon was talking, two other men came up and stood on either side of the aggravated father. They both had large mattocks in hand and appeared to be of the same stature as the father. It was apparent to Dragon that they were friends of the man, since they came up without being beckoned or called. When Dragon tried to walk away, the father stopped him with his hand on Dragon's chest. "You're in my town," he said. "Anything you do is my business, and don't make any remarks about my daughter! I think you need to be taught a lesson! Perhaps we can take you apart and find out what you are. Maybe you're an orc in disguise!"

With that, Dragon had finally had enough of the man's taunting, and his face filled with rage. What right did he have to judge and persecute him, Dragon thought. He quickly brought his hands up and punched the two men on either side of the father. With a loud thud, the men went flying back across the marketplace and crashed into some tables. Dragon then quickly reached up, grabbed the angry father by the throat, and squeezed tightly. With the overwhelming strength of Dragon's grip, the man quickly fell to his knees, gasping for air.

Dragon, still enraged and not paying attention to what he was doing, continued to choke the life out of the man. In a short time, the man's face began to turn colors, and his eyes began to roll back into his head. Suddenly, Dragon got a flash in his mind of Phanis being in the grip of his hands. Dragon immediately let go and jumped back, terrified and shocked. The man keeled over on the ground, gasping. Everyone in the marketplace cowered away from Dragon; even the young woman ducked underneath her table, quivering. Dragon, in the meantime, was looking down at his hands shaking, disturbed by the image in his mind. He then looked out at everyone with eyes filled with both confusion and terror. Letting out a dragon's roar, making everyone cower away even more, he bolted off out of the town in the direction he came from.

* * *

Dragon walked along the shore of the great lake, heading eastward. He never looked behind him to see if anyone was coming after him; to a certain extent, he didn't care. He was still shocked at his behavior in the town and the quick vision of Phanis that he received. He didn't understand what it meant or why he received it at that moment. At the same time, he was trying to understand it; he was pushing the thoughts of everyone else out of his mind as he tried to keep control of himself. He clasped his hands to his head as if his mind were in pain and looked down at the water of the lake. Looking down at his own reflection, he stood still and quiet for a moment. He could guess whose reflection it was, but for some reason, he couldn't recognize himself. Staring deep into the eyes of this stranger, Dragon knew he was lost and didn't know what to do. He felt as though he was going to cry, especially when he reached for the scale of his mother around his neck. Grabbing it tightly, he whispered for his mother, desperately needing her to be by his side. Then, as a bird passed by, quickly distracting Dragon's glance at himself, he caught sight of something else.

Looking out into the water, he saw the reflection of something greater than himself: the mountain to the east. Turning his head slowly, he peered up at the real mountain, looking at its beauty, as well as the smoke rising from the center of it. With that, he let go of his mother's scale and turned his body to face the mountain. His expression was filled with both the look of an idea creeping into his mind and the thought of vengeance. His body was then filled with rage again—this time not at humans but directed at the Creator himself. Stomping off in the direction of the mountain, Dragon was intent on finishing this conflict once and for all.

***

By the time the sun began to set, Dragon had climbed to the top of the mountain. With the town and the lake far below and behind him, he truly looked upon the mountain. To him, it was a wonder; the sides were lush and green, yet the top revealed a different sight. There was no peak on this mountain; the top was flat as though it had been lopped off, yet the mountain was hollow. Dragon saw that the top of the mountain was charred a bit as he approached the edge and looked in. He could see what caused the pillar of smoke. Deep within the mountain was a lake of fire, moving and turning. He found a good-sized ledge that overhung the edge, looking out over the lake of fire. There, he shoved Truth into the ground and walked forward, placing his feet on the very edge of the overhang. Lifting his hands high into the air, he cried out in contempt.

"Creator, I know you can hear me. Today I defy you! You have taken everything from me, especially the ones I love, and then you command me to do your bidding! I curse you for that, and I will do nothing for you until the day you give me that which is rightfully mine—my family!" Dragon stood for a moment, silently waiting for a response, even though he was sure there would be none. "You, as well as many others, say I have a destiny, and that it is to serve you and your design! Well, I refused to serve you or your design, and I cannot be a part of any destiny if I'm dead! Since you are so powerful and great, try and stop me. I challenge you to stop me! Let's see how powerful you really are when I am not the one doing your bidding!"

Dragon looked down and took a deep breath, preparing to lunge, when suddenly the earth shook furiously, making him stumble back. Then, with a tremendous explosion, the lake of fire shot up enormous burning rocks. Dragon watched, completely dumbfounded, as the burning boulders scattered in all directions. All of a sudden, one of the boulders hit right beneath the overhang, breaking it from the mountaintop and sending Dragon, Truth, and the overhang hurling high through the air. As Dragon's body was tossed end over end through the air, many things passed before his eyes. Rapidly, he spotted the sky, the sun, the lake, and then the mountain, but was unable to get his bearings. In that moment, he realized that his idea was not such a good one after all. Dragon came face-to-face with the reality that he might die, and not dying on his terms frightened him more than he had ever realized before. Finally, he got a good look up at the sky and felt something hard and cold hit him in the back, and then he remembered no more.

20

Revelations

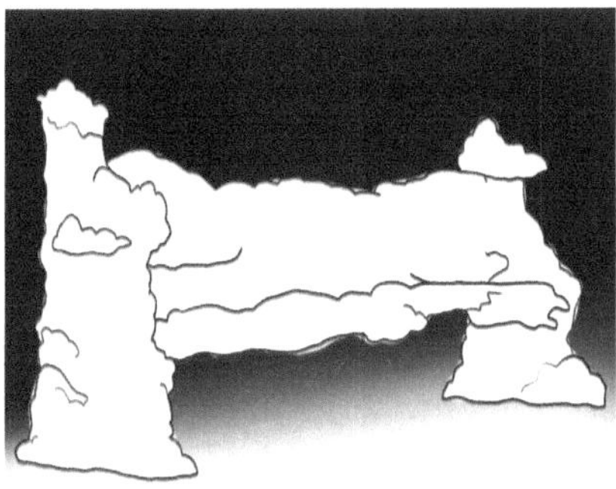

Dragon woke up and slowly opened his eyes, only to see a blur. His body was aching from head to toe; even his breathing caused his body to throb. Eventually, his eyes came into focus, and he painfully moved his head around to see what he could. He was lying on his back, two yards away from the shore of the lake. From the position of the sun, he could tell that he was on the north side of the lake. Dragon slowly realized that he was lying on thick animal fur, one of which was draped over him. He had several bandages across his chest and arms, which told him that someone had attended him. Apparently, he was completely naked, and his clothes were hanging on a nearby tree dry-ing out. There was also a well-prepared fire nearby, as well as some animals slowly cooking on a crudely made spit right above the fire. Dragon heard some noise and turned his head to see a cart and two horses unhitched and eating grass. Though he was in pain, he tried to lift himself up, only to fall back, letting out a painful moan.

"I wouldn't do that if I were you," a strange voice said.

Dragon looked around as best as he could but didn't see anyone. "Who are you, and where are you?" Dragon asked, sounding concerned. He was always taught by Marahezron that the unknown was more dangerous than the known. And Dragon wasn't fond of knowing someone was there yet not being able to see them.

"I am named Liam," the voice replied as the individual stepped around Dragon and sat down on a log beside him.

Dragon looked up to his right to see a man sitting beside him. He didn't seem important; the man was dressed in a simple hood and tunic and carried no weapons. Still, he had a peaceful look on his face; his beard and mustache were well trimmed; and he had long brown hair draping over his shoulders, with occasional streaks of gray down it. His eyes were sky blue and appeared to have much knowledge and wisdom behind them. Dragon never thought of ever comparing a human to his old mentor; nevertheless, this human had a look that reminded him very much of Ancient; more than Phanis's mother.

Because of that fact alone, Dragon calmed himself, feeling very safe for the moment. Dragon had many questions for the man. "What happened?" Dragon inquired, his voice sounding somewhat drowned in exhaustion and pain.

"You attempted to fly. However, your landing requires much grace," the man answered with a composed, level voice.

"What's that supposed to mean?" Dragon once again tried to move, making another sharp pain shoot through his body.

"It means you landed in the water, and that is the only thing that saved you from dying on impact. As for the rest, if it wasn't for me pulling you out of the water, you would have drowned. I bandaged you up as best as I could. Still, you're pretty badly bruised, and you won't be going anywhere for several days. It is a good thing you're half dragon, or else it would be months," Liam commented as he checked Dragon's bandages.

Dragon quickly stiffened and looked at the man, beginning to get concerned again. "How do you know I'm half dragon?" he carefully asked.

Liam, seeing Dragon's concerned look on his face, answered as simply as he could. "I saw what you did in the town and got a glimpse of your eyes, a little unusual for a human, if you ask me. I believed that I knew you, so I carefully followed you. That's when I saw your flying stunt. It wasn't until I undressed you and bandaged your wounds that I saw the scale on your right shoulder, verifying your identity to me."

"And who am I?" Dragon asked the man, not willing to give away too much information before he knew who this stranger was.

"You are Dragon, son of Kirianadréth, queen of the dragons, and son of Jorn, the leader of the Army of Light." Liam said that boldly and confidently, showing that he definitely knew more about Dragon than Dragon thought he did.

Dragon began to get a little aggravated by the man's answers. "How do you know that? How do you know me?"

"I know many things about you and your parents, perhaps more than you do," the man replied with a smirk.

"I doubt that old man," Dragon grunted, feeling a pain in his chest. His aggravation was on the rise, making his body tense, which caused him more pain.

The man then leaned forward, looking at Dragon with a more serious look on his face than before. "What I don't know is what happened to Soræniya. When she was younger, she didn't seem to ever leave your side."

With that, Dragon stared deeply into the man's face. "Who are you really? The truth."

Leaning back again, the man put his hands on his knees, took a deep breath, and began to explain. "Once again, my name is Liam. I am, or was, the servant of your father. Originally, your father never wanted a servant. Nevertheless, he was a leader in the Great War, and he needed some help. Even though he was forced into having a servant, he always refused to call me that. 'My good friend,' he used to call me, and friends we were. I was with him for many years, even up to the time when you were born. That was one of his proudest days."

"Yeah, he was so proud that he left and died on me," Dragon rudely interrupted.

Liam gave Dragon a sharp glance, very upset by the comment he made, and then continued with his story, ignoring that comment altogether. "I was there in the dragon city that day, and even saddled your father's horse, as well as one for me. I was so intent on going with your father. However, he begged me to stay behind and look after you and your mother, and that I did. He said he wasn't going to be gone long and that he would be back before I knew it. I was mortified when Marahezron informed me of your father's death. Somehow, I believed it was my fault, that if I had gone with him, he might still be alive. With that thought in mind, I couldn't bear to look at your mother. Not to mention that since she had returned to her dragon form, there was no need for the humans to stay in the city. So I left, hoping to find myself since I felt broken, perhaps to find a way to redeem myself to your father, and now here it is. I can redeem myself by straightening his son out."

Dragon, somewhat annoyed by the story, became even more annoyed by that comment. "And exactly what is that supposed to mean?"

"Picking a fight in town wasn't so bad. The men probably deserved it. They weren't exactly warm and inviting to you." Liam rubbed his temple, thinking back to that interesting moment. "Still, you topped it all by going out to a live mountain and cursing at the Creator. I believe that is a cry for help, for anyone."

"I had every right to curse the Creator," Dragon began to yell, even though it hurt to do so. "Besides, how do you know what I said on the mountaintop?"

Liam had to hold back a laugh at Dragon's foolish attempts to defend himself. "As loud as you were cursing, I believe everyone heard you. Look, I understand you being upset because you lost your father, but I can see no reason to curse the Creator."

"I lost my mother and Phanis, a good friend," Dragon quickly replied, wincing at the memory of them. "And that is all because the Creator had foolish plans for mankind's redemption."

Liam was silent for a moment, and his eyes filled with tears. "I did not know about your mother's passing. Now I have two to make amends to. However, the loss of your mother and this friend of yours is no reason to curse the Creator. Any idiot or fool is smart enough to know that. No wonder the mountain spewed you out of its mouth. It couldn't stomach your disrespect for the Creator."

Dragon immediately became very aggravated and began to rise. "I'll make you pay for that!"

Liam merely put his foot on Dragon's chest, making him collapse back to the ground. He then leaned over Dragon with an enormous smirk on his face. "You're so weak you couldn't even harm an insect."

"Just wait a couple of days. I'll make you pay," Dragon moaned in pain.

"I can see you are in definite need of guidance," Liam remarked, letting out a small chuckle. "Let me tell you something that you are not seeing. If you spent time around Ancient, you should already know this." Changing to a more serious tone, Liam straightened his face to speak what wisdom he had. "Death is important, though it is still painful in many ways. Death is never about the person who left. It is about the people that are left behind. Not to mention, it all depends on how we look at it."

Liam took a short pause and gave Dragon some fresh water to drink, then continued. "We were immortal once, and so was everything else that you see. When the Creator walked among us, life was perfection, until we fell from grace. Many creatures, especially humans, wanted to blame the Deceiver, for it was his words that lured man to betray the Creator. However, that is just an excuse we tell ourselves. If we had not been so foolish and selfish, life would have been different. It was our free will that destroyed everything and is continuing to destroy everything. The Creator loved us so much he did not wish to take our free will from us, but we needed to be punished. Therefore, since we were unhappy with everything that was given to us, the Creator deemed that we needed to understand the worth of things—the understanding that we need him and that we must choose him above all. So things began to die, creating a different aspect on life. Even elves, who seem immortal, can still die by an orc's blade."

Dragon turned his head away, becoming very bored with the whole conversation. "What does that have to do with anything?" Dragon complained.

Unwilling to give in so easily to Dragon's ill attitude, Liam continued as though he had not been interrupted at all. "By life hanging on a thread, everything becomes more important. Since we could die at any moment, we learn to cherish every sunrise and every sunset. Understanding your mortality makes you watch the small things as much as the big things. Unfortunately, there are those who become too arrogant to remember that, or ones that never learned it at all. For them, the Creator allows things to be taken away in order to make them understand, sometimes more than once for the stubborn ones. Another thing is that if you let him walk with you in the troubled times, you will come out the other side stronger and closer to him."

"Why me?" Dragon cried up at Liam. He then remembered that he heard something like this before from Phanis.

Putting a hand on Dragon's shoulder in an attempt to ease him, Liam did his best to explain. "One thing forgotten by many is that the Creator is all powerful. Whether you believe in him or not, everything is made by him, for his design. He raises beings up to do his bidding, and because of our free will, if they choose not to, he will raise someone else up. Everything in your life was intended to give you what you needed, not what you wanted. Because you're so powerful, you can turn against the Creator and harm many innocent people, just like the ones who harmed the people you loved. The Creator needs you to cherish every person you encounter and love everything you see. He does not need to raise anyone else in your place. You are already exactly what he needs you to be. In that town, you could've killed that man—you had every right to be angry—but you stopped. Whether it was a conscious choice or an internal instinct, it was still a choice. Now answer me this: if your life had gone the way you wanted it to, do you think you would have stopped yourself from killing that man?"

"I don't know," Dragon answered, confused, trying to discern himself.

"I'm sure you don't, but the Creator does. All the pain and suffering that you have gone through has shaped you into a good person who cares. Your mother and your father trusted in the Creator, and if you have any spark of them in you, so would you."

With that said, Liam got up and walked over to the fire, leaving Dragon to his own thoughts. He picked up the spit and pulled the meat off it, which had finished cooking. Coming back to the log to share the food, he could tell that Dragon had many things on his mind. Liam knew that he hadn't taken away Dragon's complete hatred of the Creator, yet he did calm him down and given him some things to ponder. Liam took the time to put more animal furs behind Dragon's back and head, lifting him up slightly so he could eat.

As they both gulped down what appeared to be either a large prairie rat or a large rabbit, Dragon felt he needed to know Liam better. "Do you have any stories?" he asked earnestly. "Stories of you and my father in the Great War?"

"Aren't you a little old for stories?" Liam sarcastically responded.

"Very funny," Dragon retorted, rolling his eyes. "Seriously, you're one of the last people alive who knew my father that I know of, besides one other. I would appreciate it if you could tell me something. Please don't make me beg."

"It would be humorous to see you beg in your condition, but since you asked nicely, I will." Liam took a moment to think, leaning back, putting his hand against his chin and stroking his beard. He then quickly snapped forward again, dropping his hand to his knee with a slap as an idea came to his mind. "I've got a good one for you. I think you might like it. About five years before you were born, there was an incident that bears repeating. The Army of Light was camped in large fields, and we were plagued by goblins. On one side of the fields, there were bunches of holes in the ground, leading down into caverns. The goblins dwelt in them like field mice, making it impossible to get to them. Dragons couldn't fit in the holes, and the humans would get killed the moment they entered them. Oh, your mother tried many things. The dragons were desperate to get to the goblins. They even tried breathing fire down the holes, but since the holes went so deep, the fire did nothing.

"Every night the Army of Light was attacked, and it seemed impossible to do anything, until your father came up with a wonderful idea—and quite ingenious, I might add. He had all the dragons round up as many oversized serpents as they could. Some of the serpents were three times the size of men, so he had the dragons herd them into the goblin holes. There was silence in the fields for only an hour, until the goblins came running out of their holes screaming in fear. Some threw their weapons down and their hands up into the air and began running for their dear lives. As for other goblins, they seemed to have been bitten by the serpents and couldn't run far at all. Not far from the goblin holes, the men of the Army of Light were standing ready to attack them. Unfortunately, they never got their chance. All the dragons pounced on the goblins like cats on mice. Before anyone knew it, it was all over, and everyone returned to the camp with peace of mind.

"As for the serpents, they took over ownership of the holes and enjoyed their new homes quite well. Even though the battle seemed easy, no one wanted to admit that if Jorn had not suggested the plan, they probably would have lost."

"That's quite a story," Dragon complemented Liam.

"Yes, it is, but you haven't heard the humorous part yet," Liam quickly replied. As Dragon cocked his head to the side, interested in listening to more, Liam licked his lips and prepared for the finish. "I happen to be a coward, and I had no problem serving your father in the camp. In battle, that's another story. That day was the first and only day that I mustered what courage I could to march out with your father. I even stood by his side on the field. To my luck, the battle was won by snakes and dragons. I didn't have to lift a finger to do anything, and I still fainted."

Dragon burst out laughing, joined by Liam, upon the conclusion of that story. Then, when Dragon had finished laughing, he thanked Liam for telling him the story. Liam, on the other hand, assumed a more serious expression.

"I still have the sword your father gave me. It's too bad I gained my courage only after your father died," Liam said, wanting to burst into tears. Fortunately, he stopped himself from crying when he saw Dragon's head nod with exhaustion. He carefully put his hand behind Dragon's head and began to pull the extra furs from out behind him, leaning him back down. "You may be awake, but your body is still wounded and needs rest."

Dragon's eyes quickly shot open when he remembered something he had completely forgotten about. "Where is my sword, Truth?" Dragon shouted, all concerned.

Liam quickly grabbed Dragon, stopping him from moving and hurting himself. "Don't worry," he said, calming Dragon down. "I carefully retrieved your sword from the lake, wrapping it and completely covering it with a cloth. Your sword lies next to mine in my cart."

With that reassurance, Dragon closed his eyes, feeling very secure in Liam's care. As he began to fall asleep, Liam noticed something that Dragon did not. By Dragon's side the entire time the two were talking lay his mother's scale that he wore around his neck. Liam had removed it in order to bandage Dragon, but now it was glowing in a brilliant red. Picking it up, Liam carefully placed it on Dragon's chest and then placed Dragon's hands on top of it. He then stood up and nodded in respect at both Dragon and the scale. "It appears someone else wishes to speak to you. Dream well, young one," Liam whispered. Then he turned and headed off toward his horses. "Come on, boys. It is time to hitch you up. We have a long way to go, and we better get started."

* * *

For what seemed to be hours, Dragon was surrounded by darkness. Then eventually, light appeared all around him, yet he was surrounded by clouds. The light was peering through the clouds like the sun, giving the clouds red and orange tints. Strangely, the light wasn't coming from one angle but all around. Even the clouds were confusing. They formed a perfect, large square around him. He turned around several times, glaring at everything. Eventually, he thought of something familiar and looked down: his mother's scale touching his chest was glowing. Seeing that, he quickly looked back up and became ecstatic as he called for his mother. After a while of calling for her with no answer, Dragon became disappointed. Then suddenly, someone spoke to him from behind.

"She's not here, Dragon. It's just me," a familiar voice said.

Dragon slowly turned, and his eyes widened in surprise. "Phanis," he uttered. Dragon's heart skipped a beat and then filled with joy as he looked up at his tall, dark-skinned friend. Phanis looked well; he even seemed to have an aura of light around him. Dragon could not contain himself; he ran up and embraced Phanis. After a heartwarming squeeze and a pat on the back, he stepped back once again, looking up at his friend. Dragon opened his mouth to say something, only to have his face smacked by Phanis.

"That's for the words you spoke to the Creator," Phanis snapped.

Dragon stepped back, clutching his cheek, surprised that Phanis slapped him, as well as the fact that it hurt. With a look of shock, he sat back on some clouds behind him. After a second or two, his expression of shock turned to surprise as he looked down at the clouds beneath him. He was amazed, not only by the fact that he was sitting on clouds, but also that they were holding his weight. However, the surprises didn't stop there. As he was looking down at the clouds beneath him, something cold and wet was running down his face. He slowly brought his hand up and wiped his cheek, revealing a clear liquid. Now in complete and utter amazement, he looked back at Phanis.

"Tears. I'm crying!" Dragon stated. "I thought I could never shed tears."

Phanis slowly walked over and sat down beside Dragon on the clouds. "That is one of the gifts given to you in this place by the Creator," Phanis kindly replied.

"Only one. What's the other? Your hand across my face?"

"You deserved that, and you know it," stated Phanis as he gave Dragon a polite nudge with his arm.

Dragon missed Phanis a lot since the day he lost him. He was in no mood to argue with him, so he decided to change the subject. "So what is this place?"

"It is the same place that you go to see your mother. It is the place set aside for you to see all the people that have touched your life and died. Here in this place is where the Creator can truly influence you."

"He's doing a lousy job at influencing me," Dragon said, lowering his head. "How is this influence, letting me see you only to wake and have you taken from me again?"

"It's not meant in that way," replied Phanis as he laid his hand on Dragon's back. "Here with the Creator, I have become forever. Not to mention, I can keep a better eye on you here than I could there."

"It's not fair," Dragon said, wanting to lash out in anger.

"On the contrary, it is quite fair, more than you know. The Creator has not given anyone else under the sun a place like this. The living is never meant to speak to the dead. If anything, I would say you were spoiled." Phanis paused for a moment to smile and change his tone of voice. "And right now, I am spoiled as well. I am joyfully rejoined with my mother and Krandal. I am also spending a lot of time with your family. The greatest blessing of all is that I'm in the presence of the Creator without the pain and burdens of the mortal realm. I cannot think of any better place I would wish to be."

Dragon replied with the only thing that came to his mind: "I'll still miss you."

"Then think of this place as encouragement," Phanis spoke, more animatedly. "With the Creator, we are treated better than kings on earth, and there is even a place set aside for you. When all is said and done and the Creator has rebuilt the heavens and the earth, there will be great rejoicing. Here with us, you will feel no pain, have no hunger, and never want again."

"It sounds perfect," Dragon muttered in a slight daze over everything Phanis said.

"It is perfect, and all the years you spend on earth will seem like nothing in the presence of the Creator. All that he asks of you is that you have faith in him and obey him."

Dragon looked at Phanis with curiosity and one thought in his mind. "Why isn't my mother here telling me this?"

"The Creator thought you needed me to tell you this for two reasons: one, I was the last person you lost. You needed to know I was okay. Second, you barely listened to your mother on earth, let alone here."

Dragon smirked and let out a small chuckle, realizing that Phanis had a point. "So what now?" he asked, ever so curiously.

Phanis waited a moment for Dragon to give him his full attention before he answered. "Now you must go back and deal with your uncle."

"Isn't that what you were supposed to do?" Dragon sarcastically remarked.

Phanis looked down at his own body and nodded in agreement. "True, but as you can tell, I didn't quite succeed in that."

Dragon and Phanis both laughed at that comment, even though it was a hard subject for Dragon to stomach. Dragon returned to being serious since he wasn't sure what to do. "I'm not sure if I can face my uncle again."

"You must, Dragon. It's important," Phanis replied, patting Dragon on the back and then standing up. He turned and faced Dragon, grabbing him by his arm and lifting him up to his feet. "My beloved friend, trust the Creator, trust Truth, and trust yourself. I ask you to do those things because I trust in them. Do not feel guilty about my death. It was my choice to do what I did. I was honored to be by your side, and I regret nothing. Now I am in a better place, and I am happy."

Though he missed Phanis and still felt some guilt for letting him die, Dragon was happy that Phanis had found peace.

Phanis got a serious look on his face, knowing that Dragon would not like what he was about to say. "Dragon, there's something you need to be made aware of, especially for the future to come. In the absence of light, there is darkness. One of the Deceiver's greatest lies is that one can serve themselves. When you are not serving the Creator, you are unwittingly serving the Deceiver. Most people go their entire lives not knowing it. But there are times when one is weakened emotionally just enough that not only do they serve the Deceiver, but they also allow him to take over. They are trapped in their mind as he controls them, making then do his bidding."

"What do I do to prevent it from happening?"

"Unfortunately," Phanis started to respond, carefully choosing his words, "to stop the darkness, you must step into the light, which means you must serve the Creator. That is the only way to stop the Deceiver from taking over. You can only fight it for so long on your own. You must not let your anger and emotions control you. The Creator is the only one that can put the Deceiver in his place."

Dragon had no response to Phanis, for he knew that Phanis was right.

"Unfortunately, I must go now," Phanis stated.

"No," Dragon said as his breath caught. He then reached forward and gave Phanis another tight embrace.

"Dragon, I must go. Besides, there is much for you to do." Phanis then pulled away. Holding Dragon by the shoulders and staring deeply into his eyes, Phanis said his good-bye. "I love you, friend, brother. Do not worry. You will see me again. In the meantime, there is someone else that needs to speak to you."

"Who is that?" Dragon quickly asked, getting excited.

"I can't tell you. It's hard to explain. You will just have to see it for yourself." With that, Phanis let go and stepped back, letting his body fade into the clouds as he waved farewell.

***

Dragon stood alone for several moments, curious about who wanted to speak to him and whether they would ever appear. Then Dragon began to hear an ominous thumping slowly approaching. As strange as it seemed, the clouds he was standing on began to shake with every thud. Eventually, Dragon could see an enormous shadow approaching from the clouds. At first, he began to feel worried, since he did not know who was towering over him. As the figure emerged from the clouds, Dragon fell to his knees in awe. There standing before him was an enormous and overpowering dragon with thick black scales. Dragon knew his likeness well from seeing his stone figure in the tombs beneath the dragon city. All Dragon could do was stare at him in reverence and quietly mutter under his breath, "Grandfather."

"Yes, Dragon, it is I, Larzencarak, your grandfather," the mighty dragon said as his deep voice echoed in the clouds. He waited for a moment to see if Dragon would say anything in return, and when Dragon couldn't say anything but merely kneel there in silence, Larzencarak continued with what he needed to say. "My boy, I am extremely proud of you and how far you have come. Unfortunately, I am sorry I left behind trouble for you to deal with. I am also sorry that no one ever told you about your uncle, and that you had to find out the way you did. It is ironic the way you must face him, but face him you must. You cannot let Zyrmazonus gain any more power. I know he challenged you for the throne, and that he thinks it belongs to him. However, let me tell you that the throne never belonged to him. Since the beginning, the leadership over dragons was chosen by the Creator, and so was the heir to the throne. We are not like humans. Our birthrights are not handed down to the firstborn. The Creator chose your mother himself, and you. By aligning himself with the Deceiver, Zyrmazonus lost whatever right he had as a dragon."

Larzencarak leaned down, bringing his head closer to Dragon's. "You do not have to fight him for your right to be king; you must fight him because you are the king. Do it for me, do it for your mother and father, and do it for your people. We are all watching over you."

"If I am truly king then why didn't Truth work for me the way it should have?"

"Zyrmazonus lies a lot like his master the Deceiver. Truth did not work the way you wanted it to because it is not under your control. It has its own reasons for what it does, and it has nothing to do with your title as king. I wish I could speak to you more about that sword but someone else has been appointed for that task. What I can tell you is that you should have no doubts about your kingship. What you did not realize during your conversation with your uncle is how badly he wanted you to join him. If it was about succession then why have a family member that could take his place, it is safer to kill you. However, he needed you because he does not have the power to call the dragons back from their slumber, he is not king. He even lied about that, trying to make you believe that you and him could make the dragons stay from their slumber when that is not how it works. The saddest part of it all is that he lies to himself, and he believes his own lies, he is truly lost."

Larzencarak paused for a moment and looked off as if he could see something far away. "Before I go, I will give you some information. You will not remember it until the time is right, when you need it the most. Years from now, when you are truly overwhelmed by darkness, and you need help. Call for the messenger dragon Moahdee, and he will find you and help you."

Larzencarak then took a moment to truly look at Dragon. After a second or two, he grinned enormously, very enamored with what he saw. "You look so much like your mother, with a little bit of your father."

Dragon grinned, also looking up at his grandfather. "Believe it or not, that is the first time I've ever heard that." Dragon, of course, wanted to say something more meaningful to his grandfather, but that was all he could muster at that time.

"Well, I hope that it will not be the last time you hear that." Larzencarak brought his enormous hand down and pressed his fingertip against Dragon's cheek, softly brushing it. "I am proud of you, and I have faith in you, my grandson. Go now and fulfill your destiny."

Before Dragon could say anything in return, Larzencarak leaned back and faded away into the clouds. Once again, Dragon was alone. Sitting upon his knees, he bowed his head in respectful contemplation of what he had seen and heard. As he thought over the words that he had recently been told, the light behind the clouds began to dim, returning him to the darkness of his sleep.

21

Moment of Truth

Dragon opened his eyes to see that his surroundings had changed since he had last talked to Liam. He was lying on something more comfortable than fur, and he was clothed in something that felt like silk. Dragon was now inside and looking up at a ceiling that looked similar to the rooms at Tyrilcrysalith. With a more detailed look, Dragon realized that he was at Tyrilcrysalith.

"Liam, Liam, where are you?" Dragon began to cry out. He quickly calmed down when he felt a hand pressed against his shoulder, stopping him from moving too much in his bed. Turning his head, Dragon thought he would see Liam, but instead, he found Brenath sitting beside the bed, looking after him.

"Easy, friend," Brenath responded, showing on his face the delight he felt that Dragon was awake. "You may be healed, but if you get up too quickly, you'll daze yourself."

"How did I get here?" Dragon inquired frantically. "Where is Liam?"

"Calm yourself. You've been sleeping for several days and sleeping quite peacefully, from what Liam told me. He's a good man, and he tended to you well on your journey back to Tyrilcrysalith. Of course, some of that is probably due to your dragon blood."

"Is he here? I wish to speak to him," Dragon insisted. He didn't know how to explain it, but somehow Liam made him feel safe, and the thought of him gone startled Dragon.

The look on Brenath's face quickly turned to one of disappointment as he had to give Dragon the unwanted news. "I'm afraid not. You two arrived late last night. He took some food and lodging for the night and then left early this morning as the sun was just rising. Since it is almost noon, I believe he is far away from here. Still, he left a message with me to give to you when you eventually woke up. He told me to tell you that he feels as if he has fulfilled his commitment to your mother and your father. He also said that he had his own destiny, and that's why he couldn't stay. Nevertheless, he has faith in you and believes that you will do fine, especially since you're a lot like your parents."

Dragon sighed quietly, feeling somewhat disappointed. "I wish I could see him again."

"Well, it looks like you wouldn't have had a chance anyway," Brenath sarcastically remarked as they both heard heavy footsteps bounding their way.

As Dragon leaned up to see what it was, Sonya came bolting through the door and pouncing at the bed. She landed with a hand on either side of the bed and shoved her nose directly in front of Dragon's face, making him drop back to the bed. "Dragon!" she shouted as she puffed smoke out of her nostrils. "If you ever leave me again, I swear on your mother's good name that I will beat the dragon side out of you!"

Dragon carefully rubbed her chin and then gave her a shove to give himself some room. "I'm sorry. It won't ever happen again."

"You're right, it won't if I have anything to do with it," Voraha shouted as she too entered the room, holding her ax in a defensive posture. She then pointed it at Dragon, making a very aggressive gesture. "Don't think you can just leave us behind like that ever again!"

With that, Yolana entered the room as well, followed by Crysaia, with Malic trailing behind. Since a lot of noise was coming from the room, Cromwin and two guards also entered from another door on the opposite side of the room. Yolana came forward and tapped Sonya on the forearm, urging her to give Dragon some room. With a new-found respect for Yolana, Sonya did as she asked and moved back, sitting down quietly like a very large puppy at the end of the bed.

Yolana then gave Dragon a gentle embrace, welcoming him back. "It's a good thing Liam brought you back. You have a promise to keep."

"Keeping promises is probably the last thing on his mind," Malic rudely interrupted, upsetting everyone in the room. "As a matter of fact, I'm surprised your servant Liam stayed as long as he did."

Aggravated by that comment, Dragon sat up and draped his legs over the side of the bed. He cocked his head and glared at Malic. Dragon had a serious look on his face and a strong tone in his voice. "Liam was not a servant. He was a dear friend and an honorable man, which is more than I could say for you."

Malic stepped forward, becoming very agitated as he yelled, "You are one to talk, half-breed! I heard from your pet that it is your uncle that is troubling our lands! All along, I knew you were deceitful and that you are trouble to us! Guards, take him!" Malic snapped as he made frantic gestures with his hands.

Crysaia raised her hand and was about to say something in order to resolve this issue when Dragon suddenly grabbed her hand and shouted, "Stop!"

Everyone in the room was so startled by his yell that even Sonya jumped. "I have had enough of your words, Malic. I am not in league with my uncle, and I will deal with him on my own terms. As for you, you have a smell about you that is all too familiar." Dragon then waved to the guards with his own gestures. "Take him and confine him to his room."

"I am the queen. I make the decisions around here," Crysaia snapped, so upset that everyone was giving orders around her.

Dragon then stood up from the bed and pulled Crysaia closer. "Not today. Your city is in the middle of a war that has lasted for thousands of years, and apparently, it hasn't stopped. You may be responsible for the people in your city, but I am responsible for many more. There is a storm coming, and Malic cannot be trusted. He will stay in his room till it is over. I will go to the source and stop it there, which would be my uncle. Hopefully, I make it back in time to help." Dragon then motioned once again for the guards to take Malic, and that time, they did not hesitate.

Crysaia was so surprised by Dragon's words that she did not say anything at all, even when the guards dragged Malic out of the room, kicking and screaming in protest. She didn't want to admit it, but she liked someone else taking responsibility for once. Crysaia tried not to blush as she thought of herself and Dragon ruling together as king and queen.

"Well, you at least made Cromwin happy," Brenath commented as he pointed to an unusually large smile on Cromwin's face. "So what is going to happen now?"

"I will go and face my uncle alone. If I survive, you will see me again. If you don't see me, hopefully, you will fare better than I did." Voraha was about to say something to Dragon on the subject of going with him when he shot her down with a sharp glare and a raised hand. "Voraha will stay here and help you protect the city. I'm not sure exactly what will be coming your way. However, I'm certain it won't be dragons. Yolana, I need you to look after the queen while I'm gone. Now if all of you could go to the watchtower, I will meet you there shortly."

Everyone stared at Dragon for a brief moment, taken aback by his new attitude. Somehow, he seemed more grown-up and empowered by something they could not place. Even though no one was used to taking orders from Dragon, they all respected his wishes and left quietly, all except for Sonya. She was standing on her hind legs, with her arms crossed, while she tapped the floor with her toes. She glared at Dragon with a sincere look, as she was feeling left out. "Why do you always have to do everything alone?"

Dragon smiled for a second before he answered, understanding why she would ask such a thing. "I'm not going alone."

"But you just said that you were. Are you feeling all right?" Sonya reached down in an attempt to touch his forehead to see if he had a fever. Dragon stopped her before she did, grabbing her hand and gently pushing it away.

"How am I supposed to get there? I can't walk there," Dragon sarcastically responded. He then walked over to the end of the bed, where all his things were carefully laid at the foot of the bed. As he began to gather his things and put them on, he also took the time to explain something to her. "Sonya, wherever I go, you go. It was that way when we were born, and it will be that way up until the time that we die. I'm sorry that I thought I could protect you by staying away from you. I learned the hard way that we are the strongest when we are together." With that comment, Dragon rubbed his cheek, thinking back to his dream, where Phanis had hit him.

Sonya lowered her head beside Dragon and gave him a slight nudge, enamored by his words. He too felt the need to show his feelings for her, so he reached out to embrace her. He wrapped his arms around her snout and laid his head right below her eyes, giving a tight squeeze. Sonya enjoyed this moment and began moving her head like a cat nuzzling, and she even sounded as though she was purring.

Moments later, when Dragon and Sonya were ready, they appeared in the watchtower. However, no one noticed it because everyone was looking frantically toward the southeast. So Dragon and Sonya joined the company, looking out, only to see a cloud of dust approaching from far in the distance.

"What is it?" Dragon asked.

"We don't know," Tobin replied as he came up into the watchtower. "But whatever it is, it's trouble. Some of our scouts haven't returned, so we can only assume that they're dead. Whatever is coming will be here in one or two days."

"It is the storm, breathed from the hatred of Zyrmazonus," Dragon stated as his eyes filled with disgust. He made that statement almost for himself, as well as everyone else. "It is time that someone dealt with him. Protect your gates well, Brenath, and keep Voraha out of trouble." Dragon turned to them to say farewell, only to get a sharp glare and a growl from Voraha. So instead, he bid Brenath farewell and grasped his forearm, bringing him close and patting him on the back. Then Dragon leaped onto Sonya's back, having no more time to say goodbye to anyone. With a flap of her wings and a kick of her feet, she shot off as quickly as she could go, leaving everyone else behind watching them and hoping they would see them again.

* * *

Sonya, with Dragon on her back, flew as fast as she could toward the ring of death. They weren't quite sure how long it took—perhaps a day, maybe a day and a half. Still, they reached the mountain ring swiftly. It looked as uninviting as it had been before; the only difference was it was empty of orcs. There were only a few left behind, guarding the entrance and the mountainside to Zyrmazonus's cavern. Surprisingly, Sonya was in no mood to do things quietly. She swooped down with such speed and accuracy toward the orcs. As she flew right above them, she let loose a steady stream of fire, consuming and killing them instantly. Sonya landed with a thud on the ledge before the cavern. Dragon jumped down, immediately preparing for a fight. Strangely enough, before he could take one step, a light flickered in front of him. Looking at it carefully, he saw a familiar fairy appear before him.

"Til, what are you doing here?" Dragon asked, still standing defensively and carefully looking for trouble.

"I've come to give you a message from Phanis," replied Tilly.

"Phanis, how did you speak to him?" Dragon was beginning to admit to himself that with every day, the world around him got stranger and stranger.

"I can also go to that special place set aside for you, which is where I spoke to Phanis. Don't forget, like them, I am also watching you. Phanis says to trust in the Creator and to listen to the sword Truth."

"I thought you were never to get involved?" Even though he was sarcastically repeating her words to her, Dragon did appreciate her help.

"Speaking to a dead man and relaying a message is hardly getting involved." Tilly then flew up and grabbed Dragon by the nose and kissed it gently. "Remember, Dragon, even though you can't see me, I'm still with you, and I believe in you too. This is your moment of truth. You are the king of the dragons." With that, her body began to twinkle and slowly disappear. After Tilly was completely gone, Dragon looked over at Sonya and realized something. Dragon had never introduced Tilly to Sonya, nor had he ever mentioned her before, which was apparent in Sonya's expression. Sonya's face was filled with confusion and a small hint of jealousy. In response, Dragon simply shrugged his shoulders and said he would explain it later. Some things were more important at the moment. Which was one way that Dragon could avoid the conversation altogether.

Dragon and Sonya continued on into Zyrmazonus's domain. However, this time he entered with more confidence, hope, and courage than he had ever known before. There was still a little bit of rubble in the entrance where Sonya made the ceiling fall on Zyrmazonus. Dragon and Sonya made it halfway through the large cavern opening when they heard a dark and threatening laugh. They didn't have to look long or deep into the cavern. Zyrmazonus emerged from the center passageway and stood tall. Even though they could see him, Zyrmazonus enjoyed dwelling in the shadows and didn't bother to come any closer to them.

"Welcome back, dear nephew," Zyrmazonus gloated. "Have you come to beg for forgiveness and join me?"

"No." Dragon did not hesitate to shout back. "We have come to end your reign of evil!"

"End my reign of evil? But I have just begun, nephew, and I have so many plans." Zyrmazonus was in no way threatened by his nephew and his dragon.

Dragon was a little frightened by Zyrmazonus's response, but he had committed himself to this and was unwilling to back down. To combat his steadily growing fear, he dwelt upon the thought that the Creator was with him, and if he was with him, then who could stand against him? "Your plans end with us—either we die today, or you die."

"Dragon, you are beginning to sound like me," Zyrmazonus said with a slight laugh.

"I am nothing like you," Dragon snapped back.

"Then what are you, half-breed?" said Zyrmazonus, becoming a little aggravated at Dragon, thinking he had played enough with this speck.

"I am the king of the dragons, ordained by the Creator, and I condemn you to death for betrayal!"

Zyrmazonus began to laugh as though Dragon's words meant nothing to him. "Death, I am beyond your power. You cannot destroy me. However, if it is death you wish to speak about, I can tell you about your human friend." As Zyrmazonus attempted to taunt Dragon, he leaned closer, revealing his face.

"Lovely features," Dragon taunted back, gesturing to Zyrmazonus's face. Starting at the corner of Zyrmazonus's left eye and heading down to his mouth was a long gash.

"Oh, yes, this," Zyrmazonus responded, pointing to his new wound. "Your friend gave me this as I went to get a good bite on him. Apparently, he was quicker than I thought, getting his sword underneath my scales before I devoured him. You might say that I'm lucky he didn't get my eye; still, it was all worth it. It has been a long time since I have tasted human flesh. He was delicious. Which makes me wonder what my own nephew would taste like."

"It's unfortunate that you will never get the chance." Dragon widened his stance, realizing that something might happen soon. In the silence between words, he could hear his heart beating frantically.

"You sound very overconfident. That will only make you fall faster."

"My grandfather, Larzencarak, believes that I can defeat you," Dragon said firmly.

Zyrmazonus went silent for a moment, contemplating what he had just heard. "Speaking to the dead, are we? You don't have a need to do that since you will be joining them shortly."

"What's the matter, afraid of the truth?" Dragon shouted in a mocking way.

"Truth!" Zyrmazonus barked back. "I will give you some truth, half-breed! Patient I have been for many generations of men! Waiting for my time of vengeance; revenge against the Creator, against man, and even against my own father who banished me! It was I who helped the Deceiver organize his armies, and I who turned many dragons against the Creator! Finally, when the time was right, it was me who took the life of Larzencarak!

After they heard that truth, both Dragon and Sonya barked ferocious roars at Zyrmazonus. To them, the word traitor was a poor description for this animal.

"Yes, Dragon. I took your grandfather's life," Zyrmazonus shouted with a look of glee in his eyes. "It was even my orcs who killed your father! I thought everything would be mine until my little sister got in the way! Unfortunately, I didn't have the heart to harm her myself. So I hired an assassin, and it was his job to bring me the crown! I didn't expect that selfish lowlife to claim it for himself! I assume you took care of him for me, and now you are all that is left! When you are finally dead, everything will be mine, and there is nothing the Creator can do to stop me!"

Dragon stood there for a moment, growling at Zyrmazonus, and then returned to his serious composure. As angry as Dragon was, he surprisingly caught something in Zyrmazonus's words that made him pause for thought. "I see one truth that you have failed to mention," Dragon stated calmly.

"And what exactly is that?" Zyrmazonus growled.

"That you are a coward, and you have no strength at all. You are such a coward that you had to send others to do your bidding for you. You wouldn't even fight your father face-to-face. You had to strike him in the back."

Zyrmazonus became furious at that very comment and lunged at Dragon. As he got within inches of Dragon, the side of his face got hit, knocking him away. Sonya had anticipated what was going to happen and used her tail to strike him. From then on, the inside of the mountain rumbled with a noise that sounded like thunder.

Doing their best to remember what Marahezron had taught them about fighting, Dragon and Sonya stayed one step ahead of Zyrmazonus. As he furiously came after one, the other would come out of nowhere, striking him down and then retreating. They kept enough distance between each other so he couldn't pin both of them. Sonya used her tail and hind legs to constantly whip and kick him. As Dragon would come in fast and hit his jaw and throat, or go for his eyes.

This type of fighting went on for a long period of time, only infuriating Zyrmazonus more. Dragon and Sonya, on the other hand, were beginning to tire themselves, and no matter what they did, Zyrmazonus seemed to remain strong. The tide turned very quickly when Zyrmazonus whipped his tail at Sonya. In an attempt to dodge it, Sonya jumped, only to be kicked by Zyrmazonus's hind leg, sending her soaring out the entrance. Reacting quickly, Zyrmazonus whipped his tail, scraping it against the entrance, and then he sent fire hurling toward the entrance. The force in which he had done this had broken the entrance, making a cave in. With the entire entrance blocked, Zyrmazonus had sealed himself and Dragon in and Sonya out, which was exactly what he wanted to do.

Zyrmazonus, thinking this was his one chance to deal with Dragon, lunged at him. Dragon, however, was a little overwhelmed that Sonya was now trapped outside; therefore, he didn't see Zyrmazonus bearing down on him. At the last moment, Dragon regained his wits and moved quickly to save his life. As his uncle's jaws were inches from him, he rolled to the side and jumped up. Dragon swiftly grabbed Zyrmazonus's side horn that came out from his head and stretched down toward his mouth that passed his scarred eye. With his hands firmly pressed against the horn, Dragon then placed his feet against the side of Zyrmazonus's head. Quickly pushing with all of his strength, Dragon snapped the horn off of his uncle's head, breaking it almost at the base. Zyrmazonus, screaming in agony, retreated, kicking and thrashing, giving Dragon the time he needed to escape. Without losing a single moment, Dragon bolted off down one of the caverns. Though he didn't pay attention to the way Sonya and he escaped before, he did his best to guess which direction he needed to go.

Meanwhile, Sonya could not see through the rubble blocking the entrance, so she had her ear up to it, straining to hear anything. Once she recognized that Dragon was okay and that he had run down one of the passageways, she took flight at once. Sonya moved so quickly that, in some instances, she appeared as if she were running along the side of the mountain. Her object was to reach the hole in the back of the mountain that they had made on their last visit.

Dragon was running through the passageways so fast that on some turns, he almost smacked into the walls, unable to turn fast enough. Even though Dragon did not know where he was going, his directional luck seemed to hold up. With a quick turn around a corner, Dragon was surprised to see what he was looking for. However, his surprise quickly turned to dismay when he realized that his exit strategy had been foiled. Staring at the wall, where there was supposed to be an enormous hole that Sonya had made upon their last visit, was now blocked. Large rocks were piled up, completely blocking his exit. Dragon stood for a moment, leaning against the cavern wall, breathing heavily, and completely confused on what to do next. Then he heard a massive thud against the pile of rocks, which made one of them give way, revealing a small hole. Dragon immediately ran up to it and cried out. "Sonya, is that you?"

"Yes, it's me," Sonya cried back, frantically flapping her wings as she hovered right outside, desperately trying to peer in.

"How does it look from your side?" Dragon quickly asked. "Can you get in?"

"Get in," she snapped. "My plan is to get you out before you are eaten!"

"No," he shouted back. "We cannot leave again! This time we must finish it! I need you in here with me! Can you get in?"

"The hole is well blocked. I can get in, but it will take some time!"

Dragon then turned away, looking back at the tunnel, expecting to see Zyrmazonus at any moment. "I don't have much time," Dragon quietly muttered to himself. At that moment, he got a flashback of what happened the last time he was there in a similar situation. He stepped back from the rock barrier for a moment, trying to think of something. Then, surprisingly and quite suddenly, Dragon heard a faint whisper. At one moment, it seemed as though it came from his side. Then the next, it seemed to be right next to his ear. He slowly looked down and saw something quite bizarre. The knob of Truth's hilt, which was a dragon's head, was moving, and its eyes were glowing red. As Dragon glared down at it, the hilt stared back, which seemed to intensify the whispers. The thing that both confused and captivated Dragon was that Truth was speaking, and he could understand what his sword was saying. As Truth continued to encourage him to fight, Dragon spoke to Sonya. "It looks like I will have to face him alone."

"No!" Sonya shouted. She then began to pull and kick at the rocks as her wings held her aloft. "You can't; he will eat you alive!"

Instantly, Dragon got an idea, and with a smirk on his face, he consulted Truth. "Do you think it will work?" he strangely asked his sword. "I am part dragon. My skin is like a thick hide, so I might survive." After he received a few more short whispers from Truth, Dragon's mind was made up. He began walking back the way he came, looking for Zyrmazonus, as he shouted good-bye to Sonya.

"Dragon, no!" Sonya screamed as she now began to desperately thrash at the barrier, trying to get in.

Despite Sonya's screams, Dragon continued back into the caverns. However, Dragon was a little bit concerned himself, and he was doing his best to keep calm. His breathing grew heavy, and he even bit his lower lip as he thought his plan through over and over.

Dragon eventually reached a large intersection where many tunnels met. He stood there for a moment, listening, wondering where his uncle might be. Before Dragon took a step in any direction, Zyrmazonus appeared right before him. With his hands on either side of his tunnel, Zyrmazonus pulled himself into the large juncture.

Seeing Dragon within seconds of entering, Zyrmazonus bellowed at him. "You whelp, I will kill you for this," he shouted as he pointed to the broken horn on the side of his face. Zyrmazonus then got an evil yet gleeful look on his face. "Ironic. This is exactly how it looked just before your friend died."

Dragon assumed an open stance, but left Truth in its sheath. Taking a deep breath and mustering his courage, Dragon answered, "You want to know how I taste, coward? Come take a bite if you can!" With Dragon's eyes turning dark red, he sprinted toward Zyrmazonus, letting out a furious battle cry. Then, with his hands clenched into fists and his muscles tightened, he leaped high.

Zyrmazonus was not idle. He moved swiftly, opening his mouth as wide as he could. With one fell swoop, Zyrmazonus caught Dragon in his throat and slammed his jaws shut. Standing victoriously, he took a big gulp and then smiled. Zyrmazonus leaned against a nearby wall, very pleased with himself. "Finally," he spoke out loud to himself. "With his death, the throne is all mine." Zyrmazonus then licked his lips and began to chuckle. "I might say, my nephew tastes quite—"

Before Zyrmazonus could finish that sentence, he clutched his chest in pain, as if something had stabbed his heart. He let out an agonizing scream and fell to the ground, dead. The cavern was silent for a few moments, and then suddenly, Zyrmazonus's stomach burst in a diagonal line. Blood and acid came rushing out, covering the ground and sending up a cloud of smoke and steam. After a few more moments, Dragon himself emerged from the stomach of Zyrmazonus. He stood straight and strong, holding Truth in his right hand as it glittered, illuminating everything around him. Parts of Dragon's clothes were burnt away from the fire and acid in Zyrmazonus, yet Kirianadréth's scale that was hanging down at Dragon's chest, was glowing a bright red. Dragon's cuts and scrapes that he had received during this battle were sizzling from the fluid he was covered in. He even began to emit steam as the hot acid began to dry.

"Justice," he muttered, as his eyes returned to their emerald shade.

At that moment, Sonya finally burst through the barrier and into the caverns. Following her nose, she sped through the tunnels in search of Dragon. Needless to say, her surprise was great when she finally found him still standing and Zyrmazonus lying dead. She approached Dragon swiftly, looking him over and carefully making sure he was going to be all right. Sonya then glared at him, only inches from his face. "Don't you ever do anything like that again!" she shouted. Looking at the dead body of Zyrmazonus, she quickly deduced what Dragon's plan was. "I don't care if it worked. Do not make a habit of being eaten! If you do, I will beat the human half out of you!"

Dragon slowly walked over to a part of the cavern where the floor was still dry and then sat down, catching his breath. "Earlier, you said you'd beat the dragon half out of me," he stated. "If you beat the human half out of me, there will be nothing left," he sarcastically remarked.

"Then stop doing foolish things," Sonya replied as she took her fingernail and scratched Dragon's head. She then sat down beside him, and together they contemplated what had happened.

Dragon knew that it was a close battle, and that he might have lost. Suddenly, he had earned a newfound respect for himself and the Creator. He looked down at Truth, which was still in his hand, and marveled at the sword, which, once again, was unscratched and unstained. Dragon then looked at his uncle with odd thoughts. He could hate his uncle; he had every right. Zyrmazonus had killed Dragon's grandfather, father, mother, and closest friend, not to mention a whole lot of innocent people. However, instead of hatred, Dragon felt pity for his uncle. Zyrmazonus was so consumed by anger and hatred that it ruined what his life could have been. Dragon thought back to what Ancient told him—that when you are consumed with hatred for the enemy, you become what you hate. Dragon then turned his thoughts to himself, realizing how easy it would be for him to become like his uncle. His anger toward mankind was blinding him to what he needed to see. Upon that thought, Dragon made a silent oath to himself: that he would die first before he would ever become like Zyrmazonus. If anything, he wanted to be like his mother and his father.

Dragon took a deep breath as he stood up and sheathed his sword. "Come, Sonya, we have a city to save and friends to rescue," he said with a smile on his face. With that, the two of them went back to the opening in the mountain. Dragon climbed upon Sonya's back, and with hopeful hearts, they took to the sky, never to look upon that place ever again.

22

Final Hour

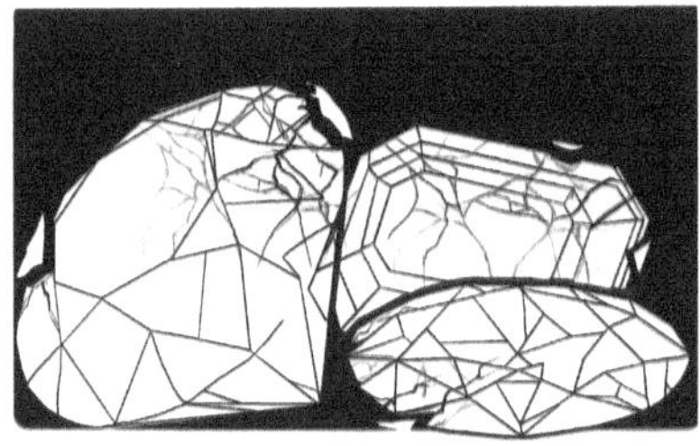

Night was upon Tyrilcrysalith, and it had been more than three days since Dragon and Sonya left to face Zyrmazonus. Tension was high in the city; even Voraha was jumpy on her feet. As for Brenath, he could hardly eat or sleep, for much stirred in his mind. What bothered him the most was that the cloud of dust that was approaching had disappeared. That thought only made him think about the calm before the storm. Brenath knew that whatever was coming wouldn't turn back, so they must be waiting for the perfect time to attack. He didn't know how or when, so he had everyone on high alert. The only thing that gave him peace of mind was that there were no dragons; whatever it was, it couldn't enter the city. Still, he was no fool, and he prepared for anything that he could. Tobin, too, was uneasy and frequently mentioned his concern to his older brother. He felt as if darkness had fallen upon the city, especially since that night the gemmed buildings collected no light, leaving everything dark; therefore, everything was illuminated only by torchlight. That effect alone intensified the fear among the people and soldiers of Tyrilcrysalith and also made it hard for the three captains to keep everyone calm.

Meanwhile, Malic felt the exact same thing as Tobin, except he had a different outcome in mind. To him, it was a message, telling him that now was the time to act. Unfortunately, Malic was locked in his chamber, one of the few rooms in the towers that had a door. The towers of Tyrilcrysalith had doors on only twenty five percent of the rooms; the doors' make varied from gold, silver, and marble. Malic happened to be staring at his silver door and listening to the voices of two guards on the outside. Then, from time to time, he would frantically pace across his room and argue with himself, whether or not he should risk his life so another could gain power. Settling on the fact that he needed to obey his master, he went to his bed and, underneath it, pulled out a cloth that was covering something. Malic carefully uncovered the object, eventually revealing the magic scepter that was given to him by Zyrmazonus. As Malic gripped its handle, the scepter's emerald glowed with a dark aura.

Needing to escape, Malic crept over to the door and held the scepter up. He stood for a moment, wondering how exactly to use the talisman. Did he need to say a word or move it in a certain motion? It didn't occur to Malic when he took it from his master that he didn't know how to use it, once again proving to Malic why he was an apprentice. Fortunately, he needed to say no words. The scepter seemed to draw upon his mental thoughts, and Malic felt its presence in his mind. As its powers emanated, Malic could swear that he saw green mist-like hands come out of the emerald and disappear into the door.

Within seconds, he could hear his door unlock and the guards snoring loudly in the hall. He opened his door slowly and peered out, realizing that his scepter had put the guards to sleep. With that being his chance, he slipped out of his room and bolted down the hall. Unfortunately, he didn't get very far, as he heard voices coming his way. Not having anywhere to duck to, he quickly hid his scepter underneath his cloak, just as three men rounded the corner and spotted him.

"Malic!" Tobin shouted as he was being accompanied by two soldiers. "What are you doing and how did you get out of your room?"

"I am a wizard; no lock or door can keep me," Malic replied smugly. "Besides, I must speak to the queen on grievous news. We are in trouble."

"That we can agree on. However, you are the trouble. You are not going to see the queen. You are to be held in your room till this crisis passes." Tobin then stepped around Malic and headed off to escort him back to his room. The two soldiers accompanying Tobin grabbed Malic by the arms right beneath the shoulders and began to forcefully drag him back to his room.

Seeing no other opportunity to escape, Malic did what needed to be done. Unwrapping the scepter from his cloak, he jabbed the diamond spike into one soldier and struck the other with the emerald. Instantly, the soldiers dropped to the ground, covered in a green substance that burnt their flesh. Before Tobin could do anything, Malic swung the scepter, releasing a bolt of lightning that pierced Tobin's chest as he turned around to face Malic. After Tobin fell dead to the floor, Malic let out a small chuckle. Looking down at the three bodies lying at his feet, he felt empowered by the scepter. In that moment, he felt as though his apprenticeship was over, and his mind filled with dreams of conquest. Then he used the power of the scepter to drag the bodies into a nearby room, so they would not be found anytime soon. Gripping the scepter tightly, Malic once again sped out into the halls, hoping to complete his task.

Carefully and quietly, Malic successfully snuck out of the towers and down to the lower city. He then crept his way into the tunnel and headed toward the gates. Malic could see two guards leaning against the gates and two against their spears, feeling quite safe and secure. Mercilessly, Malic gave them no chance to utter anything at all. He pointed his scepter and, with a wave, let loose arcs of power toward the guards, frying them. With both hands, Malic then gripped the scepter tightly and pointed it at the gates. Like before in his chamber, the scepter released a power to unsecure the gates and then forcefully pull the massive doors to swing open. Once the gates were completely open, Malic quickly turned around and ran off, hoping to reach the towers before anyone noticed what had happened.

Far out into the fields, lying low and quiet, were the orcs of Zyrmazonus. They had crawled as close to the city as they could, bringing only their armor and weapons with them. For hours, the orcs lay still and waited for their entrance into the city. Once they saw that the gates were open, they jumped to their feet and ran, letting out hideous cries of war. Like a herd of animals, they stampeded toward the city entrance.

One of the sentries on a mountainside heard a loud noise and saw movement coming fast from the fields. Without hesitation, he grabbed his horn that was by his side and blew it in desperation. The guards at the top of Tyrilcrysalith heard the horn, and they too were not idle. One man quickly took a deep breath, grabbed the mouthpiece of the city horn, and blew. The overpowering sound of Tyrilcrysalith's horn echoed across the land and alerted everyone to the presence of danger. Brenath, who was in the watchtower right below the horn, peered over the side to see what it was attacking his city. To his eyes, it looked as if the ground itself was flowing into the gates. Quickly, he turned and bolted down the stairs of the tower, letting out a cry of his own and encouraging everyone to defend the city.

The orcs funneled into the gates, running as fast as they could down the tunnel. They looked like rats escaping a sinking ship, running over one another trying to get to the other tunnel opening within the city. A group of soldiers with long spears made a line and blocked the tunnel opening as the orcs came closer. The soldiers knew their death was imminent; still, they stood fast, knowing that their sacrifice would allow innocent people to escape to the shelter of the towers. Some city archers mustered behind the line of spearmen and let fly a volley of arrows down the tunnel. Since the orcs couldn't get out of the way, many fell dead, which slowed their charge. Eventually, when the two factions of orcs and men finally collided with each other, it was like a river running over a small dam. The orcs literally crushed the soldiers. That momentarily created a blockage in the tunnel and slowed almost to a stop the orcs that were filing down the passageway. The archers took the opportunity to make the blockage higher by shooting any orcs that tried to come over the pile of bodies.

Fortunately, the soldiers' sacrifice stopped the advance of the orcs long enough for most of the lower city to evacuate to the upper city and then to the towers. Another thing that helped slow down the advance of the orcs was that this was not an open-field battle. All the orcs had to file through the tunnel in order to reach the city. Not to mention the soldiers that were on the mountain wall catwalks shot a reign of arrows down upon the orcs as they exited the tunnel. Eventually, the archers in front of the tunnel had to flee as the overwhelming numbers of orcs broke through the pile of dead and came in full force.

As people filed in through the tower opening, Brenath reached the bottom of the towers. Joined by Cromwin, Brenath found a soldier at the tower opening who was overseeing the evacuation. "What's our situation?" Brenath shouted over all the noise.

"The city is lost!" the soldier yelled back. "The orcs somehow breached the gates and have made their way into the lower city! Most of the city is evacuated to the towers, but not all are accounted for!"

"There is no time to go look for them. We must save whom we can! From what I've seen, it looks to be more than a hundred thousand against mere hundreds. We do not stand a chance!" Brenath then took a moment to think as quickly as he could of what to do next. "The city has never had to be defended from the inside. This is new ground for all of us! I believe the best line of defense now is the towers themselves! Retreat everyone down to the corridor of written walls. There is only one way down, giving us a better defense! The soldiers must fight the orcs off doorway by doorway till we are pressed to the last entryway! There we shall bravely stand and defend our people to the last possible moment!"

While Brenath was organizing the entryway defenses, he realized that someone was missing. "Where's Tobin?" he asked a nearby soldier.

"We don't know. We haven't seen him," the soldier respectfully replied.

Brenath, now filled with great concern for his brother, turned to Cromwin, his oldest friend, for support. "Things have gone ill, dear friend," Brenath stated, fighting the urge to cry. "I wish Dragon were here. We could sure use his help right now."

***

From high in the sky, something did not seem right, so Sonya landed far out in the fields. Dragon quickly jumped down from her back and glared at the gates of the city. Together, they carefully stared, wondering what was in the way of the tunnel.

"Orcs," Dragon stated. "I see thousands, if not hundreds of thousands, most likely the orcs that belonged to Zyrmazonus, the ones that infested the ring of death. However, this looks like only half of them. The rest must already be in the city."

Sonya quickly got a look of fear on her face. "Oh no, what are we going to do?" she moaned.

"I don't know," Dragon replied, scratching his head as his face was overcome with a look of failure. "Even one as great as you will surely fall to that many orcs. Still, I believe we must fight for the people, fight for our friends, even if it kills us."

"Dragons!" Sonya quickly blurted out. Her face was filled with an odd look as something peculiar came to her mind. "We can use dragons to aid us!"

"What dragons? There are none," Dragon replied, shocked that she would mention such a thing.

"Ganez said that you as king have the power to raise them to aid you when you needed it. I do not think there's any other time more justified than this." Sonya made a serious gesture as she pointed to the ongoing attack on Tyrilcrysalith.

"You are perhaps right. Still, there is a problem with your thinking. First thing is that I don't know where the dragons are. The second thing is that I don't know what call wakes them."

Seeing the sun begin to rise behind them, Sonya looked seriously at Dragon, her heart filled with hope. "Please try, Dragon—at least for our friends."

Dragon took a moment to look at the city of Tyrilcrysalith being attacked and then agreed wholeheartedly with Sonya. "Yes, if the orcs want to fight, then we will give them one! Let us give them a fight so strong that generations from now, orcs will dwell in the shadows, afraid of what lives in the light!" Dragon jumped high, taking into his lungs all the air that he could. When he landed, he landed with such force that the ground underneath his feet cracked and sent out a cloud of dust and debris. Dragon threw his head back and roared so loud that it shook the pebbles on the ground. He held that roar as long as he could, hoping that any dragon would hear him and understand his need. At the same time, his heart and soul cried out to the Creator for help.

When he was done, he took another deep breath and once again stared at the city. Dragon, for a moment, was disappointed, thinking that he and Sonya were still alone in this fight. Suddenly, he heard a strange, yet comforting sound come from behind him. That was a dragon's roar, he thought to himself, turning around quickly. In the distance, looking like a swift-moving cloud along the ground, was a large group of dragons hurrying their way. Dragon could hear their war cries from a far distance, and he did not fear them, for their roars were filled with salutes to the dragon king. With an enormous smile on his face, he leaped onto Sonya's back, and together they flew off for battle, an army of dragons following them.

***

Back within the city, the loyal soldiers of Tyrilcrysalith gave their lives defending the towers. The orcs had finally pressed their way into the main entrance of the towers and then scattered up and down the stairs in all directions. Brenath and Cromwin were doing their best to hold the entryways. They had just lost several positions and were forced to move back when Voraha finally joined their company. In spite of her short height, she was quite helpful in holding back the advancing orcs. With Cromwin and Brenath on either side of her, they stood in a doorway, fending off the orcs while archers shot arrows from behind them. They were just beginning to lose this entryway and retreat to another when a familiar sound filled the towers. A dragon's roar echoed in every corner of the city, making everyone, including orcs, pause for a moment. The company surrounding Voraha all smiled as their hearts were filled with such hope.

"Dragon!" Voraha yelled as she leaped forward and cut an orc in half. "That's my boy. I told you he'd return!" She then began to wildly and viciously swing her ax at the orcs as she taunted them. "Let's see how you like a dragon breathing down your necks, you filthy disgusting vermin!"

Brenath thought that Voraha might have been a little hasty; still, he understood her excitement and enthusiasm. Not wanting to be the one to try to stop her, he too leapt out of the entranceway, fighting furiously, doing everything he could to turn the tide. Of course, one by one, the soldiers, seeing this reckless tactic, joined in willingly.

Dragon, Sonya, and an army of dragons flew directly toward the city. At the last moment, the dragons diverted their path and flew up to enter the city from up above, as Dragon and Sonya maintained a steady course directly to the tunnel. With a deep breath, Sonya let out a burst of fire that consumed the orcs at the mouth of the tunnel. Continuing to breathe a steady stream of fire, she folded her wings straight back as she and Dragon shot into the tunnel like an arrow. The tunnel echoed of screams as Sonya soared through, leaving behind a trail of fire. The moment she hit the other side and came out of the tunnel, she lifted her back and head straight up and unfurled her wings like a sail. She slowed abruptly; still, she had to put her feet forward and stop herself by clutching on to a building. Standing on the rooftop, she roared at the orcs, making them scatter like mice. However, nothing made them scream in terror more than when they saw dragons falling upon them like dark clouds. Sonya could even see dragons coming up out of the water in the bay. Not far from Sonya, she could see a human female clutching her baby as she ran from orcs. The woman was one of the humans who couldn't make it to the towers, so she hid until the orcs found her.

In an attempt to escape, she ran through the streets, only to trip and fall as two orcs rushed upon her. Before the orcs could so much as swing their blades at her, they were crushed under the front feet of a large white dragon. This dragon apparently came up out of the bay, for he was still dripping with water. The white dragon placed his feet carefully on either side of the woman and then bent down low, shielding her and her baby with his body. He then turned his head from side to side and snapped his jaws at any orc that so much as approached them.

Sonya and Dragon continued to sit on the rooftop and watch everything happening around them. The dragons that were called from their slumber thrashed through the city, biting, eating, kicking, and stomping on any orc that moved. All Dragon could do was smile, thinking back to Ancient and Marahezron as they talked about their glory days during the Great War and what it was like. Dragon even let out a small chuckle, watching the magnificence of the dragons in battle. Some orcs continued to bravely fight, while others threw down their weapons and began screaming and running for their lives. It wasn't long before the orcs mimicked the humans and ran for the towers. Just as the humans ran through the tower entrance to escape the orcs, the orcs were now running through the entrance to escape the dragons. Hearing the ruckus at the tower entrance, Dragon motioned for Sonya to hurry to the towers. With one fluid move, she whipped around and leaped in the direction she needed to go. Jumping from rooftop to rooftop, it wasn't long before she landed upon a group of orcs trying to enter the towers. Sonya and Dragon squashed them underfoot, making sure they were dead, and then they entered the towers.

Making their way through the main entrance, while orcs scattered in all directions, Dragon leapt down from Sonya's back and drew his sword. Immediately hearing familiar voices and lots of fighting, they both darted off to the right in search of living beings other than orcs. They burst through one opening to see three familiar faces courageously holding back a battalion of orcs. Instantly, Sonya threw her body at the orcs and crushed them as she rolled over them. Any orcs that she missed were quickly dealt with by Dragon. Once the room was empty of trouble, they greeted their friends.

Voraha gave Dragon a sharp jab in his arm, showing her appreciation of him. "I'm glad to see you still alive, lad," she remarked.

Dragon smiled, overjoyed to see them, as he rubbed his arm, where it had been recently hit. "I'm glad to see you as well, all of you," Dragon replied. After he took a moment to look them over, reassuring himself that they were okay, he thought of two more. "Where is Yolana and Crysaia?"

"I don't know," Brenath replied earnestly. "While we were making the towers safe, Crysaia and her four guards were supposed to make it down to the written walls chamber. From what some of my soldiers told me, she never made it down, and neither did Yolana."

Dragon's face quickly filled with deep concern. "Then we must go look for them."

"If anything, they might be held up in the throne room," Brenath responded, still a little short of breath from fighting. "Unfortunately, the towers are now filled with orcs everywhere. If they are held up there, they won't last long."

Without saying another word, Dragon quickly turned and took off back through the towers. Sonya was right behind him the entire way, while the others trailed farther behind. Moving swiftly around corners and upstairs, Dragon was filled with anger, longing for this fight to be over and for his friends to be safe. Dragon was moving so fast that when he reached a spiral of stairs filled with orcs, he didn't slow down. He jumped up from the stairs and kicked against the wall, throwing himself over the orcs. In midair, he turned over and lopped all the orcs' heads off with Truth. Dragon then kicked against the opposite wall, sending himself farther up the stairs, where he landed on his feet. Without missing a step, he continued up the stairs as fast as he could. As Dragon continued up the towers, he terrified the orcs with every motion that he made. In some instances, he went around corners so fast that he landed against the walls on all fours and ran across them like a spider before he touched back down to the ground.

When Dragon reached the throne room, he went flying in through the entrance, with the dais to his right. He landed and skidded on all fours with Truth still in his hands, the sword scratching the diamond floor as he went. Right when he stopped, he quickly had to roll to avoid a bolt of energy shot at him. Dragon quickly jumped up, surveying the room. To his dismay, he saw Malic and several orcs controlling the throne room. Malic was standing off a bit with a strange magic rod in his hand, as the orcs held several guards, Yolana, and Crysaia, with swords and knives at their throats.

Before Dragon could do anything, Malic waved the rod at him, sending a green ball of lightning at him. Reacting like he did against the witch, Dragon swung Truth, knocking the ball of lightning away, discharging it against the wall. Malic then sent off a straight bolt of lightning, this time streaming from his magic scepter. In order to evade it, Dragon leapt out of the way and ducked behind one of the pillars in the throne room. The stream of sparking energy went right out the entrance and down the stairs, passing only inches from Sonya's head. Seeing that made her lean against the wall and stay where she was, still and listening. As for Dragon, he had his back up against the pillar, and Truth held tightly against him.

"Give it up, Malic!" Dragon yelled, trying to strike a conversation in order to give him some time to think. "Your army of orcs has been defeated by my dragons, and I have already killed your master!" Taking a short pause, he peered around the pillar, trying to figure out how many people he had to deal with all at once.

Malic then began to laugh loudly as he waved his scepter, sending small sparks of energy in different directions, showing off his power. "Fool, I have already deduced that you killed my master by your very return! However, I will not surrender to you. I have in my hands more power than my master ever had, and I will not give it up so willingly! Besides, you are a mere half-breed. What can you do against me!"

Waving his scepter in a circular motion, Malic formed another ball of lightning. With a quick flick of his scepter, it shot toward the pillar. Surprisingly, it didn't hit the pillar; it rounded the column and aimed for Dragon's head. Dragon quickly ducked and rolled straight out of the way as the orb of energy struck the pillar right where his head was a moment before. Standing swiftly, Dragon turned and faced the pillar, wondering what he would do about Malic on the other side.

"I thank you for killing my master for me," Malic said as he began to wave his scepter again. "Now this city and all its glory belongs to me, as well as Crysaia, who will be my new consort." Malic then began forming another energy ball, this time making grander gestures with his arms, trying to form a greater orb than last time.

As Dragon stood back from the pillar, he began to see a green-colored energy form on the other side. He started to breathe heavily, thinking that this time he might not survive. Then quietly, almost unheard, Truth whispered to him. Listening quickly, Dragon understood what his sword was trying to say, and he agreed with it, giving his sword a slight nod of his head. With one hand, Dragon lifted Truth over his head, and with a strong swing of his arm, he hurled his sword at the diamond pillar. Once Truth left Dragon's hand, it reacted, bending, and reforming itself. The white-dragon hilt took its guarding wings and folded them back over its head. Within a single motion, Truth became like a smooth and seamless spear. When it hit the diamond column, it melted the diamond away, like it was passing through water.

When Malic was done forming an enormous sphere of green energy, he brought it above his head, preparing to release it upon Dragon. The moment his arms were stretched high above his head, he felt something sharp pierce into his chest. With a gasp of air and the look of pain on his face, he let his arms drop, making the energy above his head dissipate. Malic then looked down to see a sword thrust into his chest. His eyes widened with the thought of his imminent defeat. Staring at the hilt of the sword, he saw white wings folded back into a guard and a dragon head hiss at him. Before Malic's eyes closed for the last time, he peered at the hole through the diamond pillar and saw Dragon's face. Malic's body fell back with a thud, adding fear to the orcs standing nearby.

With a smirk on his face, Dragon walked out from behind the column and toward Malic to retrieve Truth. At the same time, Sonya, Brenath, Voraha, and Cromwin came into the throne room to lend a hand. That, unfortunately, made the orcs holding the weapons on the captives' throats more nervous.

"Don't move." One of the orcs hissed, clinching his sword tighter.

Dragon stopped instantly right at Malic's body, yet he had not retrieved Truth. "Let the captives go. It is all over," Dragon sharply replied. He then firmly reached down and pulled his sword out of Malic, at the same time glaring at the orcs.

The orc holding his sword to Crysaia's throat gestured to Malic's dead body. "Why let them go? We are dead anyway. We might as well take them with us!"

Dragon took a step toward the orcs, only to be stopped by Brenath's cry. "Don't! There's no way to kill the orcs without harming the others!"

Dragon then looked down at Truth, hoping his sword would speak to him again. Needless to say, it didn't, and Truth's silence disheartened Dragon. He could not throw it at the orc like he did Malic because it wouldn't go through a pillar; it would go through Crysaia instead. However, in the silence of his own mind, another voice appeared in remembrance—the voice of Ancient, telling him about the sword. As Dragon remembered what he could of his old mentor's words, a plan formulated in his mind. Suddenly he threw Truth straight up in the air and yelled, "Judge!"

Suddenly, Truth stopped in midair, hovering high in the room. Everyone, including the orcs, stood in awe, just staring at it. The dragon hilt melted away, revealing the original two-winged human forms of the hilt. The sword began to emit a high-pitched ring that echoed in the room. It then began to shine with a brilliance that permeated the room. The blade was so bright that everyone, including Dragon, had to look away. The brilliance continued to grow until it became an overpowering heat.

"It destroys evil," Dragon shouted to everyone as he drew back from the sword. "Take all the evil and hateful things out of your heart and mind!"

Truth did not stop. The sword continued to let out what looked to be a fire made of light. Within moments, it melted away the orcs' swords and knives, as well as their flesh. As the orcs fell back, shrieking in pain, everyone else was left alone, even their clothes. Every-one was concentrating hard on filling their thoughts and feelings with pleasant things, all except Dragon. He stumbled back, gritting his teeth in pain as his clothes burned off him. He stood as firm as he could, flexing every muscle in his body, resisting the consuming fire. When he asked the sword to judge, he did not think at the time that it would judge him.

Crysaia, now free from the orc that held her, heard Dragon's cries. Sheltering her eyes from the light as best as she could, Crysaia looked over at Dragon and slowly made her way to him. The force of the con-suming fire was like a heavy wind, making it hard for her to move. When she finally reached him, she grabbed his shoulders, and they both collapsed to their knees. Barely able to hear anything, she placed her forehead against his and yelled, "Let go of the hatred!"

"I can't!" Dragon yelled back, his body beginning to convulse in pain. "I don't know how!" Days earlier, he had heard the wise words of his friend Phanis and his grandfather Larzencarak, and agreed to go face his uncle. Still, for some reason, Dragon blamed the Creator for taking away his mother and his father, and everyone that he loved. He even longed to see Marahezron once again. Dragon felt that if he had let it go, everything would have been done for nothing.

"Forgive. Forgive everyone and everything that has happened to you in your life!" Crysaia shouted, trying to get Dragon to come to a place of reconciliation.

Even though Dragon heard her, the pain was so overwhelming that he couldn't concentrate. Crysaia continued to hold Dragon, unwilling to let go even when his dragon flesh began to give way. She was un-willing to let him die this way; she was unwilling to lose him. Pulling Dragon close to her body, Crysaia wrapped her arms around him and kissed him. As the fire continued to pulse around them, her lips pressed tightly against his. Just when she thought it was too late, she felt his lips press back and his body relax. The light of the consuming fire rushed around them for what seemed to be ages; still, their lips and their bodies never separated.

Eventually, the noise and the light subsided back into Truth. The hilt of the sword turned back to its white dragon form as it slowly lowered and laid itself on the ground. After a quiet moment, everyone uncovered their faces and looked around. Though the room was untouched, the orcs had been burned to ash. To everyone's shock, especially Sonya, Dragon himself was badly scarred and burnt. He was still like a corpse lying in the arms of Crysaia as she cried over him. Everyone in the room was devastated at the mere look of Dragon; however, he was still alive. As his chest slowly rose and fell with each shallow breath, it made every individual person cling to that one thread of hope—that Dragon would survive.

23

The Quest Continues

Dragon opened his eyes and stirred. His whole body was aching. Once again, he could see that he was lying in a bed in Tyril-crysalith; however, this room did not look familiar. The room and the bed, as well as everything else, were extremely elaborate and beautiful. Dragon carefully tried to scoot himself to the side of the bed when he realized that it was a lot larger and more comfortable than he had anticipated. So he merely lay there, breathing deeply and contemplating much.

"There you are," Yolana softly said as she rounded the bed to his side. "I'm glad to see that you came back to us. We were beginning to worry that you would never wake up."

Dragon took a deep breath, opened his mouth, and with a raspy and shallow voice, he replied, "What happened?"

"You almost died," she responded openly. "Your stubbornness was almost the death of you, you could say." Yolana wasn't trying to be rude or mean even though it came out that way. Nevertheless, Dragon knew from the smile on her face that her concern was sincere.

Dragon's eyes moved rapidly as he tried to retrace thoughts in his mind. Though his memory was a little sketchy, some things did come back quickly. "Crysaia, is she all right?" Dragon quickly asked, stressing himself just a bit.

Yolana gently grabbed his hand and stroked it, calming him down. "She's all right, as well as the rest of us. Believe it or not, we were more concerned about you."

"Why is that? I seem fine." Though Dragon's voice was bold and filled with confidence, he could not hide the wheezing in his voice. Showing that even though he might seem fine, he still had a little bit of healing to go.

"Now you do, silly, but earlier is a different matter. As badly as your body was scorched, we almost took you for a corpse. Your dragon blood has healed you quickly. There is barely a mark left of your ordeal. Thanks to the Creator for giving you stronger skin, which lasts longer than your stubbornness. There, for a while, we weren't sure if you were ever going to wake up. As a matter of fact, Sonya, Voraha, Brenath, Crysaia, and I split up the watch over you. One of us watches you during the day, and then one of us watches you during the night."

"Day and night, huh? How long have I been asleep?" Dragon asked, wanting to close his eyes right then and there and return to his slumber.

"You have been asleep for nine days. It is the morning of the tenth day," Yolana replied earnestly. "You have been sleeping in the queen's chamber, with constant vigilance over you. If you ask me, I think we spoil you too much." Even as she said that sarcastic remark, she didn't believe it, and she knew no one else would either. From beginning to end of the whole situation, Dragon had well earned the right to be pampered, just a bit.

Dragon reached over with his other hand and held her hand within his two. "Perhaps you do spoil me too much, but I'm grateful for it, and I thank all of you for being here for me."

Both of them sat there quietly for a long moment, simply smiling and staring at each other. Then eventually, Dragon asked for her help, and in the next couple of hours, she did just that. Yolana carefully pulled Dragon to the edge of the bed and helped dress him. As she dressed him, Dragon realized that these clothes were not his own, though they fit him very well. The clothes were quite stiff and probably new, he thought. Then Yolana painstakingly lifted him to his feet and walked him about, trying to get him used to his feet again. After a long time, they returned to the bed exhausted. Still, Dragon had begun to get better use out of his limbs.

Round about that time, Brenath entered the room with a plate of food and a goblet of water for Yolana. His eyes widened in surprise and delight to see Dragon up and around. "Well, friend, you are alive," he said excitedly. "I was just bringing Yolana some nourishment during her watch. Perhaps I should go and get more."

"No, it's all right," Yolana respectfully interrupted. "I'm fine. Give it to Dragon. He needs it more than I."

"Very well," Brenath replied as he walked up and set it on the bed next to Dragon. As Dragon began to eat the food hurriedly and hungrily, Brenath could not help but stare at him. "Well, it appears that you are healing quite wonderfully," he stated. "There are only a few scratches and scrapes left from your huge ordeal. Even your hair has grown back, as short as it is. Believe it or not, it is pleasing to see you up and around again."

"Thank you. It is good to see you too," Dragon replied with a mouthful of food.

Brenath placed a hand on Yolana's back, needing a moment with Dragon. "I know it is your watch, but may I have time with him?"

"Sure," Yolana replied, thinking of what to do next. "I will go and find Sonya. She will be thrilled to know that he's awake." With that, she quickly yet gracefully left the room.

Brenath sat down beside Dragon with an earnest face. Realizing that this was a serious moment with possible bad news, Dragon finished what he was eating and pushed the plate of food off to the side. "How goes the city?" Dragon asked respectfully.

"As well as it can be, considering what we went through," Brenath replied. "The entire city owes you their lives and thanks, especially for the dragons."

"The dragons, are they still here?" Dragon excitedly inquired. He didn't want to admit that he had completely forgotten about them, but now that he remembered, he was eager to see them.

"I'm afraid not. The queen and Sonya thanked them immensely. Still, a day after you woke them, they returned to stone. However, I will say they were quite thorough. Not a single orc survived."

"The dragons didn't harm any humans, did they?" Dragon asked, concerned.

"No, Dragon. They were very protective over the humans," Brenath reassured him. "We lost several good soldiers to Malic. Seventy-five percent of the guards were lost to the orcs." Brenath took a moment before he phrased his next comment. "The last eleven to die were by you."

Dragon's jaw dropped as he took a deep breath, unable to utter any words. Seeing Dragon's reaction, especially the look in his eyes, Brenath realized he needed to explain himself, as well as ask a few questions.

"Dragon, everyone here thanks you for saving the city and their queen. Only a few people know the truth." Brenath then put his hand on Dragon's back, urging him to speak openly. "You didn't know what your sword was going to do? Also, you do not know how powerful your sword is, do you?"

Dragon shook his head in response, completely dismayed by the entire situation. He then remembered back to when Truth had killed the orcs and then tried to kill him. "What happened?" he asked, still having trouble breathing.

"When you asked your sword to judge, it sent its consuming brilliance halfway down the towers, killing any orcs as well as the ten guards that were there."

"What about the eleventh? You said there were eleven?" Dragon asked Brenath, hoping that he had made a mistake in his count as if that made a difference.

"The eleventh soldier to die was hours later. After you were brought to the queen's chamber, one of the soldiers bent down to retrieve your sword and bring it to you. The moment his hand touched the sword, its hilt arced with lightning and fire, consuming him." Brenath had trouble relating the incident to Dragon since he had known the man very well. He did not blame Dragon at all in any way, but he did want answers, or at least hoped for some.

Dragon lowered his head, unwilling to look at Brenath, feeling responsible for the whole thing. "I never have, and I believe that I never will understand the full power of Truth. I know when I first grabbed it, it struck out at me, and I never thought it would do the same to anyone else. My mentor Ancient once told me that Truth was forged the day that mankind betrayed the Creator. It was used to drive mankind out of the gardens."

"That's why it did that. Your sword was made to be against mankind," Brenath proposed his theory.

"No," Dragon softly replied, with his head still held low. "I believe it was made to guide mankind, to peel back the words of the Deceiver. No human can touch it as long as darkness lives in mankind. On the other hand, what does it matter what I believe? I have caused needless deaths. You probably hate me for it."

"I can't hate you for it, Dragon. Neither can I blame you for it," he sharply remarked, yet in a caring tone. Dragon then looked up at Brenath, very interested in his words. "You tried to save innocent lives. You didn't know what Truth was going to do. You also didn't know what the hearts of those men were like. I cannot hold you accountable for their thoughts." Brenath then brought his hand up from Dragon's back and patted his shoulder several times, encouraging him. "Not to mention the most important thing of all is that Truth almost killed you as well. You put yourself in a dangerous position in order to protect others. At least we know that Truth judges fairly—dragons, humans, and orcs alike; there is no prejudice in Truth. One of the only good things I saw was that it destroyed Malic's scepter, taking its dark magic from this world." Brenath then stood and took a more serious tone as he looked down at Dragon. "However, promise me this—that you will never ask Truth to judge ever again, unless everyone else is gone and it is your last dying breath."

Dragon nodded in agreement and then grasped Brenath's forearm and shook firmly in pledge to his word. Brenath pulled Dragon up to his feet and gave him a strong pat on the back.

"Come, Dragon, we still have much to talk about, and you need to get used to your dwarfish clothes. The walk will do you good."

"Dwarfish clothes—how did I come by them?" inquired Dragon.

Before Brenath could answer, he let out a quick chuckle at Dragon's astonished look. "Let me give you a brief understanding of what has transpired. Since most of our guards had been destroyed by the orcs and the dragons were going to return to stone, we needed some help. Sonya enlisted one of the dragons to help, and he carried a message for us. He was heading in the mountain direction anyway, so he made a brief stop at Shieldholt and delivered a message to King Ronnar. Even though the message mostly spoke of needing assistance, it did mention that you were gravely wounded and that your clothes were lost. Why that was in the message, I do not know. You'll have to ask Voraha, since it was she who wrote it. Nevertheless, before they sent any assistance, they fashioned you some of the best clothes they could ever make. I am told every bit of clothing you have, including your shoes, will last a hundred years."

"That's absurd," Dragon responded with skepticism.

"Perhaps," Brenath continued, "you will have to see as time moves on, as for now, they are stiff just like your body. So, you must move in them and get used to them. Good news, is you have a total of three sets of brand-new clothes. Yolana took the liberty of putting the other two sets into your magical traveling bag. I didn't know you had that; you will have to tell me about that sometime." Brenath then grabbed Dragon's hand, opened it, and slapped something into it. "By the way, this is a gift from Ronnar himself, with the blessings of all who dwell in Shieldholt."

Dragon looked down into his hand, only to see his mother's scale that he wore around his neck. Even though it glittered in its ruby brilliance, something else glittered beside it. It was a chain of a strange metal that he had never seen before. Dragon looked to Brenath for answers, more confused than he was with the clothes.

"That oddly enough, was another thing mentioned in the message to Ronnar," Brenath explained, seeing the look on Dragon's face. "When Truth burnt your clothes away, it also burnt the rope that was fashioned around your mother's scale. I'm happy to say that it didn't burn your mother's scale away. Unfortunately, you needed something else to carry it with. So, your scale went with the dragon and the message to Shieldholt, since we here are not exactly craftsmen, and we didn't want to fashion another rope for it. Believe it or not, in Shieldholt, Ronnar bestowed the greatest gift upon you that he ever could. Deep within Shieldholt's mines, they uncovered a new metal unknown to the world. For the last twenty years, they have been learning its secrets, as well as keeping it a secret. Recently, they have finally mastered its abilities, and they have been pondering what to make first out of this metal. All the dwarves believe that you deserve to have the first thing made of this precious ore. So, they fashioned you this chain to wear your mother's scale around your neck, in remembrance of her and in remembrance of Shieldholt."

Dragon took a moment to unfold the chain and take a good look at it. He marveled at the craftsmanship of the dwarves. Even with normal metals, this chain would be hard to make. It was made thin, and its links were small, almost seamless, yet Dragon could tell it was firm and strong. The metal looked to be a cross between gold and silver mixed, an almost whitish yet glittering look. The chain came down and hooked to a clamp that was fastened to the top of the scale and then went behind it to fasten to the bottom. Dragon carefully opened the chain up and placed it over his head. Once draped around his neck, his mother's scale, hung perfectly in the middle of his chest. He took a moment to look at its brilliance, remembering his mother, and then he placed it underneath his shirt.

"I am told that the metal is as strong as diamonds," Brenath commented, seeing Dragon's satisfaction in it. "Hopefully, if you're ever foolish enough to ask Truth to judge again, this chain might hold up against its power. The dwarves haven't completely figured out what to name this precious metal, but whatever they name it, you have the first thing ever made from it. At least that is what Drognen Hammerstriker told me when he returned it."

"Drognen, is he here?" Dragon asked excitedly, eager to see the stout dwarf.

"Yes, he is still here. Him and four hundred dwarves," Brenath replied as he waved his arms in an exaggerated motion. "Ronnar sent them to help guarantee our safety, and to help us rebuild the lower city. Most of the upper city has already healed itself. Here, come with me and stretch your legs."

Dragon nodded in agreement and had started to walk toward the door with Brenath when something came to his mind. Thinking back to their earlier conversation about Truth, Dragon remembered his sword. "Where is Truth?" he said, looking around.

Brenath grabbed his shoulder and steadied him a bit as he pointed to the door. "Your sword is still in the throne room, guarded by four men, so no one may touch it."

"Brenath, I believe I must go retrieve it," Dragon responded with a serious look on his face.

"I agree with you wholeheartedly. Let's go and retrieve it. I can use those men somewhere else. There is much to do in this city." With that, Dragon leaned on Brenath for some support as they walked out of the room.

***

With Brenath's help, Dragon painstakingly made his way up to the throne room. Once at the entrance, Dragon left Brenath and made his way in by himself. It didn't take him long to spot his sword. There in the throne room, Truth lay upon the floor, right where Dragon had asked it to judge. Surrounding Truth were four guards standing with their backs to one another. They stood several feet away from the sword, not sure what it could do. The guards were standing firm, willing to protect the sword with their lives. On the other hand, when they saw Dragon approach, they all stepped aside, faced him, and stood at attention, showing great respect. Dragon nodded in response as he walked by them to pick up his sword. Slowly, reaching down, he grabbed the hilt and lifted it up. As he did, it made a slight hum as though it were happy to see him. Dragon smiled intently, looking at the beautiful and untarnished blade, and then he sheathed it to keep others safe. He quickly turned and attempted to walk back to Brenath, not willing to stay longer than he had to. Nevertheless, one of the guards caught him with some words, which made Dragon turn around.

"Thank you for saving our city," one guard said. "You are indeed a powerful dragon."

"Don't forget, I'm also half human," Dragon replied, surprised that he said such a thing, considering his previous hatred toward mankind. All he could do was smile, thinking that he had learned much recently that had changed his outlook on everything.

Brenath waved his hand from the entrance, motioning to the guards to leave the room and attend to other things. Once the guards had left, Dragon attempted to continue to reach Brenath, only to be stopped by something else. He looked over at one of the diamond pillars surrounding the throne's dais, only to see a hole burnt through one of them. Dragon slowly walked over to it and placed his hand on the hole, feeling deeply troubled. He carefully studied it, amazed at the power of his sword. Truth had burnt a hole right through the diamond, making what it left behind look like melted wax. The only thing that confused Dragon was why it had not healed yet.

"You have scarred our city, Dragon," a soft voice spoke behind Dragon.

Dragon turned to see Crysaia, standing only a few feet from him; her face filled with joy upon seeing him, and so did his upon seeing her. "Queen Crysaia, it's good to see you," he respectfully said.

"And it is good to see you as well," Crysaia responded as she walked closer and placed her hand upon the burnt hole in the diamond pillar. "All the buildings in the upper city are almost fully healed—all except this pillar. This hole has yet to show any signs of healing, and I doubt it ever will."

"Forgive me, Queen. I did not mean to do any damage to your beautiful city," Dragon said in his defense. He took a step back, gauging her facial expression to find out where this conversation was going.

"No, Dragon," Crysaia quickly replied. "I do not mean that as a bad thing. You have touched the city and the people within it, not to mention you have saved our lives. Forever you will be in our memories, and whenever we begin to forget, this will remind us," Crysaia stated as she pointed at the hole. "Even if you leave us, you will always be with us. Which reminds me, what are your plans?"

Dragon paused for a moment, realizing that there was longing in that question. From the look in her eyes, he knew that his answer was important to her. "I'm not sure, but for now, Brenath thinks I need to walk around a bit. So he's taking me through the city to show me the works of the dwarves while we talk."

"That is very kind of Brenath, especially since he recently lost Tobin."

"Tobin!" Dragon gasped as his knees became weak. "Brenath said nothing to me about Tobin! Did I cause his death?"

"Of course not. Malic was the cause of his death," Crysaia replied swiftly, easing Dragon's nerves. "If anyone is to blame, it should be me, for not seeing what everyone else was saying about Malic. If I had sent him away earlier, none of this would have happened."

"Crysaia, you cannot blame yourself for not wanting to judge someone," responded Dragon, trying to encourage her in return. He realized from the look on her face that she needed encouragement as much as he did. "No one could tell what he was up to, as well as how much power he contained."

"Perhaps you're right. It is just so hard to be responsible for so much." Crysaia's face was filled with much trouble, yet she tried her best to keep her poise. She then glanced at Brenath, standing at the entrance, curious of their conversation. "I'm sorry that I've kept you. Go have your walk with Brenath. I hope to speak to you later."

"You will," Dragon simply answered as he turned from her and made his way finally back to Brenath at the entrance. Though they said nothing to one another, they made their way together through the towers.

*****

Coming out of a high-side exit from the towers and looking out toward the ocean, Brenath and Dragon walked on the right side of the mountain. They rounded the inside of the mountain on a high parapet overlooking the city. They stopped when they reached closer to the bay and leaned on the wall, looking over to see all the commotion. Both stared down at hundreds of dwarves scurrying about the lower city. Still, no words were spoken between the two.

After a long moment of pointing and laughing at all the dwarves scuttling about as they were fixing the lower city, Dragon needed to say something. "Brenath, why didn't you tell me about Tobin?" Even though it wasn't the perfect conversation starter, Dragon needed to know.

Brenath took a short moment before he responded, collecting his thoughts on the matter. "To me, the pain is still too fresh," he replied with a solemn voice. "Some part of me feels responsible. I made him become a warrior so that I could keep an eye on him. Little good that did him. If it wasn't for me, he might have had a family. However, he did love this city, and he always wanted to protect it with his life. I must say he died honorably, and no one can speak poorly of him."

Dragon had to admit to himself that he didn't know what to say; he knew how much death could hurt someone. Still, he longed to support Brenath and give him whatever strength he could. "Is there a tomb of Tobin so that I might go and pay my respects?"

"No, not here, Dragon," Brenath replied, still willing to talk on the subject, though Dragon could tell by the sound of his voice that it was a painful topic. "The people of Tyrilcrysalith do not fancy tombs, and the gem buildings do not fancy them as well. All those that died were laid in boats and sailed into the ocean. As they pass by the watchtowers on either side of the bay, blazing arrows of fire would join the boats. We believe it is an honorable way to be laid to rest. We even gave honor to Phanis. Yolana laid what remaining things she had of his in a boat, and we sent it with the others, for he sacrificed himself as well for you and this city." Brenath paused for a moment, taking a deep breath, and then looked up at Dragon. "I cannot tell you how much I appreciated Sonya the day we sent Tobin's body out to sea. Tobin was fond of Sonya, and she was fond of him. There were no arrows that met his boat, but from her mouth was sent a fiery kiss of farewell. I do not think that there is any greater honor that could be bestowed upon him." Even though with those words he wanted to cry, Brenath held his composure well.

"I'm sorry, Brenath; I wish there was something I could do," Dragon said earnestly.

"There is Dragon," Brenath quickly replied, grabbing Dragon by the shoulders. "Take me with you."

"What?" Dragon snapped in utter shock.

"Take me with you on your journey, your quest, or whatever it is. There is nothing for me here. At least with you, I know there will be great adventure till the end."

"No," Dragon replied strongly. "There is still much for you to do here, and you are much needed here. Not to mention, I need you to stay here and look after the queen."

Brenath quickly threw his arms down and went back to looking over the wall, very agitated. "That's exactly what your father said," Brenath complained.

"What? You knew my father? When were you going to tell me this?" Dragon snapped, becoming agitated himself. At that moment, Dragon began to question his trust in Brenath, thinking he had been lied to. Still, he did his best to stay calm, thinking that Brenath had his reasons.

"Probably never since it was something personal to me," Brenath snapped back. "Besides, it was a long time ago when I was much younger. I followed my father into the guard. At a young age, I became the third captain of Tyrilcrysalith. At that time, the war was still raging between the Army of Light and the Dark Army. Tyrilcrysalith became a staging point for gathering armies and storing supplies. Jorn, your father, needed this location as they pressed their advance southward. Crysaia's mother and father were willing to help Jorn in any way they could. They would have followed him if he asked." Brenath paused briefly as his mind drifted off in memories, thinking about his youth in Tyrilcrysalith. "However, since he never asked anyone to follow him, I asked him, hoping he would say yes and then I'd have grand adventures. Instead, all I got was an order to stay here and protect the king and queen. As the years passed on, I couldn't even do that. Still, I thought it was my duty to your father to protect Crysaia. I don't think I was ever more devastated than the day that the news reached Tyrilcrysalith about the death of Jorn. Not only did I feel as if I was a failure, but I constantly wondered what my life might have been."

Dragon leaned against the wall as well, wondering what to say next. Although he did understand Brenath's feelings about wondering what his life might have been. "I don't know what your life might have been, but I know what your life is today. You are a goodhearted man, and I believe my father would be proud of you."

"I hope so," Brenath replied as he lowered his head, almost ashamed of himself. Then he quickly raised his head again as he thought of something joyous. "I will say my youth was not all bad. I did get to meet your grandfather."

"Larzencarak," Dragon said curiously. He became more astonished by Brenath's revelations. Dragon had to admit that lately, he had been receiving plenty of strange surprises.

"Yes, your grandfather. He was here in the city for several days and nights. In spite of his rough exterior, he was quite a gentle dragon. I found myself fortunate enough to be on guard one night, at the same time that your grandfather was awake. I sat beside him down at the piers, and we discussed many things. That was the night I first learned that there was such a thing as a Creator. Your grandfather told me that no matter what we do, in the end, everything is done to the Creator's design. I've held that very close to my heart for many years and believed in it. I had hoped that the Creator put me here for a specific reason and that one day I would learn why, and it would be spectacular.

However, as the years passed, I slowly began to lose faith in it—until the day you saved my life. There, for a moment, I almost believed that Jorn and Kirianadréth had come back for me. Instead, the Creator had something better in mind. He put me in the company of Dragon and Sonya. In their company, I had a great adventure that I never could have dreamed of."

"That is a wonderful story, Brenath," Dragon said, almost sarcastically. "However, I do not believe I can share in your optimism about the Creator's design. I still do not see why he would design someone like me, and for what purpose?"

Brenath shook his head at Dragon's words. "You are exactly what you were supposed to be."

"So everyone keeps telling me," Dragon began to complain. "But I do not see it. I have no place in the dragon world, and I can barely survive in the human world. It is impossible for me to find my place in this world."

"Dragon, who you are is not a curse. You have to understand that. Even I can see your blessings," Brenath said, getting excited at the mere thought. "In your hands, you are empty, but in the Creator's hands, your life is fulfilled. Stop focusing on the things that you see and focus on the things that you do not see."

"I don't understand," Dragon stated, getting frustrated. His aggravation on the conversation made him jittery a bit, so he shifted about while he stood next to Brenath.

"Sonya tells me that because of your particular mix of blood, you have an immortality that no one else has on this earth."

"Ancient told her too many stories," Dragon sarcastically stated.

Brenath continued, ignoring Dragon's dismissal of the topic: "Even though elves and dragons look immortal, eventually, they die of old age. Men never know it because we die before they do, and because they outlive us, it gives them the illusion of immortality. Still, things fall, and no one but the Creator knows what comes after, until now. The Creator has given you gifts that I do not believe you fully understand. First of all, the knowledge itself and the time to learn it. Old and great elves could tell you that after thousands of years, they still haven't learned everything. You have time to learn everything under the sun as for the heavens that belongs to the Creator."

Brenath gave Dragon a reassuring pat on the back with that comment. "Second thing you were granted is the beauty of life and watching things grow and change. You will see a dwarven city start as a crack in the mountainside and live long enough to see it envelope the entire mountain. You will see empires rise and fall, giving birth to new ones. You will watch the mountains become seas and the seas become mountains. You will see sunrises and sunsets in cities that people will no longer see, let alone know of its existence. You will remember people and the lives that they lived when no one else will."

Dragon looked at Brenath, almost depressed at the thought. "I heard some people say that immortality is a curse because of all those things, they make you feel alone."

At that comment, Brenath simply shook his head and huffed. "Those things only make you feel that way if you're selfish. If you're selfless, and you give yourself to others and to things around you, it will open your eyes, and you will see things differently."

"Still feels like time is an enemy; sooner or later it will catch you and devour you, if not physically, it will emotionally, and spiritually."

"You're still looking at it all wrong; time is your friend and companion. It will teach you to cherish every moment on your journey because they will never come again. With the right heart, you will watch and help mankind thrive into something great."

With that, Dragon stopped listening and draped himself over the wall, suddenly feeling depressed. Twisting his head and shooting a glance at Brenath, he said quietly, "That is what I'm afraid of."

Brenath gently put a hand on Dragon's back, encouraging him to speak his mind. "What frightens you, really?"

"I fear that mankind will fail again," Dragon replied as he stood straight up and looked Brenath in the eyes. "There's too much evil in this world, and mankind thrives on it. Even after the Creator gives them a chance for redemption, I still believe they will fail. Everything that we have done will be in vain, and the dragons and the magical world would have disappeared for nothing!"

"I believe you're right. Mankind will fail again and again and again. It says so on one of the walls in the depths of the city. Your grandfather also wanted to see the walls, and I took him to see them. Toward the last couple of walls, he found the one he wanted to see. It was one of the dragon writings. Even though he was a dragon, Larzencarak could barely read it. However, when he did, it upset him, mostly because of what it said, and also because of who wrote it."

Dragon was very interested to know where Brenath was going with this conversation. "Who wrote it?"

"Someone named Ælonosanis."

"I can't believe it," Dragon muttered. "Ancient has more secrets than the mountains and the seas put together. What was written on the wall?"

"It's a prophecy of some sort," Brenath replied.

"I knew he was a seer," Dragon exclaimed. "That's how he always knew when I did something wrong. What was the prophecy?"

Brenath rubbed his chin as he thought back. "Your grandfather translated it as best he could, but he was only able to read one fourth of it and it went something like this: When the end is near, there will be a land that is a shining beacon of peace and justice. The whole world will defer to it and try to follow in its path. Nothing in history will match its greatness. But even that great land is not out of the Deceiver's reach. At the height of power, it will start to fall from the inside. The people will be consumed by their own lustful desires, and the Creator will be despised. The people will even begin to despise and hunt the Creator's servants. But at that darkest hour, when even babies are thrown to the slaughter, the Creator has made redemption for those that do not bow their knee to the world." Brenath stopped for a moment, indicating that was all of the prophecy. However, he did not give Dragon time to reply; he simply added his thoughts.

"So you see, Dragon, it has never been about mankind. Mankind has failed the Creator ever since the gardens of life and always will until the Creator is forced to send his last and final redemption. Even then, mankind will fall short of the glory of the Creator." Brenath caught Dragon's eye, making sure he was paying attention. "It doesn't matter what you believe in; there will always be those who fight against the darkness. What about those that don't bend the knee to chaos, like the people in this city who are good people? What about the individuals who serve the Creator? Are we not worth the risk? Or would you destroy the righteous with the wicked?"

"I don't know," Dragon replied honestly, surprised that he answered out loud.

Brenath put a strong arm around Dragon and drew him close to his side. "You are so concerned about mankind itself, from the beginning to the end of time. Leave mankind to the Creator's judgment and remember his design. When you lose faith in the Creator, you lose all hope. Those of us who are good and for the generations to come who are good need all the hope we can get. Because till the end of days, there will always be evildoers, and they will always outnumber us. At the same time, there will always be a person faithful to the last dying breath. For each individual, it is a personal choice. It is for them that you do this, Dragon, so that they one day may live and have the choice that you have today." Brenath then pointed a finger at Dragon, making sure he paid attention to this last comment. "Remember, the Creator was there in the beginning, and he will be there in the end. Don't worry about everything in the middle." Brenath gently patted Dragon's cheek in a loving way, almost in the way a mentor would.

"Perhaps you're right. It all depends on what I focus on," Dragon replied, considering everything.

"Of course, I'm right," Brenath said sarcastically. "I know mankind is not easy to look at, especially after all the horrendous things we do. So instead, look up to the Creator. He will steer you right."

At that moment, a soldier approached and spoke in Brenath's ear. With a disheartening look on his face, he nodded and then turned his attention back to Dragon. "Sadly enough, I have many things to attend to," Brenath spoke plainly. "I do not believe there is much more we could say to each other. So I assumed that this should be our farewell—that is, if you are leaving." Brenath then smiled and took a different tone. "Tyrilcrysalith is in need of a good king," he said, opening his arms in a welcoming gesture yet maintaining a sheepish grin.

Dragon let out a chuckle, somewhat amused by that comment. He didn't want to admit that he had thought about that. However, as quickly as his laughter came, it departed. "Yes, I believe I must go." Dragon replied, feeling somewhat depressed since he was enjoying his conversation with Brenath. "There is much in this world I must do."

"Perhaps you are right this time, although I will miss you greatly. Do not worry about this kingdom. I will safeguard it with my life. I will also look after Crysaia for you, as well as keep my promise to your father." Brenath took Dragon's hand and slapped a bag the size of his head into it.

"Here, take this. It is a gift from the city of Tyrilcrysalith. It is a bunch of broken pieces of the gem buildings that fell to the ground during the attack. Though the buildings are healed, we are left with all the broken shards. Since we have plenty of our own, I thought you could use some on your journey. You have enough diamonds, rubies, and emeralds in that bag to last for quite a while. It is the least we can do for everything that you have done for us."

For a while, there was a long, drawn-out moment of silence. Neither one of them knew what to say or what to do next. Both of their hearts were filled with such sorrow at the thought of this departure. Brenath eventually reached out his hand in an attempt of a simple farewell shake. Instead, Dragon moved forward and firmly embraced

Brenath. Even though Brenath was a straightforward man with an unimpeachable reputation, he did not mind this gesture at all, even when other guards were throwing odd glances at them. Slowly and surely, Brenath put his arms around Dragon and embraced him back like a father hugging a son who had been away for too long. For that was exactly how Dragon felt. Even though Brenath was his friend, Dragon had begun to look at him as a father figure in his life, which made this parting harder than it should have been.

At the same time, across the city, a high-pitched bellow echoed. Brenath let go and stepped back from Dragon, with a sarcastic look on his face. "Well, it looks like Yolana found Sonya, and now Sonya is looking for you. Why don't you go hide and see how long it takes before she finds you?" Brenath smiled greatly as he looked down at Dragon, staring into his eyes for one last time.

After a brief moment of Dragon taking one last look at Brenath, he nodded. Feeling much better than he did earlier that day, Dragon took off quickly, trying to make his way down to the lower city. With the help of some of the other guards, he scurried down the mountainside and jetted into the city. As he hurried through the lower city, attempting to hide from Sonya, he dodged around and occasionally jumped over dwarves. When he rounded one corner, his body was yanked to a stop by something around his waist. Slowly and irresistibly, he was lifted up from the ground by a dragon's tail. Sonya turned Dragon around, as she was slightly laughing. She then nuzzled her head against his, showing her affection and happiness that he was awake.

"You should know you can't hide from me," Sonya spoke warmly.

"I thought I would give it a try," Dragon replied, laughing as well.

"I'm glad to see that you are okay. I was so worried about you." Sonya slowly lowered Dragon back down to the ground and released her tail from around his waist.

"I'm fine now, and so are my heart and thoughts. You needn't worry about me." Dragon paused, thinking about his most recent conversation with Brenath. "I believe we should be moving on. Are you ready to leave?"

"Don't think you're going to leave without me," Voraha shouted behind Dragon. She slowly approached the two, with Drognen Hammerstriker accompanying her. "Remember, you still owe me a great kill!"

"No, Voraha, I wasn't going to leave without you," Dragon replied calmly, pleased to see the female dwarf as well.

"Good," Voraha said as she puffed up her chest in an aggressive manner. "Because I'd have to hurt you if you were going to leave me!"

Dragon then turned his attention to the dwarf standing next to her, who was in a marvelous array yet was dirty from work. "Drognen, I'm glad to see you again. Although I'm afraid this is the last time we will ever see each other."

"I'm sorry to hear that," Drognen swiftly responded. "You know King Ronnar sent a message with me for you. He said the offer to marry his daughter Felewa is still open if you care to take it. In that way, you wouldn't have to say farewell to anyone. The king's daughter, Felewa, sent you a message as well, but there's no way under the sun that I am going to kiss you."

Dragon began to laugh boldly, warmed by the thought of Ronnar Shieldbreaker's offer to marry his daughter and Felewa sending him a kiss. Dragon began to realize that the thing he would miss the most was the warmness of everyone's company. "Tell Ronnar that I thank him kindly, but I must move on. Also, take a kiss back for Felewa from me. It will be easier for you to deliver that message. Perhaps one day we might meet again, though I doubt it."

"It would be wonderful if we could, but I doubt it as well," Drognen concurred with Dragon. "Nevertheless, I'm glad to see you are doing well and that our gifts fit you well. If you will not stay with us, then a part of us will go with you and remind you constantly of us." Drognen then came forward and embraced Dragon in a strong dwarfish hug. "Farewell, Dragon, son of Jorn and Kirianadréth. May good fortune follow you on your journey." Drognen then left the three of them to discuss their plans for departure.

There wasn't much to say. Dragon asked Sonya and Voraha to gather the materials they needed. Find Yolana wherever she is and meet him on the outside of the mountain before the doors. He had some things to attend to and more people to say farewell to, and then they would be off. Sonya mentioned that it would take a while to get everything together, which was okay for Dragon for what he had in mind to do. With everyone in agreement, they separated to do what needed to be done. Dragon made his way back up to the towers, where he immediately found Cromwin at the entrance. Dragon had to admit that this was the easiest farewell to say. Since Cromwin had no tongue and could not speak, there was no need for words. They exchanged sad glances and a solid shake of their forearms. From there, Dragon swiftly made his way to the depths of Tyrilcrysalith, down to the hall of written walls.

***

Meanwhile back in the cave of Zyrmazonus, the dragon's dead body still lies on the floor of the cavern. Steam still rose from the stomach acid slowly eating away at the ground, but the blood had gone cold. The only other noise besides the acid was the sound of several goblins and orcs raiding the body. Now that he was dead, Zyrmazonus's remaining servants had only their survival to worry about. Dragon meat, they had heard, was good for eating, and also dragon scales were valuable. If anything, at least they could use the scales to make good armor for themselves. They were too busy ripping at the scales and cutting at the meat to notice anything else in the cavern.

The orcs and the goblins did not see the black mist slowly rolling in from one of the tunnels. When they finally noticed the mist, it was too late; it shot up from the ground and grabbed each of them like a giant serpent. The black mist sucked the very life out of them, reducing them to dried skin and bones. When they were all dead, the mist dissipated, dropping the bodies to the ground.

When everything went silent, footsteps could be heard coming into the cavern. In a short moment, two black–robed figures entered, their faces completely shrouded in darkness. They both walked up to the remains of Zyrmazonus and stopped a few feet from his head.

"It is true; he is dead," the tallest of the two robed figures spoke in a regal and elegant voice.

"So what do we do now, master?" the second robed figure hissed with a voice that seemed otherworldly.

"These changes do nothing to our plans; if anything, we might need to accelerate a few things."

"What of the scepter? I cannot sense its presence," the servant inquired.

"The scepter is not here; I felt its destruction in the city of Tyrilcrysalith," the master replied with a hint of frustration in his voice.

"What was it doing in Tyrilcrysalith?"

"Zyrmazonus was a fool; once again he did not understand how small he was in the scheme of things. His pride was his downfall and good riddance. He did not understand that scepter had more power than thirty dragons of his stature. He probably thought it was beneath him to wield a human scepter and gave it to his fool of an apprentice. I assume he didn't know its power either; otherwise, it wouldn't have been destroyed. I should not have entrusted it to Zyrmazonus."

"What of the other scepters?"

"Out of the seven ancient scepters, two are still missing and lost to time. Four I still have, and the fifth was just destroyed. We will need to be careful not to lose the others."

"Have we found the other wizards' tomes?" the servant asked nervously.

"No, they are still hidden from my site, but I will eventually find them," the master stated with confidence.

"What is our next move?"

"Go to each of our strongholds and make sure everything is proceeding as planned."

"What of you, master? Where will you go?"

"I must go and investigate some things. From far away I felt the destruction of the scepter and the power that destroyed it. That is what alerted me to Zyrmazonus's failure. The power that destroyed the scepter felt familiar, but I cannot place it. I feel as if our enemy has put something in motion that will interfere with our plans. I must seek it out and destroy it before it causes any more damage. Now go, and I will return to check your progress."

With that, the black mist returned and swarmed around them. It quickly disappeared, and when it was gone, so too were the black-robed figures. Leaving the cavern quiet and empty except for the corpses.

***

Dragon eventually reached the end of the hall of written walls, stopping only eight feet from the end wall that was strangely empowered. He knelt down. It was before this wall he felt closest to the Creator since he believed it was written by the Creator's hand. The wall even seemed to shimmer in the very presence of Dragon, which confirmed Dragon's belief that here was the place to do what he needed to do.

Dragon drew Truth from its sheath and placed its tip down in front of him, holding the hilt with both hands. He then lowered his head, pressing his forehead against his hands, both in respect and heaviness upon his decision. Then, with a heavy heart, Dragon began to speak to the Creator. "Your servant and my teacher Ancient once told me that there are many paths in life, and that you know the end and outcome of every one of those paths. Yet you love us enough to let us choose our own path, even though it hurts you to see us go astray. Like a loving father, you only want what's best for us."

Dragon paused for a moment, reliving that time with his mentor, and how foolish he was back then. "I was foolish enough to ask Ancient if it was just enough to believe in you and know you. And his response was swift. 'No.' Ancient then told me, 'The Deceiver knows and believes in the Creator. It is not good enough to just know of him or believe in him, but one must serve him.' So from that wisdom and the most recent things that have happened to me, I will make a choice."

With his head still bowed, Dragon fixed his thoughts deeply on his choice, making sure it was the right thing he wanted to do. There was no going back. Ancient had always told him about the importance and power of making a covenant. When he reassured himself that this was what he wanted to do, he spoke with all his heart. "Creator, wielder and maker of the heavens and earth, I come humbly before you broken and lost."

Dragon began to breathe heavily, realizing that his selfishness and anger within him were fighting the whole idea. "I ask for forgiveness on all the things that I've done against you and the hatred that I held in my heart. I ask that you guide me where you need me to be in this world of chaos. You made me what I am, so use me as you see fit. Today I surrender myself and make this covenant with you. I will serve you till the day I die."

The moment Dragon stopped talking, the room began to react. The walls began to shake, and a gust of wind hurled through the hall—but not from the entrance; the wind emanated from the end wall. The final wall and all its magnificence began to move as Dragon knelt before it, his head bowed. The walls stretched out in the shape of a mighty hand, its writings burning with light. Though the hand was big enough to crush Dragon with one squeeze, it did nothing of the sort. It simply stretched out, with its index finger pointed forward at Dragon. The moment the giant finger touched Dragon's hands, which were gripped tightly around Truth's hilt, a burst of immeasurable light exploded around him. It then rushed down the massive hall like a flood, igniting each written wall with light, adding to the surge. When the light hit the end, it stopped completely. None of it reached up the stairway, as though it was held in place by an invisible barrier. After a while of filling the hall, the light then rushed back toward the end, and once there, it disappeared, and so did the hand.

Dragon lifted his head to look up at the final wall before him. It was like a solid wall, yet some of the writings were still glowing with light. Dragon picked himself up, feeling that everything that needed to be done had been fulfilled. He then turned and walked back down the hall to the stairs. As he did, Dragon gently sheathed Truth. Something was different, Dragon thought. He could feel it. He felt a change in the air and everything around him, as if another sense had been opened up to him. Dragon even felt a change within himself, and his steps back up the stairs were lighter than when he came down, and so was his heart.

From the hall of written walls, Dragon slowly made his way up the stairways of the towers, with his hand gently brushing against the walls. As with his home, he didn't want a memory of this place to fade away. So he walked slowly, looking at everything and feeling the intricate design of the walls. As he walked, something appeared and was floating by his shoulder. Keeping pace with his stride, Tilly wished to speak with him.

"Dragon, I am proud of you, and I'm honored to be with you on your quest," Tilly said softly yet sincerely.

"I'm glad to have you with me, Tilly," Dragon responded with the same sentiment. "I'm not sure what's going to happen, but whatever it is, it should be exciting. I just have one thought for you. Talking with Brenath made me think about it. He spoke of things that I will see and be a part of when the others won't remember. I'm curious whether anyone will ever know of me in the generations to come." Dragon almost sounded arrogant saying it, but that was not at all what he had in mind, and Tilly knew it.

Tilly flew a little faster, pulling in front of Dragon and turning to face him. Her wings were flapping wildly and glittering in many different colors. As for her face, she had an enormous smirk of delight on it. "Dragon, I swear to you that when all is said and done and you have finished your quest, someone somewhere will remember you. I will make sure of that."

"I wonder if anyone will ever know of you as well," Dragon said, realizing something that he had forgotten. "I haven't even told Sonya about you yet."

Tilly gave Dragon a reassuring look, almost wanting to laugh. "It's okay. I've taken care of that for you. While you were sleeping, I spent several days with Sonya, talking to her about many things. I think we are going to get along just fine."

Dragon's face shifted to a serious look as a certain thought came to his mind.

"What's wrong?" Tilly asked, realizing his shift in mood.

"I'm scared," he said as he stared deeply into her eyes. "I need to tell you this because I can't tell anyone else, and I don't want them to worry. You are the only person I can tell, and I know you can't tell anyone else since you can't get involved. I'm scared because I remembered what the witch said to me before she died. I know you remember her words. She said, 'You have no idea what is before you. If you survive this upcoming trial, you only unleash greater perils. You have no clue what hides in the shadows that even darkness fears it. You will unleash a title wave of death and destruction everywhere you go.

"The witches words terrify me because we barely survived this ordeal. I don't know if we could survive anything greater than this. Also, did I unleash the great peril when I defeated Zyrmazonus or will I cause that later? I guess it's my destiny to find out what hides in the shadows. The unknown makes this situation so much worse. I don't want innocent people to die because of me. I know you can't warn me or give me advice. I just wanted someone to know the fear that I carry inside."

Tilly said nothing; she simply floated up to his face and kissed him on the nose. She gave him a look that meant he was going to be okay and that he wasn't alone. Tilly then sparkled and vanished before his eyes, yet Dragon knew she was still there. With a newfound smile filling his face, he continued up the stairs in search of the last person he needed to see.

Dragon finally found Queen Crysaia in the watchtower, staring out toward the east. There was no one else in there, which made Dragon feel a little bit more at ease since he knew this farewell would be the hardest. He slowly walked up to her and put his hand on her shoulder, turning her gently around. Shockingly, her face was red and wet with tears, which seemed to complicate things for Dragon.

"Why are you crying?" Dragon asked, confused, as he wiped some of the tears softly from her face.

"You know quite well why I am crying," Crysaia snapped, and then turned back around, unwilling to look at him. "You are leaving Tyrilcrysalith, and you are leaving me!"

"What am I supposed to do?" Dragon thought back to what Brenath and Phanis had told him about women, and he thought this to be one of those moments. He wasn't trying to be insensitive; he just didn't know what to do.

"Stay!" Crysaia snapped, as she threw her head into her hands and began to cry. At that moment, all the age that she had gained from being queen seemed to melt away, revealing a young woman underneath.

"Why, what reason is there for me to stay?" Dragon asked her, wanting to know her true feelings. Since she would not look at him, he walked up to her and stood beside her.

"I need you. I need a king to sit beside me and rule with me. Let us cleave together and never be separated from one another." Crysaia eventually turned to face him, desiring an answer.

"Why do you need me? You barely know me," Dragon asked, turning to face her as well.

"Very well," she snapped. "If you must know, something happened that day you asked Truth to judge. It was bad enough that I was already starting to like you, but when the sword's power was burning you and I kissed you, your entire life to this point flashed before my eyes like a vision. In one instant, I felt all your joys, your pains, everything."

"I know I saw your life too," Dragon simply responded, as if that thing happened every day.

"What do you mean you know? Why didn't you say anything?" Crysaia was so upset and frantic that she slugged him in the arm, showing him that even though she was queen, she knew how to fight.

Dragon rubbed his arm and then scratched the back of his head while thinking about the proper response. "I didn't say anything because at first I thought it was a dream. I've been having a lot of those lately."

"You should've said something," she replied as she smacked his shoulder this time. "I've been dealing with this for days. No one should ever know anyone else's life to that extent. How did it happen in the first place?"

"I believe when Truth was emanating and we were touching, everything was revealed. For nothing is hidden from Truth—that's why they call it Truth. I'm certain that since we were the only ones touching, we are the only ones who experienced it." Even though he said it and it made sense to him, Dragon realized that he wasn't too sure about it. The only thing that he would admit to himself was that he didn't understand the sword, and he left it at that.

Crysaia came closer to Dragon and touched his arms as she looked deeply into his eyes. "Dragon, I know this is strange, but I feel very strongly about this. Before this happened, I had feelings toward you, and now that all is revealed, I am certain of one thing—that I love you. Please stay with me."

Dragon stepped back with a solemn look on his face. He then walked to the edge of the watchtower and looked out. "There are several reasons why I cannot stay," he said with sorrow in his voice. "The first reason is that if I stay, many innocent people in other lands will suffer. The other reason," he said, turning back to look at her again, "is that I will be happy for only a short time. Then I will watch you age and eventually die. Also, if I stay here with you, I betray the Creator, and the place set aside for me will be taken away, and I will never see you again. However, if I go, I will always remember you as you are now, and then someday, I will see you again in an eternal place." Dragon then walked up to her, gently grabbing her shoulders, and pulling her to him. He stared into her eyes. "As much as it pains me to leave, I must for both of our sakes. However, if it is any consolation to you, I do love you as well."

With that, they both kissed in a warm embrace, almost unwilling to let go of each other. Once they let go, Dragon moved once again to the edge of the watchtower. Even though he wanted to cry, and could not, it appeared she was crying enough for both of them.

"Will I ever see you again?" Crysaia asked, a hopeful expression on her face.

"I do not think so," Dragon replied realistically. "You need to move on and find someone else to love and to help you rule."

Crysaia took a moment to gather some of her composure before she responded. "I will move on because I need to, but know this, Dragon: no matter what I do, I will love you till the day I die."

Dragon simply stared at her with a smile on his face and nodded. "Queen Crysaia of the great city Tyrilcrysalith, I say farewell. May your days be long, your rule be peaceful, and your heart be filled with joy. I will see your face again in the Creator's palace."

Dragon waved his hand at her in a parting gesture, and then he leaped out of the east side of the watchtower. With a smile on his face and his arms open wide, he plummeted toward the ground. At the last second before impact, Dragon twisted a somersault in the air and landed on his feet, sending up a cloud of dust and buckling the ground underneath him. He had landed right in front of the entrance to the city, with all three of his companions standing behind him. Dragon took a deep breath and roared in triumph over his landing, as well as bade farewell to Tyrilcrysalith. When he was done, his friends approached him excitedly, eager to start on their journey.

"What was that?" Sonya asked him concerning his reckless stunt.

"Well, I always wanted to learn to fly. What better time?" he replied.

"Showoff," Sonya snapped back. "You're lucky you didn't get hurt. Remember, I'm the one with the wings."

Dragon took a moment and looked at all three of his companions, as his heart filled with joy over the fact he was not alone. So without another word, all four of them started off to the south, wondering where this quest would lead them.

***

For the people in Tyrilcrysalith, they all paused for a moment when a dragon's roar echoed throughout the city. Strangely enough, there were no screams and no panic among the people; they all simply smiled. No one was afraid; in fact, they were all reassured by that roar. It comforted them to know that dragons were still around and that the king of the dragons would forever protect the innocent. As for Queen Crysaia, every morning she stood in the watchtower and watched the east, and every evening she watched the west. Her heart was filled with love for one being, and she always watched for his return. Whether or not Dragon and Crysaia ever met again, only the Creator and the fairy Tilly knew for sure.

Epilogue

As I sit in my home with the fairy Tilly whispering in my ear, I am filled with wonder and amazement. The sheer power of the story is overwhelming; the fact that it lasted through thousands of generations, yet remains an untold tale. I speak openly to the fairy, hoping that I am blessed with another tale. Though I cannot see her, I feel a gentle kiss on my cheek, and I hear a "thank you for listening." She tells me that there are more stories and great adventures to come. The only question I have for her is what eventually happened to Dragon.

After a moment of silence, I see something glitter out of the corner of my eye, toward the window. When I go to the window of my apartment complex and look out, I see the flickering light go three stories down to the street and stop on the other side, eventually resting upon the shoulders of what appears to be a hooded beggar. Though I cannot see his face completely, I can see his emerald eyes. Even from three stories away, I can tell that those are no human eyes.

So it is my belief today that Dragon is still among us, and he is patiently and faithfully waiting for the Creator to return.

The Dragon Child

JARED NESCHER

Learn more about
The Dragon Child Series
at
www.thedragonchild.com